ESTELLE

An Inspiring Love Story

ESTELLE

An Amazing Story of Persistent Love and the Prayers
That Produced a Great Spiritual Awakening

James W. Tharp

Christian Renewal Ministries Publishing
Bozeman, Montana

ESTELLE
PUBLISHED BY CHRISTIAN RENEWAL MINISTRIES
P.O. Box 11406
Bozeman, MT 59719
www.crmin.org

ISBN 978-0-9846712-0-5
ISBN 978-0-9846712-1-2 (electronic)

Cover photo and design © 2012 Marilee Donivan

Printed in the United States of America
2012 First Edition

CONTENTS

Acknowledgments

Each of us is a part of those who are, or have been, significant in our lives. My life has been shaped by my parents Jim and Estelle Tharp; my wives: Maxine (deceased in 2006) and Shirley (married in 2009); my siblings: Jeanette, Anniece, Burl, Russell, Carroll, Shirley, Martha, Joseph, and Paul; and my children: Deborah, Stephen, Priscilla, and Timothy.

My foremost influential mentors and colleagues have been and are my wife Shirley, my parents Jim and Estelle Tharp, the Rev. Dr. Billy Graham, the Rev. Dr. Paul S. Rees, the Rev. Dr. William M. Greathouse, the Rev. Dr. Mildred Bangs Wynkoop, the Rev. Dr. Joshua Stauffer, the Rev. Dr. Jack Taylor, the Rev. Joseph Hoffman, the Rev. G. R. Bateman, the Rev. Dr. C. M. Ward, the Rev. Dr. G. B. Williamson, the Rev. Dr. John Newby, the Rev. Joseph Youmans, the Rev. Dr. Guy Nees, the Rev. Dr. Tom Phillips, the Rev. Dr. Wesley Duewel, the Rev. Velma Hertel, the Rev. Jack Terry, the Rev. Gerald Ogden, the Rev. John K. Summers, the Rev. Dr. Michael Ross, the Rev. Fred Fowler, the Rev. Arnold Carlson, the Rev. Les Turner, Professor Amy Harvey, Mr. Charles Kercheval, Mr. Keith Stiles, Mr. Gail Fremont, Mr. John Bright, Mr. Williard Young, Mr. Larry McNaught, Mr. Mike Biggs, Mr. Steve Fowler, and my cousins George, Henry (Buddy), and James Best.

In the writing of this book, I gratefully acknowledge the contributions of the following:

Shirley Tharp, my dear wife, for her love and encouragement and her long and unrelenting months of editing.

Kathy Tyers, a professional editor, who taught me how to eliminate unnecessary information.

Susan Hill, a dear friend and prayer partner, and herself an author, who gave valuable guidance in writing.

Billy Graham, a dear friend, who—on hearing Estelle's story— insisted that I write the book.

Bonnie Hite, a dear friend, who hoped the book "might become a movie."

Ben and Ruth Ann Smith, dear friends, who have been encouragers and supporters, frequently providing conducive settings for writing the book.

Duncan and Susan Hill, dear friends and prayer partners, who have supported and encouraged the writing of the book.

Gail and Betty Fremont, dear friends and prayer partners, who have offered unfailing encouragement and support.

Marilee Donivan, a dear friend and prayer partner, who has been an answer to prayer in her guidance in writing and editing, knowledge of publishing, and talent for designing the cover for this book.

Anniece Shelburne, a dear sister and prayer partner, who is a nonfiction character in the book and very close and dear to Shirley and me in these times.

NOTE TO READERS: The author trusts the readers will not be offended by the language included in this novel. Some may deem a few expressions crude, vulgar, or offensive. Please understand that I have endeavored to portray the clearest and most accurate profile of certain characters before they experienced life transformation through faith in Jesus Christ as their Lord and Savior.

Jim and Estelle Tharp
1946

Preface

The first fifty years of the twentieth century in America was viewed by author Frederick Lewis Allen as "The Big Change" when "America transformed itself." From 1900 to 1950, America grew from 76 million people to 150 million, from a life expectancy of 49 years to 68 years, and from 13 thousand automobiles to 44 million.

Historians and journalists have attempted to portray the major changes that took place in the United States during the entire twentieth century as being amazing. They were indeed! Some ventured to list the forces behind such changes—political, educational, industrial, financial, technological, and sociological.

In this book, the focus will be on a different kind of force—not one of self-transformation—that has made America different from any other country in the history of nations. The power that we encounter in this story will take us a long way from the industrial sites of New York City, Los Angeles, Chicago, Houston, Detroit, and Dallas. We will hardly meet the great political players of the first half of the twentieth century, such as Theodore Roosevelt, Woodrow Wilson, and Franklin Roosevelt. The mighty force we will meet in this work will not be generated by such money lords as J. P. Morgan, John D. Rockefeller, the Vanderbilts, or the duPonts.

This book is about a simple, poor, unknown woman who believed that *the love of our sovereign God is the greatest force in the universe.* Estelle Tharp was not alone in believing this: Jesus Christ, the apostle Paul, Augustine, Thomas Aquinas, Savonarola, Martin Luther, Count von Zinzendorf, William Law, John Wesley, George Whitefield, Jonathan Edwards, David Brainerd, Charles Spurgeon, William Booth, Charles G. Finney, D. L. Moody, Pope John Paul II, and Billy Graham discovered this same transforming power. We will see how this woman—uneducated and unpromising—learned through prayer and faith to release the power of the Holy Spirit of God in a great spiritual awakening that changed her world. Spiritual awakenings throughout the 2,000-year history of the church have

v

been called *revivals.* God has ordained them to preserve the moral and spiritual values of the nations and as a means of purifying, preserving, and perpetuating His church.

The strange cycle of the backsliding and renewal of the people of God across the ages is a haunting phenomenon. The Old Testament church often failed to meet the conditions of its covenant with Jehovah, and the resulting apostasy wrote tragedy into its history. For over two millennia under the New Covenant, Christians through their disobedience and neglect are just as guilty of grieving the Spirit of God who lives within them. The church of Jesus Christ does not remain alive unconditionally; it experiences abundant life and lives in holiness only as it abides obediently in Christ. **If anyone does not remain in me,** warned Jesus, **he is like a branch that is thrown away and withers** (John 15:6).

The prophecy of Habakkuk addresses the mystery and manner in which a holy God deals with His delinquent children. The prophet makes it clear that God will wink at neither the wickedness of the world nor the disobedience of His church. What He condemns in the world He cannot condone in His church. It shocked Habakkuk to learn that it is the prerogative of our sovereign God to choose His own method of disciplining His people. But the prophet also discovered that even in His severe judgments God is still a God of grace and mercy. God's mighty merciful acts of judging Israel led to times of repentance, restoration, and revival. Revival has not only been God's manner of restoring His people to fellowship with Him, but it has also been His secret of preserving the nations they inhabit. Revival is His ordained method of restoring believers to New Testament life and power. With true revival comes a new healing of the land.

Every great awakening has affected both people of faith and those who are searching for the truth. This has been so true in the American experience. Three mighty spiritual awakenings have changed the course of our continent on several counts, both sacred and secular.

The First Awakening

Puritanism, legalism, and denominationalism could not hold Colonial America to her spiritual, economical, and political ideals. Long before the end of their first century, the colonies had departed from the old paths. Religious bigotry, austerity, and tradition were in great supply, but so were the evils of crime, immorality, war, and skepticism—right along with the spiritual backsliding of Christian believers.

Then in the late 1720s, the Holy Spirit began preparing a few spiritual leaders for an unusual outpouring of new spiritual life upon early America. Theodore Frelinghuysen experienced a new anointing as he preached conviction for sin to his startled Dutch Reformed congregation in Raritan, New Jersey. About the same time, Gilbert Tennent and other members of his Presbyterian family were moved by the Holy Spirit to light revival fires around Philadelphia. Jonathan Edwards, a Congregationalist, through much prayer and fasting, spearheaded a New England awakening. Then along came George Whitefield, a young British evangelist, who was used mightily to tie all of these scattered fires of revival into one mighty movement of the Spirit. Whitefield held open-air meetings throughout the Southern and Middle colonies before going on to New England, where the first great awakening reached its zenith. Several hundred thousand colonists were brought to faith in Christ as Savior between 1720 and 1744. The church once again demonstrated apostolic power and simplicity. A few historians believe that the early American awakening helped produce the quality of courageous political leadership that would prepare the colonies to sue for their independence from Great Britain.

But this great awakening subsided. Perhaps it was the rising fever of war that choked the revival fires. All too soon American believers were again trapped in complacency, their cold hearts again in desperate need of the rekindling fires of the Holy Spirit.

The Second Awakening

Beginning about 1790, God graciously blessed the new republic with another visitation of His reviving power. This time the South was included, with Methodists and Baptists playing major roles. The second revival began in Virginia, spread quickly to the Carolinas, and then extended into Kentucky, where it gave birth to the American camp meeting and produced the colorful circuit-riding preachers. These amazing heroes, such as James McGready, Barton Stone, and Peter Cartwright, would follow the growing American frontier with the Gospel of Jesus Christ and preach it ruggedly and effectively.

The Cane Ridge camp meeting in Kentucky in August 1801 attracted 25,000 people. They came by wagon, on horseback, in canoes, and on foot. From the very first service, the crowds experienced a startling release of divine power.

But this second awakening involved other human instruments in places far from the Kentucky wilderness. Timothy Dwight, president of Yale University and grandson of Jonathan Edwards, combined scholarship and evangelistic zeal to confront infidelity on the Yale campus. He was determined the Gospel of Jesus Christ would make an impact on the university. By 1802, half of the graduating class had committed their lives to Christ. Undergraduates followed in personal faith so that Yale's spiritual upheaval continued to renew itself long after Dwight's death in 1817. Lyman Beecher gave his heart to Christ during his junior year at Yale and became a leader in the second awakening. "I was made for action," said Beecher, as he launched a crusade against dueling from his Long Island pulpit, calling it "the national sin." After moving to Litchfield, Connecticut, he gained national prominence by organizing temperance societies to deal with the social evils of alcoholism. Finally, in Boston, Beecher led in one of the greatest revivals of his career.

Francis Asbury was another human instrument in the second great awakening. Commissioned by John Wesley to come to America and head the mission of the Methodist Church, the "Saddlebag Bishop" became a legend on horseback. He covered more territory and was instantly recognized by more people than any other person in all of the colonies, including President George Washington. Asbury's secret to spiritual power was rising daily at four o'clock in the morning to spend two solid hours in prayer before he began speaking to others or going about his work. He knew the source of the revivals in his own ministry, and he did not hesitate to call his preachers to the disciplines of prayer and fasting.

The second awakening died of the same causes as the first. In a combination of distractions, the revival fires burned out early in the nineteenth century.

The Third Awakening

During the early 1820s, the country experienced fresh revival fires, beginning in upstate New York under the ministry of a newly converted lawyer by the name of Charles G. Finney. Throughout more than three decades, the ministry of Finney and others penetrated the moral and social fabric of thousands of communities.

The first phase of the third awakening climaxed in the great Laymen's Prayer Meeting in the years 1857 to 1859. Jeremiah Lanphier hosted a prayer meeting in the Dutch Reformed Church on Fulton Street in New York City. At first only a few people showed up, but when hundreds started attending, the prayer meetings shifted from weekly to daily. Thereafter, the one church was no longer adequate for the crowds. Nearly all the churches in New York opened their doors and were filled. At noon each day, churches, theaters, and halls were full of people praying. The prayer meetings reached epidemic proportions when Pastor Henry Ward Beecher joined the movement. Then Horace Greeley, editor of the *New York Tribune*, supported the prayer movement with a stream of editorials and news stories. By 1858 the prayer awakening had reached Boston, Philadelphia, Baltimore, and Washington, D.C.; and by 1859 it had spread as far west as Cincinnati and Chicago.

The first phase of the third awakening ended with the threat of the Civil War. Many spiritual leaders felt that the passions and politics of the Civil War extinguished the revival fires.

But if the first phase of the third awakening began with the influence of Charles G. Finney, there is little doubt that the second phase began with the influence of D. L. Moody, a lay preacher from Chicago. By the time the Civil War ended in 1865, Moody the evangelical had become famous as an evangelist and a revivalist. He teamed up with a singer by the name of Ira Sankey, and they began filling large auditoriums in the United States and England, somewhat on the scale of the Billy Graham crusades that would be held worldwide throughout the last half of the twentieth century.

It is probably accurate to say that the third great spiritual awakening in America that began with the conversion of Charles G. Finney in 1821 ended with the death of D. L. Moody in 1899.

America's Greatest Need

A few years ago, Billy Graham asked a university professor what he considered to be the greatest need in our country. The professor replied, "I may surprise you, since I'm not a religious person, but I believe the greatest need we have at this hour in America is a spiritual awakening which will restore individual and collective morals and integrity throughout the nation."

The apostle Paul wrote about a messed-up civilization so totally insensitive to God's holiness and grace that it had given itself over to a downward spiral of perversion (Rom. 1:18-32). When a generation arrogantly closes its mind to creation's evidence of God, Paul argued, it sinks deeper and deeper into the swamps of its own sick behavior. Those who reject divine revelation are soon able to ignore conscience, and those who ignore conscience will in time refuse to listen to reason. It is this writer's considered opinion that America is rapidly approaching this dreadful point of moral insanity. Only a sovereign, merciful God can save us by sending a full-scale, historical outpouring of His Spirit that will result in His people humbling themselves in prayer and fasting, seeking the will and truth of God, and turning in repentance from their self-righteousness, unbelief, pride, lust, and materialistic idolatry.

A Novel on Revival

The Arkansas County revival that I tell about in this book is factual. But I have decided to cast it in the form of a novel. The main reason for choosing to put the story in novel form is to gain the freedom to cast a greater and clearer vision for revival for any community anywhere in the world—educated or illiterate, affluent or impoverished, metropolitan or backwoods.

I am convinced that from the present time to the return of our Lord and Savior Jesus Christ, we shall be seeing more and more outpourings of the Holy Spirit to prepare Christians for becoming more convincing witnesses to the world, while at the same time getting believers all over the world ready for Christ's Second Coming.

So, instead of setting the venue for revival in a cultured, celebrated, prosperous area of the country, we will go to southeastern Arkansas, where a transforming outpouring of the Spirit of God actually took place in the spring, summer, and fall of 1946. We go into the backwoods of the state of Arkansas and into the remote backwater areas of Arkansas County. The initial outpouring occurred in the lower part of that county in Chester township, which includes the settlements of Tichnor, Weber, Malcomb, LaGrue, Fairview, Nady, and the Merrisach Lake communities.

Estelle Tharp and Martha Honeycutt

The two principal human instruments in the Arkansas County revival of 1946 were Estelle Tharp and Martha Honeycutt.

Mattie Estelle Hughes was 18 years old when she married my father, James William Tharp, who was 20 years old at the time. Estelle's father had died when she was only five years old, and she was raised by her grandmother, Mattie Best, a born-again evangelical Christian. From the time Estelle was a little girl at her grandmother's knee, seeing her read the Bible and hearing her pray, she knew she wanted to know God with the same intimacy and power as had her grandmother. In 1930, after Jim and Estelle had been married four years and she had given birth to two children, Estelle heard the Gospel and surrendered her heart and life to Jesus Christ.

Dr. Martha Jean Honeycutt was an authority in New Testament Studies in Union Bible College (UBC) in Westfield, Indiana. In August of 1938, as she was reading the *Indianapolis Star,* she had an epiphany. In a Saturday morning edition of the newspaper, she came across the story on "The Four Most Lawless Communities in the U.S." Only one of the four was described: "In Arkansas County a woman is not safe on the country roads even in the daylight. Moonshiners and bootleggers brazenly defend their illegal operations by murdering prohibition agents and members of the sheriff's posses. Murder, thievery, rape, and all kinds of violence are so rampant that the sheriff has served notice on the governor and attorney general of the State of Arkansas that he can no longer patrol the lower end of his county. Too many deputies and posse members are being ambushed and murdered. Chester township is without churches and ministers of the Gospel."

Dr. Honeycutt laid the newspaper down, but she could not escape the impact of that story. This American community of adults seemingly had no respect for law and order and no conscience against murder, thievery, and violence. Without churches and ministers, the men, women, and children had no access to the Gospel of Jesus Christ. She knelt in prayer: *Heavenly Father, are you calling me to go to this depraved community in Arkansas and try to light a candle in that spiritual and moral darkness?* In the days ahead, she knew she would need to discuss with her college president her sense of a call to leave the comforts of her academic environment and go to that notoriously depraved county in the south.

The Greatest Need in America and in the World

I invite you to read the story of Estelle prayerfully, asking God to touch your heart, purify your faith, quicken your spirit, and allow you to envision His same mighty mercies that He poured out on Arkansas County in 1946. Then, in faith, believe that He might sweep your heart, your family, your church, your community, and your nation in a revival of grace and power.

I realize that many people, including both believers and nonbelievers, feel that the sun is already setting on Western civilization. Who can deny that deepening shadows are falling across our religious freedoms, that our sacred values of family life are eroding, and that the socioeconomic infrastructure is crumbling? This writer sincerely believes that we are now living in that late hour of human history in which God declared that He would **shake the heavens and the earth** and that such a judgment would extend to all nations (Hag. 2:6-7, Heb. 12:25-29). But the sovereign One does not leave us in the dark as to His purpose for such a sweeping judgment: *to establish His unshakeable Kingdom through His Son, Jesus Christ* (Heb. 12:27-29).

I am convinced that if Jonathan Edwards, John Wesley, Francis Asbury, Charles G. Finney, or D. L. Moody were alive today, they would find a way to tell North Americans that all of the idolatry, immorality, and irreverence of this late present darkness merely form the dramatic background and set the stage for the greatest revival in the history of the church! These anointed men of God would tell us that God has not yet given up on America and the other nations of the earth. Now, I realize that many American Christians expect nothing more at this late hour than the wrath of God to be poured out, just as it was visited on Sodom and Gomorrah. It is surely what we deserve!

But as difficult as it is for many religious people to accept, it is not our pagan society in its appalling moral darkness that prevents the mighty revival so desperately needed. Christians, let's stop blaming politicians, philosophers, secular humanists, homosexuals, abortionists, and hedonists for the delay of a needed spiritual awakening! It is the sleeping majority in the church that is responsible for the spiritual famine in the land. The Holy

Spirit is calling the church to repent of sins—division, prejudices, pride, coldness of heart, self-righteousness, hypocrisy, materialistic idolatry, slumbering spirit, and carnality. We refuse to humble ourselves and repent of our prayerlessness, slothful stewardship, and substitutions for a genuine spiritual life. Even as the world staggers toward the precipice, God is calling His people out of their slumber to prepare the way for revival: **If my people, who are called by my name, will humble themselves and pray and seek my face and turn from their wicked ways, then I will hear from heaven and will forgive their sin and will heal their land** (II Chron. 7:14).

James W. Tharp
Bozeman, Montana

1   *A Dance of Destiny*

Jim Tharp and Della Almond were the first to arrive at the Malcomb schoolhouse for the Annual Community Spring Dance of 1926. Despite a stormy April evening, couples were expected from all over the lower end of Arkansas County's Little Prairie—from DeWitt, Gillette, and Tichnor to the north and as far south as the smaller communities around Merrisach Lake. As Jim drove under the entrance overhang to let Della out, he noticed the wind was getting stronger and the rain heavier. As he moved the car, a flash of lightning reminded him to park it out in the open lot rather than under the oaks.

Finding the schoolhouse dark inside, Jim felt along the rough wooden wall until his hand hit a light switch. He then decided to light a fire in the auditorium stove where they would be dancing—"enough to knock the chill off," he explained to Della.

Glen Thigpen, the dance emcee, had arrived by that time and upon hearing several cars, trucks, and wagons arriving outside, he said, "I think they done all come at once out there." Jim and Della found a bench facing the door and sat down while Glen welcomed the musicians and others crowding onto the dance floor. Soon Glen called out, "Awright, guys, grab yore gals and get out here, cuz our musicians are gonna kick off with "You Are My Sunshine."

Della wondered why Jim was not leading the way to the dance floor. She looked at him and saw that he was staring at a couple coming down the hall—a handsome gentleman about Jim's age with a dark-haired beauty on his arm. Jim stood as they approached, and with his eyes still on the brunette, said, "Now, cousin George, where did a devil like you find an angel like this?"

"Hi, Jim!" Then turning to the brunette, George said, "Estelle, this is my cousin Jim Tharp, and Jim, this is Estelle Hughes. I found her down at Nady just a few days ago."

Jim was smiling as he reached for Estelle's outstretched hand and said, "I think I've been waitin' to meet ye!"

George asked, "Jim, don't you wanta introduce us to your lady?" When Della realized that Jim was taken up with the angel, she stepped forward and said, "I'm Della Almond, George. Glad to meet you." Walking over to Jim, she pulled at his arm, saying, "Come on, Jim; we should join the dance and allow George and Estelle to do so as well." Both couples blended into the dancing traffic.

After a few seconds, Jim said, "Della, I hope ye won't mind if I ask George to switch partners, cuz I just know I'm supposed to talk to that girl."

"Oh, really? Well, at least that means ye plan to do more than just stare at her! So, I'm gettin' dumped?"

"No, I'm just bein' up front with ye.... I need to talk with her."

"Then do what ye gotta do to get this angel off yore mind!"

Suddenly, Jim stopped dancing and led the way to George and Estelle. Tapping George on the shoulder, he asked, "George, would ye allow us to trade partners for the rest of this waltz?"

"I reckon so, Jim, if it's alright with Estelle and Della." Seeing Estelle smile and nod, George broke away and Jim moved to take Estelle in his arms.

Jim studied Estelle's face to determine whether she was pleased or disappointed with the switch and was delighted with her reassuring smile. He was glad this girl understood the roll and turn of a good waltz. She stepped, dipped, and moved with the tempo perfectly while allowing him to lead. "I'm glad yore willin' to dance with me," he said. After another few seconds, he asked, "How long have ye known George?"

"Just since he dropped by my aunt's home a few days ago and invited me to this dance."

Jim had a chance to study Estelle's face as she answered his question. He realized he was really taken with her—her looks, her voice, her proper speech, her poise. He was bothered a bit by the realization that she outclassed him in education.

Estelle whispered in Jim's ear, "Jim, you're holding me a little too tightly."

Releasing her a bit, Jim said, "I reckon I could say I'm sorry, but that wouldn't be the truth." As they waltzed on, his partial release produced one benefit that he enjoyed—the two could now look into each other's eyes. Jim wondered what she was thinking. He'd been with enough girls to tell when he could see interest, respect, and curiosity or disappointment, boredom, and unrest. *How could I help huggin' this beautiful woman too tight?*

At the end of the waltz, Glen announced a brief intermission. On their way to George and Della, Jim said, "I'd like one more dance with ye before we end here tonight, Estelle. There's somethin' I wanna ask ye." Estelle smiled and nodded. To George, he said, "Thanks, cousin! Just one more tradeoff later tonight, please."

"If that's okay with the ladies," George answered.

"Let's go find a seat," Jim said to Della. "I want us to talk while we sit out a dance or two. I owe ye an explanation, but I'll get us somethin' to eat and drink. What would ye like?"

"Just a Coke and a Snicker bar."

Jim returned to see that Della had found a bench away from the traffic. As they began eating and drinking, they could hear the rain pounding the roof. The lightning was brighter and the thunder louder than it had been at first.

After a few bites of his hotdog and a swallow of his Coke, Jim said, "Della, I think it's time I told ye somethin'."

"Yeah, I guess it is."

"I've always been honest with ye. I'm three years older than you, but we grew up together. You wuz my first date, the first girl I ever kissed. Ever time I thought of tellin' ye I loved ye, somethin' held me back—I knew I just didn't feel about ye the way a man oughta feel about the girl he hopes to marry. I wuz always open to that feelin', but it didn't happen and I could not lead ye on. But when I saw Estelle Hughes come down that hall tonight, I felt somethin' about her. That's why I asked George if we could trade again. I need to ask Estelle for a date or a time with her...so I can find out how I feel and how she feels."

"Jim, are you sayin' it was love at first sight?" Della asked.

"I don't know, but that's what I gotta find out. I think the last dance is comin' up. I hope ye'll dance with George, cuz here they come..."

"No, I'll go to the ladies room, and then I'll sit this one out. You'll find me on this bench."

3

George and Estelle approached Jim and noticed Della's departure. Jim explained, "Della thinks she'll sit this out, but she'll be back here shortly."

With excitement, Jim drew Estelle to him as they began dancing to the "Kentucky Waltz." Jim remembered her earlier request, so he released her just a bit and she smiled her thanks. "Estelle, this is the third waltz tonight, and I sure enjoyed dancin' the first one with ye. I'm glad we can have this one together, too."

Estelle said, "Jim, I believe you said there was something you wanted to ask me?"

"Yeah, I hope I can get some time with ye in a few days. I think I'm supposed to get to know more about ye and, hopefully, you might want to know more about me. Could we get together in a few days— maybe a date, a walk, or just a visit?"

"But what about Della and you?"

"That's why Della and I sat out the last two dances. I reminded her that I'd never had feelin's for her, and I told her that I sense that I'm supposed to get to know you better. Now, I'll respect ye if ye want nothin' to do with me, but I know I've gotta ask to see ye."

Estelle smiled and said, "I think that can be arranged. To be honest, I had hoped you might have some interest in further contact. So if it's really over with you and Della, I'd like you to come down to Nady and meet my Aunt Mertice and Uncle Tom some evening. We can stroll down to the pond and sit on the bench and have a good talk."

"I'd love to come! How about this Friday evenin'?"

"That should work. Why don't you come at 3 o'clock in the afternoon? We'll visit awhile and have supper at 5:30."

Jim could hardly believe that the dance was ending, but he was glad that he would get to see this marvelous lady again in just a few days. He led her to George and then asked for a few words with him. They stepped away to talk, and George asked, "What's on your mind, Jim, besides Estelle?"

"Well, yer right. I am taken with Estelle. And I've told Della about tryin' for a date with Estelle, but I also need to make this right with you, George..."

"Naw, Jim, no problem there. Estelle is nice, but we have no feelin's for each other."

"Thanks, George."

The two cousins were relieved to see that Della and Estelle were parting with civility. George and Jim decided it was time to take their dates home.

Jim and Della rode in silence most of the way to the Almond home. In the driveway, Jim said, "Della, I know things will be different now, but I want us to continue to be friends." He helped her from the car and walked her to the door.

"I reckon this is goodbye, Jim. I'll miss you, but I wish you the best. Estelle is nice and pretty. Goodnight!" With that said, Della opened the door, walked through and closed it without looking back.

Early the next morning, Jim watched his mother take browned biscuits from the oven, open a jar of pear preserves, and place a platter of fried bacon on the table. She said, "Son, pour our coffee and hold Papa's 'til he comes; he's at the barn with a cow due to calve." As Jim poured two cups, he heard his father enter the back door, so he poured his.

"Reckon it ain't gonna be right away," Boge called from the hall where he was washing up. "Be there in a minute." Boge entered the kitchen, his thinning gray hair tousled and his collar turned up against the coolness of the spring morning. After the prayer of thanksgiving, he asked, "How was the dance last night?"

"Big crowd, despite the storm. Papa and Mama, I need to tell ye about someone I met last night. Do y'all know anyone named Hughes?"

The two parents looked at each other, thinking. Boge answered, "I reckon not, son. Why?"

Before Jim could answer, Ophelia said, "Well, maybe. Seems like I remember that Alvin and Mattie Best down in the Fairview district had a daughter who married a Hughes—her name was Alma. Mr. Hughes died and left her with children, and they lived with the Bests for a long time. Why do you ask, son?"

"Well, George Tharp brought Estelle Hughes to the dance last night, and I wuz kinda taken with her. I danced a couple of waltzes with her, and I believe she likes me, too. I asked her for a date, and she's invited me to supper this Friday night. She keeps house for her Aunt Mertice, a schoolteacher who's married to Tom Miller down at Nady."

"Oh, yeah, Mertice is one of the Best daughters. Mertice is a sister to George, who BettyLee is gonna marry. She'll be up in a bit and can explain it all."

Boge asked, "But, Jim, what about Della? Y'all grew up together, and…"

"Papa, I like Della as a friend, but I've never felt about Della the way a man oughta feel about the woman he wants to marry. And I told her that last night. I told her that I was impressed with Estelle and that I wanted to find out if she's the one for me. Della and I ended it last night."

"I'm glad you were straight with Della, son," Boge said. "But the girls, especially Hollis, are gonna be sorry you won't be seein' Della anymore."

"Just leave the girls to me," Ophelia said.

"Thanks, Mama! Now I'd better get over to Marion's and see if he thinks it's too wet to plow." Jim left the breakfast table and went out into the breaking dawn to saddle Star, his four-year-old gelding.

Jim reminisced as he rode the few miles to the Derrick's place. Jim thought about the impact of the war on both Marion and his father. Boge had sold his cotton farm in Ethel and put the proceeds, plus all he could borrow, into equipment for rice farming on another man's land. He made good for four years, but he lost it all in 1919 when the bottom fell out of the rice market. Marion had played it safe and sold before the price dropped, and he had continued to prosper. Boge and many others who had ventured into rice had gone under. It still hurt Jim to remember how he had quit school at twelve years of age to help his father make his first rice crop, build a new house, and prepare for a life of prosperity after many years of barely making ends meet on their old cotton farm— then seeing his father lose it all! But Jim was proud of the way his father had played fair with his creditors and willingly adjusted to a humbler way of life—becoming a cotton sharecropper for Marion Derrick.

Boge could not have found a more generous landowner to work for than Marion. Boge and Ophelia and their four children still at home were furnished a large tenant house that was better built and more spacious than the average sharecropper's shack. Three of their children—Dee, Henry, and Hallie—were married and out on their own.

BettyLee was engaged to George Best and would be leaving the nest soon. This would leave Jim, Hollis, and Jenny. The house had electricity, but no indoor plumbing. There were outbuildings—a large barn, a tool shed, a smokehouse, a corncrib, and an outhouse. Boge had built pens for fattening and butchering hogs. Besides a large area for a vegetable garden, there was an orchard containing apple, peach, pear, and plum trees that annually produced all fruit needed for canning and making jellies and preserves.

It was known throughout the LaGrue community that Boge Tharp loved God, worked hard, paid his bills, and told the truth. It was also known that Ophelia "set a good table." Jim realized his father had given up on becoming a rich rice farmer with dreams of grandeur for his children. He knew both parents were hurting over Dee's failing marriage and Henry's liquor problem and his work with a moonshiner. But they expected Dee to return and make her home with them, and they were hopeful that Henry's wife, Oda, might be able to change the course of their oldest son. Hallie had married Bee Krablin, and they were doing well in rice farming up in the northeastern part of the state.

Jim was thankful for his good health, wished he'd finished the grades, and thought a lot about the way he would make his mark in the world. He felt that he knew himself quite well and realized his education was limited. But he believed he could make a good life in commercial fishing, trapping for mink, and working as a scout for the timber companies. Eventually, he hoped to buy land and raise cattle.

Henry Purdy, a friend of Lloyd LaFargue, Sheriff of Arkansas County, had once responded to the sheriff's inquiry about a younger man who could help him catch runaways from jails and prisons who usually made for the river bottoms for their hideouts. Henry said, "Lloyd, I want to tell you about a young man who is like family to me. Jim Tharp is still in his teens, but I'm telling you, he's a woodsman, a marksman, a timberman, a fisherman, and a man's man. I've never seen his equal in the woods or on the prairie. That boy can see where others only look— his eyes miss nothing! He catches the movements of deer in timber or thick brush 200 yards away; his ears pick up footfalls 50 yards off, and he can discern whether it's a man or a beast. By sniffing the air, he knows whether a deer, a horse, a bear, a panther, or a man is within 100 yards. He walks slowly in dry leaves, taking every step silently, which lets him get within gun range of anything he wants to kill. His dad, Boge Tharp, is a good hunter, but he says Jim is the best he's ever gone into the woods with. I've been with him when he has stopped, looked at me, and said, 'Uncle Henry, don't ask me how I know, but if ye'll follow this stream a half mile to a big stand of oaks and get behind the biggest one of 'em and stay ready, I'll make a wide circle and in about an hour from now I'll drive out a couple of deer for ye.' Shore 'nuff, I take off and find those oaks and get ready. In just 45 minutes, here comes a buck and a doe. I get the six-point buck!

"The most wonderful thing about Jim is he never misses! It's a special gift; he instinctively knows at what angle and level to hold that gun or pistol. It's something he never had to learn or train for. His brain tells him when, how, and where to pull and point and fire—no aiming, adjusting, or squinting. When he fires, there's no jerk or movement except the recoil; every time the bullet goes where he intended. Lloyd, you'll just have to see the kid work in the woods to believe it!"

A few weeks after the sheriff had met and spent time with Jim, he was convinced that his gifts were for real. The sheriff told him about a former deputy who learned how to shoot a man's ear, and he was accurate about ninety-five percent of the time. Lloyd brought him a cardboard life-size cutout of a man to see what he could do with it. Down in the LaGrue bottoms, the sheriff wanted to see what Jim could do by shooting at the ears and then the heart.

"I'll give it my best, but we gotta remember that the ear is a dangerous target—if a man is not standin' at the right angle or in the right light, it would likely be a fatal shot ever time!" Jim said.

"That's true. But when you do have the right angle and the right light, shootin' the ear is better than killin' the man. When you shoot a hole in the ear or even shoot the ear off, the man will think his head has been blown off. Now I've watched you shoot a shotgun, a rifle, and a pistol and you never miss, whether the target was flyin', runnin', walkin', or settin' still. I want you to learn to shoot ears, so we can clean up this county and save some lives. Now look it over good, then place it out there at whatever distance you want, and let's see what you can do."

Jim spent a few minutes studying the image—the ears, the heart, the height of the board. Finally he said, "Okay, I'll see what I can do at

50 yards, then 30, and then 20." After seeing that the animals were in the clear, he solidly placed the target at 50 yards. He then studied the dummy for several seconds, pulled his pistol, and fired. Both men knew the target had been hit, but they rushed to check the ear. A hole was in the center of the lobe of the left ear!

"I'm not surprised!" Lloyd said. "Now, let's see you do it in both ears."

Jim took his time, drew his pistol, and fired two shots close together. Both ears had been drilled—the right ear in the center of the lobe and the left in the upper part of the ear.

When Jim knew the sheriff was about to compliment him, he said, "Lloyd, I don't want it to get out that I'm good at this. I don't deny that I'm probably above average with a gun. But I want ye to know I'm trainin' myself, my horse, and my dog to hep you do somethin' that needs to be done. I just dread the day when I have to kill a man—when I can't see his ear or ain't standin' right so that I have to put a bullet in his heart."

"Jim, if I didn't have as much confidence in your dedication and courage to do the right thing at the right time as I have in your marksmanship, I wouldn't want you workin' for me. I just know if you can't go for the man's ear and it's a matter of life or death, you'll do what you gotta do and put the bullet in the man's heart!"

"Of course, Sheriff, ye can count on that!"

"Oh, by the way, go set up that dummy once more and let me see you drill his heart."

Jim drilled the heart dead-center five times straight!

"Jim, I've gotta go. I don't even need to see you do it with a rifle at 100 yards what you did with your Colt at 50. It won't hurt for you to practice it, though, and convince yourself. Drop by the office next time you're in DeWitt. I wanta sign you up as my deputy," the sheriff said as he headed for his car.

Jim had been working with the county sheriff for almost two years, helping him round up the runaways from jails and prisons. His marksmanship, his knowledge of the bottoms, and his way with his horse and dog impressed the sheriff greatly. In fact, Jim was not pleased with the reputation he was getting all over the county because Lloyd had written articles for the *DeWitt Enterprise* and allowed a story in the *Arkansas Gazette* with pictures of Jim and his dog. The sheriff seemed determined to make him and his horse, Star, and his dog, Buck, a legend. But Jim had told his father, the sheriff, and Marion Derrick that his work with the sheriff was only temporary.

Jim and Marion Derrick finished disking on Thursday afternoon and spent the last two hours preparing the machines for planting. Marion was putting in 1,000 acres of rice, the biggest investment he had made in farming since the end of the war in 1918.

In that third week of April, it seemed to Jim that Friday would never come. He could not keep his mind off Estelle! He wondered if he imagined her to be more than she really was. *Come Friday afternoon, would she be as pretty as he thought her to be a few nights ago at the dance? Was her facial beauty with that lovely dimple in her chin a creation of his own imagination? What will she think of me? What kind of man will she want to marry? Probably someone with a name, money, and education. Was her smile really meant to encourage me? Well, I've got one chance to find out, and I'll give it my best shot.*

It was a happy young man who saddled and mounted his frisky black horse and headed south on a warm spring afternoon. As Star cantered along, Jim hummed a few lines of "You Are My Sunshine" and whistled the tune of the last waltz he had shared with Estelle at the dance. Jim recognized the wooded area with the beautiful white house in the background, just as Estelle had described. He pulled off the dusty county road, and seeing to the east a crystal flowing stream coming from the pond that she had spoken of, he allowed Star to descend to it and drink. He urged the black on into the shade of the woods and ground-reined him in a grassy area for short-range grazing. Dismounting, Jim commanded, "*Stay!*" Looking to the gate in the backyard, Jim caught movement around the corner of the house. Estelle, wearing a bright blue dress, was walking toward the gate. She smiled and opened the gate, saying, "Hi, Jim! I see you are right on time. Is your horse okay? Does he need water on this warm day?"

"No, he drank from that stream flowin' out of the lovely pond yonder."

"Then come and have a seat in the swing there, and I'll get us a cold drink. Iced tea or lemonade?"

"How about a mixture of both, please?"

"Coming up," she announced as she stepped inside. She soon appeared and handed Jim one of the full glasses.

"Thanks, Estelle. Delicious!" Jim said after tasting it.

In a relaxed smile, Estelle acknowledged his expression. They sat in a comfortable silence for a time, and then Jim began moving the swing gently. She made an effort to match his timing. Jim noticed two horses grazing behind the garage and asked, "Who rides the palomino?"

"I do, Jim."

"Maybe we can ride together sometime," Jim suggested.

"Let's do! Next time we see each other, let's ride down and visit my mother. She lives two miles south of here with her husband and five children."

Jim was elated that she was willing to see him again. Hearing the gate close, Jim looked up to see a red-faced, bareheaded, middle-aged man coming toward them.

As the man was approaching, he hollered, "Now, Estelle who's this bright young sprout you're sparkin' with here?"

"Uncle Tom, I want you to meet my friend, Jim Tharp."

Jim stood and reached out to shake Tom's hand, noting that he extended his left hand because his right hand and wrist were missing. "I'm glad to meet ye, Mr. Miller."

"Now you just knock off the 'Mr. Miller' stuff. Just call me Tom."

As the three were standing in the yard, Jim saw a new, expensive automobile drive up and a nice-looking, middle-aged woman emerge with books under her arm. She approached, smiling, and extended her hand without an introduction. "Hello, I'm Mertice Miller. Jim, it is nice to meet you and have you at our supper table tonight. I guess you must have beaten your cousin George's time at the dance, because Estelle has said nothing about George, but she's certainly had some good things to say about you."

"It's good to meet ye, Mrs. Miller, and have this chance to get better acquainted with Estelle."

"You gentlemen just sit down now while Estelle and I finish up supper, and then we'll get to eating so you two young people can have a little time together. Come, Estelle, let's finish up what you've started, and then we'll call the men in."

Sitting together in the swing, Tom said, "Well, now, Jimmy Boy, tell me what life is like for you, where you hail from, and what you do."

Jim decided to say very little at this time, knowing Mertice would want the same information. "I live with my folks up in the LaGrue community, and I work for Marion Derrick on the rice farm. Papa sharecrops cotton for him, and I hep Papa with the cotton to pay for my room and board. I also hep Sheriff LaFargue round up runaways from jails and prisons."

"Yes, I've heard about you! You're the young feller working with his horse and dog to help the sheriff catch the bad guys!" Tom chuckled and slapped his leg.

Estelle appeared at the door and called, "It's ready, gentlemen! Come!"

Seated at the table, Mertice said, "Let me offer a prayer of thanksgiving: Father, we thank You for Your provisions in life and for Jim's presence at our table tonight. Be with us in our fellowship and guide Estelle and Jim in their friendship. We give thanks for health, freedom, and prosperity. In Jesus' name, Amen." After the food was passed, Mertice said, "Jim, tell us about your family and your interests in life."

"I live with my parents and three sisters on one of Marion Derrick's farms. My sister BettyLee is engaged to be married to your brother, Mrs. Miller. I hep Sheriff LaFargue round up runaways from jails and prisons. I work on Marion's rice farm keepin' up his machinery, plowin', plantin', and heppin' with the cattle. I do commercial fishin' in the spring and trap for mink in the winter. Also, I'm a scout for two timber companies: Anderson-Telly and Blackmon-Townsend. They pay me in timber that is downed or dyin' because of storms and disease. I log up the trees, raft 'em down the rivers, and sell 'em to the mills."

Mertice interrupted, "We've read about your work with the sheriff. It sounds rather dangerous. We'd like to hear more about it if you'd feel free to tell us."

Jim was uncomfortable for a few seconds, but he reckoned they were entitled to hear some things about his life. "We really haven't done a lot together. I'm still trainin' my horse and dog. Lloyd means to clean up the crime in the White and Arkansas River bottoms, and he's hired me to hep him. I know a lot about the White River bottoms, but Lloyd wants me to get down here in the Arkansas River bottoms and find the thickets and groves along roads and trails where runaways hide and ambush. They nearly always make for the bottoms when they break out, stealin' guns from stores, farms, or individuals on their way. My horse, Star, is learnin' to tell me with his snorts and nickers when danger is ahead. I need to watch his twitchin' ears and how he points 'em. And my dog is learnin' low growls and little low nips to indicate when somethin's ahead. It's fun to watch 'em work together."

"I saw a picture of your dog in the *Gazette*," Tom said. "I couldn't tell if he is a German shepherd dog or a wolf."

"Both!" Jim said. "His mama was a German shepherd and his daddy a wild wolf."

"I'll bet he's dangerous," Mertice said.

"Yes, he is. But that's the kind of animal we need when we get to trailin' a killer who's broke out of prison. I've tamed him some. He'll now let Mama and my sisters pet him without snarlin' at 'em. He's very intelligent, but I don't want him to become just a pet. When he bays a criminal, I want his snarls and growls to show dangerous teeth and his eyes to threaten violence. I won't let Buck tear a man apart, but I do want the guy to think that's what's gonna happen if he don't surrender."

Estelle said, "Jim, that kind of work sounds so dangerous! Aren't you afraid you'll be killed?"

"I can't afford to be afraid. Fear would mean I wouldn't be payin' attention to the horse or dog or listenin' for sounds and watchin' movements of the man who would wanta kill me."

"Do you plan to make this a lifetime career, working with the sheriff?" Estelle wanted to know.

"No, I don't. I want to buy me some land and raise cattle. I love net-fishin' the bottoms when they overflow from the floodin' rivers in late winter and spring. I plan to seine the lakes in late summer. I make good money trappin' minks and coons from December to the end of

February. But I've seen there's money in cattle, and I love to work with 'em."

"Well, Jim, you're already a busy man—rice farming, trapping, fishing, logging, and assisting the sheriff. Add cattle raising and haymaking to that, and no doubt you'll make money if you don't die a young man," Mertice said, smiling. "Say, it's time for dessert, but, Estelle, maybe you and Jim would like to be excused and visit awhile. Then when you come back, we'll serve your coconut pie before Jim goes home. Is that a good idea or not?"

Estelle nodded, and Jim said, "Sounds good to me."

"If you don't mind, Jim, I'd like to walk out with you and see your horse," Tom said.

"Me, too," Mertice said.

"Of course," Jim said.

Star snorted in recognition of his master as the four approached him. "Now, come on, boy; turn around here and meet some new friends." The black whirled, nickered, and then lowered his head to be petted.

"That's a horse of real quality," Tom said.

"Will he let me pet him?" asked Estelle.

"He'd better! Come on, Star, let the lady touch ye. Estelle, put yer hand up to his nose, let him nuzzle and sniff ye, and then ye can stroke his neck." Soon the black was enjoying her touch and smell and even licking her hand.

"Okay, Star, we'll get going but I'll visit with you later," Estelle said. Jim reached for her hand, and they entered the path that led to the pond. Jim judged the sun was still two hours high as they slowly approached the pond. He could see an arched bridge over the water and a row of weeping willows beyond the levee. Jim stopped on the bridge and leaned on the rail looking to the west. Under the willows, he could make out the bench Estelle had mentioned. He felt Estelle's arm slip in his and, almost in a whisper, she said, "I'm so glad you've come to visit me. And may I tell you that I enjoyed dancing with you a few nights ago?"

"Thanks. That's the way I feel, too!" Jim said. "How about if we go to that bench over there on the levee and sit and talk awhile? You heard about me at supper. I want to know about you—that's why I'm here."

"Jim, I hardly know where to start."

14

"Tell me about yer parents, yer early childhood, why ye're livin' with the Millers, if ye have a boyfriend, yer likes and dislikes, and anythang else ye wouldn't mind tellin' me."

Estelle began with a smile, "Well, I was born up in the Fairview community. My father was Harry Hughes, and my mother was Alma Best. My father died when I was five years old, leaving Mother with four children and nothing but a debt on a small farm. The sale did not even clear the mortgage, so the bank had to foreclose. I have three siblings— Mabel, Theo, and Mertice, named for my Aunt Mertice. With no money, Mother and we four children went to live with Grandpa and Grandma Best in the Fairview area. Grandpa Best raised cattle and hogs and farmed some. Being a justice of the peace, he was in court a lot, married couples, and settled many legal disputes. My mother is now Alma Wallace, having married again ten years ago to Franklin Wallace. Even after Mother remarried, we four children continued to live with my grandparents. When I finished the eighth grade in Fairview, Aunt Mertice took me under her wing; she had me come and live with her and Uncle Tom. She insisted I go to high school, but I only attended one year, finishing the ninth grade. Aunt Mertice got seriously ill that summer. By fall she was still sick and couldn't teach school, and I was needed to help keep house and take care of her. She paid me to do the work." Estelle paused, sighing and looking off. Jim wondered if she would go on with her story.

"But, Jim, I'm not really happy with Aunt Mertice and Uncle Tom. They treat me fine and pay me well. I'm allowed to drive their car, go see my loved ones, and go to town and shop. I can buy clothes and sew and ride the horse when I wish. While I know of nothing better right now than being with them, I know there has to be something better somewhere. I would love to go back and finish high school, but at eighteen, I guess I'd be embarrassed to be in classes with kids fourteen and fifteen."

"Ye've got a lot more education than I have. Ye talk as proper as if ye had already finished college. Ye have a better vocabulary than mine, and I know ye use better grammar."

"Jim, you said you quit school in the sixth grade, but I think you have done well with what schooling you've had. You have a lot of common sense. I think you already know where you want to go, what

15

you want to do, and how you will make something of your life. I knew the other night at the dance that I wanted to get to know you better. You have nothing to apologize for in the way you talk or act."

"Thanks, Estelle! I had a wonderful teacher, Miss Wilson, to thank for heppin' me learn to read, spell, and figger numbers. She begged me not to quit school. I never quit cuz I didn't like it. I knew Papa needed me and Henry to help him make the rice crop. Miss Wilson even come to the house and begged Papa and Mama to keep me in school. She said she saw possibilities in me that convinced her I should get a good education and make somethin' of myself. For a long time after I quit, she'd drop off books I liked—history, geography, and others. She even wrote me notes to subscribe to the *Gazette* and 'Read! Read! Read!' That paper still comes ever day and, like me, Papa likes to read it, too."

"Jim, I'm glad you are a reader. It shows up in your conversation. You are conversant on many subjects, and I notice that for someone without much formal education, you can put interesting sentences together. I like the way you describe things. Tell me why you are working with the sheriff and how long you think your work with him might last?"

"Uncle Henry Purdy told the sheriff about my way with guns and my skills in the woods, and then he mentioned to him what I was doin' with Star and Buck. I've enjoyed my time with Lloyd, but I dread the time I'll have to kill a person in this work. I know with the right conditions I can shoot a man's ears, but that will not always be possible. So when I get started on raisin' cattle and farmin', I just may tell the sheriff I'm done with heppin' him."

"Jim, I think helping the sheriff is a noble thing. I worry about the evil people you'll come up against. It concerns me greatly that you could face terrible danger in this work."

Such moving words and the tears in Estelle's eyes caused Jim to stand up and pull her to him. "Estelle, I'm glad ye care about me. I need to tell ye that I care about ye, too." Jim tightened his arms around her and continued, "I want us to become more than friends. I want time with ye to earn yore love and trust. I've never met anyone like ye. Before we go to the house, I want to hear what ye want in life, and I need to know if ye care for someone else or if I can continue to see ye."

16

Sitting next to Jim with the sun setting behind them, Estelle looked Jim in the eye and said, "Jim, I have no one I feel about as I do you. But I must tell you, I don't think I'll know what I want to do with my life until I find the Lord!"

"What do you mean by 'find the Lord'? Estelle, if you ain't found the Lord, who else has?"

"You don't understand, Jim. My Grandma Best knows the Lord personally, and I'm sure my mother does, too. Grandma showed me in the Bible where Jesus said, **Unless one is born again, he cannot see the kingdom of God**. I want to get 'born again, saved, converted to Jesus Christ.' I want my life to be lived according to His plan. Everything I do and every choice I make I want to be in accordance with His will."

Jim was deeply moved as Estelle finished in tears. "Well, Estelle, I hardly know what to say. I just hope when ye do find the Lord that He won't tell ye to have nothin' to do with me."

"Jim, the reason I don't think He'll tell me that is because I think He is the One who brought us together a few nights ago. And I want us both to see each other until we know what He wants of us."

"Now ye're makin' me feel good. Before we go, I wanta say this: even if I'm not a born-again Christian, I'll never stand in yer way of doin' what the Lord wants ye to do."

The night sounds were growing louder, causing Jim to say, "I heard an old owl hoot, and now I hear a whippoorwill callin'. So I guess we'll walk slowly to the house." With their arms about each other, they made their way up the slight incline through the woods. Star nickered as they neared the barn.

"Here they come, honey! Serve the pie, and I'll pour the coffee," Tom was heard to say as the two entered the back door.

"I hope you two have had a pleasant time," Mertice said.

"Very pleasant, Aunt Mertice! I feel Jim and I have had wonderful exchanges of information about each other, and I look forward to a continuing relationship."

"I hope y'all won't object if I tell ye that I wanta keep seein' your niece," Jim said.

"No, Jim, I was going to say to Estelle that I think she should encourage you to return here now and then," Mertice said.

17

Tom put in his word as well. "Ah, Jimmy Boy, you already seem like family!"

On the porch as he was getting ready to leave, Jim whispered, "This is the sweetest date I've ever had."

"Me, too! Except, unlike you, I've not had all that many."

"Got anythang in mind for our next one?"

"How about your riding Star down Sunday afternoon about 2:00, and we'll saddle the palomino and ride to Mother's place so you can meet my family."

"Great! And how much farther would it be to the Menard Landin' on the Arkansas River?"

"Another hour's ride."

"Then I'll see ye Sunday afternoon."

Holding Estelle in his arms, Jim said, "Now I have somethin' to look forward to."

"And I can hardly wait until Sunday afternoon."

Jim broke away, and at the gate he turned around to see Estelle still standing on the porch in the moonlight. He blew her a kiss, and he was thrilled when she returned it.

Jim mounted Star with a warm heart and bright hope for his future that he had not known before. As he rode northward, his spirits rose in anticipation of winning Estelle. *I don't wanta be a sharecropper or a lawman all my life. Maybe I can win Estelle over this spring, continue to work for Marion, hep the sheriff some, and earn enough money to buy more traps and fishin' stuff. Just might be able to get Estelle to marry me in late summer or early fall. Papa and Mama would let us live in with them 'til I could come up with the money to buy a piece of land. Then we could pitch a tent to live in.*

Because Jim was deep in thoughts of Estelle, time had flown by as Star covered the miles northward. Jim unsaddled the black and put him away for the night. As he undressed for bed, Jim reflected on the happiest day he could remember in all of his twenty years. He slipped into a deep sleep and rushed through a few fleeting dreams that included a lovely smiling face with a dimpled chin. He awoke to a cool, clear Saturday morning.

"What's on your schedule today?" Boge asked Jim at the breakfast table.

"Well, I probably need to check with Marian to see if he thinks the ground has dried out enough to use the machinery. If it hasn't, I plan to come back and take Star and Buck into the LaGrue bottoms for some trainin', unless there's somethin' I can do for ye."

"No. But how did it go with Estelle and the Millers last night?"

"Aw, Papa, better than I had imagined! I don't plan to move too fast, but I'm pretty sure Estelle is the one."

"Fine, son. I know you'll make the right choice, but don't drag your feet when you know for sure what you want."

Learning from Marion that the ground was still too wet to work, he returned home to find the sheriff waiting for him. "What's up, Lloyd?" Jim asked.

"I just hope you're free this morning, cuz we've got a dangerous man on the loose. We'll probably catch him at White River Bridge. Bring your dog, and I'll explain things on the way."

Jim knew he'd heard all the sheriff wanted the family to hear, so he said, "Give me a few minutes to put on my boots, get my gun and shells, and put Buck in yer truck."

On the way to the bottoms, Lloyd gave Jim the lowdown. "This bastard robbed a store in Stuttgart around 5:00 yesterday, raped the clerk, beat her badly, and thought he left her dead; then he stole her car. He was seen in Tichnor at 9:00 last night with a trailer containin' a boat and motor. If that is true, I believe we'll find his rig here at the Mouth of LaGrue."

"Yeah, I see his rig now," Jim said.

The two lawmen were soon launched and speeding their way southward. About 9:00, Lloyd slowed the boat and began drifting into a pier near the Bridge. When he shut the engine down, he said, "We'll likely find our man in Barney's Hole here, a restaurant, beer parlor, and gambling joint. Barney's helped me a lot in times like this. Before we go in, have the dog set down a little way from the door. We'll look through the door window and get the layout of things. Our target will be in farmer's overalls with blue and white stripes. He was armed with a shotgun, but who knows what else? You'll follow me in, and we'll both be ready."

Near the door, Jim said, "*Buck, set! Stay!*" Lloyd pushed the door open and stepped inside with Jim right behind him. Barney was off to the left. Jim could see the killer openly armed with a pistol. Lloyd spoke loudly. "I am the Sheriff of Arkansas County. You lowdown buzzard! You robbed and raped a woman and beat her up badly! I've come to arrest you and take you to jail. You can either put up your hands and we'll come and cuff you, or you can go for that gun and we'll make quick work of this whole thing." The man just stared.

Barney called out, "Lloyd, there's another person with him..." As Lloyd turned to hear Barney, Jim saw the man pull at his gun.

Jim's gun spoke. *Bang!* The killer screamed at Jim, "Damn you! You just blowed my head off." He kept cursing, moaning, and wiping blood.

"Barney, you picked a bad time to tell me someone else is with this rascal!" Lloyd said. "Now, if you can get us a rag with some oil, we'll doctor the guy's ear and be on our way to take him to jail."

"All I meant to say is that this guy's not alone. Sorry if I butted in, but fortunately your deputy was quick to take care of him. The man's lucky he just got his ear."

"You've got that right! Jim Tharp will either drill a man's ear or his heart."

The sheriff was trying to figure out how to get the stolen car returned. "Jim, do you have time to follow me in the stolen car to DeWitt?"

"Sure, Lloyd."

"And could we get your father to follow us and bring you back? If not, I'd be willin' to drive you back this afternoon."

"Let's go by the house and see if Papa can do this," Jim said. Boge came out, and learning all that had happened, assured the sheriff he'd follow them to DeWitt.

After jailing the rapist-thief, Lloyd invited Jim and Boge to the Freeman Restaurant for the noon meal. "Jim, you did perfect on your first try at an ear," the sheriff said. "You can see how it's to our advantage to bring a man in alive to stand trial than to have to kill him— more humane, too. And I knew you were the man to do that, cuz you never miss. Even the deputy that put me on to this trick could not take the ear ever time. But you'll know when to do the ear or the heart."

20

"Sheriff, I'm glad it happened the way it did today, but I don't want the reputation of being a gunslinger. I just know people will read about me doin' this, and it'll be all they wanta talk about when I'm around."

"Never mind, Jim. You and your horse and dog are already a legend, and it's for a good cause. The whole county is proud of you! Pretty soon, the whole nation will know about you."

When the sheriff paid for their meals, he also handed Boge a twenty. "Mr. Tharp, this will fill your gas tank and allow a little for your time. I'll settle with Jim the end of the month. Thanks, men! And, Jim, thanks for savin' my life! Glad you had your eye on the man when Barney called me."

The next morning Jim slept in later than he could ever remember. He rolled over and recalled that yesterday had been quite a day—he'd shot a hole in a man's ear. Then he remembered it was Sunday and he'd be seeing Estelle at 2:00. He jumped out of bed and was soon dressed. The place was quiet—the family would be at church. He went to the kitchen for some breakfast, finding the coffee still hot and the biscuits, butter, sausage, and gravy on the table. As he ate he took time to read the *Gazette* from the last three days.

Jim decided to haul Star in his truck rather than ride him to the Miller place. He also took Buck and his gun. Why? Just a feeling. He drove in their driveway a few minutes before 2:00. After ground-reining Star in the shade, he pointed to an oak with good shade and said to Buck, "*Set! Stay!*" Before he reached the back gate, Estelle came off the back porch wearing a brown riding outfit and a matching bonnet.

"Hi, Jim! You're on time, and I see you drove. I'll get Ella saddled," Estelle said.

"You bring her out near the tack room, and while I saddle her, I want ye to get acquainted with Buck."

"Oh, you brought your dog. Will he let me touch him?"

"He will after I talk to him. I'll have Buck ready for ye when ye come back."

Estelle left Ella standing in the barn hallway and returned to where Jim and the dog were, waiting as Jim told the dog, "Now, Buck, no growlin'! Be nice to this lady; let her touch ye." Turning to Estelle he

21

said, "Come on, let him smell yer hand. Now, rub between his ears and say a soft word or two. He's okay now, so I'll put yer saddle on Ella and lead her over here."

When Jim returned with the saddled palomino, he said, "Well, I see ye've tamed my wolf," noticing that Buck was lying at her feet enjoying her nice words to him. Jim helped Estelle mount, and they were soon riding side by side on the dusty county road going south toward her mother's home, with Buck running behind.

"The Sweeney's country store and post office are just a mile down the road," Estelle said. Jim had noticed all kinds of advertisements on fenceposts and oak trees—Garrett's Snuff, Prince Albert Tobacco, Coca Cola, and Orange Crush. "The Sweeneys are fine people, but they have to be careful when moonshiners, thieves, and river rowdies come around. Several times a month there are shootings. Aunt Mertice doesn't want me to come here alone, but I know she's not worried today because I'm with you."

"Nothin' to worry about! I'm wearin' my gun, and we have Star and Buck." When Jim saw the store, he called, "Go ahead, Buck! Lead the way!" Buck ran past them and stopped at the entrance of the driveway and waited, looking the place over. As the two riders walked their horses into the driveway, Buck moved nearer the store and sat and waited. He gave a low growl and looked at Jim.

"Estelle, direct yer horse over to that gate and let her stand still with ye stayin' mounted." Jim dismounted, led Star a few feet, and dropped his reins to the ground.

Two men burst through the screen door and ran across the porch and down the steps snickering. One said, "I told ye we could do it!" They stopped dead in their tracks when they came face to face with the armed man standing in their way. Ebrena Sweeney came out on the porch and called, "Is that you, Estelle?"

"Yes, Miss Ebrena. And I'm wondering if you're okay."

"I'm glad you're here, especially at this time. These two are up to no good. When I got the items they wanted, they let me know they were not paying. When I started to put the things back, they roughed me up some and called me some ugly names. I guess I'm just more angry than anything else."

22

Jim had heard enough. "Alright, ye rascals! Drop those bags there on the bottom step." When the men hesitated, Jim said, "Buck, *gittem*!" Like a flash of lightning, Buck was in their faces snarling and growling and showing teeth. Then Jim saw one of the men reach for his gun.

When Jim's gun spoke, the man grabbed his ear and cursed. "I've been shot! Might be dyin'!"

"Shut up!" Jim said. "Ye're not dyin'. I just shot yer ear, cuz ye wuz gonna kill my dog. Go for that gun agin, and I'll drill a hole in yer heart. You fellers have to learn ye can't come here and steal and abuse people. If ye want what's in them bags, go over and apologize to that lady and pay her whatever she tells ye. Otherwise, leave them bags, get out of our sight, and don't ever come back!" The man with the bleeding ear got money from his pocket and told his partner, "Go pay her!" The man apologized to Ebrena, saying, "We're sorry, ma'am. How much do we owe you?"

"$7.00," she said.

"Here's $10.00." He ran back down the steps, saying to his wounded buddy, "Let's get out of here!" They ran past Jim, giving Buck a wide berth.

Cleve Sweeney came through the door, and seeing the men running away, asked, "What's goin' on here; I thought I heard a shot!"

"You did, Cleve!" Ebrena told her husband all that had happened, ending with, "This man with Estelle took care of them. Estelle, y'all come on up on the porch for a visit. We wanta meet this gentleman and express our thanks. Cleve, get some cold drinks for all of us."

Jim first went to Estelle and asked, "Are ye alright?"

"Just a little shaken." He helped her dismount and tied Ella's rein to the post. Estelle introduced Jim to the Sweeneys, and while the four drank iced Colas, the Sweeneys and Jim got acquainted. Cleve had read about Jim's work in the papers and said, "Well, here you are at our place, and you demonstrated that talent with a gun that the whole country is hearin' about. Reckon we could use you 'round here pretty often."

When Jim and Estelle explained that they were on their way to see her mother, Ebrena said, "Please give Alma our love. We understand that she and Franklin are happy together."

23

As the two turned their horses off the county road onto a side road to head for the Wallace place, Estelle remarked, "Oh, Jim! What a frightening experience that was! I just knew that bad guy was going to kill Buck, and then I thought you had killed the man. As bad as it seemed, I was proud of you and proud of Buck. What a dog! He does exactly what you tell him."

Jim enjoyed visiting with Estelle's mother and the children. He loved Alma Wallace right off. He wondered if Franklin realized what a quality person he had in his wife. The children—the twins, Lorene and Dorene; Bernice; Buck; and Twyla—were cute, healthy, and lively. Jim was impressed with Estelle's attachment to her two-year-old half sister, Twyla. Buck was a handsome, curly-headed lad of six. All rallied around them when Jim and Estelle mounted their horses to leave. Alma assured them they were welcome to visit any time.

After they had ridden for over a half hour, Estelle asked, "Have you heard of the Menard Mound?"

"Yeah, if ye mean the Indian mound."

"Well, we'll soon see it up here on our right."

Jim could see the mound rising over 100 feet, and he was surprised to see brush and trees growing on top and all around it. "I reckon the Indians used it as a lookout."

"Yes, and for other purposes. The Arkansas River once flowed right where the Menard Bayou is now. You'll see that the Bayou bridge is not too safe."

Jim saw what she meant—large nails were sticking up and boards were missing here and there. He suggested they dismount and lead the horses across. Once across, one road led east, the other southeast. Estelle said the one east led to Garland Lake and then on to the Arkansas River Bridge; they would take the other one that led to the Menard Landing. Halfway to the river, Jim was told the lake to their right was called the Do-More Lake. Soon Jim saw a large opening ahead beyond the woods and realized the river was probably only about another half mile. Looking down on the swift-flowing river, they stopped their horses while Jim studied the view. A large thick growth of willows decorated the space reaching almost to the water's edge. "Estelle, let's ride down to those willows and leave the horses in that grove of taller willows that I would guess are only twenty yards from the river."

Estelle agreed. They rode across the dry sand to the willows, dismounted, and tied the horses to limbs. With Buck following close behind, they walked toward the river. Estelle pointed to a large old piece of driftwood that had been sawed from the butt of a giant-sized cypress. "Jim, we're looking at about all that's left of the historic old Menard Landing. That log is where people usually sit when they come here. It's where lovers come and sit. Businessmen sit here and make deals. Sightseers gaze up and down the river from this point. Hunters and fishermen rest here. Big steamboats used to land here with supplies for stores, log camps, and anyone who wished to buy food and hardware supplies in greater quantities. Shall we sit and look upriver or downriver?" she asked.

"Upriver first." They sat close on the log, Jim placing his rifle within easy reach. He told Buck, "*Set! Stay!*" Then he reached across and took Estelle's hand. "I'm sure enjoyin' the day with ye. I was proud of ye back at Sweeney's store—the way ye took that run-in with them rowdies. You didn't panic or fall to pieces. And I loved yer mother and her children. I can see that ye love children, and I 'specially liked the way ye handled little Twyla. I even like the way ye ride a horse."

"Thank you, Jim. I love being with you, too. Since Friday night, I've hardly been able to wait to see you."

Jim sat thinking about some things he was tempted to say, but decided it would be wise to wait until later. Looking upriver, he blurted out, "The old Arkansas River! The farthest up I've seen it is Little Rock, but I know it goes on into Oklahoma and beyond."

"Jim, would you want to hear statistics on the Arkansas River from my studies in American Geography?"

"Yeah, let me hear the straight 'bout this old river. While ye talk, I'll continue to watch that speck way upriver that's still about two miles away."

"Maybe I'd better wait until you know what's coming down."

"Naw, please go ahead; I can listen and watch, too."

"The Arkansas River is 1,450 miles long," Estelle began. "It's the longest tributary in all the Mississippi-Missouri system. It begins in Leadville, Colorado, and drops 10,000 feet in its first 125 miles. It carves out a lot of beauty in Colorado, including the Royal Gorge, then winds its way through Kansas where it irrigates millions of acres of wheat, and then flows into northern Oklahoma where it is joined by several rivers—the Canadian, Cimarron, Neosho, and Verdigris. Then it comes into Arkansas near Fort Smith and finally empties into the Mississippi (Estelle turned and pointed downriver) 600 miles north of New Orleans and about 12 miles from where we are right here."

"Thank you, teacher—Miss Estelle! I really learned a lot from that. I thought ye were readin' at first, then I realized ye had really learned what ye wuz sayin'. I have a few questions for ye, teacher. But I see that paddle boat with two men will soon be even with us, and I think it's gonna pull in here. If so, just relax and let me and Buck handle things."

"Buck, go down near the water!" The dog moved and was still ten yards from the landing when Jim called, "*Stay!*" Buck sat on his hind quarters and watched the two men land their boat and pull it up on the bank a ways. Sitting back down on the boat, the men watched the man and woman on the log and studied the dog. Finally, they got out of the boat and walked back and forth on the sandbar, never getting far from their boat. Jim called in a low voice, "What ye think, Buck?" Buck gave a few low growls. When the two men split, one walking upriver and the other one downriver back and forth, they met at the boat and began crowding Buck. The dog bristled and growled louder.

Jim stood, reached for his rifle and levered a shell from the magazine. "*Steady, Buck!*" he called. The two wheeled around and returned to their boat, jumped in, pushed off, and headed downriver.

"It worked, didn't it, Jim?"

"I reckon so."

"Got any thoughts about what they were up to?"

"No tellin'—maybe a robbery, killin' me and takin' you, or it could be they wuz just tired of the river and wanted to rest awhile. It's more likely they had mischief in mind. Else they'd have looked up and saw an armed man and would have said, 'Hey, feller, nothin' to worry about. We're just gonna rest awhile and be on our way.' But I'm glad I didn't have to drill an ear or kill one of 'em."

"I am, too! But I sure do feel safe with you!"

"I'm glad. Let's turn around and set facin' downriver, okay?"

"Sure!" The two men were already disappearing around the Menard Bend.

26

"It sure is peaceful here! Estelle, I can't tell ye how much I've enjoyed these two hours. But that sun is droppin' and I reckon we'd better think about mountin' up and gettin' back outa these bottoms."

As Estelle was untying Ella's halter rope, Jim thought this was his moment. Walking up behind her, he slipped his arm around her. "There's just one thing I want to do before we mount up," he whispered.

Estelle whirled around and put her arms around Jim. "I sure want to know what that is." Jim kissed her, and when he sensed no resistance, he made it a long one.

"I guess I want to say one more thing before we go. Estelle, I'm quite sure I'm fallin' in love with ye!" Her smile and nod gave him at least some assurance he had not said it too soon.

After mounting Ella, she looked down at Jim and smiled, saying, "Thank you for what you did and for what you said; this is the most wonderful feeling I've ever had."

Jim rode alongside Estelle, holding her hand, until they reached the woods. Then he said, "*Lead, Buck!* You follow Buck, my dear, and I'll bring up the rear."

The sun was setting as they rode into the Miller place. While unsaddling both horses, Jim said, "I wanta see ye again soon. Here's what I been thinkin' about—Papa, Mama, and the girls wanta meet ye. I'd like to come for ye on Friday afternoon, say 'bout 2:00, and take ye to our house for supper. George and BettyLee will be with us. Saturday mornin' the men will hitch the mules to the wagon, and we'll take our tents and go out to the Mouth of LaGrue near White River to camp out. We could fish a little on Saturday, and I'd show ye where I net fish and trap. All of us would stay there Saturday night, and after lunch on Sunday we would break camp and go home. I'd drive ye back here on Sunday evenin' before dark. I hope ye won't mind campin' out."

"Jim, I'd love it! And I can hardly wait to see you on Friday afternoon."

When everything was cared for at the barn, Jim and Estelle walked arm in arm to the back porch. Jim took Estelle in his arms and kissed her. She caressed his face with both hands and said, "There's no doubt in my mind that I love you, and I'm so happy you are falling in love with me!"

"Estelle, I cannot tell ye how hard it is to say good night."

"Same here, but I have Friday and the weekend to look forward to."

"Good night, sweetheart, I'll see ye in a few days."

"Good night, my love, see you Friday afternoon."

Boge got up early on Monday morning hoping the weather would allow him to start plowing. He needed to break 30 acres for the amount of cotton he wanted to raise this year. He knew Marion and Jim were hoping for clear weather all week to plant their thousand acres of rice. While they'd ride expensive tractors to get their work done, Boge would plod behind mules. After plowing the ground, he would run the harrow over the clods to break them down. On some land he would need to run a float for leveling. Finally, he would use a single-row planter pulled by one of the mules.

Boge looked out the window and was glad the stars were shining. He hoped clear weather would hold, for he didn't want to wait until the middle of May to get the seed in the ground. He finished reading his three chapters in the Bible and went to the kitchen for breakfast.

"Sorry, Papa; I should have waited for you to begin breakfast, but I know Marion is expectin' me early, so I jumped ahead here."

"Fine, son. Looks like it's clear out there for y'all and me to get started. Well, how did things go with Estelle yesterday?"

"Great! We stopped by Sweeney's store at Nady on our way to visit her mother and ran into a little trouble."

"What kind of trouble?"

"A couple of rowdies had roughed up Mrs. Sweeney, had refused to pay for some stuff they got, and were gettin' away just as Estelle and I rode up on our horses. I knew they were the wrong kind when I saw 'em runnin' down the steps. Mrs. Sweeney called out from the porch that they were stealin' things. I told 'em that if they wanted the stuff in the bags they would have to go and apologize to her and pay up. When they weren't goin' to, I told Buck to *gittem*. Buck went for 'em viciously. When I saw the guy go for his gun to kill Buck, I drilled his ear."

"Well, son, that's markin' two fellers in two days. What happened then?"

28

"Just like the killer at the Bridge, he started cussin' and ravin'. I told 'em again that if they wanted to leave they'd have to go and apologize to the lady and pay up. When they did that, I let 'em go."

"How did Estelle take all of that?"

"Like a trooper. She controlled the palomino. I doubt if the horse had ever been around guns. Mr. Sweeney came out and expressed appreciation for my help. Then we rode over to the Wallace's and had a nice visit with Estelle's mother and her five children. When we left there, we rode out to Menard Landin'. It was a good day. Papa and Mama, I know I'm in love with Estelle, and I know she's in love with me. She's really pleased about the invitation to come up this comin' weekend and go campin' with us. I'm to pick her up at 2:00 Friday afternoon."

"Estelle sounds like a wonderful girl," Ophelia said.

"She is, Mama. I can't wait for you two and the girls to meet her."

Boge said, "Son, we're lookin' forward to meetin' Estelle. We're glad you've found someone who will make you a good wife. Life will be different for you now that you've found the right one. Lookin' forward to marriage gives a man energy, joy, and purpose. Mama and I want you to be just as happy as we've been in our marriage."

"Thanks, Papa and Mama." As he got up from the table, he went around and kissed his mother and hugged his father. "I thank God for ye both and all ye've done for me. I'll get goin' and see ye tonight."

Jim drove into the barn just as Marion finished oiling and fueling the tractors. "Glad you are early, Jim. How about you takin' the west section and I'll take the north. Great weather to start the week. I'll watch for you when you are empty. Just hold steady and I'll be out and refuel you. I hope we can finish midweek so you can take the equipment and finish your Dad's plowin' and diskin'."

"Marion, I can't thank ye enough for the way ye treat Papa."

On Wednesday afternoon, when Boge saw Jim coming with the new tractor, he grinned and waved at his son. When Jim shut the tractor off, he said, "Now, Papa, unhook the mules, go and unharness them, and let 'em out to pasture. Then lie down and rest and get you a good nap. I'm here to give ye a break!"

At the table that night, the girls wanted to know when they would get to meet Estelle. Jim teased them, saying that he was afraid to allow them to see Estelle, lest she wouldn't want any more to do with him. "No, I'm kiddin'. Here's the plan: Mama and Papa have invited her up for supper Friday night. We'll all go campin' Saturday and Sunday, and she'll go with us. I'll take her home Sunday night."

BettyLee said to the girls, "You'll just love Estelle. She's the prettiest and nicest girl on Little Prairie."

Jim finished breaking and disking his father's cotton field on Thursday night. At the supper table, Boge said, "I'm glad the sheriff didn't come and take you away to shoot some bad feller's ear before you got that all done. Now I can start plantin' tomorrow mornin'. I oughta be through by Monday night."

On Friday afternoon, Jim and Estelle arrived at his parent's place at 3:30. "Just you wait, Estelle! Mama, BettyLee, Hollis, and Jenny are without a doubt at the door now waitin' to see ye. Of course, ye know BettyLee, but the rest are dyin' to lay eyes on ye. They've heard so much about ye." By the time the couple got out of the pickup, Hollis and Jenny were just inside the gate. Estelle stopped before them, saying, "I just know you are Hollis and you are Jenny." She hugged them both, and they clung to her all the way into the house where BettyLee introduced her to her parents. Both Boge and Ophelia were profuse in their expressions of welcome and love. Then BettyLee had her moment with Estelle. After they hugged, BettyLee said, "You probably know that George and I are gettin' married."

"Yes, I heard. How wonderful!"

At the supper table, Boge thanked the Lord for the food and for the joy of having Estelle with the family, and he asked the Lord to give them all a great weekend of recreational and spiritual blessing. Estelle could hardly believe the quantity and quality of food waiting for them to enjoy—three kinds of meat, several vegetables, and four kinds of pie.

George Best arrived in time for the desserts. Jim and George were introduced—they had been anxious to meet. Both sensed that they would become inseparable for the rest of life.

The Tharp-Best caravan, composed of two motor vehicles and one wagon pulled by a team of mules, arrived at the Mouth of LaGrue about midmorning on Saturday. Boge picked the place for the tents and pointed out where Jim and George could unload the tables and build a fire. The men found firewood and pitched three tents, and Ophelia cooked the noon meal and called for the girls to prepare iced tea and lemonade.

Jim took Estelle for a boat ride, paddling out to White River. On the way, Jim explained, "Here in these bottoms, when the river floods, I fish with heart-and-lead nets and catch schools of fish for sellin'. But before the water floods these woods, I need to pick out my sites and clean out brush and old dead logs so the nets will rest on the bottom and the webbin' will not be tangled by limbs and bushes." When they reached the river, Jim headed upstream first.

"What towns are upriver?" Estelle asked.

"Clarendon and Des Arc—there aren't many towns upriver and almost none downriver until the White and Arkansas run together and then merge with the Mississippi. On the big river, we have Rosedale and Greenville and bigger cities for 600 more miles all the way to New Orleans."

Landing back at the Mouth, Jim helped Estelle out of the boat and promised to take her up the banks of the LaGrue later that afternoon to show her where he trapped for minks and coons and where he scouted timber for Anderson-Telly.

The campout gave Estelle a realization of how well she was received by the Tharp family, and it was a time of bonding with Jim and a deepening of their love. She was pleased with the freedom that Jim felt in sharing his plans for the future—showing her his trapping, fishing, timbering, and hunting territories and sharing with her about land, cattle, and farming. She could see that he was very realistic in planning the costs of housing, food, transportation, and equipment for pursuing all of his interests.

Estelle drank in all the information Jim gave on trapping the LaGrue Bayou and fishing the overflow and rivers. "With a carbide light fixed to my cap, I can make out the shinin' of a coon's eye over 100 yards away. I've learned the difference between that shinin' and the shinin' of a star. That's why I don't night-hunt on a clear night; I need a cloudy night to do head lightin'."

Their relationship so deepened during that day that in their good-night moment Jim held her and said, "I reckon I'd better forewarn ye that when I take ye home tomorrow night, I'm gonna ask ye a very important question." He then paused to study the effects of his remark.

31

"Oh, Jim!" she said, then grew silent a few seconds. "I'll be honest with you; I was hoping to hear something like this pretty soon. I've already lost my heart to you, so you might as well know now what my answer will be."

Reluctantly, the couple parted to retire to their respective tents. Overwhelmed with the prospects of his future with Estelle, Jim lay down on his cot before George occupied the one across from him. He soon drifted off to sleep and could hardly believe it was almost sunup when he awakened. Hearing his parents talking as they prepared breakfast, he dressed and stepped out of his tent just as Estelle and BettyLee were returning from the relief tent. "Good mornin', ladies!" he called, running up to them and hugging them both.

BettyLee said, "Brother, I'm excited about what I hope will be a double weddin' sometime this summer or fall! Of course, I understand you two are not officially engaged, but I wanta tell ye—I'll have yer hide if ye don't go through with yer feelin's 'bout this girl!"

"Don't worry, Sis. It's gonna happen!"

After breakfast, the two young couples in love went fishing and caught bass, crappie, bream, and catfish. The boys and Boge cleaned them, and Ophelia fried the fish for the noon meal. The only disappointment among them came when they learned Estelle did not care to eat fish, though she had caught the largest one.

Eight happy campers loaded the wagon on that lovely spring afternoon and headed up and out of the LaGrue bottoms. After arriving back at the Tharp place, everyone gathered around Estelle and smothered her with loving goodbyes before she and Jim climbed into his pickup and headed south to the Miller's home.

A mile down the road, Estelle slid over next to Jim, and taking his free hand, said, "Darling, I've had the time of my life with you and your dear family this weekend. For the first time in my memory, I feel I have something to live for and dream about."

"When we get to the Millers, I've got somethin' to ask ye," Jim said.

"Do I need to wonder what that will be?"

"Is this somethin' I'll need to ask yer mother first?"

"No, if it's what I hope it is, you'd better ask me first. Then we can go see Mother."

Pulling into the Miller's driveway, Jim said, "Before we unload yer things and before the sun sets, let's go down to the bench under the weepin' willows for this, okay?"

"Sure!" They hurried toward the pond holding hands. Seated on the bench, Estelle dreamily said, "Just the right place for this!"

Jim slipped to one knee, looked directly into Estelle's eyes, and said, "Estelle, I love ye, and I'm askin' ye to be my wife!"

Estelle's eyes were flooding with tears as she tried to catch her breath. "Oh, Jim! I believe God sent you into my life, and although I don't yet know Him as I long to, I want to say that I love you and will be happy to be your wife!" As the gravity of the question and her answer hit Estelle, she began shaking and sobbing. As she regained control of her emotions, they both stood and she enfolded Jim in her arms.

"Sweetheart, I hope those are tears of joy!"

"Of course they are! I know I'm the happiest woman in the world!"

"Well, I have another question for ye. Just how soon will ye be willin' to marry me?"

This seemed to sober the dark-haired beauty, and she sat back down on the bench, pulling Jim to the seat with her. "Jim, I'll tell you how I feel. You already know that I'm not happy living and working here with Aunt Mertice and Uncle Tom. My aunt will be through with her school term in a few weeks, but I don't have to wait until then. I feel free to marry you anytime, but I know we have to be realistic about finances, our work schedules, and living situations. I have $300, and I will buy material for a wedding dress and make it myself. After I pay for the material, I want us to use the rest of my money wherever it will be needed."

"I agree that we do have to be realistic. I've saved up $700. We're almost into the month of June. I'll soon be waterin' rice and walkin' levees for Marion. I'll have a week or two off in August before the harvest in September. Once we are married, Papa and Mama and the girls all want us to move in with them, and I'm willin' for us to do that for a few weeks. After the harvest, I should have enough money to make a down payment on a piece of land. If necessary, we can pitch a tent, put a floor in it, fix it where we can heat it, and live comfortably for awhile. Later on we can put up a cabin. I'll come out of the harvest with several hundred dollars. It'll only be a couple of months before I'll be trappin' mink and coons—that always brings in a few thousand dollars. Honey, I don't see any problem if ye don't mind livin' with my family for a few weeks."

"Not at all, Jim! But don't forget my small amount of money. Let's use it..."

"No! I'll have enough money to buy me a new weddin' suit, take care of a week of honeymoon in a nice hotel, pay the justice, and get some groceries. So you go ahead and get yer dress and whatever else ye want. But as the head of the house, I'll pay the other bills."

"Then shall we wait until after the harvest for the wedding?"

"I don't wanta wait that long. How about the end of August? You look on the calendar for the date, and then I'll go make arrangements with Sibley Jones, the Justice of the Peace, to do the ceremony that evenin'. After the ceremony, we'll head for what I think is the nicest hotel in Arkansas right up there in Stuttgart, just a little over an hour's drive away."

The sun was setting when the two stood and held each other for a long time. Estelle finally stirred and looked into Jim's face and said, "I don't think I've ever told you that I know you are the most handsome man and the kindest and sweetest person in all the world! And I'm so glad to be madly in love with you and can hardly wait until you are my husband!"

They walked arm in arm back to the truck to unload Estelle's things, and Jim walked her to the back porch. Embracing her, he said, "I can hardly wait until you are Estelle Tharp!"

"Nor can I! But we'll try, and we will!"

"Yes, one more kiss and I'll go floatin' away home on the cloud ye've lifted me onto tonight."

"And I'll dream about what you just said."

"Good night, my love!"

"Good night, my soon-to-be husband!"

Jim drove northward almost oblivious to his surroundings. *My soon-to-be husband, she said. Can it be? Three months ago I didn't know she existed. What a spring this has been! The dance, the date, and the hours on the levee under the willows. The shootin' at the store. The visit with her mother and family. The time on the river. Our first kiss. The campout on the Mouth. And tonight—our engagement and agreement on a time for the weddin'. Am I dreamin'? Have I moved from reality into what they call fantasy? If so, I don't wanta wake up. If ever I wanted anythang, it's to take this woman, Estelle, and love, honor, and have her for the rest of my life!*

2 *"The Highest Halls of Human Happiness"*

Alma Wallace was delighted to grant permission and give her blessing for the marriage of her daughter Estelle Hughes to Jim Tharp. The date had been set for Friday evening, August 31, 1926. As the couple left the Wallace place, Jim reminded Alma, "Now we'll expect all of you at the reception on the first Sunday night of September at the farm of Marion and Peggy Derrick up at LaGrue."

Back at the Millers, Mertice asked, "What did your mother think about your getting married? But come to think of it, you didn't ask for my permission or my blessing!"

"Well, Miz Miller," Jim said, "We want yore blessin', but since ye're not Estelle's mother, I didn't think it was necessary to get yer permission. The Derricks will host a celebration on the first Sunday night of September, and we sure hope you and Tom will be there."

Neither Mertice nor Tom responded to Jim.

As Jim and Estelle drove northward, Jim asked, "Do ye think yore aunt is upset with us?"

"I don't care if she's mad at me; I just don't want her upset with you. But let's not worry about Aunt Mertice."

Boge and Ophelia were hosting a special supper to celebrate Jim and Estelle's engagement. Guests included George and BettyLee, Marion and Peggy Derrick, Lloyd and Irene LaFargue, Jim's sister Dee, and Henry and Oda. Decked out in new outfits, Hollis and Jenny were helping their mother serve.

Boge made a glowing speech in his reference to Estelle, and he spoke proudly of Jim. After expressing delight at "the presence of folks most dear to all of us," he led in a prayer of thanksgiving. Estelle was moved by his words, and his blessing on the couple brought tears to the eyes of several there.

Jim stood and said, "I feel I want to express my thanks to God for the family members here and my wonderful Christian parents. They raised us kids to be respectful, learn, obey the law, and love the Lord. I'm thankful for their example of livin' and the sacrifices they made for us. But while I'm not the Christian I need to be, I do praise God for bringin' this beautiful, wonderful woman into my life. The first time I saw her—'bout three months ago now—I felt somethin' for her that I just couldn't shake and didn't want to. I'm so glad and thankful that she felt somethin' for me. Now we both are grateful to Papa and Mama for this gatherin'. It is so good to have my bosses and their wives—the Derricks and the LaFargues—with us, as well as my sister Dee, and my brother, Henry, and his wife, Oda. Of course, ain't no way I can tell my sisters Hollis, Jenny, and BettyLee how much I love 'em." Then, looking at George, he finished by saying, "And I feel sure I've found another brother in George Best."

Estelle felt it was her moment to speak. She was wearing the last new dress her Aunt Mertice had bought her, and her shiny black hair bounced around her shoulders as she stood to speak. "Papa and Mama Tharp, I know the Lord has blessed me in allowing me to fall in love with your wonderful son Jim and to be here in this gathering tonight with his loved ones and friends who are so meaningful in his life and who will become so in mine. There's a sweet spirit in this home, and I think we all feel it. I'd just say it's the Spirit of the Lord!—a Spirit of love, grace, kindness, and integrity. I feel so fortunate to become a part of Jim's life and yours. Thank you for your warm acceptance of me."

Hollis and Jenny went into action with Ophelia's direction, and soon the guests were filling their plates with roast beef, stewed potatoes, green beans, wilted lettuce, sliced tomatoes, and okra. The girls poured the drinks—iced tea, lemonade, or coffee. Ophelia had baked both biscuits and corn muffins and several pies—apple, raisin, coconut, and Jeff Davis.

Peggy said, "Jim and Estelle, we've brought the 1,500 reception invitations; we're expecting a big crowd. Lloyd needs 500, and we need more than 300 to mail."

Marion spoke up, "Yeah, we really expect this gatherin' to be about the biggest celebration ever held here on Little Prairie. We believe in Jim and Estelle. The community and the whole county has several reasons to celebrate—Jim's work with the sheriff, his choice of a beautiful wife, and their promisin' future. Peggy and I are honored to host this thing."

Sheriff LaFargue added, "I want to say somethin' at that gatherin' about Jim's value as a lawman helpin' me clean up the county, 'specially the violence and crime in the river bottoms. I'll try not to embarrass him, but the people oughta know about his skill in savin' my life and catchin' the bad guys."

Henry was more effusive in expressing a love for his brother and in welcoming George and Estelle into the family than anyone expected.

Jim and Estelle both expressed their gratitude to Marion and Peggy for hosting the reception and for all the hard work it represented.

On the way back to the Millers, Estelle said, "Jim, I thought I was braced for the marriage ceremony, but I didn't anticipate anything like this celebration promises to be. I can't imagine a thousand people showing up for us…for you. I know I'll agree with all they will say about you."

"I don't reckon it's somethin' we can put a stop to."

"Do you think we'll need to wear our wedding clothes?" Estelle asked.

"I reckon so. I'll just hate puttin' on that necktie again; the weather will likely be hot."

"If it's hot, you can take your coat off. Why don't we just decide to enjoy it and not dread it?"

"Might as well, I guess," Jim said.

As they kissed good night on the back porch, Estelle asked, "Was it Shakespeare or one of the other poets who said that 'parting is such sweet sorrow'? I'm feeling sweet on you, but parting is truly sorrowful. I'm just glad about our future together!"

They kissed again, and Jim pulled away with a "Good night, my love."

"Good night, sweetheart," Estelle said.

On the way home, Jim reflected on some of the things they had discussed. *Estelle wants me to meet her Grandma and Grandpa Best and then her Uncle Hay. She thinks we'll be able to borrow all the money we need from her uncle for land, cattle, and equipment for farmin'—all at a low rate of interest. And that will be okay if it comes to that. But I just might work it so that, after the harvest, we can get a small piece of land,*

*put up a tent, and buy some furniture and more traps and fishin' tackle—
all without borrowin'.*

The weeks passed as Jim worked with his horse and dog,
exploring and getting more familiar with the more salient spots in the
Arkansas River bottoms. He found time to get better acquainted with his
future brother-in-law George Best. He had gone with Estelle to meet the
Best grandparents and Uncle Hay, who assured him of loans "below
bank interest." Jim kept watching for land to buy. The third week of July
found Jim and Estelle in DeWitt buying a wedding suit for him and lace
for her dress that she was making.

Back at the Millers, Tom told Jim and Estelle that he heard Tom
Monk wanted to sell his small piece of land up in White River bottoms.
"Ross Morgan could tell you more if you're interested."

"We are definitely interested, aren't we, Jim?" Estelle asked.

"You bet! It's early; why don't we drive over and talk to Ross
now?"

At the Morgan place, Jim and Estelle were welcomed warmly.
"Mertice told me a week ago y'all were gettin' married. Flossie and I are
happy for you. Yeah, the Monk property is just north of us here, and the
Anderson-Telly land is between us and Monk's. The land he wants to
sell has 20 acres, 5 on the prairie and then 15 slopin' into the bottoms.
Best of both worlds—grass for cattle and good soil for cotton, corn, or
whatever. It's also close to good commercial fishin' territory, trappin',
and huntin'. I see it as an ideal place for you. The property has a good
large house, set up on six feet of blocks cuz of floodin'. You'll have to
drill a well and a pump likely. I would think he'd want $5.00 an acre.
Wanta go up and see it?"

"Yeah, maybe tomorrow," Jim said. "It's gettin' a little late in
the day now."

"Well, I know Estelle rides Tom's palomino, and I can have two
horses saddled for us in the mornin' so ye won't hafta haul yore horse
down. Why don't y'all come at 8:30, and we can be back in the early
afternoon," Ross suggested.

"I'll have us a meal on the table around 1:30," Flossie said.

"Thanks, Ross and Flossie. Sounds great. See y'all at 8:30 in the
mornin'."

"Jim, it will be so wonderful to have our own place, won't it?"

"It will, darlin'. 'Specially that close to my work of trappin', fishin', and timberin'. I can still work with Lloyd and start runnin' a few cattle. We'll just have to see what costs will be involved bringin' the place up to livin' standards—drillin' a well and pump, fixin' up a house that ain't been lived in for awhile, and who knows what else. Just bein' realistic."

"I know, but even if we have to borrow from Uncle Hay, let's go for it if Monk is fair in his price."

"We'll decide after we've seen the Monk property. I'll meet ye at 8:30 in the mornin' at Ross's place," Jim said, as he kissed Estelle goodbye.

The August morning was warm as Ross led Jim and Estelle on horseback through timber, then through prairie, and finally out to an opening. They stopped their horses between two large cedar trees and looked at a house setting high on concrete blocks. They dismounted, walked across the bare yard, climbed the seven steps to the porch to get to the front door, which was closed tightly but unlocked. Upon entering, they found a large room—space enough for two bedrooms and a large living room. The room had two big windows on the east and a row of four shorter windows on the west. In the southwest corner of the high ceiling, they saw an opening for a stovepipe. Walking through an opening leading to the next division of the house, they found a room that was long but not as wide as the first room—a kitchen likely, for it had a hole in the ceiling for another stovepipe. The room was large enough for a stove, some cabinets, and a long table with chairs, and there were windows on the west and north walls. At the northeast corner of the house, a door opened to steps leading to the ground. Walking around the outside, they noticed a mature, healthy pin oak tree to the west of the house and a persimmon grove on the east side of the yard.

Jim asked, "Estelle, can we make this livable?"

"Of course! With some hard work—caulking the living room floor boards, doing a lot of cleaning, and putting down a well—I see possibilities. Look to the north there; we can have a wonderful garden. We can clear out some of these persimmon trees and have a nice, grassy yard. Down there to the east, before the sloping begins, you can have a barn, a smokehouse, a tool room, and a shed large enough for cars, trucks, tractors, and other equipment. Of course, we'll need an outside toilet. It looks like you'll have to clear a lot of land for farming cotton and corn and putting in an orchard."

Jim asked Ross, "Can I raise hay on that prairie land?"

"You can!—and cotton, if you wish. But that bottom land will produce even greater cotton and corn."

"Estelle, have we seen enough to make Monk an offer?"

"I think so, Jim."

"Ross, do we have time to ride by Monk's place?" Jim asked.

Looking at his watch, Ross replied, "Yeah, it's only 9:00, and it's an hour's ride over there. I'm sure we can still get back at 1:00 even if we ride out to the boundaries east later on to show you the bottom land."

The three mounted up and Ross led the way northward. Soon he pointed to a dry slough and said, "Here's the line separatin' Monk's land from Tom Miller's. Tom raises cotton and corn on the bottom land over there." They soon passed the house in which the tenant lives—a decent place, Estelle thought. Then Ross led the way west through a wooded stretch that led to the familiar county road. He pointed across the road and up an incline to a shack with a rusty, tin roof. "There's the Monk's house."

Jim took the lead, riding up the weedy incline to the house. An old Model T coupe was parked near the rotten steps leading up to the porch of the seedy-looking place. He saw that Ross and Estelle intended to remain on their horses, so he pointed to an area shaded by a large oak. "Wait in that shade. I shouldn't be long."

Jim made his way across a porch with squeaky boards and knocked loudly. A female voice called, "Just a minute, comin'." Through the screen door he could see a stringy-haired woman.

"Ma'am, my name is Jim Tharp. I'm interested in yore small place over here on the edge of the White River bottoms. I hope it's for sale."

"I'll call Art. Just a minute." Jim waited several minutes.

"Yeah, I'm Art Monk," a sleepy voice said from the inside. "Gimmie a minute to get my shoes." Jim would have sat in the old swing while he waited if he had thought it was safe. Eventually Mr. Monk appeared, looking rumpled. "Yeah, so ye thinkin' 'bout buyin' my place over there?"

"Yes, I heard it was for sale. I need to know how many acres it has, if there's a well and pump on it, if it's in the clear or has a lien on it, and how much ye're askin' for it."

"Can't say I'm dyin' to sell, but I might consider it if the price is right. The land is in the clear, and naw, there ain't a well or pump. It's 20 acres—five on the prairie and 15 slopin' down in the bottoms. I figger it's worth $6.00 a acre."

"Mr. Monk, I'm prepared to offer ye $5.00 an acre, cash money, since the land has no well or pump and the property will need a lot of cleanin' up and clearin'. I'm gettin' married in a few weeks, and I want a place of my own. My offer is good for another month, if ye wanta think it over."

"Naw, I reckon I'll take ye up on that," Monk said.

"How about I pick you and your wife up here day after tomorrow at 8:00, and we'll go to the courthouse in DeWitt to make it a legal transaction? I'll likely be able to bring ye back here before 5:00."

"We'll be ready at 8:00 day after tomorrow."

"Thank ye, Mr. Monk," Jim said.

"Thank you, Mr. Tharp."

Jim picked his way across the rickety porch and mounted his horse, saying, "Estelle, it looks like we're gettin' the place for $5.00 an acre. Closin' the deal day after tomorrow."

"Oh, honey, I'm glad!"

"Congratulations, Jim! I think you and Estelle are investin' wisely. Now let's go back and ride through the eastern part of your place. We'd ride the northern boundary, but it's just too thorny and dangerous with only a deer or pig trail. We'll go up near the house and ride the southern boundary all the way to the southeast corner and then head for my place. Flossie will be waitin' with dinner."

As they rode through the property, Jim spied several oak, cypress, sycamore, elm, ash, and gum trees. "Virgin timber, I think."

"Yeah, all of it. It'll be tough tryin' to farm this land at first because of all them stumps to bump into with the plows. But in a year or two, it will get easier," Ross said.

Later at the Morgans, they sat down to a spread of pork chops, fried potatoes, green beans, slaw, and both cornbread and biscuits. Ross said a blessing, and they began eating. "Jim, I'm sure you two will be happy up there, and Flossie and me'll sure be glad to have you as neighbors. Now, let me help you when you get ready to buy a few cows. I know the stock barns pretty well in Stuttgart, Pine Bluff, and Memphis. We'll go there and get you some heifers, and we'll turn 'em in with my bull to get you started raisin' cattle. Then a few years down the road, you can buy a good bull and return the favor. If you want to, we'll work together on vaccinatin', brandin', roundups, and sales—even on cuttin' and balin' hay."

Estelle was taken with their children—a little boy and a baby girl. "What's your name?" she asked the boy seated near his mother.

"I five," he said with a grin.

"Our son's name is Albert, and the baby's name is Iris; she's eight months," Flossie said.

"She's beautiful! And, Albert, I sure like your curly hair!" Estelle said.

Jim and Estelle thanked Flossie for the delicious meal and expressed appreciation to Ross for his time in showing them the Monk place.

As the couple left, Ross said, "We'll see you at your reception at the Derrick's home."

After mounting Ella and before Jim went to his truck, Estelle said, "Jim, I hope you're as happy as I am about what happened this morning."

"I am," said Jim. "The place is promisin'. The only drawback is havin' to move out ahead of the backwater ever few years. But I still wanted to take the chance. Its location and possibilities suit me to a tee for what I have in mind for us. So, I'll see ye day after tomorrow at 7:30 for a trip to DeWitt?"

"Yes, see you then. I love you!"

"I love you, too! I'll wait a few minutes before I leave so as not to pass ye and leave ye in my dusty wake."

"Thank you, darling!" Estelle blew Jim a kiss, and she left putting her horse into a lope.

When Jim drove into his father's driveway, he was quite sure the large old truck loaded with a tent, tools, and personal things was his brother Henry's. When he emerged from his truck, he heard laughter in the back yard. He walked around the house to find his father and brother enjoying a good time.

After the two brothers hugged, Henry explained why all their possessions were in his truck. "I had a run-in with the old moonshiner down there. I told Oda that it's time to quit helpin' to make that old rotgut whiskey and that we'd just go spend a few days with Papa and Mama and find somethin' else to do."

Boge said, "I'm glad you quit there, son. We're glad to have y'all here with us for however long ye can stay."

"Henry, if ye're lookin' fer work, I shore need someone." Jim spent a few minutes telling them about the morning and his plan to purchase the Monk place. "I'll need a builder for fixin' up the house and buildin' a barn, a smokehouse, a tool shed, and an outdoor toilet. If ye agree to be the builder, I'll pay ye a decent wage and encourage ye to pitch yore tent over there. I'll have a well and pump drilled, but for now we can get water from Tom Miller's place just a quarter mile north."

"I'll be glad to hep ye out, Jim. Shore hate to charge ye, but I need to make a livin'. Oda and me are impressed with the woman ye're marryin'. She's real purty and nice. Y'all are gonna make it fine, I know."

Boge said, "Yes, Jim, Henry's right. Estelle is the finest, and I'm glad ye'll have yore own place. Mama and me want ye to stay here for as long as ye need to, but we can't blame ye for gettin' a home."

"Papa, Estelle and me are to pick up the Monks day after tomorrow at 8:30 to go to the DeWitt courthouse and get everythang squared away on the property. I would like to drive yore car, since there'll be four of us. My pickup will be here if ye need it."

"Go ahead with the car, son. And plan on it for yore weddin' and honeymoon, too."

"Thanks, Papa. Henry, do ye wanta go with me tomorrow to see a well driller in Tichnor?"

"Yeah, guess so."

Mr. Pearson, the well driller, could not get to Jim's job until the following week. Before he could give an estimate of the cost, Jim had to select the style of casing and the kind of roof that would go over the well and the pump. He told Jim he would require one half of the estimate at the beginning of the work and the balance when the job was satisfactorily completed. He suggested the total cost might be $300.

"Dang!" said Jim. "That's several times what I paid for the land! But I want ye to do the job."

On the way back, the brothers stopped and chatted with old Uncle Hay. Then Jim bought ice-cold Cokes to drink on their way home.

"Jim, I bet I can build them covers for the well and pump cheaper than Pearson can. I'll draw ye a sketch and see what ye think."

"Good! I'd rather pay you anyway."

The next day in the clerk's office at the courthouse, Jim took charge, explaining to the clerk their purpose in being here. While the clerk checked the records, the four found comfortable seats in the waiting area. The clerk returned and said, "Mr. Monk, you are delinquent in your 1925 taxes and the taxes for the first half of 1926. You owe a total of $48.39 in back taxes. It could be that you would like Mr. Tharp to pay your 18 months of delinquent taxes, and then you could deduct that amount from the sale price. I need to know if you two agree or disagree with my suggestion before I can continue processing your paperwork."

"I'm willin' to pay the back taxes, if Mr. Monk will allow us to deduct that amount from the $100."

Mr. Monk nodded and said, "Yes, do it that way."

"Would you like me to type up a bill of sale in two copies that both of you will sign? Each of you will then have a copy to take with you for your personal records." She waited until both men had nodded and then left to prepare the paperwork.

Later the clerk appeared and showed them where to sign the bill of sale. She said, "Mr. Tharp, I'll need a check from you for $48.39, and you'll owe Mr. Monk the balance of $51.61. It's all on this sheet for your record."

Jim asked Estelle to write the check for $48.39. When she had done this, he asked Estelle, "Don't we have $52.00 in cash? If so, just count it out to Mr. Monk—forget the 61 cents."

"Anything y'all need to buy here in DeWitt before we leave town?" Jim asked the Monks.

"Reckon not," Mr. Monk said.

"Then we'll be on our way."

They rode in silence to Tichnor where Jim said, "On a warm day like this, I think some iced Cokes would taste good. I hope y'all would like one."

"Yeah, sounds good," Monk said.

Jim ran in and got the drinks, paid Edna, and they were on their way.

Having arrived at the Monk's place, the four shook hands but talked only briefly before Jim and Estelle left for the Miller's."

Pulling into the Miller's driveway, Jim said, "I'd like us to go to our love bench down at the pond."

"Oh, I would like that!"

Arm in arm they walked slowly to the row of willows and found their bench.

"What a wonderful year my eighteenth has been!" Estelle exclaimed. In April I met you! In May I became engaged to you! In August we bought our home and will be married! Oh, Jim, I can hardly wait until we are together and don't have to go our separate ways. I believe it's exactly a week from tomorrow that we get married. Oh, darling, I can't wait for you to see my wedding dress! I've never enjoyed sewing anything more than that dress! When I was making it, I thought of you and wondered what you'd think when you saw it."

"Well, I've loved ye in everthang I've seen ye in, but I'll admit I am anxious to see ye in that weddin' dress."

"I'm excited that Henry's agreed to help us clean up and build our place. I'm anxious to see it again soon!"

"Well, I promised all my family, includin' George and BettyLee, that I'd show them the place Saturday mornin'. So why don't I come by here and pick ye up at 9:00? I'll have them meet us at our property at 9:30. I want ye with me anyway when I show Henry where we want the barn, the smokehouse, the toilet, the garden, and everthang else. We'll also decide on the location of the well and pump. It will be a good time for us to look closer at what work the house needs and help Henry and Oda decide where they'll wanta pitch their tent."

"Jim, don't you want me to pay $200 on the well and pump?"

46

"No way! But thanks. After Saturday mornin', do we get to see each other before the weddin'?"

"Aren't you working with Marion this next week doing other things with the rice?"

"Yes, but we're gettin' caught up. I'm gonna help Henry get started on our place Monday mornin'. I've told Marion that the place and our personal interests come first this week but that I would be available some. He said that's fine. I've also told Lloyd to call on me only in an emergency, but I don't expect he will call at all. Since I will be seein' ye this Saturday mornin', I guess I can wait to see ye again until we move ye up to our house, say next Friday mornin'. The weddin' will be that evenin', and then we'll head for Stuttgart!"

"Just think, Jim! In just eight days that justice will say, 'Jim and Estelle, I pronounce you husband and wife!' Darling, what sweet words! Do you realize what that will mean?"

"Yes. For one thing, it will mean that you are mine!"

"And, for another, it will also mean that you are mine!"

"And with those thoughts, I reckon I need to walk ye to the house and be on my way."

They walked slowly to the back porch, where Jim kissed Estelle and said, "Happy waitin'! See ye Saturday mornin'!"

"Happy waiting, darling! The days will pass and we'll be together!"

Jim's family expressed delight at the place he and Estelle had bought. "We know it doesn't look like much now, but with Henry's help we'll soon make some changes here," Jim said. It did not take long for Henry to agree with Jim and Estelle where the buildings should go. Henry had ideas for their dimensions that he would run past them before he started building. They agreed where the well should be drilled and the pond built. "If Marion doesn't need me too badly, I'm gonna come over and start clearin'. I wanta get some fruit trees out later this fall." With Jim working between Marion's and their own new place that week, the days passed quickly.

Late Friday morning Jim drove down to get Estelle. He seemed rather glad that both Millers were not home. Estelle was happy to see him, and after their hug and kiss, said, "Jim, come into the living room.

I've found an old waltz called "Some Enchanted Evening." I've been playing it on Aunt Mertice's old Victrola. Since we have plenty of time, would you dance with me?"

"Of course." He watched Estelle wind up the device and place the needle on the record. When the music began, Jim drew her to him and they waltzed happily to the tune again and again.

Jim made two or three trips to the truck with Estelle's things. When she announced that she was ready, she looked about the house and said, "Jim, I'm not going to miss this place one bit. But I'm not at all ungrateful for what Aunt Mertice has done for me. I just can't explain what it means to me to have you as my husband for the rest of life and to have you care for me. I love you so much!"

"My darlin', I am glad to take care of ye for the rest of life! Well, since we don't wanta be late for our weddin', we better get goin'."

"Oh, Jim, it's getting cloudy and dark; I think it's going to rain."

"Yeah, I decided that on the way down. But whatever happens, it won't stop our weddin'."

They were surprised to see George and BettyLee getting out of their car as they pulled up into the Tharp driveway. They were both dressed up. As soon as Jim and Estelle got out of the pickup, BettyLee rushed up and said, "You'll forgive us, but we jumped the gun on you two and went and got married last night!"

"Congratulations, George and BettyLee," Jim said, as he pumped George's hand and went to his sister and kissed her.

"We thought y'all deserved to have your own weddin'," George said. "But we still want to drive over and be your witnesses. Then we'll drive back here and y'all can head out for your honeymoon."

Entering the house, George said, "It's already startin' to rain, and they say it's gonna pour all night."

"Then let's leave at 5:00 instead of 5:30," Jim said. "I'll get Estelle's things from the pickup, and then we'd better start dressin' for the weddin' soon."

Even though the rain and wind brought down the temperatures, Jim and Estelle could not ignore the high humidity as they worked to get into their wedding clothes. Once Jim got his tie in order, with Estelle's help, he decided to go ahead and wear the coat in spite of the weather, especially since Estelle said how nice he looked in it.

48

Jim and all the family were in the living room when Estelle came out of the girls' room wearing her wedding dress. The girls cheered, and the men whistled. Jim embraced her and said, "I knew ye'd be purty, but I never saw ye look so lovely in the months I've known ye!"

Boge, Ophelia, and the girls gathered around Jim and Estelle, wished them a happy honeymoon, and said, "We'll be lookin' for ye Sunday afternoon. Come home in time to rest up for the big celebration Sunday night."

When they were ready to leave, George and Jim got raincoats for Estelle and BettyLee to put over their heads so they wouldn't get soaked and ruin their hairdos. They pulled out of the Tharp driveway under gunmetal gray skies, with rain driven by strong winds.

Jim saw immediately that he would have to slow down some in order not to splash mud all over the vehicle and risk skidding off the county road. At times he had to go even slower because of water washing over the road. "Estelle, I believe this is the hardest rain we've ever had around here."

"Yes, I can't ever remember it raining this hard," Estelle agreed.

"Don't worry. One more mile and we'll be at the Joneses."

As they arrived at the justice's place, Jim noticed that George and BettyLee had pulled in right behind them and Sib and Lena were on the porch. Sib had his raincoat on, and he was motioning for them to stay put.

The justice came out to the cars and motioned George and BettyLee to join him in Jim's car. He entered Jim's back seat, saying, "Stay put up there. The witnesses will join me back here, one on each side of me. You two will turn and face each other, and I'll talk to you through the opening between your seats."

When they were all positioned as he had instructed, the justice began: "Jim and Estelle, join hands and look into each other's eyes. I ask you both: Do you come here tonight clear in your consciences and sincere in your hearts to pledge your faith in holy matrimony, to love one another, and be faithful to one another for the rest of life? If so, answer 'I do!'"

After the resounding "I do's!" the justice continued. "I'll ask you to repeat your vows after me. First Jim: I, Jim, take you, Estelle, to be my wife … to have and to hold from this day on … in good times and bad, in sickness and in health, to love and to cherish … for the rest of life, according to God's Holy Word, and to this I pledge my love." Then Estelle repeated her vows.

The justice said, "Seeing then that Jim and Estelle have declared their love to one another for a lifetime together and have stated the same before God and these witnesses, I now by the authority vested in me by the state of Arkansas declare them to be husband and wife, in the name of the Father, Son, and Holy Spirit. Whom, therefore, God has joined together let no one separate. Amen! Jim, you may kiss your bride."

Immediately Jim and Estelle were in each other's arms sealing their vows with a long kiss.

"One more thing," the justice said. "Jim and Estelle, in the words of a great man of God, I welcome you to 'the highest halls of human happiness'!"

"Now, the bride and groom sign the certificate here, and then George and BettyLee sign as witnesses." The justice waited patiently for the four to sign.

Jim held out a ten dollar bill to the justice. "No, Jim. No charge! I didn't charge these two last night, and I won't charge you. The Tharps and Bests are like family to Lena and me. I actually feel honored to perform the ritual. Jim and Estelle, Lena and I look forward to your celebration at the Derricks' home in another week." After congratulating them, Justice Jones followed George out of the car and waved goodbye.

BettyLee leaned over the front seat and kissed Estelle, crying, "Honey, welcome to the Tharp family! Even as George was climbing back into the car, she pulled Jim to her and said, "Oh, my dear brother, I love you so much, and more now than ever since you've brought Estelle into our lives!"

George kissed Estelle and shook hands with Jim. "We are all brothers and sisters in the Tharp-Best family. BettyLee and I always want to be close to you two; no matter what comes or goes, we'll be together! And what Sib Jones had to say about 'the highest halls of human happiness' are pretty highfalutin' words, but I reckon that's what marriage can be—'highest halls of human happiness'—that's what we all wish for one another. Y'all have a sweet and lovin' honeymoon!" BettyLee and George climbed out of the back seat and hurried to their car as they waved to the newlyweds.

Jim started the car and turned off the windshield wipers, saying, "The rain has finally stopped!"

"Thank the Lord! I just hope the Tichnor levee will be safe to cross."

"Oh, it'll be okay. I reckon we oughta get to Stuttgart about 9:00. I hope the hotel dinin' room will still be open cuz I'm kinda hungry. How about you, my dear wife?"

"Oh, Jim! I like the sound of that! I am your wife, aren't I?"

"That's what the justice said a few minutes ago."

"Yes, he did, and he said you are my husband."

"And I'll be ready to prove it pretty soon, too."

"You asked if I was hungry. Yes, I'll be ready to eat. I think the dining room will still be open."

They drove through DeWitt in almost no traffic. Their highway turned west for a time as they drove along watching the lightning in the distance. In another 40 minutes they had turned north and could catch the lights of Stuttgart across the wide prairie. It was exactly 9:00 when Jim parked under the cover of the hotel entrance. "I'll come to yer door and help ye out, cuz I don't want my wife settin' out here in the dark alone." Approaching the clerk at the front desk, Jim said, "We have reservations for Jim and Estelle Tharp, please!"

The clerk turned a page or two and smiled. "Mr. and Mrs. Tharp, congratulations on your marriage! We had a call from the sheriff in DeWitt to place you in our lovely Honeymoon Suite and to put every hotel expense on his account. Welcome to Central Hotel! Let us know if there is anything we can do to make you more comfortable. Here is the key to room number 38 on the third floor. The elevator is down that hall on your left."

"Thank ye, sir! And where do I park the car, please?"

"Feel free to park either over on the east lot or around on the south side of the hotel."

In a few minutes, they entered the hotel restaurant where a nicely dressed lady welcomed them and led them to a comfortable upholstered booth. Estelle opened the menu and said, "Jim, here's a 12-ounce T-bone steak with baked potato and salad."

"Order it for both of us. I'll drink sweet iced tea with lemon. Now I'll go park the car."

Estelle gave the waitress Jim's order: steak cooked medium well, baked potato with butter, salad with blue cheese dressing, and sweet iced tea with lemon. For herself, she only wanted a ham-and-cheese sandwich and a bowl of vegetable soup, as well as sweet iced tea with lemon.

While Estelle waited for Jim to return, she admired the chandelier, the artwork on the walls, and the quality of the tables and booths. She was a bit surprised to find a hotel of this quality in a town—now a city, she guessed—known for its rice mills, cotton gins, and stockyards. *Did Jim know the hotel was this nice? Had he stayed here before? Wow! Lloyd must really be pleased with Jim to pick up the tab for us here. What would the sheriff say about Jim at the celebration? I'm glad the community and the county will learn something of Jim's character and reputation. Lord, I'm thankful You have brought Jim into my life! Help me make him happy. Lead me..., us..., to you! I must know You as my Savior!* Though Estelle's head was bowed and her prayer was silent, she sensed when Jim slipped into his seat across from her. "Oh, Jim, you're back so soon!"

"Yeah, I didn't take the suitcases up yet. Are ye tired?"

"Not really. I feel fine. Truth is, I had bowed my head and was thanking the Lord for bringing you into my life."

"Tell ye what: I thought ye might be prayin', so when they bring our food, why don't ye say a prayer over our first meal together as husband and wife?"

"Jim! How sweet of you! I'll surely be glad to."

The waitress brought their drinks and said that she would bring their food in a few minutes.

First came Estelle's sandwich and bowl of soup.

"Honey, why didn't ye order a steak also?"

"I don't guess I'm that hungry. I ordered what I want, thanks!"

Then came Jim's steak, baked potato, and salad. "Anything else?" the waitress asked.

"Please, some steak sauce. Thanks!"

"Coming right up," she said.

Jim reached for Estelle's hand and said, "Go ahead and pray, dear."

"Heavenly Father, our hearts are filled with praise for Your blessings! I'm so blessed to be Jim's wife and to be sharing our first meal together. Please make me a good helpmate for him, and lead us in establishing our home where You will be Lord and Master. We offer thanks for our food and our first night together. I also give thanks for the generosity of the sheriff. May both Jim and I find You soon as our personal Savior. Amen." Estelle heard Jim echo her "Amen!"

"I reckon I hadn't realized that this wuz not just another meal 'til ye started prayin'. That was shore a good prayer, and it touched me."

Estelle watched Jim cut his steak, sprinkle the dark sauce on it, and then butter his roll. She liked his table manners and the quiet way he drank his tea.

"Is your steak okay?"

"Never a better one, and never a more wonderful partner in a meal!"

"I feel the same." Estelle noticed the sparkle in his eyes as he looked at her.

Later as they entered the suite, Estelle exclaimed over its beauty and space. Jim said very little but agreed it was nice, and he was glad that Estelle was impressed.

"Come and look at this lovely bathroom," Estelle called. "What do you think?"

"Well, it's shore nicer than the old three-holer down at Papa's!"

Estelle laughed and said, "In my childhood I never knew what a nice bathroom was until I went to live with Aunt Mertice."

While Estelle was freshening up in the bathroom, Jim opened his suitcase, got out his pajamas, and put them on.

Coming out to get her night clothes, Estelle exclaimed, "Oh, Jim, you look nice in pajamas!"

"Mama bought these for my weddin' night; I never wore 'em before," Jim confessed.

While Jim scanned the *Gazette,* Estelle slipped back into the bathroom and put on her skimpy new negligee her aunt had bought for her wedding night. When she came out, Jim whistled and said, "Wow! What if I rip that thang off ye?"

"You won't have to. When it's time, I'll take it off." She came to him, and when he laid aside his newspaper, she sat in his lap. The minutes passed while the newlyweds enjoyed the closeness of each other.

After a time, Jim said, "I think I'm about ready to see what it's like gettin' in bed with my wife." Estelle's response was to return to the bathroom.

A few minutes later, Jim was ecstatically shocked when Estelle appeared from the bathroom with absolutely nothing on! She walked boldly but slowly to him, quoting, **And the man and his wife were both naked, and were not ashamed** (Gen. 3:25). She then moved to the bed and pulled a sheet over her.

"In that case, I reckon I better get nekkid, too." He pulled off his pajamas and got in bed with her.

Wrapped in each other's arms, Estelle said, "Honey, I suspect you are somewhat experienced in what we are about to do, but..."

"Well," Jim began, "I really didn't think it was the time to talk about that before now. I'll just say this: I'm not the virgin you are. But I want ye to know that even if I've had some experience with women, there's a few things I've never done—I never forced a girl against her will, I never got a girl pregnant, and I never messed around with a married woman or broke up a marriage. If ye want to know more..."

Estelle pushed back a little out of Jim's arms and said, "Now you listen to me, Jim Tharp! I don't care about your Dellas and Delilahs or your Susies and Sallys. I don't want to know about your past. I heard your pledge of faithfulness to me before the justice a few hours ago. And, Jim Tharp, I not only love you, *I trust you! It's what happens between us from now on that matters.* So I don't want to hear any more. I say let's stop talking, because I'm ready to find out if this thing's all it's cracked up to be. So, come on and show me what it's all about!"

Jim was about to laugh but thought better of it. Instead, he asked, "Do we turn out the lights?"

"No! I want the lights on until we're ready to go to sleep!"

Jim chuckled and took his bride in his arms, delighting in her spunk.

An hour later, Jim went to the bathroom and then returned to find Estelle in a deep sleep. It was 8:00 in the morning when Jim woke again. Estelle stirred, raised up, and asked, "Are we where I think we are?"

"In our honeymoon suite in Stuttgart!" Jim said. Estelle relaxed and snuggled close to her husband, whispering, "Yes, thank the Lord! Honey, our wedding night was even better than I had imagined!"

Jim whispered back, "You were wonderful." She squeezed his hand, and they both dozed off again.

At 9:30 Estelle woke up, kissed Jim awake, and headed for the shower. Thirty minutes later she came out dressed in a new pink dress. Jim got up and dressed in khaki trousers and a new blue shirt.

"How about breakfast?" he asked.

"I'm ready when you are."

Downstairs in the dining room the male receptionist seated the newlyweds in the same booth where they had eaten their late meal the night before. Both ordered sausage, eggs over easy, hash browns, toast, and coffee.

"What'll we do today?" Jim asked, as they waited for their food.

"I'd like to do whatever you want to do."

"It seems to be nice and cool for August, so I'd like to walk."

"Then I'd like to walk with my husband."

"So let's walk over to the main part of town to a hardware store and then to a department store—I wanta buy my wife a new dress. Maybe we'll be ready by then to have some ice cream and iced Cokes."

"I'm in agreement—and here comes our breakfast," Estelle said.

Two days and nights of their honeymoon had already passed, and they both realized how comfortable and delighted they were with each other. They compared their worldviews, checked out their religious beliefs, and even got into politics. As they were relaxing in the hotel lobby, Jim spied the current issue of the *Gazette* and began studying the news on the front page.

"What's going on in the world?" Estelle wanted to know.

"The editor is speculatin' on the 1928 presidential election already, and here it's only 1926."

"Does he think President Coolidge will be reelected?"

"No, cuz he thinks Coolidge won't run."

"I'm surprised. After all the Harding scandals, Coolidge filled out Harding's term so well and had such a good vote in 1924. I think he could do well in '28."

"I guess Herbert Hoover is the editor's man. He was Coolidge's Secretary of Commerce; he must be a brilliant man cuz President Wilson chose Hoover to head a program to feed the starvin' in Europe after WWI."

"Any other news?"

"Yeah, great news for my boss and all rice farmers. Our governor just made a speech and told 'em they'd be gettin' $2.25 a bushel for rice this fall! And Marion has 1,000 acres! It's nice and cool out there, too—makin' it good for the harvest in a few days."

The next day, after a visit to the stockyards to see how mules were selling, Jim asked Estelle if she would be interested in going to Little Rock. "I thought there might be somethin' goin' on there that we might enjoy—a picture show or somethin'."

Back at the hotel, Estelle searched the newspaper for movie ads. "Honey, I don't see much that I'd care to watch. I like Mary Pickford, but I don't care about the more modern Clara Bow with her feministic arguments; yet she seems to be replacing Pickford."

"What do ye mean, feministic?"

"Well, it seems women want to be as free as men nowadays—they're entering business and politics and taking over management. Also they are swearing, drinking, and smoking in public. For me, they're coming on too strong; I guess I'm just too conservative."

"I shore like ye that way, darlin'. But I reckon there's some women who can run a farm, a factory, and even a state or the nation better than any man. So I guess they ought not be held back too much just because they're women."

Estelle continued to look through the paper. In a few minutes she looked at Jim and said, "Now here's something I'd like to go to Little Rock for: The famous WWI hero Sgt. Alvin York will be speaking tomorrow night at 7:00 at the Park Plaza Mall at University & Markham Streets. It says he'll give 15 minutes of his war experiences and 15 minutes of his Christian testimony; then an offering will be taken for the Christian Academy he's sponsoring in Jamestown, Tennessee. There's no admission charge for those who contribute to his project at the door. A $5 donation is suggested per person."

Jim's reaction was positive. "Yeah, I've read about him. So far I've made him out to be genuine, simple, humble, and trustworthy. I'd like to go and hear him."

They enjoyed the drive to Little Rock. Rice fields on both sides of the highway drew Jim's attention as the rice crop waved in the breeze, ripening, drying, and hardening for the cut.

"A penny for your thoughts," Estelle said.

"Aw, I was just thinkin' 'bout next week's harvest and how fortunate I am to be married to a woman like you and to be workin' fer a man like Marion; I've been able to earn his confidence to manage men, work on machinery, and get paid for what I like to do."

"I think Marion is the fortunate one to have someone like you."

"We'll stop up here in North Little Rock, gas up, get us iced Cokes, and cross over the river. I know right where York will be speakin'." Jim had no trouble recognizing University Street, and the Park Plaza Mall was clearly marked on their right. He paid 50 cents for a 3-hour parking permit, and they crossed the street to the auditorium. At the door, Jim gave the hostess a $10 bill and they followed an usherette down into the center section close to the front.

After a few minutes of quiet with only the sound of people gathering, Jim started to say something to Estelle but noticed her head bowed as though she was meditating. It caused him to think more seriously. *This honeymoon is more fulfillin' than I expected. Estelle is even more wonderful than the girls I dated—more down to earth, more intelligent, more helpful, more gracious, more everthang! Whatever she's lookin' for from the Lord, I hope she finds. Then I'll bet she'll share it with me without pushin' too hard. I think I just need to relax and let happen what will. I know I couldn't have found a better wife, cuz she's everthang I need!*

The lights suddenly came up, and microphones and banners were out announcing THE STAMP-BAXTER MELODY BOYS. The audience clapped its welcome, and they came on with a hymn, "Power in the Blood." It was a toe-tapper, and Jim could tell Estelle enjoyed the Gospel in the song. After a few numbers, the quartet closed with a soft, convicting song they called "Draw Me Nearer." The refrain each time would touch Jim deeply, and he knew it was having a powerful effect on Estelle: *Draw me nearer, nearer, nearer, blessed Lord, to the cross where Thou has died. Draw me nearer, nearer, nearer, blessed Lord, to Thy precious bleeding side.*

After the quartet sang, a tall, brown-headed, middle-aged man stepped out proudly to the microphone and saluted the audience. "Good evening, ladies and gentlemen," he said with a Tennessee drawl. "I feel honored and very proud to be here in this wonderful city of Little Rock and greet this good crowd tonight. Your great spirit makes me proud to be an American, and in hearing the Stamps-Baxter Quartet, I want you to know that I am very proud to be a Christian and serving in the army of our Lord Jesus Christ.

"Thank you for comin'! You know, I wasn't plannin' to have any part in the war. Fact is, belongin' to a great holiness church, I wuz at first a conscientious objector. I even went into trainin', plannin' to apply for services other than fightin' and killin' Germans. I come from a poor, uneducated Tennessee family, and at first I didn't understand the meanin' of that commandment, 'Thou shalt not kill.' But after I done so good there in Camp Gordon, Georgia, in rifle shootin', the Major said, 'York, yore so good on that rifle, I think it's a shame you've listed yoreself a C.O. Now I ain't claimin' to be a great authority on the Bible, but I want to give you a furlough home to spend a month— if need be— to visit yore pastor, yore mama, and anyone else to check out and see if that commandment doesn't really mean THOU SHALT DO NO MURDER. See, York, even in the Bible, there was an understandin' that under some circumstances, it's right to kill a bad man. Why, a policeman is not arrested when he has to kill a feller who's tryin' to kill him. I'll bet you'd shoot an evil man who was tryin' to rape or hurt yore sweetheart.'

"Well, they let me leave for several weeks, and my good pastor in Pall Mall and my Mama shore agreed with the Major. I went back to camp free to go to war. I'm not here to brag about what happened in that Argonne Forest. I had prayed to be courageous, accurate, and able to do my duty. When I learned to kill Germans, it did bother me some, but I soon realized the skill God give me to shoot was to save the lives of my American comrades. So shore 'nuff, that mornin' I cleaned out them machinegun nests and killed them Germans and captured all them prisoners, I knew the Lord hepped me save lives and hepped bring the war to an end." York was interrupted by a great applause from the audience, including Jim and Estelle.

Then York began his personal testimony. "I was a rowdy young feller there in Wolf Valley around Pall Mall. I'd get liquored up, shoot my pistol outside the church, and fight a man at the drop of ye hat. My dear Mama tried to change me. But it took the Holy Spirit of God to convict me, bring repentance, and transform my heart. It happened one night in a preachin' service in the old Church of Christ in Christian Holiness. I walked that aisle without shame and knelt before God and confessed my sins, and God gave me a new heart. Fokes, I got more than religion—I found peace with God and become a new person in Christ Jesus."

The famous soldier then began his appeal for others to join Christ's army. He pointed out where he'd be standing to pray with anyone who came forward as the quartet came back on to sing, "I Am Thine, O Lord."

Jim observed Estelle, wondering if she'd go down. But she leaned over to him and asked, "Why don't we slip out quietly to get ahead of the crowd?" They were the first to leave. Soon they were crossing the river and back on U.S. 70 heading east.

"What did you think about York, honey?" Estelle asked after a few minutes of silence.

"I liked him! I think he was sincere, humble, genuine, and interestin'. What did you think?"

"I agree with you about him. I've never felt so hungry for the Lord as I did on that last song by the quartet, "I Am Thine, O Lord." But I somehow knew it was not the time for me to go forward. I so want us both to be ready at the same time."

"Don't wait on me, dear. I felt somethin' in York that I ain't felt before. I now know I don't have to get religion to get saved. But don't hold up on my account when ye're ready."

By the time they turned off U.S. 70 and headed south for Stuttgart, Estelle was asleep leaning against the door of the car. When Jim parked at their hotel, she awakened and asked, "How long have I been sleeping?"

"About 20 minutes."

"Sorry, I'm such poor company, but thanks for going to hear that wonderful testimony to God's saving grace!"

The next few days remained cool and clear as the honeymoon continued. Jim and Estelle ate, danced, shopped, listened to the radio, and dreamed about fixing up their home, farming, raising cattle, trapping, fishing, and hunting. Spiritual things were also very much on the mind of Estelle.

Sunday morning dawned as clear and cool as the preceding six days. They ate breakfast, checked out of the hotel, and headed south. The only stop they made before reaching LaGrue was at Tichnor to get iced Cokes. They had an hour to rest before heading for the celebration at the Derrick farm.

Both were amazed at the cars, trucks, wagons, saddle horses, and motor bikes parked for a half mile in both directions near the Derrick farm. Boge and George with their carloads were ahead of them, no doubt looking for a place to park. Marion had been watching for Jim and motioned him into his barn lot where he had reserved places for him, the sheriff, and other close friends. He and Peggy welcomed the newlyweds with great excitement, introducing them to many people all the way into the large living room where special seats awaited them. The couple was amazed to see that their loved ones in both families were seated in a special section. Nearly all were waving and blowing kisses.

So many couples and individuals made their way to Jim and Estelle—L. A. Black and his daughter, Cleve and Ebrena Sweeney, Sib and Lena Jones, Tom and Mertice Miller, Press and Edith Whitman, Dr. and Mrs. Whitehead, Sheriff and Mrs. Jefferson, Sheriff and Mrs. Westin, and Barney Stevens.

About sunset, with lights on and fans stirring the cooler air, Marion called out "May I have everyone's attention? We are here to honor and congratulate a young couple dear to all of us here in Arkansas County, Jim and Estelle Tharp, who just returned from their week of honeymoon." He had to pause for a minute because of the loud applause of about a thousand people. "Of course, I'm prejudiced, but of all the people who have ever worked for me, Jim Tharp is the hardest working, most reliable, and most efficient hand I've ever had—the best mechanic, the wisest manager of men, and the most compassionate person I've ever met. I am proud of him as a friend, a neighbor, and an employee. But I am also proud of him for the choice he's made in a wife. As you can see, Estelle is beautiful…" He paused and motioned for Estelle to stand—she blushed and smiled as the crowd cheered, whistled, and clapped for more than a minute. Estelle sat down, and Marion continued, "She's gracious, kind, and wise, and already Peggy and I have grown to love her. I'll now ask Jim's parents and Estelle's mother and stepfather to stand." After the applause, he said, "And let's have every relative of these two please stand." Again there was a round of applause as nearly fifty people stood.

"In a little while, there will be refreshments, band music, and dancing in the yards around us. You'll then have an opportunity to meet and greet Jim and Estelle personally if you'll join the line and be patient. We've read about some of Jim's work in the Little Rock, Stuttgart, DeWitt, and Gillette newspapers. But right now I want to present a man who knows Jim well and who wants to say a word about him and the service he renders this county. I present to you our good, brave, and much-loved Arkansas County Sheriff, Lloyd LaFargue!"

When the extended applause ceased, Lloyd LaFargue stepped up on the riser where Marion had stood. He was dressed in full uniform along with twin pearl-handled pistols, a ten-gallon white Stetson and light gray Western boots. He began, "Dear people, I'm so proud to see so many of you here tonight. We hoped there would be several hundred, but I hear that well over a thousand people are here to indicate their love and respect for Jim Tharp and to congratulate him on his choice of a beautiful wife in Estelle! I'm here to join you in showing my appreciation for how this young man is helping me not only to clean up Arkansas County from crime and violence but also to restore civility and respect for law and order in our communities. I don't want to embarrass Jim, but I want you to know I owe him my life. Twice now he has saved me by beating killers to the draw and wounding them slightly rather than killing them. What you've read about in the papers is not a myth. Jim's the real deal! He has been retained as my special deputy. Since the county can only pay him a token salary, I've already been to several of you more prosperous citizens—people who already bear heavy tax burdens—to ask you to contribute to Jim in order that I might with good conscience continue to have his services. He has trained his horse, Star, and his dog, Buck, to scent an outlaw a half mile away and signal to him their presence and location. In my twenty-five years of law enforcement, I've never seen a marksman as perfect as Jim, whether it's a flying, running, walking, or sitting target. He never misses! But he's a life saver—not a life taker. He's the most conscientious, most humane person that ever sought to enforce the law. He could put a bullet through the heart of any criminal he had to shoot, but he prefers to drill a hole in his ear. Most of the time, that's what he does.

"So tonight, I'm asking us all to show our appreciation for this man's gifted service. Why, he with his horse and dog are worth more to me than any posse I could assemble. I sincerely ask that you consider writing a check or dropping a meaningful amount of money into those stations outside there to show your appreciation for Jim's help. Now that Jim and Estelle are married, they want to add some buildings on the land they have bought, buy some furniture for their house, raise some cattle, and make a life for themselves. Please, let's help them! So, once more, let's hear it for Jim Tharp, a legend in his time!" After the sheriff motioned for Jim to stand, the lively applause was a great climax for that part of the evening.

Farmers, businessmen, fishermen, loggers, salesmen, merchants, and scores of common people swarmed Jim and Estelle inside the house and then on the couple's way to the head of the refreshment line, as directed by Marion and Peggy. The two could not figure out why they were being celebrated and honored and made over on such a scale. They watched dozens writing checks and even more dropping bills and coins into the boxes scattered around in all the yards.

When Jim got a chance, he asked, "Estelle, are ye okay?"

"Oh, yes, dear! I'm so proud of you and the way people are responding to you. I believe everything Marion and Lloyd said about you. The people are with you and for you, too!"

The greeting line moved slowly, lasting for nearly two hours. Jim and Estelle were tired from standing so long, but they tried to not show it. As the crowd thinned out, Peggy came and escorted them to two chairs set back a ways. "I'm filling two plates with food and bringing two glasses of sweet iced tea. Please relax and be ready for the finale in a bit; then we can release you to go home and get some rest. Marion and I haven't forgotten what an important day tomorrow is for you."

After the couple enjoyed the refreshments and greeted a few lingerers wanting a close-up visit with them, Peggy and Marion brought a large bag to Jim. "Now Jim, Peggy and I only counted the checks that came in before tonight. We know there is over $1,000 in checks, but I wouldn't be surprised if you find three times that for the total. Now, listen, friend! You're worth every penny of it. Take it and enjoy spending the money for the things you need and want. Now you know where your car is parked, so with our love and blessing, go and have a good night's rest, and we'll see you in the morning!"

"Marion, you've always been so generous with me. And, as I've told you before, I appreciate the way you treat my parents. It's such a privilege to work for you. We'll never forget this evenin'. Thank you both for all you've done for us."

Estelle said, "Peggy, you're a tremendous hostess! I don't know how you fed so many people, and, Marion, thank you for all your kindnesses!"

On the short drive home Estelle said, "Honey, what a beautiful moonlit night! If we weren't so tired, wouldn't it be good to have a waltz together under that harvest moon?"

"Yes, but let's go home, shed these fancy clothes, put on somethin' more comfortable, and get a glass of iced tea. We'll have the girls help us count our money, and then we'll get to bed."

The girls were almost in awe of their brother and his bride when they came in. "Girls, Estelle and I will change clothes, and then we want you to help us count the money."

"You mean you'll let us help you do that?" Hollis asked.

After Jim and Estelle had slipped into the clothes they would put back on in the morning, Jim emptied the bag of money on the bed. He gathered all the checks and asked Estelle to take the bills and coins to the dining room table and let the girls help her count the cash.

Estelle held up two $20 bills and said, "Do I have your permission to give these to Hollis and Jenny when we are through?" Jim smiled and nodded his answer. Estelle continued, "I think I should take $100 and buy something nice for your mother; I hope you will do the same for your father." Again Jim nodded and smiled his agreement.

Estelle went to the dining room to count with the girls, and Jim began adding up the checks. He was amazed at the total of the checks: $3,475! He wrote the figure on a card and went to check on the progress in the dining room. He could see that they were well organized—Estelle counted the coins and each of the girls counted half of the bills. Estelle took Jim's figure, added the cash figure of $570, and announced a total of $4,045!

"Jim, you didn't know that horse and dog would make you rich, did you?" Jenny said.

Watching the process from the sidelines, Ophelia said, "I don't think it's just Star and Buck that make Jim appreciated, but they do hep him and the sheriff in their work."

Both Hollis and Jenny squealed with delight as Estelle handed each of them a $20 bill.

Boge and Ophelia wiped tears as Boge said, "I never enjoyed seein' anybody get gifts like I did tonight. I was thrilled with the way all them people piled their love on you with their money. We're shore proud of ye both!"

It was a few minutes past midnight when Jim crawled into bed and drew Estelle into his arms. "I was so proud of ye tonight! And, sweetheart, I enjoyed our honeymoon. I just can't thank the Good Lord enough for the joy of havin' ye as my wife!"

Estelle responded in tears, "Honey, I realize how happy and fortunate I am to have you as my husband. And the words the justice quoted have been going through my mind all evening: *Welcome to the highest halls of human happiness!*"

"Yeah, it's been about ten days now, and we've walked a tiny way down them halls."

The two drifted off to sleep, overflowing with happiness.

3 *"Home, Sweet Home"*

Jim greeted his parents about an hour before sunup with a hearty "Good mornin'!" as they were about to sit down to breakfast. "Come on and sit down, son. Even though you had a short night's sleep and have a hard day ahead, you look ready for the day," Boge said.

Jim helped himself to biscuits, sausage gravy, and scrambled eggs. "Yeah, I'm not only excited about today but also the whole fall season of harvestin' and gettin' Henry goin' on cleanin', clearin', and buildin' over at our place. Papa and Mama, I feel like a new man—with Estelle, with y'all, Henry's help, my work with Lloyd, and the great offerin'. Now I don't wanta get too big for my britches or get to feelin' too frisky, but it shore feels good!" Jim said.

"Ain't nuthin' wrong with feelin' good about life, son," Boge said. I'm excited, too—ain't even dreadin' the cotton patch. I just don't want Mama out there all the time."

"Papa, count me in on helping to pick cotton," Estelle said, as she walked into the room and sat down near Jim.

"Well, look who's here!" Jim said. "I slipped out on ye, but I wuz comin' back in 'fore I left to kiss ye goodbye."

Ophelia said, "Now Estelle, we don't think ye oughta be in the cotton patch gettin' ye hands all bloody and sore. Papa and the girls and me can get it all done before the end of October, I'm sure. Ye can hep me in the kitchen and 'round the house here so I can get out there more, but the cotton ain't fer you."

"Now, Mama, I'll help in the kitchen and wherever I'm needed, but I really want to pick cotton; I don't mind if my hands get sore and bloody. They'll heal up just as your hands do."

"Thanks, sweetheart," Jim said. "Ye look good this morning; hope ye rested well."

"I slept well and didn't even know when you got up. I'm glad I caught you before you left."

"Well, I'm off to the harvest." Jim got up from the table, kissed Estelle, and went over and kissed his mother and hugged his Dad. "I love y'all so much and 'preciate all ye've done for me! Estelle and I wanta pull our weight 'round here."

"We love you and Estelle, son," Boge said. "It means everything to Mama and me to have y'all with us."

Jim waved and was gone.

"Shore makes me happy to see Jim so happy," Ophelia said, after she heard the door close. "Estelle, ye've brought joy to our son's heart, and we thank ye! Now, Jim ain't never been mopey or downcast, but he's shore perked up since you come into his life."

"Mama, he's brought joy into my life, too. I love him for who he is—genuine, good, sincere, thoughtful, and gracious, and I just want to be a good wife and be worthy of such a great person."

Boge said, "Y'all will excuse me, ladies, and I'll get to readin' my Bible and then do the milkin'. When the sun comes up, I'll get out there and check the fields."

Marion came out of the implement shed when Jim drove in. "Late to bed but early to rise, huh, Jim? But you look okay this mornin'."

"Yeah, I oughta feel good after all y'all done for Estelle and me last night— the offerin' was a little over $4,000!"

"Hot dog! I knew there was over $1,500 in checks before last night. You deserve it, man! Maybe ye'll not have to borrow much for fixin' up your place and buyin' cattle."

Ben Morgan and Kelly Jones, neighboring rice farmers, arrived and asked Marion where to start. "Jim, you know as much as I do what all has to be done. Put 'em to doin' what you think we need done first, cuz I'm gonna be loadin' the binder." Jim asked Ben to fuel the tractors and Kelly to gas up all the trucks. By sunup, ten men had reported for duty. Jim put Ben Ellis on the binder, for he was an experienced rice farmer. He took the other men out in the field to work behind the binder, showing them how to stack up the shocks to dry, an operation called "shocking." Most of them were experienced at it, but he saw two or three who might need some instruction on how to balance a shock so the wind would not topple it. The shock would have to be topped off with bundles having the heads exposed to the sun.

Marion came out and told Jim, "I'm leavin' it all to you and the men; I'm gonna help Peggy clean and straighten up the house and yard from last night. Don't count on me much for the rest of today, but if ye need me, just call."

Ben got off the binder to see if Jim agreed that the bundles were spitting out of the binder in good shape or if adjustments were needed. "They're perfect!" Jim said.

Jim asked Kelly to go to the barn and tell the latecomers they were needed in the west section and to "come a-runnin'." Jim watched the shockers for awhile, and deciding that two of the twelve needed help, he stuck with them for a half hour. Looking at his watch, he saw it was 11:00. Before taking his leave to report to Marion, he told the workers, "In an hour y'all will hear the bell ring for chow time. Come quick, wait in line for the blessin', load yer plates, and find ye a seat over in the shade where the chairs are. When ye get through eatin', stretch out on the grass 'til the bell rings again and then get back to work. I wanta see this 200 acres all cut and shocked out by sundown. Then if the weather holds, we'll complete the east section tomorrow. Oughta finish cuttin' and shockin' by Wednesday night."

Just before Marion rang the bell, Peggy walked over to the barn to speak to Jim. "Marion told me about the amount in your offering, Jim. Oh, how wonderful!"

"Like we say when we catch a good bunch of fish in the seine, we had 'a great haul'! We're grateful, Peggy!"

Eight other women besides Peggy had loaded the tables with food—four kinds of meat, a variety of vegetables, pickles, jellies, jams, preserves, and plenty of cornbread, biscuits, and iced tea. Off to the side were cakes, pies, and cobblers. When Marion took the hammer and hit the silver triangle hanging down from the barn, Jim looked across both fields and saw about 25 men running toward the table. Marion called on Kelly to give the prayer of thanksgiving, and then Marion and Jim led the way through the food line. The ladies held back until the men had served themselves.

Before Marion rang the back-to-work bell, he commended Jim for the progress made on their morning of harvest. "We'll be done before Friday at the present rate."

"Yeah, and if we get along well, I think I'll need Friday afternoon off to go over and see how Henry's comin' on my new place."

"Of course, Jim! Just let me know when you need some time."

When they finished cutting and shocking on Wednesday night, leaving the shocks to dry for the next phase of threshing, Jim asked for Thursday and Friday off. He and Estelle drove to DeWitt on Thursday and opened a checking account at First National Bank. Before they left the bank, L. A. Black, president of the bank, recognized them and wanted to visit. "I sure enjoyed the gathering at Marion's last Sunday night. I'm proud of couples like you in this county. And I'm interested in the work you do with Lloyd, Jim. By the way, many years ago my father was the sheriff of Arkansas County. I'm backing you and Lloyd all the way. And anytime you want to venture in land, cattle, or anything else, see me personally and I'll assure you the lowest interest rate of any bank in our county."

"Thanks, Mr. Black. We appreciate that."

Leaving the bank with cash for Henry's wages and building supplies, Jim and Estelle went to their new place. Jim and his brother discussed putting in an orchard and plans for watering it.

"Jim, my brother, it shore is a joy to be with ye here, dreamin', plannin', workin', and heppin' ye."

"And we're glad to see the fine work you're doin', Henry! Shore 'preciate it."

Later that evening as they sat down to Ophelia's delicious supper, Jim and Estelle both realized how hungry they were. Jim asked, "What's the cotton like, Papa?"

"Great, son! Good healthy bolls startin' to open, showin' a lotta white fluffy stuff—it'll be a good crop."

On the second week in September, the cutting and shocking crews moved to Ben Morgan's farm, which was half the rice acreage that Marion had. Jim knew they could finish in just a few days with only half the crew.

Things moved along so well at their property that Jim began looking forward to the end of the harvest when he and Estelle could move over to their own home. Pearson had finished both the well and the pump in a week. The total bill ran $275, but it would have been $400 if he had also built the covers. Henry would soon be through building both of them.

Estelle learned to pick cotton right alongside Boge and Ophelia. At first she couldn't pick as much or as efficiently as Jim's sisters who were accustomed to the task. Her fingers did get sore and bled a little as she expected. But she kept them treated with lotion, and in two weeks they were adjusted to the sharp splits of the bolls. Soon she could lift the fluffy stuff right out and into her cotton sack and then quickly move on to the next stalk. However, she found that she did tire from pulling the eight-foot cotton sack—the fuller it got, the more her back hurt.

The first phase of the harvest, cutting and shocking, was completed at the end of September. All three farmers—Derrick, Morgan, and Jones—were pleased with the yield and were looking forward to the finishing phase of threshing, drying, and marketing. They all agreed that with good weather they should finish by the end of October.

Using Marion's big truck, Jim took time to help his father with loading and hauling cotton to the gin. There was still some picking to do, but they would finish with the cotton by the middle of October. Both Jim and Estelle spent a day each week with Henry and the projects at their place. Costs were adding up, but they were thankful for the resources to cover everything. Estelle thought that Jim's income from the harvest would probably restore most of their expenses on the house, well, and pump, as well as Henry's labor. Jim was discovering some timber down that he could claim for himself. He would have Henry's help in logging and rafting, and that income would be welcome. She saw no reason to be concerned about finances. Jim enjoyed clearing ground on his place, even chopping, sawing, and burning the thorn trees. He decided Henry was right in putting the orchard north of the house. Marion had given Jim a catalog from which he ordered 50 assorted fruit trees—apple, pear, peach, and plum. He followed the directions on planting, watering, and fertilizing, and within a few weeks, he could tell that they were taking on life.

As the threshing phase began in October, Jim was as excited about it as he was the first phase. Things had gone well with nearly all the hands, and Henry was making good progress on his work. He and Estelle were getting anxious to buy furniture and move into their home.

The weeks slipped by, and during the last week of October the threshing was finished on the Derrick, Morgan, and Jones farms. Since Marion engaged Jim to run all the operations on those farms, Morgan and Jones settled with Marion on Jim's compensation.

On the final evening, Jim performed his own little ritual of taking his bar of Ivory soap that floated, stripped off his clothes in the dark, plunged into the cold canal, and scrubbed from head to toe. When he felt he was clean, he dried off, slipped into fresh clothes free from the scratchy rice chaff, combed his hair, and went to the Derrick kitchen for coffee and a piece of pie with Marion and Peggy. It was time for Marion to settle with him for his work during the harvest on all three farms.

When they were through with their pie, but still sipping coffee, Marion said, "Well, Jim, all three of us, with your leadership, completed the work in record time and with less expense than in previous years. We had the greatest yield and sold at the best price ever, makin' this the most lucrative harvest in all of our years. We're not only thankful to God but also to you. Now, we have you down for 62 days of work. Is that what you have?"

"No, Marion, you let me off a total of 2½ days. That makes it 59½ days."

"Never mind that, Jim. We three agreed on payin' you for 62 days. At $12 per day, that comes to $744; but we are unanimous in decidin' to pay you $800 for what you have done for us in the harvest of 1926. I'm writin' you a check, but do you need some of this in cash?"

"No, just a check; Marion, I feel you three men are being too generous with me. But I am grateful!"

"You are welcome, my friend! By the way, how are things comin' over at your place?"

"Just fine. Henry is turnin' out to be a good carpenter, and he's teachin' me a lotta things. We'll be ready to buy furniture and move into the house in a week or so."

"Well, if you need a big truck for anything, come and get one of mine."

"Thanks, I'll need it in a few days. It could be that when we take the last of Papa's cotton to the gin, we can bring back the furniture at that time and save a trip back."

"Whether that works for you or not, you're welcome to a truck when you need it. Take the new one."

Jim and his father hauled the last load of the cotton crop to DeWitt the first day of November. Estelle went along and they shopped for furniture, buying a bedroom set, a sofa, two chairs, and two stoves—one for heating and one for cooking. Since they had the large truck, they also decided to buy several items from the hardware store. Back at the house, Henry helped Jim unload their purchases and Estelle gave directions for placing the furniture.

After breakfast the next day, the sheriff knocked on the door and asked Jim, "Could you be free to help me for several days?"

"What's up, Lloyd?"

"Trouble at the Arkansas River Bridge. Two fishermen camped on the north side of the river were robbed and murdered night before last. That puts the crime in our county. As yet we have no witnesses to identify the murderers. If you can, let's drive down today and investigate."

"Yes, I guess ye've caught me at a good time. We've finished with Papa's cotton, and I'm through workin' with Marion for the season. Estelle and I were plannin' to go over to our place and get settled in there, but we can do that later." Estelle was understanding when she heard about Jim's leaving.

Lloyd said, "Then get your things and put 'em in my truck. Take Buck; if we need Star, we'll come back for him. Estelle, I'll return Jim to you as soon as I can."

The two lawmen arrived at the Bridge about 11:00 o'clock. Lloyd told Jim, "Drive over to that cabin yonder. The Burns couple will know what went on if anyone will. Lloyd knocked, and George Burns opened the door. "Howdy, Sheriff. Been expectin' ye," the redheaded, wrinkle-faced man said.

"Tell me what ye know and what ye suspect."

"I know two fine men have been murdered. My wife and I liked them. They come here, set out some nets, and caught some fish. 'Bout midnight Bets woke me and said she heard shootin'. I jumped outa bed to look out the window, but it was so dark outside I couldn't see nothin'. I stepped outside quiet like and heard someone headin' down to their boat on the river. I'm shore there wuz two, cuz when they pushed their boat off the bank, a man's voice said, 'Joe, you get in front and paddle, I'll steer back here. We're gonna make a clean getaway!' I can't tell you who they wuz or where they went, 'cept they went downriver and one of 'em's named Joe."

"And then you went over and found the bodies?" asked Lloyd.

"When I knew the men had got away, I got my flashlight and went over to the shack to see if anyone wuz hurt or dead. Both men were in bed; they had been shot in the chest and were already dead. I didn't sleep much that night, and at daylight I went across the river and told the telegraph man to wire you and the Desha sheriff. I give him the names of the dead men—Shorty McGraw and David Wilkins—don't know their address, but I know one of 'em lived around Yancopin. Sheriff, their old truck is over there by the shack. The plate on it oughta tell ye the county."

"Their bodies have been removed by now, I guess," said Lloyd.

"Yesterday afternoon late a deputy sheriff and a Watson funeral home man came and took the bodies away. The deputy told us not to clean the cabin 'til you or the sheriff from Dumas said it would be okay."

Burns accompanied the lawmen to the shack just up from the river bank. There had been very little disturbance inside that would indicate a struggle. The men's trousers were still in the corner of the room; their pocket linings were exposed, showing that the robbers had probably taken whatever was in their pockets. Two empty wallets had been thrown on the floor. "Hope we can get some prints off these," Lloyd said, as he dropped the billfolds into a small bag.

"George, you can go ahead and clean up the shack. Thanks for the information. We'll see if we can get on the trail of those killers. I'm sure you'll hear the story later."

"Jim, now we'll go over to the railroad shack to send a message to the Desha County sheriff." A telegraph operator was on duty and cooperative, but having no telephone all he could do was send the telegram that Lloyd dictated: "Just finished investigating the scene of the murder of Shorty McGraw and David Wilkins here at Arkansas River Bridge. Will be callin' ye to see if I should come there to assist in the search of the killers. Signed, Sheriff Lloyd LaFargue."

"Jim, I'll drop you off at your Pa's place, and then I'll go over to Marion's to use the phone. I'll call Wilbur in Dumas and see if we can help."

After making the call, Lloyd returned to Boge's home and reported to Jim that the Desha County sheriff was on the trail of the killers. The house in which they were staying was being watched by a prominent family in the community, and they would notify the sheriff's office when the killers returned.

"Jim, I think we ought to go down tonight. The sheriff has a cabin where you can stay, and I'll stay in his home. He has a place for your horse, but he doesn't think we'll need him because he has horses we can use. I think we should take Buck though. Maybe you should drive your pickup in case I have to stay for legal reasons—no point in your bein' stuck down there with nothin' to do. If I understand Wilbur right, it's a waitin' game. The two killers usually come in early mornin's, usually before daylight. So why don't you come late afternoon or even after supper. Come to Dumas on 165; when you get to U.S. 65, turn left and go two blocks where you'll see Bing's Grocery; turn right and go behind it. You'll see the sheriff's office, and I'll be waitin' for you there. Can you get there at 8:00? What I'm thinkin' is we'll stand guard under cover each night from about midnight to daylight. Sooner or later, we'll have a showdown with 'em. When we do, I shore want you with me. Jim, I'll go ahead down, and if you can, come on down later tonight and meet me at the sheriff's office."

"I'll see ye tonight around 8:00, Lloyd."

Overhearing Lloyd and Jim's conversation, Ophelia decided she needed to serve an early supper. After they had eaten, Estelle told Jim they should spend some time in their room. "Honey, I have an unusual sense that this will be a dangerous mission for you and Lloyd. I'll admit that things aren't clear in my mind. But I know I need to pray for you both, so that the outcome does not involve taking your lives. I know two people will be killed! I'm very disturbed, but I have a deep assurance that one of them is not you and that you'll come back to me—very heavy in heart. I'm glad you're taking Buck. He'll be important in your showdown. Now, let's pray: Heavenly Father, You know our heart's concern for the three lawmen in Dumas. You know the whereabouts and schedules and intentions of the two killers. Bring about the information and wise decisions that will result in justice. And please keep Lloyd and Jim safe. Use them for Your glory. Help me to be faithful and watchful in prayer until this case is ended the way You want it to be. In Jesus' name, Amen."

On his way to Dumas, Jim developed some of the sense of pending tragedy that Estelle had shared with him. Even during her prayer, his spirit was opened to the possibility of death and the heaviness of having to kill or be killed.

Lloyd welcomed Jim and introduced him to Sheriff Wilbur Weston, who received him warmly and said, "From what I hear, you're the man to ride the river with." The two sheriffs briefed Jim on the trace put on the killers. Sheriff Weston said, "It's Joe Blackburn's house, and he's one of the murderers. Walt Kerstein, a rice and cotton farmer who lives close to Blackburn, is watchin' the place for us and keepin' us informed. Walt said the killers returned yesterday mornin' an hour 'fore daylight. Now we can't be certain that schedule will be the case from here on, but we're thinkin' to divide shifts, startin' at midnight and runnin' through the daylight hours. Jim, we both decided we want you on the last one." The sheriffs had already gone to the house and studied the layout, and then they dragged limbs and materials to make the covering to camouflage their presence as they watched the house.

Wilbur said, "Lloyd and I'll take you to our cabin and get you settled so you can get some sleep." Turning to Lloyd, he asked, "When do you want Jim to come on guard?"

"Well, it's 8:30 now, so why don't you go watch as soon as you get Jim settled, and Jim and I will come at 11:30. We will both stand guard from 12:00 until after daylight. Even if I fall asleep before daylight, Jim and Buck will not miss anything."

Jim kept Buck in the cabin with him. He had three hours of good sleep before the call at the door let him know it was time to go. On site, Jim made a few suggestions for changing the covering, because he doubted that some of their layout appeared very permanent and natural. He was glad for the grove of oaks in which they were to hide. He took a position that put him closest to the front door of the house, while Lloyd would be 20 yards to his left and a little more exposed. Jim looked at his watch—it was 12:05. As he settled back against a tree with tree branches as his cover, Buck's head was resting on his leg. Lloyd was expecting

Jim to go back to sleep but counting on Buck to awaken him if something happened earlier than expected. Jim planned to be wide awake from 4:30 on.

Jim could see stars shining here and there, promising a bright sunrise. The same heaviness of spirit he had experienced while driving down to Dumas now revisited him. *What's goin' on with me tonight? Buck, I'm glad you are here. Am I about to be killed? Is this the way the Creator deals with a man just before He calls him to judgment? Will I have to kill one or both of these murderers? God forbid! Will Lloyd be killed? Will I? I'm afraid I'm not prepared to meet the Lord. I'm glad Estelle is prayin'. I better not put off gettin' right with God too long.*

Buck stirred, and Jim slowly fought his way to consciousness, realizing the need to be awake but not knowing why. It then dawned on him that the darkness was slowly fading and in a few minutes he'd be able to make out objects and see whether Lloyd was awake or sleeping. Buck looked at him expecting a signal or a word. Jim heard a loud whisper from Lloyd and then a louder whisper.

"Hey, Jim! You awake?"

"Yes. Don't ye wanta go get some sleep, Lloyd? I'll stay."

"No, Jim, I'm stayin' with ye; I'm thinkin' they'll show up any time now." Jim was afraid Lloyd's loud whispers might be heard by the killers.

A few minutes past 7 o'clock, Buck stirred and looked toward the house. He sniffed, his ears forward. Jim heard what sounded like a stuck door opening, and he heard a low voice utter a word or two. He couldn't see anyone. Were the two killers entering the house from the back door beyond which was a wooded area offering more cover than the front? Of course! Why hadn't Lloyd and Wilbur realized the killers might park their vehicle a good ways away and slip in through the back?

Something was definitely taking place in that house, indicated by Buck's interest and the sounds Jim had heard. Apparently Lloyd thought so as well, for both Jim and Buck heard Lloyd stirring. Jim made his escape from his coverings and with his rifle in hand stepped quietly toward Lloyd, who was motioning toward the house. Jim nodded and then realized Lloyd was indicating that he was going to rush the house and Jim was to cover him.

"No, Lloyd!" Jim pleaded, as Lloyd bolted from his covering and dropped to one knee, pointing his rifle. Jim dropped his rifle and pulled his pistol, feeling he would be too late. He saw the front door open just a crack and then wider as two men stepped outside. Then he heard Lloyd's rifle go *snap!* Jim knew the sheriff's rifle had failed.

Jim stepped out into view and saw that the two killers were shifting their attention from Lloyd to him—just what he wanted! Jim's pistol spoke twice—*Bam! Bam!*—and both men folded. Had he waited another half second, Lloyd, kneeling helpless, would have been killed.

Shaking his head in amazement, Lloyd went forward to the two bodies. "Jim, they're both shot through the heart, just like you intended. You saved my life! Boy, that's the first time a gun ever failed me in all my years as a lawman. Thank you for being there for me."

"Sure! That's what I'm here for." Later as Jim was walking around, he began feeling the gravity of what had happened. "Lloyd, I know I did the right thang. If I was to do it over, I'd still kill 'em just to save yore life. But, man, I shore hate I had to take a life—even worse *two* lives. I know I'll get over it, and Estelle will hep me."

Lloyd watched his deputy pace and realized how seriously he was taking the killings. He went to Jim and put his hand on his shoulder. "If it's any comfort, I'm grateful you saved my life and did what I couldn't do because of a jammed rifle. If you hadn't, I'd be layin' back there dead instead of those two."

Lloyd let Jim pace and hurt for awhile before he spoke again. "Jim, let's go to Wilbur's office to get his rig, and then we'll load these bodies. Then you can head home; I think you need to be with Estelle."

Jim packed and loaded his stuff and drove away from the cabin. In Dumas, he had the feeling he should go by Wilbur's office again and reassure Lloyd he'd be okay. "Glad ye decided to stop, Jim. I just told Wilbur that I've worked with a few men who were good with guns, but I don't know anybody—lawman or criminal—who could have got off two perfect shots as quickly as you did a couple of hours ago! *And I'm so grateful you saved my life!*"

Wilbur also tried to reassure him. "Now, Jim, don't let this dampen your spirits. It's bound to happen again if you stay in this business with us. We're fortunate to have a man like you alongside us."

As Jim shook hands with the two sheriffs, they thanked him profusely for his help. They both noticed his downcast spirit as he drove away.

"Wilbur, Jim's not in the business to kill, not even the worst kind. But I know he cares enough about me to protect me against anything. I think I'll call a friend of mine and a neighbor of his, who loves him like family, and have him check on Jim tonight."

"Give me his number, Lloyd, and I'll put the call through for you." Wilbur gave the operator the number, and when it began ringing, he handed the phone to Lloyd.

"Marion, this is Lloyd LaFargue."

"Yes, Sheriff. Is Jim okay?"

"He just left for his dad's home, and he is why I'm callin' you. We got the two killers in our sights this mornin' just a bit after daylight. I attempted to shoot 'em, but my gun jammed. Jim stepped out quickly and took both of them out in lightnin' speed. Shot right through the heart, both of them. Jim and I both knew this day would come, but he left here sick at heart over what he had to do. Course, he's not sick about savin' my life. Marion, Jim Tharp is the most humane person who ever went into our business. I know you and Peggy love him. You might wanta check on him in a day or so. I've got a feelin' that his spirit will improve when he gets back with Estelle."

In the meantime, Jim had arrived back at his parents' home, where Estelle was waiting anxiously for him to return. She rushed outside to greet him. "Oh, honey, I'm so glad to see you! I haven't slept since midnight. I knew you were in great danger." She looked into Jim's eyes as he pulled her into his arms. "Something went wrong, didn't it, sweetheart?"

"Yeah, it was bad! Lloyd's gun jammed when he tried to shoot the murderers. I stepped out and shot twice, killin' both of them, but not a second too soon…" Jim broke off, turned his head. and sobbed softly. He was soon able to get his emotions under control. "The way I was standin', I couldn't get their ears, so I had to shoot to kill."

Estelle was crying, not over the news that two men had been killed, but that Jim was forced to do the killing. "Well, honey, I'm sorry! But what you had to do in the line of duty does not make you a murderer. You weren't about to let them kill Lloyd, your friend and a good, decent lawman. Consider the character of the men you shot. They murdered two men in cold blood and robbed them of their money. Who knows what else they have done? And, sweetheart, you knew a time would come when you couldn't just drill a hole in their ears. I'd guess that both men were shot right through the heart and died instantly!"

"That's the way it was. And I couldn't wait to … *come home to you!*"

"Oh, my dear one! I'm going to help you through this. While you fill Buck's dishes with food and water and check on Star, I'll go in and make you a good breakfast. After we eat, we'll go to our room and you'll strip down so I can give you a massage until you fall asleep. I want you to stay in bed and rest until this afternoon."

Inside, Estelle told Boge and Ophelia all that Jim had told her. "Now, please wait in the kitchen for Jim to come in. Just let him say anything he wants to, and while you listen and talk to him, I'll fry bacon and eggs and make toast and fresh coffee."

Jim hated being smothered with attention, but he had to admit that there was something comforting about feeling his parents' love and watching Estelle cook breakfast, often looking at him with a loving smile. He realized that things could have gone the other way. He might be lyin' dead down in the Dumas area and his parents and Estelle would be sobbing their hearts out. Or he might be delivering Lloyd's body to the DeWitt Mortuary and then his wife, Irene, and the family would be mourning.

Jim got up from the table having eaten a delicious breakfast, hugged his precious parents, and walked arm in arm with Estelle to their room. "Sit there on the bed for a minute, dear." With her head in his lap, she prayed, "Dear Lord, I thank You for protecting Jim and Lloyd this morning through the skills of my dear husband. You know his regret and his sickness over having to kill those two men. Now, come in a special visitation on him and bring comfort, reassurance of Your presence, and protection in all of this. May he learn to prayerfully turn all of his sickness and regret over to You. And help us both to turn to You very soon for the free gift of salvation by grace. Help Jim sleep and rest and recover. Amen.

"Honey, let me help you get undressed down to your shorts. Now, lie down on your stomach." Estelle began applying lotion and soft hands beginning with his neck and shoulders and moving down his back. Soon Jim was asleep. She covered him with a sheet, blessed him with a silent prayer, closed the door, and returned to Boge and Ophelia.

Jim got up at 3:00 and told Estelle and his parents that he felt like a new man—hardly able to remember the killing that morning. Lloyd came by a few minutes later, even though he had asked Marion to check on him. "Thought I'd better check on you, Jim. Glad to see you lookin' better than when you left Dumas several hours ago. Thanks again for savin' my life." Then the sheriff turned to Estelle and Jim's parents and sang his deputy's praises before saying goodbye.

To continue her son's therapy, Ophelia made sure that George and BettyLee, Marion and Peggy, and Henry and Oda, along with the girls, were all at their supper table. No mention was made of the shootout in Desha County until Marion and Peggy were ready to leave a good while after supper.

George and BettyLee broke the news that they had a new job— managers of the Little Rock Hunting Club on the lower end of Merrisach Lake. They were pleased that George would be paid a good monthly salary, receive gratuities from each hunting party, and be furnished a nice roomy house rent free. His job would be to guide the hunters when needed, keep the club supplied with firewood, build a new duck blind during the summer when no hunters were around, and see that the buildings were kept in good repair.

When the Derricks were leaving, Peggy pulled Estelle and Jim together at the door and said, "We know you two, especially Jim, have been through quite an ordeal. But Jim, we are proud of you for what you did. You saved a dear friend's life—a good sheriff and a wonderful man. You did your duty, and you should have no regrets. And Estelle, we know the Lord is using you to help Jim climb out of any downcast spirit into which he might have fallen. Look up, Jim; you both have a lot to look forward to, and we are with you all the way." She kissed both of them.

Marion said, "We love you two like family. Keep up the good work. The whole county is proud of you, Jim, but none more than Peggy and me. God bless you both!"

The rest of the people in the house had quietly listened to the Derricks' remarks. Then they expressed their thoughts with Jim and

Estelle, knowing they were intimately involved in Jim's recovery. George and BettyLee were the first to speak. "We feel so close to you two that when you hurt we do, too. Jim, you did what needed to be done this morning." Henry and Oda were the next ones to comment. "Brother, feel good about whut ye done! Just realize the Good Lord give ye the skill to knock off them kinds of evil people." The girls each came and kissed their brother and hugged Estelle.

"Now, Jim and Estelle, Henry and Oda, and Papa and Mama and girls, we want y'all at our place for Thanksgiving dinner in a few days," BettyLee said, with George agreeing. "We shore do! And Jim and Henry, bring ye shotguns and we'll go huntin' in the early afternoon. Reckon we'll eat about dark, so we can hunt right up 'til then."

After the dinner guests had left and before retiring, Boge prayed for Jim's healing and thanked God for Estelle's love for Jim and her tender support.

The next day Jim and Estelle loaded their personal things in the truck to move to their own house. It was a cool November afternoon, and they were pleased that Henry, anticipating their arrival, had built a fire in the heating stove. "I'll get curtains and blinds when we go to town," Estelle said, "and I'll make a list of other things we'll need. I think I have about everything I need for the kitchen. But I guess there are a lot of things you need, aren't there, dear?"

"Yeah, I'd better make me a list, too. We'll go to the bank and make a deposit of my harvest pay. I need to get some cash to buy the things we want, catch up with Henry's wages and expenses, and have some money to live on."

Jim decided to get his traps ready for setting the first week of December. He needed to clean the rust from the old ones and oil both old and new. He planned to set 200 this year—a hundred in the bottoms here and another hundred up in LaGrue bottoms. From what he had heard, the price for fur would be the same as last year.

While getting settled in their home, Estelle noticed Jim was recovering well from the sadness over having to kill two murderers. He was delighted to be able to settle with Henry, have the fruit trees paid for, pay for the well and the pump, and still have a few thousand dollars in the bank.

When Jim was getting ready to leave for the Thanksgiving hunt with George, Estelle noticed Jim looking at his gun. "I've been huntin' with this old double-barrel shotgun since I wuz nine years old. Reckon I'm gonna hafta get me a new one—this one is so outdated."

"What kind will you buy?"

"Most hunters now shoot a Browning Automatic. They cost over $100. But I want me a Winchester Pump, Twenty Gauge, Modified Choke. It'll only cost about $45."

"Then that will be your Christmas present, and I'm paying for it with my money! Wish I had known about your need the day before yesterday when we were there in the hardware store buying things for the house. Listen, I'd be glad to buy the Browning Automatic if you'd let me."

"No, thanks; I'd prefer the Winchester Pump."

"Well, we'll be going to town before Christmas, and I want you to pick it out."

On Thanksgiving Day, BettyLee greeted Jim and Estelle at the door. "Nobody in the world I'd rather welcome to my house than you two. Come on in, and I'll show you around. Halfway in the tour she blurted out, "Oh, Estelle! I'm gonna have a baby! Jim, you're gonna be an uncle!" George appeared just then and joined in on the rejoicing.

An hour later, George and Jim, each with a guest in his boat, paddled out to two duck blinds. Jim's guest was Dr. Ed Williams and George's, Roger Fulton. After getting set in the blind, Jim said, "Now, Doc, I usually blow the duck caller, but if ye prefer…"

"No, young man. I'm not even a good duck hunter; please do the calling."

They'd only been in the blind ten minutes before two mallards flew over fairly low. Jim blew the caller, and they circled and came back, descending lower as though they would land. Jim told Doc to get the one on the left. He fired and missed. Jim shot the one on the right and it folded. When he saw that Doc was not going to shoot again at the flying duck, Jim killed that one too. "Now, Doc, sit down and rest a minute. I'll get in the boat and fetch the ducks."

Back in the blind, Jim assured the doctor that they would get another flight of ducks soon. "Now, Doc, don't fret over a missed shot.

Just take a little lead on ducks flying across your field of vision, and let 'em fly into your shot."

Several flights gave Jim and the doctor opportunities for action. Jim killed his limit of eight, and he killed three for the doctor so that he had his eight.

When George and Jim arrived back at the Club House, Boge, Ophelia, Henry, Oda, Hollis, and Jenny were all there to enjoy Thanksgiving Dinner. First though, they celebrated BettyLee's pregnancy.

"Who'll be next for a pregnancy?" George asked, "Oda or Estelle?"

"We're tryin'," Oda said.

"And we are, too," Estelle said.

Dinner was called and, looking at the table filled with food, Henry exclaimed, "What a Thanksgiving Day feast before us!" After George had prayed a blessing on the meal and the family, he began carving the turkey as the rest of the meal was passed around the table. BettyLee had prepared potatoes, sweet potatoes, gravy, blackeyed peas, corn, cranberries, and both cornbread and biscuits. She had also made apple and minced pies, and Estelle had brought her great coconut cake.

While they were eating, someone discovered that it was snowing outside and growing colder. BettyLee declared, "There's room for y'all to spend the night with us," but everyone thought they should return to their own places.

On their way home that night, Estelle said, "I'm happy for George and BettyLee's pregnancy. And, by the way, Oda whispered to me that she thinks she might be also. She said she did not want to announce it yet, fearing that Henry might not be happy about it like George was or you would be. How do you feel about it, honey?"

"The only way it would make me unhappy is if it did not make you happy," Jim said.

"We'll just keep trying, and I believe it will happen soon," Estelle said.

By the time they arrived home, snow was falling heavier and the temperature had dropped nearly to zero. Jim built a fire, and soon the room was comfortable. "Estelle, I'm glad we came home tonight, for if we hadn't, I wouldn't be able to get my traps out until another week with this cold spell. I'll begin tomorrow over on Elbow Slough and then the next day at our set on LaGrue Bayou. I'm glad to hear that the price for mink fur will be the same as last year—for coon, though, there will be a little drop in price."

On the first day of December, Jim mounted Star and set out to see what his traps held. Just before dark that night, he returned with 12 mink hides and 20 coon hides. "A good haul," he said to Estelle, rejoicing over their prospect of getting ahead to his dream of buying cattle and clearing more land for cotton and corn.

Late one evening after he had finished stretching several mink and coon hides, Jim called Estelle over to him. "Life is good with you, sweetheart. I love ye so much, and I thank ye for heppin' me out of that mental and emotional sinkhole I fell into after killin' them two fellers."

"And I want to tell you that I'm thankful for the joy and privilege of being your wife and living with you here in our new place. I enjoy cooking for you and cleaning house, and I can't wait for you to come home each evening. I'm hoping to have your baby. The Lord is blessing us and meeting our material needs. But, honey, I think often of our need to get saved and have God's Spirit in us, to have the assurance of eternal life and to enjoy praying and reading the Bible together. I would love to see people all over this community come together and form a body of believers so we can go to church, sing, pray, reach the lost, and be a people of God."

Jim listened respectfully to her words. "I'm in favor of all that. I just don't know how to get there."

Bob Hibbard came by on the second week of December to look at Jim's and Henry's mink and coon hides. "These are the best hides I've seen in a long time. Well, I'll give $30 each for all 30 mink hides and $10 each for the 11 coon hides. That comes to $1,010. If you decide today, that's what I'll pay you. I can't promise that even next week."

"I'll take it, Bob."

The next day the snow and ice had melted, so Jim and Estelle decided to go to town. They went by Jim's parents home to see what they might need. Ophelia got the list of groceries she needed and added two or three things to get from the hardware. When she tried to hand Estelle a $20 bill, it was rejected. "No way, Mama! We want to take care of this for you. And by the way, this will be our first Christmas, so we want to have you and Papa and the girls, Henry and Oda, George and BettyLee, and Dee all at our house on Christmas night to share dinner and a wonderful time together. Please come!"

"We surely will come and celebrate with you," Boge promised.

"What can I bring?" Ophelia wanted to know.

"Two or three Jeff Davis pies, please, Mama!"

After they left for the store, Estelle thought about the Christmas gifts for the family. "Honey, I want us to buy everyone a nice gift. We'll get yours today. I think I know what I want to buy Papa and Mama, Oda and Henry, George and BettyLee, and Hollis and Jenny. I also want to get a nice gift for Dee."

"And what would you like to have?" Jim asked, trying to figure out what her smile meant.

"I'll be pleased with whatever you decide to get me."

"I'm thinkin' of a silver or pearl necklace for ye."

"I'll confess that I'd like one or the other, whichever doesn't cost so much."

"Since I'll be goin' to the hardware store to pick out my gift, I want ye to go to the jewelry store with me to pick out yores."

After making their bank deposit and visiting with L.A. Black for a few minutes, Jim and Estelle headed for Schellhorn's Hardware. Jim went straight to the guns and found his desired Winchester Pump. Mr. Schellhorn came over to the display to see which gun Jim was examining. "You're lookin' at an awfully popular gun there. They tell me you shoot a pump better and faster than most guys shoot an automatic." Jim was not surprised that his way with guns was common knowledge.

"I'm wantin' a twenty gauge, modified choke."

"Mr. Schellhorn, I'm buying this gun for my husband's Christmas present. How much, please?"

"Well, it would normally cost $45.95, but since you're buying it for Jim Tharp, it will be $36.76—that's a discount of 20 percent. That discount will always be available for anything either one of you buys here in this store for as long as I own the store!"

"We thank you very much, Mr. Schellhorn," Estelle said as she handed him two $20 bills.

"What else for you two?" he asked.

"A case of 20-gauge Peter's High Velocity shells, number 5 shot," Jim said, handing him a twenty.

"And I need to buy a roasting pan." Estelle headed for the section that displayed pots and pans.

At the jewelry store, Jim thought the silver necklace looked nicer than the pearls that had taken Estelle's eye. But she convinced him she wanted the pearls.

At Young's Department Store, Estelle bought items for most of the others. Before they drove home, Jim thought they had better run by Lloyd's office.

"Yes, Jim, he'll want a look at you, and he'll see you are looking well."

Lloyd saw them drive up, and he met them at the door. "Welcome, Jim and Estelle. Been wonderin' 'bout you, Jim. Hey! You look like yer old self."

"Yeah, Lloyd, I'm doin' fine. Give this woman credit for pullin' me out of the hole. I'm ready for anythang ye need me for now."

"That's good news, Jim! I was sure it would work that way, because I knew Estelle would be able to bring you back in good shape. Oh, say, I'm droppin' a nice Christmas check in the mail for you in a day or two, and I wish you both a very Merry Christmas! Thanks for stoppin' by. It's startin' to snow a little, I see, so be careful," Lloyd said.

While Estelle shopped in Tichnor for Christmas baking supplies, the normal groceries, and the items on Ophelia's list, Jim visited with Uncle Hay, who wanted to know how things were coming at their new place—buildings, well, clearing, orchard, cattle. "I haven't bought cattle yet, because I hear so many warnin's about a 1927 flood. I might wait on that. Because I did so well workin' with Marion in the harvest last fall and I'm doin' great in trappin' minks and coons, I might not have to borrow much money from ye, Uncle Hay."

"That's good, Jim, but whatever you need, I'll see that you get it when you are ready."

"Thanks, Uncle Hay. Estelle and I do 'preciate that."

Trapping proved even more profitable for Jim in the days leading up to Christmas than it was during the earlier season. Estelle and Oda spent hours in the kitchen preparing for the Christmas celebration. Both women were pleased with the excitement their husbands were manifesting in the coming season—like talking about the gathering and even cutting Christmas trees for both places.

Two days before Christmas, Estelle asked Jim to go with her to Sweeney's store for a few needed items. The roads in the woods were white with a few inches of snow, but the frozen ground assured them they would not get stuck. It was inspiring to drive slowly through the winter wonderland, especially when a buck and two large does darted across the road in front of them. After both had exclaimed delight in seeing the graceful animals, Jim said, "That reminds me, we're gettin' a deer season in 1927, which means I can kill us a deer for Christmas or Thanksgiving next year. And maybe I'll kill us a couple of wild turkey gobblers."

"You'll use the Winchester for turkey, won't you?"

"Yeah, but I'll start usin' the Winchester in January when we go to George's for New Year's Day."

At the store, both Cleve and Ebrena greeted Jim and Estelle warmly. Estelle told Ebrena she needed sweet potatoes, raisins, sage, and baking powder.

"I'll bet the woods were beautiful up your way this morning," Ebrena said.

"Indeed they were, and the deer we saw made our trip here even more exciting," Jim said.

The next day while Estelle and Oda baked and cooked for the Christmas party, which was now only one day away, Estelle played Christmas carols on their new large radio. Just before dark, Estelle called Jim to come and look with her at the two large cedar trees in their front yard decorated so beautifully with snow. "Isn't that a beautiful picture! Honey, I'm so thankful for our place here whether it is snowing or raining or we're baking in the sun!"

As Henry came in for a piece of pie, Estelle said, "Henry, I thank you so much for this large table, but I think we're going to have you build us a large dining room that runs the full length of the kitchen, and we'll add it on to the north here."

"Well, I reckon I could do that, come spring or summer."

When all of those invited had arrived and the Christmas meal was on the table, Estelle called everyone to come and sit down. As Jim carved the turkey, she shared a few sentiments with them. "You'll all need to forgive my tears of joy. This is Jim's and my first Christmas, and we're so happy that you've blessed us by coming to be with us. I thank the Lord for allowing me to become a part of this family. I owe Grandma Best so much, and I have a wonderful mother. Now I have a home of my own and the greatest husband in the world, and Papa and Mama Tharp here, and all of you…" Estelle paused to collect herself and wipe tears. "Jim, do you want to say something and then call on Papa to pray over our food and this gathering?"

"First, I wanta thank the Lord for bringin' me this beautiful, lovin' wife. I always knew I wanted to marry a wonderful woman, but I never dreamed any girl could be so sweet, wise, lovin', and hardworkin' as this dear person. She's heppin' me to want to know the Lord, too. I ain't claimin' to be a Christian, but I have a feelin' her prayers are gonna lead us both to the Lord purty soon in a born-again way. Now, Papa, would you lead us in a prayer of worship of the Christ Child and in gettin' into this glorious season?"

Boge was definitely gifted in expressing thanks to Almighty God for Jesus Christ and His gracious salvation for sinners. He rejoiced in forgiveness of sins and fellowship with God through the Spirit. He thanked God for Jim and Estelle and the goodness of God that brought them together and for their hospitality in bringing the family together for the evening and a delicious meal. He thanked God for George and BettyLee, Henry and Oda, Dee, Hollis, and Jenny. He prayed for "a sense of the presence of God on all as we share this food and express love to one another."

The feast lasted almost an hour. Ophelia asked, "Estelle, do we cut this great coconut cake and these pies, or do we get our breath and eat dessert later?" Estelle put it to a vote and announced that those wanting to wait won. She said, "Now, we'll ask the men to carry chairs into the living room, where we'll sing some Christmas carols and maybe even allow Santa Claus to make an appearance."

"What a meal!" Boge said, as he followed his daughters into the living room. Estelle turned on the radio and found carols immediately. "Sing along," she urged, as she led out. "Silent Night," "Joy to the World," and "Away in a Manger" played one after the other, besides a few more carols they were familiar with.

When the radio program ended, Estelle decided it was time to open the gifts she had wrapped for the guests. "Jim, why don't you be our Santa and see if you can find something over there under that tree for everyone." Groans and protests were heard by some who felt embarrassed, not knowing of any plans for gift exchange. "No," Estelle said, "We don't want any of you feeling badly because you didn't bring a gift. This was my idea, and we weren't expecting any gifts from you. Jim and I are simply expressing our love for our family because the Lord has been so generous with us all through this year. Please receive these gifts as tokens of our love."

Jim began with "gifts for Papa and Mama and two precious young sisters, then for a dear brother Henry and his wife, then for a dear sister BettyLee and her husband—who truly has become my brother—and then for our dear sister Dee." Once Jim had distributed the gifts, Estelle instructed them to take turns opening them starting with the young girls.

Hollis and Jenny squealed with delight in receiving gifts of lingerie. Ophelia was delighted with her "navy blue dress and brooch." Oda held up her "brown dress and a beautiful matching wool sweater to keep me warm." Henry said, "Jim, you musta seen I been wearin' a worn out old jacket, so you bought me a new Duxbak huntin' coat and a hat to match!" Boge stood up smiling, slipped on a leather jacket with its dark brown fur collar, and held up a pair of leather gloves to match, and remarked, "I'll be the best-dressed man in town." Dee, delighted with her gift of a light green cable-knit sweater set and some hosiery, said, "Estelle, this sweater set will fit perfectly, and you've only seen me twice. How did you know my size?"

Without answering Dee, but smiling, Estelle jumped up and walked over to the tree. "Well, that's not all!" She reached behind the tree and brought out a beautifully wrapped, narrow elongated box and handed it to Jim, saying, "For my loving husband on our first Christmas together!" Everyone clapped when Jim opened the box and drew out the shiny Winchester Pump gun. Standing, he threw up the gun and began pumping and clicking with the touch of the trigger several times. Going over to Estelle, he pulled her into his arms and kissed her long and meaningfully, to the delight of all.

Jim then found the small package he had for Estelle, which he handed to her, saying, "For the prettiest and sweetest wife in the world!" It took little time for her to open the box and adorn herself with a genuine white pearl necklace. The family clapped and whistled and called out, "Beautiful Estelle!" In tears, Estelle embraced Jim and said, "I'm so grateful, darling!"

Estelle called on all to stand and asked the men to put the chairs back to the table so they could enjoy dessert and coffee.

About 10:00, Boge called Jim and Estelle to him. "Children, we've all felt the presence of the Lord here in your home tonight. My own spirit is inspired by being here with y'all. We wish you a lot of happiness. Thank you for the gifts to all of us! It's late and we'd better get our young girls, Mama, and head through the snow to our home. Good night all! Are you ready, Dee?"

"Since I came with you and Mama, I'd better leave with you before I miss my ride."

George and BettyLee were next to leave, "Gotta get my mama-to-be home and in bed for her rest."

Henry and Oda, who lived in their tent only a few yards from Jim and Estelle's kitchen steps, lingered awhile and reflected on the past year. They expressed their delight and joy in helping Jim and Estelle build up their place and in living so close to them.

"Estelle, I'm going to have a baby! And the best news is, Henry is happy about it!"

"Wonderful!" both Jim and Estelle exclaimed at the same time.

"Well, it hasn't happened to me yet, but Jim and I are not giving up."

"We're shore tryin' hard!" Jim said, and all laughed.

No sooner were Henry and Oda gone than Estelle said, "Honey, I truly am happy for George and BettyLee and Henry and Oda. But I pray for a baby every day and then I cry every month when my period comes. But I believe about three days ago that I got the assurance from the Lord that I will get pregnant some time in the new year of 1927! And I'm so happy about it!"

"Estelle, that's wonderful! I've known you now about nine months, and I find that you usually get what you pray for. The things you count on the Lord to do usually develop. So I'm quite sure in my own mind that you will get pregnant in the new year. Not that it couldn't happen tonight and durin' the few days and nights left in 1926!" Jim paused, and then with a great smile, said seriously, "Sweetheart, I feel in my heart that you will make a great mother!"

"Oh, thank you, darling. I know you will make a loving, caring father!"

"Well, since we have our home and I'm makin' a little money and gettin' it together, I reckon we're not doin' too bad."

"Well, honey, I'm not only praying and hoping for a baby; I really want us to think seriously about finding the Lord in saving grace and living a life of faith!"

4   *Family and Faith*

The first week of 1927 was a prosperous time for Jim. The ice and snow were melting, the wild animals were on the prowl, and he could never remember catching as many minks in his traps in one week.

In late February, Jim and Henry worked hard in the bottoms clearing out logs and brush to set their heart-and-lead nets for catching schools of fish. Now that Jim's brother would be working with him, they would need to make greater investments in fishing tackle, boats, and motors. Since Henry had no accumulated resources, it was up to Jim to buy this equipment. Henry agreed to forego a portion of his share of the fish sales to repay Jim. Estelle felt the brothers should venture out together, since they were fond of each other, very compatible in their dispositions, and not afraid of hard work. Estelle supported their agreement to purchase a large truck for hauling the fish long distances to get better prices.

When Estelle gave Jim the news in March that she knew she was pregnant, they rejoiced together. They talked often about what it would mean to become parents—it would bring joy, change their lives, and be costly. Estelle was fortunate in escaping the morning sickness that had overtaken BettyLee and Oda in the third month of their pregnancies. She was able to garden, work in the yard, and help Jim with feeding and watering the orchard and the animals at the barn.

Both Tharp families were not pleased with the increasing forecasts of flooding that would drive them from their comfortable abodes. Henry and Oda assured Jim and Estelle that their large tent would have plenty of room for both families wherever they might have to relocate. The brothers agreed to move the tent to the LaGrue community near Papa and Mama Tharp's place. The relocation allowed them to divide their time between net fishing in the bottoms and helping Marion and Boge plant their rice and cotton.

Estelle was saddened to know that her garden was inundated with water, but she enjoyed time working in Ophelia's garden. She missed living in her own house, working with the animals at the barn, and seeing improvements in the land as the men cleared out thorn thickets and planted grass in the yard. Even in her disappointments, she learned to pray and trust the Lord to use all interruptions to strengthen her and Jim. Each week she realized the increasing size of the baby she was carrying and was filled with joy over the prospects of giving birth and nurturing the little one.

When the crops were in and the waters had receded, Jim and Henry decided that the seining season was not far in the future. Instead of moving back to their place, they thought it would be wiser to relocate the tent on some high ground down near the lakes they would be seining. The first of August they moved the tent to the banks of Mill Bayou, about three miles south of the Nady store. They had both done well in net fishing, and Marion was generous in paying Jim for his labors. However, Henry felt he should donate his labor in working for his father. After relocating the tent, Jim and Henry spent a week cleaning up the house, the other buildings, and the entire area around their place. Jim and Estelle planned to move back into their house in the fall.

Living in the tent was not as uncomfortable as Estelle had thought it would be. The tent had a solid and smooth wood floor, and their sleeping areas were separated, allowing both couples privacy. Even though they needed mosquito bars for their beds at night, she and Jim were happy with the setup. Years ago, a pump had been driven, so they had pure, cool water for drinking, cooking, and washing.

One night after supper, Estelle asked, "Jim, have you thought about a name for the baby?"

"Not much. Do you have a name? Guess we don't know if we'll need to name a boy or a girl."

"If it's a girl, would you agree to our naming her Frances Jeanette?"

"I reckon so, but why that?"

"I want her to have the name Frances after my sister Mabel Frances. And I love hearing Jeanette McDonald sing on the radio. Sometimes she does duets with Nelson Eddy. I like the sound of Frances Jeanette. I hope you do."

"Yeah, that will be okay. But what if it's a boy?"

"Then I'd like to name him after you—James William Tharp, Jr."

"Wouldn't that be a little confusin'? I'd be pleased for him to have one of my names, but…"

"It's done all the time, and I think you will be proud to have your son named after you."

"Of course, I would! Thank you."

Jim and Henry got licenses for enough lakes to keep them seining all through September. With their large new truck, they profited from driving the distances to market in Pine Bluff, Stuttgart, and Memphis. When they had settled with their workers and divided their profits, Henry was elated and yelled out, "Eat ye heart out, John D. Rockefeller! I've got more filthy lucre on me than I ever had in my life!" He was able to settle with Jim on the equipment they had bought and buy groceries and other supplies to prepare for moving their tent back up on Jim's place.

When it was time to move back, Estelle admitted to Jim that she did not feel as well as she had a few days before. She feared something wasn't right with her pregnancy.

"Then let's go see Dr. Whitehead in DeWitt." The doctor could not give Estelle a reason for the way she felt. "Get plenty of rest, and don't work too hard—only get a moderate amount of exercise and no lifting and straining."

Jim decided on the way back home that Estelle should be moved to his parents for the remaining time of her pregnancy. "Mama and Dee and the girls can see to your every need. And we'll be only two miles from a telephone if we need one." Estelle agreed.

Boge, Ophelia, and the girls were elated over Jim and Estelle moving back in with them. They looked forward to the baby's arrival. Jim was helping Marion overhaul a pumping engine on a bright October day when Boge drove over to give Jim the news that Estelle's water broke about 11:30. After phoning Dr. Whitehead, Jim said, "Papa, Marion and I will be through with the engine in an hour, and then I'll be home by the time the doctor gets there."

"No, Jim," Marion said, "Go out and show me which gaskets go where, and I can finish up. You belong with your wife, not here helpin' me."

"Well, if you insist, I'll go to Estelle."

Boge and Ophelia were relieved that Jim had returned home. The labor pains were mild so far, but Estelle needed her husband to be there as the labor progressed. "Oh, honey! I'm so glad to see you!"

"Are you in a lot of pain?"

"Just every now and then, although I know it will worsen and probably the contractions will hit me more often soon. Have you eaten lunch?"

"Yeah, we'd finished when Papa come."

While Jim was rubbing Estelle's back, they heard Ophelia welcome the doctor. He kissed Ophelia's cheek and she took him to Estelle's room. After kissing Estelle, he slapped Jim on the shoulder. "Hey, looks like my old huntin' buddy's gonna be a daddy!" He turned to Ophelia and asked, "Got plenty of hot water and towels?"

"Yes, Doctor, and the towels are all washed, dried, and ready when you call for them."

"Now that's the kind of midwife I like. I don't expect any problem in the delivery, because the baby was in the proper position the other day when you came in for your appointment. Your contractions should start getting closer together and stronger. Now, I'll let you know when it is time for you to start pushing. So rest up and get ready!"

On October 12, 1927, at 2:32 in the afternoon, Estelle gave birth to Frances Jeanette, described by Dr. Whitehead as "a perfectly healthy baby girl." The doctor left after he made sure baby and mother were fine and he had given instructions.

Jim knelt by Estelle's bedside and patted her arm. "Honey, I'm so proud of you! I'm grateful to you for all the sufferin' you endured to give us this precious baby girl. Mama's got her now, but I can't wait 'til I can see and hold her again! When she gets hungry, will you breast feed her or put her on a bottle?"

"I really want to breast feed her. If I can't, Dr. Whitehead said to call him and he'll tell me what formula to use."

Jim felt an inner melting as Ophelia lay the baby girl in his arms. *I'm just not worthy of the honor of bein' a daddy. Lord, You'll have to hep me.* When Frances Jeanette started fussing, Estelle reached for her, thinking she was hungry and needing to be fed. Jim watched as the baby nestled against her mother and, guided by Estelle, began nursing.

The next morning, Estelle said, "I can't dismiss the feeling that we need to check on our mail down in Nady. And I know you are missing the *Gazette.* Also, Mama may need something from the store. And would you please go tell my mother about the baby?"

Alma rejoiced at the news of another granddaughter, and she loved the name. "I hope Estelle did not have too difficult a time and that she'll soon have her strength back."

"Mother, Estelle's doin' fine and enjoyin' nursin' the baby. The baby was born up at my folks' place in LaGrue. We had to move out of our home for awhile 'cause of the floodin', but we'll be movin' back when Estelle is strong enough to be up and about."

"When Estelle is able to make the trip, please bring her and the baby to see us. Tell Estelle we love her, that we are all well. The children are growing like weeds, and Twyla jabbers about 'Stell' every now and then. We can't wait to see Frances Jeanette!"

At Sweeney's Store, Ebrena was elated to hear that Estelle had given birth to a baby girl. "When you get moved back to your place, maybe Cleve and I will drive up and see this precious new person."

"Well, why don't y'all drive up to Papa's Sunday night and be part of a gatherin'—Marion and Peggy, George and BettyLee, and Henry and Oda will be there. Estelle would be so pleased. Please come!"

"Jim, we'll be there. It's our best time to get away; we close the store early on Sunday. Now let me get your mail back here." She handed Jim a whole armload of papers and letters.

"See you and Cleve Sunday night. Come in time for supper!" Jim said. He could hardly wait to get home and see Estelle and the baby. Would it be this way from now on?

Ophelia was pleased to hear that the Sweeneys would be a part of the Sunday night supper. She had a late garden to draw from, and Jim had kept her pantries filled with food and supplies. She would miss Jim and Estelle and that little one when they moved out in a few days, but she understood their longing to be home.

It was a joyful gathering on Sunday evening around the Tharp table, with Estelle seated next to Jim for her first table meal in almost a week. She was feeling strong and looking fine. Everyone showered her with congratulations, expressions of love, and gifts for the baby daughter. After supper, Jim brought the sleeping baby into the dining room so she could be viewed by all. Cleve jokingly said, "I can't understand how that baby can look so much like Jim and still be beautiful." Ebrena countered her husband's remark by saying, "Well, I happen to think Estelle married one of the nicest and most handsome gentlemen on all of Little Prairie!" Jim was uncomfortable with that, but lifting his daughter up higher said, "She is beautiful alright, but I know she gets it from her mother." Everyone nodded or agreed verbally when Peggy said, "No, this darling baby gets her beauty from both her father and her mother. Look at that glossy black hair and that dimple in her chin."

On Monday, Jim and Estelle and the baby moved back to their place. On the way, Estelle had a request. "Honey, I wish we would give our place a name and not have to say 'the place' or 'over there on the edge of the White River bottoms.'"

"Well, what do you have in mind? I don't reckon we can call it 'The Eagle's Nest' or 'Falconcrest' even if we do see eagles flyin' 'round now and then. We certainly can't call it 'The White House!'"

"No, it's just something we might want to think about. I'd be pleased to just call it 'The Haven,' since it represents a place of safety and peace for us. Well, here we are and doesn't the place look good? How wonderful to be bringing our baby into our home!" Inside they found that Oda had the place looking spic and span with everything in place.

"Estelle, where does the crib go?"

"In our bedroom on my side of the bed."

Ross and Flossie drove up after Jim and Estelle had eaten supper. They rejoiced with them about the condition of their place after the water had receded. "Yes, we just moved in today along with our new baby," Estelle said, as she left the room to get Jeanette from her crib. Flossie took the baby and exclaimed, "For being a week old, she is very alert. She sure is a beautiful child!"

"We think so," Jim said. "She sleeps most of the time, as I reckon all newborns do."

Ross cleared his throat and said, "Jim and Estelle, we've come to talk about spiritual things, and we hope you'll be interested in what we have to say. The other day in DeWitt, I met a preacher by the name of Frank Fox, who has been associated with a Bible college in Westfield, Indiana. He belongs to the Friends Church, and he's scoutin' around DeWitt and Gillette and over in Desha County—around Dumas, Watson, McGhee, and a little community called MacArthur—to see if he can begin some preachin' points that will develop into churches. He asked about our community around Nady. I told him that I know we are in need of spiritual life, with havin' no church in our community. He wants to either come himself or send someone down in our parts to hold a meetin', preach the Gospel, and get some folks saved—then see if there's possibilities for a church. Now, Estelle, I've talked to your mother and Franklin Wallace, your sister Mabel, and Wesley and Morgan Tharp. I'm thinkin' George and BettyLee might be interested and maybe Henry and Oda. I wanta get Estelle's and your ideas on this."

"Oh, Ross and Flossie, something like this is what I've been praying for! Jim and I both know we need to find Jesus as our Savior. I want the new birth, like Grandma Best has. I've told Jim that this is my main passion in life. I also want Jim to know the Lord, and we'll want to raise our children in a Christian home, teach them about God's love, read the Bible to them, and take them to church on Sunday. Yes, indeed, we are interested!"

"This Rev. Frank Fox gave me his name and address. If I can stir up enough interest for a community meetin', I'm to write and invite him or someone else to come down for a week of meetin's each night. As people get saved, he'll meet with them, explain the doctrines and conditions of membership, and maybe organize a church while he is here."

"Well, why don't we have a prayer meeting and invite the ones you've already mentioned plus those we think might be interested. We can see what everyone is feeling. Jim and I would be willing to host this at our place. Just give us time to get the word out."

"That's good! Flossie and I will help you two decide who to invite and who'll do the invitin'."

"Can we make it a month from tonight? You and Flossie invite those you mentioned. Jim and I will invite Tharps, Bests, Sheltons,

Sweeneys, Cooses, and others we can think of. A month away will put us on the Friday night after Thanksgiving. Let's make it the last Friday night in November. How does that sound?"

As the Morgans were leaving, Ross asked, "Jim, have you thought of buyin' cows yet?"

"Not much lately, but I'm still interested."

"Well, I know where there are five heifers for sale at a fair price. Oughta have calves in the spring. Let me know if you're interested."

"Thanks, I will let you know."

After the Morgans left, Estelle asked, "What did you think of our meeting here tonight?"

"I think it was fine! I'm glad somethin' might be startin' to shape up that you've been prayin' for. And I'm with you in this. Glad you opened our home for the prayer meetin'. Don't know if Henry will wanta come, but I bet Oda will. Same with George and BettyLee, but we can invite 'em and see."

One beautiful fall day, Estelle decided to leave Jeanette with Oda while she and Jim walked around their property. They took in the yard and went down around the outbuildings and north to the orchard. Returning back by Henry and Oda's tent, Henry said, "Y'all come in and have a glass of iced tea." While they drank their tea, Jim talked about his trapping plans. "I always try to set my traps the last week of November. I need a few days to sand and scrape the rust and do some oilin'. I'm plannin' to set 200 again this year—100 here and 100 up in LaGrue."

Henry let everyone know what he planned to do. "I'll set at least 100, mainly 'round Honey Locust, Deep Bayou, and Buckhorn, I guess. I wanta do some headlightin', too. But I gotta get into them minks, cuz that brangs in the dollars."

"Henry, how about heppin' me get the honey from three trees I've got marked?" Jim suggested.

"Shore will! Wanta do that next week?"

"Yeah."

Jim and Henry were delighted that their harvest of honey was abundant. After that task was done, they spent one day finishing the barn; the smokehouse, tool shed, and outdoor toilet were already finished. Then they devoted a few days to clearing land.

To Jim and Estelle, so much talk of a coming great depression did not seem to be based on reality. Yet they both felt they must operate economically and watch their spending throughout 1928.

One night after supper Estelle said, "Honey, unless you have something urgent on for tonight, I want us to sit down and talk about some things on my mind."

"Alright, and if there's somethin' I ain't doin' right, let me have it straight," Jim said.

"No, dear. You are not what this is about—not entirely. You are not to blame for what is bothering me. In fact, I've never loved you more or been more pleased with our life together than I am now since the baby came. Darling, do you realize we have bought land, built buildings, paid for a well and a pump, furnished this house, bought half interest in a new truck and equipment for fishing and trapping, and have the money set aside to buy a few head of cattle. All this and we have not borrowed one dollar. Everything is paid for, and we have $7,000 in the bank and about $500 cash in hand. So why am I concerned? Because time is slipping by and neither of us yet knows the Lord in saving grace. Yes, He has answered many of our prayers. I'm also concerned that even in our prosperity we have not begun to tithe our income and give to the needy. I'm glad we are going to have this prayer meeting here in a few weeks and consider having a Gospel meeting to which we can contribute. I want us to really push for a church and a pastor, and I want us to begin tithing and giving."

"Sounds to me like you think our spiritual life should include our pocketbook and bank account."

"Yes, I do!"

"Well, I don't disagree. We have been blessed, and I want us to be generous with the Lord's work. But I don't like the idea of walkin' up to some self-ordained, jackleg preacher and handin' him a lotta money. But I do agree that we ought to give accordin' to the way the Lord blesses us financially. And we certainly will be generous in gettin' this preacher here Ross is talkin' about."

"Honey, I remember how Grandma Best had to argue with Grandpa for every dollar she gave in the Campshed Methodist offerings. I thank God you are not like that. I look forward to helping finance the

Gospel meeting coming to Nady. Thank you for listening to me and being so understanding."

Because of unforeseen circumstances, the prayer meeting at the Tharp's home in the interest of holding a Gospel meeting did not take place until March 20, 1929, Jim's 23rd birthday. Ross called the meeting to order with 15 people present: Ross and Flossie Morgan, Jim and Estelle Tharp, Morgan Tharp, Oda Tharp, Alma Wallace, Ebrena Sweeney and her son Spencer, Garland and Tassie Coose, Wesley and Mabel Bennett, and George and BettyLee Best. Ross shared with the group what he had told Jim and Estelle a few weeks before. Again, he expressed his deep concern that the Nady and lower prairie community needed to have a spiritual center. He did not propose to explain the doctrines and policies of the Friends Church, but he liked all that Rev. Frank Fox had told him. If there was sufficient interest, he felt contact should be made for a week of Gospel meetings to hear the Word preached and to allow people to respond as the Lord led.

Estelle moved that Ross write the letter of invitation to Rev. Frank Fox to arrange for a Gospel meeting sometime in the fall. The vote was unanimous. A question was asked as to the whereabouts of such a meeting. Ross said that since the Menard schoolhouse served most community interests, he assumed that would be the site.

Estelle announced Jim's birthday and welcomed all to remain for cake and iced tea. During the birthday celebration, they also rejoiced that they had something to look forward to that the Lord could bless.

After their guests had left, Jim asked Estelle how she felt about the meeting.

"Good! I feel like we've taken an important step toward the Lord answering my prayers. I thought everyone here expressed a sincere interest, and I'm sure there are more who are concerned. I hope this Rev. Fox will respond and send the right preacher for the meeting. I'll be praying about that, too."

Coming in from the barn one afternoon, Jim noticed Estelle hanging out clothes on the line he had stretched for her a few days before. He stopped a few yards from her and gazed at her, admiring her quick movements of reaching down into the basket, shaking out a sheet or a dress, and pinning it to the clothesline. She turned and saw him.

"How long have you been standing there?" she demanded.

100

"Long enough to enjoy seein' my beautiful wife workin' hard. He went over and kissed her, and said, "Take a break and come in the house, please. I've got a few thangs I want to run by ye. Then I want to come back out here and have ye show me how to do what ye're doin'. And I'll order ye back inside to lay down and take a nap or at least rest!"

"Well now, aren't you sweet! I think I'll just do that."

After Estelle had poured them both a glass of iced tea, Jim said, "Let's go in the livin' room to talk." Once they were seated, Jim began, "We don't really know what the economy is gonna do since the election. But I been thinkin'... it's not right that we just set around here frozen in fear of a comin' depression and not venture out on opportunities that come up."

"What opportunities are you referring to, honey?"

"I'm thinkin' that with the money we've got in the bank, plus what we could borrow from Uncle Hay and L.A. Black, we could buy the 500 acres Walter Campbell wants to sell, buy 100 more head of cattle, and go into corn and hay farmin' in a bigger way. And with the timber on our land plus what I come into with the two timber companies, we oughta install a big sawmill and wire it for electric power that the REA promises to come next year. Instead of raftin' stuff down the river, we could saw it and sell it to the lumber companies in DeWitt, Gillette, and even Pine Bluff and Stuttgart. We could get your brother-in-law Wesley to run it for us. I'd buy a Caterpillar tractor for loggin' and workin' around the mill and put in a timber-dryin' buildin'; I could go into the lumber business and retail right there at the mill. Then over there on the county road before ye get to Tom Miller's place, among them pretty oaks and the only pine trees on the prairie, we'd build us a nice big house, cuz I know we'll want more children. Havin' more land, more cattle, and the mill would allow us to put more people to work down around Nady and up on the prairie. I'd still be close enough to trap, hunt, and fish these bottoms. I think we'd have the best of both worlds." Jim paused, studying Estelle's face for signs of agreement or hesitancy. He couldn't be sure how she felt.

Estelle stood, came to him, knelt at his knee, and said, "Honey, I'll respond to your dream after I've prayed: Lord, I thank You for my husband, Jim! For our daughter, Jeanette. For our place here and all You've allowed us to accumulate. Thank You for our good health.

Thank You for the venturous spirit You have given Jim. Lord, I must not stand in his way nor discourage him with my own fears and lack of faith. Help me to know how to express to him my sincere opinion of the opportunities he sees before us. Amen!"

"Amen!" Jim echoed. Estelle began wiping tears and looked at Jim and saw that he was weeping, too.

"What's wrong with us?" Jim asked. "I feel alright and yet, like you, I can't help bawlin'."

"I don't think anything is wrong, dear. I just know we were supposed to have this discussion. I thank you for confiding in me and sharing your dream of greater things. And now that I'm feeling something definite about it, I must tell you what I think."

"That's what I expect and want—just the way ye feel and how ye look at it."

"I want us to go ahead and plan and think through the things you see as opportunities for us to move ahead in life. If you wish to go ahead and move on these important steps, I shall not stand in your way. However, my dear one, there's something I feel deeply—I don't feel close enough to the Lord to claim this feeling is from Him—but I do know we are to wait until early next year to begin on your dream to even go a step further than planning. Let's see, it's now the middle of May— let's say, the middle of March 1930—so that's 10 months from now. When that time comes, if everything's right for our dream, we'll go for it!"

"You bet we will!" Jim said, pulling Estelle to her feet. "But, for now we'll wait. After hearin' yore thoughts, I realize that's the thing to do. Let's get back to the clothesline, and ye can show me how to hang up the clothes like ye do it. Then get back in here while the baby is asleep and get some rest." Chuckling, he said, "I'll hurry so I can finish before someone catches me doin' a woman's work."

After showing Jim how to shake the clothes and pin them to the line, she left Jim to himself. He felt good about helping her. It started to dawn on him how hard Estelle worked—cooking, cleaning, doing laundry, working the garden, caring for the baby, and helping him with anything he called on her for. He also admired the way she took time to read her Bible and other literature and pray and talk to people about spiritual things.

When he was finished with that task, he went in the house and filled his glass with more tea. He had only taken a few sips when he heard the baby stir. He hoped he could lift Jeanette from her crib without disturbing Estelle, who was in a deep sleep. Their seven-month-old daughter saw him and smiled, reaching both hands toward him. He was deeply moved as he lifted her up and into his arms. She grabbed his nose and reached for his ears as he took her into the living room. He'd already changed her wet diaper a time or two, so he decided to do that. She seemed playful, so Jim got a quilt and spread it on the front porch. He lay down flat on his back, allowing Jeanette to lie on his stomach while he talked softly to her. She came alive in playing with her daddy's mouth, nose, and ears, and he was pleased that the little thing was full of joy. This went on for a few minutes before a familiar voice spoke.

"What a lovely picture! A handsome father playing with his pretty daughter!" Estelle said, standing at the front door. "That little girl is learning to love her daddy, for sure! She plays with me pretty often of late, but this is the first time I've seen her play with you like that!"

"To tell ye the truth, I'm gettin' a bigger kick out of it than she is. Even if she is ours, I gotta say, this is the purtiest baby I've ever seen!"

"I agree! She's a beauty alright."

Estelle went in the house to get a chair so that she could join them on the porch. She heard a car drive up and Jim say, "Come up on the porch, Lloyd. You caught me entertainin' our little daughter. I'll turn her over to her mother and bring us out some chairs."

Jim met Estelle coming out the door with two chairs, and once they were placed, he handed her the baby. "What's on ye mind today, Lloyd?"

"I'm sorry to interrupt your family time, but I do need your help right down here in these bottoms, not too far away, I think. There's a loggin' operation over here on Elm Ridge. I think it's not far from where you trap on Elbow Slough."

"Yeah, I have to ride over Elm Ridge to get to my traps on Elbow."

"Well, the operation is on the highest part of Elm Ridge. It started back in the spring when the water was still pretty high."

"I know where the highest part of the Ridge is. What's goin' on?"

"A feller was sent last night to notify me of a shootin' death over there on that job. Eight tents have been pitched. Four saws have been cuttin' and two teams and two wagons haulin'. They were raftin' out to White River 'til the water went down. They've been bankin' logs to haul out when things dry out. But the report is there was fightin' and gunplay. A man has been shot to death. The man in charge of the operation left last night, too, and sent this feller to report to me. He warned me that there are nine people left over there in their camp, and he said the killer threatened that no one—not the owners, not the bosses, and *not the law had better come around!*"

"Lloyd, I know you well enough to know they shouldn't have said *not the law.*"

When Estelle brought the lawmen iced tea, the sheriff apologized to her. "Estelle, I know you hate to see me comin', but I sure do need Jim's help."

"I overheard your conversation, and the situation sounds very dangerous."

"Jim, the man said there are four armed men in that camp. I need you to go there with me today!"

Jim asked, "Got somethin' real quick for lunch, Estelle?"

"Sure! Ham and cheese sandwiches and potato salad, with iced tea."

"I 'preciate that, Estelle. Jim, could we get goin' as soon as lunch is over?" Lloyd asked.

"Yeah, we're fortunate that all the water's gone between here and Elm. The ground should be dry enough that our horses won't bog. What if these people have left camp though?"

"If they have, what route would they take?"

"I'll bet they've been haulin' logs to Wild Goose Bayou and raftin' out to the Mouth. But they may still have boats at the turn in Wild Goose where it heads straight east for White River. I know we have to go and check the camp, but they may all be gone. If not, we'll have to be prepared for a fight."

"Yeah, that's where you come in, Jim. Lay out a plan here before we eat. Then let's saddle up and head out."

"While the tea is brewing, honey, let's go into the kitchen and have prayer. Invite Lloyd," Estelle said. Bowing her head, she prayed, "Lord, You know what all awaits Lloyd and Jim this afternoon over on Elm Ridge. I know that my spirit is heavy because they are going on a dangerous mission. Help these servants of Yours and the animals. Help them come away from this mission victorious in every way. Amen!" Both men echoed Estelle's "Amen!"

Jim was glad for a clear afternoon as they left the front yard, urged their horses to a canter, and moved down the slope into the bottoms. Buck knew to take the trail from Jim's land straight east to Honey Locust. Wading across Honey Locust, Jim signaled Buck to take the southeast direction toward Elm Ridge. After 15 minutes, Jim called on Buck to stop and the lawmen dismounted. "Lloyd, we're at the edge of Elm Ridge. But the high point is a mile and a half straight ahead. Now here's what I'm thinkin': Another mile straight ahead, I want us to stop. I'll leave the horses with you, and Buck and me will move to the right a little and find the road they've been usin' to haul logs to Wild Goose Bayou. Buck and me can tell if they've been over that road lately. If they haven't, we'll come back for you and I'll suggest a plan for attackin' the camp. So just relax here for maybe an hour. The sun is high yet, so even in these bottoms we can see what we'll have to shoot at."

Lloyd nodded. The two mounted, and Jim said, "Straight ahead, Buck!" Jim marveled at the straight line Buck always walked whether in the bottoms or on the prairie. Even in going around a tree or a clump of brush, he always turned right back to the exact direction he had been going before the detour.

Jim called Buck to "Stay!" The men dismounted. After taking ammunition from a pocket, Jim shucked his coat and threw it across Star's saddle. "I've a hunch that Buck and me better stay in the woods a bit before goin' out on the road they've been usin'. Cuz we just might catch 'em on their way out. In case we don't find any tracks or run into 'em, we'll be back, probably in a hour." Slapping the black gently on the neck, Jim said, "Stay, Star!"

"Good luck, Jim."

Jim nodded and pointed Buck in the direction he wanted to go. After ten minutes, Buck stopped, his ears forward and turned slightly to the east. Somewhere Jim caught the low murmur of a voice. Buck hearing it, too, sniffed and looked at Jim. A louder voice was heard, and Jim knew two men were walking slowly together in the woods but not on the road, which was still 200 yards ahead. If Jim and Buck remained hidden, the men would likely walk across in front of them probably within rifle range, hopefully even in pistol range. The largest elm on the Ridge was to Jim's right and ahead just a few yards. He quietly walked over and took his waiting stand behind it, signaling Buck to join him.

Jim could now hear their footfalls. He knew they would come into view at any time. Buck gave a growl that only Jim could hear. "Yeah, Buck. Quiet!" He could see two men armed with rifles, each with a pack on his back. They apparently had chosen to stay in the woods for cover rather than walk the road running parallel and be spotted— probably expecting to be arrested, Jim thought.

As the men drew closer, Buck sniffed while looking behind the men, and Jim caught a glimpse of two more men. Jim could see they were also carrying rifles. But he'd have to watch the two nearer him and then manage the next ones. But how many more were on their way? The two nearest were close enough that Jim decided to lean his rifle against the tree. If it came to fireworks, he could make faster work of it with his Colt. When they were even with him, he called, "Halt!"

Jim watched them stop, drop their packs, and train their rifles on him; simultaneously Jim's .38 spoke: *Bang! Bang!* Both men folded and sprawled headlong on the ground and lay still. Jim crouched and looked a bit to his left to see the reaction of the other two. They were obviously shaken in their inability to see where the shooting originated, and Jim could see they were startled. He saw one of them turn around and heard him call back to others, "Y'all stay there!" With both men turned with their backs to Jim and talking to a third group, Jim stepped out in the open and called, "*Freeze where you are, men!* Drop your guns if ye want to live! Put yore hands up! Turn around and face me!" Buck growled. With the men not immediately responding and whispering to each other, Jim sensed that the men were going to take a chance on shooting him. Both men whirled with their rifles up at the same time. Before they could fire, Jim's Colt spoke: *Bang! Bang!* The two folded, fell forward, and lay still.

Jim reloaded his Colt and stepped behind the big elm once more, watching Buck. "Where, Buck?" The dog's ears went forward and his head shifted leftward. Jim could see three people, but they had no guns that he could see. As they drew nearer, he stepped out where they could see him.

"Don't shoot, mister!" a woman's voice called. "We don't have any guns. We want to come to you."

"Come on, with yore hands up! Walk slowly and come forward." When the dog started to growl at the three people approaching with their hands in the air, Jim commanded, "Quiet, Buck!"

When the three were only 20 yards away, Jim said, "You may stop there and put your hands down. I am the special deputy of the sheriff of Arkansas County, and I'm told that someone was murdered in yer log camp yesterday. The sheriff is with me, and we are here to investigate. So talk to me and tell me what's been goin' on." Jim heard Buck's sniff of friendliness and saw him turn around and bark a friendly bark, and he knew Lloyd was coming.

To the three he called, "Come on up a little closer, and you can tell the sheriff himself what we want to know."

"What's happenin' here, Jim?" Lloyd asked.

"I'm sorry to say that I was forced to kill four men in self-defense. I dropped 'em a split second before they got me. These three here seem to be unarmed and friendly. They're comin' closer, and I'm expectin' 'em to tell you their story. We'll keep an eye on 'em, lest they have a hidden weapon."

"No, Sheriff," said one of the women. "We left our weapons back in camp. We'll tell you anything ye wanta know."

"I want to know why a man was killed over here in your log camp yesterday. I'm the sheriff of Arkansas County. Now why has someone been killed?"

One of the women took another step closer and said, "My name is Maggie Price, and for the last several days the first man yore deputy killed a while ago—his name is Chancy Poole—had been tryin' to force me to pay attention to him. I warned him I would tell my husband. He said if I did he would kill my husband, but before he killed me he'd do ugly things to me. Yesterday about noon, Chancy come in for lunch at the shack, and then come over to our tent and started makin' advances. My husband come at him to fight him off, and Chancy shot him down in cold blood. My husband had gone to them other men yore deputy shot and tried to get 'em to help him deal with this evil Chancy Poole. Nobody would help. My husband went to the boss and told him whut wuz goin' on. When the boss found out whut happened to my husband, he took off. I ain't got no idea where he went, but I'm shore glad y'all come out here. We shore don't regret anythang that happened to those four men. Wished you'd come before my husband was murdered."

Lloyd said, "Well, Miz Price, we're shore sorry about what happened to your husband. Of course, we knew nothin' about this timber project over here until a man sent by whoever heads the operation here, probably the boss, came and gave me a report of the murder. Do you know when he is comin' back?"

"Nawsir, I can't say. I thought he might've gone and told the company what happened."

"Where were the seven of you headed here today?"

"I can't say where those four men were goin'. But if the three of us could get to one of them boats out here at Wild Goose, we wuz hopin' to get out to a railroad bridge and get a train to Elaine, where I live. My sister and nephew here wuz gonna go with me, cuz they ain't got no place to go. They wuz heppin' to cook and gather wood fer the log camp."

"Alright, I'll suggest somethin': My deputy here lives about three miles from here out on the edge of the prairie. Do y'all think ye could walk that distance? I'll deliver y'all to Elaine tonight, or we might find lodgin' for you in DeWitt."

"Sheriff, that would be wonderful! But can we make the people deliver my husband's body to Elaine? I shore don't want him buried out here in these wilds."

"I have authority to force people in charge here to be civil and accommodatin' up to a point in situations like this. I'll try and get them to deliver your husband's body to Elaine, but I reckon they'll bury these four bodies here on the Ridge."

Lloyd had brought both horses with him so Jim offered to allow both women to ride his horse, if they weren't afraid to ride and didn't mind riding double. They both declined, saying they were used to walking.

"Son, what is your name?" Jim asked of the teenage boy.

"They call me Bud."

"Well, Bud, if you wanta, you could ride behind me."

"Nawsir, thanks, I'll walk with Mama and Aunt Essie."

"We'll walk the horses slow, so as not to make you have to walk too fast," Lloyd said.

"Thank you. I believe we'll all be able to keep up. We're in pretty good shape," Mrs. Price said.

Halfway to Jim's place, Lloyd pulled the horses to a stop and pointed out a log where the three could rest if they needed to. They sat down, but in five minutes they said, "Let's go."

They arrived at Jim's house as the sun was setting. Estelle welcomed the women and the boy and prepared a meal for all of them.

Just before Estelle called supper, Lloyd took Jim out on the porch and said, "You know, Jim, it would save me lots of drivin' if the boy could stay here with y'all tonight. I wuz thinkin' of drivin' the women to Elaine tonight and bringin' the boy back here if you had room for him. Then, I need you to take him over to the log camp tomorrow and represent me in dealin' with the boss about gettin' Price's body to Elaine and heppin' the boy with the personal things belongin' to them and his aunt."

"Sure, we'll bring a cot in for the boy. Tomorrow we'll wait 'til after lunch to go to the camp, cuz they ain't likely to be there 'til afternoon."

"Well, play hardball with 'em if ye have to. Get Price's body to Elaine, and try to get somethin' for burial expenses."

Mrs. Price agreed with the sheriff that Bud could stay and then go back to the camp the next day. "Jim will try to make the boss there responsible for gettin' Bud to the train so he can get back to Elaine tomorrow night," Lloyd said.

It was late evening when Lloyd left with the two women. Jim got Bud's cot set up so that he could go to bed.

Estelle was finally able to ask Jim about the encounter. "Am I wrong in believing that you had another shootout?"

"Estelle, I had to kill four men, but I somehow don't feel as bad about it as I did in havin' to kill those two men in Desha County. I don't understand it."

"I'm sorry you had to shoot them, but I'm so glad you aren't downcast about it. You did what you had to do."

"Yeah, I got 'em just before they woulda got me."

"Thank the Lord you're back here safe with me and Jeanette!"

In the early afternoon the next day, Jim and Bud arrived at the campsite. The owner and the boss were there, and they had engaged a half dozen men to help with livestock, tents, and equipment. Jim told them he was a deputy sheriff and that he had killed four of their men out there in the woods and had witnesses that he did it in self-defense. He also told them the four bodies would need to be buried. He informed the owner that the sheriff was holding him responsible for delivering Mr. Price's body to Elaine. When the owner hesitated, Jim said, "Sir, I don't want to do this, but if you refuse to deliver this body to Elaine and pay $300 toward his burial expense, I have the order to arrest you and take you to jail in DeWitt. The decision is up to you."

"Guess I will do it if I have no choice in the matter."

"Fine, I'm glad." Before Jim left for home, he helped Bud pack their personal belongings and made sure the owner would see that Bud got on the train to Elaine.

At the sheriff's office two days later, Lloyd said, "You handled those heads of the loggin' operation just right. Mrs. Price was able to get her husband buried for the $300 by buyin' a cheap casket and still gave the mortician about $50. She was grateful and said to tell you how much she and her sister appreciated that good supper and the nice way you treated her son. Jim, you'll get paid well at the end of the month for all you did there."

"Well, Lloyd, you've always treated me fair, and it's good to be workin' with ye."

"I'm glad you don't seem so downcast over killin' those four guys as you did over those two earlier."

"No, Estelle noticed right away that I didn't mope around about it this time."

"That's good, Jim. And it doesn't mean you're developin' a hard heart or that you'll ever get to where you enjoy killin' a man. It shows you're growin' into your work and gettin' more mature. I'm shore pleased with ye, man. I need you with me, and we'll take care of each other."

Ross rode up in July and told Estelle that Rev. Frank Fox had discussed the invitation with Dr. Smith, president of Union Bible College, to have someone come to Nady and conduct a Gospel meeting. It had been decided to send Rev. and Mrs. Homer Rich possibly sometime in the fall of 1930. Ross said, "You can read the letter, but I sure like the part about Homer Rich being 'a powerful preacher of the Gospel, has pastored a church for a few years, and graduated from Union Bible College.' The letter also says his wife is a good pianist and singer and they are anxious to come."

Estelle said, "I sure like the thought of sitting under a powerful preacher. I just want to get saved so I can be at peace with God! Sometimes I feel Jim is hardening against the Lord; at other times, he seems to be closer to getting saved. Well, it's sure good news that we'll have a Gospel meeting, even if it is over a year away. Ross, where do you think the preacher and his wife might stay?"

"Flossie and I probably have more room in our house than any of the families represented at our prayer meeting. Flossie says they can stay with us."

"Well, I'm glad. With you and Flossie, I know they'll sleep in clean beds and eat good food. I know we all want to take good care of them. Jim and I will want them to eat with us a time or two."

"Estelle, we are so glad for the way the Lord is blessing you and Jim. Your place is fixed up so nicely here, and your orchard is growing and developing so well you'll have fruit from it in another year or so. Your few head of cattle will be multiplying, and Jim told me he was planning to get more. Then I know the last time I talked to Jim he said he had also been doing well in trapping and fishing."

"Ross, the Lord has really blessed us. But I know some hard times are ahead, according to what we read in the *Gazette* and hear on the radio. Still, we look forward to tithing and giving and supporting the revival. And we hope a church will be organized after the meeting. We want to do our part."

"That's great, Estelle! With several families showing interest, we ought to be able to support a pastor and buy the supplies we need for Sunday school and worship. I expect we can get the Menard schoolhouse, with Jim and me both being on the board of directors. I doubt that Jeff Wallace will object. He's our other board member. We'll pray that he and Jewell will become interested in getting right with the Lord."

"Ross, there are a lot of people in the Nady community and up on the prairie for whom we will pray and hopefully lead to faith in Jesus. I guess we don't need to wait for another year to begin to talk with them. We must pray and trust that the Lord will prepare their hearts to get saved in the meeting. I sure want to get saved then, if not before."

Jim came in before Ross left, and he seem pleased about the report of the coming Gospel meeting in the next year. "We'll sure pitch in and do our part. You can count on us, Ross."

"Thanks, Jim. And I believe others will, too. We'll be prayin' for all of you who need the Lord. Flossie and I both want to renew our spiritual life and draw closer to the Lord."

After Ross left, Jim picked up the newspaper and read awhile. "Estelle, I been readin' here, and I'm beginnin' to see how right you wuz to caution us against launchin' out into bigger things. I was disappointed that Coolidge didn't run. For awhile there, it looked like Hoover was gonna lead this country to prosperity. Even Will Rogers, my favorite philosopher, cracked, 'You can't not like this prosperity thing. Cuz even the feller that ain't got anything is all worked up over the idea of gettin' it!' I reckon that was the way I was for awhile 'til you spoke some wisdom into me. Now it shore looks dark. Speculation has got out of hand, and the market is already headin' down fast. Course we ain't got anything in the market, cuz that just ain't our way. Thangs don't look good."

When Estelle knew Jim was through talking, she said, "The Lord will see us through, no matter what presidents and industries and rich people do. We need to be thankful for the way He has blessed us already."

The next day, Jim listened to the radio as it brought news of the stock market crash and read about it in the Business Section of the *Gazette*. He laid the paper down, went into the kitchen where Estelle was working and said, "Honey, after readin' and seein' all the bad things happenin' to the American people these days, I'm thankful for two thangs this mornin'."

"What's that, darling?"

112

"First, I'm thankful that I listened to ye weeks ago when ye felt my ventures should not happen right away—I was ready to take the plunge then. And, second, that we did not have one dollar in the stock market. I'm glad our land and house and everthang else we got is paid for. We can make a livin' from traps, nets, and saws, and we can eat what we raise in the garden or kill in the woods. And, too, we have each other, our baby, and our health! I'm rarin' to praise the Lord today!"

"Wonderful, honey! I'm with you!"

Jim had a note in the mail from the sheriff. "Jim, I'm very sorry to tell you that our budget is being cut, and I'm forced to lay you off for about a year. But when emergencies come and I really need you, they told me I could hire you by the job. I hope you are willin' to work this way. Soon as possible, I want you back on the payroll and available at any time. Sincerely, Lloyd."

"Well, Estelle, when I see Lloyd, I'll tell him not to feel bad about my layoff. I understand thangs are tight all over the country. I'm thankful I can make a livin' without that job."

"Dear, I'm glad you are not worrying. There are probably people around who will need our help. I've got more stuff canned than we'll use. We're going to make it fine throughout this depression and come out alright."

"You always help me, honey." *How is it that just a few sentences from this dear wife can change my thinkin'? Of course, she's right—we are blessed. Look where we live, how we make a livin', what all we can grow and catch and kill! I guess I oughta ask the Lord to forgive me for worryin' and doubtin' and gettin' afraid of the times.*

After hearing from Bob Hibbard that fur prices would drop drastically in the coming season, Jim was surprised that he didn't feel down. The depression was taking its toll—people were losing their houses, farms, cars, and jobs all over the country. Even if he only got half price for his fur this coming winter, he was sure they could make ends meet.

Jim set traps the last day of November. During the month of December, he caught the same amount of marketable hides as in the previous December. Hibbard came to buy the hides, and his earlier prediction was correct—Jim received half as much for the hides as he had the year before.

Noticing Jim's upbeat spirit and attitude, Estelle rejoiced and continued to encourage him.

"I just reckon the Lord is usin' you to hep me see thangs through different glasses. I do know I'm trustin' in Him more than in my own ability. I ain't runnin' scared no more!"

"Perhaps that's the reason the Lord is allowing this depression— to teach us Americans to rely less on money and material things. Now I don't believe God causes depressions, sickness, tragedy, and poverty, but I do believe He will use such things to help us find a stronger faith and become less dependent on what we can see and do ourselves. God is not going to waste these hard times that He's allowing to come almost everywhere. I'm looking forward to hearing the Gospel preached in a few months. I can hardly wait until that preacher comes and the meetings begin," Estelle said.

"Yeah, I'll admit that even I'm lookin' forward to the meetin's."

Henry and Oda appeared to be quite worried over the low price of fur and the effects of the depression. They seemed to want to spend more time with Jim and Estelle. "Estelle, I think you've got me more interested in this comin' Gospel meetin' than I can understand. Maybe the Lord will do somethin' for us that will change our hearts, our thinkin', our ways, and even our attitudes. Henry and me—we just ain't gettin' along like we ought. I'm comin' to believe it's like you say—we all need the Lord!"

The Menard School Board of Directors learned that those who had the contract to paint the building could only work during the dates that had been set for Rev. and Mrs. Homer Rich to come and conduct the Gospel meeting. The Board called a meeting of the more interested families, and they decided to put up a "brush arbor" in which to hold the October meeting.

With his usual generosity, Ross Morgan offered to furnish some cull lumber from his sawmill and, with the help of eight or ten men, erect a temporary setting for the meeting. His idea was a rectangular arrangement of sturdy timbers, a roof of several crosspieces piled with brush to keep out the sun, and slab board seats with no backs. A platform would be built with a long altar bench across the front for seekers. He'd put up a makeshift structure for a pulpit desk. The "brush arbor" would be something long remembered in Nady, Arkansas. Just the appearance of it had the community talking about "that meetin' still nearly a year away." As time drew nearer, Ross had some men help him move the piano from the schoolhouse to the platform. He covered it with quilts and, in case of rain, a tarp. Ross called for someone to donate two upholstered chairs for the platform on which the preacher and his wife could sit comfortably.

On October 16, 1929, Estelle gave birth to a baby boy. With some reluctance on Jim's part, he was named James William Tharp, Jr. Jim's objection was, "It'll be confusin' as he grows up. Even though he'll love his daddy, he won't feel good about sharin' the name."

"Then, Jim, we can call him by his initials—J. W."

Jim wasn't completely pleased. "I'm proud that the boy will have my name, but I hope he'll appreciate it instead of feelin' he's been cheated. But let's go ahead with the "Junior" part."

It so happened that Homer and Helen Rich began the "Brush Arbor" Revival Meeting on October 16, 1930, when the Tharp baby boy was one year old. Ross introduced the Riches to a crowd of about 80 people.

When Ross introduced "Brother Homer Rich," the crowd stood and clapped and cheered. The distinguished, well-dressed gentleman began, "Thank you for this warm welcome to Helen and me. We feel so blessed to be here in Nady, Arkansas, with you. We've come with the Gospel of our Lord Jesus Christ! We feel it is an honor to preach and sing His good news of salvation to all who will repent of sin and believe in Him as Savior and Lord. We know God loves this community, and He wants to start a great work of salvation and Christian love and fellowship among you. You are a wonderful people, and all you need to complete you is a personal saving faith in Jesus Christ. This experience will enable you to read and understand the Bible, which is the Word of God, and give you wisdom to follow the leadings of the Holy Spirit on how to live the Christian life.

"Before I preach to you from the Bible text God has laid on my heart, my wife, Helen, is going to play and sing a few Gospel songs. Then I'll lead us in a few familiar hymns, after which I'll preach. Okay, Helen, it's all yours!"

Helen first spoke a few words about "the joy of being down here in the south with you wonderful people;" then she began singing "Amazing Grace."

Jim, sitting several rows back with Estelle, was moved inwardly. *My, what a voice! And she can play that piano, too. Why are those words so powerful? Will Homer be as good a preacher as Helen is a singer and musician?*

After the congregational singing of "Power in the Blood" and "Blessed Assurance," Homer announced his text and read it: **For I am not ashamed of the gospel: it is the power of God for salvation to every one who has faith, to the Jew first and also to the Greek. For in it the righteousness of God is revealed through faith for faith; as it is written, 'He who through faith is righteous shall live'** (Rom. 1:16-17).

Homer closed his Bible, stepped down off the platform, raised his voice, and said, "I didn't come to Nady, Arkansas, to present a religion. I came to preach the Gospel of Jesus Christ—to tell of a God who loves all human beings everywhere, loves us so much that He found a way to not send us all to Hell, even though we've all sinned and deserve to go there. In His gracious nature, God found a way to forgive our sins of not obeying His Word and seeking to be independent of Him. For as the apostle Peter put it, **God is not willing that any should perish, but that all would come to repentance** (II Peter 3:9). Now the apostle is not telling us that all will be saved. What he is saying is that a God of love doesn't want us to be lost. He does not want us to miss Heaven. He does not want us to burn in Hell for eternity. But it does grieve God that anyone might reject His Son as their Savior, the only One God has designated to save us from sin, from a wasted life, from eternal damnation.

"Now it doesn't seem to make sense that anyone in his or her right mind would choose not to believe in, trust, and rely upon Jesus as their Savior. But we all know that millions of normal people are walking around, going about life, choosing not to trust in the saving grace of our Lord Jesus Christ. Why is this? If you are not a Christian, why aren't you? If you have not decided to become a Christian, why haven't you? Let's hear the answers from the Bible.

"In Ephesians 2:8-9, we read: **For by grace you have been saved through faith; and this is not of your doing, it is the gift of God—not because of works, lest any man should boast.** Notice that we are saved by grace (God's goodness and kindness bestowed on us who are undeserving) and that by *faith* (our part is believing, trusting, relying on God's provision of His Son Jesus). When His Word says we are saved because we believe, we must count on that! We exercise faith when we hear the Gospel, believe it, pray the sinner's prayer, confess our sins, and then claim Jesus as our Savior in confession.

"Many people are not trusting Jesus because they are too proud to make their confession before others. They are ashamed to allow their family and neighbors to see them or hear them deciding for Christ. Jesus had something to say we'd better all consider: **If any man** (any person) **would follow me, let him deny himself** (that is, be willing to let others think you are foolish) **and take up his cross** (this means to be willing to be made an object of ridicule) **and follow me** (make up your mind to obey the Word of God as Jesus taught it).

"Friends here in Nady, I've come a long ways from Indiana to tell you that God loves you, that He offers to forgive your sins here tonight. But you'll have to believe in Jesus as the only way provided for you to be saved. Jesus said, **I am the way, and the truth, and the life; no one comes to the Father but by me** (John 14:6).

"Helen is going to sing. Some of you here need to be saved. God's love is calling you. His Holy Spirit, an invisible Presence, is prompting you even now to come and bow here at this sacred bench and pray the sinner's prayer. I'll give you direction and quote some Scripture to help you understand. Come and thank God for sending Jesus to save you. Do not reject God's Son; come tonight and let Him give you His peace and His forgiveness and manifest His love in your heart. Please stand as Helen sings the invitation."

Estelle was deeply moved as Helen began singing. She leaned over and whispered, "Jim, I know it's my time, but I surely don't want to go alone ... without you." She suddenly knew he was not going with her. *Lord, how can I stand to go without Jim?* Just as she had known it was her time, now she was given the inner strength to go without him. She started to give the baby to Jim, but she decided to leave their baby son with her mother on the front row just in case Jim might have the urge to come later. She stood and said, "Honey, I'm going. Please come!"

"You go ahead, dear." Jim nodded, but did not promise to come.

Estelle walked to the front seat and leaned toward her mother, saying, "Mother, I want to give my heart to Jesus. Please hold my baby."

"Oh, yes, dear! I'm so glad for you! Bless you!" She took her grandson with joy and started praying for Jim.

Estelle was the first to go forward. Soon Oda, BettyLee, Vivian Shelton, Alice Plant, Perry and Nellie Plant, Allen and Dorene Freeman, Lorene Malcomb, and Tom Proctor were responding to the invitation.

Homer gave instructions to those kneeling at the altar. "Just pray out, telling God you believe that because of Jesus' atoning death on the cross, you now have forgiveness of sin and that you, with His help, will obediently follow Christ as your Lord. Thank Him for giving you a new heart, for adopting you into His redeemed family, and for giving you the Holy Spirit by whom you will find strength and wisdom to live the Christian life. And when you have prayed this way, please stand when you believe that God has forgiven you, that He has changed your heart, and that now His Holy Spirit lives in you."

All eleven new believers stood. "I want you new believers to please turn and face this congregation. Now, dear people, whether you are a professing Christian or not, I think all of you owe these eleven people the respect to stand and applaud their decision to go with God. As they endeavor to live the Christian life, they will try to win loved ones and others in their communities so as to see the power of God bring the changes so desperately needed here in this part of Arkansas County!"

Estelle's eyes were on Jim, and she was pleased that he was the first to stand and begin clapping. The applause lasted for a meaningful period. Then Homer said, "Before you sit down, I just wonder how many of you realize that you should have made the same decision these eleven made and you are willing to request the prayers of the praying people here tonight, including your loved ones who have made this important decision. They will be praying for you that you'll have the courage to step out for Christ some time during the next seven nights of this Gospel meeting. Now this will not save you, but it will allow the Holy Spirit to prepare you with hunger and courage to come and make your decision."

Estelle was watching Jim, and again his hand was the first to go up; then George, Henry, Oscar, Earl, the Plemmons brothers, the Wallaces, and several others raised their hands.

As Homer prayed a closing prayer, Jim knew he should have gone. As the prayer ended, he was the first one forward to embrace Estelle and compliment her for the decision he should also have made.

Jim was quiet all the way home. He was the devoted husband and father in assisting Estelle and carrying both children into the house and helping her put them to bed. He actually got into bed ahead of Estelle, knowing she'd probably want to read her Bible and pray as usual.

Estelle began in the Gospel of John, as Homer had suggested to the eleven converts. She prayerfully concentrated on the Prologue (John1:1-12). She realized it had to do with Jesus and His preincarnation and then in His coming, God incarnate. He really is the **Word sent from God. In Him is the light to shine in the darkness and overcome the darkness, and the Word became flesh and dwelt among us....** *"Thank You, Father, for calling me to eternal life. For giving me a new heart, for giving me Your Holy Spirit, the Spirit of God, the Spirit of Jesus, the Spirit of life, the Spirit of grace, the Spirit of holiness, the Spirit of love. Thank You for writing my name in the Book of Life. Lord, I wondered if I would feel anything, and I did, and I do! I don't know what to do about Jim. I confess disappointment, but not despair. I thank You that You love him and will draw him to You without my nagging and pleading. Continue to speak to him and to George and Henry and all the others who raised their hands indicating their need to be saved. Do help them to yield at some point during the next week of meetings."*

Jim was not sleepy and waited patiently for Estelle to come to bed. When she finally did, he drew her to him and repeated some of the things he had said after the benediction earlier. Before he released her, he said, "I love you, Estelle! I'm proud of yore decision for the Lord. I meant it when I raised my hand that I do want to give my heart to Christ. Don't give up on me, and let's get a good night's sleep."

"Thanks, darling! I love you, too! Good night."

Estelle woke up at daylight. By the time Jim dressed, she had coffee ready and biscuits and gravy on the table. He waited for her to say the blessing. Although they ate in silence for most of the meal, she did not sense any tension between them. Estelle asked, "Honey, would it be okay with you if we invited Homer and Helen, Ross and Flossie, Henry and Oda, and George and BettyLee to have a meal with us Sunday noon?"

"Yes, but wouldn't that be quite a crowd for you to prepare for?"

"I'll ask Oda to help me. She's a great cook, and I know she'll be willing to prepare a dish or two. What do you have planned for today?"

"I'm gonna ask Henry to help me clear some more ground—gotta get more bottom ground ready for the corn and cotton crops, and then I wanta find someone to help me put in those crops next year. George told me about a black man over close to the Merrisach who is tryin' to farm some land he bought off Walter Campbell a few years ago. I heard he's a good man with a nice wife and some children. I thought of seein' if he might be able to farm my place on shares while he's workin' at his own place. George didn't think he had the equipment—tractor, plow, disk, cultivators, and all that to work with as he needs. I'd be willin' to invest in all that if necessary. Of course, if I furnish everythang—land, equipment, seed, and fuel—his share of the cotton crop would be less."

"That's something to pray about, dear. Why don't you talk to the man. What is his name?"

"George said his name is Bird Washington, and they call him Birdie."

"Maybe as a family we oughta call on them. I don't like it that our community seems to look down on black people, even calling them 'niggers.' Let's teach our children to respect people regardless of their color. We'll need to set a good example for them."

The Gospel meetings were well attended all week. Estelle enjoyed every service. When Homer called on some of the new Christians to give a word of testimony, Estelle shared freely and passionately what the Lord had done for her. "This meeting has made a dream come true—ever since I was a little girl at Grandma Best's knee, I've longed to become a born-again Christian! That happened to me right here at this altar last Sunday night. Thank you, Brother and Sister Rich, for coming to Nady and sharing the Gospel of Jesus Christ and telling us how to trust Him as our Savior!"

The Sunday dinner with the Riches and loved ones turned out to be a tremendous blessing for the saved and unsaved—Jim, Henry, and George were drawn into the fellowship with the charm and wisdom of the Riches. Estelle could see the respect developing in all three men for the preacher and his wife. In fact, the people attending the revival services could see that the preacher and his wife were first class—warm, educated, professional, spiritual, and forthright.

Henry asked, "How in the world did two wonderful people like you ever find yore way down here into these barren prairies and ugly swamps?"

Helen replied, "We felt sure that the Holy Spirit was leading us to come to these parts and share the Gospel and then, hopefully, see a church body organized."

After the closing service Sunday night, Jim asked Homer and Helen if he might have a few minutes of their time. They graciously consented. Near the platform, with most of the crowd leaving, Jim said, "I think y'all know that I work with the sheriff of Arkansas County as his special deputy."

"Yes," Helen said. "We've heard a lot about you, Jim. You're a well-known figure in these parts. Ross showed us some clippings from the *Gazette* of stories about your heroics. Several here in Nady have remarked about your marksmanship and the times you've saved the sheriff's life."

"Well, one thang I got to settle: In my service as a deputy, includin' shootin' people—tryin' to wound rather than kill 'em, is it possible to be a Christian and stay on in this work? It seems out of keepin' with livin' a Christian life to me. Then there's one more thing: I smoke cigarettes, not around my family but when I'm in the woods or out in a duck blind huntin'. I know some folks around here think that's a sin. Well, I been smokin' for 12 years—ever since I wuz 12 years old! I know it ain't gonna be easy to quit. I know Estelle is disappointed I didn't get saved in this meetin'. I just want y'all to know that I plan to give my heart to the Lord. And if it takes stoppin' smokin' and givin' up my work with the sheriff, I will when the time comes. But I shore ask for ye prayers!"

"Oh, Jim! Homer and I are so excited about what the Lord is going to do in the lives of Jim and Estelle Tharp. She has made her decision, and you will make yours in time. But you two people were ordained of God to become a man-and-wife team to be the premier influence in these prairie-bottoms communities for advancing the kingdom of God in leading people to Jesus Christ, laying the foundation for a strong church to influence hundreds of families for Christ, and for populating Heaven. With your wife's talents and your leadership, marvelous things are ahead for you.

"As for your work with the sheriff, we urge you to see your role as a policeman on duty or a soldier on the front line in a battle. When a policeman has to shoot a man to either wound or kill him, he is never arrested as a murderer. When a soldier kills the enemy in a war, he is more likely to be decorated than arrested. Please understand the commandment 'Thou shalt not kill' to truly mean 'Thou shalt not murder.' Jim, the thousands who read about you in the *Arkansas Gazette* consider you a hero, not a murderer. It's time you understood that God has gifted you with abilities to put the right kind of fear in the wrong kind of people. As for smoking, I don't see it as a sin. I see it more as a health hazard, an abuse of the body, which in reality and according to the Scriptures is the temple of the Holy Spirit. I will tell you the same thing I tell others who have addictions and habits they can't seem to break; just don't try to clean up your life *before* you come to Jesus. Come to Jesus and let Him help you clean up *after* you've received Him into your heart."

"Sister, you've shed a lot of light on my situation. Thank you for tellin' me all that. I really do plan to give my heart to the Lord and let Him hep me do what's too much for me to do by myself. And, if I may ask, Homer, when do y'all plan to leave?"

"Jim, we have the special meeting tomorrow night with all who are interested in organizing a church. So we plan to leave on Tuesday morning. Why?"

"Estelle and me want you to come to our place for breakfast on Tuesday mornin'. We've already invited Ross and Flossie to join us. You set the time. I'm sure you'd like it early."

"We'll come! How about 8:30?"

"That's good. I hope we'll see you tomorrow night at the meeting, and we'll look for you at 8:30 Tuesday morning."

Estelle thought her heart would break when the Gospel meeting closed without Jim going forward and making a commitment to Christ. However, even on the way home, she settled it in faith that the Lord would help her to continue to pray, be faithful, and encourage him to not procrastinate.

"I guess you'll wanta be in the meetin' tomorrow night, won't you?" Jim asked.

"Well, will you go with me tomorrow night if I decide to go?"

"Of course! I'm interested, too, even if I'm not a Christian yet. I wanta know about the doctrines and plans of what would be a church if enough join. I had a good talk with Homer and Helen about my work with the sheriff and my smokin' habit—the two things that bother me. I reckon they look at it about like you do. They don't think my work as deputy oughta matter, and they say come to Jesus and let Him hep me clean up my life with such things as smokin'. Helen made it clear I oughta get right with the Lord, so we can do what God has—what she called 'ordained'—for us to do here on the prairie and down in the bottoms. If she's right, it scares me a little."

"Honey, I doubt if you realize what God could accomplish through you in all the lower part of Arkansas County if you will totally surrender to Him!"

"It ain't gonna be no halfway surrender when I do!"

"Praise the Lord! May He hasten the day!"

Thirty people turned out for the Monday night meeting to hear Homer present the beliefs and policies of the Friends Church. He spoke of George Fox, the founder, told what he believed and how he suffered in England for his beliefs. He laid out ten to twelve main points that agree with most evangelical denominations—the Bible as the infallible Word of God, the Holy Trinity, Jesus Christ's atoning death on the cross, salvation by faith, the Second Coming of Christ, the Judgment including rewards for the righteous and retribution for the unbelieving—Heaven and Hell. Then he spoke of the responsibilities of believers—praying, studying the Bible, worshiping both privately and corporately, witnessing to the lost, bringing up children in the faith, living holy lives, and tithing and giving. He passed out an application to all who knew they were born again and were interested in membership. He gave out the name and address of Rev. Frank Fox, to whom the completed applications would be mailed. He explained that Rev. Fox was commissioned by the National Organization to secure a charter from the Secretary of the State of Arkansas in order that the Friends Church might establish congregations throughout the state. He assured them that when Nady had sufficient numbers, they could organize, call a pastor, elect officers, and function as a church.

Estelle asked, "Brother Rich, in what way is the Friends Church different than, let's say, the Methodist Church?"

"Well, let me make a general observation about the spiritual condition of the Methodist Church. In past decades, it has grown more modern and liberal, and its founder, John Wesley, would hardly recognize many of the Methodists throughout the world today. I do want to say that I personally know some Methodists who are deeply dedicated to our Lord Jesus Christ, and I do not want to slander all Methodists as liberal and backslidden. Now, in doctrine and practice, there is one difference that I should mention that sets us apart from most evangelicals. Friends do not practice the two ordinances of the Lord's Supper and Water Baptism. As a pastor in the Friends Church, I'm not personally prepared to defend that as of now, but I do not administer these sacraments."

Estelle felt a disappointment with this view on the sacraments. She recalled their pastor at the Camp Shed Methodist Church referring to both ordinances as "a means of grace." However, she chose not to register her disappointment at that time.

In bed later that night, Jim asked, "Estelle, did the meetin' go as you had hoped?"

"Not really. While I didn't feel like making an issue of it, I wish the Friends believed in the two sacraments of Water Baptism and the Lord's Supper as means of grace. But I don't want to lessen the importance of a good beginning in establishing a Bible-believing church in our community."

When the Riches, the Morgans, and the two Tharp families were gathered around the breakfast table on Tuesday morning, Jim surprised them all by saying, "Well, folks, I may not have gone forward to pray in the meetin', but I do want to ask the blessin' this mornin'." He began, "Heavenly Father, thank You for sendin' Homer and Helen to Nady to preach the Gospel. Thank You for drawin' so many to Jesus and for the effects of Your Word on those of us who did not respond for a prayer at the altar. Bless in organizin' a new church. May we all pray and give and worship as we ought. Do be with Homer and Helen on their long drive back to Indiana. Keep Your hand upon them and supply their every need. Bring 'em back to us in Your plan for their lives. Bless this food and our fellowship this mornin'. Amen."

"Thanks, Jim, for that wonderful prayer," Helen said. "Amen," Ross, Henry, and Flossie responded in unison.

After most were through eating but still sipping coffee, Helen surprised the Tharps and the Morgans by saying, "Folks, Homer and I have discussed something a little bit, and we haven't felt free to announce anything on it, but with the three families present, I think we should ask you all to make it a subject of prayer. We love you very much, and we love the Nady and upper prairie people we have met. Homer and I would be open to the Lord leading us back here to become your pastor."

All present received the announcement of that possibility with great joy. Henry first spoke, "Why, Brother Homer and Sister Helen, if y'all come back down here to pastor, this old sinner will just about shore 'nuff give his heart to the Lord right alongside my dear wife."

"My! What an incentive!" Helen said. "Homer, that makes us want to go back to Indiana, take a few weeks to get our affairs in order, and come back and see what the Lord might do with us here in this part of the south."

"Estelle and I would welcome your comin', and we'd do all we can to help ye live here as good as ye lived in Indiana. I do believe that with yore leadership, ye'd get half of Little Prairie saved and be able to help those needy lives down in the bottoms," Jim said.

Homer was asked if he would have to delay organizing a church in Nady until Rev. Fox got the legal okay from the state. "No way. Frank is serious about getting a church organized in DeWitt. We'll proceed with the understanding that when the charter is granted, we'll simply affiliate with the Friends Church and have Quarterly Meetings according to their bylaws. Otherwise, we'll operate like any other nonaffiliated independent congregation."

"That's good," Ross said. "Homer, I feel it is important meanwhile to have guidance concerning services from leaders, such as you and Pastor Fox. Hopefully, we can have services at the Menard schoolhouse. I believe we need gifted teachers, such as Estelle and others, giving lessons; and when Pastor Fox and other reliable, trustworthy ministers are available, we need to have worship services as regularly as possible. I know Estelle is gifted in explaining the Bible. I imagine her mother, Alma, is as well. Uncle Morg Tharp, who for a time was my stepfather, is a good exhorter. My guess is that Garland Coose and Spencer Sweeney would be good for an occasional Bible message or lesson. Anyway, my point is that we don't want the fruit of this Gospel meeting to go to waste because of no gathering of believers and others. What do you think?"

"Why don't we make some arrangements this morning before Helen and I get in that nice car that has been loaned to us and head for Indiana. Ross, I believe that you, Alma Wallace, Estelle Tharp, and Oda Tharp should become what we'll call a Steering Committee for promoting worship services, using the various gifts and talents of the people who've given their hearts to the Lord. I'll write Pastor Fox and encourage him to give this committee oversight. Now I don't feel I have exceeded my authority in simply appointing these four to this committee. Will you—Ross, Estelle, and Oda—accept the responsibility for meeting as often as Ross, whom I am appointing chairman, feels you need to? Alma is not here, but I trust Ross can see her and let her know she's been chosen to serve on the committee and get her agreement. You'll probably want to discuss and decide on meeting times, select people to bring the message or teach the lesson, recruit those who can sing songs and play music, and make it what you think an anointed worship service should be. Is there anything anyone wants to say before we adjourn? Alright, I'd like to lead a prayer and bless this home and all present here and pray for the four who will make up the Steering Committee for the new Body of Christ in Nady, Arkansas. Let's stand.

"Father, we are grateful for all You have done in Nady over the past ten to twelve days, for every person who found the Lord, and for stirrings in all hearts for interest in the things of God. Bless Jim and Henry and George, and scores of others who are close to the kingdom and hungry for a relationship with God in which they shall know that they are forgiven by the blood of Jesus Christ and ready for Heaven. Thank You for those who have given their hearts to You and showed up at our meeting last night. Do lead Helen and me in our decision whether or not to return here as the pastor. Provide every need. We ask Your blessing on Ross, Estelle, Alma, and Oda. Give them unity and harmony in their important meetings of steering this community in the things of God until that responsibility falls on others. In Christ's name we ask these things. Amen."

All present followed Homer and Helen to the car. Jim slipped a $100 bill in Homer's coat pocket as he got into the car. After all waved and the car pulled away, Ross explained, "By the way, that beautiful new Dodge Sedan is a loan from an Ohio businessman who is interested in spreading the Gospel and starting new churches. Homer and Helen are people who have almost nothing of this world's goods; they live by faith. Jim, I just saw you slip Homer a bill, and I appreciate that. That's what they depend on—the Lord supplying their needs. They are the kind that I think can make a go of it here in this part of the country. Estelle, you drive a car, don't you? I'm thinkin' of having a meeting of our Steering Committee on Wednesday night at our place, say at 7:30. It shouldn't last for more than an hour. Oda, you could come with Estelle. I'll contact Alma in the meantime." Oda and Estelle, sensing some of the responsibility that Ross felt, assured him that they would be there.

At their meeting, Ross stressed the importance of having regular Sunday morning worship services at the schoolhouse. "People need the opportunity to get adjusted to attending worship on Sunday mornings. I don't think we have a better preacher-teacher in our community than you, Estelle. I don't want to overload you, but I think we should begin getting the word out to the Nady community that we'll have worship at 10 o'clock every Sunday morning. I would like to ask Estelle if she'll teach a Bible lesson this week."

The three were in full agreement. Estelle said, "I remind you that for a week we listened to an educated man of God who had graduated from a Bible college. I only went through the ninth grade, didn't finish high school, and have only been saved ten days. I do feel the burning in my heart to do this, but I don't want to fail in properly teaching God's Word. I feel honored that you would even trust me enough to ask me. The only way I can possibly do it is to know you'll be praying for me."

Ross requested the privilege of introducing Estelle as the Bible preacher-teacher the next Sunday morning. Then he asked the committee to come up and lay hands on Estelle as he prayed for her.

Jim was encouraging when Estelle told him what happened in the committee meeting. "Them committee members know what's what! You're the person to teach the Bible and get these new Christians established in the Lord. I'm backin' you 100 percent!"

Fifty people gathered in the schoolhouse at 10:00 on Sunday morning. R. H. Searcy played guitar as Alma led the congregation in "Standing on the Promises" and "Blessed Assurance." BettyJean sang a special song, "The Love of God," and Allen Freeman prayed a prayer.

Ross then called the committee up to the front and introduced them as "The Steering Committee" appointed by Rev. Homer Rich just before departing for Indiana. He explained the job description given the committee and asked for prayer for them. "Now, we the committee have assigned an important job to Estelle—we've asked her to bring a lesson from the Bible this morning. I don't know of anyone in the community more capable of explaining the Bible than Estelle. So, Estelle, as committee members, we want to lay hands on you and pray for the Spirit's anointing as you give the Word to us. Please don't hesitate to share all that the Spirit has laid on your heart. Think of us as little birdies in the nest waiting for the mother bird to drop the worms in our mouth. Will the congregation please stand and join the committee in prayer as we intercede for Estelle's ministry of teaching not only today but perhaps many times in the future?"

Everyone present, saints and sinners, seemed to feel the need to lift Estelle before the Lord to plead for her freedom, boldness, and clarity in teaching. When the prayers ended, Ross dismissed the committee and thanked the congregation for the way they participated in the prayer time. "Estelle, would you come forward, please. Jim Tharp has a wife he can be proud of. And as far as I'm concerned, this community has a person in Estelle that we also can be proud of—her love for God, her love for Jim and her family, her love for people, her wisdom, and her God-given ability to make the Bible come alive. I want you to greet her this morning as if she were a fully ordained minister of the Word. Estelle, may God bless you as you speak to us!"

Before she began, the crowd was very expressive of their appreciation of Estelle in their applause. She bowed to them and said, "I'm not worthy of this honor, but I promise you I'll do my best to obey the Spirit, and I just pray I can say something that the Lord will use to touch our hearts."

Estelle's Scripture lesson was the Parable of the Sower, the Seed, and the Soil. She read from Luke 8:5-15: **A sower went out to sow his seed, and as he sowed, some fell along the path, and was trodden under foot, and the birds of the air devoured it. And some fell on the rock; and as it grew up, it withered away, because it had no moisture. And some fell among thorns; and the thorns grew with it and choked it. And some fell into good soil and grew, and yielded a hundredfold. As He said this, He called out, "He who has ears to hear, let him hear."**

And when His disciples asked Him what this parable meant, He said, "To you it has been given to know the secrets of the kingdom of God; but for others they are in parables, so that seeing they may not see, and hearing they may not understand. Now the parable is this: the seed is the Word of God. The ones along the path are those who have heard; then the devil comes and takes away the word from their hearts, that they may not believe and be saved. And the ones on the rock are those who, when they hear the word, receive it with joy; but they have no root, they believe for a while and in time of temptation fall away. And as for what fell among the thorns, they are those who hear, but as they go on their way they are choked by the cares and riches and pleasures of life, and their fruit does not mature. And as for that in the good soil, they are those who hold it fast in an honest and good heart, and bring forth fruit with patience."

Estelle began by saying, "We were listening all last week to an ordained minister of the Gospel, a man educated in theology and experienced in preaching. And I remind you this morning that I am an uneducated woman who did not even finish high school. I've only been a born-again Christian a little over a week. But I've been asked to give a Bible lesson, and I'll do my best. If any good comes from this, it will be due to a God of mercy and grace who helped us understand His Word today.

"Jesus gave this parable about a Sower, some Seed, and the Soil. I'll mention three thoughts: the *Nobility of the Sower,* the *Quality of the Soil,* and the *Responsibility of the Hearer.*

"First, the *Nobility of the Sower.* Jesus was faithful to sow, and He had confidence in the seed he planted and his hope that the soil he invested in would produce.

"Jesus Christ came to earth and taught. He was the Primary Sower, and His Word was the Seed. The Gospel of Jesus Christ is God's love for the world providing a Savior to die an atoning death for our sins. This is the Word of salvation and the hope of the world. We are told in Romans 1:16 that the gospel is **the power of God for salvation to everyone who believes.** This means that it is potent, powerful enough to transform a heart, change a life, and bring light to dispel our darkness.

"But notice that even the fruitfulness of the seed of the Gospel depends on the *Quality of the Soil.* The soil represents the life of an individual—his mind, his heart, and his will. Look at the various responses people may make to the Gospel.

"Some seed fell into *Unprepared Soil.* The seed fell on the roadside where people walked; the soil was packed down and hard and unreceptive to the truth. A lot of people hear the Gospel, but Satan comes immediately and distracts their minds and hearts from allowing its seed to sprout. Their minds are on business or pleasure or their problems, but not on the fact that Jesus died for them.

"Often the seed fell into *Shallow Soil.* Jesus said the soil was full of rocks mixed with soil, but the rocks crowded the seed and even though a little bit of soil allowed the seed to sprout, the rocks prevented the seed from taking root and going deep in the Word of God. Soon, the new plant withered away because the roots did not reach down where the moisture was.

"Sometimes seed fell among *Polluted Soil.* This soil was predisposed to weeds and thorns. The seed did sprout and grow a bit, but the weeds and thorns also grew in that same soil and choked the Gospel, so that the seed could not develop as was intended. Rather than attaining heart purity, to which the believer is called, the result is an impure heart.

"Finally, we see the *Responsibility of the Hearer.* Last week many of us responded to the Gospel. Time will tell what we will allow the Lord to do in our hearts. Will we let Him keep us tender and humble and hungry for His will and Word so that Satan cannot pluck the

Scriptures out of our minds? Will we allow Him to deepen us with trials, tests, and experiences that will strengthen us and remove the rocks of hindrances to His will? Or will we grieve Him by not denying our selfish urges and interests that would choke our praying and worshiping and telling others about Jesus? May we allow the Spirit to take the seed of the Word and bring forth a marvelous harvest in our lives!

"I hope you have received something from the truths illustrated in this parable to help you through the week. Thank you for your attention, and I'll turn the service back to Ross."

Ross made comments of gratitude to Estelle and told the people that "as we pray for Estelle and encourage her, we will no doubt hear a lot more powerful messages from God's Word through her. I, for one, feel we are fortunate to have her ministry." He prayed a closing prayer, and many of the congregation swarmed Estelle with words of gratitude and expressions of confidence in her ability to *rightly divide the Word of truth* as the Holy Spirit helped her explain the passages He inspired God's messengers to write. Ross and the committee agreed that, while others who are gifted in teaching and preaching should be used, Estelle would become the mainstay for the regular Sunday morning messages.

On Sunday night after putting the two children to bed, Jim and Estelle sat and talked about the future direction of the Nady and prairie communities spiritually. Jim was most effusive in his comments on Estelle's ability to become the spiritual leader of the community, even if it was only for a brief interim. "We'll need to get someone to live in with us to help you with the children, the house, and the garden, so you'll have her when you need her. You'll need time to pray and study and see people who'll need you, almost like a pastor. Until we find someone, I want to take burdens off you and help you in any way I can."

"Thank you, dear! I have a joy and peace in my heart, even though I never dreamed the committee would lay such a heavy assignment on me. But I'm thankful for you, for the children, and for the way God has blessed us financially. Let's put the Lord first, and He will help us take care of our family the best we can. He will also help you to come to know Him, and then we can grow in grace and faith together."

5   The Clash of Two Kingdoms

Homer and Helen Rich made it back to Nady, Arkansas, to pastor the Friends Church in the fall of 1932, two years after they had held the Gospel meeting. On their first Sunday, more than 100 people were present to greet them.

In his opening remarks, Homer acknowledged the faithfulness of the Steering Committee, chaired by Ross Morgan. He expressed appreciation for the inspired teaching of Estelle Tharp and others across the months that had fed the flock and resulted in a number of new converts to Christ.

A few weeks after their arrival, Homer announced a special meeting featuring the Vice President of Union Bible College, Dr. Simeon Smith, and his wife LaVaun. "Smith is a well-known theologian, a much-loved professor of Christian Apologetics, and an excellent preacher. He and his wife are talented singers and musicians, and they are bringing with them a trio (two young ladies and a young gentleman, students of UBC) well-known in the Midwest for their sacred concerts.

"We will be fortunate to have this kind of talent here in Nady, and we ask everyone to come and enjoy their presentations of the Gospel in sermon and song." Homer assigned the committee the responsibilities of getting the meeting advertised, arranging for housing, and making known to the more prosperous people of the communities the need for financial support for the Indiana group.

The event was to begin on the last Sunday night of October and end on the first Sunday night of November—"eight great days and nine powerful services of hearing the Gospel of Jesus Christ in a time of bringing us all together in the unity of the Spirit. Let's get the word out to other churches and the people in surrounding communities and share the good news with all who wish to come and enjoy this wonderful occasion with us."

The October Sunday night came with a golden Fall sunset, and at least 200 people filled both rooms of the Menard schoolhouse. An additional 200 on the outside listened to the service through raised windows. Enjoying the accompaniment of piano, accordion, and guitar, the congregation sang such hymns as "Power in the Blood," "Amazing Grace," and "Blessed Assurance." The trio was composed of two well-dressed young ladies in their twenties, presented as "Mary and Martha," and John, a striking young man who might have been borrowed from Hollywood, judging by his looks and trained voice. Following an offering, a prayer, and announcements, Simeon and LaVaun played their guitar and accordion, respectively, and sang "The Ninety and Nine," a powerful tribute to the Savior's extravagant love for the lost, made even more impressive by the harmony of their trained voices.

Simeon Smith took his text from Hebrews 9:27: **It is appointed for men to die once, and after that comes the judgment.** "It will be a dreadful thing following death for any human soul to stand before a just and holy God not having confessed Jesus Christ as his or her personal Savior, the only one Almighty God has designated as our means of salvation.

"But tonight the Holy Spirit is in this place—inside and outside this building—working the crowd, stirring hearts, sobering minds, and giving tenderness, humility, and hunger to approach God through Christ and repent of sin. Don't wait for others to begin. You who feel the tug of God at your hearts, come on. *Today is the day of salvation.* Tomorrow might be too late. Come as the trio sings "Softly and Tenderly Jesus Is Calling."

On the first stanza, several from inside the building came forward to stand in front of the preacher. During the second stanza, twenty came from outside. Simeon congratulated them on their choice of a Savior who never fails and led them in the sinner's prayer.

"Now, as we all stand for a closing hymn, these new converts will be given some materials to help them in the beginning days of their new walk with God. The trio will distribute these materials, so please read, even tonight, what you are given. Do come back tomorrow night and plan to attend each service this week."

On the way home, Estelle commented, "I would say that was a powerful sermon." She was in the back seat of the car holding Alma Anniece, their eleven-month-old child, who was born November 23, 1931. On either side of her was their five-year-old daughter, Jeanette, and their three-year-old son, J. W.

"Well, I agree," Jim said. "But wasn't the singin' both by the Smiths and the trio awfully professional, cut-and-dried, showy? Or is it just me—an old country boy who prefers simple, down-home, old-fashioned music and song? I'm quite sure this kind of talent goes over big up in Indiana and most other places."

"Honey, the Lord is in this meeting, and we just need to forego our own tastes and preferences for the time and rejoice that people are getting saved."

The first two nights of the meeting were orderly, and many responded to the invitation. Then on the third night, the outside crowd was invaded by rowdies from down in the bottoms. The noise outside was so bothersome that Ross, Jim, and George slipped out of the building and moved among the 200 or more people, most of whom were orderly and listening to the singing and preaching on the inside. But Jim noticed three young men who seemed to be there for other reasons. They yelled a few obscenities and elbowed their way through the crowd in a bullying manner, insensitive to the men and women around them.

Jim worked his way to the tallest and noisiest of the three until they were face to face. "Buster, I don't know who ye are or why ye're here. Most of us are here to hear the Gospel. But I'm warnin' ye, either ye calm down and behave decently, or I'll see to it that ye leave this place one way or another."

Ross and George saw the confrontation and moved in behind Jim for support. "Why, you little half-pint, scrawny religious hypocrite! You think you can make me behave! I just might as well put your lights out right here and now." Jim saw the bully raise his fist and brace his feet. When he swung, Jim was ready for him—he turned his shoulder in a hunch, caught the man's arm at the wrist, twisted sharply, throwing him over his shoulder. The man's arm snapped loud enough that everyone outside heard it. Curses flew from the bully's mouth as he lunged at Jim. But Jim's fist slammed into his mouth, shutting him up and bringing blood and teeth spilling out on the ground. Jim was ready to finish him off, but he saw him stagger and fall to the ground, howling about his broken arm. Ross and George found the other two and brought them over to the man on the ground.

"Is this man with you fellows?" Ross asked.

"Yeah, this is our buddy. We call him Big Boy. What's goin' on here?" one asked.

"Well, Big Boy just got too big for his britches and too loud with his cussin', and this is what happened to him. We are in a worship service here. We are glad to have anyone here who comes to worship and behaves himself. But we don't tolerate Big Boy's kind of behavior. This man here who took Big Boy on is the special deputy to the sheriff of Arkansas County. Either you take Big Boy outa here or Jim Tharp will arrest all of you for disturbin' the peace and then take you to jail in DeWitt."

By this time another member of the mischief-makers' party came up and grabbed Big Boy, calling to his other pals, "Help me get him outa here!" The people stepped aside and watched as the three carefully carried their bloodied partner away while trying to protect his broken arm. From a distance one of them called, "We ain't forgettin' what you done to Big Boy. Jim Tharp, you'll regret this!"

The run-in with the rowdies put a damper on the meetings, and the next night the crowd outside was smaller, but orderly. On the fourth night, however, things really got bad. Jim had told Estelle to drive their car and take Oda and the children and go ahead to church. Jim and Henry had been working with cattle on their horses all day, and they would ride their horses to the service after they cleaned up.

Arriving at the schoolhouse, Jim had tied Star's halter rope to a tree limb and had told Buck, "Stay!" Right at service time, he was climbing the steps when he met Ross, who was pale-faced and wild-eyed.

"What's wrong, Ross?"

"Man, am I glad to see you! Some rowdies are back, and they just kidnapped Martha, one of the girls in the trio. Someone saw two rascals take her and drag her kickin' and screamin' to their old truck; then they headed down toward Garland Lake. Estelle said you rode here tonight on your horse."

"Yeah, I'll head out there, and you drive yore truck behind me." Jim rushed to Star, buckled on his gun, and said to Buck, "Lead!" Jim pointed eastward toward the bottoms. He did not want to travel too fast until Ross caught up with him. Down in the bottoms it would be darker than on the prairie. Jim could now see Ross's headlights, and they were about to cross Deep Bayou bridge. A few miles beyond the bridge, Jim could make out a tent and through an open flap he could see a dim light. He decided to rein up, motioning Ross to stop a ways back. Outside the tent was an old dirty truck. He was pretty sure he would find the girl here. Would he be too late?

Ross came walking up, asking in a low voice, "Whadda we have out there, Jim?"

"It may be what we're lookin' for. We'll soon find out. Take my rifle here; it's loaded and ready. Buck and I will go through that flap yonder, hopefully not too late to save that girl. If someone runs by ye, shoot a leg off! Come, Buck! Bad men!"

Ross watched Jim throw the tent flap open wider. Then he heard the girl screaming, "No! No! Don't do this to me!" He could see a naked man standing over the naked girl lying flat on her back on the ground inside the tent. He heard Jim call, "*Freeze!*" A second later he heard *Bang!* Immediately he heard screamin' and cussin', then "Damn you! You've shot me!" Ross heard Jim call to someone in the tent, "Bring yore shirt over to the girl! ... Come on, honey, ye're okay. Ye're safe, we're gettin' ye outa here."

Jim turned to see Ross enter the tent. "Ross, do ye have a blanket in yore truck to wrap around her?"

"I have a quilt; I'll be right back!"

"Now, I'm a deputy sheriff, and I'm arrestin' ye two men for attempted rape and takin' ye to jail in DeWitt. Martha, we'll have ye back out safely in just a few minutes. I believe I got here before they did anything to ye."

"Yes, thank God!" the trembling, pale-faced girl said, as she allowed Ross to drape the quilt around her.

"Now Ross, go to my saddlebag, get two sets of cuffs, and come and cuff these two." Jim held his pistol in hand as he talked soothingly to the girl, while keeping an eye on the two criminals.

Back at the schoolhouse, Ross rushed inside and found LaVaun. She and Flossie came out and rejoiced when they saw Martha in the cab wrapped in a quilt. "Praise the Lord!" LaVaun said.

"Yes, thank God! Mr. Tharp got to me before they had their way! Praise the Lord!"

Ross said, "Flossie, go with me to the house. We'll take Martha to her room there, and Jim and I will take these two rascals chained in the back of the truck to jail yet tonight."

On the way, Flossie said, "Ross, Simeon and LaVaun are talkin' of closin' the meetin' and headin' back to Indiana."

"I think that would be a mistake, given what Jim's accomplished during the last hour. I'll try and talk 'em out of it when they come home tonight."

When the two were locked in jail and Jim and Ross were on their way back, Ross said, "Jim, I just don't see how we can have a civil and decent community without you. I'm sure Lloyd would have long ago given up on this end of the county if he didn't have you."

"Well, I guess I see the area as worth fightin' for. The Lord has given me some abilities, and I ain't plannin' to use 'em in the wrong way. So I'm just doin' my duty." Back at the Morgans, Ross immediately began trying to persuade Simeon and LaVaun to reconsider and stay the course of the meeting. Jim could see they were willing to reconsider.

"I believe the worst is over," Jim said. "Let's allow the Lord to take what has happened, and let's all learn something. I'm thinkin' Estelle is right—that evil forces we can't see or hear are gangin' up on the community tryin' to prevent what the good forces want to accomplish. Let's don't back off and turn it all over to the devil." Jim could see his words were having an effect, so he said good night and went to get Star and Buck down at Ross's barn.

Estelle was waiting up for him. She agreed completely with what Jim had expressed at the Morgans a half hour before. "Yes, we've got to allow the Lord to help us find a strategy for defeating Satan. I know our secret can be found in the Bible! May the Holy Spirit give us direction and faith to discover it and put it to work so our Great God will be glorified and the devil defeated!"

It was clear to the average American that Herbert Hoover would go down in defeat in the 1932 election. He had labored for the last few years under the dead weight of the deepening depression. Most voters were ready to take a chance on Roosevelt's New Deal, believing he would bring back happier days. When the Democrat took the oath of office on March 4, 1933, the stock market had already begun an upswing. In his inaugural address, he asserted his firm belief that "the only thing we have to fear is fear itself—nameless unreasoning, unjustified terror which paralyzes needed efforts to convert retreat into advance."

Most Americans couldn't remember a new leader making such a difference in the mindset of the country as had Roosevelt. Even Will Rogers wrote, "America hasn't been happy in three years as they now are. They've got no money, no banks, no works, no nothing, but they think they got a man in there now who is wise to Congress, wise to our so-called big men. The whole country is with him."

Estelle laid the *Gazette* down and said, "Well, not the whole country! Though I pray for our new president and wish him well, I know we have more to fear than fear itself. We need to fear the Lord, because that **is the beginning of wisdom**."

"I'm impressed with Roosevelt," Jim said, "cuz he has a winsome way, and I hope he can turn thangs around and open up trade and get us venturin' again—heppin' us think smart, support one another, and work hard."

"But Jim, I'm concerned about the spiritual leadership of the country also. I think we'll miss the moral and spiritual influence of President and Mrs. Hoover. But that's no excuse for our little prairie community here. God wants us to pray, worship, love, witness, help one another live for the Lord, and make it financially. I'm feeling things about the country in general and our own region in particular that's causing me to consider another reason for the way people think, act, and live as they do, especially when it comes to immorality, murder, irreverence, violence, and all other kinds of crime. I want us to talk more about this when I've prayed and read more."

"I don't know anybody who thinks better than you. I don't reckon I can be much help to ye, but I can listen."

"I'm afraid you might think me off mentally when I tell you that I believe there are invisible forces of evil—**hosts of wicked spirits operating in the heavenlies**. I think these unseen forces are spiritual beings that have access to our minds and are able to urge us to think and do things contrary to what is good, things that result in hurt, wrong, confusion, sickness, poverty, and evil. I'm convinced that even most Christians are obsessed with the visible, the sensual, the material—**the lusts of the flesh, the lust of the eyes and the pride of life**—to the extent that the heavenly hosts seeking to capture our minds to think appropriately, lovingly, and helpfully are repelled by our bent to selfish ways. May the Lord help me **to take every thought captive to obey**

Christ, and so **destroy arguments and proud obstacles** the devil would hurl at me.

"But right now, I'd better tend to some things I can hear and see—like a calling child and dirty dishes." She first went to check on Jeanette and calm her, and then looked in on Burl Harlan, their fourth child, who had been born on December 18, 1933.

About a year after the meeting with Simeon and LaVaun Smith, Homer and Helen visited Estelle, feeling there was something urgent they needed to talk to her about. "We don't know who to mention this to, except you. We are convinced that Satan is targeting this area for defeat. Ever since the meeting in 1930, and especially since you've had such a good ministry here before our return, our praying has been opposed like no other time we can remember in all our ministry! We've been drawn to Ephesians 6:10-18 and feel it is for us to live in and preach on. It has to do with spiritual warfare. I'm sure you know what we are talking about."

Estelle said, "Yes, and you are confirming my discernment and verifying the very things I've been talking to Jim about. So far he has not called me crazy. But I do know the enemy is fiercely attacking this area. One evidence of that is the attempt to break up the meeting and send the Smiths and the trio back to Indiana in defeat. And, Satan is not through with us. The worst of his efforts are yet ahead. But we must find a strategy, a plan, and an approach to defeat him or this entire area will be lost!"

Helen spoke, "Estelle, we agree with you! We feel we should contact UBC and have materials sent here on the subject. Brother Fox is unable as of now to secure the charter for churches in this state. We are all fighting against opposition that can only be explained by the opposition of supernatural evil."

"I'm going to be preaching on this passage in Ephesians for several Sundays," Homer said.

"Good! I'll be taking notes. And I'm willing to buy books on spiritual warfare if there are some you recommend," Estelle said.

Estelle decided to begin spending an hour each morning in prayer before the children needed attention. It would mean getting up earlier, but with the Riches confirming her sense of Satanic attacks, she knew it was essential that she be fortified in prayer.

Jim had other things on his mind. Lloyd had come by and told him that the Feds had called his office and reported that two prohibition agents had been killed; their bodies were found a long way down the Mississippi River. Lloyd suspected moonshiners in the White River bottoms might have had something to do with these murders. He wanted to talk with Henry to find out what he knew.

Lloyd came back a few days later, and while he and Jim were drinking coffee, Henry dropped by. Lloyd asked, "Henry, when did you quit working for Reddon?"

"Let's see, just about a week before Jim got married—toward the last of August, 1926."

"Tell me about him. What he was like?"

"Old Reddon did shoot at some of the 'snoopers' one afternoon. I heard the shots, but I was workin' on the still. Early the next mornin' he sent me for supplies. A day or so later, I wuz out cuttin' wood and saw where somebody had dragged somethin' to the bayou. But them woods are full of stuff like logs and limbs people drag from here to there. I wouldn't put it past old Reddon doin' whut ye think, but I can't say he did. He wanted me to shoot anyone snoopin' around. When I told him I'd be willin' to shoot to scare 'em but no way was I gonna shoot a lawman, he didn't like it and said so. I knew my days with him wuz numbered, so I just quit."

"What caliber rifle did Reddon shoot?"

"He shot a .30.06, just about like Jim's."

"Soft-nosed bullets?"

"Definitely! I saw the shells on the table. He boasted of what they would do when they hit."

"The two men the Feds found were in bad shape, but they could tell they had been shot with a .30.06. Then just a little later they found two more who'd been hit with .00 buckshot."

"Now, that's somethin'! On the same table with the rifle shells wuz a box of twelve-gauge .00 shotgun shells."

"Is Reddon still operating in the same place?"

"As far as I know, he is."

"I can't arrest a man because he shoots a .30.06 rifle, but I would like to meet him, look him over, and scout around his operation some."

"Sheriff, I would caution you not to go messin' 'round that place! He'd rather kill a man of the law than cripple or scare him. He's mean! Don't crowd him!"

"Jim, I'll bet you could come up with a plan to get up with Reddon," Lloyd said.

"I probably could sneak up on him, get behind a tree, call him, and then have to kill him in self defense, if he's as anxious to shoot lawmen as Henry claims."

Lloyd said, "Let me tell you the rest of the story, Henry. I didn't even tell Jim, but the official who called me from Washington, D.C. the other day said they suspected a man here in our county is responsible for killing 14 agents, 12 with a .30.06 soft-nosed bullets and 2 with 12 gauge .00 shot."

"It shore sounds like Reddon alright. But Sheriff, I know of more than 20 other moonshiners who shoot a .30.06, the most popular high-powered gun for wild hogs, deer, bear, and panther. Now I shore ain't defendin' Reddon, but I reckon in a court of law ye gotta have more than suspicion."

"I know, Henry. That's why I wanta go down there and eyeball the man."

"Sheriff, ain't nobody, includin' me, gonna get close to that operation and live unless Reddon's away."

"I guess you haven't seen your brother in action."

"Don't try it, men!" Henry begged, looking at both Jim and Lloyd.

"How close can we get to the operation, Henry?" Jim asked.

"Go to Garland Lake, and park yer truck. Walk a mile northeast to a slough, turn a little to yer right, and follow the slough a half mile. Come to a grove of white oaks and stop! Ye're within Reddon's rifle range. Hide behind the biggest tree, watch, and listen. Decide if Reddon or anybody else is around before you go any closer. Maybe yer dog can hep ye decide."

Estelle, overhearing the conversation, said, "Sheriff and Jim, I'd like to ask you to reconsider trying to go to Reddon. I can't explain this feeling, except to say I'm getting negative vibrations from a source that I've come to trust."

"Estelle is right," Lloyd said. "I'll go back to the office and call the agent in D.C. and see if he has anything at all on Reddon. Anyway, thanks, Estelle. We'll give this more time."

Estelle was glad when Homer announced that his Sunday morning merssage would have to do with Spiritual Warfare. He went on to say, "Even those who recognize the kingdom of evil as headed by a fallen Lucifer, now known as Satan or the devil, are reluctant to acknowledge such reality lest they be accused of reverting back to 'medieval theology.'" Homer then read his Scripture from Ephesians 6:10-18, and declared, "The apostle was setting forth a conflict between two kingdoms—the kingdom of God and the kingdom of Satan, the kingdom of salvation against the kingdom of destruction, the kingdom of light against the kingdom of darkness. In this age of grace, it is God's purpose to deliver human beings from the kingdom of darkness and translate them over to the kingdom of light.

"Our Bible gives us the revelation of the two opposing kingdoms. God is the Head of His own kingdom, but we are told in the Scriptures that He gives this kingdom over to His Son, Jesus Christ. Throughout the Bible, we have a revelation of the attributes of Almighty God as revealed in the Holy Trinity. Jesus Christ shares equally all these attributes with God the Father and God the Holy Spirit.

"In the Scriptures we also see the nature of the evil one who heads up the kingdom of darkness. Satan is a fallen angel. The Bible does not list in narrative form all the details leading up to Lucifer's fall, but we are given to understand something of his evil nature in his hatred and jealousy of a holy God. Most Bible scholars agree that Lucifer was of the highest order in all the angelic hierarchy. It appears that he was given the task of coordinating their worship among the celestials in offering praise to Almighty God. Isaiah and Ezekiel reveal that Lucifer grew jealous of God's glory and became obsessed with the passion to take the place of God. That's when Lucifer was thrown out of Heaven. When he became Satan, the god of this world, he tempted Jesus by offering Him the kingdoms of this world if He would but **fall down and worship me** (Matt. 4:9). The apostle Paul tells us that when the time comes in the end for Satan to manifest himself as **the man of lawlessness, the son of perdition, ... he will exalt himself against every so-called god or object of worship, so that he takes his seat in the temple of God, proclaiming himself to be God** (II Thes. 2:3-4).

"It is from the four Gospels that we get the true picture of Satan from Jesus. Our Lord said that Satan is a *liar, murderer, destroyer*. As followers of Christ, we need to be aware of the five main things Satan is out to do on planet earth. As a created being, he cannot possibly achieve a higher level than that for which he was created by an omniscient, omnipotent, eternal God. He infected a third of the angelic world with his evil spirit, and this great number met swift judgment right along with him. God knew all along that Satan would organize the fallen angels into a hierarchy of evil and relentlessly oppose the Creator in five ways:

"(1) *To seek to prevent the glory of God.* Since there is nothing noble and grand in the nature of Satan, but only a negative power of degradation, he seeks to take advantage of the vulnerable human race and deceive and divert them from their divinely ordained purpose of reflecting the glory of their Creator. He lies to human minds, impressing them with their own abilities to reach their highest potential by living independently of the will and purpose of God. All through the ages he has perpetrated the lie of humanism. He was successful in the Garden of Eden, but he still seeks to divert every individual from bringing glory to God in finding his or her fulfillment in the will and power of God.

"(2) *To seek to blind human minds to the Gospel of Jesus Christ.* Satan hates the Gospel, because **it is the power of God for salvation to everyone who has faith** (Rom. 1:16). When a sinner believes in the Risen Christ and confesses Him as Savior and Lord, he is translated from the kingdom of darkness over into the kingdom of light. That believer is no longer a child of Satan but he becomes an adopted child of God. It's no wonder that Satan hates the Gospel; it makes him a loser. So**, the god of this world has blinded the minds of the unbelievers, to keep them from seeing the light of the gospel of the glory of Christ** (II Cor. 4:4).

"(3) *To seek to perpetrate all manner of evil, suffering, and destruction.* Satan cannot create, so he seeks to destroy. He loves death, disease, poverty, confusion, war, division, rebellion, ignorance, violence, and suffering of every kind. When a third of the angels fell with Satan, God could have consigned them immediately to the Lake of Fire. He chose instead to demonstrate His power over them by taking the evil they would work in the lives of mortal beings to test and strengthen them morally and spiritually for His plan for their lives. In the end, these evil forces would be cast into eternal punishment.

"(4) *To seek to rob Christians of their divine calling.* The apostle Paul tells all of we believers that we are **predestined to be conformed to the image of Jesus Christ** (Rom. 8:29). This is why God saves us and why He sanctifies us—so that we might become like Jesus. God sent

Jesus to us in our own likeness in order that He might make us into Jesus' likeness. The context here is a reminder that God requires our cooperation—our surrender to His will, our yielding to the leadings of His Spirit—in shaping us into a life of Christian holiness. Let not one of us mistake Satan's efforts to rob us of this our destiny.

"(5) *To keep the church in ignorance, or violation, of its call to militant warfare praying in opposing the kingdom of darkness.* Jesus' parting instructions to His followers did not contain emphases on organization, public relations, fundraising, or theological content of preaching and teaching; He simply ordered them back into Jerusalem *to start praying in order to be filled with the Spirit*! They were to be **endued with power from on high** (Luke 24:49). It is believed that over 500 believers heard this command, but Luke tells us that only 120 obeyed (Acts 1:15). We are left to wonder—is it any different today? Most pastors would be satisfied to have one-fourth of their membership committed to intercessory prayer for the fullness of the Holy Spirit and all that He would have happen in our congregations! But there is good news: *An unbelieving, uncommitted, indifferent majority cannot prevent an outpouring of the Holy Spirit on a congregation where there is a believing, committed, obedient minority!*

"The truth is, behind the violence, evil, and spiritual backsliding going on in our communities, there is an invisible war raging in the spirit world. Something sinister is going on throughout the prairie and river bottoms communities. Behind the symptoms of murder, rape, thievery, lying, violence, and unbelief there is a cosmic battle. Invisible armies are in conflict contending for the destiny of our communities. The fallen forces of darkness headed by Satan, the god of this age, are rallying to oppose all that God has planned to do in these critical years.

"Some time ago Helen and I felt the Lord speak to us through Brother Frank Fox to come to Nady and hold the "brush arbor" meeting. We felt God wanted to take this obscure community and make an example of His marvelous power in redemption and transformation of human hearts and lives and show the world the miracle of revival.

"But there is the human factor in spiritual warfare that we must face. In closing today, I want to urge everyone here, saint and sinner, to concentrate this week on the Scripture found in Ephesians 6:10-18. The apostle Paul closes this great passage by mentioning *prayer* as our *ultimate weapon* in this battle. I close my message by asking every believer here to make this week a time during which you will pray every day for an anointing of the Holy Spirit in praying for the communities in Arkansas County, beginning with the members of your own household."

As Homer prayed with great emotion, Estelle felt her eyes fill with tears and her heart strangely warmed to know how to pray in power against the kingdom of darkness that Homer had been speaking about. She only had time to hug her mother and a few others before she and Jim gathered their little family and headed home.

After the noon meal and the children were napping, Jim asked, "Estelle, did it seem to you like Homer was declarin' war on evil today?"

"Yes! And I'm glad. I need to let the Lord help me to get around to being a warrior like Homer talked about. I hear that Brother Fox in DeWitt and Homer here in Nady are trying to get some of us to go and attend a special meeting at UBC in Westfield, Indiana, in August. I keep feeling that we ought to go. I don't think we'd need to drive, because Al and Dorene are thinking of taking a load in the pickup. Would you consider leaving everything in Henry's care here and being gone for a week?"

"Maybe it wouldn't hurt to go away for a time. I guess we have the money, don't we? How much will it cost? Who'll care for the children?"

"We can afford it. We'd actually be gone eight days. We could probably get Dee to come and live here, and I know Oda would help. Couldn't Henry take over for you?"

"Yeah, let's see if he will. It might be good for both of us to get away for awhile."

Upon arrival in Westfield, Jim and Estelle were assigned a room in the dorm. The next morning they walked across the lovely college campus and sat down at a picnic table under a large elm. It wasn't long before a lovely young woman came along who looked familiar to Estelle. She was about to pass them by when Estelle stood and asked, "Aren't you Martha?"

"Yes, that's my name," she said as she drew nearer trying to identify them.

Jim recognized her as the girl he had rescued from a rapist a few months before.

"Oh! You're Mr. Jim Tharp, aren't you?" the smiling girl asked. "You're the one who saved me from that terrible man!" She grabbed Jim and hugged him, saying, "Thank you, sir!" Then she turned and hugged Estelle. Turning to her parents who were not far behind her, she said, "Mother and Daddy, come meet Jim and Estelle Tharp from Nady, Arkansas. This man saved me from ... that bad situation in Arkansas! These are my parents, Robert and Grace Boyden."

"Oh, thank you, Mr. Tharp, for coming to Martha's rescue!" Robert said.

"Have a seat, folks." Jim said, as he pointed to the empty bench across the table from them. All three were profuse in their gratitude to Jim. Martha said, "I'll be in debt to you for the rest of my life."

"I'm glad I could reach you in time. Actually, I was only doin' my duty."

"Tell us about yourselves," Estelle said.

"We are from Findlay, Ohio, in the steel business," Robert said. "Several years ago we were in a formal, cold church. But the Friends came along, preached the Gospel, and we got saved. We helped start a Friends Church in Findlay, and it has been growing. Since the Lord has prospered us, we decided to do more than tithe—we started giving generously to the Friends' desire to launch out into other states. So we financed Brother Frank Fox's going into Arkansas, and we've also helped down in South America in some missions work. You might remember that Brother Rich drove a nice car down your way for the meeting; that was a loan from us. And we felt greatly repaid when our daughter was rescued by you when she was with the trio down there a few months ago."

When Simeon and LaVaun Smith came along and added to the gathering, the Boydens excused themselves and allowed the Tharps and Smiths to visit awhile.

Later in the bookstore, Dr. William Smith came to them and introduced himself. "Mrs. Tharp, we have talked together on the phone a time or two, and Dr. Honeycutt and my son Simeon have had some wonderful things to say about both of you." Jim and Estelle enjoyed the older man's kind words for a few minutes until someone else sought the famous theologian's counsel.

In the first service of the Annual Spiritual Renewal Week, Estelle and Jim listened to a rousing orchestra and heard Simeon and

LaVaun sing "The Ninety and Nine," once again. Then Dr. Ernest Jones, president of Cleveland Bible Institute, preached a message on "The Sanctifying Spirit."

Estelle wrote furiously in her notebook, while the preacher made it clear from the Bible that "No one can live a holy life, pray in the Spirit, and be the man or woman for God they are called to be until they have allowed God to cleanse their hearts and fill them with the Holy Spirit!" When he had finished his sermon, he invited all who truly and earnestly wanted God's cleansing and power in their lives to come and surrender to God.

Estelle leaned over and whispered to Jim, "Darling, this message is for me! I can't wait another day to go forward and surrender my heart and trust God to sanctify me. Will you come with me and trust Jesus to save you?"

Jim shook his head and said, "Go ahead, honey. I reckon when I do get saved, it will probably be in Nady, or maybe just you and me together in our livin' room. But you go ahead; I think you should."

At the altar, among others, Estelle surrendered her heart and will and life to God. "Please, Lord, cleanse me from all unrighteousness, purify my heart, and get me ready for Your will."

Dr. Jones gave instructions to the seekers, saying, "Now, what you have asked God to do, please don't offend Him by doubting that He's giving you what you need and what He wants you to have—purity of heart and a readiness to do His will."

Estelle felt faith come as a rushing gift to her. She stood with her hands raised in praise and said, "Lord, I know You have sanctified my heart. Now I go out of here to pray, worship, live, and witness in Your grace and power." She walked back to the seat and told Jim, "The Lord has done a cleansing work in my heart, honey! I believe He'll help me to pray and live better."

Estelle enjoyed all of the services for the rest of the week. Jim was sociable and pleasant and didn't complain about the food and services that he tolerated but did not particularly like. Dr. and Mrs. William Smith invited Jim and Estelle to have breakfast with them on Monday morning before returning home. When they went to pay the bill for their room at the dorm, the clerk informed them that Mr. Robert Boyden had already paid their bill. Learning that the Boydens had left the evening before and they wouldn't be able to thank them in person for their kindness, Estelle secured their address so that she could express their appreciation in a note.

On the fourteen-hour trip back home, Estelle told Jim, "Honey, I thank you for coming with me to make this trip. I truly believe I have received the sanctifying presence of the Holy Spirit in my heart, and I learned so much from Drs. Stauffer, Wilson, Jones, and Smith! And I was able to buy some books on spiritual warfare which I can't wait to begin reading!"

Back home, it was a joy to reunite with the children and feel their love. Jim and Estelle both expressed their appreciation to Dee, Oda, Henry, and George for their help during their absence.

When it became apparent that Homer and Helen could no longer make it financially on the amount the congregation was paying them each month, Homer shared their concern with Jim. "I do believe the Lord brought us down here, and I'm willing to become bivocational—work at a job to earn the amount I need to live on and still preach here and pastor." Homer confided that if they couldn't raise a few hundred dollars to pay off their car, they would lose it.

Jim shared with Estelle what Homer had told him. "Jim, I think it's time we hired someone to take over your venture into farming. You are doing well fishing, trapping, and timbering. And it appears you are going to do well with the cattle. Since you are planning to put in cotton on the ground you have cleared, I think it's too much for you take on that, too. Why don't you see if Homer would be interested in sharecropping your cotton?" Jim said he would think about it.

"Jim, I'll go to prayer and find out from the Lord how much we ought to give on the Riches' car. Then let's think of four or five others we might consult to join us in paying that car off." Jim thought it was a good idea. One night after supper, Estelle said, "I think we could give $100 and never miss it. Who else should we consult to join us?" The two came up with the names of Ross Morgan, Cleve Sweeney, Uncle Morg, and George Best.

On a Friday night, after adding their $100 to the others' hundreds, Jim said he would drive down and give the money to Homer and Helen. When he started out still wearing his gunbelt, Estelle said, "I don't think you'll need to take that thing," pointing to Jim's pistol. Jim started unbuckling the gunbelt and then, leaving both himself and Estelle puzzled, refastened the buckle and headed for his car openly armed.

Jim was approaching the home of the Riches when he saw Homer returning from the Massey farm. Suddenly, Homer bolted and ran for his back door. By the time Jim had parked his car, he heard Helen screaming and then noticed a man running out the front door toward him. When the runner saw Jim, he bolted to turn and jump over the yard fence.

"Hold it, buster!" Jim called. "What are you runnin' from?" He looked at the young man who had fallen on the ground and waited a second for his answer. "Somethin' tells me you've tried to harm that lady in the house. Now, stand up! And stand still!" The man obeyed his command. "I happen to be a deputy sheriff, and I know somethin' ain't right here." He could now hear Helen sobbing, so he pulled his gun and motioned to the man, "Come around through the gate and have a seat on the front porch steps there! I'm gonna look into this matter if you don't talk." When he saw the man was about to bolt for the road, he shot a hole in his ear.

Again, the man fell to the ground and began screaming, "I reckon you've killed me, and I'm dyin'."

"No, ye're not dyin'. I've shot yore ear to remind ye that ye can't go 'round violatin' other people. Next time I might jus' kill ye."

As the man left, Homer came to the door and said, "Jim, did you just shoot that man?"

"Just shot his ear and marked him good. Is Helen alright?"

"Yeah, I just reached her in time. She beat the guy off. He didn't have his way, but I got here just in time. Come on in."

"Homer, I do want to talk with you and Helen, but maybe I oughta come back another time."

"No, come on in. She's getting dressed after that guy about tore her dress off. It'll do us both good to have you here with us for a few minutes."

Jim went to the car and unbuckled his gunbelt and then went in to join Homer and Helen in the living room. To Helen, Homer said, "Well, Jim just took care of your attacker by marking his ear." All three laughed, and Helen said, "Good enough for him; maybe he'll behave now."

"I'll go and make some coffee," Homer said.

When Homer returned, Jim said, "Homer and Helen, I know we, your congregation, haven't been comin' through with support for ye like we should. Estelle and I have been talkin', and we've decided somethin' oughta be done to pay off yore car, then somethin' else oughta be done in a permanent way to help ye over the long haul. So here's what I've done—I went to several in our congregation, and we want to pitch in and pay yore car off. So here's $500."

After both expressed their appreciation, Jim went on, "Now, ye said ye might be willin' to work at somethin', and I have a proposition for ye. I'd like to hire ye to clear the rest of the ground we need to put in a cotton crop. I pay fifty cents an hour for my workers, and I like when they can give me ten hours a day. But since ye've got to prepare for preachin' and takin' care of people, I'd let ye work yer own hours—a few hours at a time or all day when ye can. Then after the ground is clear, I'd like ye to consider sharecroppin' cotton for me. And if ye don't know anything about cotton farmin', maybe we oughta get ye a partner who does. I heard Birdie Washington, over near the Merrisach, wants to extend his cotton farmin'. They tell me he's good. Y'all could work by the hour for clearin' the rest of the ground we need. Then on farmin', if I furnished the tools—the tractor, seed, fuel, and everythang, I'd be willin' to deduct all costs and let the two of ye divide the profit on the cotton."

"But that way, you don't realize any profit from the crop," Homer said.

"Naw, but you two would have an income, and we'd do that for a few years 'til things are better."

Estelle gave birth to her fifth baby on September 20, 1935—a boy she named Russell Dexter. Dee and Oda kept the house in order and the children well cared for, and Jim tried to spend special times with Estelle. Before long they were all back to normal.

When Estelle was stronger, she told Jim that she felt they should get the children ready and go visit the Washington family. Besides making it a social visit, they would also see if Birdie might be willing to join Homer in raising cotton on their place. Estelle prepared the children for visiting with the black family. "Now, children, even though some people in our community, and even some of our loved ones, refer to black people as 'niggers,' we don't do that. It's demeaning, disrespectful, and not the Christian way to speak. When we go over there, be nice to them and play with their children."

Birdie was pleased to not only help clear ground but also join Homer in raising the cotton. Jim and Henry joined the two men in clearing ground over the fall and even into early winter. After Jim and Henry went to trapping, Homer and Birdie finished the clearing so that they could put in at least five acres of cotton in the next season.

George and BettyLee moved into the Tom Miller place just north of Jim and Estelle in May. It became a blessing to all parents and children to live so close. George joined Jim and Henry in the business of trapping and hunting. George came by one afternoon and told Estelle that he had been feeling like it was time for him to give his heart to the Lord. She questioned him, read Scripture, and led him in the sinner's prayer. She gave him material to read and promised to be available anytime he felt he needed to talk about spiritual things.

BettyLee soon came over and rejoiced in "a transformed husband" and thanked Estelle for helping George find the Lord. "You've been such a blessin' to me, and I know you'll help George grow in grace, too."

A few weeks later, the sheriff came by with a situation he felt he needed to share with Jim. The son of a wealthy oil man in Odessa, Texas, was a concern to Sheriff Jefferson up in Pulaski County. "Here's who we gotta watch, Jim: Billy Don Jackson is the son of Joel Jackson. Billy Don lived for awhile in Little Rock, but he now lives in your community over near Merrisach Lake; he bought land from Walter Campbell, and he'll bear watchin'. He has been in trouble in a dozen places—disturbin' the peace, drivin' drunk, gettin' underage girls pregnant. Jefferson is sure that he'll be a problem to one of the men who works for you. Billy Don has built a house near Birdie Washington. And he has this thing against black people. He attacked an old negro man in North Little Rock because he wouldn't answer him when he told him to stand up when he walked into a gas station. Then, he assaulted a young black employee of a supermarket when he went in to exchange a busted watermelon for a fresh one. When the colored boy said he'd better get the manager, Billy Don slapped him across the face several times and bloodied his nose. The store manager insisted the boy file charges. When he wouldn't, the manager filed charges; this is the only case in which

Billy Don had to pay a fine. His daddy has a big influence all around it seems, and judges seem intimidated by him. Another charge was filed when Billy Don grabbed a *Gazette* out of the bag of a black delivery boy. The case was dismissed.

"Jim, all I'm sayin' is, keep an eye on this fellow. Sheriff Jefferson is very concerned and wants to bring the Jacksons to justice. I thought ye oughta know about it."

"I'll go visit Birdie and see if the jerk's been around."

The joy of having another baby helped offset a foreboding that had been pressing in upon Estelle ever since she overheard the sheriff tell Jim about Billy Don Jackson. She was glad it was bedtime, that she could slip in beside Jim and feel the love, comfort, and security of a faithful husband, whatever might be lurking in the future. Her night was filled with dark dreams. As she awoke in the morning, she was glad to hear Jim stirring.

Jim noticed that Estelle had been restless during the night. "Did you have bad dreams, honey?"

"Not only bad dreams, but a vision. I'm sure it's about the fellow who moved in over near Birdie and Susan. I believe it's a warning."

"Maybe we'd better drive over and check on them."

"Let's do. I've been wanting to take their girls, Polly and Sally, some nice dresses our girls have outgrown. Let's take the children with us."

A little past the turnoff to the Washington's home, Jim drove on to the next driveway where he could see a tent with piles of lumber and concrete blocks behind it. No vehicles were around, so they turned around and drove back to the Washington's.

They received a warm welcome from Susie, and soon the black mother was introducing Polly and Sally to Jeanette and Anniece and her son Harry to J. W. Estelle was pleased to see Jeanette take Polly's hand and Anniece respond to Sally's invitation to go see her dolls. J. W. and Harry stood grinning at one another, until Susan said, "Harry, why don't you go show your new frin yo' puppy?" Harry led the way out the door and the two scampered off to the barn.

When the room was emptied of the children, Jim asked, "Birdie, are you gettin' a new neighbor?"

"Yessir, we sho' is. Some feller from Little Rock. Say he gonna farm cotton."

"I hope he'll be friendly and no bother to ye."

"Sue, she fears 'im, cuz he come by, kept knockin' and hollerin' loud at the doah. I heerd 'im from de barn and come a-runnin'. I say, 'Whudda ye want, suh?' He whurl 'roun and say, 'Didn't expec' no nigga heah. I'm buyin' land near ye. Name's Billy, whut's yorn?' I say, 'Birdie.' He say, 'Now don't get smaht wid me, nigga.'

"'Naw suh,' I say, 'I ain't smahtin' ye—my name be Robert Bird Washington.' I puts my han' out to shake, and he say, 'Be seein' ye, nigga.'"

"Well, I'd say he wasn't very friendly. Keep me posted about him; if he pulls something bad, I'll need to know, Birdie!"

"Susan, you be careful, too," Estelle said. Be sure the door is kept locked, and keep an eye on the children."

"Miz Stelle, I sho' hate to 'fess it, but I'se downright scaid uv dis man!"

"Well, I should say, and we're concerned about you! Before we go, I want to lead a prayer for your safety concerning your new neighbor."

"Ah, please do, ma'am," Susan begged.

Estelle felt the Spirit help her pray for the Washingtons. She prayed for each one's protection against the neighbor, for the Spirit's conviction of his intentions, and for Birdie's and Homer's prosperity in working the field of cotton for Jim.

"Please come over and visit us," Estelle said as they left.

The next morning, Estelle was awakened by Jim. "Wake up, Estelle! What's wrong? You were cryin' and hollerin'. Been havin' a nightmare?"

"No honey, not a nightmare. Something more about Birdie. It's a vision like I saw the other night. But this time it was clearer. It was a Sunday morning, bright and clear, and we were on our way to worship. We got to Sweeney's store, and there were saddle horses in the driveway. Over under the sycamore tree out in front of Cleve's blacksmith shop, four men were stringing Birdie up to a rope to hang him!" Estelle stopped and began crying. "Honey, this is a vision from the Lord! You've got to check on him. We can't just sit around and let this happen."

"Did you recognize any of the four men who had Birdie?"

"No, they were all strangers to me. The rope was hanging from the lowest big limb, about 20 feet from the ground. Two of the men were tying the noose around Birdie's neck; he was not saying a word—just letting them do it. Honey, are you taking me seriously?"

"Of course, I am! Birdie's supposed to be here at 8:30, but I think I'll go ahead and drive over there."

"Please do! Thank you for checking on him."

Jim put Buck in his pickup and drove quickly to the Washington farm. Outside he found Harry playing with his pup. "Daddy's gone!" the boy said, with a worried look.

"Good mawnin', Mista Jim," Susan called from the doorway. "Sho' glad yo's heah. Don't know what's happen' to Birdie. Ain't seen 'im since 'bout sunup when he went out to feed de mules."

"Susan, I'm sorry! Would ye get a piece of Birdie's clothin' and come with me and my dog to the barn where ye think Birdie wuz when he disappeared?"

Susan looked through the dirty laundry and brought out a piece of clothing. "Birdie's underpants he pulled off las' night to take a showa—ain't been washed yet."

"Good! We'll have Buck sniff this, and we'll see what we can make of what happened in the barn," Jim said. Jim and the dog followed Susan to the barn.

"Here, Buck!" Jim said as he allowed Buck to sniff the clothing. He had Buck jump up into the box where Birdie had fed the mules. Buck was already onto the scent and led the two across the pasture to the main road. Buck was sniffing, telling his master where the scent ended. Jim could see the crushed grass where a vehicle had parked on the side of the road.

"Well, Susan, I'm quite sure Birdie has been taken by two, maybe three, people. I think ye know who I suspect, and I'll stay on this 'til we find him! Meanwhile, you and the children are welcome to come over and stay with Estelle." Seeing her draw back from the thought of leaving, he said, "Or I can get someone to stay with y'all here."

"Yahsir," dad's whut I'd ruther, just stay heah."

"Then either Estelle or Helen will be here later this mornin'."

"Mista Jim, I sho' do thanks ye."

154

Jim drove down to the Riches and told Homer and Helen about Estelle's vision and Birdie's disappearance. They both insisted on going to be with Susan.

At home, Jim told Estelle he would go have Lloyd authorize a posse. He was sure Lloyd would have them be ready Sunday morning for the showdown in front of Cleve's blacksmith shop.

Lloyd asked Jim to name the most reliable marksmen he knew.

"Me, you, George Best, my brother Henry, and Ross Morgan. Maybe Cleve Sweeney."

"This is Friday," Lloyd said, after he and Jim had ordered a steak dinner at the Freeman Restaurant. "You go back and round up the other four and have them at Sweeney's store tomorrow night. I believe in Estelle's vision. You and I will find hidin' places for the four of us before daylight Sunday mornin'. I'll swear the four in, and hopefully we'll head off a lynchin'."

Jim returned to the Washington's and found Estelle and the Riches there. Jim told them that he would be contacting the other four men for the posse and that someone should be with Susan all night and remain until midmorning. Helen and Homer volunteered to stay.

Jim made the rounds and all four men were delighted to be a part of the watch and be ready for action at Jim's and Lloyd's leadership. Lloyd and Ross were to be across the road from the blacksmith shop within easy gun range. Jim and George would work from the tall weeds just north of the blacksmith shop, coming in on the lynching men in time to save Birdie. Jim would get permission from Cleve to cut a hole in the fence through which he and George could crawl. Cleve was to decide whether he would be in the store or over at his house and when to come on the scene without revealing their presence.

George and BettyLee and their children spent the night with Jim and Estelle. At 2:30 in the morning, George and Jim ate a light breakfast, drank coffee, and loaded Buck. They drove halfway between Tom Miller's house and Cleve Sweeney's blacksmith shop and parked Jim's pickup in a grove of oaks 100 yards off the road.

Under a starlit sky, Jim and George climbed the fence and Buck jumped over it. They waded through the weeds for a good 100 yards and tramped down the weeds where they chose to spend their watch.

"George, I'm wide awake and won't get sleepy," Jim said. "Please, lie down there and go to sleep and get some rest. I'll shake ye lightly when and if there's sign of their arrival."

Jim could tell when George was breathing like a sleeping man. At 5:14, Jim heard horses. He could count four or five horses in the predawn gray, and he could see that someone was thrown over the saddle of one of them. Two minutes after the horses stopped near the blacksmith shop, a large car drove into the Sweeney Store driveway.

Jim awakened George and whispered, "The four just brought Birdie in. They're dismounting now, and Billy Don Jackson just drove in the drive to probably pay them off and give them the final order on what to do. I borrowed Cleve's wire cutters and cut a hole in the fence for us to crawl through. We'll wait 'til it's lighter, and I'll be able to see when it's time to interrupt this necktie party."

Both Jim and George could hear a cough and a clear voice saying, "Boys, here's your money. Now make sure this nigger is left hanging for everyone to see, but don't leave until you know he's not breathing." Soon they heard the car start, back out of the driveway, and pull slowly away up the road.

The next sound was unmistakably Birdie's: "O, Lawd, do be wid my sweet Suzie, Polly, Sally, Harry! Lawd, hep me, hab mercy! Jesus, I thanks ye fah salvation! Les' ye interfere, I'm a comin' home!"

"Bless old Birdie's heart! He knows Jesus, and he's ready to go!" George said.

"Accordin' to Estelle, he's ready, but he ain't goin' this time," Jim said, and George nodded.

At 5:23, Jim crawled to the hole and stuck his head out and searched the hanging area. It was not light enough to see well, but he knew the pully had not been thrown over the limb and the hanging was still a quarter hour away. Jim just rolled over, lay on his back and watched the dimming stars. *Lord, I do believe Ye're gonna answer Birdie's prayer. Ye've already hepped him by givin' Estelle a vision. We wouldn't be ready here if Ye hadn't showed her where, when, and how; and it's takin' place just like she saw! Now, hep me be accurate in my shootin'. Hep us kill the right men and wound and capture the one we need to put this Billy Don away. Do comfort Birdie. Hep his wife and children. Hear Estelle's prayers this mornin', even if Ye can't hear mine.*

Sounds were coming from the shop, only a few yards from Jim and George. "Awright, nigger, git ready to meet yer Maker purty soon." Another voice said, "Ain't no last supper fer ye, darkie. Ye're gonna go out and meet yer Maker on a empty belly." Something Jim could not make out was followed by laughter from at least three voices. Growing angry but not reacting, Jim kept his head near the hole in the fence. Even though it was definitely getting lighter, he realized it would still be a few minutes before the hangmen would emerge from the shop.

Jim knew he would be ready. *Why am I so confident? So sure I'm gonna hit that inch-wide rope without aimin'? Why do I know I will kill the men I need to before they can get Birdie connected to the hangin' rope and hoisted high enough. Where does this kind of skill come from? Lloyd says no one else has this? Why me? A nobody, unknown, uneducated, just a common, poor man. I reckon God must have somethin' in this. I reckon I need to try and see to it that the devil never controls it.* How long had he been in deep thought, Jim wondered.

"Sounds like they're movin', George." Jim saw three men dragging a ladder to the suspended rope dangling from the sycamore. The medal ring could be seen easily. Two men dragged Birdie out by his feet and dropped him under the rope. All three would have the ladder braced against them, while they held Birdie up as the fourth man tied his noose to the ring. Seeing that all four were obsessed with their work, Jim slipped through the hole, followed by George. Before they stood, Jim whispered, "Walk two feet away from me but even with me. When I shoot the rope, kill the first man that escapes to your right. I'll kill two of them and cripple a third."

Jim stopped. *Bang!* Birdie dropped onto the three men who had been holding him. One of the four stretched to run toward the shop, but George's bullet caught him and he dropped to the ground. As the men scrambled to get free from Birdie on the ground and stand up, Jim fired twice in swift succession, and two men dropped. He somehow knew the third man was the one to cripple, so he fired into the leg of the third man, amazed that he had been so sure about which one to spare.

By the time Jim and George got to Birdie, he was wide awake and crying, "O, Lawd, I do thanks ye! Iffen it ain't Mista Jim! Jus' whut I figgered! I sho' thanks ye, frin!"

"Yore shore welcome, Birdie! We're gonna have ye home within the next hour. Don't worry, some of our women and Homer are over there with Susan and the children," Jim said.

Ross, Henry, Cleve, and Lloyd came running over to watch Jim free the noose from Birdie. Cleve said, "I told 'em all you'd do it just like you did, Jim!"

"Birdie, you're one fortunate soul to have Jim Tharp on yore side!" Ross said.

"Yahsir, I sho' is!"

"If you ask me, the Lord helped Estelle have the vision so that we could all be here and rescue Birdie," Ross said.

All six men said, "Amen!"

Jim walked over to the groaning wounded man and asked, "What's yore name?"

He mumbled something about not wanting to tell his name.

Jim pulled his gun and said, "Well, a few more shells in this thing might change yore mind!"

"Hold it, please! My name's Punkin, Punkin Simpson."

"Alright, Punkin," Jim ordered, "Look over here at these two dead men. What's the name of the leader here?"

Punkin stopped groaning and stretched up his head to look, still holding his left knee. "The one with the black hat—name's Hump."

"Is he related to any of the three dead men?" Lloyd asked.

"Naw, just pals a few years."

Pointing to the dead man George had killed, Jim asked what his name was.

"'Hot' from Little Rock."

"Well, Punkin, you're under arrest for attempted murder by hangin'. You'll be cuffed and jailed. A doctor will look at your wound and give you medical care. I've gotta tell ye somethin': even if you escape the electric chair over this, you'll spend a long time in prison. That is, unless you're willin' to talk and tell us who paid you to attempt this awful hangin'. Now don't think for a moment that because it was a black man you were tryin' to murder that it won't be a serious thing with the court. Cuz you picked a black man who is considered a fine gentleman, a valued citizen of his community, and a hard workin' man with a nice wife and good family."

Turning to the men, Lloyd said, "Gentlemen, if you'll help load the three dead men in my pickup there, I'll see if our prisoner wants to ride up front with me or in back with the dead. George, thanks for takin' care of the man escapin'. I had a bead on him when you dropped him." All, including Cleve, wanted to follow Jim and George to the Washington home and witness Birdie's reunion with his family.

All vehicles drove into the lane and parked in a circle. Lloyd and Jim assisted Birdie as he walked weakly to his own front door where Jim knocked loudly.

When Estelle answered the door and saw Jim and Birdie, she exploded into praises to the Lord. She unlocked the door and called for Susan as she fell into Jim's arms.

After Homer led a prayer of thanksgiving for Estelle's vision, Jim's gifts for shooting, and the outcome of Birdie's rescue, Susan asked, "Miz Stelle, my Birdie ain't had nothin' to eat for three days! Whut do I feed 'im?"

"Fix him oatmeal, Susan," Estelle said. "And give him milk to drink. He'll probably enjoy some hot coffee, too."

Lloyd said, "I think we all should clear out. Jim, come to DeWitt early tomorrow, and we'll plot a plan to capture the man behind all this."

Taking Estelle to visit Susan and Birdie the next morning, Jim noticed Billy Don Jackson's car parked in his driveway. He was tempted to go over and take him to DeWitt then, but he decided to follow Lloyd's instructions. An hour later in DeWitt, Lloyd said, "Well, Jim, you took care of the four men who carried out the crime; now go get the man who was behind it all."

"Yeah, shoulda done that an hour ago when I took Estelle by Susan's, but I thought you might have somethin' else in mind to tell me to do."

"No, just go and get the bastard! Now, bring 'im in alive if ye can. Hope you can do it without killin' 'im. Maybe take an ear, but I'd like to give Jefferson the pleasure of seein' the fool fry or at least go to prison for life." Yet in his heart he was grateful for Estelle's vision and the support of the men who stood with him in the rescue.

Jim parked at Birdie's place and walked across to Jackson's house. To Buck he said, "Bad man! Quiet! Crawl!" Buck led the way. Just before reaching the porch of the house, Buck stopped and sniffed as Jim heard what sounded like the scrape of a chair on a floor. "Go slow!"

Jim said. Buck eased forward, his ears pointed toward the door that was open. The screen door was shut, but Jim could see a man sitting in a chair with a gun across his lap.

With his right hand on his Colt, Jim knocked on the door with his left hand. He saw the man lunge forward immediately, but he didn't position his gun to shoot. After two seconds, the man stood, focused on Jim, and began slowly raising his rifle and getting ready to aim.

"I'm the deputy sheriff, here to arrest a Mr. Jackson for plottin' the murder of Mr. Washington. You either put that gun down, or I'll shoot." Jim heard the safety snap on Jackson's gun. *Bang!* Jim's gun spoke.

"Oh! Mercy! You done shot me!" the man screamed, dropping his gun and wiping a bloody ear.

"I warned ye! I coulda killed ye, but I want to see ye fry in the electric chair for tryin' to hang a friend of mine, a wonderful neighbor in our community here." After dragging the younger man out on the porch, Jim cuffed him and led him to his pickup. On their way to DeWitt, Jackson railed about "uppity niggers and nigger lovers."

Jim was silent with his anger until turning Jackson over to Lloyd, who said to the prisoner, "You stupid ignoramus! Did you think you'd get away with hangin' a black man who is loved by his neighbors and friends in a community where Jim Tharp is a threat to any evil bastard like you! You're in a lotta trouble, boy! The kind yore daddy can't do a thing about! Come on, we'll find a little cell for you!"

Jim was glad to find Estelle at home when he got there. She reported that Susan was surprisingly calm and filled with praise to God. Birdie went to sleep after eating oatmeal and drinking coffee. He was snoring away a few hours later when Helen was ready to drive Estelle home.

That night, just as they were ready to sit down to supper, Oda cried from the door, "Oh, Estelle! I gotta come in and tell you somethin' bad!" Inside, she said, "Henry just come in liquored up and hit me. He's leavin' me and the kids and goin' back to the bottoms to work for Reddon's nephew, who took over the still." Oda broke down and sobbed. Estelle saw the welts on her red face and the tears flowing from her eyes.

"I know it hurts to be rejected and abused like this by someone you love! The devil's at work, but God's love will overcome and win out, dear! I think God will let Henry have his way awhile and get buried

160

in deep darkness; then He'll bring about salvation, a mighty deliverance, and you and Henry will be happier than ever before. Now, let me clean your face and put some lotion on it, and then I'll come over and pray for you and the children."

The next day, BettyLee came to see Estelle, reporting, "Estelle, George is backslidin'. He's been cussin' and drinkin' and actin' mean with me and the kids." Estelle told her about Henry, and then said, "Sit down there! I'm going to pray for Henry and George right now and for you and Oda and all the children." Estelle sobbed her way through a five-minute passionate intercession for "our backsliding, disobedient loved ones," asking God to comfort the wives and children and to deal with Henry and George in His wisdom and love.

Jim had entered the room while Estelle was praying. When she was through, he asked, "What in the world is goin' on?"

"The kingdom of darkness is attacking the kingdom of light, and we are caught in the violence of the warfare. But the light will dispel the darkness. **The light shines in the darkness, and the darkness has not overcome it**. Satan will not have the last word!"

6   *A Strategy Summit in Spiritual Warfare*

Estelle gave birth to her sixth child, Carroll Wayman, on January 19, 1937. This time it was Dr. Davis from Gillette who attended her. Her mother, Alma, and her neighbors Tassie Coose and Maime Plemmons assisted her in caring for the children and trying to make her comfortable during her first week of recovery.

The trapping season ended with greater success than Jim had anticipated. He would go into the fishing season with hope. However, there was a problem on the horizon—everyone was expecting another flood in 1937 equal to the one in 1927.

Alma told Estelle that since Franklin had died, Lorene and Dorene had married, and Bernice had decided to remain in Indiana, her house at Nady seemed empty. By moving Buck and Twyla into her bedroom, she felt that her home was large enough for Jim and Estelle and the children to move into her living room and the other bedroom. She also insisted that the living room was large enough to partition into two or three bedrooms for them.

In February, just before the backwater took over their yard, Jim and Estelle moved into her mother's place. Jim would still fish the White River bottoms, and he would be closer now to the Arkansas River for net fishing in the summer. The children would also be closer to the Menard schoolhouse.

One day Jim went over to the Sweeney Store to get the mail. Ross was there, and he approached Jim with a concern. "I'd rather show you than tell you, Jim," he said. "But if you're in a hurry…"

"No, Ross, I'm not in that big of a hurry. If ye're talkin' 'bout somethin' at yore place, just ride on home on yore horse and I'll be headin' there as soon as I've got my mail and filled up my gas tank."

"Thanks, Jim. Just meet me at my barn, and I'll show you what I'm up against."

At Ross's barn, someone had written with black crayons, "We'll burn ye out, kidnap ye girls, and string ye up."

As Jim and his cousin stood looking at the words, Jim asked, "Ross, do ye know someone who wants to hurt ye, get even with ye?"

"I suspect some rowdies that the flood chased out of Garland Lake, who are now camped here at the Menard Mound. They tried to steal a few cows from me two weeks ago when we had to let them drift while we went back for more. I took a couple of shots at 'em to scare 'em off. They didn't return the fire. I tracked 'em out to their camp down there."

"When did ye discover this writin'?"

"Yesterday, 'bout two o'clock."

"I'll scout their camp tonight. Just where are they near the Mound?"

"Do you know where the pear trees are just this side of the Mound?"

"Shore."

"A little this side and north of the pear trees."

"I'll check 'em out tonight. I'll ride up tomorrow, and we'll make a plan. We can't ignore this threat here on the wall."

"Shore 'preciate it, Jim!"

In the darkness a half mile north of the Mound, Jim reined southwestward. Eventually he dismounted and told Star, "Stay!" To Buck he said, "Lead! Quiet!" A few yards closer to the two tents, Jim whispered, "Stay!" He sat down on the ground beside Buck to watch and listen. He could see a dim light through a slight opening in one of the tent flaps. Jim heard voices. One voice said, "The three of us will be ready tomorrow evening. Do we kill him?" Another voice said, "Naw, just snatch the older girl. Kill only if we have to."

Jim whispered to Buck, "We'll go back home." Jim mounted Star and walked him quietly by the corral, where he counted four horses. One of them snorted, having scented Star. "Quiet, Star!" Jim whispered. Jim then gave the two tents a wide berth before putting Star into a lope. Instead of going home, he decided to visit Ross again.

Finding Ross standing guard with his gun in the front yard, Jim stopped at the gate but did not dismount. When his cousin came over he told him he had learned that three men would visit Ross's place the next evening, but he didn't know what time. "I'll be here at four, and we'll wait 'em out. They'll no doubt enter your barn gate, and we'll be ready."

"Thanks, Jim!" Inside the barn driveway at 4:15 the next day, Jim said, "Ross, we need to take the top board off that stall where I've put Star, so I can watch his ears."

"No problem." Ross got a hammer, straightened the nails, and jerked them out.

"Buck and me'll be in the stall across from Star. Now I need to see where ye'll be between the barn and the house."

"See that corded wood yonder piled eight feet high? I'll be behind it."

"Good place! Ross, like I told ye yesterday, there'll be at least three men. I'm quite sure none of the three will get to ye here. But if one does, shoot to kill the man who's tryin' to get to yer house! I know ye won't let him get to yore yard!"

Ross felt Jim's seriousness meant for him. "The man won't make it! Count on it!"

"I know, Ross!"

At the barn Jim went to his horse, rubbed his neck, and whispered, "They're comin'. We need yore help. Look! Listen! Move yore ears! Quiet! I'll be watchin' and listenin'!" The black licked his master's hand and nudged his shoulder. The dog followed Jim across the driveway, with Star watching them intently.

An hour passed. Jim couldn't see the sun, but he guessed it could be another hour before they heard horses arriving. Even tonight, after the sun set, Jim knew he could still see quite well. How many times does this make that I've been waitin' in a situation like this? *Is Estelle prayin' for Ross and me? Will I have to kill another man here tonight? I just can't let them get to Ross. He's needed by Flossie and those kids. He's needed in the church and in the community.*

Jim stood up from the sack of oats he'd been sitting on. Buck moved from his stretched out position to a standing one. Star's head suddenly went higher with his ears forward, and Jim knew he had heard something that made him curious. Jim started to sit back down, but Buck gave a nip meant only for his master. Soon Jim could hear the clip-clop of more than one horse. He was glad the entrance to the barn allowed the stalls to be inset about two feet; from the road the riders could not see Star or Buck or him. Jim watched a stocky man dismount and unlatch the gate and motion the other two to ride through. Leaving the gate open, the man mounted again to ride the twenty yards to the barn.

When the three on their horses were only 20 feet from the barn, the man on the roan, who seemed to be leading, called, "Hold here!"

Dismount! Let's see what's in the barn, tie up someone maybe, then hit the house."

They had not reached the barn when Jim and Buck were in their path. "Hold it where ye are! I'm the deputy sheriff of Arkansas County, and I've seen yore threatenin' words on the barn! Now either back outta here slowly and be on yore way, or go for a gun and I'll kill all three of ye before ye can draw and shoot."

Jim sensed that one of them didn't believe him. For a second, no one moved. He watched the man holding the sorrel's rein. His left hand twitched, but his right hand started for his gun. Jim's gun spoke: *Bang! Bang! Bang!* Screams were heard from all three men. The third man's ear was bleeding heavily, but he seemed to be ignoring the blood. When the man went for his gun, Jim decided to drill his other ear. By this time, Buck was snarling at the third man.

Hearing Ross arriving behind him, Jim said, "Alright men! Listen up! Ye're lucky y'all aren't dead! Here's the man whose family you threatened. I had hoped ye might wanta put up a fight so I could kill all three of ye; then we'd be rid of ye forever. Now as a lawman, I'm orderin' ye out of the county. All three of ye—right now!—throw yore guns on the ground. Mount yore horses, go through that gate, and don't look back 'til ye're in yore tents at the Mound. By ten o'clock in the morning, all of ye had better be gone with all yore stuff. Don't stop in DeWitt or Stuttgart or anywhere else in Arkansas County. We don't want the likes of ye around here! *Get outa here!*"

All three dropped their guns, walked their horses through the gate, spurred them southward, and were soon out of sight.

"Good work, Jim! I'm obliged."

"Them three don't deserve to live. But at least we don't have three bodies to haul to DeWitt. But that third man would be a corpse if I hadn't realized in a flash that I was in the right position to take that other ear. First time I've had to drill two ears on the same man."

The cousins hugged and slapped each other on the back, and Jim rode away.

The Annual Camp Meeting for the Central Yearly Meeting of Friends took place on the campus of Union Bible College in Westfield, Indiana, in August of 1937. The featured speakers were Dr. Paul S. Rees, of Minneapolis, Minnesota, and Dr. Charles Carter, Professor of New

Testament Studies at Indiana Wesleyan University, Marion, Indiana. Dr. Rees was considered to be the leading expositor of Wesleyan theology in the United States. He was pastor of First Covenant Church in Minneapolis, the largest congregation in America embracing the teachings on Christian Holiness as taught by John Wesley, the founder of Methodism. Rees was also the President of the National Association of Evangelicals.

Before the camp meeting, Pastor Frank Fox of DeWitt, Arkansas, and Pastor Homer Rich of Nady, Arkansas, had spoken to Dr. William M. Smith, President of UBC, about having a meeting to discuss the unusual spiritual and moral darkness of Arkansas County. The president seemed sympathetic with the two pastors' consensus that the areas in which they pastored were under strategic attacks of supernatural evil. Dr. Smith seemed supportive in their appeal for guidance from authorities in the areas of theology, Satanic strategies, and revival intercessory prayer.

Dr. Smith promised to announce a meeting in which he would invite his son, Dr. Simeon O. Smith, the vice president of UBC, and all faculty members in New Testament studies. "Of course, we will invite Drs. Rees and Carter, our special speakers in this year's camp meeting. Both men have earned doctorates in spiritual matters. Among the faculty members invited will be Dr. Martha Honeycutt, our new Chairperson of New Testament Studies. She has a doctorate in Wesleyan teachings on the deeper life, and she is considered one of America's foremost authorities on Revival and Spiritual Warfare. When Dr. Ernest Jones invited her to Cleveland Bible Institute for a full term, I learned of this gifted woman, and we were able to secure her for three years here at Union. I know she will be invaluable to all of us in a meeting like this. There are others pastors and theologians not far away who might respond to my invitation to a meeting such as this. Gentlemen, allow me to talk with some of these people before I announce the date and time of this meeting during this eight-day camp."

Dr. William Smith was presented on Wednesday night of the camp meeting by Dr. Simeon Smith to make an announcement. Dr. William Smith rose to say, "The announcement I wish to make is of such importance that I request the prayers of all here who know the Lord. This coming Friday afternoon at 3:00 o'clock, right here in this auditorium,

166

there will be a gathering that I am calling 'A Strategy Summit on Spiritual Warfare.' We have two pastors from our association here who've gone into the south to open churches, and they have met with serious opposition. Now, we know that Satan is at large all over our planet. But Satanic reactions to their efforts are of such violent measures that they are convinced—and as I listen and learn, I am in agreement with them—that supernatural evil is at work in these territories. Several authorities will come together Friday afternoon to plot a course against the principalities, powers, and rulers of this present darkness. We believe our Lord Jesus Christ disarmed Satan and his hordes of evil spirits and put them to open shame in His victory at Calvary. But we believers in every age are called upon to enforce this victory by fighting— **contending against principalities, powers, rulers of darkness and hosts of wicked spirits operating in the heavenlies.** This meeting could be of interest to many of you pastors and prayer warriors in various parts of the world. Both of our speakers, Drs. Rees and Carter, will be in the meeting, as will Dr. Martha Honeycutt and other authorities on spiritual warfare. Please pray for this meeting that the Holy Spirit will give us light and understanding on how to put on the whole armor of God and stand our ground in these areas of outbreaks of demonic darkness. Thank you."

Dr. William Smith caught up with Frank and Homer after the service and asked them to come into his office. There, he laid out an approach to the problem for the coming meeting. The three decided to hear first from Frank, who had been sent to open the charter for the Friends Churches in Arkansas. He would describe the opposition he had met in seeking to get a church opened in DeWitt. Homer would then explain the spiritual darkness, depravity, and Satanic violence he had met in Nady, the lower region of the county—murder, thievery, lying, gambling, rape, and no respect for law and order. He would describe what Sheriff LaFargue and Jim Tharp were up against in their seeking to keep order. Homer would give a report on Estelle Tharp—her unusual results in witnessing for Christ, the miracles she has seen, her visions, and her tremendous effectiveness as a teacher of the Word.

Then Dr. Smith would introduce Dr. Honeycutt and have her give counsel and admonition as to how to proceed. It was thought that perhaps Drs. Rees and Carter, and even others, might wish to add to the guidance that had already been offered.

The campus was buzzing about the coming meeting on Spiritual Warfare the rest of the time leading up to Friday afternoon. Judging by the full car lots and the crowd on the grounds on Friday, it appeared that the auditorium might not hold all the people.

Since his founding of UBC in 1911, Dr. William M. Smith had not seen this auditorium so packed. As he opened the meeting, he greeted the people enthusiastically, observing that the subject of Spiritual Warfare was obviously of great interest to all evangelicals and particularly to those who were of the Wesleyan persuasion. He then introduced Rev. Frank Fox.

Pastor Fox made his way to the platform lectern. He declared he had never encountered such opposition to ministry as he had experienced since applying for a certification of charter for the Friends Church in the State of Arkansas. Attorneys, clerks, and employees of the state had reported failure after failure, all claiming "strange circumstances" holding up their petitions. "We still do not have our charter, but we have been assured that it will be in hand by the end of 1937. All I can say is, that given our opposition in DeWitt and that which Homer has experienced in Nady, I believe we are launched on a course that the forces of Hell have sworn to defeat. Therefore, I am grateful to Dr. Smith and to all of you for coming to listen to our endeavor to make a case for intercessory prayer for a breakthrough for the Kingdom of God in the State of Arkansas."

Homer then went to the platform lectern and continued to appeal for prayer for Arkansas County. He described the people on the lower end of the prairie as "honorable, law-abiding, decent, hardworking, upright citizens, though uneducated, plain talking, and poor." He reported that since the "brush arbor" meeting in 1930, in which scores were saved, services have been held on Sunday and on Wednesday night in the Menard schoolhouse.

"There is, however, another element in the lower part of Arkansas County that we are greatly concerned about." The pastor went on to describe the people who lived in the White and Arkansas River bottoms located east of the prairie communities of Nady and Tichnor. "In those bottoms live fugitives from justice—murderers, thieves, rapists, liars, gamblers, and other kinds of outlaws. With the passing of the eighteenth amendment in 1919, another kind of people came to join the evil men and women who had no regard for others. Thousands of job hunters suddenly became self-employed in a manner that gave organized crime a tidal wave of growth. The White and Arkansas River bottoms offered innumerable places for secret whiskey stills. In the 20s and 30s, "moonshiners" came from far and near with their equipment to make liquor. By the mid 20s, at least twenty-five "moonshiners" were making liquor on such a grand scale that they hired "bootleggers" to help them market their product to distant places up the Mississippi River as far north as Memphis and down the river as far south as New Orleans. These "moonshiners" became the richest men in Arkansas County. They hired men to guard their operations with orders to shoot to kill anyone snooping around, whether a probation agent or a local person who just happened along. Villages sprang up along the Arkansas and White Rivers that soon became inhabited by loggers, fishermen, railroad workers, and curious wanderers. Very few of these communities had post offices, but there were general stores, hardware stores, restaurants, hotels, blacksmith shops, liquor stores, gambling joints, and prostitution houses.

"The sheriff of Arkansas County is an honorable man who seeks to maintain law and order even in this wicked part of his assignment. He has hired another honorable man in our community to help him. Sheriff LaFargue has made Jim Tharp his special deputy. Now Jim Tharp is an exceptionally gifted man, and he is the husband of an unusual Christian woman, Estelle Tharp. First, let me tell you about Jim. No one shoots a gun like Jim. He is the fastest man to ever draw a pistol, and he never misses. He doesn't strain to sight or take aim on his target; he simply shoots instinctively and has never missed. He has developed a practice, whenever possible, of shooting a hole in the ear of a killer instead of putting a bullet in the killer's heart. He is a legend in his time. Even up here in Indiana, it is likely you've read about him—how he hates to kill, had rather shoot a man's ear and make him think he has been killed than to actually kill the man. But of course, saving the man by shooting his ear requires more than great marksmanship. It simply can't be done unless there is ample light to see the man's ear and unless Jim is standing at an angle from which he knows he can take the ear instead of the man's face. Jim has killed—put a bullet in a man's heart—when he has not been able to shoot the ear. He has killed only in cases of self-defense or saving his sheriff's life. Jim has shot 32 ears, and he has killed eleven murderers.

"And now a word about Estelle. She was saved in our "brush arbor" meeting at Nady in 1930. She was sanctified right here at this altar in our 1934 camp meeting under the ministry of Dr. Ernest Jones. She has the spiritual gifts of discernment and teaching, and she is a woman of prayer and fasting. Her family and neighbors and close friends report lights on her head and radiance in her face quite often after a season of prayer and fasting. Recently she had a vision of four evil men lynching a wonderful black man in our community, a man who worked the farm of her husband. Her vision included the time and place of the hanging. The sheriff, Jim Tharp, and their posse were hidden and prepared on the very morning Estelle's vision specified, and by the grace of God they were able to prevent the hanging and either arrest or kill the would-be hangmen.

"I thank God for Jim and Estelle Tharp. Estelle knows that, sooner or later, her husband Jim will give his heart to Jesus Christ. We probably would have no order or protection for our services were it not for Jim Tharp. A few years ago, Dr. Simeon and LaVaun Smith came down to Nady for evangelistic services, bringing with them a wonderful trio of singers—two young ladies and a young man. Evil men kidnapped one of the young ladies. Fortunately Jim had ridden his horse to church that night, and along with his dog, he trailed and captured the kidnappers and recovered the young lady from the outlaws, just before they planned to rape her.

"Something strange, eerie, and heartrending is happening in the lower end of Arkansas County. Supernatural evil is waxing bolder and bolder as my brother Frank Fox and I attempt to launch a beachhead for the Kingdom of God in that deepening darkness. I'm glad all of you are here this afternoon as we appeal to you for your prayers and moral support in working with the sheriff and Jim to see that part of our world changed. We are convinced, however, that the answer is not guns or even courts of law. We are fighting spiritual forces of principalities, powers, and rulers of this present darkness—invisible, strange, supernatural forces of evil. We need prayer, but we also need counsel to know how to carry on this warfare. I shall return the meeting to Dr. William Smith."

Dr. Smith returned to the lectern and said, "I sense a tremendous interest in this large crowd about the subject of Spiritual Warfare as we have listened to two of our wonderful pastors describe the frontlines of ugly spiritual warfare in an area that we are beginning to recognize as being under Satanic attack. I am not unaware of the controversies surrounding this subject and our need to be very prayerful, biblical, and wise in this meeting today as we seek to come to a strategy for continuing to wage war against evil. Next, I wish to call on Dr. Paul S. Rees, the wisest, deepest, and most gifted man in spiritual matters that I know. I urge him to come and talk to us about how to proceed against evil. Dr. Rees…"

With dignity, humility, and directness, Dr. Rees stood and began, "My brothers and sisters in Jesus Christ, I feel we are gathered here this afternoon in what we might look back upon and realize was a critical hour in the course of spiritual warfare for the Holiness Movement in America. I feel the need to acknowledge that our Pentecostal friends for over three decades now have been preaching and writing about Satanic warfare, demonic possession, and other spectacular things. I for one am not writing them off as being extremists, sensationalists, or fanatics. While I have my disagreements with some Pentecostalists, I confess that we Wesleyans have been too slow to acknowledge the invisible war that is raging here in the Western world. We've heard of supernatural demonic activities going on in Africa, Asia, and South America. But our education, affluence, and organization do not exempt us from the wiles of Satan. He is out to keep us ignorant of his ways and means of dealing with saints and sinners. Deception is his trump card. Yes, he will resort to violence and threats, but he seeks to work covertly.

"All I feel led to say at this time is that I agree with the assessment that Dr. Smith, Pastor Fox, and Pastor Rich have made: that Arkansas County is under Satanic attack and that we need to organize prayerfully to counter this present darkness. But I also warn us that a thousand communities in both metropolitan and backwoods places alike are under the evil one's scope for attack. We can no longer sit comfortably, indifferently, and idly by! We must heed the call to spiritual warfare! Thank you!" Dr. Rees turned and sat down.

Again Dr. Smith came to the lectern. "Dr. Carter, would you come and say anything that's on your heart."

Dr. Charles Carter came forward from his seat on the platform. "My friends, I'm glad to be in this meeting. Thank you, Dr. Smith, for inviting me to come. I believe the Lord is speaking to me about this present darkness we are in here in America and all over the world. I'm glad that we in the Wesleyan Holiness Movement are recognizing at last the nature of our opposition and will speak openly and boldly about the biblical way of conducting our offensive and defensive operations against the Kingdom of darkness.

"It's one thing to foolishly imagine a demon behind every bush. But it's tragic when Christians bury their heads in the sand and ignore the biblical call to the Spirit-filled life of Holiness and power for spiritual warfare. Only then can we become equipped with the whole armor of God and go out to conquer our enemy in the glory of our Lord and Savior Jesus Christ.

"Dr. Smith, I'm grateful to be in this meeting, and I shall be praying that the Holy Spirit will lead us to know how to respond to the wickedness in Arkansas County, as well as show us how to wage the spiritual war all over America and to the ends of the earth. I am attending this summit in prayer, in humility, and in readiness to arm for battle! Thank you!"

Dr. Smith came to the lectern again. "Before I open the meeting to any brother or sister who definitely feels a word from the Lord, I call upon our Professor of New Testament Studies here at Union. We are fortunate to have Dr. Martha Honeycutt in this institution. Her knowledge of the Word of God and her studies in sanctification and the Spirit-led life have given me hope in so many areas in these times. I feel confident that not only because of her academic background but also because she is a woman who prays in the Spirit and receives understanding from the Lord, she will have something sound and relevant for us this afternoon. Dr. Honeycutt..."

A petite, wiry lady came forward with a smile on her face and spoke clearly and authoritatively. "Well, Dr. Smith, I am glad you invited me here. I listened carefully to our two Arkansas pastors as they clearly made the case for spiritual warfare. And I listened intently to my two colleagues Drs. Rees and Carter as they humbly acknowledged the conditions of warfare we face and clearly recommended that we make the kind of preparation for battle that the Word of God prescribes. And I heartily agree with them.

"I wish to read Ephesians 6:10-18." After reading the classic New Testament passage on spiritual warfare, Dr. Honeycutt said, "In my opinion, it is high time that believers everywhere consider seriously what the apostle Paul means here when he speaks of **this present darkness** (v. 12). More and more people are recognizing that we truly live in **perilous times** (II Tim. 3:1). The truth is that behind the violence and evil and suffering here on planet earth there rages an invisible war. It is raging in the **heavenlies**, meaning "in the spirit world." Something sinister is going on. Behind the symptoms of our times, such as those operating in southeastern Arkansas, we are in a fight of cosmic dimensions. Invisible armies—the heavenly hosts of the celestial world—are contending against the Satanic hordes of Hell for the destiny of our planet. The **principalities** and **rulers** selected, trained, and commissioned by Satan, **the god of this age**, are planning the strategies to be executed by the **hosts of wicked spirits operating in the heavenlies**. These forces must be opposed in biblical measures! We need to know that everything God has planned for the end times will be opposed by the enemy; so we must have God's plan for our response.

"And what is God planning? *To show His mighty glory in this midnight darkness, even as He plans to involve His people by raising up millions in mighty spiritual armies to fight the good fight of faith. Such Spirit-filled men and women are called upon to enter boldly and bravely against the one who* **makes war against the Lamb and His Church**.

"I call attention this afternoon to Rev. 12:12: **But woe to you, O earth and sea, for the devil has come down to you in great wrath, because he knows that his time is short!**

"For the rest of the twentieth century and perhaps extending into the twenty-first if our Lord delays His Coming, the saints on earth will be called to face the most violent opposition we have known since the persecution of the saints under the Roman emperors Nero, Domitian, and Diocletian. It is a strategy of our Sovereign God to allow the **earth to be shaken**, as we read in Heb. 12:26-29: **Yet once more I will shake not only the earth but also the heaven.... Yet once more indicates the removal of what is shaken, as of what has been made, in order that**

what cannot be shaken may remain. Therefore let us be grateful for receiving a kingdom that cannot be shaken, and then let us offer to God acceptable worship, with reverence and awe; for our God is a consuming fire.

"The call must go out for an army of saints to form all over the world. The Spirit's most urgent call at this crucial time in history is the call to prayer, the call to be filled with the Spirit, the call to be sanctified holy, the call to be anointed of the Holy Spirit for the awesome ministry of warring against evil. We are children of light, and never will the saints of God shine more brightly across the ages than they shall in these end times with the glorious anointing of the Spirit upon them as they pray intercessory, militant, prevailing prayers against the forces of this present darkness.

"Back again to Rev. 12:10-11—Here, we are told how to pray: **And I heard a loud voice in heaven, saying, 'Now the salvation of our God and the authority of his Christ have come, for the accuser of the brethren has been thrown down, who accuses them day and night before our God. And they have conquered him by the blood of the Lamb and by the word of their testimony, for they loved not their lives even unto death.'**

"The praying armies that God raises up in these last days will, just as the saints across the ages, overcome Satan and his evil hordes by remembering three things as they pray: (1) *They will plead the blood of the Lamb.* Those of us who pray will have to remember that it is the blood of our Sinless Savior offered at Calvary that atones for our sins. As we plead the merits of that precious blood, we remind the evil one that it was that very blood that **disarmed him and his minions and put them to open shame, that they have no authority over the body of Christ or even over the communities that we claim for Christ's Kingdom.** Yes, Christ won the victory at Calvary, but we here and now in this age must go out to defend the victory He won. By pleading the blood, we call Satan's bluff in whatever we discern that he is up to. Our word spoken to him **in the strong name of Jesus sends him fleeing in trauma from the conquest of Calvary's blood against his dark kingdom.** (2) *They will overcome by the word of their testimony.* What is meant here is that we must have praying men and women who not only declare they believe the Word of God; their daily living must be brought under the rule of Christ's Word. The written Word must become our testimony, so that we pray His promises against evil forces, even addressing evil spirits and quoting the Word of God, as Jesus did in the wilderness of temptation (Matt. 4:1-11). As Satan seeks to capture our children, destroy our marriages, cool down our churches, dry up funds for Kingdom work, rob believers of their fire and fervency and anointing for prayer, we must learn to pray against Him with the testimony of Jesus' Words. (3) *By becoming living sacrifices.* The Scripture for this reads, **they did not love their lives so much as to shrink from death**. Self-promotion, self-coddling, and self-assertion are so common in the lives of professing Christians today, but we surely know by now this kind of selfishness will lose us the victory. May we come to pray as Jesus, '**Not my will but Thine be done, Father'**! As the apostle Paul resolved, **I do not count my life dear to myself, so that I may finish my race with joy** (Acts 20:24). The call here is to die to a life of sin and selfishness. There must be commitment, surrender, and prayer. We must become **crucified with Christ**.

"In closing, my prayer is that this institution here in Central Indiana shall become a center for training an army of last-days prayer warriors who will go out to not only proclaim the Gospel of Jesus Christ but who will also invade the kingdom of darkness by Spirit-anointed prayer. Down in Arkansas and out there in hundreds of other places, we must become armed for militant warfare in the Spirit.

"Someone—perhaps Pastors Fox and Rich, or others—must go into Arkansas and teach the kind of praying that will dislodge principalities and powers and shake the present darkness. We must teach people like Estelle Tharp the principles of genuine revival and see the glory of God overwhelm the darkness until entire communities are swept into the Kingdom of God!

"Let us pray!" Dr. Martha Honeycutt wept her way through a five-minute prayer to which nothing that anyone could remember would compare. Everyone—professors, preachers, and all the people—were dissolved in tears and caught up in the inspirational hope of a new invasion against the Kingdom of darkness.

Dr. Smith made his way back to the lectern with his glasses off and wiping his eyes. "My people, we have heard a message from the

Lord. I know the hour is late, but someone else here may have something to say."

A tall, distinguished gentleman made his way to the lectern, and Dr. Smith returned to his seat on the platform. "My name is Robert Boyden. I'm from Findlay, Ohio, and I am in the steel business. God has prospered me and my wife in a far greater way than I ever dreamed. As I've listened to Drs. Smith, Rees, Carter, and Honeycutt this afternoon, I've felt the Lord speaking to my heart about Arkansas County. I have supported Pastors Fox and Rich in their endeavors in that part of the south. Our family has felt firsthand the wickedness of that community. A few years ago, Dr. Simeon and LaVaun Smith went down to Nady and conducted a revival meeting, and they took with them a trio of singers. Our daughter Martha was one of those singers. One night just before the service began, three wicked men kidnapped our daughter and carried her off into those river bottoms and were about to rape her. But Jim Tharp had ridden his horse to church that night, and when he learned of Martha's kidnapping, he mounted his horse and rode hard into the darkness of those bottoms. With the instincts of his trained dog, he came upon the men with Martha. He shot the ear of the would-be rapist, rescued Martha, and arrested the men. My wife, Grace, and I shall be forever grateful to Jim Tharp. I had the privilege of thanking him personally when he and his wife, Estelle, attended the camp meeting here a few years ago.

"Now, what is on my heart is this: Someone must go down to Arkansas County and work with our two pastors and perhaps through Estelle Tharp teach militant warfare praying and see the kind of revival God wants to bring to that community. And I'm here to pledge the start of a fund for that purpose. Dr. Smith, before this camp ends Sunday night, the Lord has told me to write a check for $50,000 to be expended in whatever manner you, or those you would designate to oversee this fund, determine to be appropriate. We can't let this cause drop with this meeting today. I believe it was Pastor Homer Rich who said that things in Arkansas County would not be settled with Jim Tharp's guns or in a court of law. They will be settled by Almighty God's response to an army of praying intercessors! I pledge to pray daily for that part of the world, but I want to give financially to make it possible for someone to go down there and teach the people to pray and see the glory of God in that dark place. Thank you!"

Dr. William Smith came to the microphone and said, "Well, thank you, Mr. Boyden! I'm sure others will respond also, but it is time now for us to adjourn, go to dinner, and be ready for the service tonight. I'll ask my son, our vice president, to close this meeting in prayer." Most of those who attended the Spiritual Warfare meeting left with the feeling that its importance eclipsed all the other meetings, even though many had expressed the feeling that this year's camp was by far the greatest one they had experienced.

In mid-August of 1937, a larger crowd than had been expected attended the Sunday night meeting at the Menard schoolhouse when both Frank Fox and Homer reported on the significant gathering in Westfield to pray and plan against all that Satan was up to in Arkansas County and elsewhere in the nation. Pastor Fox said, "Dr. Smith heard Homer and me out on our opposition down here. Drs. Paul Rees and Charles Carter recognized the need for an awareness of the serious intensified strategies of Satan to oppose all God has in mind for the last days. Then Dr. Smith introduced a lady he called 'the foremost authority on spiritual warfare in America,' Dr. Martha Honeycutt. She gave a serious message and said the only answer to what Satan is trying to do in Arkansas County is for believers to organize for a greater kind of militant warfare praying that most comfortable Christians know nothing about. For a small woman, she gave a great message!

"Then a businessman got up and spoke. He was the father of the girl Jim Tharp rescued from the feller who had kidnapped her and was planning to rape. He is evidently pretty well off, because he said God told him to write a check for $50,000 to help finance someone coming down here to teach people like Estelle and others. I think the teacher may be Dr. Martha Honeycutt. This same man helped Ola and me financially in coming to Arkansas a few years ago. He also loaned Homer and Helen a new car to drive down here and hold that Gospel meeting in Nady.

"Now I want to report that our people up in DeWitt are getting serious about prayer. I've been preaching on prayer a lot, and the Holy Spirit is helping me learn to pray in a new dimension of power and passion. So I'll turn the meeting back to Homer, and I think he might want to take some pledges for stepping up our battle against the darkness of Satan here in this part of our county through a more intensified prayer life."

Homer stood and asked, "Are we getting this? Do we realize the importance of the battle we are in and what's at stake? I believe it's the salvation of our children, the transformation of our culture—both here on the prairie and down in the bottoms—and a new vision of the Kingdom of God."

When he paused, Estelle stood and said, "Pastor, I know that I'm to pledge an hour a day in the kind of praying the Lord is leading me into in these times."

Homer recognized that the Spirit was moving on the people. He asked Alma Wallace to list the names of all who would follow Estelle in pledging an hour of intercessory prayer daily for people in the communities here and for revival. More than half of the crowd stood to pledge.

Several months after the summit on Spiritual Warfare in August of 1937, Dr. Martha Honeycutt was reading the *Indianapolis Star* one Saturday morning. She had read past the editorials and was about to reach for the next section when she noticed a small caption on page 12, "Anarchy in America" by Reuben Malcomb—an article that had been picked up by the Associated Press. The first paragraph listed four counties considered to be the most lawless in America: a county in Kentucky, in Arizona, and in Montana, and Arkansas County in Arkansas.

The reporter commented only on Arkansas County. He had been staying a few days and nights in a hotel in Little Rock. Reading the *Arkansas Gazette*, he had learned of the violence in the southeastern part of Arkansas County. One article was a story about the courageous work of Sheriff Lloyd LaFargue and his Special Deputy, Jim Tharp, down in Chester Township, the southern end of Arkansas County. The reporter decided to drive down to the two county seats of Stuttgart and DeWitt, about 125 miles from Little Rock, and ask a few questions and feel out the communities. At the courthouse in Stuttgart, he was told by a clerk, "The roughest stuff in our county is down below DeWitt, another forty miles from here. Go talk to Sheriff LaFargue there." Malcomb drove on to DeWitt and found the sheriff to be open and free to admit the wickedness, lawlessness, and danger in his county; but he insisted, "Most of the bad men are down in the river bottoms east of the Nady community. Those people in Nady, for the most part, are fine folks. They are law-abiding, and they love and respect one another. But, yes, there are murderers, thieves, rapists, and liars down in those bottoms. They'd as soon shoot you as to speak to you, some of them anyway." The reporter visited the Nady post office and general store and found the owners friendly and informative. But they were open and honest about the dangerous people in the bottoms. "We've had gunplay right here inside the store as well as on the porch and in the driveway," the owner said.

"Does the sheriff come around and confront these people?" the reporter asked.

"Yes, we have a very brave and attentive sheriff," answered Cleve Sweeney, the owner of the general store in Nady. "And he has one of the best men in the world as his special deputy; his name is Jim Tharp, who lives right here in this community. He's so accurate with his pistol or rifle that he never misses. Not long ago, I saw him shoot a hanging rope out yonder to save the life of a black man that four rascals from the bottoms were trying to hang. Then in a flash he killed two of the men before they could return his fire. He intentionally wounded a third man, because he wanted his testimony to convict the rich guy who was paying the four men to hang this black man. You stick around in these parts very long and you'll hear plenty about Jim Tharp—all good. He's not a killer. He shoots holes in fellers' ears, and they think they've been killed. That way he saves their lives and still gets his man. Our sheriff depends on him and knows better than to go into those bottoms without Jim Tharp." Dr. Honeycutt continued to read as the reporter described the "moonshiners" and "bootleggers" in the White and Arkansas River bottoms. But he painted a nicer picture of the prairie community citizens.

Dr. Honeycutt had not been able to dismiss the passion of the two pastors she had heard report in the summit meeting nearly a year before. And now, here was a report from a secular witness. She had been praying for DeWitt and Nady since the meeting. She'd even prayed a few times for the people in the bottoms who were walking in darkness. She prayed for Pastors Fox and Rich and for Estelle Tharp and her husband, Jim.

She reread the story, and felt the Holy Spirit speaking to her. *Lord, it's true that I have been asked to come to Union here to teach on Spiritual Warfare. I do believe You were in that summit meeting about a year ago; You not only helped me speak but also helped me listen. I can't get that woman, Estelle Tharp, off my mind. Is she the key to your merciful and gracious transformation of those communities including those people in the river bottoms? Am I to go and pour my life and vision for revival into her? If so, Lord, make it clear to me.*

Martha Honeycutt tried to finish the rest of the newspaper, but she had read and felt too much to continue. After she had prayed, she knew she was to talk to Dr. and Mrs. William Smith. When the clock in her apartment struck nine o'clock, she decided to walk the three blocks to the Smith home.

Annie answered the door bell. "Why, Sister Martha, come right in!"

"I hope I might have a few minutes with you and Dr. Smith."

"I'll call my husband. Please have a seat."

Soon, the aging president came shuffling in, clearing his throat and stroking his gray beard. "Well, good morning, Dr. Honeycutt."

The esteemed theologian rose and shook hands with the president. "I'm fine, Dr. Smith. I hope to have just a few minutes of your time to discuss something that the Lord might me laying on my heart. I'm reminded of the caution the inspired Word gives us to 'try the spirits,' to test and see that the enemy isn't trying to mislead us."

"Yes, of course, we must always do that. I'm glad you are free to share your concerns with us."

"Well, ever since our summit meeting on Spiritual Warfare during the camp last year, I've been passionately praying for our two pastors down there in Arkansas County and their burden for revival. Now, this morning, I was reading the *Star,* and here on page 12 is a story from a reporter who visited the Nady community and verifies a lot of what the pastors told us."

"Sister Martha, Simeon and LaVaun know something about the wickedness and lawlessness down there. You heard Mr. Boyden tell about his daughter being kidnapped and almost raped and how Jim Tharp, having trailed the bad men with his dog, stuck his head in their tent and shot a hole in the ear of the man about to rape her."

"Yes, the reporter in the *Star* mentioned this Jim Tharp."

"Just a few years ago Jim and Estelle Tharp attended the camp here, and Annie and I had them in our home for breakfast on the morning after the camp closed. After breakfast and a brief visit, they went out and got in the truck that brought them here and headed back to Arkansas. They are certainly fine people. As far as I know, Mr. Tharp has not yet given his heart to the Lord, by his own admission. But Estelle Tharp is one remarkable believer in our Lord Jesus Christ. She was saved in the Brush Arbor meeting that Pastor Homer Rich held at Nady in 1930, and she was sanctified at the altar here in the first Sunday night of the camp that year—1934, I believe. Given time, I'm quite sure she will be the key to the great revival God will give that community."

"Dr. Smith, that's what the Lord might be dealing with me about. Now I know I've agreed to be here at Union to teach Prayer Warfare and to be a counselor to the New Testament faculty members. But I'm just sharing this thought—and it hasn't really been settled in my mind at all—but here it is: If we are serious about teaching Spiritual Warfare and there are communities under Satanic attack, such as in Arkansas County, should we not focus on those places with both students and professors and do some holy experiments? Is there a better way to teach Spiritual Warfare than on-the-job training right on the frontlines of the battle?"

"Wow! Dr. Honeycutt, you might have something there! I had thought of getting Pastors Fox and Rich to guide our thinking and maybe send someone down to teach prayer warfare a few nights and then hold revival services. But I am feeling with you that we need to have some faculty/student leader meetings and get the mind of the Lord on this."

"Dr. Smith, if the Lord is leading and you feel free to approve, I believe I should make myself available and go down and do some training that would, I'm sure, need to include Estelle Tharp."

"I'm glad to hear that, Sister Martha," said the president, "but for now, let's just make it a subject of prayer. And I don't think there's any doubt that our purpose in emphasizing Spiritual Warfare here at Union just might find its fulfillment in what happens down in Arkansas County."

"I wonder if Sister Annie could lead us in prayer before I go?"

The three got on their knees, and Annie began, "Lord, we thank Thee for Thy marvelous leadings. For speaking to our hearts about *how* to pray, about *what* to pray, and about *where* to pray. We thank Thee for bringing Sister Martha to Union. O, I thank Thee for giving her such power and inspiration in speaking to us during the camp on our vision and call to militant prayer for coming against the kingdom of darkness to see revival! Now, give us wisdom and direction concerning Arkansas County and Union's role in that spiritual battle that is raging. If Sister Honeycutt is to go down and minister, show her and us. Continue to work through Pastors Fox and Rich and Estelle Tharp. Be with Jim Tharp and spare his life. Continue to convict him of his need of a Savior. Continue to anoint Estelle in teaching, praying, and winning souls. Help her with her visions and revelations to be obedient. Show us the plans to make and the personnel to involve.

"Heavenly Father, we believe Thee wants to send a mighty revival to that terrible darkness of Arkansas County so that hundreds of men and women and boys and girls will be saved. We believe Thee will call young men and women from that transformed community to go all over the world and preach the Gospel! We thank Thee for the funds that are coming in for this special ministry. Continue to lead us, we pray. In Jesus' name, Amen!"

Martha Honeycutt left the Smith home with the inner comfort and peace believers feel when they have obeyed the voice of the Holy Spirit. The rest of her day was spent in praying, singing, studying, and trying to envision Jim and Estelle Tharp and the goings on in that needy southern backwoods community.

Jim decided to get down to Garland Lake where George and the seining crew were camped. So far, George had reported good catches, but low prices. The depression was definitely affecting their labors this year more than any previous one. Fortunately, fishing tackle, gasoline, food, and even labor were lower in cost as well. Jim hoped that cotton prices would hold up. He had already made up his mind to deduct his fuel, seed, and fertilizer costs from the crop and allow Homer and Birdie to divide the rest of the profit. As Estelle had pointed out again and again, "Honey, we are so blessed! Your fur, your fishing, your few cows, and your timber have all brought in far more than we've spent. I'm so thankful for your willingness to give and to be generous with those who work for us."

Jim had brought Star and Buck with him to the Garland Lake camp. Seeing that George and the men had everything under control, he said, "George, I'm gonna be gone 'til about dark. I'm gonna ride north here and try to find Henry. I know it's dangerous, foolin' around that young Reddon's operation, but I'll get close enough to see if Henry is around. I know he won't like it that I'm nosin' 'round, but if I can get his attention I know I'll be safe. I wanta tell him that Oda and the kids are fine, but they miss him. I wanta tell him we love him and we all want him back home."

"Yeah, Jim! Tell him BettyLee and I feel the same way, that we miss him, and we love him."

When Jim reached the slough a mile north of the lake, he drew Star to a halt. Then he said to Buck, "Thataway, Buck! Slow and easy! Lead!" The German shepherd-wolf dog sniffed that he understood and slowly led the way in the direction his master had pointed. When they came to the giant red oak that Jim recognized, he whispered to Buck, "Stop!" Jim dismounted and dropped Star's reins in a position that put the giant tree between his horse and the liquor still to the east. Buck responded to Jim's hand signal to come to him behind the tree. "Shh! Listen!" Jim called to the dog and the horse. It grew quiet. Jim soon heard voices and then hammering—like metal on metal. When Jim would slowly lean out from behind the tree to catch a glimpse of any movement, Buck did the same.

Buck sniffed once, indicating that he either saw or smelled someone. Jim patted his head and neck and said, "Atta boy!" For thirty minutes, Jim could see no one. Finally, when Buck gave a low and short growl, Jim carefully peeked and saw Henry examining a fallen tree, probably planning to saw it up for wood. Turning to Star, Jim said, "Stay, Star! Be back soon!" He signaled to Buck to lead the way, and they got within forty yards of Henry before he realized someone was coming. Henry whirled, threw down his saw, and reached for his gun. "Henry, it's me, Jim!" Henry lowered his gun, began motioning to his brother to go back, and pointed to himself, signaling that he would come to him. Jim called, "Buck! Let's go back!" Immediately the dog went around Jim and headed straight back to the red oak and Star, with Jim following. Jim could see Henry slipping slowly and noiselessly through the brush, carrying his rifle but leaving his tools.

"Whudda ye doin' out here, Jim? Tryin' to get yeself killed? This young Reddon ain't no softy; he'd ruther kill ye than speak to ye! Now, let's hold our voices to a whisper, and I'll hear ye out. What ye doin' here?"

"Henry, I've missed ye so much and just wanted to see ye! I wanted ye to know Oda and the kids are fine. They shore miss ye. Henry, Miriam, and Reba come over the other night and asked, "Uncle Jim, would you go find our Daddy and tell him we love him and miss him and want him home with us and Mama so bad? Henry, I just had to come and see if you wuz okay and if there's a chance ye would come back. We're camped at Garland Lake, seinin' Garland and Johnson before we go out and do Mill and Do-More. George told me to tell ye that him and BettyLee can hardly wait to see ye and that they love ye and want ye home again!"

All the time Jim was speaking, Henry was looking down. When Jim stopped talking, Henry said, "Brother, I admit I'm one miserable fool. I ain't fit for Odie and them kids, but I love 'em and miss 'em. But you know who I think about a lot, cuz I know she's thinkin' of me and prayin' fer me? Estelle! I reckon as long as that woman lives and prays, I ain't gonna be able to make it out here or anywhere else as an outlaw. But I ain't never made the money I'm makin' here. And, yeah!—I wanta send some home with ye fer Odie. Dang it! I ain't got it on me. Stay right here, Jim, and keep hid behind this tree. I'm gonna slip in the back way and brang ye money for Odie." Jim squatted down, rubbed Buck's neck, and waited. He listened to the birds singing and heard a squirrel fussing at a woodpecker. When he heard Henry coming through the brush, he stood up so he could find him.

"Here's $2,000, Jim, for Odie and the kids in this gunnysack. And here's $1,000 for you," he said, as he tried to hand Jim a brown paper bag.

"Naw, Henry. Oda'll get it all. I haven't been out that much money on your family. Besides Oda has helped Estelle so much when the baby was born and when she's out in the smokehouse prayin'. And lots of times they come over and Oda cooks the meal. We love your kids like our own, and they play good together; all that's missin' is you. We all need you, Henry—Oda and your children, Estelle and me, George and BettyLee, and Papa and Mama!"

"Well, I ain't fit fer any of you." Henry choked with emotion, paused a second, then just blurted out, "But, Jim, tell Oda I'll be comin' home in a few months!" With that he grabbed Jim in a bear hug, and they weaved back and forth a few seconds. "Thank ye for comin', brother! But ye better not come back in these parts. Reddon hates ye guts and so does just about everbody in these bottoms! It's too dangerous for Jim Tharp to be seen in these bottoms! The next time I see you, I'll be home."

Jim led Star a long ways, just thinking, before mounting. *Lord, I wish I wuz a prayin' man and could ask You right now to dip into Henry's heart and let him be overcome with Your love for him and his family. Course, I know I oughta be prayin' for me. I reckon, from what Estelle says, I'm as lost as my brother Henry. But I'm shore thankful for Estelle and them kids and fer Ye heppin' me make a livin' and brangin' me through a lotta shootin' scrapes alive and well. Show me when it's time to get saved, and don't let me be lost.*

Estelle rejoiced at Jim's report on Henry. Oda and the children broke down with sobs of joy at the promise that Henry would be home.

In a few days, Homer came by with two things on his mind: a meeting with Estelle to report on both the Westfield meeting and a strategy in spiritual warfare for Arkansas County; and the need for a truck to haul the cotton to the DeWitt gin. Homer wanted to know if Sunday night would be a good time for the meeting. Jim thought so.

Oda overheard the conversation concerning the truck; knowing that Jim's new truck was being used for hauling fish, she said, "Jim, our truck is in your barn. Use it if you can get it started. I reckon the battery is dead." They took the battery from Jim's pickup and got Henry's truck started. Jim told Homer to purchase a new battery for his pickup at Jack's Auto as he came out of town.

Jim's prosperity with cattle and his success in fishing, trapping, and logging prompted him to suggest to Estelle that he build a nice log cabin on their place. He could host some of his hunting friends from Little Rock, Memphis, and Hot Springs—businessmen who were not interested in joining either one of the hunting clubs over on Merrisach Lake. Estelle encouraged Jim to build it just beyond the yard on the east side. Jim expected Henry home sometime in the fall of 1938 and planned to have him build the cabin.

"But does the cabin have to be used strictly for hunters?" Estelle asked.

"I guess not, but why do ye ask?"

"Because I need a place to pray!"

"Well, I know ye pray in the smokehouse now, but I reckon ye could use it for prayin' when I don't have hunters usin' it—which would usually just be during huntin' season."

As Jim planned the cabin, Estelle made suggestions regarding the quality of flooring, dimensions, and materials. She said nothing about what she felt to be the main purpose of the cabin.

In late August of 1938, Estelle told Jim she wanted him to clear an evening when they could sit down and talk over some things she was concerned about.

"How about this Friday night?"

"Good! I'll look forward to it."

On Thursday, Estelle had another thought. She would prepare a picnic for them, and they would go to the river and celebrate their first trip to the river together twelve years ago. They would sit on the same old driftwood log and recall the time they realized that they were in love with each other.

Jim supposed they would drive to the river in the pickup. "No," Estelle said. "I want us to ride the horses as we did in 1926."

"Are you sure you can still ride a horse?"

"As good as you can." And she proved it by mounting Ella for the first time in several years. At the river, she spread out the food, prayed a blessing, and they began eating.

"Well, Jim, a lot has happened since we were here twelve years ago."

"Yes, but I can say that you're the best wife in the world. In fact, you're the best person in the world!" He said it so seriously that she knew he wasn't trying to be funny.

"Thank you, dear husband! I know that came from your heart, even if it might not be true. I can honestly say that I love you more every day, and I thank God that I am privileged to be your wife." Estelle went on talking about the children, the place they had bought, the changes they had made, the people who'd come into their lives, her spiritual journey, and the blessings of the Lord.

"Estelle, I want to interrupt ye long enough to say I'm ready for my pie. Then ye can go right on talkin', cuz I've learned to respect yore wisdom. Whatever is on yer heart, I'm ready to hear. I do know some changes need to be made in our lives, and I'm ready to hear what ye think."

After Estelle served the pie and refilled their glasses, she took a few bites and decided to begin. "Honey, no one works harder than you do. You work all the time. Even after church, you are off to see about the cattle or ride down to see what Ross thinks about this or that. You take no vacation time between trapping, fishing, seining, and timbering. I'm looking forward to moving back up to our Haven this summer before school starts, even if it does mean that our four children will have three miles to go to school. We have the car, and I can drive them when you don't have time. I know you did the right thing to turn the farming over to Homer and Birdie, and they've done well. Now I want to suggest that you turn the orchard over to Birdie. And I want you to hire more help during seining—you only need to oversee the jobs. Please take more time off. You can afford to—I just showed you the other night that we are ahead of where we were two years ago. I want to spend more time in prayer. I also want you to consider allowing me to hire someone who can help manage the children, drive them to school, and help me with the garden and various other chores. I'm serious when I say that I must spend more time in prayer. I'd like to remind you that I want to use the cabin for prayer. Of course, that won't mean you can't allow guests to stay in it from time to time during hunting seasons. I do think we ought to buy a new family car, and I feel you need a new pickup. We can pay cash for both. And one more thing. I believe we should give more to the Lord."

"Don't ye think ye're takin' spiritual warfare a little too seriously?" Jim asked.

"No, I don't." I doubt that you can understand it yet, but I agree with Homer and Pastor Fox that Satan is intensifying his evil efforts to take over our part of the country—there's more violence, more spiritual attacks, and more backsliding among believers. And, mark my word, unless we can see more praying, things will get worse. Homer just received a letter from Dr. Smith to the effect that the Committee on

Spiritual Warfare is planning to send Dr. Martha Honeycutt down to Nady and DeWitt to teach. I know this would not be in your thoughts, but I happen to think it would be great if we could move her into that new cabin when it is finished. Now, am I upsetting you with that suggestion?"

Jim thought a moment and looked away. "No, I'm not upset, but I'm not promisin' anythang. I do think I have to give ye credit for all ye've done—the good thangs ye've prayed to pass, the prophesies and visions that have come true, and the good ye've done. So, I might just have God to contend with if I don't consider lettin' ye have that cabin for prayer and for the thangs ye feel it ought to be used for."

"Thank you, darling. You're so kind to listen to me this evening and to consider all I've suggested."

Both were standing, gathering the picnic leftovers and supplies, and preparing to depart. When they had returned to the horses, Jim saw Estelle was almost ready to mount. He said, "Wait! I wanta do what I done twelve years ago right about here before ye mounted up that time." He drew her to him and kissed her. Then after helping her mount, he looked up and said, "And if ye'll remember, that wasn't all." She remembered and leaned down for another kiss as she had years ago.

On the day before Thanksgiving, Jim left the house midmorning with his shotgun and came in around noon with two wild turkeys. Estelle was having all the Tharps and the Bests for the big dinner. She had hinted a time or two that Henry just might appear at their Thanksgiving table. Despite Estelle's record of having her prayers answered and prophesies fulfilled, Jim wrote off her remark as wishful thinking.

Nineteen members of the Tharp and Best families had finished their delicious dinner on a snowy Thanksgiving evening when there was a knock at the door. Estelle flew to the door. "Well, praise the Lord! Henry, get in here to your wife and children and loved ones!" A chorus of praises rang out as Oda and her four ran across the room to take their turns welcoming their returning loved one. As he threw down two bags on the floor and grabbed and hugged Oda and then each of the children, Estelle noticed his bloodshot eyes. After them came Boge and Ophelia and then Jim and finally Estelle. Everyone made him feel welcome!

"The Prodigal has returned!" Henry said. "And I shore am glad for the love I feel in this room. I don't deserve it, but..." looking at Oda, he continued, "I've missed my wife and chilluns, but more than anythang, I know it's time for this old sinner to get right with God! Ever since Jim come down and found me, I've wanted to come and let Estelle hep me find the Lord."

Estelle said, "Well, Henry, that's wonderful! But right now we're all so joyous over your return that we've almost forgotten that you are hungry. BettyLee, help me clear the end of this table, and I'll set a place for Henry. We still have plenty of turkey and vegetables and more pie or coconut cake. Let's leave Oda, the children, and Papa and Mama with Henry as he eats. The rest of us will take our chairs and go into the living room. Then when they're through eating, they can join us and we'll all lead Henry to Jesus."

It was easy, it was moving, it was glorious! Henry was ready in repentance, believing in his heart, and Estelle guessed that it had never been easier for anyone to lead another person to Jesus Christ. She knew that not only twenty people were rejoicing but also the angels in Heaven as Henry Tharp shouted for joy that his sins were forgiven and he was back home with his family and loved ones.

Henry's transformation was more than George could hold out against. After rejoicing over Henry's newfound faith, George asked Estelle and his loved ones to lead a prayer for God's grace in restoring him from his backsliding. Again, BettyLee and the Best children found themselves experiencing the same emotions that Oda and the Tharp children experienced a few minutes before.

Estelle led all in the Doxology before the families left that Thanksgiving night. In bed that night, Jim said, "Well, I reckon ye feel like it's been a great Thanksgivin'."

"It has indeed! I can think of only one thing lacking to make it perfect. I was hoping after Henry found the Lord and George returned to Him that you might feel it was time for you to make your move of putting your faith in our Lord and Savior Jesus Christ."

"I really thought about it and even wanted to. I'm not sure I can explain why I didn't turn to ye after George did and tell ye that I, too, wanted to give my heart to the Lord. I reckon it could be pride, maybe a little stubbornness, or even a grip the devil has on me. I think I'm more prone to say it just ain't my time yet and just leave it at that."

Estelle felt checked in pursuing that challenge. "I'll keep praying, believing, and waiting for a time when you will definitely and sincerely place your faith in Jesus Christ as your personal Savior." She felt it was time to go to sleep after a great day of spiritual victories.

A few days after Thanksgiving, Estelle was returning home after taking the children to school and gathering up a few small items they had left at her mother's place. It was almost eleven o'clock when she drove up to their gate and noticed a woman knocking on their front door. Hearing the car drive up, the woman turned around and was waiting. As Estelle made her way toward the front steps, she could see that the young woman was shabbily dressed and her hair was disheveled.

"Hello," Estelle called. "May I help you with something?"

"Howdy, ma'am," the woman said, seeming a bit shy and afraid. "I shore hope so!"

"Well, please come in and we'll talk. I'll get rid of these things and fix us a glass of tea and cut us a piece of pie. Sit down in that chair here in the living room, and I'll call you into the kitchen when I get things prepared. Then we can get acquainted."

After a few minutes, Estelle looked into the living room and noticed the girl finger-combing her hair, taking out sprigs from her hair and putting them in a pocket of her ragged coat. "Come into the kitchen, and let's eat a bite together. I want you to tell me about yourself and how I might help you."

"I shore thank ye, ma'am. I come from White River Bridge, left 'bout daylight this mornin and got lost a time or two. I'm purty wore down, but I wanta talk with ye and then get back."

Estelle set a tall glass of iced tea and a ham-and-cheese sandwich before the woman. Then she realized she was hungry as well, and she added a dish of potato salad for both of them.

"Well, I hope I might help you some way," Estelle said. She noticed the girl hungrily ate the sandwich and the potato salad, so she began preparing another sandwich and warmed up some vegetable soup. Estelle thought about the girl's needs—a bath, clothes, food, spiritual help, comfort, guidance, prayer. *Lord, help me with this girl. She is precious in Your sight, even if she doesn't look like much the way she is now. Give me love and wisdom and the right words.*

The girl looked hungrily at the pie Estelle set before her. "Honey, I think you are in need of a good meal, so I'm warming up some soup and fixing you another sandwich."

"Yes'm, I reckon I am. I just hate to be a bother. But, I thank ye."

After the girl had finished everything Estelle had set before her, she pushed back from the table and started talking. "Ma'am, I'm Patsy Simpson from the White River Bridge. My man and me is on hard times. He jus' got outa prison and can't find work. He's scared to come out here on the prairie, cuz yore man shot and crippled him when they wuz tryin' to hang a nigger. We done hit such bad times—nuthin' to eat or wear and no friends to hep us. So I went over to see Barney—I reckon ye know Barney at Barney's Hole at the Bridge, cuz he knows yore man."

"Yes, I've heard my husband speak of him."\

"Yeah, Barney say I hafta come see ye. Cuz Punkin hepped put Jackson in prison, Barney say ye jus' might not turn us away."

"Well, Patsy, we just might be able to help you. Does your husband know anything about fishing, trapping, cattle, or timber?"

"Fishin' maybe, nevah done no farmin' or hepped with cattle."

"Patsy, I wonder if you would like to take a bath and put on some clean underclothes and a dress I want to give you? I'll fix some food to take back with you, enough for you and your husband to have a pretty good supper tonight. Then I'll have my husband come to the Bridge and talk to your husband about work to see if he can offer him a job."

"Aw, no ma'am! Punkin ain't wantin' to see yore man! He'd be scared."

"But, Patsy, you don't understand. My husband is a good man. He could have killed your husband, but he wanted him alive to testify against Jackson. I'm sorry Punkin got mixed up with the bunch who tried to hang our friend, Mr. Washington. But if my husband comes down to talk with him, he has nothing to worry about or be afraid of —he'll be glad Punkin's out of prison. I just believe if my husband can use him at all, he would hire him and we could put you up in a tent out here. You could live nearby, and it might be we could put you both to work."

"Well, ma'am, I could use a good bath; then I reckon I'd better be on my way back. It's a long ways, and I don't want it to get dark on me in them deep woods."

As Estelle got things together for the girl's bath, she prayed silently that Jim would return before the girl left and be interested in helping them. Maybe he'd even saddle another horse and ride back with her, meet her husband, and feel like hiring him.

Estelle left Patsy to bathe, while she fixed more sandwiches and salad. Then she laid out underclothes and a dress she had been planning to send to Bernice. She could hear the girl scrubbing up and rinsing off and taking her time drying off. When Patsy finally emerged wearing the dress, which fit her perfectly, Estelle was glad to see that she had also washed her hair.

"My goodness, ma'am! I feel like I'm a-goin' to church!"

"You look nice, Patsy!"

"Can we just throw my old duds away? They ain't fit to carry home."

"That's up to you, but I could find a bag for you to put them in."

"No, ma'am. Let's trash 'em."

Estelle heard a horse lope in and knew it was Jim. "Just sit there, Patsy. I want you to meet my husband. He just came in. Excuse me while I go and tell him about you and your husband."

When she could tell that Jim was interested, she said, "Honey, do you think you might like to talk to Punkin and see if he is someone you could use? I know Patsy is rough and uneducated, but I might be able to help her and, at the same time, train her to take care of the children and help me with housework and the garden. But I think it's too soon to be able to tell. If you would saddle Ella and let her ride back with you, you might be able to talk to Barney and get some insight on their character and reliability. What do you think?"

"Well, I think it's worth a try. Think she can ride a horse?"

"I'll go and see."

"Patsy, Jim would like to go back with you and see if Punkin would be interested in working for him. Can you ride a horse?"

"Yes'm, I can ride. And if your husband can use Punkin, that'd be a dream come true."

"Ella is my horse, and she's easy to ride. She'll just follow Jim's horse, and I don't think you'll have any trouble with her."

Estelle fixed Jim lunch, and they were off into the bottoms. After riding for two hours, Jim asked, "Now, which one of these cabin boats do ye live in?"

"That old one across there under the bank from Barney's."

192

"Then ye go in and tell Punkin I want to see him, makin' sure he understands that I ain't mad at him and that I shore wanta hep him any way I can."

Patsy dismounted, leaped onto the pier, and went into the old listing cabin. She was gone several minutes and then reappeared with Punkin, who seemed afraid.

"Hi, Punkin. Glad to see ye again and in different circumstances than the last time I saw ye. Glad ye're out of prison. Whata ye say we three go over to Barney's, have a burger and a Coke or something else to drink, and talk awhile before I head back?"

Both nodded, and after Jim tied Ella and ground-reined Star, they made their way over to Barney's. Barney greeted Jim warmly, saying, "Glad ye come back with Patsy. Jim, this couple just might make you and your wife someone you need and have been lookin' fer. What can I get y'all? It's on the house."

"A burger and a beer," Punkin said.

"A burger and a Coke," Patsy said.

"A cold Coke for me and a piece of apple pie," Jim said.

The three found a table by the window where Jim could look out on the river and watch the horses. "Punkin, tell me what kind of work ye've done and what kind ye'd like to do. Now I don't know if I've got what ye're lookin' for or not, but I raise cotton, run cattle, and work some in loggin' timber. I also do commercial fishin'."

"I can shore hold my own with a crosscut saw in the timber. I can drive a tractor and plow behind a mule. Don't know nuthin' 'bout fishin', but I could learn. I have picked cotton. Patsy here is good at pickin' cotton, too."

"Now, Punkin, I don't wanta hire anyone with a drinkin' problem. I'm not talkin' about someone who has a beer once in a while. But we got six children, and we'll have more I'm purty sure. I don't want drinkin' and cussin' and fightin' goin' on around 'em."

"I get it, Mr. Tharp," Punkin said. "You'll never have to worry 'bout us gettin' drunk or cussin' or fightin'. I really do need some work, and I would be willin' to live in a tent and try to prove myself if I could get a chance. Ain't very many fokes ready to hire a guy who's been in prison. I've learned my lesson runnin' with the wrong crowd. Maybe yore shootin' me was a blessin'."

"Well, Punkin, I'd shore like to put that behind us and start over new. How soon would y'all wanta move outa here?"

"The sooner, the better," Punkin said.

"What all in the way of furniture and personal things would ye have to move?"

"We can get everthang we got in a couple of small bags," Patsy said.

"Got any debts ye need to settle?"

"Nawsir, we owe Barney less than $10. Patsy and me been down on our luck, but he's been good to us."

Barney, overhearing what they were talking about, said, "Jim, if ye can use them out at yore place, their debt is cancelled."

"Alright, Punkin and Patsy, give me a few days to go back, buy ye a new tent, and put some stuff in it—stove, table, chairs, a bed, and things you'll need. I'll be back for ye a week from today unless it's real bad weather. If it's stormin', I'll be back the first nice day after a week from today. I'll be here on a horse and leadin' two more for y'all to ride back on. We'll have an understandin' 'bout what I'll start ye out doin' and how much an hour I'll pay ye. I wanta be fair with ye and hep ye get started on the right path."

"We'll be ready, Mr. Tharp." Punkin and Patsy both grinned with pleasure.

Jim handed Punkin a $20 bill and said, "Somethin' to hep ye for a week."

Jim reported to Estelle that he felt both Punkin and Patsy could be helpful to them. He wanted her to go to town with him to buy a tent and other items for making the tent reasonably comfortable for them. On the way, Estelle thought of some things Henry and Oda had stored in their barn that they might be willing to loan for awhile. They had moved to DeWitt to work for Bill Patterson in his store and chose not to move all their furnishings.

"Yeah," Jim said, "Let's go out and see how Henry, Oda, and the children are doin' and get permission to use their things for awhile. Ye know, that Punkin, he shore hepped put Jackson away—couldn't get him the electric chair, but he'll be in the cooler for a long time. So it might be good that we are tryin' to get them two on the right track before he is released."

Punkin and Patsy were excited and grateful for their new home. On their first day, Jim loaned them money for groceries and agreed to put Punkin to work and pay him fifty cents an hour for clearing ground, helping with the cattle, and sawing logs. Right away, Jim was pleased to note that the young man enjoyed his work. After teaching Patsy how to drive and giving her some training on cleaning and cooking, Estelle was quite certain that she was her answer for helping her care for the children, including driving them back and forth to school, and working in the garden.

On a warm afternoon, Estelle sat in a chair in the shade of one of the large cedar trees in their front yard and overheard her five older children discussing their names while at play.

Jeanette asked J. W., "Why don't you like your name?"

"Because I feel cheated!" her brother replied. "I really like the name Jim, but that's what they call Daddy. I would rather be called James than J. W., and it's not right for people to call me Jim—that name already belongs to Daddy, and he's a famous man."

"What would you like to be called?" Anniece asked her brother.

"I don't know, but I don't like the initials. Whatever we could come up with to honor my true name, James William, but I don't want to be called William. And as sure as I take on the name of James, people will start to call me Jim. So, why don't y'all help me come up with a name we could take to Mama and Daddy for their approval?"

Estelle called, "J. W., come here, son." He went to his mother and stopped a few yards away, wondering if she was angry with what she had overheard.

"My dear boy, I never realized that you don't like your name. When you were born, it was my idea to name you after your father. He felt proud to let you have his name. I do recall that he wondered if making you a Junior might not cause some confusion. Anyway, he consented with pride. Several other boys that you know have initials— J. L. Shelton, J. H. McKay, R. H. Searcy; and the richest man in Arkansas County has initials—your Daddy's friend, L. A. Black." Estelle raised her voice and called to the other children. "So, come on over and let's talk about your brother's name. Any suggestions?"

Anniece was the first to speak, "I like the name of Jake—it seems to be a good name for James."

"Maybe you would prefer the name of your first initial spelled out J-a-y," Jeanette said.

Estelle waited for the two younger ones to respond. Finally, Burl with a grin said, "How about Jock, Joke, or Jerk?"

Both Jeanette and Anniece yelled, "No way!"

Estelle looked at her oldest son and asked, "Have you heard anything here that you would prefer over your initials?"

"I could live with either Jay or Jake, but I think I like Jake better."

"Then I'll take it up with your father tonight, and if he approves, you children can inform your cousins and playmates at school. I'll write the teacher a note that you are to be called Jake instead of J. W. from now on."

Homer and Helen and Ross and Flossie drove up to visit Jim and Estelle on a winter evening after supper. They had the news that Dr. William Smith of Union Bible College in Westfield, Indiana, had approved the Committee's sending Dr. Martha Honeycutt in a few months to Nady for a year and then to DeWitt for a few months.

Where would she live in or near Nady for a year? When there seemed to be no answer, Jim looked at Estelle as if he expected her to answer.

Then Jim said, "Well, I know Estelle would like for her to live over there in our cabin. Henry had it almost completed when he moved away to DeWitt. I could find a finisher somewhere, and it could be ready in a month or two, I guess."

That seemed to relieve everyone, so it was agreed that the cabin would be available for Dr. Martha Honeycutt if the Committee sent her.

On a warm, sunny afternoon in late April of 1939, Estelle was experimenting with the new washing machine Jim had bought her when Homer and Helen drove up to the front gate. Estelle knew immediately that the woman in the back seat of their car was Dr. Martha Honeycutt. She shut off the washer and untied her apron, flinging it on the shelf there in the smokehouse. She ran out to greet the woman she had been waiting to meet for more than a year.

Martha Honeycutt stopped in her tracks inside the front gate, politely pushing Helen on ahead of her to greet Estelle. She motioned for Homer to go on also so she could watch the woman she had heard so much about from Dr. and Mrs. William Smith, Dr. Simeon and LaVaun Smith, Pastor Fox and Ola, Pastor Rich and Helen, and so many others. She listened to her voice responding to the Riches' questions as to her readiness for a guest. Watching and listening, the professor's spiritual gift of discernment connected strongly with the present situation. *O, Lord, thank You that at last I get to meet Estelle Tharp! There she is! Please let us bond! Let her find the confidence in me that will allow her to believe the word You have sent me to give her. Let her become so committed to Your word that she will fulfill Your calling on her life as she becomes Spirit-cleansed, Spirit-filled, and Spirit-empowered to wage the war on this culture of darkness that she lives in. Now, Lord, get me ready mentally and emotionally for this—the most urgent meeting I can ever recall in all my thirty years of ministry! Help me, Lord, for here she comes.*

Now led by Helen, Estelle came smiling. "Helen, let me look at this dear woman a few seconds before you introduce us." The two stood searching, smiling, thinking, rejoicing, and praising the Lord silently.

Finally, Helen said, "Estelle, please say hello to Dr. Martha Honeycutt, who will be your guest and teacher for the next year or for as long as the Lord leads! Dr. Honeycutt, you've heard us talk about this dear lady, without whom I doubt very much if Homer and I would still be pastoring in Nady."

Estelle moved first, and then Martha moved quickly to meet her halfway. Estelle allowed her guest to signal how the greeting would go— a handshake, a hug, or simply some formal, traditional words. Miss Honeycutt whispered, "O, my dear Estelle!" Her arms were around Estelle, and she was pulling her closely. "I've been waiting for this moment for over two years!"

"Likewise!" Estelle said, as she clung to her long-awaited teacher, releasing her only as she felt Martha release her.

"Praise the Lord!" Homer said. "We've just reached a milestone on the road to spiritual warfare as we've witnessed the star student welcome her long-awaited master teacher in the things of God."

"Please come upon the porch here," Estelle called as she led the way. "Patsy, would you bring five chairs. Jim will soon be here, and he'll want to join us. Dr. Honeycutt, this is Patsy, our neighbor and helper. Patsy, this is Dr. Martha Honeycutt, from Westfield, Indiana. She is a professor of New Testament studies, and she'll be living here with us out there in our new cabin." The two ladies smiled, nodded, and both said, "Hello!"

"Now we have iced tea and hot tea. Which shall it be?" Estelle asked.

"Iced tea for us," Helen said.

"Hot tea for me," Martha responded.

Estelle was glad that she remembered what Helen had said about most of the people in Indiana—"They hardly know about iced tea; they take theirs hot, but some like it unsweetened and some like it sweet."

"Dr. Honeycutt, would you like your tea sweetened with honey and a bit of lemon?" Patsy asked.

"Oh, my dear, that would be perfect!"

Patsy nodded, and Estelle knew she was prepared.

"Are the children sleeping?" Estelle asked Patsy when she served the hot tea.

"Only the baby."

"Then bring them all out here, please," Estelle said.

"Oh, two sweet little boys!" Martha exclaimed, as Patsy led them to her. She stood and then knelt in front of the bug-eyed boys and hugged them, even though both boys seemed uncomfortable.

"Now, don't be afraid, for this is Dr. Honeycutt from Indiana, and she's going to live in our new cabin."

When Patsy went in to get a pitcher of tea to refill their glasses, Estelle heard Jim come in the kitchen door and say something to Patsy. She excused herself and went inside to bring Jim out.

"Dr. Honeycutt, this is my husband, Jim Tharp," Estelle said.

Holding his glass of tea in one hand, Jim extended his right hand. Looking directly into the professor's eyes, he said, "Doctor, we are all glad you are here. We've waited a long time to have you come to this needy community."

"It is so good to meet you, Mr. Tharp," Martha said warmly.

"Now, ma'am, I'm just Jim, and that name will do."

"Alright, and you and Estelle can drop the doctor with me, if you will."

"We hope ye can adjust to our poor country ways," Jim said. "Estelle and I were in Indiana a few years ago, and we know ye have a better style of livin' up there than we have here. But we'll do our best to make ye comfortable." Turning to Estelle, Jim asked, "Have ye showed our guest where her quarters are?"

"No, but we'll all walk over there in a bit. She hasn't been here long, and we're enjoying getting acquainted."

"Homer and Helen," Estelle said, "I want you to know that Patsy and I are planning to have you stay for supper. And, of course, we want Sister Martha to have her first meal here with us. Later on, we'll take her to the store and stock her place with the food she'll want."

"Thank you," Homer said. "We'll be glad to stay. Sister Honeycutt, no one in these parts can cook like Estelle."

"I'm looking forward to her cooking," the professor said.

"Well, Patsy is a good cook, too," Estelle said. "She learns fast." We just hope we can come up with the kinds of food Sister Martha is used to and likes."

"Not to worry, honey!" I lived in Alaska for three years. I've not been in the south very much, but I'm truly looking forward to some of your southern dishes and hoping I might learn how to prepare them myself."

"Estelle's a good teacher," Helen said. "She's taught me how to make biscuits, cornbread, gravy, and pies. She taught me how to fry chicken and potatoes and how to cook okra and black-eyed peas, too."

"It all sounds delicious to me," the professor said.

Martha Honeycutt entered into what would become her new home, as Estelle held the door open for her. "I believe this is a new cabin! My, what a lovely bed and beautiful cabinets and drawers. And, oh, these shiny hardwood floors! The kitchen's nice too, and I'll have an inside pump! I see an icebox, too."

"Yes, Sister Honeycutt, the icebox—we meet the ice truck two or three times a week, and we'll get your ice and place it in your icebox. The only problem with an icebox is the need to empty the ice melt from the floor tray once every day or else you'll have a wet floor. If you're like the rest of us, you'll let it run over a time or two before you remember to do the emptying in time."

Helen interrupted, "Estelle, I insisted that Dr. Honeycutt leave her personal things at our house and give you a few days to get ready for her. We'll bring her back up when you're ready."

"Then why don't you bring her up midmorning on Thursday, and we'll take her to Uncle Hays at Tichnor for groceries and other things she wants. I should have everything ready by then. I'll finish the curtains for the east windows there, and I want to get a rug to put by her bed for her to put her feet down on when she gets up of mornings. I think there might be another item or two that I need to get for her cabin. I've got them written down so I don't forget."

"Oh, Estelle, this is so nice! I do appreciate all the trouble you've gone to, and I know I'll be happy here. I see you have a comfortable chair and a nice kerosene floor lamp there for me to read by. That's important to me, and I'm grateful. Thanks also for bringing in a bookcase. I didn't bring all that many books with me, but books are so important to me."

"I'm sure they are. I'm learning their importance, too," Estelle said.

"Jim, would you please show Miss Honeycutt around the other buildings. She might want to see the horses, so take her to the barn; then, pull the flap back on the tent and let her see how close Patsy is if she needs anything. Patsy will be back with the children soon, and I'll get supper on the table."

"Let me help you," Helen said.

"Alright, I'm going to fry chicken, so I'll let you cream the potatoes. Thanks, Helen."

"Of course. What can Homer do to help?" Helen asked.

"Not a thing! He and Jim can entertain Miss Martha for a little while, and we'll be ready to eat soon after Patsy comes with the children."

Jeanette, Jake, and Anniece were in awe of Dr. Honeycutt, but Burl seemed casual and unconcerned. Miss Honeycutt made much over all of them. They were "beautiful, precious, and promising," she declared.

After Homer's blessing on the food, the six adults and five children began filling their plates with fried chicken, mashed potatoes and gravy, green beans, corn, fried okra, and candied sweet potatoes. The professor asked, "Estelle, do you usually put on such a feast, or is this a display for my education in southern foods?"

"Maybe a little of both."

"Well, I'm impressed! In fact, I'm delighted with everything I'm eating. And I see some pies over there that await us. I can hardly wait!"

After the evening meal, the six adults returned to the porch, and Patsy would return periodically to check on the children playing in the yard. Later on, the three older children whispered to their mother that they wanted to join the adults on the porch. Estelle consented, and they made her proud when they merely listened and did not interrupt. They hardly took their eyes off their new guest.

Helen led a prayer before the Riches and Miss Honeycutt departed. "We'll see you Thursday morning," Helen called as they got into their car.

After the Thursday morning shopping trip to Tichnor for groceries, Estelle could see that they needed to go on to DeWitt to get the small rug and other items Miss Honeycutt needed. So it was almost sundown when they drove home, only to find that Patsy had, by herself, fixed a lovely meal and had everything in readiness for them. They had driven Helen's car so that Patsy could transport the children to and from school. Jim had spent the day in the garden planting and tending the vegetables that were already growing.

After supper, the professor said, "Estelle, I wonder if you and I can have an hour together for prayer and for laying out our study plan? Could you come over to my cabin about 9:00?"

"I'll be there!" Estelle said with joy.

"This will be my first night in my southern cabin—my home for we know not how long," she said as she told Helen and Estelle how much she enjoyed the day. Patsy volunteered to help her carry over the things they had bought.

7 *The Ebb and Flow of Battle*

Estelle was as apprehensive as she was eager to meet with her new teacher. Would she still be able to learn as she had in the grades and in her one year of high school? Could she understand theological, Biblical, and spiritual terms as used by her teacher with her graduate degrees? She knew her hunger for spiritual knowledge matched her need for it. Therefore, she would trust the Lord to help her grasp what it meant to become militant against the invisible demonic forces that the apostle Paul insisted were real.

"Please come in!" Dr. Martha Honeycutt called as she opened the door to Estelle's knock. She embraced her and then pulled back to gaze into her student's eyes, finally saying, "Estelle, you are all and more that I prayed you'd be! Please have a seat there on the couch, for as of now we are not teacher and pupil; we're sisters in Christ, both learners at the feet of Jesus, where the ground is level.

"We do need to decide what two hours each day, Monday through Friday, will be best for you. You'll need a notebook, much like you had in high school. You'll bring your Bible to every session. I'll furnish some textbooks from time to time.

"Estelle, we'll begin by studying the Holy Spirit! He is the Spirit of Truth, the Spirit of Revelation, and the Spirit of Illumination. Apart from His work in us revealing truth, we simply are not going to understand spiritual truth. Now we can learn science, mathematics, history, geography, and even philosophy without the Spirit's indwelling; but we can never understand most of the Bible and absolutely nothing about spiritual truth or spiritual warfare without His illuminating presence. We'll spend much time on the subject of the Holy Spirit.

"Then, we'll study prayer, and we'll practice prayer. We'll also test ourselves on how we are doing from time to time. Prayerlessness is the greatest sin of the Christian. It's the reason most believers do not go on into sanctification—into spiritual fullness and power. Because of this failure, the kingdom of darkness has taken over Arkansas County. Because of prayerlessness, Satan has gained on Christians to such an extent that most believers are frightened, frustrated, confused, and filled with doubt. You and I are seeking to learn the truth as to how we can become empowered by the Holy Spirit to trust Him to turn all this depravity, darkness, and defeat into a release of God's revival power on this community. This empowerment can turn darkness into light, abominable sins into righteous living, and the stench of sin into the glory of God throughout this part of the world!

"Next, we'll study the great revivals of history, beginning with the Pentecostal Revival in Acts, chapter two. And we'll learn God's conditions for revival—the kind that will turn the tide of evil into an avalanche of divine power that will sanctify believers and redeem sinners on a scale unimagined by nominal Christians!"

Estelle could hardly keep her seat. She knew she was hearing what she needed to hear. Her facial expressions and body language kept pulling the thoughts out of her teacher. At the end of the orientation that evening, she felt like she was on cloud nine, except for being drained, tired, spent. She believed she was about to begin a new chapter in her spiritual life and ministry as an intercessor, as an agent of power, and as a witness to the power of God.

After they had gone to bed, Jim remarked, "Ye seem awfully pleased with yer teacher."

"I am indeed! She's been sent by the Lord. I'll do what I can for you and the children, but I do beg for your understanding as I throw myself into this course on spiritual warfare. I've asked Patsy to give us more hours, and because of the extra work I'll be putting on her, I want us to raise her pay."

"Honey, let there be no doubt—I want ye to put yore total self into this course. Ye'll have my full support! I'll also try to spend more time with the children, even though Patsy will be givin' them added attention."

On the opening day of their studies, Martha remarked about the wonderful orientation session they had experienced the night before. "We meet the Holy Spirit on the first page of our Bible (Gen. 1:2), where we find Him as the Spirit of Creation bringing order out of chaos, turning darkness into light, and bringing reality from nothing. Then we find Him on the last page of the Bible (Rev. 22:17) where He is drawing thirsty hearts to Jesus Christ our Savior. The Spirit of God of the Old Testament is the same Holy Spirit of the New Testament. Throughout the 66 books of the Bible, the Holy Spirit is like a river winding its way through the entirety of divine revelation. The river becomes wide in places, narrows down in others, and even goes underground at times. But the Holy Spirit is ever-present—creating, revealing, convicting, cleansing, refining, reviving, renewing, and leading."

"In our New Testament, there is a book that is more uniquely The Book of the Holy Spirit. Traditionally, it is called "The Acts of the Apostles," but it really should be called "The Acts of the Holy Spirit through Apostles, Deacons, Evangelists, and Other Believers.""

"The book of Acts opens with a *command* and a *promise* (1:4-8). Jesus commanded His disciples to go back into the city and begin a prayer meeting. They were not to leave the city of Jerusalem until they had been **clothed with power from on high** (Luke 24:49). During this 10-day prayer meeting, the *command* was obeyed and the *promise* was fulfilled—the 120 **were all filled with the Holy Spirit** (Acts 2:4).

"Six times in the book of Acts there are accounts of how the Holy Spirit was poured out on believers (Acts 2:1-4; 4:31; 8:14-17; 9:17-19; 10:44-48; 19:1-7).

"In His three years of teaching His disciples, Jesus taught more on the Holy Spirit than on any other subject. He made it clear that the coming of the Holy Spirit into their lives was their most urgent need. If they missed the coming of the Spirit, they would miss His will, fail in their purpose of getting His Gospel to all nations, and betray their calling. The disciples were not to leave Jerusalem to carry out their mission until they had been filled with the Holy Spirit.

"The Holy Spirit is not a mere theology; He's a Person, a member of the Triune Godhead. He's not a thing, an it, or a mere blessing. He is a personal God, and Jesus commanded that we have a relationship with Him. We are commanded, **be filled with the Spirit** (Eph. 5:18). We can love Him or spurn Him. We can receive Him or reject Him. We can obey Him or grieve Him. We can warm to Him or quench Him. We can yield to His sanctifying power or ignore Him and go on in our carnality, selfishness, and worldliness. We can cry out for fullness or continue to operate in our weakness and failure.

"Let none of us attempt to enter into spiritual warfare until we have asked God to fill us with the Holy Spirit.

"The Holy Spirit is *the Spirit of Holiness*—He purifies our hearts.

"The Holy Spirit is *the Spirit of Power*—He empowers us for prayer, worship, and ministry.

"The Holy Spirit is *the Spirit of Grace*—He enables us to love, forgive, and persevere.

"The Holy Spirit is *the Spirit of Truth*—He strengthens us to recognize the truth and distinguish it from deception, heresy, and fantasy. He gives us courage to face the truth, to tell the truth, and to speak the truth in love.

"The Holy Spirit is *the Spirit of Freedom*—He delivers us from the bondage of lust, greed, pride, fear, and malice.

"The Holy Spirit is *the Spirit of Wisdom*—He reveals to us the will of God and guides us in paths of righteousness.

"The Holy Spirit is *the Spirit of Prayer*—He *enlightens* our understanding so that we pray according to the will of God; He *energizes* our human spirit so that we do not faint or fail in our ministry of prayer; He *emboldens* our faith so that we refuse to be denied, but continue to ask, seek, and knock." The teacher had noticed that her pupil seemed to have taken everything seriously. After years of teaching, the professor knew when she had a true learner.

"Estelle, what have you learned from what you've heard this morning?"

"Oh! Sister Honeycutt, I've heard you give the most wonderful truths about the Holy Spirit this morning! A few of the things you've said I already knew. But I learned some new things! And I'm telling you here and now: I am hungry to be filled with the Holy Spirit! Will you be telling me how I can be filled with the Spirit?"

"Honey, our first hour in the morning will be helping you get filled with the Spirit! Take this booklet home with you, and try and read it tonight. I'm going to predict that by this time tomorrow you will be joyfully filled with the Holy Spirit!"

"Oh, praise God!" Estelle said. "That's my greatest need! It's my greatest desire!"

That night after all the children were in bed, Jim asked Estelle, "What are ye all caught up with there?" He pointed to the book she was reading.

"Sweetheart, I'm preparing myself for getting filled with the Spirit in the morning!"

"Just what does that mean?"

"It will mean spiritual power!"

"I thought ye already had a lot of that."

"No, I'm a spiritual weakling. I need to be filled with the Spirit in order to stand up against the power of Satan."

"Seems to me like ye've been doin' a pretty good job of that ever since I've known ye."

"But we are up against evil forces in this county, the kind of which I'm almost totally unprepared to counter. When I'm filled with the Spirit, I'll have discernment! I'll know how to pray! I'll pray with a bold faith! I'll be able to invoke the strong name of Jesus!"

"I've heard ye do that before now, and I've seen ye get answers. Ye had that vision of Birdie bein' kidnapped and their tryin' to hang him."

"Yes, I don't deny that the Lord has used me some, but I've got so much to learn. I feel like a child in over my head when it comes to spiritual warfare. I know the Lord sent Sister Honeycutt to lead me into life in the Spirit."

"Well, more power to ye!" Jim said. He kissed her and went off to bed. Estelle read the 82-page booklet and was so excited about what might happen the next day that she had trouble relaxing and going to sleep that night.

Estelle was so thankful for Patsy's help; she could leave the breakfast dishes and other household chores and count on her to get the children to school. She could hardly wait to get over to the cabin and experience what the Lord had in store for her.

"Estelle, **this is the day the Lord has made; we shall rejoice and be glad in it!**" was the professor's greeting as she opened the door upon hearing Estelle knock.

"Yes it is! And I'm ready, too!"

"I believe you are, my dear. I don't feel it's going to be difficult at all getting you filled with the Holy Spirit. The Lord has been preparing you now for ... let's see, when did you say you and your husband went to Westfield and you went forward to pray for the sanctifying experience?"

"In 1934."

"Estelle, I do not question that you are sanctified and have a pure heart. If so, then the way has been cleared and the stage has been set for **the baptism with the Holy Spirit and with fire**. Too many Christians who ask to be sanctified do not go on to ask for the baptism, or fullness, of the Holy Spirit. And according to Jesus, we are supposed to **ask** (Luke 11:13)."

"Well, I'm sure ready to ask and then receive that baptism!"

"Yes, I believe you are. Put your Bible down and have a seat, and I'll prepare you with just a few questions."

"Dear Estelle, I sense that you have already surrendered everything to the Lord—your pride, your hopes and dreams, your husband, and each one of your children. Total surrender is essential to receiving the fullness of the Holy Spirit."

"Sister Honeycutt, God being my Judge, I cannot think of anything I would want to hold back from the Lord!"

"Then you should be on believing ground! When you ask, you can't afford to insult the Lord by doubting that He will fill you. I don't want you to base your knowledge that you have been baptized with the Holy Spirit and fire on anything but faith—faith in the promise of Jesus that if we ask, the Father will grant our request. I don't care how high your emotions are, I want you to settle it in your heart and mind that God has given you the fullness of the Spirit *by faith,* not by feeling. Don't expect an angel to come and tell you it's happened. Don't expect to feel a tingling in your spine or go into a quaking spell. Now sometimes joy is an immediate accompaniment to the fullness of the Spirit. But I don't care what your feelings are—I urge you to trust your heavenly Father to do what He has promised. Your faith is what is critical here, not how you feel."

"Alright! My heart says *Amen!* to everything you are telling me. I feel sure I am ready to ask, to believe, and to receive."

"Then, I shall lead a prayer for you, Estelle; then, in your own words you'll ask the Lord to fill you with His Spirit." Then Martha prayed, "Father, we have come to a very salient moment here on the second day of this course in spiritual warfare. Estelle is about to make her request for the baptizing fullness of Your Holy Spirit. Clear her heart and mind, fill her with faith to believe that she shall receive what she asks for. Let her rest in the knowledge that anything she asks of You in

Jesus' name she will receive. Grant her the assurance—with the witness of the Spirit to divine fullness right here this morning! In Jesus' name, Amen!"

"Now, Estelle, in your own words, just ask for what your heart longs for and for what the Lord will delight in giving you."

"Okay, Sister Honeycutt. But before I do, I want to ask one thing. What does *salient* mean?"

"Oh, honey, it means 'the point of significance, the place of importance.'"

Estelle slipped to her knees; seeing her student humbling herself touched her teacher so deeply that she went over to the couch and knelt also.

"Dear Heavenly Father, I am so thankful that You have used Dr. Honeycutt to bring me to this significant moment in my spiritual life. Oh, how I thank You for saving me, for cleansing my heart from sin, for helping me learn a few things about You and Your Word and Your will over the last eight years. I've made lots of mistakes. I've fallen short of Your will so many times. Lord, I've been so weak. I'm so ignorant of spiritual truth. But when I've asked Your forgiveness, I know You have kept Your promise to forgive me of my sins and cleanse me from all unrighteousness.

"So, I feel You have prepared me now to come before You and ask You to **baptize me with the Holy Spirit and with fire**! Lord, I want this more than anything in the world. Just as You filled the apostles and disciples in the Upper Room so long ago, just as Jesus had promised, so now I'm trusting You to do the same for me. Thank You for doing it, Lord!"

Estelle heard her teacher say, "Amen! Give her the witness to it, Lord, the assurance!"

Estelle remained in a kneeling position, losing awareness of the passing of time. *Lord, I'm just waiting on Your witness. I'm in no hurry to get up. I'm not ready to think about anything else but what I've asked You to do. I know it's coming. Oh Lord, how I thank You for this peace!* A flood of tears fell on the handkerchief in the chair. *Lord, I believe You have heard my plea. Wow! I know the joy that now floods my soul, my consciousness, is Your witness to my baptism with the Holy Spirit and fire! I'm so unworthy of this! I never knew what I was missing. Lord, I don't want to ever get over this. I'm so grateful for what You are doing in me right now. I'm not sure I understand all that You are doing. But I know this burning in my spirit is my witness. Maybe I'll understand it better in the days and weeks to come. How I praise You for doing for me exactly what I asked.* "Thank You, Lord, for the baptism of the Holy Spirit and fire and for the assurance and witness I'm receiving even now," Estelle said with emotion, as she stood up and looked at her kneeling instructor.

Martha Honeycutt wiped the tears from her eyes and stood up with a heavenly smile. "My dear Estelle, I know you have the witness of the Spirit Himself that you have been baptized with the Holy Spirit and fire! And I praise the Lord that He has witnessed to me also that you are now in His fullness and power—power to learn, power to pray, power to think God's thoughts, power to prevail in spiritual warfare, power to stand against the evil forces, power to love the lost, power to love the saints, power to reap a spiritual harvest, power to do whatever the Lord commands, and power to experience a mighty revival in this county!"

The more her instructor talked, the more Estelle felt the joy of the Lord increase in her heart. She found herself walking around the cabin shouting praises to God while Martha continued to rejoice and prophecy many things that would come to pass as a result of what the Lord had done for Estelle that morning! Estelle felt it strange that she was able to both express her own heart to God in praise and, at the same time, catch most of the prophecies her instructor had uttered.

The two hours had been taken up in prayer and praise. Estelle could hardly believe where the time had gone when Martha said, "Well, Estelle, it's eleven o'clock. But what a morning with the Lord! His will has been done, and school is out!"

The two women hugged and praised the Lord together. Then Estelle got her Bible and notebook and headed for her house.

Estelle spent the rest of the day in a state of contemplation, even as she worked in the kitchen. In preparing supper for the Riches, Washingtons, Sweeneys, and Dr. Honeycutt, Estelle decided to cook a rump roast and several vegetables. She put the roast in the oven about 3:00 o'clock and then went to the garden to gather lettuce, onions, okra, green beans, and cabbage. She also prepared her famous stewed potatoes; she cut them in quarters, put a good amount of lard into a large black cast-iron pot, added salt and pepper, covered the potatoes with water, and set the pot on a back burner to cook slowly. Throughout the afternoon, she sang praises to the Lord and thanked Him for filling her with the Holy Spirit.

Since breakfast, Jim had been working with the cattle and helping Ross with his early branding. Knowing they were having several people coming for dinner that evening, Jim came in earlier than usual, put up his horse, fed the stock, and took his shower in the barn.

The Riches drove in about 5:45 o'clock, having invited the Sweeneys to ride with them so they could get better acquainted. The Washingtons and Dr. Honeycutt arrived just in time for dinner. At the table, Jim called on Dr. Honeycutt to pray God's blessing on the meal.

"Thank you, Jim. I shall in a moment, but first I want Estelle to tell us about the filling of the Holy Spirit she experienced today."

"I would be glad to. The greatest blessing I've had since becoming a Christian several years ago happened to me just a few hours ago. I knew when God sent Sister Martha our way to teach on the Holy Spirit that I would need to be filled. When she spent time on *Who the Spirit is* and *What the Spirit does,* I knew I was a candidate. I met the conditions: I was a believer, I made a total surrender, I asked, and I believed! Dear family and friends, I'm telling you, *God filled me with His Holy Spirit!*" She paused and wiped tears. Praises were expressed by all, except Jim; but he had a bright smile of approval on his face.

Ebrena said, "Estelle, you've always radiated the love of Jesus; but I'm glad you've reached a new level in your relationship with God."

When it seemed all were ready, Martha led the prayer. As they passed the food, Homer said, "Sister Martha, I feel impressed to ask you to speak on "The Fullness of the Holy Spirit" Sunday morning, and I think it would please the Lord if we made Estelle's testimony a preliminary to your message."

"I accept the invitation, and I trust Estelle will also."

Ebrena said, "Cleve, I'm glad we turned down our daughter's invitation to join them in their Sunday plans. Now we can hear both Estelle and Sister Martha. We'll encourage Spencer and Agnes to come with us."

Tom and Dee Miller drove up to see Jim and Estelle on Saturday morning. About two years after Estelle's Aunt Mertice died, Tom

210

married Jim's sister Dee. It appeared their marriage was going well. As the four sat on the porch, Tom said, "Jim and Estelle, I'm renting my place just north of you here to a fine young couple who moved in from Reydel. They are Jack and Linda Buchannon, and they have three children. I think you'll like them. When I told them a little about you, they said they'd read about Jim in the paper. They're anxious to meet y'all. But there's another reason we dropped by this morning. I've decided to sell that property over there. It has 80 acres of rich soil, mostly bottoms like yours here, a large barn in good condition, and a house with a new roof in fair shape. We wondered if you would be interested in buying the farm."

"Estelle and I will talk about it and let ye know, Tom. Have ye set a price on it yet?"

"A thousand dollars."

The next week, after a late Saturday morning breakfast, Estelle said, "Let's take the three oldest children, leave the younger ones with Patsy, and go over and meet the Buchannons."

"Yeah, let's do. Wanta drive?"

"No, let's walk. We need to let the children walk with us." On the way Estelle asked, "Have you given any thought to buying Uncle Tom's farm?"

"Yeah, we need to talk about it. I think it would be a great investment if we are in good enough shape financially. Where do we stand?"

"We have several thousand in the bank. I know you said you wanted to buy a big flatbed truck with high sideboards and a trailer for hauling fish, cotton, and logs. And we do need to buy a new family car. And one other expense is coming up—we need a large dining room built the full length of our kitchen on the north side of the house. I know the Lord wants to use us in having people over and getting them saved, and having Christians over and getting them filled with the Spirit and into growth and service for Him. But to be honest, I do think we ought to buy the farm."

By this time, the family was already approaching the Miller farm. The house was now in view, and they could see that it was not in shambles, but solid and in good condition. Two children about Jeanette's and Jake's ages were playing tag in the front yard. When the youngest disappeared in the house, the mother soon came to the front door. "Hello, there!" the pretty young woman called. "You must be our neighbors, the Tharps."

"Yes, we are," Jim said. "Thought we oughta come over and welcome ye to our area."

"Well, come around back where my husband, Jack, is settin' up some chairs."

"Annie, Robert, Janet! Y'all come and meet the Tharp children!"

Estelle introduced, "Jeanette, Jake, and Anniece."

Jack was a nice-looking young man and very friendly. "Are you a farmer, Jim?"

"I have 20 acres over there, and I've got a couple of men who sharecrop cotton. I trap coons and minks in the winter, fish the overflows in the spring, and seine the lakes in the summer and fall. Then I run a few cattle. Also I do some loggin' and raftin' downriver to the mills. I've got a lotta irons in the fire. On top of that, I'm special deputy to our county sheriff."

"Yeah, I read about you now and then in a couple of newspapers! Sounds exciting all that you do. I'd like a look at your horse and dog sometime."

Jim asked, "Are ye gonna be farmin' Tom's place here?"

"Naw, I reckon not. I'm lookin' fer somethin' to do to make a livin' though."

"Jack, I might be able to use ye—clearin' ground and workin' cattle once in awhile. When ye need some work, come over. My orchard needs some attention in late summer and fall. I pay fifty cents an hour."

Looking at Jack, Linda said, "That sounds good, Jack—better than around Reydel."

"Jack, Tom Miller is my brother-in-law, and I'm buyin' this place here. If ye think ye might wanta farm, I'd be glad to work somethin' out with ye," Jim said.

Linda wanted to show Estelle some new furniture they had bought, so they excused themselves while Jack and Jim visited about farming, clearing land, trapping, fishing, and running cattle.

On the way home, Estelle said, "Honey, Jack and Linda are in real need of a job. They had to borrow money to buy a stove, a bed, and some cabinets. I hope you can use Jack to help you so they can buy groceries and make payments on their loan. Linda shared that they had a few potatoes and Jack is a hunter. They were beat out of their last crop they made for a farmer in Reydel. So I guess he might be a bit hesitant to start sharecropping again. I did invite them over for the noon meal next Tuesday. I hope you can be with us about 12:00. I want some time with both Linda and Patsy to present the Gospel, and I thought maybe you'd watch the children for about an hour."

The attendance was good on the third Sunday morning of June when Dr. Martha Honeycutt was introduced by Homer. Word had gotten around that a special speaker would be there for that Sunday service. It had been awhile since the partition had needed to be removed in the Menard schoolhouse in order to fill both rooms. Today both rooms were packed.

"Sister Honeycutt is here on a ministry of teaching "Spiritual Warfare." She began meeting with Estelle this past week, and before Sister Martha comes to speak to us, we want Estelle to tell us about an experience she had on the second day of their sessions."

It took Estelle only five minutes to express her heart. Her face was radiant, her voice was clear, and her testimony was powerfully convincing. Most of those who knew her well realized that something very dynamic had happened to her, though they had known her as an inspiring Christian. She closed with her wish that "every Christian here this morning will become a seeker of the fullness of the Holy Spirit." Following Sister Martha's 15-minute message on "Divine Fullness," twelve people came forward immediately on her invitation.

On Tuesday morning, Estelle reminded Jim of the noon meal with Buchannons as their guests. He would be there and attend the children for an hour after the meal.

The session with Sister Martha was an inspiring one. Estelle asked her to come have the meal with them and then to pray as she presented the Gospel to Patsy and Linda.

When the three women were situated at the table, Estelle gave a few words of testimony, telling about her desire to know Jesus since she was a little girl hearing her Grandmother tell about God's love and power to save. She told how in 1930 she gave her heart to Jesus and the difference Christ had made in her life. She then read Romans 10:9-10: **If you confess with your lips that Jesus is Lord and believe in your heart that God raised him from the dead, you will be saved.**

"Linda and Patsy, before anyone can get saved, there are a few things they will need to feel seriously about: one, that they need a God who loves them and wants to forgive their sins and adopt them into his family; two, they need to believe that God loves them so much that He sent His Son Jesus to die and pay for their sins by shedding His blood; and three, they need to know that they must confess their sins to Him and then believe they are forgiven. I want to lead you in a prayer in which you will ask God's forgiveness and confess your faith in Jesus. But first, is this something you are ready to do, and are there questions you wish to ask before we pray the prayer of salvation?

"Linda, I believe you seem to want to say something or ask a question," Estelle said. "Go ahead."

"I do know I need God's forgiveness. I do want to get saved and be ready to go to Heaven when I die. And I wanta be able to pray for Jack and the kids to get saved. I guess I thought you got saved by joinin' the church, gettin' baptized, and then just livin' a good life."

"Honey, joining the church and getting baptized will likely come later. We get saved and God puts His Spirit in our hearts to enable, strengthen, and help us live the Christian life. We all need to be born again, and that's what happens when we pray the prayer I will lead us in.

"Patsy, do you have questions about going into the prayer now?" Estelle asked.

"I just know I ain't right with God, and I'm glad to hear God loves me and doesn't want me to go to Hell, but that He wants me to go to Heaven. I really do believe Jesus died for my sins, and I want to confess Him as Lord and Savior."

Linda nodded that she was ready, too. Estelle explained the prayer she would give in short phrases, which they would repeat after her. As they began, Estelle was delighted that both girls prayed with feeling and sincerity.

"Linda and Patsy, I congratulate you both for allowing Jesus to come into your hearts, for confessing Him as your Savior. Now I have Bibles I want to give you and a small booklet to read that will help you to live the Christian life. Remember, I am praying every day for each of you, and anytime you have a question or a need, feel free to come to me. We'll pray together, and the Lord will help you live the life He wants you to live."

On Sunday morning after the congregational singing, Scripture, and prayer, Homer called on Estelle to introduce the two new believers she had led to the Lord that week.

Linda said, "Miss Estelle told us that God loved us and gave His Son Jesus to die for our sins. When she asked if I wanted to confess Him as my Savior, I felt I just had to do that. She led us in a prayer. Jesus came into my heart, and I feel His peace and presence this morning."

Patsy apologized for not being able to speak in public, but she smiled and said, "I'm shore glad Mr. Jim and Miss Estelle let Punkin and me come work for 'em. Ain't nobody ever hepped us like they do. But Tuesday I knew when Miss Estelle said whut she did, I needed to know God like she does. So I said the prayer she gave, and Jesus is now my Savior."

The sincerity and faith of the two new converts drew a loud and long applause from the congregation.

On the first Monday in July, Estelle went to class to hear her teacher say, "Estelle, we are going to get into truth on Holy Warfare for a few weeks. I know this is why the Lord sent me to you. We must get the picture of the battle that is before us in your community and learn how we are to win this battle for the glory of God and the liberation of this area. Since you've been filled with the Spirit, I know it's time to begin with this. We're now ready to learn the nature of the enemy and how to approach him. It is amazing how much authority we have over the enemy when we are walking in the Spirit and clothed in His power.

"Satan is a brilliant deceiver. This master deceiver has been leading people astray for thousands of years. Regardless of the great experience you may have gained in the baptism with the Holy Spirit and fire, just remember that Adam fell from a place called Paradise. Our knowledge of God and the Bible must not make us too overconfident or presumptuous. Let us recall that Solomon, the wisest king of Israel, was taken down into idolatry by the strategies of the devil. And, no matter how profound, mystical, and sincere your worship, don't forget that Lucifer himself was cast out of Heaven even after he had led the heavenly hosts in divine worship.

"We need to remember that our enemy's first line of attack is usually through the mind. From personal experience and from hearing some of my close colleagues relate how they were defeated, I have to conclude that Satan has access to our thought life and can influence our thinking. He certainly understands the power of suggestion. He prompts thoughts of self-pity, attempting to influence us to exaggerate offenses we have suffered and seeking to keep us brooding over our hurts and needs.

"How tragic that so many of God's childen fail to discern the source of their thoughts that are leading them right into the devil's trap of spiritual defeat. Of course, Satan never begins his appeal by announcing, 'This is the devil speaking.' Even after being filled with the Spirit, we must purposely learn to think and walk in the Spirit so as to discern what is going on in our minds. Just before Jesus' temptation (Matt. 4:1-11), He had been anointed with the Holy Spirit following His baptism by John in the Jordon. After fasting 40 days and 40 nights, he was hungry; and there came the thought of turning stones into bread. But His sensitivity to the Spirit prompted Him to recognize the tempter behind his thoughts. So He addressed the tempter with the Word of God: **'Man shall not live by bread alone, but by every word that proceeds from the mouth of God'** (Deut. 8:3-4). Now Jesus knew He was the Messiah, but how many people believed in Him? Maybe two—His mother and John the Baptist. How was He to get a following? Satan is always ready to help us meet our 'needs.' Thoughts began forming about going to the temple during a great feast in the plaza below. He could leap down, the angels would form a parachute, and he would land intact, thus impressing the people to recognize Him as the Messiah. But it dawned on Jesus that the devil was messing with His mind. His response was: **'You shall not tempt the Lord your God'** (Deut. 6:16). Jesus knew He was the King of kings, yet He did not have an earthly throne. No single nation honored Him. Soon it was as though He was looking through a telescope of time, seeing **all the kingdoms of the world and the glory of them, and hearing a voice saying, 'all these I will give you, if you will fall down and worship me.'** Again, recognizing the source of the appeal, Jesus answered, **'Begone, Satan! For it is written, You shall worship the Lord your God and Him only shall you serve'** (Deut. 6:13).

"Estelle, we are not helpless against the enemy when he invades our minds, planting thoughts that tend to contaminate our stream of consciousness for hours and days. Consider II Cor. 10:3-5: **For though we live in the world we are not carrying on a worldly war, for the**

weapons of our warfare are not worldly but have divine power to destroy strongholds. We destroy arguments and every proud obstacle to the knowledge of God, and take every thought captive to obey Christ. In our battle against thoughts planted by Satan, we follow Jesus in rebuking our enemy, saying with Jesus, **'Begone, Satan!'** And He must flee. Until we learn to defeat Satan in his assaults on us mentally, we will not be able to defeat him in his attacks on us physically, relationally, morally, and spiritually.

"We must understand the power of the weapons God has given us: **the blood of Jesus, the Word of God,** and **Spirit-anointed prayer**."

A letter came from Oda revealing that things were not working well between Henry and Bill Patterson. If Jim and Estelle would give their permission, they wanted to move back to the tent near them. "Please pray for Henry. I feel he is slipping back spiritually. He even talks about going back to work for Reddon. I know some of it is because we are so far behind financially. But I know the Lord will help us if Henry will completely yield to the Lord."

"Write 'em and tell 'em they can move back," Jim said. "We'll replace all we've used for Punkin and Patsy. And let Henry know I've got work for him the rest of the summer. He'll know, no doubt, that he'll be paid as much as Bill paid him. He can then seine with me this summer and fall, if he wants to."

Estelle mentioned to Sister Martha that Jim's brother was slipping back spiritually and was talking about going back to work for a moonshiner in the bottoms. "Sister Martha, do you think we might practice some of the spiritual warfare we've been learning and see Henry accept Jim's offer to work with him and turn back to the Lord soon? I just feel like God wants to show us a breakthrough of His mighty power!"

"I'm in agreement!" Martha said. "In fact, let's hear Jesus in Matt. 18:19-20: '**I say to you, if two of you agree on earth about anything they ask, it will be done for them by my Father in heaven. For where two or three are gathered in my name, there am I in the midst of them**'.

"Now, Estelle, we are agreed that it is the will of God to reclaim Henry from his backsliding, aren't we?" When Estelle nodded assent, she went on, "And we are also agreed that it is God's will to decline the offer from his former boss and remain with his family, aren't we?"

"Most certainly, yes!"

"Then I'll lead a prayer and you will close our praying, putting before the Lord our petition."

"Praise the Lord!" Estelle said. "Sister Martha, we aren't merely studying spiritual warfare, we are practicing it. And I feel sure that in a short time we shall see a victory in this."

The rest of the session was taken up discussing Matt. 18:18 on **loosing and binding**. Martha noted in Matt. 16:19 that Jesus said, '**I will give you the keys of the kingdom of heaven, and whatever you bind on earth shall be bound in heaven, and whatever you loose on earth shall be loosed in heaven**'. "Estelle, let's think of keys as instruments of locking things up, securing something valuable; they are also instruments for unlocking, releasing, and making available something powerful or precious. Now God has promised His Holy Spirit to believers who will surrender their lives to Him and allow Him to cleanse and purify their hearts and fill them with the Holy Spirit. It makes sense to me that He can entrust **the keys of the kingdom** to those who are filled with His Spirit, and He will give them power to discern His will and know how to use the keys."

Henry and Oda moved back in August, and Jim put him to work right away building the dining room that Estelle wanted. Oda said she believed Jim's offer to give Henry the job of adding on the room and seining with him in the fall had kept Henry from going back to work for Reddon.

Sunday morning was the first Sunday that Henry and Oda and the children were back in the Nady services. Estelle invited them, the Buchannons, and Sister Martha for the noon meal. After Estelle blessed the food, Henry said, "Folks, it shore feels good to be in y'all's presence here. I felt God speakin' to me this mornin' about my backslidin'. I know I need to get back close to God. Just pray for me that I will!"

Estelle and Martha exchanged glances and smiled in silent praise that God was working a victory in Henry's heart just as they had prayed. Then their silent rejoicing deepened when Henry went on to say, "I ain't even told Odie yet, but I know in my heart I'm to turn Reddon down on that job and stay right here and work with and for Jim." Looking at Oda, he said, "And, honey, that's what I intend to do." Oda got up and hugged her husband, and Miriam said, "Daddy, that's the most wonderful thing I've heard you say in a long time!"

Not able to restrain herself any longer, Estelle burst out, "Praise the Lord! Henry, you bless our hearts in your decision!" All around the table several more were praising the Lord, even Jim.

"Estelle, have you had time to look over the plans I drew for your dinin' room?" Henry asked.

"Yes, and I like them. Please go ahead with that."

"Well, Henry, I plan to have Jack, Birdie, and me hep ye on it," Jim said.

"I think we can have it all done before winter," Henry said.

The next Sunday as Homer was closing his sermon, Estelle looked across the room and saw Oda whispering to Henry. When she saw Henry wiping tears, she slipped over and laid her hand on his shoulder, whispering, "Henry, I know the Lord is gently drawing you back to Him this morning. Come and surrender it all to Him so He can give you peace and freedom and the faith you need." Like an obedient child, Henry stood, saying aloud, "Yes, it's time. I'll go and turn it all over to the Lord!" With Oda on one side and Estelle on the other, he knelt and wept his way back into fellowship with His Lord.

Homer was about to pronounce a benediction when he saw Jack Buchannon coming to the altar of prayer. Linda came and knelt beside him, as did their three children. Helen, already at the piano, sang, "Softly and Tenderly Jesus Is Calling." Three more adults and two teens came and surrendered their hearts to the Lord.

After a few minutes, Jack stood and said, "Dear people, I just can't tell y'all how good it's been to know Jim and Estelle and Henry and Oda Tharp. The only thing that's better is now to know the Lord! This mornin' I just wanta thank God for His salvation for me and my family and for what it means to work for Jim Tharp and to be in this fellowship of Christians."

It was one o'clock before Homer felt clear to pronounce the benediction.

The 1938 Chevrolet pickup was quite an improvement over Jim's older 1925 Model T Ford pickup. Estelle had been impressed with a luxurious Dodge sedan she had seen. She told Jim about it and said she thought they should buy a family car, one that was comparable to the

Dodge for its space, comfort, and efficiency. "Well, one of these days we'll drive one that suits us and see what it costs," Jim promised. Estelle was pleased that Jim never seemed to draw back from buying what was needed. He was not a big spender, but he seemed to always be willing to purchase needed clothing for Estelle and the children as well as durable, quality equipment for trapping, fishing, farming, and running cattle. Nor did he object to giving the tithe Estelle was certain was a biblical principle that true believers must observe to advance God's kingdom and prevent materialism in the believer's heart.

Tom Miller agreed to turn the 80-acre farm over to Jim in October. Jack was delighted to accept Jim's proposal to sharecrop the greater part of the farm in cotton and corn. Since Jim would furnish all tools, fuel, seed, and fertilizer, Jack would get a third of the income from the yields. Meanwhile, Jack would work for Jim by the hour in clearing ground, working the cattle, and helping with the orchard. With Henry, Jack, Punkin, and Birdie, Jim had the most reliable and productive crew any employer could ever expect.

When Jim told Estelle that, with the greatest success in any seining season he had known and with the coming sale of the cattle the next week, he believed it was time to look at a modern sedan for the family. He asked her to ride to Stuttgart with him the next Saturday morning to look at two different cars he had been considering.

"First, let's go look at the 1938 Dodge ye've had yore eye on, Estelle." It was truly luxurious, and they both enjoyed driving it. The dealer told the salesman and Jim that his bottom dollar was $1,000.

Jim and Estelle got back in their Chevrolet pickup and drove over to the Pontiac dealer across town. "I like the Pontiac, and ye like the Dodge. If ye don't like the Pontiac better than the Dodge after we drive it, we'll go back and buy the Dodge," Jim promised.

"We'd like to drive that 1938 maroon Pontiac 4-door sedan there," Jim said. He insisted Estelle drive it, and she was not to give in to his preference if she honestly preferred the Dodge. She insisted on Jim driving it back to the dealer's. She said, "I'm hoping we can get this Pontiac for the same price as the Dodge."

Jim said, "Well, I prefer the Pontiac also, but I won't pay the $1,100 they want for it."

"Let's buy the Pontiac anyway, honey! You are right, this is the one we should buy."

When the dealer said his bottom dollar on the Pontiac was $1,100, Jim said, "I was hopin' you would not make me go across town and buy a different car for $1,000. I'd rather give $1,000 for this one and drive it home today."

"$1,100, please!" the dealer said.

Jim took Estelle's arm and was turning away, when the dealer called, "Wait! I'll split the difference—$1,050!" Jim again took Estelle's arm, and without saying a word, headed for their pickup.

"Alright, Mr. Tharp! $1,000 it is!" Jim and Estelle turned back, and Estelle wrote the check.

Driving his pickup, Jim looked in the rearview mirror and saw Estelle smiling as she followed him home driving the Pontiac. She finally passed him before they got to DeWitt. Beating him home, she had already put the children in the car to give them a short ride when he drove in.

On a Monday morning in mid-October Estelle arrived at class to hear Martha say, "I shall read you something. Don't take notes just yet. Just listen: 'The reaches of all man's faculties are limited ... extensive but limited. The strides of science in the past few years have been nothing short of astounding. Our children are passively nonchalant about some things that would have frightened most of us ... But there is a limitless reach that has been given man. It is as infinite as God, for it links human life to God. It is limitless in space, touching three worlds. It touches Heaven, earth and Hell simultaneously and instantaneously! It touches God as no other endeavor. It moves man as nothing else can do ... It is not confined to the laws of space. It knows no limit in time. It belongs to the principles of a transcendent dimension.'"

Martha walked around to the side of the table where Estelle was seated and asked, "You know what that power is, don't you, Estelle?"

"Yes, Dr. Honeycutt. Whoever wrote that was writing about the power of prayer!"

"Yes, Estelle. And that's what we are going to discover right here in this room over the next few weeks. But we'll go out and test it in the homes, in the Menard schoolhouse, out on your prairies, and down in these bottoms."

Estelle felt such a forceful thrill in anticipating what she and others were about to discover that she could hardly restrain verbal praises to God. *Oh, praise the Lord! Glory to the God who ordained prayer and graciously gave to His children this mighty force to pray His will to pass here on earth and see His glory fulfilled!*

The teacher simply smiled, nodded, and joined her pupil in pouring out her own thoughts in praise and worship. Both raised their hands in worship, allowing tears of joy to flow down their cheeks.

After some time had passed, Martha went on to say, "Estelle, the church in general has overlooked the kind of praying we are leading up to. In fact, many nominal Christians would consider believers mentally unbalanced or religious fanatics for entering into an agreement in prayer such as we did that your brother-in-law would turn down an offer to work in the liquor business, remain home, find other work, and give his heart to the Lord. But in the leadings of the Holy Spirit, we agreed to accept Jesus' promise; we proved the power that is available to any of God's born-again, sanctified, Spirit-filled prayer warriors. For Jesus promised His followers who would be filled with His Spirit, **Whatever you ask the Father in my name, He will give to you** (John 16:23-26).

"Now, I want to spend the rest of this session on this urgent subject—that of *Prevailing Prayer.* But we must face the truth and realize that few believers prevail in prayer; therefore, not many Christians get YES answers to their praying. Why is that? In Rom. 12:1, God calls us to **present ourselves as living sacrifices, holy and acceptable to Him, which is our spiritual worship.** Those who do not take this call seriously will not go on to a meaningful life of powerful prayer. They will not seek the Lord fully, die to their selfishness, surrender to God completely, cry for His sanctifying power, or hunger for the filling of the Holy Spirit. But a few Christians will not stop around the shallows; they will go on into the depths of grace, of God's Spirit, of God's promises, of God's will.

"So I am saying that across the centuries the failure of the church and Christians is caused by *the failure to pray, pray in faith, and pray in the Spirit—praying the will of God to pass in their lives, in their homes, in their churches, and in their world.* We need look no further than this."

Estelle left the session not only with a burning heart but also with a holy fear lest she fail to remain full of the Spirit; lest she *grieve, quench, ignore, or disobey* Him; and lest she fall short of becoming **a living sacrifice in prayer**. However, even before she climbed the steps into her kitchen, a wave of reassuring faith swept her inner being, causing her to resolve, *O Lord, I shall by Your grace live in such fellowship with an ungrieved, unquenched Holy Spirit that He will be free to enable me to pray Your will to pass in my life, my family, and in my sphere of influence!*

Estelle told Patsy, "After you bring the children home from school tonight and we have had supper, we'll have a little party with cake and ice cream to celebrate Jake's tenth birthday. I've made a coconut cake, and I've bought him a gift. The Best, Shelton, Morgan, and Buchannon children are coming. Sister Martha will come over later when Anniece goes to get her."

When he became the center of attention, Jake was more uncomfortable than he realized he would be. Estelle saw his shyness and said, "Now, son, you need to realize how much God loves you, and He wants you to respond to our love. Your Daddy and I, your sisters and brothers, and your cousins here love you. And I know your neighbors, the Buchannon children, love you, too. Your friend Fontaine there loves you. And Dorothy and Roscoe love you, as well. All nodded their agreement with Jake's mother, and some said, "We do!" Jeanette and Anniece broke away from the circle in the living room and went to their brother and hugged him. When Anniece kissed him on the cheek, Jake blushed and grinned. After singing, "Happy Birthday," all the other children lined up to hug him as well.

Jim called to his son, "Jake, I want ye to know that I'm proud of ye. I think yer a fine boy and a trustworthy lad. Sit right there while I go and get the gift I've bought for ye." Jim returned with an item that Jake found incredible—a gun! "Son, I trust ye to use this gun carefully and safely. It's a 20-gauge, single-barrel shotgun. With this gun, ye can hunt squirrels, turkeys, or ducks. It's good for deer, too, but we'll have to buy ye slugs to use when huntin' deer. When yer older, we'll get ye a multiple-loader, like a pump or an automatic."

When Jake reached out to take the gun, tears of joy welled up in his eyes. He quietly and brokenly said, "Daddy, I know I'll never be the perfect man with a gun that you are. But I'm proud of this gun, and I promise to be careful with it."

When Jake returned from standing his gun up in the cabinet alongside his father's Winchester Pump, he went to his mother and hugged her. Then Estelle said, "Well, son, there's something else we'll need to do before we cut your birthday cake and serve ice cream. Sister Martha wants to come over here with a gift for you, and she has something very special to say to you." Estelle turned to Anniece and said, "Honey, go tell Sister Martha we are ready for her."

When Anniece returned with Martha Honeycutt, all were impressed with a new white dress the teacher was wearing, one that no one had seen her in before. Estelle thought that she looked so dignified, so awesome. Even her face was shining. Miss Martha went straight to Jake, who Estelle had made sure was seated in the center of the room for this very purpose. She held out to him a small gift wrapped in bright red. "Jimmy, I know you like to be called Jake. I know your name is James, a very wonderful name. I happen to think a good substitute for the name James is Jimmy. And if you don't object, I'd like to call you that. So, Jimmy, unwrap your gift, please, and then I am supposed to tell you something the Lord told me this morning to tell you."

Jake nervously untied the white ribbon around the red package. Anniece helped him when he couldn't easily untie the knot. Inside the red package was a black leather King James Version of the Holy Bible. He opened the cover with a grin on his face, then turned the cover and first page to find His name printed "James William Tharp, Jr., a gift for Jimmy Tharp, Messenger of the Lord Jesus Christ. Given October 16, 1939, on his tenth birthday, from Martha Jane Honeycutt." Jake looked at the smiling teacher standing in front of him and quietly said, "Miss Honeycutt, I thank you, and I'll read this. And I'll try to keep it all my life."

"Jimmy," Miss Honeycutt said, as all ears were attuned to her every word, "What I have to tell you might be a disappointment. I really don't know what you have planned to do with your life. Do you know what you want to do when you are out of school?"

Jake didn't hesitate, but said, "Well, ma'am, I think about it a lot, and I reckon I'll raise a buncha white-faced cattle, like Daddy. Seems like the only people who have any money in this part of the world, except for people who make whiskey or kill and steal, are the cattlemen. I think I oughta buy land and raise cattle. I know my Daddy will help me, and our Uncle Hay has already told me he'll help me with all the money I'll need to get started." Jake had said it with excitement, but out of respect for his questioner, he looked to see if she was pleased with his answer.

"Well, Jimmy, I'm sure the Lord is not unhappy with people who raise cattle as long as they please Him when they do it. But the Lord wants me to tell you something wonderful. I don't often get words of prophecy from the Lord to give out, but I know that I'm supposed to prophecy over you on this your tenth birthday. Something glorious, something supernatural is going to happen throughout this entire community in a few years—and in a great part of Arkansas County—that will change hundreds and thousands of lives, including yours. You and all in this room are going to give your hearts to Jesus Christ! *Jimmy, a while after you are saved and before you finish high school, the Lord is going to call you to become a minister of the Gospel. You're going on to higher education after high school to learn the Bible. My dear lad, you will become a man of prayer and preach the Gospel all over the world. You'll see mighty revivals!* And I promise you that for as long as the Lord allows me to live, I shall pray for you every day! And may I pray for you now?"

Jake, though greatly embarrassed, reached for her hand and said, "Thank you!"

"Heavenly Father, I thank You for the privilege of delivering Your message to Jimmy here tonight. Thank You for his life, for his parents, for his mind, and for his future in Your will. Bless him as he loves and obeys his parents and as he is kind and good to his brothers, sisters, cousins, and friends. I thank You that one day You will sweep this community with Your saving presence and power, redeeming hundreds, **causing them to renounce ungodliness and worldly lusts and to live holy lives in this world, awaiting our blessed hope in the appearing of the glory and coming of our Savior Jesus Christ!**" Martha Honeycutt bent over and kissed the red-faced boy on the cheek, and said, "May God bless you, Jimmy!"

"Alright!" Estelle said. She intended to say more, but all in the room began a loud and long applause. So when this had subsided, Estelle went on, "Miss Martha, thank you! Please have a seat over there and join us in celebrating our son's birthday. Patsy, come help me serve the cake and ice cream."

Martha Honeycutt told Estelle on the first Monday morning of November that their entire month would be spent on prayer. "I want to try and answer the question: 'What is Prayer?'

"First, it is *worship*. It is not just crying out to God for His help and getting our needs supplied. It is by prayer that we come to *know the Lord!* When we worship God in prayer, we are recognizing His worthiness and putting Him in proper perspective. Someone has said, 'Prayer is not only the shortest distance to the Throne of God; it is the only way in which we come to Him through our Great High Priest, Jesus Christ.' God is never more than a prayer away. We come into His Presence by prayer, and there we discover the wonder of worship—that all true praying is done in worship. This is its primary essence. Only the praying believer can get to know God, get to know Him intimately, and get to know His will.

"Then, prayer is *work*. I agree with Oswald Chambers, who said, 'Prayer does not just fit us for the greater work; prayer *is* the greater work.' Jesus said, **'Truly, truly, I say to you, he who believes in me will also do the works that I do; and greater works than these will he do, because I go to the Father. Whatever you ask in my name, I will do it, that the Father may be glorified in the Son; if you ask anything in my name, I will do it'** (John 14:12-14). So much Christian activity in our times has little evidence of being the work *of* God, even though it may be work *for* God. We need to understand that we must follow Jesus in such prayerful obedience that God is at work in what we do—in our praying, in our witnessing, in all our works. Jesus is telling us in this passage that prayer is work and that without prayer our works won't matter in the sight of God.

"Jesus considered prayer as His greatest work. After being anointed of the Holy Spirit, the Spirit led Him into a six-week prayer retreat—for forty days and nights Jesus fasted and prayed, during which time He was tempted by Satan. We are told by the Gospel writers that Jesus would sometimes spend all night in prayer.

"In Luke 5:15, we are told that Jesus **withdrew to the wilderness and prayed.** Then two verses later Luke reports that **the power of the Lord was with him to heal.** The historian here intends his readers to make the connection between *cause* and *effect*. Because Jesus prayed, the power of God was present to heal! The miracles of healing came out of Jesus' works of prayer.

"God has ordained prayer as the means by which He releases His Spirit of power to do all He has planned for the church to do. This is why John Wesley declared, '*God does nothing except by prayer.*' He simply will not pour His Spirit out on a prayerless church, nor will He trust His power to a prayerless servant.

"Jesus tells us the secret of His success in ministry when He said, **'Truly, truly, I say to you, the Son can do nothing of his own accord, but only what he sees the Father doing; for whatever he does, that the Son does likewise. For the Father loves the Son, and shows him all that he himself is doing; and greater works than these will he show him, that you may marvel. For as the Father raises the dead and gives them life, so also the Son gives life to whom he will.'** Since we believe that prayer was the main work of Jesus while on earth, we know that it was in prayer that Jesus learned what the Father was doing and what the Father wanted Him to do. The same goes for us today; we give ourselves to prayer, and we learn what God wants done. Prayer is the main work of the Holy Spirit in us.

"Finally, prayer is *warfare*. In the classic warfare passage of Ephesians 6:10-18, we hear the apostle Paul calling for strong and courageous followers of Jesus Christ to get ready for battle. The front line of battle is no place for cowards or weaklings. **Be strong in the Lord and in the strength of his might** (v. 10). Note that we are called to *wrestle* against **principalities** (evil spirits given authority over certain territories and gifted in deluding); **powers** (demons commissioned to take over human thoughts and passions); **the world rulers of this present darkness** (the cosmic forces trained by Satan and armed with strategies for capturing human thoughts, emotions, and purposes for deepening the end-of-the-age darkness); and **hosts of evil spirits operating in the invisible realms** (a reference here, I think, to the ground troops at the disposal of these evil cosmic masters to carry out the wickedness, violence, and depraved conditions that will lead to divine judgment).

"Estelle, let's go back to verses 10 through 12 and note that Christians, **strong in the Lord and in the strength of His might** are to

stand against the wiles of the devil. We are to **wrestle against** these wicked spirits.

"We are called to *intercession*! Oswald Chambers, D. L. Moody, and E. M. Bounds all believed that intercessory prayer requires the highest sacrificial energy of which the human heart is capable. There is no doubt in my mind that it represents the most intense form of spiritual warfare! My dear sister, prevailing prayer could well be the most difficult work you and I will ever do here on earth. The apostle made it clear in the beginning of this passage on spiritual warfare that because we are pushing against the heavy, threatening forces of spiritual darkness to get through, around, or past the forces of evil to the very Throne of Grace, we must be armed **in the strength of His might**! Wrestling against such opposition is demanding, taxing, and draining on mere human strength because we are moving beyond human understanding and human ability. Such praying is not a natural science; we can only be led into such periods of struggling against cosmic forces by the promptings and leadings of the Holy Spirit. That is why the apostle finishes this classic passage on spiritual warfare by saying, **'Pray at all times in the Spirit, with all prayer and supplication. To that end keep alert with all perseverance, making supplication for all the saints...'**(v. 18). We need to be aware that even though intercessory prayer is driven by the anointing of the Holy Spirit, it still takes a heavy toll on the human mind, body, and spirit.

"Listen to how Jesus interceded: **In the days of His flesh, Jesus offered up prayers and supplications, with loud cries and tears, to Him who was able to save him from death, and He was heard for His godly fear** (Heb. 5:7). Jesus was praying in the Spirit. He was praying in faith. He prevailed in prayer and prayed the will of God to pass in His own life and ministry. He was a divinely anointed intercessor.

"Jesus practiced what He preached and taught. In Luke 11, where Jesus is speaking on persevering in prayer, He says, **'And I tell you, Ask, and it will be given you; seek, and you will find; knock, and it will be opened to you.'**

"Estelle, the kind of spiritual warfare we are up against here in Arkansas County will not be won by mere *asking* (just filing a claim, stating our need). Nor will it be won only by the second level of *seeking* (committing to a course, taking it by the job). No, we must reach the place in seeking God's outpoured Spirit upon communities by praying as Jesus did—we must *knock!* Knocking entails burdened praying, crying out, shedding tears, pleading the blood of Jesus Christ, and fasting. It's the kind of desperate praying Jesus did in Gethsemane. Most Christians consider agonizing prayer extreme, fanatical, and foolish.

"But, oh! Estelle, because we know we are praying the will of God, this kind of boldness comes to us from the Holy Spirit and we refuse to be denied!—this persistence comes to us from the Holy Spirit! And it only comes to those whose hearts are pure, who are full of the Holy Spirit, who are sensitive to His assisting presence in prayer. While doing it, we come to realize that He is doing it through us. We are bearing His burden. The Holy Spirit is shedding Christ's tears through our eyes!

"Remember the parable of the persistent widow (Luke 18:1-8). This widow would never have been heard by the unjust judge if she had not been willing to knock and to keep on coming and knocking at his chamber door every day. Nor will we see a rending of the heavens on these southern communities unless we make revival in these parts the most serious, sacrificial, desperate, consistent, prolonged project we've ever thought or dreamed of!

"Are you with me, my dear sister?" Martha asked with tears.

Estelle nodded, and said with great emotion and tears, "Oh, yes! May the Spirit help us reach the stage of *desperation* in which we *knock, cry, beg, fast, believe!*"

"*Amen!*" said Martha. "The Lord has been talking to me, my sister. I won't have very many more months with you. I'm to go to DeWitt early next year, where Brother Fox believes he will have a dozen people to study with me on spiritual warfare. But, I feel the Lord is leading me to form a Prayer Pact for Revival in Arkansas County with you and others who will join us. After a few weeks of teaching in DeWitt, I'll invite you, Brother Rich, and all who wish to join us in that prayer pact. Then I plan to go back to Indiana and resume my position on the faculty of Union Bible College. I'll encourage hundreds of believers in Indiana to join this prayer pact, and together we shall not stop praying *until God invades this county and hundreds, even thousands, turn to Jesus Christ*! But this kind of spiritual power always requires *prevailing, persevering prayer.*

229

"Before I let you go today, Estelle, I want to say a few things about *prevailing prayer.* This level of praying always requires someone who is full of the Holy Spirit, strong in the Lord, totally committed to a specific prayer goal, and determined to see a glorious supernatural invasion of the Holy Spirit. Estelle, I believe God can trust you with a prayer burden. One reason such praying takes time is because the Holy Spirit will often need to take us through several emotional stages in order to prepare us for His answers. Let me mention a few of these.

"*Desire.* God may feel that He needs to test the depth of our desire for what we are asking. In Jeremiah 29:13, He says, **'You will seek me and find me, when you seek me with all your heart.'** Any time we are satisfied to go on without His answer, then we may be sure the answer will not be coming. But if we do not grieve the Spirit's working within us to develop stronger desire, it will soon come.

"*Pure motives.* I have a friend who is a powerful prayer warrior, and I've heard him say that 'wrong motives can block our praying, even if we are praying according to the will of God.' Then he quotes James 4:3: **You ask and do not receive, because you ask wrongly, to satisfy your own desires.**

"*Fervency.* Desire and fervency are related, and each supports and strengthens the other. Desire has more to do with hunger and need; fervency has more to do with passion and zeal. Desire is born in need; fervency is born in love. We need eyes that see the needs, but we must have hearts burning in love. Evangelist Charles G. Finney pointed out that in prevailing prayer, 'We must have so much of the love of God in us that as we pray the Holy Spirit helps us to pray with the love of God.' Andrew Murray insisted, 'It is the very nature of love to give up and forget itself for the sake of others. It takes their need and makes it our own. It finds real joy in living and dying for others. This kind of love in us will become intercession, for this kind of true love must pray.' And Missionary pioneer Adoniram Judson wrote, 'A travailing spirit, the throes of a great burdened heart, belong to prayer. The Spirit, the power, the air, and the fuel of prayer is in such a spirit.'

"We must ask the Holy Spirit to give us the kind of love for souls and the kingdom of God that these great prayer warriors are talking and writing about. And as He does this, we must practice praying immediately as we feel Him pouring love into our hearts, so that we do not quench, grieve, or ignore the help the Spirit is offering us for prayer warfare. We must welcome and cherish any drawing of the Spirit to prayer at any time. With E. M. Bounds, let us acknowledge that a praying spirit is not in our power. We cannot create this fervency of spirit on our own. But as God begins to do it, we must not turn to other things and wait too long to go to prayer and see how He will then deepen our desires until we are praying passionately and boldly."

Several times Martha suggested to Estelle that she felt they should join Jim some day and go down into the bottoms and visit some of the people. Jim had mentioned to the sheriff Dr. Honeycutt's interest in the bottoms, and he said, "Well, let me know when y'all are ready. I'll get the speedboat and take ye. I think the world of Estelle, and I wouldn't mind meetin' this woman who means so much to her."

"Well, bring Irene along," Jim suggested.

On a lovely Friday afternoon in November, the five, along with Buck, landed at Barney's Hole at the Arkansas River Bridge. Getting out of the boat, Estelle pointed to an old listing cabin boat and asked, "Is that where Punkin and Patsy lived?" Jim nodded in the affirmative.

"Sit, Buck!" Jim ordered as the five entered Barney's place. Soon the bearded owner emerged from his private quarters, saying, "Lloyd and Jim! What in the devil are you two lawmen doin' here with these nice women, brangin' 'em into this ungodly hole?"

Lloyd said, "Barney, we knew your place could use a little class for a change. Meet Jim's wife, Estelle; and this lady here is Dr. Martha Honeycutt, a professor from Union Bible College up in Indiana; and I'm not sure you've met my wife, Irene."

Barney bowed and said, "Welcome to you beautiful ladies! Shore 'nuff, they're first class alright! Y'all have seats over there at that nice table in the corner. I'll find Syl and she'll brang y'all iced tea or coffee or Cokes. Estelle ordered iced tea, Martha wanted hot tea, and Irene joined the lawmen in ordering cold Cokes. After the drinks were served, Jim noticed that Barney disappeared.

Syl came to take their orders. "Estelle, how about sharing a ham-and-cheese sandwich with me?" Martha asked. Estelle nodded. Irene ordered a bowl of vegetable soup. The lawmen both wanted steaks.

Jim could see Buck out under the elm and noticed that he was restless about a large boat being tied up at the pier. Two men and a woman were heading for Barney's.

Lloyd told Syl to call Barney, and he appeared at the same time the three stepped through the door. "What can I do for you folks?" he asked.

"One room for three, with two beds for one night," the taller man said.

"I just got a two-room cabin down on the river, $20," Barney said.

"Little high, ain't ye?"

Barney shrugged, "Take it or leave it."

The taller man turned to his two associates and said, "Now ain't he actin' like a smart son of a bitch!" When the man opened his mouth and turned where the sheriff could get a full view of his face, Lloyd thought he had never seen an uglier human being. One of the man's teeth turned down like that of a vampire.

"Hold it there!" Barney said. "Watch yore talk! We've got fine Christian ladies in here. Ye ain't talkin' ugly like that so long as they're around. I'd just as soon all three of you'd move on up the river!"

"Aw, so ye got some holier-than-thou hypocrites here, and we're heathen bastards. We ain't welcome! Is that it?"

"Let me tell you who these gentlemen at this table are: this man is the sheriff of Arkansas County, and the other one is Jim Tharp, his special deputy. These ladies know God in a powerful way, and you'll have Almighty God to reckon with if you start callin' them bad names like you just done."

Before Lloyd or Jim could respond, Martha stood to her feet. Every person in the room stopped breathing. She searched the eyes of all three of the newcomers, and her eyes came to rest on the tall, ugly one. "Mister, I beg you to listen to me! I am a born-again child of God, a 53-year-old virgin, a professor of New Testament in an Indiana Bible College. And this my dear friend," pointing to Estelle, "my Spirit-filled sister in our Lord Jesus Christ. She has great power with God in prayer. And I am impressed to warn you against the kind of ill-chosen words you just used to describe two of God's children."

Since the room was electrified with a sense of a frightening power, Martha went on to say, "I want to tell you three people something, and this goes for Barney and Syl as well as Lloyd, Irene, and Jim. God loves you all. He is holy and just, but He is also a God of grace, full of mercy and forgiveness. I sense that all eight of you need to fall down before Him, repent of your sins, call on Jesus Christ as your Savior, and let Him come into your hearts to help you live according to the Bible. He prefers to forgive you rather than to send judgment on you and send you to Hell. There's nothing more that Estelle and I would rather do right now than to lead all eight of you in a prayer of repentance and faith in Jesus Christ." For several seconds the silence was awesome.

Then the tall man exploded with curses on Barney. He told the two others with him they were getting out of there, but not before he would "shoot this damned hole all to Hell! And if Barney so much as opens his mouth, I'll put a slug in his worthless gut!" When he pulled at a pistol, Jim's gun spoke: *Bang!* Blood poured from his ear, and he fell across the table. Turning to the shorter man, he hollered, "Eddy! Dammit! Can't you take care of that murderer who just shot me?" Jim was ready for Eddy, but he knew from his eyes he was not about to attempt to avenge what had happened to his partner.

Barney was grinning and said, "Feller, you just come up agin' the wrong man! He happens to be the husband of the woman you just called a 'holier-than-thou hypocrite.' I got a kick outa seein' Jim Tharp drill that ugly ear of yours. If y'all don't clear this place shortly, I hope he drills your hearts like he's apt to. I'm orderin' you three outa here. I refuse to serve such low-down jerks as you. Get outa here and *never come back!*"

The three cleared out and gave Buck a wide berth on their way to their fancy boat.

When Lloyd tried to pay Barney for their food and drinks, Barney said, "No, and I do apologize to the ladies for what that rascal said!"

"It's alright, sir," Martha said. "We'll pray for all of you, asking God's Spirit to draw you to His Son, Jesus Christ."

"Thank you, ma'am!" Barney said. "I reckon we won't ever forget the sermon you gave us in such powerful words."

"Well, Barney and Syl, let me tell you what Estelle and I truly believe: In a few years, because of a prayer pact we have made with the Lord, the Almighty God of Heaven, the God of Eternity, the God of salvation and judgment of all mankind is going to send His powerful Holy Spirit across Arkansas County like an invisible army, and people who do not know the Lord will never guess at first what has hold of them. There will be an overwhelming conviction for sin, and hundreds will fall to their knees and repent of sin and call on the saving name of our Lord Jesus Christ. Hearts and homes will change. People converted to Jesus Christ will start to live holy lives. And, oh, Barney! I pray you and Syl will be among those who will be saved!"

Barney's face was as white as a ghost, and Syl was in tears as the five left. When all five were settled in the boat and Lloyd had hit the starter, they headed upriver leaving their own remarkable wake behind.

8   The Armies of God

Between Christmas and the New Year, Martha emphasized spiritual warfare with different analogies. She said, "Estelle, you can call me visionary or weird, but I feel God is calling forth an army of prayer warriors to prepare for the mighty invasion He wants to make on your county here. I don't want to feel self-important, but I believe He has called me to help train this army. And I'm sure you are being called to train for leadership in the coming battles. You see, revival is a mighty work of God. It will come from the heavens. Perhaps I should say it will come from the *heavenlies*, meaning from the unseen spiritual world."

Estelle wasn't sure at first that she understood what her teacher meant. But her inner being cautioned her to listen carefully. Soon she would start to grasp new truth about spiritual warfare.

"Let's go to Joshua, chapter 5, for what is on my heart," Martha said. "God is preparing Joshua for capturing Jericho, the first battle the Israelites will fight after passing over the Jordon. Also it's Joshua's first time to serve as leader since Moses was taken from the scene. In v. 13 it appears that Joshua is out walking in the evening before the battle. **He lifted up his eyes and looked ... a man stood before him with a drawn sword in his hand; Joshua went to him and said, 'Are you for us, or for our adversaries?' And he said, 'No; but as commander of the army of the Lord I have now come.' And Joshua fell on his face to the earth and worshipped, and said to him, 'What does my lord bid his servant?' And the commander of the Lord's army said to Joshua, 'Put off your shoes from your feet; for the place where you stand is holy.' And Joshua did so.**

"It is significant that God the Father chose to call His incarnate Son **Jesus.** *Jesus* is the Greek form of 'Joshua.' We know that Joshua was the Hebrew general chosen to lead his people into battle to take the promised land. Without the meeting with this **Commander of the army of the Lord**, or **Captain of the Lord of hosts**, Joshua could never have become a conqueror. Estelle, those of us who are preparing for the spiritual battle that will result in a mighty revival must have a greater revelation of Jesus Christ than we have ever known. We prayer warriors must behold our Lord Jesus Christ with His drawn sword, a Holy Warrior, dressed for battle! A militant Savior! **The Lord is a man of war** (Ex. 15:3). **Who is the King of glory? The Lord, strong and mighty in battle!** (Ps. 24:8). And the kind of battle we are called to engage in demands that we keep in mind that it is **Not by might, nor by power, but by my Spirit, says the Lord of hosts** (Zech. 4:6).

"Joshua had his vision of the Lord of hosts at the close of chapter 5. But the Jericho victory did not come until later in chapter 6, because the Heavenly Joshua must tell the Earthly Joshua at least three things before he can see the victory that is promised: (1) *Joshua, taking Jericho is not your idea; it is God's command;* (2) *Joshua, Jericho will not be taken by your weak army; it will be taken by divine, invisible forces;* (3) *Joshua, Jericho will not be taken for your glory; it will be taken for the glory of the Captain of the Lord of hosts.*

"Estelle, the kind of army you and I will be a part of will not impress the world. In fact, it will not impress most who call themselves Christian. But it is the only kind of army that can rise against the tide of evil that Satan has planned for the end times that Jesus describes in Matthew 24 and Luke 21. We go to Ephesians 6:10-18 to be reminded of our call to battle, the kind of preparation we must make, and the nature of the fight we are in—**we wrestle against principalities, powers, rulers of the present darkness, and hosts of wicked spirits operating in the heavenlies**. Paul is speaking here of intercession, not a casual approach but a passionate one as we see in the parable of the persistent widow (Luke 18). She kept on knocking and would not accept a negative answer.

"The intercessory prayers of the great Laymen's Prayer Meetings of 1857-59 were persistent, as were those leading up to the great Wales Revival of 1904 and the Colonial and Wesleyan revivals. Estelle, God requires this kind of intense intercession for the great awakening so desperately needed here in Arkansas County."

During January, Sheriff Lloyd LaFargue sent Jim notice that Sheriff Jefferson had evidence that Joel Jackson had individuals sneaking around in the lower end of Arkansas county. "Jim, it could be he knows Punkin is working for you. Keep an eye out for trouble."

For three mornings straight in early February, Jim had heard Buck howling as though someone was snooping around. The first morning he heard the howling, Jim went outside to check and took Buck with him. "Where!" Jim asked. Buck looked east, both ears pointing that direction. "Lead!" Jim ordered as he followed Buck down the slope 50 yards from the barn. Buck stopped. Jim squatted down in the predawn to wait for more light. Watching where Buck was looking, Jim could finally make out a brush pile that he and his helpers had built for burning limbs and thorn branches. It would soon be light enough to determine if someone was hiding there. Thinking he saw movement behind the pile, which was 75 yards away, he was tempted to put a bullet there, but that was not his way of operating. As the sun was rising, he said, "Come, Buck! Let's go see if someone is or was there." Boots had crushed grass and pushed sticks into the ground, but Jim did not believe it had been done recently. He and Buck returned to the barn.

Jim could hear Punkin building a fire in their heating stove. Jim called, and Punkin opened the tent flap. "Punkin, don't start feedin' 'til it's good light anymore. I'll be by after awhile and explain."

Later on Jim was at the barn to take care of the horses. He asked, "Punkin, have ye heard anythang around the place early mornin's lately?"

"Naw, just heard Buck cuttin' up a little, howlin' and yippin' now and then."

"Well, I shore don't wanna scare ye, but the sheriff thinks we need to take precautions lest Jackson might have someone 'round here who would try to get a shot at ye. So don't go out any after dark or too early before light of mornin's. I don't want anythang happenin' to ye."

Ten mornings later, Jim and Estelle had only been up a few minutes when they heard Patsy screaming and knocking at the door. Jim overheard her tell Estelle, "Tell Mr. Jim to come quick! I think Punkin is dead! He's layin' there bleedin'. Before Jim could get to the door, Patsy was back at the entrance to their tent. Without grabbing his coat, Jim ran out in the cold February morning to kneel down by Punkin, whose face was pale, and his eyes were set in death. "Oh! Punkin!" Jim sobbed, as he saw several stabs the young man had taken. "I'm so sorry, Patsy!" Estelle had hurriedly put on a coat and run to the tent to comfort Patsy. Jim stood up and remarked, "Someone will pay for this, but it won't bring Punkin back to us! I'll take him into the smokehouse and come back and cover the blood with a shovel or two of sand. Estelle, you and

Patsy need to either go over to the house or step into her tent where it is warm."

Jim drove to DeWitt to report the crime to Lloyd and to have the mortician pick up Punkin's body. Lloyd was as angry as Jim about Punkin's murder. "You say he was stabbed five times?" Lloyd asked. "Probably so a bullet wouldn't waken you!"

"Yeah, I guess. I could only find one set of tracks. The murderer hid behind the barn, accordin' to the way Buck was lookin'. Then when Punkin went to the toilet just before daylight, he caught him. It looked like Punkin had took several steps before fallin' almost into the openin' of their tent."

Estelle had her hands full comforting Patsy and the children. When she prayed, the children all wanted to say a prayer for Patsy. Estelle insisted that Patsy lie down on her bed, where she slept most of the day. Henry thought Homer and Helen should know about Punkin's death, so he drove Jim's pickup down to inform them. They both would be coming up that evening to pray with Patsy. Jack and Linda also came over to comfort her and the Tharps.

After eating lunch, Patsy said, "Miss Estelle, how I thank God that you hepped me and Punkin both find the Lord! Ain't it good that Punkin is in Heaven with Jesus?"

"Oh, what comfort for all of us, Patsy! What do you want to tell Pastor Homer about a funeral service?"

"Oh! Hadn't even thought about that yet."

"Since we worship the Lord in a schoolhouse, we usually schedule funerals on Saturday. I know Jim and I will take care of the mortician charges. You will need to pick out a casket, and you can bury Punkin at Hockenberry Cemetery. We'll buy the plot; it doesn't cost much. Mr. Essex will want to know how you want him dressed. You might just want to have him wear something he'd normally wear to church. But, if you want him buried in a suit and tie, we'll take care of that, too."

"I don't think Punkin would want to be dressed up."

"Then just take Mr. Essex the clothes he would wear to church."

Saturday was a cold, clear day. The crowd was the regular worship crowd. Homer read from the Gospel of John and the 23rd Psalm, and Leora Brown sang "Amazing Grace." Estelle told about the joy of leading Punkin to Christ, following the time that Patsy gave her heart to

Jesus. "Punkin and Patsy have been like family to us. I know we all rejoice with Patsy today that Punkin is with Jesus and out of all sorrow and pain." Homer gave a good Bible message directed to the living about preparing to meet the Lord. Almost all present went to the brief service at the cemetery.

Lloyd asked Jim to allow him and the county to share the funeral expense, especially since Punkin's testimony had helped to put in prison the man behind the effort to murder Birdie. Both felt it was very likely that same man had arranged to have Punkin murdered as well.

Martha sat on the couch, looking across at Estelle, and said, "I think I should tell you how the Lord is preparing me to wind up my time in Arkansas. I had a letter from Dr. Smith a few days ago, and he's invited me to be one of the speakers at the Annual Camp Meeting this August. I believe you and Jim attended one of these events a few years ago. I was hoping you might pray about the two of you attending this year. Here's what I feel like projecting as of now: ask Pastor Rich to allow me to preach the Sunday mornings in March to prepare the people for a special commitment to intercessory prayer on Easter Sunday and finish here with you in April. Then in May, I would move to DeWitt and begin classes with those who Pastor Fox can rally for studies.

"I'm thinking that perhaps on the first Sunday evening in August, I'll ask Pastor Fox to allow me to have the service. I'd like it to be a combined service with the DeWitt and Nady churches coming together. We'll have those from Nady come forward who will be committed to praying daily for revival. Then with the Nady prayer warriors already standing, we'll see how many commitments we can get from the DeWitt congregation. Estelle, we must have the Spirit's help to recruit prayer warriors for *the armies of God*!

"With Jim's and your permission, perhaps I can return to this cabin for my last week in Arkansas, during which you and I will have some special times agreeing to ask God for certain things to happen in Arkansas County. Then I want us to make a Prayer Pact, which I'll explain more about later. The following week, I hope we can leave for Westfield, Indiana, and the camp meeting."

"Oh, Sister Martha! I just know it would please the Lord if Jim and I could attend another camp in Westfield! I'll talk to Jim about that tonight. And if we go, we would love to have you ride with us in our

Pontiac! I'm quite sure my mother would want to go to see Bernice and attend the camp as well. And I do like the thought of your preaching on Easter Sunday and getting pledges from prayer partners for revival! Oh, the Lord is increasing my faith for the long haul in intercessory prayer leading up to the time of a mighty historic outpouring of the Holy Spirit on this county. Praise God! Yes indeed! I want to know more about the Prayer Pact and enter into it with you.

"Now, Sister Honeycutt, the only sad part in all this is that I only have three more months of sitting under your wonderful teachings! But I'll always be grateful. And already, the Lord is helping me practice what I've been learning."

"Yes, Estelle, that's the promising part of this our first effort to get Spirit-filled Christians in Arkansas County skilled and trained in spiritual warfare and teach them what it means to **put on the whole armor of God** and to **pray in the Spirit.** The Lord is helping you to do it already. As I see it, you and Pastor Homer will teach and model militant intercession as faithful prayer warriors for all the believers in Nady who volunteer for God's armies."

"Sister Honeycutt, I'm glad to tell you that you, Homer, Helen, and I are not the only ones in this community learning to prevail in prayer. I'm quite sure that my mother, Alma, my sister Mabel, Uncle Morg, Oda, BettyLee, Tassy Coose, Flossie and Ross, Blanche McKay, Vivian Shelton, and even Linda are all learning to really get into prayer! And I know that Thelma Bonner up in the Fairview community is a powerful prayer warrior."

"That's great to hear! And, Estelle, since God has given you the gift of communication, I believe He'll direct Pastor Homer to use you to instruct and gather all who make pledges to come together periodically to practice group intercession. During that early week of August, you and I will discuss group intercession and do 'agreement praying,' like we did about Henry's returning to the Lord and declining the job in liquor."

"I do look forward to that," Estelle assured her.

Martha spent the rest of the morning session reviewing the earlier material she had given Estelle on the Holy Spirit and Prayer. "Now tomorrow and throughout our remaining weeks and months together, we'll study the subject of *Revival*."

"Well, I do believe my heart is ready," Estelle said, as she slipped back into her boots, donned her heavy coat, and went out into the deep snow. She returned in the trail she had already broken and was soon home. Jack had parked their old car out front and had left a note on the front door saying he'd be over at four to get the children from school. No doubt, he knew that Jim would be busy most of the day checking his traps and tending cattle.

Star had waded through deep snow all day carrying Jim and a dozen mink hides, but he delivered his load at sundown. After putting out grain, hay, and water for Star, Jim rubbed him down, dried him off, and talked with him a few minutes before going to the house for a warm supper and an anticipated restful evening with Estelle and the children.

"How did it go today, Dad?" Jake asked.

"It couldn't have gone better, son. I reckon the 12 minks I caught will bring us over $300. I can't complain about the weather with such a catch."

After the children were all in bed, Estelle told Jim about Martha's desire that they attend the camp in Westfield in August. "Honey, I really feel the need of attending another meeting like that. And I think a break in August away from cattle, cotton, fishing, and timber would do you good. I know you can trust George, Henry, Jack, and others to go ahead with the seining. No doubt Ross, with Jake's help, will keep an eye on the cattle. And we'd be gone less than two weeks."

"I guess it would be a nice trip to test our Pontiac, wouldn't it?" Jim said, smiling as though he would agree with his wife.

"It sure would! Sister Martha would want to ride up with us, and I know Mother will want to go and see Bernice. Sister Martha won't be coming back after the camp."

"Ye're gonna miss her, ain't ye?"

"Oh, honey, you know I will!"

"Well, ye'll still have me," Jim said with a grin.

"Thank goodness! I've had you all along, and I'm so grateful!"

Martha Honeycutt's final sessions with Estelle focused on revival. "Revival is a phenomenal thing. It is a divine thing, but there is a human factor. The strange cycle of the spiritual and moral backsliding of the people of God and of the nations across the centuries is a haunting

241

reality of history. The Old Testament church often failed to meet the conditions of its covenant with Jehovah, and the resulting apostasy wrote tragedy into its history. But Christians under the New Covenant are just as guilty of grieving the Spirit of God who lives within them. The New Testament church does not remain alive unconditionally; it experiences abundant life only as it is faithful to obey the teachings of its Lord and Savior, Jesus Christ, who said, '**If a man does not abide in me, he is cast forth as a branch and withers**' (John 15:6). We have so many dried-up, withered professing Christians in our churches today all across America!

"The prophecy of Habakkuk addresses the mystery and manner in which a holy God deals with His delinquent children. The prophet makes it clear that God will wink at neither the wickedness of the world nor the disobedience of His church. What He condemns in the world He cannot condone in the church. Let us listen to the prophet's prayer: '**O Lord, now I have heard your report, and I worship you in awe for the fearful things you are going to do. In this time of our deep need, begin again to help us, as you did in years gone by. Show us your power to save us. In your wrath, remember mercy.**' (Hab 3:2)

"It seems that Habakkuk was shocked to learn that it is the prerogative of our sovereign God to choose His own method of disciplining His rebellious people. He would use the violence of a plundering Babylon to get the attention of Judah. And yet the prophet also observed that even in His severe judgments, God is still a God of mercy.

"Habakkuk's prayer should inspire our faith today in praying for revival. We should not doubt that God will use the increasing plagues of our times to bring America to repentance. If Charles G. Finney were alive today, I think he would argue that such awful judgments can actually set the stage for the drama of revival. I think Finney would say that if America would humble herself and plead moral bankruptcy before a God of holiness and justice, we could yet experience the greatest awakening in the history of our country. The prophet's prayer reflects his memory of God's merciful acts of reclaiming Israel many times, and it becomes his hope that He will do it again.

"From the beginning, Estelle, revival has been God's secret of preserving His people. And this has been so true in the American experience. Three mighty spiritual awakenings have changed the course of our continent on several counts, both sacred and secular.

"Before we get into the history of the American revivals, I want to spend time giving you *definitions* of revival as stated by some of the leaders.

"Charles H. Spurgeon, who experienced a 25-year revival in the London Metropolitan Tabernacle: *A special move of the Spirit of God on His people, drawing them upward to their power and privileges in the purpose and grace of God—holiness, prayer, evangelism, vision, miracles.*

"Evan Roberts, who was God's youthful leader in the Great Wales Revival of 1904-05: *God's marvelous way of bringing the church to its knees in order to draw the world to His heart.*

"Charles G. Finney, a prominent American evangelist in the nineteenth century: *A supernatural invasion of the church by the Holy Spirit, bringing believers to a new beginning of holiness in life and power.*

"J. Edwin Orr, an outstanding revival historian: *A divine supernatural move of God on His people, restoring them to New Testament power as modeled in the book of Acts.*

"Jonathan Edwards, a Calvinistic Puritan Pastor in New England, who was a prominent leader in the earliest American awakening: *God's major means of extending His kingdom.*

"But now, Estelle, I wish to give you my own definition of revival: *A mighty move of God upon indifferent, powerless, fruitless, professing believers, in response to their hunger, humility, honesty, and deep repentance, restoring them to New Testament power and authority for holiness and evangelism.*"

Estelle, Homer, and Martha all agreed that Easter Sunday of 1940 was indeed "a most significant day in strengthening and preparing the armies of God for the violent spiritual warfare ahead for Southeastern Arkansas." Never had Homer Rich heard such a powerfully penetrating message on anointed, sacrificial, prevailing prayer as Dr. Martha Jane Honeycutt delivered to a schoolhouse full of people on that bright morning. The atmosphere was charged with both holy fear and excited faith. So many believers tried to fill the altars until the speaker directed "all who will pray one hour each day *until an outpouring of the Holy Spirit comes to Arkansas County* please stand where you are. Now, let's think about what we are doing. Don't stand merely because many others are. Be sincere and plan to carry through on this promise. This is a sacred vow you are making to the Lord. You must not break it!" Despite the caution, 77 people stood and remained standing for several minutes while Mabel Bennett wrote down their names.

Martha Honeycutt certainly deserved the week of rest following the weeks of praying and teaching that she had shared with Estelle. Beginning on the Monday morning after Easter, she and Estelle agreed to pray together daily for one hour, from 8:00 to 9:00.

Estelle had never known such praying, not in herself and not in another. She felt that their anointing by the Holy Spirit might have been like the anointing that had been experienced by Moses, Abraham, Samuel, and Daniel. *Or maybe it was even like the praying of Jesus, or Stephen, or the apostles Paul, Peter, James, and John. Or perhaps she and Martha were praying like Polycarp, Savonarola, Martin Luther, John Wesley, George Whitefield, Francis Asbury, Jonathan Edwards, David Brainerd, Charles G. Finney, John Hyde, and Evan Roberts.* If so, time would tell, *for revival will come*!

Estelle felt good about the way she could go from prayer to her garden to work the soil, plant the seed, and remove the weeds—and still continue to fellowship with the Holy Spirit in worship, honor, praise, and thanksgiving. Never had she been so certain of revival—*Jim will get saved, and Jake will also. God will sweep this county just as we have envisioned. Those river bottoms will be cleaned up. Jim will no longer need to kill or shoot men's ears. Blasphemy, drunkenness, cursing, murder, adultery, rape, stealing, and lying will disappear from this community. Churches will be built and filled with worshipers and seekers of God. Singing, shouting, rejoicing, and worshiping will replace cursing, hatemongering, whoremongering, murdering, stealing, and lying all over these prairies and down in the bottoms. Yes, we'll go from mourning to dancing. God, let us see Your glory, Your power, Your salvation! Oh, Lord, please let it be*!

During the spring season, Estelle discovered the power and peace of fasting. She cut out meat and ate only vegetables—and a limited amount of them. She also gave up coffee and tea during that period. She had never felt better or more energized. And, oh! How she looked forward to prayer—prayer alone, prayer with Martha, prayer at the table, prayer with the children individually, prayer with all of the children at bedtime, and prayer with Jim.

Late one morning, Jim rode in from tending cattle, unsaddled Star, and put him away with water and grain. Spying Estelle in the garden picking lettuce, he could hardly wait to join her. "My! Ye sound happy out here singin'!" he said as he bent over to receive her offered kiss.

"Well, honey, I am happy! I'm happy with the Lord! I'm happy with you! I'm happy with our children! I'm happy with what God has done, is doing, and is going to do. But, are you happy?"

"Well, I'm not sad. I may not be as happy as you are, but I'm thankful for you and the children and for the way life is goin'. I saw Ross this mornin', and I'm thankful for what he told me about cattle prices this fall, … and somethin' else."

Estelle stopped picking lettuce and raised up to look at her husband. "What else?" she asked.

"Oh, somethin' good—cattle buyers for President Roosevelt's CCC camps and his other conservation projects are increasin' the price of cattle this fall. And what's more, cattle buyers are organizin' here in Arkansas and they'll send out fleets of trucks and trailers right to the farms and ranches to buy and haul the cattle to the market places. No more havin' to haul them ourselves!" Jim said with excitement.

Estelle was pleased with the excitement in Jim's face and voice. "Praise the Lord!" she said softly, as she stooped to resume picking lettuce. "I'll pull some onions and radishes and come in and prepare your lunch in a few minutes."

Over lunch, they talked about various farming responsibilities and how much they appreciated those who were helping them handle the many tasks involved. Estelle asked, "How is the cotton looking, or haven't you had a chance to check on it?"

"I like the looks of it. We used seed from our own crop last year, and we may do it agin next season. We save a lot of money when we do that. We don't get that much for the seed we sell, but we sure pay a lot for the plantin' seed we buy."

"I guess you're pleased with both Homer and Birdie doing your cotton."

"I shore am! They know what they're doin', and they work hard. I can trust 'em with the equipment and with money."

"And what about Jack?"

"Ah, he's the best. He's able to get more outa that orchard ever year. He knows how to spray the trees, how to get his help to handle the fruit carefully, and what markets to go for first. In his first year with us, he had less fruit ruined by careless handlin' than I did when I took care of it. Yeah, he's even better than Birdie was, but we're fortunate to have all three men on this place. And I'm thankful for George and Henry to work with in fishin', trappin', and huntin'. Ross is a great help in runnin' cattle and huntin' wild hogs, and he even knows better ways of farmin' cotton than I do, things Homer and Birdie catch onto right away. Yeah, Estelle, I wouldn't be into cattle at all without Ross's help. Ye know, Cleve and Ebrena have been very nice and helpful and encouragin' to both of us. We really do have a lot to be thankful for in the people we have around us."

"Yes, and don't forget our good neighbors, Oscar and Vivian Shelton, out there on the county road. That Vivian is one wonderful neighbor, and I can tell now that she's making a good Christian, as is her husband. They're raising a fine family, too."

"You're right. Os Shelton is a fine man, a sincere man, and a smart man. He can carry on an intelligent conversation on a lotta things."

"Well, I love them all, and I'm praying that when the Lord sends the great revival, others who don't know the Lord will just be swept into the Kingdom of God by being born again. As they grow in the Lord, the Spirit will lead them into a life of holiness and power."

"I'm not sure I understand all ye mean by revival," Jim said.

"Oh, honey, revival is a mighty work of the Holy Spirit when He moves on hearts both individually and community-wide. People begin to feel their need of getting right with God and calling on the Lord in repentance. Sister Martha and I have been studying the revivals that have come on various parts of the world since Pentecost, when the Holy Spirit was poured out on the 120 believers in Jerusalem. As the revival spirit spread over the city, thousands repented the first day, were born again, baptized, and added to the church. It's coming, Jim! Brace yourself.

246

You're going to be one of the first ones to get saved in the great revival here in the Nady community!"

"Now, you just wait a minute! Ye're gettin' carried away with this thing. I ain't gonna become no shoutin', prayin', hollerin' hypocrite!"

"Of course you're not! You're going to repent of sin and yield your heart to Jesus Christ. You're going to experience the miracle of the new birth and be adopted into God's family of the redeemed. At the same time, you're going to receive the power of the Holy Spirit within you to help you live the Christian life. You will begin to understand spiritual matters that you've never understood before. God is going to make a wonderful Christian man out of you, and you will be an example to your sons and daughters and to the men and women of this community. You're a wonderful husband now, but you'll be even more wonderful when you've yielded your life to Jesus."

"Well, I reckon I've heard your sermon, so I'd better go spend a little time with our children. I think they're all playin' in the yard."

"They'll be glad to have you play with them, I know."

Just as Jim went out the front door, Jake came in from playing with his siblings. "Mama, can I talk to you?" he asked hesitantly.

"Of course, son. Sit down. Would you like a glass of tea?"

"No, ma'am. Thanks. I just wanted to talk about the service with all of us kids a few weeks ago."

"Yes, what about it?"

"Well, I know you are probably disappointed that I didn't go forward to pray."

"I'm sorry you didn't, but I thought maybe you weren't ready. I also thought maybe you wanted to, but you held back because Fontaine was with you and he didn't want to."

Estelle's growing, maturing son looked down in embarrassment as he said, "Well, Mama, I think there are two reasons: first, I don't know what's holding Daddy back from confessing Jesus as his Savior; then, too, I reckon I did let Taine hold me back from going to the front with the rest of 'em."

"My dear boy, the Holy Spirit deals with us as individuals, and I pray that you will not let your dear Daddy's reluctance to yield to Christ keep you from that important decision. I know you and Fontaine are good friends, but I am confident that when you feel the Spirit of God calling you to Jesus, you won't let anyone stand in your way—not your dear father nor your best friend."

"Mama, I love you! And I believe in you! I'm proud of you…" Estelle noticed there were tears in her son's eyes now, as he went on, "…I want Daddy to get saved. I think when he does, it will be easier for me to make up my mind."

"Come here, son." Estelle stood and let the tears flow as she drew her son to her. "I love you, too. I'm proud of you also. And I believe what Sister Martha told you on your last birthday—that God has His hand on your life and will use you in some special way. I pray for you every day that you will come to love and know Jesus and follow Him, no matter what others do."

"Mama, I think that's part of my fear of confessing Jesus—I want to raise cattle like Daddy. I don't want to fish like he does, and I don't care whether I farm cotton or not. I know I'll need to raise corn and hay, but I don't think I want to preach…. And that's something I've been wantin' to tell you, but I was afraid you'd be so disappointed in me."

"Now, son, let's put first things first. First will come your call to salvation by the Holy Spirit. I think He was calling you a few weeks ago at that service. You declined His call, but I don't feel you slammed the door on Him. I believe He will call again, and I think you'll say yes to Him. After you've been walking with the Lord awhile and you hear the voice of the Holy Spirit calling you to preach, then you'll be able to respond. But if you don't feel a call to preach, you can go right on and finish the grades, go to high school and, hopefully, go to college. If when you are through school, you still haven't received a call from the Lord to preach, I'd say you can begin your herd of cattle. In fact, I think I overheard your daddy tell you that you ought to start a little herd of cattle when you get into high school. And I think that's okay."

"Yeah, and I will, too! Daddy's going to show me how to catch minks, and I'll use the money to buy a few cows. He also told me if I worked with him, he'd pay me in young heifers that would in a year have their first calves. And like him, I'll sell the steers and keep the heifers. Maybe when I get through high school, I'll already have twenty-five or thirty head of cattle."

"Son, I am sure glad we had this talk. Now you just know that I'm praying for you every day. Whether the Lord wants to call you to preach the Gospel or raise cattle, that is not for Sister Martha or your mother to say. I just urge you that when the Spirit is calling you to Jesus, don't let anyone keep you from trusting in Him as your Savior, okay?"

"Yes, Mama!" Jake stood up and gave her a smile that warmed her heart. He held out his arms to embrace his mother in a big hug, whispering, "I love you so much, Mama!"

"And I love you so much, too, son! May God bless you!" After Jake went out to join his father and his siblings, Estelle wiped her tears and prayed, "Lord, bless my boy. Deal with him in Your time and way. Let nothing stand in his way from the life You want him to live. Thank You, Lord, that he came to me for a talk that was long overdue. Help me to know how to influence his life for You without trying to control him."

Jim and Estelle asked Jack and Linda to take their five children to church on the first Sunday in May and feed them the noon and evening meals so that they could take Dr. Honeycutt to DeWitt to begin her ministry there. She would preach in both services in the DeWitt Friends Church and announce her schedule of teaching on Spiritual Warfare during May through July.

Estelle and Jim were warmly greeted by Frank and Ola Fox. They were invited to join them and Dr. Honeycutt for the noon meal and to stay over for the evening service. The attendance was encouraging, as the DeWitt congregation was larger than the one at Nady. Preaching a powerful message on the subject nearest to her heart, Dr. Honeycutt warned the believers that we were in for dark days that required courageous, self-denying soldiers. She used the evening service to explain the curriculum she would be using in the classroom over the next three months. Then she closed the service, explaining what she expected of the students. She called for those who would commit their all to learning how to become a true soldier in spiritual warfare to come forward for a prayer of dedication. Estelle was thrilled to count nine people, five women and four men, who knelt at the altar for the prayer.

Before Pastor Fox pronounced the benediction, Martha called Estelle to come forward and tell the nine, as well as the congregation, what her three months of study with Martha had meant to her. Estelle was surprised at the freedom and excitement she felt as she expressed her joy over learning about, and being filled with, the Holy Spirit. She told them that she knew that experience prepared her for learning about prayer and for then entering into the anointing of the Spirit for prayer. "My prayer life is far different now than it was before I studied with Sister Martha. Oh, but you nine people are also in for some transforming hours in the presence of God as you learn from the teaching by this great woman of God."

Patsy had taken over the care of the Tharp children after the evening meal and had seen to them being in bed at the proper time. When Jim and Estelle arrived home about ten o'clock, they found Patsy asleep on the couch. "I didn't hear ye drive up or come in the house," she said apologetically.

Seeing Patsy getting ready to head for her tent, Estelle said, "Why don't you stay and have a piece of pie with us, honey?"

"Sure," the girl said. Estelle cut three pieces of raisin pie and poured them glasses of cold milk from the refrigerator.

"Yer sure gonna miss Miss Martha, ain't ye?" Patsy said to Estelle.

"Of course, but I've got Jim and the children, you, Henry and Oda and their children, and, of course, the Buchannons. And I'll pray a lot for Sister Martha. We had a good meeting in DeWitt today, and she'll have nine people to teach up there instead of the one she had here."

"Well, I reckon it'll take that many to match the one she had here," Patsy said.

Estelle smiled at the compliment and said, "Thanks, but I'm afraid you're wrong."

"I've learned so much from you, Miz Estelle. I feel like I'm a part of your family. Y'all are so good to me! You pay me too much and feed me too much. You let me drive your cars and take care of your children. When I need somethin', y'all see that I get it, just like I'm an important somebody."

"Honey, you are somebody important! You are a child of God. You are a part of our family. We need you more than you need us, but we are surely glad to help you when you need it. I'm proud of the way you are growing in the Lord, praying, reading your Bible, testifying in church, and witnessing to some of the women down at Nady who haven't yet given their hearts to the Lord. I'm also glad for the way you are learning to write your letters and numbers and improve your vocabulary and grammar."

"You and Mr. Jim took me and Punkin in from the first and made us feel like we belonged. Ye never made us feel like the trash we had been before we come here." Patsy started to weep softly.

Estelle patted her shoulder and said, "We knew you were not trash. You and Punkin had good hearts, good minds, and good manners. You are a joy to have in our lives and in our home. Without your help, I know I couldn't get everything done that I need to. You are always here when I need you, and I've never heard you complain about anything. I know the Lord is pleased with your life. We surely are!"

As Patsy started to leave, Jim said, "Wait here a minute, and I'll go turn the light on in yore tent and make sure ye're safe." He returned saying, "Everything's fine in your tent, Patsy. Good night."

"Good night, Mr. Jim and Miz Estelle. I shore do love y'all."

"We love you, too, Patsy," Jim and Estelle said in unison.

Martha Honeycutt sensed she was off to a good start with her nine students, most of whom she felt were hungry to know the biblical truth of the mystery of spiritual warfare. She was committed to patience, prayer, and faithfully expounding the Scriptural emphases the Spirit laid on her heart. Now and then, a forceful testimony, an insightful question, or even an emotional outburst would come from one of the nine to indicate they were grasping more than she supposed.

Once in June and again in early July, Estelle and Jim drove up on a Saturday. Oh, how Martha enjoyed the radiance and faith of this woman who had drunk in her every statement in their months of training together! When Estelle asked what day they should return to take her back home with them, she replied, "If you and Jim could be here with all the rest of the folks from Nady who will attend the Commitment Service on the last Sunday night of July, I'll be prepared to return to the cabin with you."

"Praise God!" Estelle said. "We'll be here! Having you with me for a week or ten days before we head for Indiana will be heavenly!"

"Indeed it will!" Martha agreed, as she hugged her prayer partner goodbye.

The night of the Commitment Service, the Friends Church in
DeWitt had the largest crowd in its five-year history. Pastor Fox and his
custodian had electric fans stirring the inside air. Thankfully, a cool
breeze was blowing through the open doors and windows from a cold
front coming down from the northeast. Over 90 people from the Nady
church were in the congregation, including every one of the 77 who had
stood on Easter Sunday in the schoolhouse and pledged *to pray one hour
each day until revival comes to Arkansas County!*

After words of welcome by Pastor Fox, he acknowledged "a
great crowd of people from the Nady Friends Church, just about as many
as we have from here in DeWitt." He prayed God's blessings on this
special service, saying, "and we trust, Lord, You will honor us with Your
presence, and that the kind of praying we engage in during the months
ahead will result in a mighty **rending of the heavens**, bringing a tidal
wave of revival and salvation to Arkansas County." A dozen or more
"Amens" were heard during the closing words of the prayer. Pastor Fox
then introduced "Brother and Sister Rich, with their talented voices and
music." Homer led the congregation in "Revive Us Again," after which
Helen sang a solo, "Pentecostal Power." After an offering was taken, Dr.
Martha Honeycutt was presented for her special message on "Militant
Intercession for a Full-Scale Historic Spiritual Awakening."

Estelle felt she had never heard such an anointed indictment of
the American professing Christians for their betrayal of the Holy,
Faithful, and Merciful God. She was reminded of reading Jonathan
Edward's historic sermon, "Sinners in the Hands of an Angry God,"
preached in Enfield, Connecticut, in 1741, in which he declared that "the
wrath of God is like great waters that are dammed for the present; they
increase more and more, and rise higher and higher, till an outlet is
given; and the longer the stream is stopped, the more and rapid is its
mighty course, when at once it is let loose."

Now Sister Martha was declaring the wrath of God would be let
loose on the church's *apostasy, hypocrisy, apathy, self-righteousness,
prayerlessness, unbelief, and materialistic idolatry!* She went on to
declare that American professing Christians were as much in fearful
danger as were the sinners Jonathan Edwards preached to 198 years ago.

"Oh, let's understand something here tonight: the reason our
country is rampant with the brazen sins of atheism, idolatry, immorality,

and irreverence is not to be blamed on politicians, philosophers, scientists, manufacturers, or financiers. Please, let's not blame President Roosevelt, William James, Thomas Edison, Henry Ford, or Andrew Carnegie. No, beloved, the Bible places responsibility for revival on the people of God. Hear it in II Chronicles 7:14: **'If my people who are called by my name humble themselves, and pray and seek my face, and turn from their wicked ways, then I will hear from heaven, and will forgive their sin and heal their land.'**

"You see, those of us who are professing Christians need to understand that Christ is as sick of our apathy, coldheartedness, spiritual laziness, and unbelief as He was with the Laodicea church! Yes, I know it's hard for us to believe our God of love is sick of us, but He is! And because He is, He will not hear our prayers until we repent of our indifference, unbelief, and worldliness!

"Some of us don't understand an angry God, because we only want to know about a God of love, compassion, and forgiveness. And thank God, He is just that! He promises that if we will come and call upon His name, He will abundantly pardon us and cleanse us from all unrighteousness. Then He can fill us with His Spirit, after which He can call us to sacrificial praying, worshiping, witnessing, and believing for the mighty revival He wants to send. It is the delinquent Christians who are holding up revival, not the atheists, thieves, harlots, and murderers who have never claimed to know God.

"The revival must start within the hearts of professing Christians who have repented of their hardness, unbelief, unforgiveness, backbiting, self-righteousness, and failure to attend the means of grace. We've come into this service tonight to pledge ourselves to sacrificial, militant, intercessory prayer for a mighty revival to be poured out on Arkansas County. But many of us are not ready to pray that way. Some of you have come prepared to make that pledge. But before we come to this important moment, I want to ask everyone to bow your heads and listen carefully to the Holy Spirit as He searches your hearts. How many of you Christians are living holy lives daily before the Lord? How many of you husbands and wives are fussing, fighting, and accusing one another even in open conversation before your children? How many of you go for days, even weeks, without praying or reading your Bibles? How many of you are failing to share a tenth of your prosperity with the Lord through

253

tithing into the church storehouse? How many of you are judging and finding fault with your brothers and sisters in Christ and criticizing the pastor and lay leaders of your church behind their backs?

"Well, it's my duty to tell you that you are not ready to enter into intercessory prayer for revival. You, yourself, need revival. And you can experience it right here tonight if you will humble yourself and come and kneel publicly at these altars and ask God's forgiveness. He is merciful, and He will hear your prayer, forgive you, and take away your guilt and condemnation. You can go out of this service at peace with Him and ready to obey Him. Then you will be ready to pray for revival in your own heart, in your family, in your church, in your community, in this county, and in this nation.

"Brother Rich, please be ready to lead us in an invitational song after I have prayed. Now, Lord, You have been present in this service tonight in a mighty way! You've been speaking to Your backslidden children, and they've been listening. You really don't want them leaving this service the way they are feeling right now; You want them to come and confess their sins of disobedience so that You can forgive them and empower them to live out their faith in power, and joy, and blessing. Draw many of them to You tonight.

"Stand, please!" Martha Honeycutt called. "Come right on down to these altars and humble yourselves, and confess to God what He already knows that needs to be forgiven in your life. Step right out.... Yes, many are coming. It's our night to get right with God and to have a spiritual housecleaning in our hearts, homes, and families. Just obey God, and prepare the way for revival."

Already the altars were filled, and Martha was kindly asking all on the front seats to vacate them and allow people to kneel. When the front seats were occupied with seekers, Martha motioned to the second row to do likewise. Estelle believed 60 people were seeking the Lord!

Martha did not hurry the altar service, but gave seekers direction to repent and then believe that God has heard. "Trust His promise to forgive if we confess! Go, standing on that promise that you're forgiven, free, having faith and unity with God. Begin obeying, loving, serving, witnessing, worshiping, and praying."

People kneeling at the altar and the front rows were rising with joy on their faces. Homer led a praise chorus, "Thank You, Lord, for saving my soul; thank You, Lord, for making me whole." They all joined in, and the congregation could sense the relief that the seekers felt as they all returned to their seats.

Martha then said, "All of you who are prepared here tonight to stand before God and this audience and pledge to pray one hour each day *until revival comes to Arkansas County*, come forward now, please!" Estelle led the way as 76 others from Nady and 54 from the DeWitt church followed her.

Martha asked the seated members of the congregation how many of them would join the 131 prayer warriors who stood before them in offering a daily prayer for revival. "Maybe not for an hour, but daily, you'll call on the Lord for revival in Arkansas County and say a prayer for those who are wrestling an hour a day against the powers of darkness and pleading with God for a mighty awakening."

Nearly all those who were seated stood! Pastor Frank Fox went to the platform and commented, "What a significant night it has been as we have seen trained and courageous and dedicated soldiers of the cross pledge their efforts and energies in spiritual warfare. Together, we shall prevail with God and see a glorious revival in Arkansas County! God will bless this mighty spiritual army He is raising up in this county."

When Pastor Homer Rich had given the benediction, the DeWitt and Nady believers mingled together in warm fellowship for awhile. Since Jim and Estelle were moving Martha back to the cabin, Pastor Fox helped Jim transfer her personal effects from his car to Jim's.

On the drive home, Estelle commented, "Sister Honeycutt, I must tell you that tonight *you preached the greatest message I've ever heard!*"

"Thank you, Estelle. The Spirit was on me, and I was impressed to say what I did."

"Of course, He was on you, and that's why it was so powerful."

The Tharp house was quiet when they arrived back home. The children were all in bed and asleep. Having anticipated that Estelle, Jim, and Sister Martha would be hungry, Patsy said, "I've got soup and sandwiches ready if ye wish them; and then there are three different kinds of pie for ye to choose from. I've got Sister Martha's cabin clean, the windows are open, and the house is airing out. After she has eaten something here, she might want to close some of the windows, because the colder air has come and the wind is still blowing."

"Sister Martha, let's sit down and eat something before we take you to your cabin," Estelle said.

"Yes, thank you. I am rather hungry," the preacher admitted.

"When ye're ready, I'll back the car up to yore cabin door and unload yore thangs, Sister Martha," Jim said.

Inside the cabin later, Martha turned to Jim and Estelle and said, "Folks, of all the places I've tried to call home—California, New Jersey, Kentucky, Ohio, Alaska, and Indiana—this is the most restful, beautiful, and blessed place I've ever lived. I've lived where there have been mountains, oceans, deserts, and plains. But here I've worshiped. I've prevailed with God. I've communed with a true sister in Christ. I've had visions and seen miracles. Oh, how I thank you for letting me live here!"

"It's been our pleasure to have ye, Sister!" Jim said.

"Yes indeed!" Estelle agreed. "And Sister Martha, I'm looking forward to the time we'll have together in the next several days."

"Well, Estelle, from the calendar it appears that we'll have 10 days before we need to leave for Indiana. Would you like to meet me here each morning at 8:00 o'clock, beginning tomorrow, for an hour of prayer for the next 9 days?"

"I certainly would!" Estelle assured her.

"Then go home and get some sleep and rest well. I'll see you in the morning!"

Estelle felt tired and somewhat drained from the exciting service in DeWitt, but she was so filled with joyous anticipation of the upcoming prayer times that it was past 1:00 a.m. before she finally fell asleep.

Martha welcomed Estelle at exactly 8:00 on Monday morning. In preparing for this prayer time, she had marked passages of Scripture concerning **praying in the Spirit**. She read Luke 10:21, Eph. 6:18, and Jude v. 20. "Estelle, what do you believe it means *to pray in the Spirit*?"

"In a general way, Sister Martha, I think it means to allow the Holy Spirit to help us pray, rather than thinking we know how to pray on our own. Did not the apostle Paul teach that when it comes to the matter of prayer, we are all weak? Let me read Rom. 8:26-27: **Likewise the Spirit helps us in our weakness, for we do not know how to pray as we ought, but the Spirit himself intercedes for us with sighs too deep**

for words. And he who searches the hearts of men knows what is the mind of the Spirit, because the Spirit intercedes for the saints according to the will of God. You taught me that the Spirit helps us pray in three ways: (1) He *enlightens* our understanding so that we pray according to the will of God, (2) He *energizes* our human spirit so that we don't faint, and (3) He *emboldens* our faith so that we refuse to be denied!"

"Oh, Estelle! What a memory! Thank you! How did you come up with all that so perfectly?"

"Well, Sister Martha, when you hear something which you know to be the truth and you start practicing it, I think it's easier to remember. I know the Spirit does all three of those things in my prayer life, and I praise Him for it!"

"Well, do you remember what we discussed about *two or more people agreeing in prayer*? I'd like to hear you express your feelings about the most urgent matters we should agree on in prayer."

Estelle bowed her head in prayerful thought for a minute. Then she looked up at Martha and said, "Number one is *a mighty, historic, full-scale, spiritual and moral awakening in America.* Number two, *the conversion of my husband, Jim Tharp, my daughters Jeanette and Anniece, and my son Jake.* Now, I fully expect that it will be during the answer to the first request that my husband and children will find the Lord."

"Well, I think you are correct in that, Estelle. I have two urgent matters to add to your two: My first concern is that sometime this fall—in a matter of weeks—*a terrible world war will erupt in Europe.* It will last several years. Our nation will not be involved for awhile, but before it is over, America will be involved. All the nations involved in this war will lose millions of people, both military and civilian. We must pray! We must pray for (1) President Roosevelt and his advisers and generals and admirals, (2) the brave men and women who face the violence and tragedy of war up front, and (3) the faith and morale of the people in all of the nations that will be involved in this horrible tragedy.

"My second concern is that *beginning in Westfield next week and continuing for months to come, we shall be able to see the armies of God increase at an even greater rate than we have seen here in Arkansas County over the past months.*"

"Yes," said Estelle, "We will agree on these four important and urgent matters, and they will frame just about all that the Spirit brings to our minds and hearts across the coming years. For, Sister Martha, I believe these wars—I mean both the spiritual battles we are already fighting here and throughout the world and the military battles that are going to last into the years—could tax, drain, and *deplete both the armies of God and the armies of our allied nations, unless we persist in prayer, and pray in the Spirit.*" So, Sister Martha, could we get right to prayer for the inspiration, direction, and anointing of the Holy Spirit about these matters? I feel impressed to pray that the armies of God might increase in numbers as well as in power and that the allied military armies might experience unusual, even miraculous, protection of our merciful God."

"Yes, my dear! It's now 10:30. So let's spend the rest of our morning practicing what we've just agreed to and resolved to carry out with the anointing of the Holy Spirit. Perhaps you would like to lead out, and as the Spirit directs me, I'll join in. I know you'll not be disturbed or distracted if I pray aloud and weep before the Lord even as you may be doing the same. Let's forget the clock and simply pray until our hearts are free and we know the Lord has heard us."

Estelle knelt at the couch, and no sooner had she opened her prayer by calling upon the Lord to receive their praise and hear their supplications than she felt the divine Presence fill the cabin. She hushed her praying and waited in holy silence. *Lord, You are here! Oh, please touch my mind to think Your thoughts concerning intercession for revival, for Jim and the children, for the Westfield Camp, and for a recruiting of the armies of God.* Estelle waited for what seemed a long time, then she began feeling and seeing in a dimension she had never experienced before. A peace swept her soul and body. A joy flooded her total being. She burst out in psalms and hymns. She quoted many of God's promises from the Word back to Him and said, "Lord, I'm holding You to Your Word!" She saw visions of battlefields, bombs bursting, men falling, strafing planes flying over villages with men, women, children, and farm animals being slain.... Then, she saw prayer meetings all over the nation—two or three here and hundreds and a thousand over there. She saw the heavens open and innumerable hosts of angels hovering over the earthly intercessors and then descending on them, gathering their prayers into vials and larger vessels. She was amazed, but when she entertained a doubt that this was only her imagination or a self-induced fantasy based on things she had read or things Martha had said, a quiet darkness settled over her spirit. *Lord, forgive my unbelief! Here You were answering my prayer for inspiration and direction for intercession for revival. Forgive me for misinterpreting Your answer in visions as my own silly imaginations. Now, Lord, I thank You for these visions and thoughts. Oh, by Your grace, I shall receive more and more of these. Then I shall know how to offer up sacrifices of praise and enter into fellowship with You* **when in the days of your flesh you offered up prayers and supplications with loud cries and tears..., and you were heard because of your godly fear**.

On Tuesday, both Estelle and Martha seemed to lack the inspiration for prayer they had known the day before. At midmorning, Martha called for a conference. "Let's think now—the enemy is countering our efforts, Estelle. Oh, how he hates prayer! Remember, there are a few things he dreads most—*the blood of Jesus, the Word of God, a Spirit-filled believer, and prayer. So we can expect to be opposed in our efforts to pray in the Spirit. You just listen and meditate on a Scripture or two while I rebuke the enemy. I'll order those invisible opponents out of this cabin and forbid them in the name of Jesus to return for the time of our praying together over the next few days!*"

Estelle listened in amazement as Martha called out in a clear but not loud voice, "Evil spirits, in the strong name of Jesus Christ and by the authority given me in His sovereign name, I command all of you to *depart these premises now. Go into the regions of darkness and never return here!*" Estelle heard Martha begin praising God that Christ possessed complete power and authority over all, **having in his death on the cross disarmed all principalities and powers and made a public example of them, triumphing over them**! She continued to plead the blood and praise God for Jesus' death on the cross, for giving **Christ dominion and authority and power over all, exalting Him above every name, that He has put all things under His feet and made him head over all things**. As Martha sang "He Is Lord" and then "Power in the Blood," Estelle joined in. Soon the atmosphere changed from bondage and restriction to freedom and glory.

Throughout the rest of the week, the same freedom, inspiration, and holy boldness continued in their praying. Estelle had learned a valuable lesson in being delivered from Satanic attacks on her praying. She would simply need to summon the courage and boldness, as Martha had, to come against evil spirits who seek to prevent the praying of Spirit-filled believers. She knew the evil spirits would fight to keep them in bondage. She had learned from her mentor a powerful method of invoking the name of Jesus. *O, Jesus, let me never misuse that holy name of Jesus, but breathe it in worship and invoke it with authority over anything that I discern Satan or his minions are doing or are about to do!*

Estelle was busy washing clothes for their trip to Indiana and instructing Patsy on caring for the children for the ten days she and Jim would be gone. Jim, Henry, and Jack were on horseback, planning where to position the pens and chutes where the cattle being sold could be penned and then loaded onto the big trailers the buyers would bring. Jim had already studied Ross's corrals and pens to get ideas on how to build them. Ross had volunteered to draw plans for the pens and chutes, and he was present to explain the proposed plans to the men and make suggestions on the dimensions and kinds of posts and braces needed. Jim would put Jack and Birdie to work right away cutting the timber and making posts, and he expected to see the finished work when he returned from Indiana.

As always, both Jim and Estelle were saddened to leave the children. Estelle had wanted to take Carroll along on the trip since he was the youngest and still her baby. However, Oda, Henry, Jim, and Patsy talked her into leaving him behind, along with the other children. Jeanette would soon be thirteen and she would help Patsy and Oda with the smaller ones, providing familiarity and keeping them from getting too lonesome for their parents. Jake would help Ross and the men with the cattle.

Henry said, "You have wonderful kids, Jim and Estelle! Shore, they'll miss you, but they're in good hands; they'll have somethin' to look forward to—Mama and Daddy comin' back! Besides, me and Oda and Miriam and Jack and Linda will give Patsy a hand anytime she needs us. Y'all go on to Indiana, forget about all of us, have a good time, and bring a carload of blessin's back for all of us ole country folks."

On Tuesday, Jim asked Jack to wash the Pontiac, brush out the carpets, and remove anything from the trunk they wouldn't need on the trip. They were taking Sister Honeycutt's belongings from the cabin and luggage for all four, so every inch of space would be needed.

That evening, Henry volunteered to go down to Nady and bring Estelle's mother back to spend the night so that the travelers could leave early the next morning. Patsy and Estelle fixed an unusually good dinner, and the Washingtons, Buchannons, Riches, both Tharp families, and Martha sat down to a feast. Homer prayed an inspiring prayer of blessing on the food, the trip, and the camp meeting in Westfield.

Before daylight, Henry and Oda, Miriam, Reba, and Jack and Linda and their three children joined with Patsy and the six Tharp children to see the four off. Jim had loaded the luggage and boxes in the spacious trunk, rejoicing that he had managed to get it all in after rearranging everything for the second time.

Estelle said, "Henry, I was impressed with your prayer for us at dinner last night, and I feel this morning you are the one to offer a prayer for God's protection over us and all of you we are leaving behind. And would you also pray for the camp meeting and give thanks for allowing Dr. Martha Honeycutt to be with us for these many months, please?"

"O God, we're so blessed," Henry began, becoming emotional but continuing, "You by Your mercy and grace have saved us. Some of us was fit for Hell, but You stooped way down and lifted us up, and put Heaven in our hearts. I thank You for the peace and joy and love that's made a new man outa me. I know I've got a long piece to go, but here I am, Lord, and I'm on my way. Lord, we are thankful that You allowed Dr. Honeycutt to come off down here in this hellhole and bring us the glorious Gospel of Jesus Christ. I thank You for what she's taught Estelle and all the rest of us. Hep her preach powerful up in Indiana and extend Your great army of prayer warriors. Give 'em all safe travelin', includin' the preachers and their wives. And make 'em all a blessin' to that camp. Bring 'em back safe with the glory of God on their lives to share with us. And, Lord, hep us take good care of these little-uns here. Hep Jim and Estelle not to worry about any of us, hep 'em forget things they've worked so hard for. Let 'em have a good rest from the farm, the cows, the fishin', and the timber. Keep us all prayin', Lord, for that great revival You're gonna send! Amen!"

Tears flowed as the six Tharp children lined up to be hugged and kissed by their mama and daddy. They were followed by the other children who wanted the same. Then came Henry and Oda, Jack and Linda, and finally Patsy. "I love y'all so much and feel so blessed to care for your precious children. Don't worry 'bout nothin'," Patsy said, as she kissed Estelle.

After Jim pulled the car onto the county road heading north, Jim asked, "Ladies, do you want to have breakfast in DeWitt or Stuttgart?" All three women thought they should wait until they reached Stuttgart, when it would be getting light.

They rode in silence for awhile until Martha asked, "Jim, if you go by Memphis as you said, do we not go through three states including Indiana?"

"Yes, after Arkansas comes Tennessee and Kentucky and then Indiana."

"Well, if you don't mind, tell us when you're almost to the Tennessee state line. As you continue to drive, I'll lead a prayer for God to call Christian believers in that state to become filled with the Spirit and begin praying for revival. Then, please do the same at the other two state lines; Estelle can pray for Kentucky, and Alma can take Indiana. Alright?" Everyone was in agreement, including Jim.

Jim pulled up to the hotel in Stuttgart where he and Estelle had spent their honeymoon fourteen years before. The fragrance of fresh coffee brewing and bacon cooking made them realize how hungry they were, and they all ordered a good breakfast. When it was served and the waitress had departed, Estelle asked Martha to offer thanks. When she had finished her prayer, she addressed Jim and Estelle in serious tones, saying, "I've never needed to ask a lot of favors from you two, because you've been so generous and thoughtful during the whole time I've been with you. But I am asking something of you on this trip. Before I left Indiana, I was given money for any expense I would incur on this mission. I still have most of that money left. So I beg you, please allow me to cover all automobile, restaurant, and lodging expenses on this trip!"

Jim was about to open his mouth to object, but he held his peace when he felt Estelle nudge his arm. "Sister Martha," she said, "God has blessed Jim and me financially, and it would be no hardship for us to cover everything, including your and mother's expenses. But I do sense you are speaking about this with real conviction." Turning to Jim, she continued, "So, honey, I think we should allow Sister Martha to do what she feels is God's will. It won't hurt us to let others do something for us."

"Oh, thank you, Jim and Estelle and Alma! I am blessed doing this, even though it is not my money. I've made a decision that pleases the Lord."

When they had finished breakfast and were settled in the car, Martha handed Jim two $100 bills. "No, Sister, not that much!" Jim protested.

"Yes, this money is for both going to Indiana and returning home."

"I doubt if we'll need this much," Jim said.

"Well, it won't hurt to have a little left. Your nice car might need to be serviced after this long trip."

Before leaving home, Jim had studied the map for a route around Indianapolis to connect to U.S. 31 that would take them to Westfield. He watched for the cutoff as they passed Bridgeport and were about to see the welcome sign to the capitol city. He found it, and as he turned on it, Estelle asked, "Don't we stay on 40 until we come to 31 in the heart of Indianapolis?"

"We could, but I've found a quicker way to 31."

When Jim turned the car onto 31, Martha said, "Well, if I remember correctly, we'll be in Westfield in about 30 minutes. And Alma, I want you to stay with me in my apartment. I think you'll be more comfortable there than you would be in the dorm. I've written ahead to Martha Boyden, whom you will remember is the girl Jim rescued. She wanted to study Greek when I came to the college, so she's returned to Westfield after graduating. I felt I needed someone in my apartment while I was gone, and she's been living there. She's a wonderful cook and housekeeper, and I don't know what I'd do without her. She'll have both of our bedrooms ready, and she'll sleep in the dorm while the camp is on. So, Alma, don't argue with me—just come as my guest, please!"

"Oh, thank ye, Sister Martha! I'll be glad to."

"And now, Jim and Estelle," Martha continued, "I know you stayed in the dorm the last time you were here. But I don't know how comfortable Jim feels around all that praying, testifying, and witnessing. And I'm not sure if you enjoyed the food over there. So here's what I insist on: just north of the traffic light in downtown Westfield, still on 31, is the Royal Inn, the only quality public housing establishment that I know of this side of Indianapolis. I want to pay for your lodging there. Adjacent to the Inn on the same side of the street is Mary's Café, a small, clean place to get breakfast and lunch. Please don't object to this offer; I want to cover the costs of your motel and food for as long as you will stay with us, even after the camp!"

"But, Sister Martha, ye've already done enough. Estelle and me can pay our own way while we're here, but thank ye."

"No, you won't, sir! I insist! I'm returning with almost all of the money I was given for my mission. Estelle, here's another $200 for your expenses while here. If any is left over, spend it on some books and materials you'll no doubt find in the bookstore at the college." She handed two more bills over the seat to Estelle, and Estelle received them with a smile.

"Thank ye, Sister!" Jim said.

"Home, sweet home!" Martha almost shouted, as Jim turned into the driveway to UBC. "Drive past the dorm, and turn right on the first street. Now, pull into the drive of that third house. That's my apartment on the first floor. A sweet couple from Kansas did live in the upper floor. I hope they are still with us."

Jim unloaded the luggage for Martha and Alma and carried it into the living room. As he set the two large cases down, a lovely young woman rushed to him and gave him a hug, saying, "Here's the wonderful man who saved me from tragedy!"

"Hello, Martha!" Jim said, patting her on the shoulder. "It's shore good to be welcomed by such a lovely young woman as we come back to Indiana." Then he turned to Sister Martha and said, "I'll get the rest of your items from the trunk now." When Jim told Estelle that Martha Boyden was inside, she got out of the car and went in, and gave her a hug.

Sister Martha said, "See what a wonderful housekeeper this young lady is?" Turning to the girl, she added, "It's so good to be home and have you here, darling!"

"Oh, I've been looking forward to seeing you again, Sister Martha. I'm also happy to see the Tharps and Alma again. I know you all are weary from that long two-day drive."

"No, we really aren't. Jim and Estelle have a very comfortable car. Last night we had a nice motel down in Kentucky and a good night's rest. I'd say if any one of us four is tired, it would have to be Jim. He did all the driving, and I think he's the best and safest driver I've ever ridden with."

As they prepared to return to their car, Jim and Estelle received hugs from all three women. "Now, you rest tonight," Sister Martha ordered. "Don't bother with us at all. Have some quiet time to yourselves. Oh, Estelle, I might want to call you up front at a particular point in my message tomorrow night—as part of my emphasis on our training. Please don't be embarrassed. I won't call on you to say anything. However, if the Lord puts something on your heart, don't think you will be interrupting if you express it."

Estelle nodded her approval. "Mother, tomorrow morning, Jim and I want you and Bernice to have breakfast with us at the café. Can I come for you at 8:00? We'll pick up Bernice wherever she is staying."

"Yes, that will be fine," Alma said.

Jim had no trouble finding the Royal Inn, and he pulled his car into the spacious drive and parking lot. "Now, how many nights are we stayin' here?" he asked Estelle, as she gave him one of the bills Martha had given her.

"Five nights," Estelle said, as Jim tried to decline the $100 bill.

"No, take it Jim, and I'll buy teaching and training supplies with the other $100."

The clerk said they still had a few vacancies and she could give them a nice room on the ground floor for the five nights they requested. "You don't have to pay for all five nights now, just pay each morning, please."

"No, I'd prefer to pay for all five nights now!"

"Well, thanks. With tax, that will be a total of $66.

Jim and Estelle were pleased with the room. "Oh, this is just as nice as the one we stayed in last night in Kentucky!" Sitting on the bed, she exclaimed, "And the mattress is firm, too!"

"Estelle, I saw the *Indianapolis Star* in the lobby. I'll go get a paper.

"While you read the *Star*, I'll lie down. Then later this afternoon, let's take a walk up and down that beautiful tree-lined sidewalk, okay?" Estelle asked.

"Yes, let's do. We ain't walked together for awhile," Jim said.

Estelle woke up the next morning while it was just turning light. She could hardly believe Jim was still sound asleep, breathing softly. She slipped out of bed, put on a robe, and went into the bathroom and combed her long hair. After putting on her slippers, she went to the lobby to pick up the newspaper. She drew two cups of coffee from the large urn and returned to their room. Jim stirred as she entered, saying, "My dear woman, where have you been? It must be sunup already!" He rolled out of bed, pulled on his trousers and shirt, and started putting on his shoes.

"No, it's 6:45, and it hasn't hurt you one bit to sleep all night without waking and get an extra hour or two of rest. Now, drink your coffee and read your paper. About 7:45, I'll drive down and get Mother and Bernice and we'll come back to have breakfast with you. You can read for as long as you wish."

Bernice was already at Sister Martha's place when Estelle drove up. The girl ran out to the car to hug her older half sister. "I've been hoping you and Jim would come up and bring Mama!"

Estelle could see that Bernice had matured both emotionally and physically. No doubt she had learned a great deal before graduating from the academy, and now she had finished her second year at Union Bible College.

When Alma came out, they went back to the motel to get Jim. When Estelle knocked on their hotel door, Jim was ready to go eat. Bernice had gotten out of the car to greet and hug Jim, and when he saw her, he said, "Now, don't ye look great, young lady!"

"Thank you, Jim. I'm ready for breakfast. Let's go and eat."

During breakfast, Bernice was excited to tell them about the things she was learning about the Bible. Also she was taking music under LaVaun Smith and learning to play the piano.

"Well, how 'bout the boys ye've met?" Jim asked, grinning.

"Now, Jim, I didn't come up here to study boys!"

"Yeah, but I'll bet they've been studyin' you. Do ye have a date about every night?"

"Nope. It's not allowed when you live at the dorm."

"Well, then, I wouldn't be surprised if ye find somewhere else to live," Jim teased.

Early on the Friday night of camp meeting, Jim and Estelle were getting ready for the service. "My, but ye look pretty tonight!" Jim exclaimed, as Estelle came out of the bathroom. She had styled her black hair up in a chignon, and she was wearing the new dress she had bought especially for tonight's occasion.

"Well, you look quite handsome yourself!" Estelle responded. "I like it when you put on a suit and tie."

"I'd rather not, but I knew ye would want me to."

"Now, that's my man, doing what pleases me."

By 6:30 on Friday evening, the UBC parking lot was filled, and Jim and Estelle had to park in the field nearby. A farmer had given Simeon Smith permission to use it if they had an overflow crowd. Inside the auditorium, Estelle and Jim were fortunate to find the row Martha had reserved for special guests. They were seated near an aisle so that Estelle could exit easily to make her way to the platform. Jim thought the auditorium was cool, considering that it was almost the middle of August. The lower level was packed, and all now entering were climbing the stairs to the balconies. An orchestra had begun to play "Holiness Unto the Lord." Drs. William Smith, Simeon Smith, Martha Honeycutt, and Paul Rees were taking their places on the platform. Martha smiled at Estelle and Jim and gestured to them with a small wave. They both waved back. A tall, young man stepped to the microphone and welcomed the large crowd and then led the congregation in the song the orchestra had been playing. Simeon welcomed the people and then called upon "our faithful Spirit-filled layman from Findlay, Ohio, Brother Boyden, to lead us in prayer." The same trio that had accompanied Simeon and

LaVaun to Nady several years ago sang a beautiful song about the love of God.

Dr. William Smith introduced, "Dr. Martha Honeycutt, who has spent the past year down in Arkansas training an army of prayer warriors for the last-days battles in spiritual warfare. Some of her recently recruited and trained warriors are with us here tonight, and I hope she introduces some of them. Many of you will recall Dr. Honeycutt's convicting challenge given right here a few years ago on a needed awakening in the Church of Jesus Christ across North America if we are to be prepared to meet the tidal wave of evil planned by the Antichrist to paralyze the people of God. We believe that tonight she comes prepared to report a partial awakening and some extensive preparations being made on the part of increasing numbers to enter the battles awaiting us. Please welcome Dr. Honeycutt as she comes." Estelle sensed in the applause that her own love and respect for this unusual teacher was shared by many others, and this pleased her.

"A few years ago, I spoke to you here on what I believe to be the Holy Spirit's most urgent call to the church in North America—the call to intercessory prayer. God's people need to stop playing church and religious games and become sanctified holy and filled with the Holy Spirit in order that they might hear that call and answer it in sacrificial, systematic, militant intercession! If we start praying in the Spirit, the Lord of hosts will move Heaven and earth in our times and bring our nation back to God.

"Now, on the counsel and commission of Dr. William Smith and others, most of whom are present here tonight, I have spent the last year in southeastern Arkansas beginning the work of recruiting and training men and women who will go into action against the kingdom of darkness with prevailing prayer! I wish we had here all 131 of those prayer warriors from Nady and DeWitt who stood at the altar of the DeWitt Friends Church about two weeks ago and pledged to pray a minimum of one hour daily in the power of the Holy Spirit for the great revival God wants to give!

"But we do have three of those committed prayer warriors with us here tonight. I want to ask Pastor Frank Fox, Pastor Homer Rich, and Estelle Tharp to join me here on the platform for a few minutes. As they come, I want you to know that they represent the beginning of a mighty, powerful, anointed army of prayer warriors across America whom God will use to revolutionize the Church of Jesus Christ and bring a sweeping revival of Holiness Evangelism to our country. These three people are not strangers to this crowd of people. These two pastors attend this camp nearly every year. And a few years ago, Estelle was sanctified at these altars. And, oh, what a powerful witness she has become in the community of Nady! She prays the will of God to pass in her own family. She witnesses and wins souls to the Lord Jesus consistently—her own children, and her neighbors, as well as strangers that she meets. God gives Estelle visions and revelations. Angels visit and minister to this dear woman. God speaks to her in dreams. She is seeing God perform miracles more that anyone else that I know. She lives much like the miracle-working apostles that we read about in the book of Acts! Now, I've had the privilege of teaching spiritual warfare and prevailing prayer to several hundred students, but the months I spent in private sessions with this sister represent the most exciting period in all my 30 years of teaching!

"Thank you, Pastors Fox and Rich and Estelle! Now as they return to their seats, please express your appreciation for these exemplary soldiers whom we hope to see multiplied in Arkansas, Indiana, Ohio, and all over this nation!" The crowd not only clapped loud and long, but hundreds stood in appreciation for what they felt was the beginning of something significant. At long last, they were going to see something besides an orderly church service every Sunday morning. Perhaps dead churches would live again. Maybe there would come another historic spiritual awakening.

Martha began with her scriptural text from the latter part of Ephesians 5:14: **Wake up, O sleeper, rise from the dead, and Christ will shine on you**. "So many of God's children have lost the glow," she began. "Most North American evangelicals are getting so accustomed to grieving the Holy Spirit that they are losing the image of Christ, losing the shine of His glory, and taking on the likeness of this world. What we need is a turnaround, a period of repentance, a turning from our self-worship in the forms of materialistic idolatry and moral compromise. Before we can recruit, train, and refine an army of spiritual warriors here in America, we must have the kind of awakening that brings us to realize our deadness, our unreadiness, and our desperate need for a new touch of

God on our minds, hearts, and spirits. We must be brought to the light. The apostle has told us in our Scripture read tonight, **it is the light that makes everything visible**. Some of you here tonight cannot stand the test when you come under the light of God's searching presence and begin to see what He sees. Until you come under the white heat of His omniscient gaze, you will remain blind to your own needs and deceived about your condition of unpreparedness. Right here in Hamilton County, Indiana, may God raise up His armies of praying men and women who will fast and pray until the light of the Spirit's searching presence convicts us of our shallow, cheap, religious pretensions! May we wait before the Lord for His cleansing, sanctifying power and allow His Spirit to wring the truth from our hearts and lips in confession as we tarry before Him in humility, repentance, supplication, and prayer and see His glory in the kind of revival He longs to give us!

"My dear people, I'm convinced that many attending this camp meeting need the kind of confrontation with God that the prophet Isaiah experienced. Hear it from his own lips: **In the year that King Uzziah died, I saw the Lord seated on a throne, high and exalted, and the train of his robe filled the temple. Above him were seraphs, each with six wings: with two wings they covered their faces, with two they covered their feet, and with two they were flying. And they were calling to one another: 'Holy, holy, holy, is the Lord Almighty, the whole earth is full of his glory.' At the sound of their voices the doorposts and thresholds shook and the temple was filled with smoke. 'Woe to me!' I cried. 'I am ruined! For I am a man of unclean lips, and I live among a people of unclean lips, and my eyes have seen the King, the Lord Almighty.' Then one of the seraphs flew to me with a live coal in his hand, which he had taken with tongs from the altar. With it he touched my mouth and said, 'See, this has touched your lips; your guilt is taken away and your sin atoned for.' Then I heard the voice of the Lord saying, 'Whom shall I send? And who will go for us?' And I said, 'Here am I, Send me!' He said, 'Go and tell this people...'**

"I must tell us here tonight what God is saying to me to tell His church at this critical hour. *He is putting on my heart to sound the Spirit's most urgent call at this hour—the call to sacrificial, bold, militant intercession.* We must pray for the lukewarm, indifferent, preoccupied people who call themselves followers of Jesus Christ. I may sound like an alarmist and an extremist, but I must tell you that unless there is an awakening in *our times*, the American church and the American nation will tragically miss their divinely appointed destinies. And we shall give an account at the Judgment Seat of Christ. But I believe some of us will face a kind of judgment even before that awesome time when we shall all stand before Jesus Christ as our Judge. God calls His people to proclaim His Word and will to every generation. We have failed to proclaim the Word of God in America, and we evangelicals have been more concerned about earning a living than surrendering to the Lordship of Jesus Christ. Therefore, we have not seen a full-scale revival in this country since the phenomenal Laymen's Prayer Revival of 1858-1860 just before the Civil War. Consequently, our culture reveals its moral sickness and spiritual apostasy. A gracious God will still reach us with His mercy and miracles if we will catch the vision with Isaiah and confess our undoneness. Then we can experience His forgiveness and cleansing and surrender to Christ's Lordship!

"What does this mean? First, it means *repentance*. Now, we know that sinners—murderers, liars, thieves, and whoremongers—must repent. But professing Christians who lose their devotion to Christ, turn to materialistic idolatry, hold grudges, resent others, fail to forgive, fail to practice what they preach, or refuse to go on to a life of holiness and power—these kinds of religious sinners must also repent!

"When we repent and then ask for a new filling of the Holy Spirit to enable us to *pray, worship, witness, obey, and become living sacrifices*, then we are ready to answer the call that Isaiah answered: **'Here am I, Lord; send me!'** *Send me* to a meaningful *life of prayer* that will become for me the lifestyle of *a living sacrifice. Send me* to the secret closet daily to open my heart, mind, and soul to God and to confess to Him every act of disobedience, all acts and attitudes that have grieved the Holy Spirit, and every sin of commission and omission. Let me not stop until I have fully accepted God's forgiveness and cleansing. *Send me on to asking for a fresh filling of the Holy Spirit.* And then *send me* out to live in the continual consciousness of Christ's presence and power.

"Dear people, I am obeying the Holy Spirit in preaching repentance to God's people here tonight. So I shall continue to mind Him in closing this service by calling on those to whom He is speaking to come publicly and unashamedly to call upon His name in confessing all the sins He is convicting you of. And know ahead of time what this must lead to: *You must answer the call to become a soldier in God's armies.* You must learn how to put on the whole armor of God, how to prevail with Him for the revival He longs to give, how to weep before Him for the souls of men, and how to **wrestle against principalities, against the powers, against the world rulers of this present darkness, against the hosts of wicked spirits in the heavenlies**.

"Some of you have almost no kind of prayer life. Some of you have never won another soul to Jesus Christ in all of your years as a professing Christian. Some of you know nothing of sacrificial giving—even complaining over tithing and then falling short, stealing from God. Some of you have an attitude of unforgiveness; you don't even love your fellow Christians, let alone lost souls living next door. Some of you are a poor example of the Christian faith; it's no wonder those who know you want nothing to do with the religion you claim to have or the church that you attend.

"You need to repent!"

Martha then gave the sign to the song leader to commence the invitation. She urged those to whom God was speaking to move out of their seats and make things right with God, to come clean, and not stop until they had a new filling of the Spirit. Estelle was greatly moved at the hunger demonstrated as scores left their seats and tearfully knelt and began calling upon the Lord in open confession. The rising roar of repentance from the hearts and lips of God's people, she felt, must have been pleasing in God's ears. She felt her own heart aching more deeply for the revival so desperately needed everywhere, especially on the prairies and down in the bottoms of Arkansas County. She felt led to join Martha, several pastors, Dr. Smith, and Dr. Rees at the altars as they prayed with penitent, seeking believers for the renewing, cleansing, and filling of the Holy Spirit. By the time most of the seekers were standing with shining faces and free spirits, Estelle felt a new hope sweep over her that true revival was on its way in Indiana, down in Arkansas County, and all over the nation!

The second service became an amazing departure from the normal order in the annual camp services. Following a lively song service and a powerful prayer by a local pastor, Dr. Smith approached the lectern and, wiping tears, said, "Dear friends, we are in the presence of God here tonight. Last night, we witnessed a mighty breakthrough to spiritual victory in the lives of nearly 200 men and women of God! Now, I feel the Lord would have us hear what God is doing in the lives of those who have found a new anointing. If Dr. Honeycutt and those who plan to sing here tonight will forgive me, I'm asking our technicians to come and set out two more microphones on stands here in front on the floor level. Then I believe the Spirit will lead dozens of you to get in line to speak into these microphones and tell us what the Lord is doing in your hearts and what He is speaking to you about. This camp meeting will undoubtedly result in hundreds of people from here in Indiana, over in Ohio and Pennsylvania, out in the Midwestern states, and down in Arkansas and in other places in the south *joining the armies of God for prevailing prayer for the kind of revival we so desperately need.*"

The two technicians quickly set up the microphones. Right away, lines formed at the microphones and excited witnessing began. One would tell with tears and shouts what had happened the night before and then return to his seat while the crowd shifted their attention to a witness at the microphone on the other side. An hour passed while the glory of the Lord settled on the people as they rejoiced with "Amens" and other expressions all over the building. More than 100 had reported their experiences and newly-formed convictions for holy living and sacrificial praying. Dr. Smith rose again to ask Dr. Honeycutt to address the congregation with an admonition to those God had spoken to as they listened to their fellow Christians.

Dr. Honeycutt was quickly on her feet and expressed joy over what the Lord was doing and would continue to do as others sensed their need. She nodded to the singers to begin. A repeat of the night before was seen in the response. Jim and Estelle left the service hearing amazing expressions about what God was doing.

"I reckon that was some service, wasn't it?" Jim asked, as he locked the car and they made their way into their motel room.

"Oh, darling, it really was! I'm so glad we came! What Sister Martha has taught me is being rekindled and deepened as I see what has happened these last two nights. Honey, we are going to see God move all over this country! Even down in Arkansas County!"

"Maybe so," Jim said. "I guess ye can see and feel things that I can't. But I do know that some kind of awesome power was at work on those people tonight, and I know it must be encouragin' to ye."

Very few changes came in the order of services all week until the closing Sunday. Martha felt that more than a thousand people were ready for a public declaration of their intention to join the armies of God. So in both services she was gratified to see her feelings confirmed. The camp would close with hundreds returning to their churches to request that their pastors call Dr. Martha Honeycutt to sound the same call to their communities as they had heard in Westfield, Indiana.

Martha and a team of singers and musicians would spend the next year and a half covering 30 states calling believers to repentance, to the fullness of the Spirit to live in holiness and power, and to enlist in the armies of God for Spirit-anointed prayer.

After delivering Alma to her house down at Nady, Jim and Estelle returned to their home. The children were playing in the front yard; when they saw their parents' car pulling up to the front gate, they started jumping up and down with joy. Before Jim could open the gate and drive into the yard, they ran toward their parents to meet them. Patsy stood on the porch smiling at the beautiful scene. *Oh, how they love one another! Where would I be today if I had been raised by parents like Jim and Estelle? Thank God, He led me to them!*

After everyone had been hugged and kissed, they all went into the house. "Patsy, you've got this house so clean that it's shining! And the children all look clean and happy. Honey, I love you," Estelle said as she rushed across the living room and hugged her young friend and housekeeper. "The Lord sent you to us."

"Yes'm, and the Lord sent y'all to me, too! I have no idea what would've happened to me if y'all hadn't took me and Punkin in like ye did."

Estelle spent nearly an hour giving presents to all her children and Patsy. She laid out the gifts she would give Jack and Linda and their three, Birdie and Susie and their three, and George and BettyLee and their four. Then she, Patsy, and Jeanette took a load of presents over to Henry and Oda and their children.

As darkness began falling, Jim was still at the barn with the stock. He spent extra time with Star and Buck, who seemed especially glad to see their master. For many years, they had been faithful companions and most useful in helping Jim track down and capture outlaws in his work as special deputy to the sheriff. Both animals were aging and would not be able to continue much longer in that role. A sad thought crossed Jim's mind when he realized he couldn't have them with him much longer. Although Jim hated to part with them, at Estelle's suggestion he decided it would be best for those two animals if they could eventually live out the remainder of their lives on Uncle Henry Purdy's farm. Estelle's palomino, Ella, had already died from old age and Prince was slowing down, so Jim knew he needed to begin looking for two young horses.

By the time Patsy had the table set and all the food on, Jim came in and joined the family at the table. Estelle gave thanks for the good trip, a great camp meeting, multitudes added to the armies of God, the joy of being home with the children and Patsy, and the coming great awakening.

9   *"This Present Darkness"*

Throughout 1939 and 1940, Jim and Estelle read the *Gazette* daily and listened regularly to their favorite news commentators—Gabriel Heatter, H. V. Kaltenborn, and Walter Winchell—and realized that dark clouds were gathering over the world. What Martha Honeycutt had prophesied about Adolph Hitler was coming true. A few years before he had denounced the disarmament clauses in the Versailles Treaty and later entered the Rhineland. Nobody did anything to resist him. Italy, an ally of Germany, went to war with Ethiopia. Emperor Haile Selassie went into exile, and the country was annexed to Italy. Hitler and Mussolini then established the Rome-Berlin Axis. About the same time, General Franco began a civil war in Spain. Japan was aggressively engaged in an undeclared war with China.

In all of these evil portents of global conflict, the most sinister seemed to be the rise of Adolph Hitler. The grip of that uneducated maniac over the German people, with their long tradition of culture and decency, was a mystery that the most brilliant statesmen could not explain. Perhaps Dr. Honeycutt came closest when she described him as "demonically inspired."

By midsummer the stage had been set by Hitler and his top generals for conquest throughout Europe's heartland. He had invaded Austria early in 1938, and since he met no opposition, his next victim was Czechoslovakia. Neville Chamberlain, the British Prime Minister, had visited Hitler three times in September 1938. Completely deceived by the German leader, he had returned to England announcing "peace in our time." Hitler would also turn against Russia and France with whom he had made agreements.

While all the fires were being kindled in Europe, Asia, and South America, the majority of Americans were holding to the ideal of neutrality. Of course, they hoped for the defeat of Hitler and his satellites, but they wanted to keep out of war even more. President

Roosevelt and Congress would later relent somewhat in passing the Lend-Lease Act in 1941, which allowed the President to "sell, transfer, exchange, lease, or lend any defense articles to the government of any country whose defense the President deems vital to the defense of the U.S.A." The act made the U.S. the "arsenal of democracy," the President said. Under its provision, America not only provided the enemies of the Axis with $50 billion in arms, food, and services, but also geared her own production to war needs and officially abandoned any pretense at neutrality.

Things moved swiftly after the passing of the Lend-Lease bill. The U.S. seized all Axis shipping in American ports. After the sinking of an American freighter came a proclamation of an "unlimited national emergency." All Axis assets were frozen and all consulates closed.

President Roosevelt and Prime Minister Churchill would later meet in Newfoundland and draw up the Atlantic Charter which proclaimed "The Four Freedoms." In the coming months, Congress passed the first peacetime conscription in its history, providing for registration of all men between the ages of 21 and 35 and the induction into the armed forces of 800,000 draftees.

After reading the *Gazette* late one evening in 1940, Estelle turned to Jim, who was knitting a new net, and said, "Honey, Congress has passed a law that all men in this country between the ages of 21 and 35 must register to be summoned for physical examination to see if they are able to train for combat service. The President wants a million men in all the branches of service—the Army, Navy, Marines, and Coast Guard. He'll get 800,000 by drafting them, and he's hoping for 200,000 volunteers."

Estelle paused, giving Jim time to consider what she had told him. Then she said, "Sweetheart, you are 34, and this means you'll have to register. The article here says that once the U.S. is actually in war, the ages will change to 18 through 38 or maybe 40. Oh, I do hope you don't have to go to war!"

"Well, I ain't no better than Jack and Birdie. I reckon that age range don't catch Henry, George, Homer, and Ross, at least for now," Jim said. "Yeah, thangs are in a mess over there, so I'm not surprised that we can't stay out of the heat of war any longer. Well, if I have to go,

I'd shore like them to let me take my guns, but I don't reckon they will. I'd really like to take a crack at that devil, Hitler! I'd do more than put a hole in his ear!"

"Now, honey, don't you think the sheriff would be willing to appeal to the powers that be to get you exempt, because he needs you here as his special deputy?"

"He won't if I have anythang to say about it," Jim said with firmness.

"Don't tell me that you want to go to war!"

"I don't really want to, but I'm not gonna shirk my duty."

"Please! Just talk it over with Lloyd before you decide."

"Naw, I know what he'll say, but he ain't the one to decide. But I ain't been drafted yet."

"No, but you will be," Estelle said with concern.

While Estelle and Patsy were still preparing breakfast the next morning, Jim went out to saddle his young horse, who nuzzled him and snorted his welcome several times. He had been fortunate to find a frisky, black gelding and a spry, attractive buckskin that either Estelle or Jake could ride. After a few days of riding the black gelding, he decided to name him Flash.

Today Jim had a number of things on his mind—he'd need to check the cattle, find out from Oda where the men were seining that day and check on them, see about the cotton crop, and have a look at the orchard. Jim called to Jake, who was taking trash out for his mother, "Hey, son, how about saddlin' the buckskin and ridin' down with me to check on the cattle after breakfast?"

"Yeah, Dad! I'd like that. I think Mama and Patsy have breakfast ready," the boy said.

The women served pancakes, scrambled eggs, and bacon. Patsy poured coffee for the three adults and then went to get the other children up, knowing that their parents wanted them all at the breakfast table.

When Jim entered the kitchen, he saw Estelle looking at the children with pride. Turning to him she asked, "What's on for today?"

"Jake's gonna ride with me to check the cattle, and then we'll ride on down to see Ross. Then I'll find out from Oda where the men are seinin'. I'll check on the cotton and the orchard. This afternoon I'll go down to either Garland or Johnson Lake or wherever George and Henry and the men are at work to see how they're doin' and what they need. But, tomorrow let's go up and see Papa and Mama and Hollis and Jenny."

Flash seemed to be determined to lead the way, but Jim motioned to Jake to come alongside with the buckskin. He felt a pride in seeing how his son took control of the hesitant pony and spurred the animal on alongside the black. The boy was learning to make sure the animal he rode knew who was in charge.

When the new corrals, chutes, and gates were in sight, Jim felt grateful for the progress being made in his cattle business. Riding their way slowly through the grazing herd, Jim could not find a single animal that looked gaunt or sickly. After circling the inner bunches and examining the entire herd, Jim said, "They're lookin' good, Jake!"

Ross wanted to know how the camp meeting went, and what progress had been made in recruiting prayer warriors in God's armies. Jim answered, "Well, Ross, ye'll get a better readout on that when ye talk to Estelle. But I will say there was a spirit on that camp meetin' like I ain't never felt in any other meetin'. This ole sinner shore felt somethin' up there!"

After letting the brief report sink in, Ross finally said, "As you know, if you've had time to keep up with the news, things are lookin' bad in the world. But some good news is that we're gonna get great prices for our cattle this year, and we can start sellin' next week. They'll come to our pens and buy either by the head here or by the pound at their scales. They'll come any weekend in September that we want 'em to or twice in October. Mine are in good shape, and yours are the same from what I've seen. Wanta sell next week?"

"Might as well; but should we sell by the head or by the pound?"

"Well, why don't we have 'em look over our cattle and make an offer by the head? If we then decide we might do better to sell by the pound, we'll ask how much they will pay. If we agree on the price, we'll follow them to the scales. They'll figger the total amount, and then we'll know which offer to accept.

"Jake, you look good on that buckskin. I reckon you're gonna make a fine cowboy," Ross said, admiring the tall lad.

Jake just grinned and said, "I do enjoy ridin' this horse. And I like to work the cattle with you fellows."

On their ride back to the house, Jim asked his son, "Wanta help us with the roundup on Thursday?"

"I sure do!"

"With Ross and Jack and the two of us, we should have enough help. We'll probably do our cattle first, and then we'll help Ross. I think we oughta finish early Thursday afternoon. When we get the cattle sold on Friday, how about goin' quail huntin' with me?"

"Dad, I'd sure like to go, but I've never shot a quail. I know I can kill a squirrel sitting still, but I'll embarrass you if I miss those quails. I know you never miss."

"Ye ain't never gonna learn to shoot a flyin' bird 'less ye're willin' to try. I ain't gonna razz ye none; if ye miss, ye miss. So plan to go with me. I think I've got both dogs, Better and Best, ready to point 'em and retrieve 'em for us," Jim said.

"I'd like to go, Dad!"

"Good! We'll have us a good time!"

The roundup was enjoyable for all, and Jim was especially pleased, because he was able to sell the largest number of steers of any year since he had been in the cattle business. Thursday morning, he and Ross both decided to accept the buyers' offer by the head, receiving the best price per head in all their years of selling cattle.

Not having to spend the rest of the day on the road with the cattle buyers, Jim and Jake had an enjoyable quail hunt that afternoon. They stayed on Jim's property, but worked out of range of the grazing herd of cattle. Right away Better went down on point. When Jim told Jake this would be his shot, he also added some instructions. "If the bird flies away from ye, put the bead right on him; then if the bird is still risin', raise it an inch or two and pull the trigger without jerkin' the gun. But if the bird is flyin' to yore right or left, lead him at what looks about five or six inches and, without jerkin', pull the trigger."

Jake nodded agreement, but Jim knew he was tense.

"Flush!" Jim told the dog. Better lunged, and up came the bird in a frightening flutter. Jake already had his gun pointed. Seeing the bird going to his right, he led it as his dad had instructed and then fired. He had hesitated a little too long, however, and the bird flew on.

"Shucks!" Jake said.

"Don't worry about it, son. That's the way it went for me on my first quail shot. Two thangs went wrong for ye. First ye waited too long to shoot. Second, I think ye shot too far ahead of the bird. Ye'll do better next time. Don't be discouraged."

The next action came on the flush of a whole covey. Jim killed three birds as fast as he could shoot. With his single barrel, Jake missed again.

"Jake, yer doin' one thing right, and that's very important—yer holdin' steady when ye shoot, no jerkin'. I was so busy with that covey gettin' my three shots in that I couldn't watch ye. But I'd bet money that when Best starts pointin' singles now for awhile from that scattered covey, yore next shot will be a kill!"

"I sure hope so, Dad!"

Best soon came down on a point, and Jim said, "Walk that way a few steps, for I think the bird will rise into the wind and keep risin' to fly for cover way over yonder. I think ye'll figger out just how far to lead 'im on his rise. Kill 'im while he's still risin', for once he levels off he'll fly so fast that he'll soon be out of shootin' range."

"Flush!" Jim called to Best. At the lunge, the bird rose so close to the dog that it barely escaped the dog's leap in the air to grab it by the tail. Just as Jim had predicted, Jake fired, and the bird fell, prompting Best to quickly retrieve it and return it to Jake as the shooter.

"Now, son, take the bird from Best's mouth rather tenderly, then pat the dog and talk to him. He'll know ye're pleased with his work. Did you notice that he didn't bring the bird to me? Cuz he's aware of who killed the bird!"

"Dad, I'm amazed at that! He's your dog, but I guess you trained him that way."

"I did. But I need to help Best with a few other things."

Before sundown, the hunt ended with Jim killing his limit of ten birds and Jake killing four. Jim was sincere in bragging on his son, saying, "Ye did good, Jake! On my first hunt I killed only one, but shot five times. I wasn't as steady in my shootin' as y'are. I predict that when ye learn how to lead yer bird and let it fly into the shot, ye'll get to where ye don't miss either. I think ye already know when a bird is out of gun range, and that's important. There's no need to waste a shot, and we certainly don't wanta cripple a bird with a shot that wasn't fired within killin' range. In my estimation, ye'll make a good quail hunter. This winter, we'll see how well ye do shootin' those big fat mallards out of a duck blind. I'll teach ye how to call 'em down, too.

"We'll do a turkey hunt next spring and let ye learn how to call a gobbler right up to yer hidin' place. But ye'll learn that the turkey is the easiest creature in the field to scare off; they can see farther and hear better than any other thang we'll ever hunt. Deer are gettin' more plentiful now, so we'll soon have a deer season. This area is becomin' a paradise for hunters. I guess it's time to try to talk Mama into our makin' the cabin into a guest house for hunters."

One November evening after darkness had fallen, Jim returned from scouting out trapping sites to find Estelle and Patsy worried about him; he was usually home before dark. That day he had decided to take Star, rather than Flash, but he left Buck at home. He explained that he had been fired on while crossing Deep Bayou and that the bullet came very close. "I can't figure out who would wait so late to waylay me if they wanted to kill me."

Estelle reached for him and drew him to her. "Oh, sweetheart! I'm so thankful you are safe! You know there are people in those bottoms who'd like to kill you. So please promise me you'll be more careful!"

"Well, I watch Star close when I'm unable to see the landscape. He gave no snort nor any movement of his ears that signaled trouble. I guess I've jes' gotta face it; Star may be gettin' too old to do the job. I only know the direction the shot came from, and I can guess the clump of trees where he was hid. But I'll have to visit the site in daylight to see if I can find the empty shell. All I know is that the weapon was a high-powered rifle. But it's not the end of the matter—you can count on that. Tomorrow I'll ride Flash and take Buck along to check out the site.

Just before sunrise the next morning, Jim gave a wide berth to the clump of trees from which he was quite sure his would-be killer had fired at him the night before. He slowed Flash's gait and called to Buck to sneak. He didn't think the man was still around, but he had learned that being sure was the safest policy. Neither Buck nor Flash gave any indication of anyone being there. Among a stand of oaks, Jim waited for the sun to rise. Since it was a clear, quiet morning, Jim would be able to hear a footfall at 50 yards or the snap of a twig even farther. A few minutes after the woods were lighted with the rising sun, Jim ground-reined Flash, took his rifle and Buck, and eased slowly toward the clump of trees, stopping often to listen. It was easy to see that whoever had stomped around for awhile in this setting had been chewing tobacco. Jim could see several reddish brown leaves splattered with spittle. He picked up a tightly-wadded piece of paper and found it to be the wrapping for a Brown Mule block of chewing tobacco. By raking leaves back with his boot, Jim found a .30-.30 shell casing and pocketed it. Discovering an oversized-boot track, Jim was quite sure it was a western boot. Studying the tracks, he was able to discern that the tracks went in a southeastward direction; Buck soon picked up the trail confirming the continued course. After following the boot tracks for about 200 yards, Jim saw evidence that his would-be ambusher had mounted a horse and headed east.

"Stay!" Jim told Buck. He went back and mounted Flash, and returned, letting Buck lead the trail, which soon angled north toward the Mouth of Wild Goose. Jim knew of a houseboat at the Mouth, just a stone's throw from White River. Charlie Ade, the owner and builder of the boat, had been a friend of Jim's. After Charlie died, it was not unusual for people to occupy the old boat-shack from time to time. Before reaching the heavy timber near the Mouth, Flash snorted softly. Jim looked ahead of them and could make out a corral containing two horses. Buck tracked the suspect right up to the corral. Jim studied the two ponies, one a roan and the other a sorrel, and could find no brands. He smelled smoke and then spotted a tent near the old hut that was built on the water-soaked logs in the Mouth. He dismounted, left Flash in the cover of the tall brush, and motioned for Buck to sneak slowly. Buck stopped every time Jim did; no sounds were heard. Fortunately, both Buck and his master were dead still and waiting when a man appeared from around the tent and went inside. The man carried a rifle, and he wore boots with his trouser legs tucked in them. Had he been on the other side of the tent by the fire watching the river? Was he expecting company? Jim realized that many times he had depended on inner hunches and unproven theories to determine a course of action. He believed the man who had just entered that tent was the one who had tried to kill him. But before any showdown, he needed to be more certain than he was now. With no one in sight, Jim got behind a good-sized sycamore and called to Buck, "Bark!"

Buck's three loud barks brought the man back through the opening in the tent, where he froze, seeing the dog standing and bristling. The man was wearing a mackinaw and a western hat, an Open Road Stetson much like the one Jim wore. In fact, Jim figured the man to be about his own age and height. He stood still watching for any move or sound from Buck that would indicate he needed to level his rifle on the man or go for his pistol. The man pulled a package of tobacco from his coat pocket and bit off a big chaw. He continued to stand and gaze at the dog, working the fresh tobacco in his mouth. Soon he spat a mouthful toward the dog and began walking toward him, mumbling something Jim couldn't make out. Buck, not hearing any direction from his master, began snarling low and inching toward the stranger. When the man and the dog were only about ten steps apart, the man stopped and started to pull his pistol.

"Hold it!" Jim called, as he stepped out from behind the tree. "Stay, Buck!" The dog quieted and sat, watching the stranger and listening for orders from his master. With the man's hand still on the handle of his pistol, Jim continued, "Mister, ye go ahead and pull that gun and ye're a dead man. I'm comin' closer to look ye over good and to find out why ye tried to kill me while I was crossin' Deep Bayou last night." With his eyes on the man, Jim walked straight toward him and stopped even with Buck. "Now, I want ye to know that my name is Jim Tharp, special deputy to the sheriff of Arkansas County. I order ye to brace yerself against the low limb of that tree near ye there and lift yore right foot up and hold it there a minute for me to examine." The man obeyed Jim's order, all the while keeping his hand on his gun handle.

"What the hell is this all about?" the man protested.

"It's about identifyin' my would-be killer! And if ye don't do what I tell ye, I'll arrest ye here and now and take ye in for further questionin'." Seeing the suspect hesitate a few seconds, Jim said, "Or maybe I'll have to kill ye." The man reached back for the limb and started lifting his right foot. Jim walked on up to the man, calling to Buck, "Come!" Jim examined the western boot with the horizontal bars on the sole, and he judged the heel to be of standard height.

"Put yore foot down," Jim said. As he did so, Jim watched him move his hand again toward his pistol. Jim fired, blowing the pistol out of his hand and seeing parts of the damaged gun flying to the ground. Whether the man would have pulled the gun or not did not matter to Jim. He was convinced that this was the man who had tried to kill him, so it was time to make it a serious case. "Hand me yore rifle!" he ordered. Jim took the gun from trembling hands. At first glance, he saw that it was a .30-.30 Remington. He pulled the empty casing from his pocket and said, "Here's what's left outa yore shot at me last night. I'm takin' ye in. Turn around and put yore hands behind ye so I can put the cuffs on ye." The man obeyed, and Jim snapped the cuffs. "Alright, are those two horses yonder in the corral yers?"

"The roan is."

"Who owns the other one?"

"My brother. He caught a train to McGhee last night, and he's supposed to come back in a couple of days."

"Who else is in the tent there?"

"Nobody."

"Where's yore saddle?"

"Inside the tent."

"Then come with me to the tent. We'll get yore saddle and then yore horse, and we'll ride out. I'm takin' ye to the DeWitt jail. But before we go, tell me why ye want to kill me!" Jim ordered.

"I didn't … I don't wanta kill ye!" he said.

"Now that may be the first lie ye've told me this mornin'! I know ye took a shot at me as I was crossin' Deep Bayou last night. This mornin' I examined yore hidin' place and found this spent shell, yore tobacco splatterin's, and yore boot prints. And my dog trailed ye right to that corral over there. Come on; I'll unsnap yore cuffs and ye can do yer own saddlin'. Hurry, and don't make a wrong move or ye won't make it into the saddle." Free of the cuffs, the man swiftly bridled and saddled his horse without a questionable move. "Before we leave, go put out some extra oats and water for that sorrel."

Three hundred yards before arriving at his place, Jim told his prisoner to dismount. "I'll tie ye to that tree over there and take yore horse with me to my barn. I'll return to ye in about 45 minutes. Yore horse will be okay with me until after yore trial. When ye go to prison, ye can tell me or the sheriff what ye want done with the roan."

On the way to DeWitt, Jim said to the securely chained man, "I'd still like to know why ye want to kill me. I reckon they'll get it out of ye during the interrogation, but I'm curious to know, myself." The prisoner was silent, so Jim let him be. In town, the sheriff listened as Jim described what happened the night before and then what took place at the Mouth of Wild Goose that morning.

"Good job, Jim!" Lloyd said. "Let's go out and get the would-be murderer. I'll bring him in for questioning while you are here, and then we'll make our charges." The prisoner was not as sullen with Lloyd as he had been with Jim. He told them his name was "Dan Haskins from Lake Village, Arkansas. I been doin' some fishin' and huntin' and cuttin' logs fer the mill down at Watson. Figgered there'd be a good place to trap this winter around the Mouth of the Goose."

"But, Dan, why do you wanta kill Jim Tharp? Has Jim killed, wounded, or arrested someone you know and you're mad at him?" Lloyd could not get an answer, so he asked him, "Will you admit that you want to kill Jim?" When the silence became ridiculous, Lloyd continued, "Will you even admit that you shot at him last night?"

"I reckon I might as well confess that I shot at him, but I shore didn't kill him, did I?"

"No, but you'll be in jail until there's a trial, and I'm quite sure you're gonna serve time, mister. Jim, I'm gonna jail this man, and then we'll go have a bite of supper before you leave town."

Jim went on over to the restaurant and was having a conversation with the owner, Mrs. Freeman, when Lloyd arrived. When she asked if they wanted "their usual," both men nodded, knowing they would get a delicious steak cooked medium well, along with a baked potato, a crisp tossed salad, and hot coffee.

"Well, Jim, I finally got that joker talkin'. He coughed up the name of the one who promised him $1,000 to take you out."

"I guess I ain't worth all that much, huh?"

"I imagine a thousand bucks is a lotta money fer that guy."

"Do you think he'll say that to a court?"

"It looks that way. I've got him pretty scared, and I think I've convinced him it's the only way to stay outa the electric chair. But then, he ain't seen a lawyer yet."

Both men enjoyed their supper, and Jim wondered out loud, "How do we get to this Jackson who's behind all this—the big Texas oilman, of course!"

"Yeah, but findin' proof is somethin' else. Reckon we'll visit ole Barney agin."

On his way home, Jim reflected on how well Buck had performed in helping him apprehend his would-be killer. But he realized that both Star and Buck were well past the normal age of being able to do the things he had been requiring of them. *I think Estelle has the right idea—I must talk with Uncle Henry and see if he is willing to take care of them through their remaining years.*

The very next day found the sheriff and Jim sitting across the table from Barney in his Hole at the White River Bridge. "I figgered the day would come when you two would be here again to learn what I know. Yeah, fellers, y'all oughta been here a few weeks ago when a big fancy streamlined boat that looked like it might belong out on the Atlantic or down on the Gulf pulled up out there. This fancy highroller stepped out and walked in here like he owned all of this country. I pegged him right away as the oilman Jackson. But, course he didn't interduce hisself. Jes' stretched, preened, and highbrowed all the time he drunk his beer, and he ast about some fellers I ain't never heard of. Then he walked down the river a ways. He come back and ast iffen I thought he'd be able to navigate his boat off the river to the Mouth of Wild Goose. I told him I reckon he could if he stayed in the middle of the channel all the way, but I couldn't be sure he could turn his boat around there in the Mouth. He'd probably need to run in reverse all the way back to the river. He said that'd be no problem. He ordered a steak dinner, paid for it, and left."

"Did he go upriver or down?" Lloyd asked.

"Up."

"Thanks, Barney! As always, you've been helpful," Lloyd said.

After Lloyd paid their bill, Jim asked, "Barney, I don't reckon ye've seen a guy about my size around here, have ye? He keeps a big chaw of tobacco in his mouth most of the time."

"Yeah, a guy 'bout yore size that chews tobacco pitched a tent out back here for awhile; a few days ago, him and another guy loaded their tent and left."

"Did you hear their names?" Lloyd asked.

"One of them called the other Puck. I never heard the name of the one that looked about Jim's size."

Lloyd cranked the engine and headed the craft upriver. "I guess we know who paid off yore would-be killer. I'll get the Pulaski County sheriff in on this, and we'll see what we can do about Mr. Highroller, the oilman. I'm sure the sheriff will put a tail on Jackson. If we can get our jailbird to talk on the stand, we might be able to put Jackson away for another few years. That'll make two Jacksons behind bars."

"Well, I hope so, but that Texas oilman might own about as many politicians and judges as he does oil wells. I wouldn't be surprised if he wouldn't try to pay off the jurors, too."

Before Jim left town, Lloyd reminded him that he'd need to be careful while out anywhere, especially in the bottoms. He'd let Jim know when the trial for Haskins would come off.

Jay Reddon drove into Jim's place on a warm Sunday afternoon. "Where can I find Henry Tharp?" he asked Patsy, who had just come in from a walk down to the orchard. The way the man looked at her made the young woman uneasy.

"Over in his tent, right around there, I guess," Patsy said, as she started up the steps to see Estelle.

Inside she called, "Miz Estelle!"

"Here in the kitchen, honey. What's wrong?"

"Maybe nothin'. Some feller just drove up out there and asked for Mr. Henry. But it's the way he looked at me that made me nervous." Estelle embraced the nervous girl, patted her shoulder, and said, "Well, calm down. Just go sit down over there, and I'll get you a cup of hot tea. Did the man go over to see Henry?"

"Yeah, I pointed the way to the tent."

Feeling that Patsy needed more from her, Estelle asked, "Did the man say anything to you except asking for Henry? Have you ever seen him before?"

288

"No—to both questions. But I don't feel safe with him around here. I hope he leaves real soon." She shivered as she drank the tea.

"Jim will be in shortly. He's stretching some mink hides, but I don't think he'll be long. I hope he gets a good look at this man."

"Yeah, I'd feel safer if Mr. Jim seen the man. He'd figger him out real soon, I know. Miz Estelle, ye're a nice-lookin' woman, and even iffen ye're in yore thirties and bore some children, do ye ever feel like a man is undressin' ye when he looks at ye?"

Estelle would have laughed if the question had not come from a frightened girl that she loved like her own daughter or a younger sister. "I guess not, Patsy, but I think I know how you feel. Perhaps as a Christian, your fear is a message to your inner being to stay clear of such a man. Why don't you take a break and lie down on the girls' bed and rest awhile?"

When Jim came in, Estelle told him that someone was visiting with Henry and that his presence and leering at Patsy had frightened her. She told him that he ought to go over to Henry's and learn more about the man who had frightened Patsy. "You know, honey, we've got three beautiful young women on this place—one is our daughter Jeanette, another is your niece Miriam, and the third is Patsy here, and she's like a member of our family. Now we need to be on our guard against strangers snooping around here."

Jim stood outside the tent and heard enough to understand that this was Reddon, the nephew of the moonshiner-killer who was now in prison. He was trying to persuade Henry to come back and work for him. Jim heard the outstanding salary he offered, but Henry stood his ground and answered, "No way! I'm done with that kind of life."

Realizing that Reddon was about ready to leave, Jim walked toward the barn a few steps until he heard the "so long" to Henry. He turned around and found Reddon staring at him. "You've gotta be Jim Tharp," the man said.

"You got that right. What about it?" Jim stood ready, the bright afternoon sun revealing his gun, his bright eyes, and his anticipation of challenge. He was glad to be able to size up the man, concluding right away that the man was probably more dangerous than his uncle, faster with a gun, and more clever in his evil ways.

"I reckon you're the gunslinger everyone's talkin' about in this part of the country. Shootin' people's ears, huh?"

"Sometimes, and once in awhile I just drill their hearts. Wanta make somethin' of it?" As Jim positioned his right leg a few inches more apart from his left, he moved his right hand near the handle of his gun. Waiting as he watched Reddon's angry and fearful eyes, he knew there would be no fight.

Reddon mumbled, "Some other time, I guess," as he turned toward the front gate to go to his car.

"Hold it!" Jim called, as he walked rapidly to close the distance between them. A few steps from the moonshiner, Jim looked him in the eyes and said, "Don't ever come on my place agin! Stay away from here and from my family! Get goin'!" Jim watched him drive away, remembering his threatening sneer and mumbled expletives.

That night, Jack and Linda Buchannon drove over and asked if they might come in and talk about something. Estelle said, "Please come in! Where are the children?"

"Oh, they're home. We left them, cuz we wanta talk some business with y'all," Jack said.

"Well, have a seat," Jim said. "Estelle, ye've got the table cleared in there, ain't ye? Let's go in and talk business around the table with a cup of coffee."

"Now, what's on y'all's minds?" Jim asked.

"Mr. Jim, we're wonderin' iffen ye might be willin' to sell us the place over there that we been farmin' fer ye?" Jack began. We reckon it's time we owned our own place and tried to get ahead a little. The Lord's been good to us since we come to work fer ye, and y'all have been good to us. Would ye consider sellin' that eighty acres? I know ye ain't made a lot off it, cuz ye've allus give me the best end of things. But we'd shore be willin' to give ye a decent price for it."

"Well, Jack and Linda, I've never considered sellin' that little farm. I've been pleased to have ye work it for me. Ye're a good cotton farmer, and ye've made my orchard pay off. Ye've been a big help with the cattle, too. But I can't blame ye for wantin' yore own place. I might talk with Estelle about it and see what she thinks. I would like to see y'all get ahead in life and have yore own place." Jim turned to Estelle, and asked, "Whadda ye think, sweetheart? Would we be willin' to sell the eighty acres to Jack and Linda?"

"Honey, I wouldn't want us to sell it to anyone else in the world except them. But maybe we oughta pray about it a few days and then tell them what we would be willing to do. We could give them an idea what we would price it at, or maybe they'd want to make an offer," Estelle said.

"Mr. Jim, I don't know what ye give for that farm about ten years ago, but land has gone up, like everthang else, so I'd expect ye to make a profit on the sale. Ye let us buy yore pickup and pay on installments without interest, but Linda and me wouldn't expect that on the farm. Now, we'd like to buy it with so much down and make payments monthly or even twice a year, but we would expect to pay ye interest."

"Well, Jack, I don't wanta get nosy, but do ye have a few hundred dollars saved up that ye could pay down? Then if ye could make a payment once a year after ye harvest each fall, we would charge ye interest as ye're requestin'."

"Mr. Jim, we've been savin' half of our income from the fur this winter and livin' off the other half. We could pay ye $500 down when we sign the deal, and we'd pay ye half the cotton crop ever fall 'til we get it paid off. Oh, yeah, and I'd like to buy the tractor, plow, disk, and planter, too. So iffen ye decide to sell the farm to me, figger out what ye want fer the farm and the equipment together." Turning to Linda, Jack said, "Honey, I think we've said all we need to. We need to give 'em time to pray and think about this fer a few days, so let's go."

"Well, just a minute," Estelle said. "I'd like to lead a prayer before you go ... Lord, we thank You for the pleasure of having Jack and Linda and the children as our neighbors these few years. Oh, thank You that they've given their hearts to You and You are helping them live the Christian life. Lord, they've meant so much to Jim and me and to our children. Lead us now in this business proposition. May we know if it is Your will for us to sell the farm to them and still have them as our neighbors. Continue to bless our fellowship and give Jim and me an understanding; if we are to sell, may we be fair in the price we ask from these dear ones who are like family to us. In Jesus' name, Amen."

All said "Amen." The women hugged, and Jim and Jack shook hands. Jim said, "We'll get back to ye in a day or so." The younger couple left in smiles, feeling it would go as it should.

Before they retired, Jim and Estelle had agreed that they should sell the eighty acres for $1,200 and ask $300 for the equipment. They would accept the $500 down and charge 2 percent interest on the unpaid balance each year. They would ask Jack to continue his management and marketing of the orchard and to help when possible with the cattle, paying him well for both jobs. He could take cash for the extra jobs or apply the amount to his debt, whichever he chose.

The very next day, Jim and Estelle went to the Buchannon's home and made known their decision and spelled out the terms. Jack and Linda were ecstatic with the conditions and rejoiced as Estelle wrote out the agreement on bond paper for them, making a carbon copy for themselves. Jack counted out five $100 bills for the down payment and shook hands with Jim while the women embraced. Estelle wrote a receipt for the down payment, annotating the balance owed.

Jim and Estelle left feeling almost as happy as the buyers did. "I feel like this farm is still in the family," Jim said, as they drove across the slough and up the hill to their place.

"Now, honey, you and Jack will need to go to the courthouse and let the clerk make note of the sale. We'll need to pay our part of the taxes this year, but Jack will be getting the tax bill every year after that."

"Yeah, we've gotta make it legal. I'm glad ye made a copy of the agreement for us. Well, we know by now that Jack and Linda meet their obligations, and we have nothin' to worry about."

Two weeks later, Jack knocked on the front door and called, "Hey, Jim! It's Jack! Ye got a minute?"

Jim came to the door and said, "Come in, Jack. Of course! What can I do for ye?"

"Well, I might be out of order here, but I felt I oughta report somethin' that happened over at the house a few days ago. I was out at the crib oilin' a saddle, and Linda was outside hangin' out clothes. She come arunnin' to me kinda scared, tellin' me a man was sittin' in his pickup out on the road watchin' her. She was pretty shook up. When I went out where the guy was, he got out of the truck and said he was Jay

Reddon. He told me he was lookin' fer a worker for his liquor operation down in the Arkansas River bottoms, and he really made me a great offer. I told him I'd have to think about it for a few days. I didn't like the looks of the guy, and Linda said she felt undressed the way he had eyed her."

"Jack, I'm glad ye told me this. This feller is a bad character. He was here a few days ago makin' Henry a big offer too. See, Henry used to work for Jay's uncle before he turned to the Lord. Jay came up on Patsy here and scared her the same way he scared Linda. We had a little showdown before he left. When he got a little pushy with me, I called him out and he backed down. I told him to beat it and never show up here again. If ye want my opinion, Jack, yer better off workin' fer yerself even if he paid ye ten times as much. I'm afraid we'll have to keep an eye on this Reddon. He's got more in mind around here than a hand to work for him. He'd better not lay a hand on Patsy or Linda—or Miriam or Jeanette—or I'd probably have to kill him."

"Yeah, we both better keep an eye out for him. I expect he'll be back in a day or so to see what I've decided."

"Meanwhile, don't leave Linda alone over there. If ye're gonna be gone, have her come over here and stay with Estelle."

The very next day was the last day of trapping season, so Jack drove Linda over to stay with Estelle while he went to pull his traps. He left, saying, "Honey, I'll come for you in time to go and pick up all the kids at school."

Jim was also gone to pull his traps. After lunch, Estelle said, "Linda, let's go over to the cabin and build a fire and warm up the place. Then Patsy, Oda, you, and I can have a prayer time before the men come home. We can be through in time for you and Jack to pick up the children."

All the women were excited about having a prayer meeting together. They each read a scripture and mentioned certain concerns that needed prayer. Estelle led out and then each one prayed. They ended the meeting by singing "Sweet Hour of Prayer" and "Tell It to Jesus." Patsy and Oda left, but Estelle asked Linda to stay a few minutes to help her clean a soiled spot in the rug over near the stove. With both women on their knees, Linda applied the cleaning fluid as Estelle rubbed the area with an absorbent cloth to remove the spot. Suddenly, the door flew open with a crash and a red-faced man came rushing in calling, "Stay right where ye are, bitches!" Pointing to Linda, he ordered, "Start takin' yore clothes off, girl!" Then to Estelle he ordered, "Git outa here and into yore house over there." Touching the gun on his hip, he said, "If I see ye come out, I'll kill ye!"

Seeing the man moving toward Linda, Estelle knew it was time to act quickly. *O Lord, I've never done this, but I have to trust You! Lord, You must help me!* She pointed her finger at the attacker and ordered, "In the name of Jesus Christ, *Stop!*"

The man stopped—frozen. When he strained to take a step and couldn't move his foot, he looked shocked and angry. But looking at Linda, he started spewing out filthy threats and describing the ugly things he would do to her. Once more Estelle pointed a finger at him and said, "In the name of Jesus Christ, *shut up!*" The man's jaws locked, and all he could do was groan and shake his head. Estelle saw the color of his face change from red to white, and then back to red. She assumed he was angry, but she silently praised God that their attacker could neither move nor speak. She called, "Linda, stand up, honey. Go and get Oda and Patsy." Linda moved around Estelle, giving their attacker an even wider berth. As she ran out into the cold with no coat on, she heard Jack's truck drive up and called to him as he got out of the vehicle, "Come quick, Jack! Hurry up!" Jack came running, asking, "What's wrong?"

"That Reddon man is in there with Estelle. He was comin' at me to rape me, but Estelle stopped him in the name of the Lord, and now he can't move or speak. He's just froze in there. Get him outa there, honey. Please!"

Jack hurried into the cabin and was amazed to see Jay Reddon as white as a sheet and frozen in a position with one foot in front of the other, just as Linda had said he was, after being stricken by the power of God at Estelle's word of command. "My! How amazing! Miz Estelle, what should I do?" By this time, Linda, Oda, and Patsy had entered the cabin to share in the amazement. While Jack waited for a word from Estelle, the women were all praising the Lord for divine intervention.

"Just wait a few minutes, Jack," Estelle said. "I'm about to give the man permission to walk over and sit in that chair yonder, but I don't think I'll release him to talk until Jim comes!"

"No, don't!" Linda said. "Don't let him say them ugly words again with us women around."

"Okay, girls, all three of you go over and sit on the couch. Jack, you stand across over there with your pistol ready to shoot this man if he makes for the door." Then Estelle looked into the eyes of the man frozen in an awkward position, and said, "Mister, you see that chair there in the corner?" Reddon's eyes followed where she was pointing, but he said nothing. "I now give you permission to walk to that chair and sit down!" Looking relieved at freedom to move, Reddon staggered at first, regained his balance, walked to the chair, and sat down. He appeared to be frightened and was probably wondering what would happen next. "Jack, would you see if the door is damaged, or if it will shut, please? Let's keep this man a prisoner until Jim comes and decides what to do with him. He can't talk until I permit it, but I'm going to ask the Lord to paralyze him again so he can't move. Jack, would you build up the fire and guard him until Jim comes? We women will go to our houses, and Patsy can then go for the children at school. Until you've built up the fire, we'll stay right here to watch him; then we'll go. But don't you turn your back on him!"

The women were glad to get out of the cabin. Patsy bundled up and started the Model T sedan and headed for the schoolhouse. The other women joined Estelle in her house, none of them feeling like being alone.

When Jim finally came in and discovered what had happened, he had to get control of the rage that was rising in him. When he left the women in the house and went over to the cabin where Jack was guarding Reddon, he wondered at first why the prisoner did not answer his questions.

"Jim, I think ye'll have to get Miz Estelle to give him permission to talk," Jack explained. "Ye see, she commanded him to shut up in the name of the Lord! Just take over with guarding him, and I'll go get her. Then, I need to go pick up the children from school."

In just a short time, Estelle entered the cabin. Looking at Reddon, she said, "Now, I release you to answer my husband's questions. Speak up!"

Reddon shook his head back and forth several times as though he was trying to wake up. He looked around, moved his hands and his feet, and then fixing his eyes on Estelle, asked, "What kind of witch are you?"

"I'm no witch! I'm a servant of the Lord Jesus Christ and filled with His Holy Spirit. God hears my prayers and will not allow evil men, such as you, to rape or abuse His children. Now, excuse me!" She started to leave but turned around and continued, "If you know what's best for you, you'll answer truthfully everything this lawman, my husband, asks of you. And you'd better obey him!" With that, she went back to the women over in her home. "Ladies, let's get supper started, and we'll all eat together. Linda, Jack just arrived with the children. Oda, would you go and get Henry and the children, or at least have them here in an hour so that we can all eat together? I expect Jim will take this Reddon to jail after supper."

After he tied Reddon's hands, chained his feet, and then locked him to a post outside, Jim went in to eat supper with the rest. Henry went out later to tell Reddon that he was ashamed of the way he had acted with Estelle and Linda. Reddon dropped his head and refused to speak. "Ain't but one hope fer ye, man! Ye gotta beg God's forgiveness and turn to Jesus as yer Savior." Henry went back in the house and asked Jim if he wanted him to go with him to the jail in DeWitt.

"Naw, Henry. Please stay here with the women and children for awhile. I know they're outa danger, but they're all shook up," Jim said.

"Yeah, me and Jack, we'll calm 'em down some, I reckon."

"Well, Jim, ye're shore busy bringin' me the trash outa them bottoms, ain't ye?" the sheriff said, when Jim told him who he had outside in his pickup. "We'll charge him with assault and threatening behavior, and we'll ask the women to testify when the trial comes up. They won't have to repeat the ugly words the bastard used, I don't think. But that oughta be enough to put him away for awhile."

"Hey, Lloyd, what happened to the guy who tried to kill me a few months ago? I never did find out."

"Aw, he got a light sentence—just 10 years. But there's a big hunt on for the oilman in Texas. I'm leanin' on the Little Rock sheriff to help me with that. This Jackson is all over the world, so if he gets wind of our efforts, he might stay off over in Africa or Europe or somewhere else. The sheriff up there reports to me about every week. I'll try and keep you posted on it."

The first spring thaw began the last week of February as Jim finished pulling his traps. He knew Flash was tired from carrying the load of steel traps, especially since his four feet were laden with the buckshot mud formed by the moisture on the ground. Back at the barn, Jim was glad to remove the canvas bags from the black, spray his hooves with a hose, and rake off the pounds of black mud before leading him into his stable for grain, hay, and water. Inside the house a joyful greeting from Estelle and the aroma of ham, fried potatoes, cabbage, okra, and cornbread caused him to forget the labors of the day. The children found their places around the table, and Estelle offered thanks to the Lord for food, family, freedom, and faith. Jim realized once again how blessed he was to have Estelle and the children.

"Honey, you are so tired! I think after supper you should do your outdoor chores and retire early tonight!" Estelle said. "You don't have anything else you have to do, do you?"

"I have a lot I could do, but I guess yer right. It's been a tough day in the bottoms with the thaw and all that mud. Poor Flash, he made it, but he's one tired horse. I'll go out and talk to him when I do the rest of the stuff out there. It's shore good to have Jack takin' so much of the workload off me."

"Yes, I don't know what we would do without Jack and Linda."

While Jim was doing the evening chores, Henry came out where he was working and asked what would happen to Jay Reddon. Jim said, "Lloyd don't know just yet. I hope they can put him away before I have to kill 'im. I've had all I can take from that varmint."

When the children were all in bed and Jim was still reading the paper, Estelle decided to share what was on her heart. She began, "Jim, I feel the spiritual darkness deepening in this part of our county. In recent weeks, your life has been threatened, Linda and I were assaulted, and attendance is falling off in our services down at the Menard schoolhouse. Of course, weather has been bad, but I sense that Satanic forces are seeking to strike against what the Holy Spirit has in mind for our community. While you and Lloyd probably have a way of dealing with the criminals, I believe God wants us who are interceding daily in prayer for revival to intensify our praying and allow Him to deal with those men His way."

"Well, what do ye think His way is?"

"To send the kind of spiritual awakening that will cause such men to realize their wickedness and, on hearing the Gospel, repent, believe, and be saved. Then when their hearts are transformed, they'll come clean in confession and trust the Lord to help them reform and live the kind of lives they are supposed to. Instead of being a threat to their community, they will turn out to be blessings."

"Well, it would be nice if that happened before we have to deal with those varmints in a shootin' match, but don't hold yer breath."

"Well, I'm going to ask Homer to allow me to appeal to our prayer warriors Sunday morning. I know we have a number who are being faithful to the pledge they made before the Lord to Sister Martha. But I want to admonish all of us to come together for a half night of prayer—six hours of tarrying before the Lord, taking before Him these attempts of wicked men to kill, rape, and steal. I know that the road to revival is humility, prayer, passionately seeking the Lord, and repentance on the part of Christians; and then God promises to **hear from heaven, forgive our sins, and heal our land**. I'm not giving up! He answered prayer when I prayed and commanded Jay Reddon to *stop*! Jim, that man froze! He couldn't have taken another step. Then, he mouthed all those ugly threats to Linda and I ordered him to *shut up!* His jaws locked, and he couldn't say a word! Honey, I wish you could have seen what the Lord did. You saw he was still in that frozen position when you got there. And he couldn't talk until I gave him permission. Now, that was God's doings, not mine. Yes, I was used of the Lord to take authority and order Reddon to do something, but it was God who stopped him and then shut him up. So I need to emphasize to our prayer warriors our need for praying to take authority and to issue commands that we feel the Lord is laying on our hearts. Tomorrow is Saturday, and I think I'll drive down and talk to Homer and Helen. I need several things from the store, and we haven't gotten our mail in three days. Both Patsy and Linda are busy helping me with a half dozen things around here. So I'll leave here midafternoon, talk to Homer and Helen, and get the mail on the way home."

"Come on, Estelle. Let's go to bed. Ye're as tired as I am."

Homer gave all of his time for a sermon over to Estelle on the last Sunday of February of 1940. The weather was nice, and a large crowd listened to Estelle's concern that "the prince of darkness, Satan, is at work in our community. There was an attempt on Jim's life late one evening two months ago—someone tried to ambush him in the bottoms as he was crossing Deep Bayou, just barely missing him. Many of you have heard of an ugly assault on Linda and me only a few days ago. And I sense that many of you who have given your heart to the Lord have been under serious attacks from our spiritual enemy, even to the extent that some of you have yielded to temptation, slacked off in prayer, and developed discouragement and spiritual depression. The enemy is battling you and seeking to cause you to withdraw from faith in Christ as your Savior and Lord.

"Now, when such things occur on a large scale, as I suspect is going on in our community, it is Satan's strategy to seek to oppose the attempt on the part of prayer warriors to counter all that he is trying to do to sink us deeper into spiritual darkness.

"Just as there is the ebb and flow of battle in military efforts, the same is true in spiritual warfare. Sometimes we move ahead; at times we are forced back. We are in a declining period here in this end of our county. I have asked our pastor for the privilege of addressing you today. I am asking you to join me here for a six-hour season of prayer this coming Friday night starting at six o'clock. Now, I know this might impress you as asking too much. If it does represent a sacrifice, I would ask this: Aren't we willing to make a sacrifice for our Lord? Just remember what He has done for us! We are told in Romans 12:1-2: **I appeal to you therefore, brethren, by the mercies of God, to present your bodies as a living sacrifice, holy and acceptable to God, which is your spiritual worship. Do not be conformed to this world but be transformed by the renewal of your mind, that you may prove what is the will of God, what is good and acceptable and perfect.** *Some* of us will want to come fasting. Oh, if you are afraid of getting too weak and won't be able to go the six hours without food, then eat something—and we'll pray until midnight.

"Now, here's how I feel the Lord wants us to begin this half-night of prayer: I'll read some Scriptures on renewal, and we'll pay close attention to what the Lord is saying to us through His Word. The first wave of our praying will be *an upward look*—the look of worship, adoration, praise, and thanksgiving to a God who has saved us, cleansed our hearts, and empowered us for prayer and for living a holy life in this old sinful world.

"The second wave of our praying will be *an inward look*—we'll pray with the psalmist, **Search me, O God, and know my heart! Try me and know my thoughts! And see if there be any wicked way in me, and lead me in the way everlasting.** And again, **Create in me a clean heart, O God, and put a right spirit in me. Cast me not away from thy presence, and take not thy Holy Spirit from me. Restore to me the joy of thy salvation, and uphold me with a willing spirit.**

"The third wave of our praying will be *a roundward look*—we'll bring all of our difficult circumstances before the Lord; we'll **cast our cares on Him, for He cares for us**. Whatever we are struggling with in life—relationships with family members, a problem with a neighbor, a financial deficit, a son or daughter not doing well in school, or anything that's bothering you. Get it before the Lord. Make a list and bring it Friday night. It's for no one's eyes but yours and the Lord's.

"Then our final wave of praying will be *the Kingdom look*— we'll ask the Lord for a special anointing in prayer to join with Jesus, **who in the days of his flesh, offered up prayers and supplications with loud cries and tears, to him who was able to save him from death, and he was heard for his godly fear.** We'll seek a Kingdom anointing by the Kingdom Spirit, the Blessed Holy Spirit, to pray for a Kingdom outpouring of revival on our community, to revive our weak hearts, and to save our unsaved loved ones and neighbors. Bring your lists, beginning with members of your own family and the names of your neighbors; ask God to help you offer prayers filled with love and faith for their salvation. Then don't forget those poor, darkened souls down here in these river bottoms who murder, rape, steal, and lie. Remember, God loves them, too! We must see them saved! I want that man who shot at my husband saved! I want that man who tried to rape Linda saved! I want those moonshiners and bootleggers down there in the White and Arkansas River bottoms saved! And I know you do, too. And I know we all want everyone on this prairie—the good and the bad—saved!

"Oh, beloved, God wants to send a tidal wave of His saving grace and power on Arkansas County that will change the very nature and direction of these entire communities. But with all of His wisdom and power to send it, God puts a responsibility on us to prepare the way for Him in intercessory prayer!

"Are you with me?" Estelle asked in closing. And she was inspired by the loud "Amens" and "Yeses" she heard in the audience.

Homer came up and prayed a powerful prayer, and then said, "I've asked Helen to play and sing, "Sweet Hour of Prayer," after which you are dismissed."

Estelle sensed the Holy Spirit settling on both saints and sinners as Helen sang all three verses. She was encouraged especially by the message in the final verse: "Sweet hour of prayer, sweet hour of prayer, Thy wings shall my petition bear to Him whose truth and faithfulness engage the waiting soul to bless; and since He bids me seek His face, believe His Word, and trust His grace, I'll cast on Him my every care, and wait for Thee, sweet hour of prayer." *O Lord, let it be six sweet hours of adoration, introspection, petition, and intercession. Come, Lord! Come with anointing, freedom, faith, blessing, and answers! Don't let our prayers fall to the ground. Don't let us pray in vain. Please, Lord, send revival!* At the end of the song, Estelle was swept into the arms of many waiting believers. She listened to their confessions of weakness, their vows to join her in confession and intercession on Friday night, and their expressions of faith that God is up to something glorious in a few months or years.

Estelle was both humbled and thrilled at the turnout on Friday night. The south room of the schoolhouse was full, and Homer instructed the ushers to open the partition. When the lights were turned on in the north room, over forty people were seated there.

Estelle began by acknowledging the encouraging attendance, crediting those present with the realization that "the kingdom of darkness is on a vicious counterattack, and I believe those of us here tonight are in agreement that our only hope is to comply with the Word of God, which declares in Ephesians 6:10-18: **Finally, be strong in the Lord and in the strength of his might. Put on the whole armor of God, that you may be able to stand against the wiles of the devil. For we are not contending against flesh and blood, but against the principalities, against the powers, against the world rulers of this present darkness, against the spiritual hosts of wickedness in the heavenly places.**

301

Therefore, take the whole armor of God, that you may be able to withstand in the evil day, and having done all, to stand. Stand therefore, having girded your loins with truth, and having put on the breastplate of righteousness, and having shod your feet with the equipment of the gospel of peace; besides all these, taking the shield of faith, with which you can quench all the flaming darts of the evil one. And take the helmet of salvation, and the sword of the Spirit, which is the word of God. Pray at all times in the Spirit, with all prayer and supplication. To that end keep alert with all perseverance....

"Now, dear fellow prayer warriors, it has been on my mind of late that if we really heed this call to become strong in intercessory prayer, as God is calling us to, we might be looked upon by loved ones and neighbors in this community as extremists and fanatics. But I know God wants me to intensify my praying, begin *calling out, weeping, and begging* as we read about Jesus doing in Hebrews 5:7. I think some of us should add fasting to our praying.

"So here's what I feel we should do tonight: during the first portion of our six hours, I think we should be praying for the Spirit to help us exalt the Lord in expressions of adoration and worship. Like Jesus did in Luke 10:21, we need to **rejoice in the Holy Spirit**! We'll call this *the upward look.* Then will come the *inward look,* during which the Spirit will help us to search our hearts and reveal what there might be in our lives that hinders God from answering prayer. But we'll not be looking just on our own; we'll appeal to the One who *searches our hearts.* God tells us in His Word, **The heart is deceitful above all things, and desperately corrupt; who can understand it? I the Lord search the mind and try the heart, to give every man according to his ways, according to the fruit of his doings**. And we are told specifically in Rom. 8:27 that our Helper, the Holy Spirit, **searches the hearts of men**.

"So, what does this mean? It means that we don't always know our own minds or hearts, and that it takes the Holy Spirit within us to turn on the inward lights to reveal the things we need to confess and clear up before the Lord if we are going to get our prayers answered. Now, I want to lead a prayer in a moment, asking the Lord to do that. Then as I get quiet, let's all wait before the Lord for a quiet time while the Holy Spirit brings to our minds things we need to confess. Very likely, those things will include unbelief, spiritual and mental laziness, and unforgiveness toward someone who has disappointed us, maybe a husband, or a wife, or a child. Perhaps we have neglected to pray and study the Bible as we ought. It could be that some of us are living with known sin in our lives; let us not think our prayers are going to be heard until we repent of it and begin to obey the Lord!

"Now, let's be serious, as we pray. "O Lord, quiet our hearts and clear our minds to think with the Holy Spirit, even now as You move on this Friday night prayer meeting. Show us the things that You want us to acknowledge in our own hearts and lives, things that keep us from the fullness of the Spirit's power, and joy, and peace. Lord, we wait for You now in quietness; as the Spirit reveals our hearts, may we each confess and believe that we are forgiven and that we are cleansed from unrighteousness, just as You promise." For the first two minutes, the crowd was quiet. Then a few began weeping softly, as increasing murmurs of confessions were being heard. This went on for several minutes. Estelle sensed that she should allow the praying and confessions to continue for awhile longer. Finally, she felt impressed to say, "Now, all who have confessed specific sins, shortcomings, or situations of disobedience, believe you are forgiven on the basis of God's promise that *you are forgiven*! Begin thanking Him now for His grace and mercy, and then ask the Lord for a fresh filling of the Holy Spirit and believe that you receive it, never doubting it. For here is what Jesus said in Luke 11:13: **If you then, who are evil, know how to give good gifts to your children, how much more will your heavenly Father give the Holy Spirit to those who ask him**!

"Helen, please lead us in that hymn "Wonderful Peace." And as we sing it, just lift your hands and allow the Spirit to witness to your heart that He has washed, cleansed, and filled you afresh, giving you His assurance that you are ready for greater power in prayer!"

Helen led right out on the chorus, and it seemed everyone picked it up: "Peace, peace, wonderful peace, coming down from the Father above. Sweep over my spirit forever, I pray, in fathomless billows of love." Helen felt the momentum building, so she repeated it several times and the crowd readily responded.

Estelle nodded to Homer, and he came to the lectern, saying, "Oh! Thank God, He is here tonight! And, Estelle, I think we are not yet ready to enter into our third period of the *roundward look.* Let's return for a time to the *upward look of adoration* with freedom and praise to the Lord for salvation, for health, for families, for prosperity, for God's promises, and all that the Spirit brings to our minds. Let's praise the Lord for His holiness, grace, mercy, compassion, forgiveness, provisions, wisdom, faithfulness, and power. Come on, let's pray in one accord. Don't be confused or inhibited by all the praying going on around you. It will be a joyful noise unto the Lord."

Estelle noticed that the clock showed it was 10:55. The volume of prayer was decreasing, and she was glad there would be nearly a full hour for the main course during the night of prayer—that of *intercession.* She called on Homer to prepare the people for this final segment.

Homer began by saying, "In all of my experiences in corporate praying, I've never felt such freedom and faith for all that we've been asking God for as I have experienced in the past five hours we've spent in worshiping, heartsearching, and casting our cares on the Lord. In this closing segment, remember that we are appealing to God for revival; we call it *the Kingdom look.* We must have Kingdom anointing for this—the Holy Spirit. We must have Kingdom faith—holy boldness to address the evil spirits in the strong name of Jesus, order them to back away from the community, and go off into the regions of darkness. We must demand that they retreat from this prairie and these river bottoms. Then we must invite the heavenly hosts to replace them and the Holy Spirit to come in great power of conviction, salvation, deliverance, and revival! Let us plead the Scriptures now, as the Spirit directs us."

Estelle came forward to lead the final prayer period of the night, and she was delighted to see even more people present than there were five hours before when they started the meeting. She led off in a burdened cry for God to "come upon these prairie and bottoms communities with a mighty sweep of Your Spirit and transform our darkness to light! Lord, do a new thing in our midst; let the old pass away and all things become new. Have You not promised to **give power to the faint, and to him who has no might**? Yet You have said that **they who wait upon the Lord shall renew their strength, they shall mount up with wings like eagles, they shall run and not be weary,**

they shall walk and not faint. Lord, we are here tonight to claim Your promise that You **will make a way in the wilderness and rivers in the desert,** that You **will pour water on thirsty land and form a stream on the dry ground,** that You **will pour Your Spirit out upon our offspring and Your blessing on the inhabitants of our land.** O Lord! That Arkansas County might **see the glory of God, Your glorious majesty, and power! Come, Lord, strengthen our weak hands and make firm our feeble knees. Let blind eyes be opened, the ears of the deaf unstopped, and sinners** *all over these prairies and down in these bottoms wake up to their need of God, repent, believe in Jesus Christ, and be saved!"*

As Estelle paused to catch her breath, she realized that the Spirit of prayer, inspiration, faith, and freedom was moving on all ages in the building. The Lord may have used her to "prime the pump" of inspirational praying, but great volumes of prayer were ascending to the Throne of Grace in sobbing sounds of desperation. Kneeling, she thanked God for the miracle she was hearing as the marathon of supplication continued to the midnight hour.

At 12:00, Helen's sweet penetrating voice started singing "Amazing Grace," signaling the end of the greatest prayer meeting and most anointed service anyone present had ever attended. As she began the last stanza, the congregation joined her in singing the familiar words.

The next morning, Jim asked Estelle, "Well, what did ye think of yer six-hour cry?"

Estelle, sensing some cynicism in Jim for the first time, said, "I was very pleased with what I felt, heard, and saw! But, tell me, what did you think of it? I noticed you stayed for about an hour at first and then you returned for the last few minutes."

"You shouldn't ask me," Jim said with a brief smile. "I thought it was just a bunch of hooey, a lot of religious noise, and a bunch of silly emotion. I reckon ye think ye mighta moved God to take a hand in all the bad things that's been happenin'."

"Well, if He doesn't, I think things will get beyond you and Lloyd and your ability to control the evil things that Satan has in mind."

"We might have to organize some posses and get us a few small groups trained to invade a few camps. But I don't foresee anythang too bad for us to handle. A few of us might get shot, but the law will prevail." Jim showed a trace of disgust against Estelle's taking another approach to a cleanup of the bottoms.

"Honey, I'm not about to give up on a mighty invasion of the Spirit of God on this part of our county," Estelle said. "I have been grateful for your support of me and my praying and teaching on intercessory prayer. And I have been grateful for your respect for Sister Martha, Brother Fox, and Pastor Homer. I'm glad you have not objected to the money we've poured into the ministry of Sister Martha and the church here as well as the one in DeWitt. But I have sensed a hardening of your heart. And I know you are almost out of patience with me. But as much as I love you and thank God for keeping you safe through your dangerous moments, I'll not let up in what we call spiritual warfare. I don't suppose you are the only one in this community who feels that most of us in that crowd last night are fanatical, extreme, and half crazy. But you'll just have to laugh at us, dismiss us, or even curse us—we are determined to see a divine takeover of this community!"

Jim did not feel good about all that he had said to Estelle as he left the house without embracing her and kissing her goodbye. Even so, he regretted that he had not said even more. As he saddled Flash on that cold, clear, spring morning, he felt frustrated over his own feelings. *Still, I know enough about Estelle, Homer, and Martha Honeycutt to know that the prayin' last night was not a bunch of hooey. But why do I feel a disgust about the way they carried on all those hours? Should I try and gather the courage to apologize to Estelle for what I said to her? I'm glad I can count on her patience with me, but I'd better not push her too far. How can I be sure I won't pay for my resistance to the spiritual call I feel at times to yield to the urge to pray, confess my sins, and ask God to hep me live a different kind of life? If He can hep Henry, George, Ross, Birdie, and Jack, I reckon He could hep me, too.*

Flash's inquiring nicker jolted Jim out of his thoughts. He mounted up and said to the black, "Okay, fella, let's make some tracks across the prairie and check on the cattle. Then we'll gather the traps over on Deep Bayou and Elbow Slough that we keep puttin' off."

Riding his frisky mount, Jim crossed the sunlit prairie. But the sight of his cattle having survived the cold winter in good shape did not remove from his conscience his regret for the way he had talked to Estelle earlier. *I guess when it comes right down to it, I don't think the way they prayed the other night is a bunch of nonsense. I might never see things like Estelle, or Martha Honeycutt, or Homer Rich, but I've seen enough to know that they aren't crazy. That vision of the attempt to hang Birdie and the way it all came off, the account of her and Martha agreein' in prayer over Henry's rejection of employment with Redding, and Estelle's orderin' of Redding to halt in his approach to Linda and then to shut up when he was spewing ugly words…, well, I can't deny there's a mysterious authority given to those who pray right, live right, and then obey the way they are led.*

Jim had covered all the herds, so he pulled on the reins for Flash to stop. Suddenly, Jim had a feeling that he should ride on down to see Ross, rather than head into the bottoms. Checking on his traps could come later.

Flossie poured two cups of coffee and carried them to the two men as they conversed about the coming war. When would the U.S. get into it other than in furnishing tanks, guns, and ammunition? Had Jim registered for the coming draft yet? How many men would need to register from their immediate community?

Then Ross changed the conversation. "Jim, I was glad to see you at Estelle's special prayer meetin' the other night. I couldn't tell if you were comfortable with that kind of thing or not. I want you to know that I think she and Homer are on the right track and that we will see a difference comin' over our community. Estelle hit it right on the head when she called on those of us who have cooled off some and have failed to pray as we promised to repent, come clean, and resume our commitment to the Lord. Well, I did just that the other night! And, Jim, I'm prayin' for you."

"Thank you, Ross. I reckon that's one reason I come down this mornin'—I don't feel right about the way I talked to Estelle when she asked what I thought about the prayer meetin'. I said it was just a bunch of hooey. But, I know that's not true. I've seen too much spiritual authority out of Estelle and Martha Honeycutt to write everthang off as fanatical or crazy."

"I'm glad you feel as you do, Jim. I hope you'll set it straight with Estelle. Of course, I know her well enough to believe that she'll love you and pray for you just as earnestly whether you apologize or not. But I think you owe it her to tell her how you really feel."

"Yeah, I don't plan to sleep tonight 'til I have done just that!"

"Good! Jim, you're a good man. I reckon only a few of us down here realize what a valuable man you are, how gifted you are with a gun, what instincts you have for prosperin' and helpin' people, and how much you give to the Lord's work. Jim, I do pray for you spiritually. I want you to come to a place where you honestly and sincerely want to give your heart to the Lord, live in total obedience to God, and support Estelle one hundred percent."

"Thanks, Ross. I mean to do just that. I hope I ain't put it off too long already."

When Jim said he needed to leave, Ross asked if he would mind a short prayer. "Go ahead, Ross." Jim listened to his cousin pray, and he felt an inner warmth which he took as assurance that he had not sinned away God's time of grace. But even as he hugged Ross and said goodbye to Flossie and thanked her for the coffee, he sensed an inner warning that he must not keep putting off his surrender to Christ.

After mounting the gelding, Jim headed home to take care of a matter that should ease his conscience. On his arrival, Linda was letting the children out of the car.

Jake waited for his father's approach. "Dad, let me unsaddle Flash for you. I'll rub him down, feed him, put down the hay, and see that he has fresh water."

"Thanks, son. Then I'll go in and visit with your mama a little while before supper. I'll bet she's in the kitchen."

Estelle was returning to the kitchen from the smokehouse, where she had gotten a large ham. Jim could smell potatoes frying and cabbage cooking. "Hello, darling!" Estelle called with a smile. "Sit down and I'll pour you a cup of coffee. I'd offer you a fresh piece of apple pie, but I don't want to ruin your supper."

"Naw, I'll wait 'til after supper for my pie. But there is somethin' I don't want to wait for," Jim said, looking at Estelle. He was glad to overhear Estelle giving orders to Jeanette to take care of the two younger children while the school children got busy on their homework.

"Now, what is it you want right away?"

"I want ye to sit down across the table here from me while I ask ye for somethin'."

Estelle obeyed immediately, looking into Jim's eyes for a clue to what might be on his mind.

Jim leaned forward and said, "Honey, I ain't felt good all day about the way I answered ye at breakfast this mornin' when ye asked me what I thought about the prayer meetin'. And I need to tell ye, I know that kind of prayin' ain't a bunch of hooey. Please forgive me! Ross helped me to see how wrong I was today, and he even prayed for me before I left him and Flossie a while ago. I want ye to forgive me, please!"

Estelle wiped tears, then rose from her seat opposite Jim, came around to his side, and put her arms around him. "Darling, of course I forgive you! Thank you for talking to me about how you feel. I'm so glad you don't think our praying is outrageous or fanatical. I believe we'll see the fruit of it even if it isn't immediate." Estelle kissed Jim's cheek and then went to the sink to rinse the curing salt from the ham. "Honey, would you mind slicing the ham? I want to fry ham steaks for supper."

As Jim got up and began helping her with the ham, he said, "I was hopin' for some ham steaks from one of these big ones. How many more are there?"

"Oh, we still have three big ones and two small ones left."

"Well, I guess we'll make it through 'til our first cold spell in November."

After supper on a windy March evening, George and BettyLee drove in. Even as the women hugged and the men shook hands, Estelle could sense something of a serious nature. They all went in the living room to visit while Patsy and Jeanette took over the kitchen for cleanup from supper.

Tearfully, BettyLee began, "Estelle and Jim, we just learned from Dr. Whitehead today that George has a bad case of tuberculosis and will be goin' away for several months to the Booneville sanitorium."

"Oh, we're so sorry to hear this," Estelle said. "George, are you in pain?"

"No, just weak and feverish, but I do have a little pain every now and then."

"Well, George and BettyLee," Jim began, "I know Dr. Whitehead knows what's best for ye. And anythang ye need that I have or can do, it's yers—all ye need to do is ask."

"Jim, I hate to go away and leave BettyLee and the kids. But Doc says if I don't, I can't live very long. I just ain't ready to die and leave my loved ones yet. Yeah, I'm gonna need Henry's and yer help, like lookin' in on BettyLee and the kids. Because of y'all, I feel I can leave with the assurance they'll be in good hands. Course, I know y'all got yer own things to look after, but now and then, please drop by and check on 'em to see if they need anythang."

"George, I promise!" Jim said. "And I don't want ye worryin' none about yore family. They ain't gonna want fer anythang! If it's money, a trip to town, or help on yer farm, either me, Jack, Homer, or Birdie will see that they have whatever they need."

George wiped tears, and said, "God bless ye, Jim and Estelle! I knew we could count on ye, and it means so much to know they'll be cared for."

Estelle spoke to Jim, "Honey, go over and get Henry and Oda, because they need to know about George. We'll have a time of prayer for George, and then we'll have coffee and pie—I've got apple and coconut."

Henry and Oda came in and offered their expressions of concern for George's health. There was not a dry eye in the group when Estelle had praised God for the blessings the Lord had bestowed upon them so that they would be able to supply any need BettyLee and the children might have in George's absence. She asked that God's healing hand might be upon George, that the doctors and specialists in Booneville would be successful in their treatments, and that George might not have to be away for as long as Dr. Whitehead had thought. She asked the Lord to comfort George and BettyLee and each of the children in their loneliness during the period of waiting and prayed that all would be safe.

A spirit of hope settled over George and BettyLee as all of them joined in sharing the pie, drinking coffee, and listening to one another's thoughts of all that they might do to help their loved ones through a time like this. As she hugged Estelle goodbye, BettyLee whispered, "O, Estelle, I'm gonna have to lean hard on you during the time George is gone. I don't know what I'd do without you!"

"Of course, dear! We're here for each other. You've always been there for me, and I want to be there for you. I'll be over at least once a week; just count on that."

After the Bests had gone, Estelle noticed Jim remained pensive. Finally he said, "Ye know I feel like George is just as close to me as a brother-in-law as BettyLee is as my sister."

"Yes, dear. I've always known you and George were closer than brothers. And I feel more close to BettyLee as my sister than I do to George as my uncle. We'll pray often and every day for them. And I know the Lord will help us to help them."

"Yeah, we're able to do it; even if we didn't have it to help BettyLee, we'd find it somewhere, cuz she ain't gonna lack anythang she needs while George is gone. I'll help George Alvin get in wood and put out some of George's nets. I plan to put in George's corn and cotton crops, and I'll have Jack and Birdie over there helpin' with the crops as needed. We'll make sure they have groceries. And ye can check on Betty Jean and Jeanell and take care of their needs. We're all family. If I was down in bed or off somewhere, George would be right here to hep ye with the work and the kids."

The Pulaski County sheriff and the Arkansas County sheriff were having a steak dinner in the Freeman Restaurant in DeWitt and discussing the coming Haskins trial.

"Lloyd, do you think Jim Tharp is suspicious of Jackson bein' the one behind the plan to kill him?" Sheriff Jefferson asked.

"Of course he is!" Lloyd said. "He told me that the night he brought Haskins in. He was settin' right in your chair there and named Jackson right out, sayin' he figgered he'll pay off the jurors as well as the judge."

"How long have you known Jim, Lloyd?"

"Aw, I reckon it was about 1922 or 1923—when he was only a teenage kid. One day Henry Purdy, a rice farmer down here south of town, come by sayin' he had a nephew he thought I oughta meet, a young feller 'bout 17 years old who had a way with horses and dogs that would make you think he was a miracle worker. He told me that the boy was the best shot he'd ever seen, and old man Purdy is quite a hunter hisself. Said if I wuz ever interested in breakin' in a new deputy, I oughta go down to LaGrue and talk to Jim Tharp. Well, I liked the kid the first time I laid eyes on him. Medium height, quick, and as strong as a panther cat! Them eyes went right through me. He called out 'Here, Buck!' and his half-breed German shepherd-wolf animal showed up. When he called 'Star!,' his horse whinnied. Out of the stable pranced this shiny jet-black animal, and Star put on a show at his master's coachin'.

"Then he said I oughta see the two work with him in the woods. Well, we went into the LaGrue bottoms, and he proved to me that no lurkin' outlaw would ever have a chance of ambushin' him or even gettin' close enough to shoot at him. Well, I felt him out about joinin' me occasionally to catch some runaways. He seemed interested, so I made it a point to go huntin' and fishin' with him. I ain't never had a deputy or posse member who can shoot like him—whether it's a fast-flyin' quail or a small wild hog runnin' through the brush, *Jim Tharp never misses*. It doesn't matter if he's shootin' with a shotgun, a rifle, or his .38 Colt revolver!"

"Yeah, well, I've read three or four stories in the *Gazette* about him, and all the reporters said that he never misses what he shoots at—man or animal. How many men do you reckon he's killed?"

"I've been with him when he's killed … let's see…" The sheriff paused and took a minute to figure. "I'd say he's killed 12 men when I've been either *with* him or *near* him—so close I heard the shots. Every fatal shot was either to save his life, my life, or someone else's life. And I know he's killed a few men who he warned to not try and outdraw him. He begged them to save themselves. But the fools went for their gun, and no sooner was their hand on their pistol handle than a bullet pierced their hearts."

"But how many ears has Jim drilled?"

"Well, during the time I've known him…, let's see, from 1922 to 1940…, during those 18 years, I reckon he's shot 30 or 40 ears. Beats anything ye ever saw! No one could see how he could shoot at some angles and get an ear without tearin' up the man's face, but he put a neat little hole in all of 'em. He prefers that to puttin' one in their hearts. Ah, Jim hates to kill a man. Ye ought to have had to deal with him on his first kill. Took him a long time to get over it."

"But, Lloyd, don't ye worry 'bout him bein' shot one of these days?"

312

"I do worry some. But, listen! Jim ain't no ordinary guy. For several years he took those two trained animals, Star and Buck, with him most of the time. They had uncanny ways of givin' him the whereabouts of his would-be killers; and the man hisself has mysterious gifts of discernin' the presence of evil. I've seen it time and time again. He can hear a footfall through the woods 100 yards away, and he can tell whether it's a man or an animal. He can study the behavior of squirrels and birds and tell if another human being is around. He's saved my life so many times, I can't even name all of 'em.

"And, Sheriff Jefferson, there's that wonderful wife of his!" Lloyd said.

"Yeah, what about her?"

"Well, she's a prayin' woman and she gets things from God. Like when we knew young Jackson's gang had that black feller down there in Nady, Estelle woke up one mornin' with a dream or a vision. She told Jim who had him and where and when to find him. She said he was being hanged by four men before sunup on a Sunday morning on a certain tree near Sweeney's country store. We wuz all a-waitin', and shore 'nuff there they were! Jim shot the rope in two they had him hangin' from, and he fell to the ground. Jim killed two of the men—shot 'em through the heart. Then he wounded a feller on purpose in order to have him for testimony in court. Jim's brother-in-law George Best killed the other hangman before he could take cover. I saw it all! It wuz all wrote up just like it happened in both our DeWitt paper and in the *Gazette*."

"Yeah, I read it, too. So, would you say Jim is fearless, or will he break down one of these days if he doesn't get killed?"

"I can't see him weakenin' one iota, Sheriff. I pray he don't get killed. We need him. The thing I worry most about Jim is that the Army might draft him. I could try and keep him out for good reasons, but he won't hear to it. I don't think he actually wants to go to war, but he realizes he has special skills with guns; and I know he doesn't want to shirk his duty to his country. But I think he also knows huntin' Germans wouldn't be the same as trackin' down outlaws in them bottoms."

"I'll bet that, under the right conditions and setup, a man like Jim Tharp turned loose on those Germans or Japs could come home much like Sgt. Alvin York of WWI—highly decorated for bravery and efficiency in combat!" Sheriff Jefferson said.

Sheriff Lloyd LaFargue nodded his agreement.

Jim knew that Jack was excitedly preparing his own acreage for cotton and corn this spring. Homer and Birdie were equally busy on Jim's place. Jim was working even longer hours than they were—tending nets and catfish trotlines, riding both in the fields and in the bottoms looking after cattle, and checking tracts of timber for both companies, Anderson-Telly and Townsend-Black. It looked like a good year as far as promising markets were concerned. Fish, cattle, fur, and timber all showed increases projected for the future. To Jim and Estelle, it seemed a shame to require an anticipated world war to break the nation out of a depression and launch it into a period of prosperity.

Estelle was still concerned about Jim having to go into the military and train for the combat that she felt surely America would have to face. George Tharp, Jim's cousin, who escorted her to the dance where she met Jim, had a great deal of experience with political authorities and had shared with Jim that America would need to be prepared for war with Japan at some point in 1941. As a celebrated naval officer in charge of shipping war equipment overseas, George addressed a group at the American Legion Club in DeWitt, at which time he predicted that America would play a major role in WWII and that it would not end until late 1945.

Jim received his notice in June to report for a physical examination in Little Rock. If he met the physical conditions, he could expect to be called for training within 60 days. Looking to be in military training at least by the first of September gave Jim mixed feelings—he dreaded leaving Estelle and the seven children, counting the one Estelle was expecting; he would miss hunting, trapping, fishing, farming, tending cattle, and logging. He also wondered how the sheriff might handle alone some of the dangerous flare-ups in the bottoms. He was concerned about BettyLee and the children—the fishing and hunting her boys were involved with, though they seemed to be doing well with the farming. He knew he would still have sufficient funds for Estelle to see that BettyLee and her children had everything they needed. He would no longer have Jack to look after the cattle, because Jack had already completed his military training and, without a doubt, would be one of the first to be shipped into combat areas when America entered the war. He knew Ross would be available to help Jake when needed, but even the small herd of cattle he now had was an awful lot of responsibility to place on the shoulders of a young boy.

On the other hand, Jim found the prospects of a demanding daily physical routine of exercise and periodic brainstorming sessions regarding strategy and tactics for battlefield action all a bit challenging. He considered himself to be in very good physical condition. Despite his limited book learning, he felt that his daily reading of newspapers and magazines and listening to the radio had helped him with the current thinking of the times. He had no aspirations to become an officer, but if and when the occasions came, he did look forward to relating to officers and possibly even matching wits with them.

When Jim ran all of his concerns past Estelle, he found her wisdom amazing and her attitude reassuring. "Honey, if you are drafted, we'll miss you terribly; but I've soaked this matter in prayer now for over a year, and I doubt that you will need to leave us and all of your interests behind to go to war. I think your place will be right here at home with us and continuing to do all that you have been doing for your family, your community, and the nation. But if you are called into the military, I know the Lord will have a plan for all of us through that. Don't be worrying about us. The Lord will take care of us, and He'll provide the help we need for the farm, the fishing, and the cattle—Jake and Ross will take care of all those cattle. And I'll bet George Alvin will be glad to help them out when they need him. I think you have noticed how Jake and George Alvin get along so well and really seem to love each other like brothers. Even Homer and Birdie would give Jake a hand. Just don't worry! Maybe you ought to talk to the sheriff about someone to replace you. This war might last a few years, maybe even longer than your cousin George thinks."

Homer drove Jim to DeWitt to catch the special bus that hauled those called to go to Little Rock for their examinations for military training. As they sat in the car at the bus station, Homer prayed for Jim—to give his heart to the Lord and that his examination for military duty would turn out just as God had planned. The 10 men on the bus arrived at the Induction Center in the capitol city in the early afternoon and in time for Jim's group to complete their preliminary physicals that day.

A Dr. McKenzie stamped Jim's papers in late afternoon, and said, "Well, Mr. Tharp, according to your preliminary physical, you are in perfect condition for military training. Congratulations, sir! Here is your round-trip bus ticket to the hotel where they'll assign you a room, and here is the slip to give to the receptionist right over there in the morning. We want to see you at 8:30. Now tomorrow will tell whether or not you are fit for combat. First, you'll see a cardiologist, who will examine your heart. In the afternoon, you'll be tested by other specialists. After tomorrow's tests, you will go back home for a few weeks to put everything in order. If you pass everything, you'll be told where and when to catch a train to report for training. Any questions?"

"No, sir!" Jim said. "Thanks for the information, and I'll see ye in the mornin'."

"One more thing," the doctor said. "When you get off the bus at the hotel and give the clerk this paper, you will receive two meal tickets—one for supper tonight, and one for breakfast in the morning at the hotel restaurant. You won't have to go downtown Little Rock to eat unless you just want to."

That night after his meal, Jim lay in the comfortable hotel bed, thinking about what military life might be like. He realized the doctors and personnel at the examination center might not be military officers, but he wondered if taking orders from army officers might be like working with county sheriffs. He had only worked with three—Lloyd, Sheriff Jefferson, and the Desha County sheriff. Already, he missed Estelle and the children and realized being separated from them would be his heaviest cross to bear if he happened to pass everything and be inducted into the service. He knew the children would not only miss him greatly but they also needed the presence of a father at their ages. *I wonder if I will survive the war. If I am killed, will it be on the Atlantic in a sinkin' ship that's been torpedoed by a German U-boat? Or on a battlefield, with a bullet in my chest? Or in a buildin', blown to bits by explodin' bombs dropped by enemy aircraft? Or in a foxhole, mortally wounded from a hand grenade thrown by a German soldier?*

Deploring his negative mental wanderings, Jim ordered his mind to shift in another direction. *I really don't believe the kind of prayin' that*

Estelle does is a lot of nonsense, but will it make any difference in my situation when I'm in a hot spot in the war? Had it made a difference on Elm Ridge when I killed those men, all of whom were raisin' their guns to kill me, even as my bullets pierced their hearts? Was God respondin' to Estelle's prayers that early mornin' near Dumas when Lloyd's gun jammed and I instinctively caught both killers just split seconds before they got me and Lloyd? Just how many times had there been supernatural interventions that saved me, all because of Estelle's prayers? Ross made me feel that I do need to get right with God pretty soon. I wonder what might need to happen to give me the signal that it is time for that. What if I should wait too long? Is Hell a reality? Does a person take his final breath, lose consciousness, and then wake up in the flames of Hell or wake up to the glories of Heaven, like Estelle, Homer, Frank Fox, and Martha Honeycutt declare in their preachin' and teachin'? I just don't know if I really believe that. How can anyone really know before he dies? Estelle says that she has an assurance—that she has the witness of the Holy Spirit that she will go to Heaven when she dies. I reckon she's closer to God than anybody I know, so I guess I ought to believe her. I'd rather trust her view of things than those of anyone else. I guess I ought to admit that time is slippin' by, and what Estelle, George, Jack, Linda, Birdie, BettyLee, and even Henry claim the Lord has done for them is real. It ought to be enough for me to take a step of faith. I think I will, but I hope I don't put it off too long.

Jim slept soundly, wakened at six o'clock, showered, shaved, and brushed his teeth. He was among the first few men to show up for breakfast, which consisted of bacon, scrambled eggs, toast, and hot coffee. He read the *Gazette* in the lobby while waiting for the bus. The front page was filled with pictures of Hitler's violent invasions of European countries, and the pages following reported the shipments of weapons of war—Jeeps, tanks, guns, and ammunition—by the United States to England and France. Jim remembered that his cousin George had something to do with these ships loaded with weapons that crossed the Atlantic to England and France. The editorial emphasized that our participation already in the European theater gave the lie to our claim to be neutral. "Thousands of American men are now being drafted to train for executing the most violent and costly war in human history."

At the end of the day, Jim was surprised to learn that he would need to return the next day for a continued examination by the cardiologists. No one was present to explain what they had found, and he returned to his hotel with some disappointment.

The second day found him being examined and tested throughout the whole morning by four different cardiologists. After lunch, which was served to him in a waiting room at the Center, he was told by the same Dr. McKenzie, "Mr. Tharp, we are rejecting you because of questions about your heart. Now, I'm not a cardiologist and can't explain their reasons for rejecting you. I do know that they feel they cannot verify through their testings and findings that you would be able to stand up under extreme violence of combat. Please don't take this as a mark against your character or a doubt that you would purposely fail to carry out orders under adverse conditions. From my understanding, their technology—the instruments they use to learn the conditions of the human heart—just can't reassure them that you ought to be asked to go into combat."

"That's strange, Doctor, and very surprisin'! Ye see, I'm a special deputy to the sheriff of Arkansas County, and more than twenty times I've had to shoot my way out of a crisis while tryin' to arrest someone. And Sheriff LaFargue would tell these cardiologists that he has never once seen me fail to stand up under fire."

The doctor sympathetically replied, "Mr. Tharp, you look to me like a man we could trust all the way in helping to win this war against the Nazis, but I suggest you return to your family and to the job with your sheriff. But perhaps you do need to visit a cardiologist to find out if there's something they need to do about a heart condition that we can't seem to diagnose fully."

Jim left the Center to catch the bus to DeWitt with mixed emotions. He was disappointed that something might be wrong with his heart. But he would be glad to get home to Estelle and the family. Hoping the sheriff had a free evening, he would call him from the bus station and ask him to drive him home. Jim wondered if he should tell Lloyd that he had been rejected because the cardiologists' equipment could not confirm a strong and healthy heart. But he knew he had never had any symptoms of a weak or defective heart. So he would do as Dr. McKenzie suggested—return home to his wife and family and keep doing his job with the sheriff. Of course, he was relieved to know he could still keep on with his hunting, trapping, fishing, farming, logging, and running cattle to make a living doing all the things he enjoyed.

Over a steak dinner at the Freeman Restaurant in DeWitt, Lloyd comforted Jim over his rejection for military service. "Look at it this way, Jim—maybe the Good Lord heard Estelle's prayers and would rather you help me catch criminals in the White and Arkansas River Bottoms than to kill Nazi Germans in the war. Also, you can go right on supportin' Estelle and the family while fishin', huntin', loggin', savin' my life, and helpin' me keep them moonshiners and bootleggers under control. I know your wife will be glad to see you." Lloyd glanced at his wristwatch and said, "I bet we can get you home before they all go to bed if we pay the bill and get outa here right away."

"Let's go."

Estelle was awake before daybreak the next morning, and noticing Jim stir, she turned over to him and whispered, "Sweetheart, could we sit up and talk before the children get up?" Giving him time to wake up, she continued, "Please don't be discouraged over being rejected by the military. I knew in my heart that God did not want you to be a part of the war in Europe. Now, I want us to go see Dr. Whitehead in a few days so that he can examine you and listen to your heart. Then he'll probably set up an appointment for you to see a good cardiologist in either Little Rock, Memphis, Hot Springs, or somewhere else. Leaving the children in good care, we'll drive there, spend a night or two, and enjoy a little break from things here. Even though I'm just sure you don't have anything to be concerned about with your heart, it will be good to hear qualified specialists pronounce you in good health. Meanwhile, promise me that you will tell me if you ever feel any pain or heaviness in your chest area, okay?"

"Sure, honey! I will. But meanwhile, I'm plannin' to go right on with my life as usual—ridin', huntin', fishin', trappin', loggin', and the whole nine yards."

"Of course, dear! And I think you'll see no decline in your health whatsoever for several years. Eventually, of course, our age will catch up with us; we'll slow down some and feel a few aches and pains—just as the Lord intended for all of us, saints and sinners alike. If we continue to work, eat healthy, and get the rest we should, I think we could live well into our eighties or maybe even into our nineties," Estelle said with excitement and in faith. "And I'll just say this even if it scares you a little—I think I'm still good for a few more babies, even after I give birth to the one I'm expecting!"

10 *"Weeping through the Night"*

From several letters Patsy had brought in from the mailbox, Estelle selected Dr. Whitehead's to read first. He had made Jim an appointment for September 11 at 2:30 with Dr. Martin Bonnhoffer, a cardiologist in Hot Springs.

"What's the chance of our staying overnight?" Estelle asked. "I'd like to do some shopping for the children and myself."

"I reckon the odds are pretty good," Jim said with a grin.

A note in the mail from BettyLee was good news. George would be released from the sanitorium in time to be home for Thanksgiving Day.

Jim and Estelle checked into the Hot Springs Inn, a lovely hotel, the night before Jim's appointment. They enjoyed a delightful meal in the dining room and a good night's rest. The next afternoon, Estelle dropped Jim off at Dr. Bonnhoffer's office, and then she drove downtown to shop at Janie's Women's Store.

Dr. Bonnhoffer, a tall, pleasant-faced, middle-aged man, greeted Jim warmly and asked, "Aren't you the Jim Tharp who is special deputy to the sheriff of Arkansas County?"

"I am, Doctor. I reckon ye've read about me some in the papers."

"Yes, and I'm delighted to meet you. Is it true that you never miss what you shoot at?"

"I ain't missed anythang, whether it's flyin', runnin', hoppin', crawlin', or standin' still, since I was 10 years old."

"You know, Mr. Tharp, I'd like to see that country over there where you're from sometime. I'll bet you have a lot of deer, ducks, and turkeys. Any quail?"

"All of that, Doctor. Maybe ye'd like to come over and quail hunt with me."

"Well, now that's exciting to think about. But I guess we'd better get to the reason you're here, and maybe we could set up a hunting date before you leave. Tell me, do you have any pain in your chest? And just what did they tell you when they rejected you for the military in Little Rock?"

"They just said I passed everthang with flyin' colors, 'cept my heart. Didn't say what was wrong, but they said their instruments couldn't assure 'em I'd be able to stand up under some battle conditions. But Doctor, I'm in shootin' scrapes several times a year workin' with the sheriff—have had to kill men, been shot at, and shot fellers' ears so as not to kill 'em. Except for the noise of bombs, planes, and tanks, I can't imagine anythang in the war that would be more stressful than what I often face over in our county helpin' the sheriff."

After listening to Jim's heart and running an EKG, Dr. Bonnhoffer said, "Mr. Tharp, I want you at the Medical Center in the morning at 9:30, not to be admitted, but to have two highly trained specialists run tests on equipment that I don't have here in my office. My guess is that you have nothing to worry about, but let us put you through some tests that will be studied by the greatest heart doctors in the business down in New Orleans and over in Houston. We won't have the answer tomorrow, but as soon as we learn the results, you and Dr. Whitehead will hear from me.

"Now, Mr. Tharp, about a quail hunt. What would a week from this afternoon be like for you?"

"I believe I'm in the clear. Doc, why don't ye come in time for a hunt on Thursday afternoon? That night ye can eat supper with us and spend the night in our cabin. We'll hunt the next day, mornin' and afternoon, and then the second day if you wish."

"Mr. Tharp…"

Jim interrupted, "Just Jim, please!"

"Fine, Jim! I'll see you in the morning a few minutes before 9:30 in the main lobby of the Medical Center, which is just six blocks on this same street going east."

The next day, Estelle dropped Jim off at the Medical Center, and then she spent the rest of the morning in a few department stores in Hot Springs. As Jim had suggested, she returned to pick him up at two o'clock, but she had to wait in the lobby for an hour before he appeared with Dr. Bonnhoffer. Upon being introduced, she was impressed with the doctor's appearance and demeanor. Jim told her he had invited the doctor to their place for a quail hunt the next week. After Jim gave him directions to their house, he said, "Doc, we'll see ye next week on Thursday afternoon." The two men shook hands like warm friends.

On the drive home, Jim told Estelle that he had also invited Dr. Bonnhoffer to stay at the cabin and eat supper with them Thursday night. So the first of the week, Estelle left the baby in Patsy's care and went to the cabin to clean and make it ready for Jim's hunting guest. While she worked, she prayed for the doctor. "Lord, the thought came to me yesterday when I met the doctor that You might be in his coming here for more than a hunt. Help me be sensitive to Your leading, and perhaps You'll give me a chance to witness to him and pray for him." It was then that her heart was strangely warmed! A verse came to mind: **Sing praises to the Lord, O you his saints, and give thanks to his holy name**. But she knew there was more to the passage that she must get now! She reached for her Bible she kept on the table in the cabin and turned to the Scripture: **Weeping may tarry for the night, but joy comes with the morning** (Ps. 30:5). When she reread the passage, God spoke to her heart that she was being called into a season of weeping. He was taking her up on her surrender to **present her body as a living sacrifice**. "O Lord, I thank You for speaking to me and calling me into a weeping season. I do long to be faithful. And I long to know more about how and when to weep within your perfect supervision. Prepare me for ministering to Dr. Bonnhoffer."

Estelle's eyes filled with tears even before she became conscious of anything specific to weep over besides the needs she was already praying about. Of course there was Jim's lostness, a wicked community, some believers losing the faith, and a nation on the verge of war. As the tears rolled down her cheeks, she began praying for each person or situation that came to mind. She was amazed that her praying was now with deeper passion—a greater strength and quality of emotion was being imparted to her. Something told her that *she was now by the power of the Holy Spirit weeping the tears of Jesus.* She turned to Hebrews 5:7: **In the days of his flesh, Jesus offered up prayers and supplications, with loud cries and tears, to him who was able to save him from death, and he was heard for his godly fear.**

In her prayer time the next morning, the Lord impressed her with the need to make a list of all the people she knew, beginning with her immediate family, all of her relatives, and all of Jim's. She walked back to the house to get one of the children's school tablets, and as she wrote each name, she began praying for that person. It was noon when she ran out of names, but she was sure the Lord would add to her list later.

Jim was on the porch reading the *Gazette* when Dr. Bonnhoffer drove up about 2:00 on Thursday afternoon. He greeted him at the gate and took him over to the cabin. Jim was already dressed for the hunt, but the doctor needed a few minutes to change into hunting gear. In the meantime, Jim put the two dogs, Better and Best, in the back of his pickup, and they were soon off to Jim's favorite quail hunting area. Along the way, Jim directed the doctor's attention to his hayfields and cattle. Pulling up under a grove of white oaks, Jim pointed to the first field they would hunt. After both had loaded their guns, Jim said, "Doctor, take the right, and I think we'll flush a covey just this side of that red oak yonder. Take what swings yore way, and I'll take what comes my way."

Just before they reached the location Jim had suggested, Best froze on a point. Jim said, "We'll walk slowly now and stop ten feet before we get to the dog." They stopped, and Jim said, "Flush!" Best almost leaped at the command. Bobwhites exploded into the air, and Jim's guest shot first and the bird folded. Jim shot twice and two birds folded.

"Good shootin', Doctor. Let's hold here until Best retrieves for us." Soon the dog ran up to the doctor and waited while the bird was gently removed from his mouth. The doctor patted the dog's head, and Best and Better hurried off to retrieve the other two birds for Jim.

By holding to the south edge of the hayfield, the two continued to hunt eastward. On all the singles, Jim deferred to his guest. The doctor never missed on his first twelve shots. He asked, "Jim, when do you go into action again?"

"On the next covey rise, and when both dogs go down on a point."

It happened within the next ten minutes. The covey rose with a sound like thunder, with 20 to 30 birds flying up. Jim's gun fired three times, and three birds fell. At the same time, the doctor went into action; he fired twice, and two birds fell.

"Jim, what a pleasure to watch your dogs work and see your accuracy in shooting!"

Throughout the trip back to the house, the doctor talked excitedly about the hunt. Jim asked, "Doctor, would ye mind if I invite my oldest son on the hunt with us tomorrow? He's not as seasoned as you, and he shoots a single. He's only been on one hunt with me."

"Sure! Let's have the lad join us."

Jim was pleased to see that Estelle and Patsy had gone all out for a great meal that evening—ham, stewed potatoes, wilted lettuce, boiled cabbage, and okra. Jim knew the women had also baked raisin and coconut pies.

As they gathered everyone to the table, Jim said, "Doctor, my wife has a strong Christian faith, and she usually leads a prayer of thanksgivin' at mealtime. I hope ye'll not feel uncomfortable if she does that."

"Oh, not at all! In fact, I'd appreciate it. But just before she prays, Jim, I need to tell you something. I was so excited about the hunt that I forgot to tell you that the results of your tests are absolutely negative—nothing could be found wrong! I knew Mrs. Tharp might want to include that in her prayer of thanks."

Estelle burst out, "Oh yes! Thank You, Lord, for the privilege of having Dr. Bonnhoffer as our guest and for the good report he just gave us about Jim's tests. Bless the men as they hunt, and give us thankful hearts for Your many blessings on our lives. Bless this food to its intended use and all of our lives to Your glory, Amen!"

"Amen!" the doctor echoed. His head remained bowed for a few seconds during which time no one stirred. Then, looking at Estelle, he said, "Miz Tharp, thank you for that prayer. Ever since meeting you for just a moment in Hot Springs and now this afternoon, something tells me that before I head home tomorrow afternoon I need to sit down and talk with you about spiritual things—if you have the time."

"Doctor, it would be a pleasure to share my faith with you."

Jim started passing the food around. The children were so taken with the guest that they almost neglected to eat. After filling his plate, the doctor still wanted to talk. Looking at Estelle, he said, "There's something about you that reminds me of my people back in Germany. They were believers in the great Martin Luther reformation, and they grieved greatly over the direction Germany took under the Wilhelm II. At least those people have gone on to be with the Lord and do not have to suffer the humiliation that many of us feel over Germany's present maniac."

When the doctor paused, Estelle said, "Well, Doctor, I feel led of the Spirit to pray often for the good people of Germany who are embarrassed by their evil leader Adolph Hitler! I do not judge the German people by their wicked leader. I know that he will be brought to a violent end, and I pray the people will be able to endure to the dreadful end."

"I do thank you, dear woman, for those kind words. I'm almost ashamed to be of German descent since Hitler has been doing all the horrible things to the Eastern European nations. But I'm certainly not ashamed of my Christian heritage in my German parentage."

"Of course not!" Estelle said. It was clear that the doctor was enjoying the food and his iced tea. He was delighted with Estelle's raisin pie and said so.

After dinner, the doctor turned to Jake and said, "Jake, I think you should join us in the hunt tomorrow." Jake seemed surprised and looked at his Dad, who nodded his approval. About 8:00 o'clock the doctor said he was feeling tired from the hunt, excused himself, and walked over to the cabin to relax and retire for the night.

Friday morning seemed an ideal time for a quail hunt. By 7:00, breakfast was on the table for the hunters, and 30 minutes later they were on their way. Jim parked the pickup in the same oak grove, but he led them to a different field to hunt.

Jim had positioned the doctor on the right, Jake in the middle, and himself on the left. "I'll only shoot at the birds that fly off to the left. Doc, ye'll shoot those that swing right, and Jake will shoot those in the center." Jake felt good positioned between his father and the doctor. The dogs friskily made their way eastward in the middle of the field, and suddenly both dogs came down.

"I'm quite sure this is the covey, and when I give the word to the dogs, the birds will start risin' on the installment plan. When Jim said, "Flush!," eight birds flew up, all swinging to the left. Jim shot twice and three birds fell. The dogs quickly retrieved one each; Best brought his bird to Jim, and then Better did a rare thing—he found the third bird and brought his two to Jim.

"I'm amazed!" declared the doctor. "I can hardly believe the two things I just saw—Jim, you killed two birds with one shot, and that Better retrieved the second bird, with one already in his mouth."

"It happens ever once in awhile on a covey rise when a hunter is shootin' "scatter loads" and two birds get close and sometimes even cross each other. Once or twice, I've even killed three in one shot. But this is the only time I've ever seen any dog retrieve a second bird with one already in his mouth."

As the three hunters were riding back to the house for lunch, the doctor exclaimed, "This has been my greatest quail hunt ever! Thank you for a very enjoyable time."

After the noon meal, while Jim, Patsy, and Jake dressed, cleaned, and iced the birds, Estelle and Dr. Bonnhoffer spent over an hour in the cabin. Right off, Estelle told the doctor, "I would be glad if you called me Estelle instead of Miz Tharp." She spent a few minutes giving her testimony of how she had found Jesus only ten years ago and how through Dr. Martha Honeycutt she had learned how to pray. Then she presented the Gospel, finishing with the question, "Doctor, where do you stand with the Lord? Have you ever invited Him into your heart, surrendering your will and life to Him and allowing Him to impart to you His Holy Spirit?"

The doctor decided to be totally honest with this sincere, discerning woman. He sensed that she would not put pressure on him to do exactly as she had done to experience what she knew. But he had never before wanted to know Jesus Christ like he craved peace with God at this moment. "I'm ready! I'm hungry! I'm desperate!" the man almost shouted.

Estelle found it easy to lead the doctor in the sinner's prayer.

"May I embrace you?" the doctor asked, as he finished his prayer. Estelle's answer was to open her arms. He walked right into them, saying, "Thank you, Estelle! Now I know why I wanted to come and hunt quail with Jim—so I could meet you, find the Lord Jesus Christ as my personal Savior, and begin a new life in His grace. I hope it might be possible for us to communicate with each other so that you can help me learn more about the true way."

"Doctor, we don't have a phone, but here's my address. I hope you will come again and bring your wife, whether you are coming to hunt or not. This cabin was built for Jim's hunting guests, but I also use it as a prayer room when we don't have guests. So write and come to see us anytime."

The doctor promised to do that as they walked back to the house to join Jim, Jake, and Patsy, who had finished cleaning and packing the birds in ice and were sitting on the front porch. Jake went in and got two more chairs, and the five visited for a few minutes before the doctor said he needed to leave for home. "Well, folks, this has been a most significant weekend, one I shall never forget—I've found Christ as my Savior, made some very precious friends, and had the best quail hunt of my life."

"Congratulations, Doctor!" Jim said. "Ye've done somethin' I ain't got around to doin' yet—gettin' right with the Lord."

"Well, don't keep putting it off, Jim," he said as he stood, shook hands with Jim, and patted Jake on the shoulder. After smiling warmly at Patsy, he embraced Estelle and kissed her cheek. "Thanks, dear lady!"

Jim and Jake carried the ice chest full of quails to the doctor's car and lifted it into the trunk. Jim refused the $100 bill offered him, saying, "No, Doc, I do sometimes accept money from some of my guests, but I ain't seen a medical bill from ye yet."

"There won't be one, Jim!" Looking back at Estelle standing on the porch, he called, "Thanks for those delicious meals, the comfortable cabin, and the spiritual ministry. I shall not forget y'all!"

When the doctor had gone and the kitchen was clear, Estelle said to Patsy, "My dear girl, you are such a blessing! I'm turning the children over to you for the afternoon. I'll be in the cabin for several hours. Just knock on the door if you need me."

While raising the windows, Estelle heard a message—it was silent but certain—*go lie down on the couch and get quiet, preparing to receive my thoughts so you'll be able to share my heart, my concerns, and my tears.*

Even as a rush of fresh cool air came into the room, Estelle almost flew to the couch, removed her shoes, and stretched out fully.

Already the tears were flowing freely, but she did not bother to get a towel to wipe them. How easy it was to think and pray. She prayed for Jim, her six children, Patsy, all of her loved ones, all of Jim's loved ones, Dr. Bonnhoffer, and Dr. Whitehead. Then she grew sleepy and knew this, too, was a part of God's plan.

Estelle awakened from a dream, her tears still flowing. She was aware that her neck was wet with tears and the upper part of her dress soaked. Then she was startled as she began to recall her dream. An angel of judgment had flown over the prairie communities, then turned eastward and southward over the river bottoms, and floated above all the streams and bayous, dropping objects that remained a mystery to Estelle. She remembered visions of battlefields—strafing airplanes, exploding bombs, fire-spewing tanks, falling soldiers. She saw funeral processions in many communities arriving at the Hockenberry, Malcomb, and many other cemeteries all over the land. Other scenes in her vision included the Menard schoolhouse with a dozen believers on their knees and flames of spiritual power rising to the heavens from them; women from the Nady community fleeing rapists and murderers, screaming for their husbands to help them; mothers and fathers all over the country weeping for their fallen sons in battle; dozens of dead cattle lying in pastures with the familiar J T brand; and a bereavement wreath hanging on their own front door.

Estelle began sobbing. When she sought to rise from the couch, it seemed an invisible, unfelt hand pushed her back down; she knew this was part of her weeping season from which she was to make no effort to escape. She would continue in quiet submission. She knew she should resist the temptation to become morbid and restless over the vision of the wreath on their door. *Will it be Jim, one of the children, or me?* She felt the help of the Spirit release the worry from her mind. A comfort came, and her sobbing ceased, but the tears continued to flow. *My tears, His tears ... O how blessed I am that I might share His suffering ... I am* **to consider that the sufferings of the present time are not worth comparing to the glory that is to be revealed**.... As Estelle was released from the spirit of sadness, a sweeping peace cleared her mind and spirit which seemed to affect her bodily. She got up from the couch and washed and dried her face, allowing the towel to absorb most of the wetness of her neck.

Feeling refreshed, she stepped out of the cabin and into the company of Jim and Jake heading from the barn to the house. "I bet ye've been in that cabin all afternoon," Jim said.

"Yes, and I've had a most interesting time with the Lord." Estelle felt that she shouldn't say anymore. Inside, Carroll was sitting on Jeanette's lap, and he broke into a smile when he saw his mother.

"Supper's ready!" called Patsy.

The attendance on Sunday morning hinted of a partial fulfillment of Estelle's vision—a small, weak, subdued atmosphere. Homer made known to the congregation that the Spirit had released him and Helen from their ministry in Nady. He felt that with Estelle's anointing for prayer, teaching, and leading people to Christ, the Committee would want to consider inviting her to take on the responsibilities of Sunday morning services. He had Pastor Frank Fox's support in making the suggestion, and Ross, as chairman of the Committee, would present the matter to the other members.

After a brief farewell message and a lovely solo from Helen, Homer called on Ross to dismiss the service. Ross knew he faced a disappointed crowd, but he rejoiced in the wisdom of Brother Fox to put the congregation under the spiritual leadership of Estelle. He called on Estelle to pray the closing prayer. She first thanked God for all that had been accomplished under the ministry of Homer and Helen. Then, the Spirit helped her to pray for the enablement of the Spirit to rightly divide the Word of truth, that God might show His strength in her weakness, and that the small group might grow close and be united lest the enemy come in and divide, discourage, and defeat. Estelle was encouraged by the people expressing confidence in her and pledging prayer and faithfulness.

On the way home, Jim said, "Well, with the job of pastorin', how much more do ye reckon ye can stand?"

"The Lord will provide the strength, the will, and the help that I need, so I will trust Him. I think it'll be about three more weeks before the baby comes. I'll line up testimonies from Henry, George, and J. H. McKay for the Sunday I'll miss."

George was able to ease back into work, having recovered from tuberculosis. He had the children to help him with the farm, and Jim saw to it that he had the help he needed in setting nets and hauling fish to the market. BettyLee often assisted him with setting and raising nets. George had been able to pull his weight in the seining season, and he looked forward to a profitable season of trapping fur.

George and BettyLee were growing in their spiritual lives. Estelle was pleased with Linda's progress and very happy to hear her tell of Jack's letters filled with spiritual testimonies. Henry and Oda and many others who had been saved under Estelle's ministry were also growing spiritually, but not without some struggles.

Attended by Dr. Whitehead, Estelle gave birth to Shirley Ruth, her seventh child, on October 1, 1940. For several days after delivery, Oda and Patsy served her faithfully, with the help of the three older children.

Estelle anticipated that Thanksgiving Day of 1941 would be a time of spiritual renewal among those she would invite to initiate her new dining room—all of Jim's family, all of her's, including her brother Theo and his wife Elsie, the Buchannons, Sweeneys, Cooses, Morgans, LaFargues, and Bonnhoffers. During their time of fellowship, the doctor gave his testimony, Betty Jean sang "Great Is Thy Faithfulness," Jake read both an Old Testament and a New Testament passage, and Dr. Bonnhoffer spoke for several minutes. Estelle read prophecies by Sister Martha that she had written in a long letter. The *Indianapolis Star, Chicago Tribune,* and *Boston Globe*, as well as other newspapers, published the prophecies: (1) A great falling away of believers, (2) A sneak attack on America by a strong Asian power, (3) America would be a major participant in a world war that would last five years, and (4) An unusual passion would develop among evangelicals for another great historic spiritual awakening. Estelle closed the evening with a burdened prayer for such an awakening to break out in their communities.

Jim spent the first Sunday afternoon in December skinning and stretching coon and mink hides. Excited about his first week's catch of the season, he washed up at the barn, visited briefly with his animals, and then went to the house. As Jim entered the room, he found Estelle in tears. "Honey, what is so terribly wrong?"

She looked up from her Bible and ran to him. "The Japanese attacked our American Pacific Fleet out in Pearl Harbor, Hawaii, early this morning! Gabriel Heatter reported that their airplanes bombed and torpedoed our battleships there in the harbor and airplanes on the airbase, killing more than 2,000 military people and wounding over 1,000. He said it was a sneak attack that had been in the planning for months!" She stopped to weep and wipe tears, while Jim sought to come to grips with the significance of the news.

Estelle continued, "This is what Sister Martha prophesied! An Asian nation would make a sneak attack on us. So, according to her, I guess this is the beginning of a five-year war. And to think Jack might be in the middle of it very soon!" Jim walked over and turned on the radio to learn that all stations out of Little Rock and Memphis were reporting in various ways what he had just heard from Estelle.

A few days later, Jim rode in at noon from his trap line, ate lunch with Estelle and Patsy, and then skinned and stretched hides for three hours. A little past four o'clock, he went to the house and drank a cup of coffee and seemed quite nervous to Estelle.

"What's wrong, dear? You seem upset about something."

"Well, I don't really know what's got me on edge or what I'm so uneasy about. I don't feel sick or like there's somethin' wrong in my body. I've got the best bunch of hides I can ever remember to sell to Bob. He said he'd be here at 3:30—and that was nearly an hour ago. Do you feel uneasy about anythang?"

"I didn't want to mention it, but I've felt strange all day, like something terrible is about to happen. For some reason I felt the need to pray with Patsy before she left to get the children from school about an hour ago. She went early to get some things at the store and to take a few things to Mother."

"Did Patsy seem afraid or upset over anythang?"

"If she was, she didn't act like it, but she sure clung to me when she hugged me goodbye. She said she appreciated all we had done for her. But now that you've brought it up, I think we might have reason to be concerned."

"Well, I probably should drive down and check on her, but Bob oughta be comin' any time now. He has never been this late before."

"Let's wait to see if he comes in the next few minutes. If Patsy and the children aren't here in the next half hour, we'll go see about them." Thinking she heard a car drive up, Estelle said, "Maybe that's Bob now."

Jim knew something was wrong as soon as he saw Bob jump out of his pickup and run to the gate. He met him at the porch steps. Looking at his friend's white face and pursed lips, he asked, "What's wrong, Bob?"

"Ah, Jim! A few minutes ago I come up on the ... uh, ... ghastliest scene! A woman—I think she's yore helper here, ... Patsy."

"Yeah, Bob. What about her?"

Bob had turned his back to Jim while he coughed, blew his nose, and wiped tears from his eyes. "Man, Jim, I hate tellin' you this! She's been murdered and probably raped. Her body is tore up, ... there's blood all over her from her head to her feet. It probably happened more than an hour ago; whoever did it left her body out in the weather uncovered. I knew it was yore car; the door was open, and the motor was still runnin'. I turned the key off and shut the door. I reckon it's a case for you and the sheriff. Jim, I hate to tell this to Estelle. Let me stay out here and try to get my breath while you go tell her."

Jim was weeping when he opened the door to the living room to tell Estelle. She was sobbing, having already heard what Bob was saying. "Oh, why would the Lord let this happen and take her this way? Honey, please go get the children. I don't think I can stand to drive around the sight where Patsy's body is. Would Bob be willing to stay here until you come back with the children? And, please drive another route home— don't let the children see what has happened to our dear Patsy!" Jim held her close and tried to comfort her as she began sobbing again. As soon as she calmed down, Jim went back outside to talk with Bob.

"Bob, I would appreciate it if ye would stay with Estelle while I go pick up the kids at the schoolhouse. I shouldn't be gone long. As soon as ye get home, would ye phone Lloyd in DeWitt and let 'im know about the murder and where the body is located? Tell the sheriff I'll go to the crime scene in a couple of hours and wait for 'im there. Since it'll be quite dark by then, Lloyd will need to bring lights. He'll take Patsy's body to the coroner in DeWitt. I'm sure sorry for what ye had to see! I know it had to be upsettin'. While I'm gettin' the children, why don't ye go in the house so that Estelle will feel safe."

Bob knocked on the front door lightly so that he wouldn't startle Estelle. "I'll stay with you 'til Jim gets back; then I'll leave so that I can get back to Tichnor and make the call to the sheriff. While Jim is picking up the children, he wants me to go ahead and look at the hides and give you the check. So I'll do that now."

Both teachers, Mrs. Bass and Mrs. Sweeney, remained with the four Tharp children, knowing that sooner or later either Jim, Estelle, or Patsy would show up for them. They heard Jim's pickup arrive, and both teachers followed the children out.

"Ladies, I'm sorry to be late." Jim decided it was best to reveal the tragic event even in front of the children. "Patsy was on her way to pick up the children, and she met with a terrible death. We don't know yet who done it. We just know she's been murdered." The children began to cry, and Jim could not hold back the tears. Each teacher had two of the crying children in their arms, and Jim just stood and choked back the tears. When the four noticed that their daddy was also crying, they all ran to him. Jim dropped to his knees, folding each child into his arms, one after the other. Nothing as traumatic as this had ever hit Estelle and him.

Ebrena Sweeney spoke, addressing Jim and the children. "Well, dear ones, I knew Patsy well enough to know that she loved the Lord. And regardless of the ugly thing that happened, we know that she is now with the Lord—removed from all hurt, and tears, and worry about life. Jim, you and Estelle and the children took her in when she had no home, no future, no hope. You've cared for her like she was your very own."

"Yes, Ebrena, she *was* our own. We loved her and took her in when her husband, Punkin, was killed, *murdered.* She has sure been a blessin' to us. Well, children, we'd better get back to the house. Bob Hibbard found Patsy, and he's pretty shook up, too. I asked him to stay with Estelle while I come to pick up the children. Thanks, Ebrena and Miz Bass, for stayin' late and takin' care of my children."

"Oh, Jim, you are welcome! We'll be praying for all of you. Let us know if we can help in any way."

"Thanks, ladies! Don't expect the children to be at school for a few days. I think Estelle will need them home with her for awhile."

"Of course, we understand." Both teachers hugged each of the children again before they got in the pickup to go home, and they waved as Jim drove away with all four in the cab with him.

Anniece was the first to speak as they drove northward. "Daddy, why would the Lord let this awful thing happen to Patsy? She was *soooo sweet!*" She sobbed out her last words.

"Honey, I think yore mama will have a better answer to that than I can give," Jim said.

He had decided to drive north a ways and take the long route home to save the children from being exposed to the murder scene.

"Oh, Daddy, I know Mama is just hurting something awful!" Jeanette said.

Jake and Burl kept their hurts to themselves for awhile, but when they were back home the two boys were the first to run to their mother. They buried their faces in their mother's side and wept out their grief. Then the girls took turns receiving amazing comfort from their mother, who said to all of them as they listened intently, "Children, our dear Patsy whom we all loved so much has been called home to be with Jesus. Let us not think that the terrible tragedy she met with is any cause to believe that God was absent or any less loving with her in receiving her spirit to Himself in great love and comfort. We'll pray for whoever hurt her and ask God to have mercy on him or them. We all need the Lord's help, and we'll believe God to come and comfort us."

Turning to Bob, who had put on his hat, overcoat, and gloves to leave, Estelle said, "Uncle Bob, this was hard on you, too. We love you like family, and I thank you for staying with me and the little ones. You were a great comfort! You drive carefully going home, and just know we love and appreciate you."

"That's right, Bob. Tell Lloyd I'll meet him at the scene later tonight," Jim said.

Bob wiped tears again as he drove away and headed for Tichnor.

Jim told Estelle that he was proud of how the children handled hearing about Patsy's murder and that both teachers had been very comforting and understanding. Then he remembered they had asked him to tell Estelle that they were praying for the family.

Estelle finished the meal that Patsy had planned before leaving the house a few hours earlier. She had been such a meaningful part of the family that it would be difficult for them to sit down and eat without Patsy. While praying before the meal, Estelle thanked the Lord for all that Patsy had meant to them and asked Him to comfort the family. She prayed for His guidance as Jim and Lloyd investigated the crime. She even prayed for the perpetrators and for God to deal with them as He saw fit. She heard a few sniffles during the blessing, but as the food was passed, their natural need for satisfying their hunger took over. When he had finished eating, Jim said he guessed he ought to saddle Flash and be on his way "out there to wait for Lloyd. I shore hope we can come up with some solid evidence—maybe they dropped a glove, a knife, a cigarette, or somethin' else that would be a clue about who and what we are to look for."

As Jim rode out, the night was dark, cold, and cloudy, seeming to promise snow; but only a small flake here and there was hitting his face. A snow wouldn't help a thing right now, Jim thought. From the way Bob had described the scene, it included three or four large oak trees, so Jim guessed that he knew the exact spot where he would find the car. As he was nearing the site, Flash turned slightly and Jim could barely make out the vehicle under the trees. Reining the black to a stop at the car, Jim dismounted and placed his hat on the front seat of the car. He lit the carbide headlight and attached it to his hunting cap that he had removed from his hunting coat. Turning his light on bright, he walked over to the corpse and saw what Bob had seen a few hours before. He was thankful, though, that no wild animal had picked up the scent of blood and found her body. Aloud he spoke, "The bastards! They never even threw her clothes back over her!" Anguish washed over him. Thinking he might get sick, he stepped away.

Hearing Flash snort and seeing him turn his head southeastward, Jim turned the gas up higher on his headlight. Looking in that direction and about 30 yards away from him, Jim was quite sure he was seeing a pair of human eyes shining dimly. He knew those eyes did not belong to any beast he had ever seen.

"Don't move an inch!" Jim ordered, as he levered a shell into his rifle loud enough to send a message. "I've got my gun on ye. If ye turn and run in any direction, I'll put a bullet in yore heart! Come toward me slowly!"

"Don't shoot! I'm comin'," came a male voice. "But I ain't the one that killed her." Jim watched as the man approached and stopped about 20 yards away. Jim could see that he was dressed in a soiled tan Duxbak hunting outfit and his gloved hands were hanging at his side.

"Don't move!" Jim said. "I'm comin' closer, and if ye make a move or go for a gun, I'll kill ye! Drop yore huntin' coat. Slow now, unbutton it, and shuck it off. I'll know if ye go for a gun, and ye'll be dead." Jim reached up and turned up the controls of his headlight for a stronger flow of gas and brighter light. As the man was unbuttoning his coat, Jim could make out the bulge of a gun on his hip, but he saw no sign of a rifle or shotgun. When the coat was on the ground, Jim moved closer. "Now, slowly unbuckle yore gun belt and throw it, with the gun in it, over here to where I'm standin'." When it was done, Jim said, "Now turn around and put yore hands in the air. I'm comin' over to frisk ye." When he had obeyed, Jim frisked every part of the man and removed a knife from a boot holster. He figured that since the coat had fallen heavily, it probably contained items he should check. Believing the man to be totally unarmed, Jim said, "Now, turn around and face me!" He was surprised to see a young face with a Roman nose and something of a daring look. "Look now at where I'm pointin', and walk around me and stop over there when ye get to the body." Maybe the guy was not as daring as he had thought, because he stopped just before he got to the body. Jim shone the light on the victim's face and hair now smeared with dried blood. "Are ye denyin' that ye done this?"

"I swear, man! I never done it!"

"But ye know who did, and ye had some part in it!"

"Naw, I never touched her!"

"Then why are ye back here at the scene, about five hours later?"

"Cuz the feller who done it used my knife. I've looked ever'where, and I ain't found it. I reckon it's gotta be 'round here somewhere."

"Are ye sayin' the knife I took off ye is not the one that was used?"

"Naw, I use that knife for skinnin' hides and dressin' my kill."

"Okay, mister, I hear the sheriff comin', so I'm gonna tie yore hands and bind ye to that tree over there. We're gonna do an investigation here and try to get some answers about what happened to

Patsy and why. Any information we can get from ye will shore help yore case. But ye ain't ruled out as havin' a part in this murder yet. So put yore hands down slow-like and put 'em behind ye." After Jim had tied the man's hands, he said, "Now, head for that tree I'm pointin' at, and I'll see to it ye don't run off." Again the man complied and Jim tied him to the tree.

The sheriff had parked in the road facing Jim's car and was walking toward them. "Whudda we got here, Jim?"

"Well, Sheriff, I just got here a few minutes ago. Shore didn't expect anyone near the scene of the crime this time of night, but Flash indicated someone was around. I caught this man's eyes shinin' in my headlight. I disarmed 'im and tied 'im up here. He claims he didn't kill Patsy, but he's gotta know who did, cuz he says he come back to find his knife that the killer used. Why don't ye talk to him while I go check on my horse."

"Jim, I'm so sorry about this. Patsy was like one of your own family, and I know this has got to be hittin' you and Estelle and your children pretty hard. I remember Patsy—she served us some fine meals when I was at your place. How's Estelle takin' it?"

"Well, ye know she's a strong woman, but it couldn't have hurt her more if it had been one of our own girls."

"Yeah, of course. But she'll be a comfort to the children and everybody else who's grievin'."

"Be right back, Lloyd." Jim went to Flash, who was still where he had been left. Jim stroked his neck, finger-combed his mane, scratched between his ears, and talked to him. The black nuzzled his master's coat and sniffed, obviously uneasy about the scene. Jim again dropped Flash's reins to the ground, allowing the horse freedom to step around if he wished, and he returned to where Lloyd was questioning the stranger.

"Jim, this guy claims he's Preston Hill and that he's been trappin' and huntin' on some of your territory like Wild Goose and Elbow Slough. He won't say who killed Patsy, but he knows him. He says he's a buddy of his, but he took off this afternoon and is long gone from these parts. Preston is sure he used his knife, but he can't find it. We'll look around here for evidence tonight and wrap the corpse. I'll take it to the morgue in DeWitt and have the coroner check the body for rape and determine what they used to kill her. The body is in bad shape; anyone can see that. It hurts me to think of all she suffered before she died. I hope to God we can find the ones who killed her! We've already got one of 'em. We'll jail Hill until he can prove he's innocent. It's hard for me to believe he'd come snoopin' around the murder scene five hours after the crime if he was not a participant. I'm glad Flash helped you get him.

"Go look in your car, Jim, and see if everything's in order. Check the front and back seats, and look in the trunk. Bob said the car was left runnin', and he shut off the engine when he got here." Jim checked the Pontiac and could find nothing that would give them any clues. He removed the keys and locked the car, planning to drive it home the next day.

The sheriff moved Hill from the tree to his pickup, handcuffing and chaining him securely. When Jim returned to the crime scene, Lloyd was wrapping the corpse in a blanket. "Jim, I know this will be hard for you, but you pick up the end with her head there. I'll lift this end, and we'll carry her to the pickup. I'm sure the Essex people will clean her up good and make her presentable for the service whenever and wherever you and Estelle wish. One thing though…, this guy claims he and his buddy have a camp somewhere near Buckhorn. Do you think you could ride over there tomorrow and see if you can locate it? Look around and learn all you can about how they live and who might have seen 'em. Note anything around there that might tell us somethin'. Then come to town."

"Shore, Lloyd. I'll go tomorrow morning to see what I can find. I know Estelle will wanta go see Patsy in the evening. Hope they'll have her cleaned up by tomorrow night."

"Surely they will, Jim. Well, I'll get goin'. I hope you can find out somethin' 'bout the killer."

As soon as the sheriff pulled away with his prisoner and the corpse, Jim got his hat from the Pontiac. As he mounted Flash, he realized that snow was falling lightly. The black picked his way through the darkness, never veering once from the road.

The next morning Jim was up early, but not ahead of Estelle. He was dressed for cold weather when he sat down to a breakfast of bacon, biscuits and gravy, and hot coffee.

"Estelle, be ready to leave for DeWitt about three o'clock this afternoon. Lloyd thinks they'll have Patsy cleaned up and ready for ye to see her by then. See if Oda and Henry can stay with the children, cuz I don't wanta leave 'em here alone. I'm ridin' this mornin' to where the killers are supposed to be camped down on Buckhorn. I oughta be back by noon."

Flash was eager to go, and Jim decided to leave at first light. Two hundred yards before reaching the regular trail crossing Buckhorn Slough, Jim reined Flash off into a familiar clump of oaks and dismounted. He would wait for better light—at least all the light that would be available on this cold, snowy day. His horse gave no sign that Jim would find a live body in the camp over across the slough.

After an hour, Jim decided it was as light as it was going to get. He mounted Flash and started looking for the camp. He found it exactly where most tents were pitched on the bluff bank, and where several years ago he himself had driven a pitcher pump to have clean water for cooking, making coffee, and watering his animals. There was very little in the tent of interest to Jim, except a Bowie knife. Was this the knife that had been used on Patsy? If so, it had been cleaned. Had Hill overlooked it here and thought it had been left at the scene? Jim studied its sharp edge and its back edge curved to a very sharp point. Had this ugly thing he now held been the weapon used to take the life of one who was like family to him, Estelle, and the children? Jim wrapped the knife in an old towel that was lying on the table and put it in his Duxbak coat pocket. He decided to take one of the .38 pistol shells, noting that it was exactly the same as the soft-nose kind he used.

It was getting dark when Jim and Estelle arrived at the sheriff's office. Lloyd suggested they go on over to the funeral home to view the body. Estelle was nervous as they followed Lela into the viewing room. When the casket was opened, Estelle said softly, "O, my dear Patsy! Bless you, dear! I never realized when you hugged and kissed me yesterday before you went for the children, it would be our last time together." She wiped tears, then turned to Jim and said, "Well, she sure looks better than I thought she would after being treated so cruelly."

"Yeah, honey, they've done a good job cleanin' her up. I'm shore glad ye didn't see the way them murderers left her!"

"Well, they can't hurt her anymore. She's with Jesus and Punkin now. No more tears or worries. We'll sure miss her. I don't dread for the children to see her now, but I know it'll hurt them to have to say goodbye."

"Yeah, but they'll need to see her to have closure." Did ye bring the checkbook to pay for the funeral?"

"Yes, and we need to talk to Mr. Essex and set the time for the funeral, too. I think I oughta ask Brother Fox to officiate. You know, he lives right across the street from here."

After Jim and Estelle had selected the casket, answered several questions about the deceased, and paid the bill, they walked across the street to see Brother Fox. Ola and Frank welcomed them warmly, and Ola expressed her condolences. "We're all so sorry and shocked over what happened to Patsy. We remember her; we know she worked for you and that you led her to Jesus!" Frank added, "We remember how lovely Patsy was and how real her testimony rang."

"Brother Fox, Jim and I would like for you to speak at Patsy's funeral."

"I'll be honored, Estelle, but I do think it appropriate that, after I open in prayer and Betty Jean sings, you tell how Patsy and her husband came into your life. Don't hesitate to tell how the Lord saved Punkin and then how she gave her heart to Jesus. This funeral service can be a Gospel message to the living."

When satisfied that all arrangements for the funeral were complete, Jim took Estelle to Freeman's Restaurant, where he and the sheriff often went when they met for various reasons in DeWitt. Lloyd and his wife were to meet them there for dinner.

Lloyd and Irene came in, and Lloyd made introductions. Mrs. Freeman said, "Dorene will serve you, and it's all on the house tonight!" When Lloyd protested, she said, "No, Sheriff! You've given us all kinds of business on a regular basis. We're so glad Estelle is with y'all tonight! She's family; you know, she and Dorene, who works for us, are sisters. No arguing, it's all on the house tonight." Lloyd expressed his thanks, and Mrs. Freeman excused herself to greet some folks just entering the restaurant.

Lloyd said, "Jim, isn't it good to have Estelle and Irene with us? Jim and I have been in here a lot, but never all four of us together." Irene asked about Patsy and expressed her condolences. When their Swiss steak and vegetables came, Dorene freshened their coffee and left them to enjoy their meal. She returned later to announce apple, raisin, and coconut pies were available for dessert.

In their goodbyes, Estelle told Mrs. Freeman, Dorene, and the LaFargues that it helped the sad occasion to be less painful because she got to be with them and share such a lovely meal. Driving home, Jim said, "Surely this snow and ice will all be melted by Saturday so that we can have a nice afternoon for the funeral."

"Yes, Jim, I hope that's true, but we'll have to take whatever weather we get."

The Saturday afternoon of the funeral turned out to be cold, but clear. Pastor Frank Fox welcomed an attendance of over 100 people in the funeral chapel, prayed a short meaningful prayer, and read a brief obituary of Patsy. Betty Jean sang, "God Be with You 'til We Meet Again," and then Estelle gave the sketch of Patsy's life as she knew it from the time she first saw her at their door several years before, desperately looking for some meaning in life. She went immediately to Patsy's and Punkin's confession of Jesus Christ, then of Punkin's murder, after which she dwelt on the spiritual growth and blessing that Patsy had been to the Tharp family and to the Christian community in Nady. Pastor Fox's message emphasized the need for those who do not know Christ to act immediately while there is time, saying, "Patsy is proof that we can die young." Many of the people lingered and expressed their love and sympathy to Jim, Estelle, and the children.

On the way home, a tearful Anniece spoke from the back seat. "I miss Patsy so much it hurts! But just like you said this morning, Mama, when all of us kids were crying, she's with the Lord and even happier than when she was with us. I know she liked us and loved us, and I'm so glad God let her live with us!" The 10-year-old girl's remarks brought tears to everyone's eyes.

Estelle braced herself to go through Patsy's personal things on Sunday afternoon. In her purse was an envelope marked "Burial." Estelle found six $20 bills. The dear girl had probably planned to add to this amount in the months and years to come, so her burial costs wouldn't be a burden to others when her time came. Estelle thought, *Oh, sweet Patsy, it was a joy for me and Jim to pay that $1,100 for your funeral. You were* *like one of our own. We'll find a use for the $120 you left that will be like a memorial to you. I don't think I told you often enough how special you were. The Lord sent you and Punkin to us. Punkin helped us bring those evil people to justice, and the Lord helped us lead both of you to Jesus. O, my dear Patsy, I shall never forget the day you came to our door. I knew instantly we were to open our heart and home to you. You shall not be forgotten!* Several questions went through her mind: What should I do with her clothes? What can I do with her Bible and other books that she had striven so hard to learn to read? How can I know who to contact and inform of the girl's passing? How can I help Jim, the children, and myself cope with the hurting emptiness of Patsy's tragic death?

Throughout December, Estelle spent early mornings from 6:00 to 7:00 at the cabin in intercessory prayer. Jim insisted that Jake accompany her, regardless of the weather. The 12-year-old lad could either go inside or stand guard on the outside. In his adolescent pride and immature worldview, he silently wrote his mother off as a religious extremist because she wept when she prayed. She would often cry out in different biblical expressions, making him think she was fanatical. At times he even wondered if his mother might be mentally unstable.

But Mama had that vision about Birdie being hanged, and Dad said it was exactly like she described all the circumstances to him, the very time and place. So he was able to save Birdie from a horrible death and bring the murderers to justice. And what an influence Mama has in this community and beyond. The way this Dr. Bonnhoffer took to her, listened to her, and allowed her to lead him to Jesus. And the way I feel when she talks to me about the Lord! But, really now, is this thing she calls revival ever going to hit this part of the country the way she thinks it is? Why, I can't bring myself to believe anything like that has ever happened or ever will…the way she claims Dad and I are going to get saved.

Jake was always glad when his mother was through praying. But as she emerged from the cabin, always in tears, he could never bring himself to follow through with his plans to say what had come to his mind. His love and respect for her would quickly cancel out all his disappointment in her. Occasionally, he would discuss her praying and her spirituality with his father. Even Jim would shake his head and often say, "You gotta hand it to her, son, she's got somethin' goin' with the Lord that we ain't gonna ever be able to figger out—unless she happens to win us over and we turn to the Lord with a zeal that matches her own!"

One night a week, usually Thursday night, after supper dishes were done and she had spent an hour with the family, Estelle would depart for the cabin to pray until midnight. Jim or Jake would walk over with her, stand guard awhile, and then return to the house. One of them would go out several times during the next three hours to listen for any signal from the animals that they detected a problem or to make sure she was safe. One or the other was always there at the door when Estelle emerged from the cabin. Neither Jim nor Jake realized when she started this praying schedule—an hour every morning and every Thursday from dark to midnight—that it would last for another four years.

The new year of 1942 came in with low temperatures and snow affecting sections of several of the southern states, including all of Arkansas County. Jim did not make his trap run during the first part of January. Taking advantage of the zero temperatures, he butchered several hogs, including a few wild ones that he, Henry, George, Ross, and Jeff were able to find and kill in the bottoms by tracking them on the snow. He and Henry also enjoyed some duck hunting with two of the clubs over on the Merrisach. During the week that school was dismissed, the children enjoyed playing games and skating on ice with their cousins and the Washington and Buchannon children.

When Linda came on the tractor pulling a small cart to pick up her children, Estelle could see that she was crying. When she met her at the door, Linda rushed into her arms, exclaiming, "Oh, Estelle! Jack's dead! His ship was blown up!" As Estelle held Linda, she wept with her. Finally able to continue, Linda said, "His ship went down and hundreds drowned in the Atlantic. Oh, how will I be able to tell the children?"

Estelle was glad to see that Oda was gathering the children around the table for a meal of venison stew. Jim noticed that Linda and Estelle were upset about something, and he told Oda to go ahead with the meal and they would join them soon.

Estelle drew Linda and Jim aside where the children could not hear her and said, "Jim, Linda just got word that Jack's ship sank in the

Atlantic and hundreds drowned. Jack's gone. She hasn't told the children yet. Linda, I know it's hard for you to tell the children, so I think we should let them enjoy supper and then Jim and I will tell them. I think you and the children should all stay here with us tonight."

"Thanks, Estelle, but we've got to face up to Jack never coming home, so we might as well face it tonight by ourselves…no, you're right, we do need y'all tonight. I think we'll go home tomorrow."

"Yeah, stay with us at least tonight," Jim said. "I think it will help yer children to be with ours even through the night. It's still snowin' outside, so I'll go put yore tractor in the barn. I'm glad ye didn't try and drive over in yore pickup. Don't think it woulda made it up the incline comin' over here." As Jim drove the tractor to the barn, he could see that it was snowing hard and he figured the temperatures were hovering near zero. His heart was sad that his friend and neighbor, Jack, would not be coming home. *But maybe Jack is still alive and aware somewhere. Maybe he even knows he's with the Lord, like Estelle believes and teaches… she taught Jack about the afterlife. Jack even warned me to not put off yieldin' to the Lord. So maybe Jack right this minute is happy with the Lord.* Jim decided to shut the thought of Jack and his fate out of his mind.

The next evening, Gabriel Heatter reported that the Germans had opened a costly U-boat offensive against the Atlantic sea-lanes and many American ships had already been sunk. He named three of the sunken vessels loaded with American military men going to England for an eventual invasion of the continent. As the news program was interrupted for a commercial, Estelle said to Jim, "Well, honey, what Sister Martha predicted up at Camp Doughboy last fall is surely coming to pass. It just hurts that we have to lose Jack here in the early part of the war. I feel so badly for Linda and the children!"

"Yeah, I do, too. We'll hep 'em all we can, but I know we can't take the place of Jack. He was a good man, a great neighbor, and a hard worker. I know he'd have made a good soldier, too! It seems a greater tragedy that he had to drown gettin' to the war."

"We're going to lose many more, a lot of them from right here on the prairie!" Estelle said with a sigh in her soul. "O, Lord, help them to be ready to meet you!"

Jim turned to her with a serious look and said, "I could've been aboard one of them ships that was sunk if those doctors had read my heart condition as Dr. Bonnhoffer did. Course, I'm glad I didn't go down that way. But I ain't no better than them poor boys who drowned. Maybe they'll recall me one of these days. I shore ain't rarin' to leave y'all, but I don't feel quite right with thousands goin' to war and me stayin' home."

"Now, honey, we've been over this before. You aren't supposed to go to war! Just feel sure that the Lord is sparing you for His own purposes. We'll all see this in due time. Don't think or worry about it!"

Jim and Jake had slept over at the cabin to give Linda and her children plenty of room in the Tharp bedrooms. Linda and her daughters slept together in one bed the earlier part of the night. Around two o'clock in the morning, Linda slipped over and got in bed with Estelle. About daylight Estelle roused, hearing Linda weeping softly. She put her hand on her shoulder and prayed, "Lord, You know Linda's breaking heart over the loss of her dear husband. But Your Word tells us, **Precious in the sight of the Lord is the death of his saints**. You foresaw Jack's death, and You were there to comfort him and escort him to his heavenly home. Now with Your great comfort, come this morning and be with Linda and her three children. Just now give Linda strength for this day, and touch each of the children's hearts, so that when they wake up and remember with sadness that their father is gone they'll sense Your comforting presence also. Make us all a blessing to these grieving hearts whom we love so much."

Linda echoed Estelle's "Amen," and she whispered, "Estelle, you continue to be the Lord's comforter to the Buchannons. When we first moved onto your farm, you and Mister Jim came over and welcomed and comforted us. Then you led us all to Jesus, and here you are this morning again being the Lord's voice of comfort to us. Thanks!"

"Try to get some more sleep, dear. Stay in bed awhile, at least until the children are stirring and you feel they need you. I'm going to slip out and get breakfast. Jim and Jake will be over in a little while. Don't get up until you are good and ready. It will do you good to go back to sleep now."

Estelle had coffee, bacon, eggs, and biscuits and gravy ready to serve when Jim and Jake came in. She spoke in a low voice, "Go ahead and sit down and eat your breakfast. I've urged Linda to sleep awhile." Jim nodded as he and Jake began filling their plates.

"Guess the children won't be goin' to school for a few more days," Jim said.

"Probably not for another week, even if it doesn't snow anymore. But I think it's still coming down out there, isn't it?"

"Yeah, hard enough that I don't think we'll venture out to the traps or to the cattle today. Tomorrow, I'll load several wagons with hay, hitch them to the tractor, and go throw out hay to the herd. Today, Jake and I will just patch some harness, shoe our ridin' horses, and make use of ourselves inside during this bad spell. I hope Linda and the children decide to spend a few days with us. If she needs somethin' done over at their place, we'll go by tractor and take care of it. I know we've enough food to feed all of us durin' this cold spell, even if it lasts a month."

"I'll see if there's anything Linda needs from home and if something is needing attention over there," Estelle said.

The days passed with news reports that the U.S. government had mobilized a lot of scientists to find efficient ways and means of tracking and sinking U-boats. Inshore and offshore patrols were organizing and destroying enemy vessels increasingly, a comfort to the captains of those ships carrying American troops to England.

Linda was grateful for Jim's and Estelle's kindness in allowing her and the children an extended stay. For their convenience and to give them more privacy, Estelle directed that a cot be moved into the cabin so that Linda and her children could be together as a family. She insisted that they take a small battery radio with them for music and news. They were invited to take their meals with the Tharps, which Linda was thankful for, because she realized her children needed to spend time with the Tharp children. Estelle seemed to know exactly when they all needed to pray and sing together; she would read a Scripture and pray down the comfort of the Holy Spirit on all of them. Jim and Jake kept the path cleared between the two dwellings, even though it was like a tunnel with snow piled up about six feet on each side.

One evening before Estelle had begun preparing the evening meal, she was pleasantly surprised to have the Washingtons drive in on their tractor and wagon. Susan brought a large kettle of beef stew and cornbread she had just taken out of the oven. They had learned about the loss of Jack and wanted to be with Linda and the children.

While all three ladies were setting the table and pouring the tea, Susan exclaimed, "It sho' ain't the same since Ms. Patsy and Mr. Jack be gone from us! I'se been a-prayin' hawd fo' all of ye who's been grievin'. We just needs to be wif ye, so I tell Birdie, les go tonight!" Estelle and Linda both responded with their thanks for the food they had brought and their thoughtfulness in coming to see them.

In early February, Estelle realized that Linda was truly allowing the Holy Spirit to help her emerge from the deepest levels of grief. She displayed periods of joy and wanted to join Estelle in prayer and Bible study more often. She volunteered to drive the children to school and to pick them up in the evening. She also helped in cooking and cleaning, volunteering to grocery shop and get the mail. In the middle of the month, she insisted that she was ready to take the children and return to their place.

In early March Estelle was pleasantly surprised to receive a letter from Dr. Martin Bonnhoffer. He desired to come and spend a weekend the last of March if the cabin was available and if his coming would not interfere with their plans. He would hope to have some time with her to report his spiritual progress, to study certain passages of Scripture, and to learn more about prayer. He was not expecting to have any hunting time with Jim, but it would be a pleasure to visit with him and maybe even ride horseback with him or Jake, or both. He would expect to pay for all the meals he would share with them and the lodging for three nights. He would like to arrive on Thursday afternoon about 4:00 and depart Sunday afternoon at 3:00. "Please write and let me know if this is possible. I shall understand perfectly if it is not a convenient time." He signed it "Martin Bonnhoffer."

Jim agreed with Estelle that the dates would be fine. "Maybe he'll go to worship with us on Sunday mornin' and hear ye preach before he leaves. I hope the weather will cooperate so we can have a pleasant horseback ride. We probably won't have time to hunt since he wants to spend quite a bit of time with ye. It looks like ye have a follower in the doctor. He wants to know more about what ye know."

Linda and Jeanette helped Estelle clean the cabin and get it in readiness for the doctor. Estelle had not missed a day praying for him.

She'd written down several Scriptures she wanted to share with him when it was possible. She was quite certain his coming was of the Lord. *Wouldn't it be good, Lord, if Dr. Bonnhoffer could meet Sister Martha and really learn from a scholar? But I am here to be used to the extent of my capability, though I know I am limited.* She, Linda, and Jeanette drove to Tichnor to purchase groceries and other supplies. She planned to serve the dishes the doctor had seemed to enjoy when he was with them the previous fall.

Jim was on the front porch reading the *Gazette* when the doctor drove up and parked outside the gate. After he had greeted Jim, Estelle, and the children, he said, "Jim, how have you been feeling? Noticing anything about your heart?"

"Naw, Doc! I feel fine!"

"Well that's good. I brought my stethoscope to listen to your heart, but I don't figure I'll find anything significant."

"Doc, if it's this nice tomorrow, why don't ye ride over with me to check the cattle? It'll probably take an hour or so. I know you and Estelle wanta spend some time together. I'll jes' let ye set the schedule."

"Yeah, a ride would be nice! How about my riding the buckskin?"

"Shore, Doctor! He's a good ridin' horse."

Since it was a pleasant spring evening and the mosquitoes did not seem to be around yet, Jim and his guest sat on the porch to visit for awhile, finding each other pleasant to converse with. They talked about the war and the recent sinking of ships, some fairly close to the New York and New Jersey shores. Jim told the doctor about their loss of Jack on one of those ships a few weeks ago and that he'd meet the widow and her three children at the supper table.

"Oh, that's too bad she lost her husband! Is she the young woman who was helping Estelle when I was here last?"

"No, that young woman was Patsy, who was like one of our family; she met an even worst fate." Jim explained the horrible end to which Patsy had come. The doctor listened with a mixture of sympathy and anger. When he asked if the perpetrators had been found and dealt with, Jim explained that he had captured an abettor that night, about five hours after she had been raped and murdered. After Sheriff LaFargue had questioned the man extensively, he had revealed the name of the murderer. Jim told the doctor he had arrested the murderer a week later over in Mississippi, and he was sentenced to life in prison last week in DeWitt.

"Great work, Jim! I'm pleased to hear it, and I'm very proud of the work you do!"

"Well, thanks, Doc. I enjoy workin' with Sheriff LaFargue, but seein' what happened to Patsy shore took a lot outa me—how she had been abused, mangled, stabbed with a knife, and left naked to lay out in the cold night. It shore made me sick and so angry that I was ready to turn mean in dealin' with the bad guys!"

"Yes, I can understand, Jim!"

Estelle called supper, and both men were glad to change the subject. At the table, Estelle introduced Linda, Annie, Janet, and Robert. The doctor greeted them warmly. "I'm so sorry to hear what happened to your brave husband and father!" All four nodded their thanks.

Leading a prayer of thanksgiving, Estelle included petitions that the Lord would comfort Linda and the children and make their time with Doctor Bonnhoffer one of edification and a clearer understanding of the things of God. Then she thanked God for the food and asked His blessing on their fellowship.

"Jim, since it's so nice out now, I think I'd like for us to ride at least for an hour. Then I can check your heart. If Estelle and I could spend an hour together later tonight, that would sure be fine with me."

"Jake, how about goin' out and saddlin' Flash and the buckskin? It's only 4:45, so we will have about an hour and fifteen minutes to ride before it starts to get dark," Jim said. Jake headed for the barn, followed by Burl and Russ. Estelle, Linda, and Jeanette began clearing the table and preparing to wash dishes.

Not long after the men returned from their ride, Estelle walked with the doctor to the cabin. She praised the Lord silently, rejoicing that God had answered her prayers and had led Dr. Bonnhoffer to **grow in the grace and knowledge of our Lord and Savior Jesus Christ**. She also thanked God that she felt calm and confident as she anticipated an anointed time sharing with him the Scriptures the Holy Spirit had led her to use.

Realizing that it was warmer in the cabin than she had expected, Estelle raised two windows to get some cooler air. "Please sit in that comfortable chair, Doctor, and I'll sit here on the sofa. It will be nice to see you sitting where my mentor, Dr. Martha Honeycutt, usually sat when we studied right here in this place for over a year. Now, I'm glad you have your Bible with you, and I notice you have a notebook. Well, the Holy Spirit has given me several passages that I know we are to study. So I feel prepared.

"First, let's turn to II Peter 3:18." Seeing the doctor find the book, chapter, and verse with little effort made her realize that he was already familiar with the Bible. "This verse is about *growing in grace.* Would you be willing to share with me how you began your early spiritual development, even as you left here last fall. I'd like to hear how you dealt with some of the doubts and struggles that you encountered when you came to the experience of prayer and what efforts you made to get to know the Bible. Maybe you had some disappointments in people who failed to understand your new interest in spiritual things."

The doctor smiled and leaned forward. "You know, Estelle, I rejoiced in the Lord and prayed nearly all the way home last fall. By the time I got to our house, I knew just how to tell Maureen what had happened in my heart and life. But before I got a chance to tell her of my newly found joy in the Lord, she said, 'Honey, you're different!' I told Maureen, 'Yes, the most wonderful thing that happened to me over there in Arkansas County was not my quail hunt with Jim Tharp; his wife, Estelle, a born-again evangelical Christian, led me into a heartfelt, heartwarming relationship with Jesus Christ. I'm no longer just a nominal church member; when Estelle told me that I must prayerfully confess my sins and personally confess Jesus Christ as the Son of God and my Savior who died on the cross for my sins, I did just that. And when I did, the Holy Spirit assured me of a personal faith, warming my heart with a confidence that I was a new man in Jesus Christ!'"

"Oh, Doctor!" Estelle interrupted, "I hope this did not upset, threaten, or cause her to challenge the reality of your knowledge of the Lord."

"Not at all, Estelle! In fact, she said, 'Martin, I can already tell you are different, and I want you to tell me more about this. I have felt there ought to be more to the Christian faith than what we have known— reading the Bible only a bit now and then, never praying except during the rituals at church, only going to church a few times a year, giving a little money now and then. I am glad you have found something real. Help me to know it, too!'"

Estelle interrupted again, "Dr. Bonnhoffer, this is wonderful! In fact, this is what I prayed for."

"Well, I didn't know any better than to suggest right then and there that we follow the same procedure you had led me in. She repeated after me the same prayer that you led me in. Even though she reacted a little differently than I did, I know she is filled with the same peace, joy, and knowledge that she is forgiven and a new creation in Christ. Every morning, we have the most wonderful time studying the Bible and praying together. Our marriage has never been so happy, although we've always been in love and shared our hearts with one another. Both of our children are away in college right now—Jeff is studying medicine at Yale up in New England, and Shirley is at the University of Arkansas preparing to teach. We are looking forward to sharing our newfound faith with them when they come home on the spring break!"

"Doctor, I shall be praying for Jeff and Shirley as you and Maureen witness to them about your own spiritual lives. But I'm also interested in how your colleagues in medicine and Maureen's friends have responded to your new way of life. I hope they are supportive and not critical."

"Actually, I want to tell you about that. I told the two doctors who work with me in cardiology that I've had a new experience with the Lord. I don't know if it's because I'm their senior in the work there or if they really are interested, but neither of them has been critical or acted skeptical. They both show an interest, maybe even a hunger. Also, I wanted to tell you that I made an appointment with Dr. Baylor, pastor of Faith Presbyterian Church, where we have our membership. I told him that I'd found Christ as my Savior. Actually, he's the only person I've talked to about my spiritual birth who's been a bit negative. But even he said he knew people who were 'strongly evangelical,' who seemed to take on a new strength for the battles of life. He did make one encouraging remark when I left his office—he said, 'Martin Luther would have been proud of you.' When I told Maureen about our pastor's reluctance to rejoice with me in our newfound faith, she said she thought we'd better look for a new church home. However, we have both been checked by the Spirit on this impression. I might be following an illusion, but I have hopes that what you describe as revival might come to Faith Presbyterian if Maureen and I stay and pray and witness to our friends there. We trust that, through prayer, our pastor will sense a need to get into a deeper walk with the Lord. Also, Maureen thinks that she and I should get our friends together and have you come and speak to them. We want to make your trip to Hot Springs a great witness for the Lord. Estelle, I just know the Lord wants to use you in our area. Would you pray about this?"

"Of course I will! You know, Doctor, I'm not an educated woman. But I do know the Lord has given me a gift of communicating His Word as I depend on His strength and wisdom. I'm willing to go anywhere He would lead me and tell what He's done, and is doing, in our lives. Jim would be happy to drive me over when you wish to set it up."

"Good! I'm thinking of having you speak at the Hot Springs Businessmen's Club some Saturday morning. I'm the chairman; I believe after a few months of my laying a good foundation, a lot of the members will be ready to listen to what you have to say. Then if I can get Dr. Baylor to agree, we want you to speak in our worship service the next morning. What do you think?"

"Doctor, I feel honored and blessed to have those opportunities. I know the Lord will give me something meaningful to say. And when I have a word from the Lord, I don't get frightened or intimidated, no matter who is in the audience. I certainly do not want to embarrass you in any way."

"Oh, please, Estelle! In no way can you possibly do that. I've heard enough and learned enough from you that I'd be willing to put you up to speak before any audience anywhere."

"Well, Doctor, time is slipping by, and I've certainly enjoyed our session tonight. But I think in tomorrow's session we'll take up the Scriptures I had laid out for you. But before we go over to the house, I'd like to ask you to pray—pray for Jim, pray for our community here, and pray for a number of our young men from the prairie who are, or soon will be, in harm's way in both Europe and the South Pacific."

Estelle was so very pleased with the doctor's prayer. He seemed to understand just how to pray for Jim. He asked that Estelle's dream for a mighty spiritual awakening in Arkansas County might soon be a reality and that it spill over into surrounding counties. He asked God to comfort the Tharps and all who knew Patsy and to especially be with Linda and her children in their grief. He prayed that Estelle would have the direction and anointing of the Holy Spirit to continue her ministry of intercession.

When they returned to the house, Jim was listening to the radio. "Doctor, it's time for Gabriel Heatter's news report. Do ye mind listenin' to him for a few minutes?"

"Not at all; he's my favorite reporter."

Heatter came on with his regular greeting and then quickly went to the good news that the tide was turning against the German Navy in the Atlantic. He reported the number of vessels sunk this month as compared with last month, stating that two-thirds of all sinkings had been German vessels. American men and materiel were now getting to their destinations on a large scale so that the enemy forces would soon be facing overwhelming odds.

When the news report was over, Jim turned off the radio and turned to Dr. Bonnhoffer. "Are ye of the opinion that the war in Europe will be a long one…say, four or five years?"

"Jim, I'm convinced that it will take until 1945 to finish off Hitler; then, it may take another year to defeat the Japanese. I fear that none of our political and military leaders have come close to realizing the hundreds of thousands of casualties our allies will suffer. I trust Roosevelt and Churchill, but I can't feel good about Stalin. He's a butcher, and no doubt he will invest heavily against our enemies along with us. But toward the end, I wonder if the president and prime minister can handle him. I just don't trust him."

"Well, Doctor," Estelle spoke up, "Sister Martha, whom I hope you can meet one of these times, gave a prophecy last fall that nearly one million casualties would be suffered by the allies!"

"I fear she is close to being accurate," the doctor said.

Since it was getting quite late, they thought they probably ought to leave the subject of the war, decide what they would do on Saturday, and then get some rest. Jim and the doctor wanted to ride the horses out to check on the cattle on Saturday morning. Then after the noon meal, Estelle and the doctor would meet at the cabin for another session of Scripture study and prayer. The doctor expressed a desire to worship with them on Sunday morning and then head back to Hot Springs after the noon meal. He realized he needed to sit under Estelle's teaching in a worship setting to learn what he and the people in Hot Springs could anticipate hearing when she visited there.

The doctor enjoyed seeing the cattle, thinking he had never seen so many before. Jim suggested they ride down to the Morgan place so he could introduce the doctor to his cousin Ross. After enjoying an hour of discussing politics, the war, and the anticipated revival in Arkansas County, Jim invited Ross to ride along while he showed the doctor some of the White River bottoms. He explained that since the backwater had not completely subsided and returned to the river, they could only ride a few miles into the wooded areas where the land had had enough light to dry out. But he pointed out Deep Bayou, Wild Goose, and Honey Locust. They were able to climb part of the way up Elm Ridge. After Jim showed the doctor where he had killed his four would-be murderers, they turned back westward, reaching home in time to sit down to a pork roast dinner with plenty of vegetables, iced tea, and Jeff Davis pie.

Estelle and the doctor had not been in the cabin very long before she explained to him that, before his arrival, she had been feeling she should share with him about God's call to all of his redeemed children to an intimate relationship with the Holy Spirit. The doctor seemed ready and anxious to hear all that she could tell him.

"We'll study the Gospel of John, chapters 14 through 16," Estelle began. "There are a few salient or key passages in these Paraclete Passages, as New Testament scholars call these three chapters of John. They are also called The Last Supper Discourses on the Holy Spirit. Just about all Greek scholars point out that the term *Counselor*, as used here as a title for the Holy Spirit, comes from the Greek *parakletos*, which comes from two words: *para*, meaning "with" or "alongside"; and *kaleo*, meaning "I call." So *parakletos* literally means for us today "one called alongside to help us."

"Doctor, I'm sure you've read enough Scripture since being saved that you know Jesus pointed out to His followers that they must not miss the "Promise of the Father"—the coming of the Holy Spirit. He emphasized that only in their receiving the Spirit could they carry out His commands. Failing to receive the Holy Spirit's power would mean tragic failure.

"Here in these Paraclete Passages we see why: because He is our *parakletos*, one come alongside to help us. Jesus said of Him, **I will pray the Father, and he will give you another Counselor, to be with you forever, even the Spirit of truth, whom the world cannot receive, because it neither sees him nor knows him; you know him, for he dwells with you, and will be in you** (John 14:16-17). Jesus is here describing a daily, continual Living Presence to be realized by His followers. Never are we to think of the Christian life as being impersonal, mechanical, or automatic. Life in the Spirit is far from institutional, routine, or abstract. Our faith in Christ and in His Spirit will save us from all of this.

"Please note, Doctor, that Jesus seemed to have a favorite title for the Holy Spirit—**the Spirit of truth**. Now, I'm sure He did not mean merely theological truth or scientific fact. The Holy Spirit's assignment to the attentive follower of Christ is to internalize the truth that Jesus taught His disciples, the eternal Word of God, the Scriptures. He who inspired the holy Scriptures is present with each of Christ's obedient followers to illumine these same holy Scriptures and help us understand them. While I'm indebted to the gifted teaching of Dr. Martha Honeycutt, my ultimate reliance must be upon the Spirit's faithfulness to help me understand the Bible. Let us grasp the importance of Jesus' promise in John 16:12-14: **When the Spirit of truth comes, he will guide you into all the truth; …he will declare to you the things that are to come. He will glorify me, for he will take what is mine and declare it to you**. How reassuring these words are, for Jesus had declared His departure. He pointed out that it was to His followers' advantage that He go away physically in order to return spiritually in the power and presence of the Holy Spirit. He explained that He and the Spirit were one in nature and disposition, just as He and the Father were one.

"Well, Doctor, I hope these thoughts are helpful, but there's something more urgent on my mind now before we return to the house and to the others. I want to point out once again that while it is good to *learn about* the Holy Spirit, we are commanded by our Lord Jesus Christ to *ask for Him—for His much-moreness, His fullness*! Now, you were given the Holy Spirit when you were born again, but are you ready to be filled? Do you feel you are ready and willing to ask and receive His cleansing, filling, and empowerment?"

Estelle was pleased with Martin Bonnhoffer's serious pause before answering. He closed his eyes for two or three seconds and then opened them, leaned forward, and spoke with emotion, "Dear lady, I've listened with my ears and my heart. I believe I am ready to ask and receive what you once referred to as "the baptizing, sanctifying fullness of the Holy Spirit." And ever since you used that expression, it's something I've longed to experience. Yes, I believe I am ready. Will you lead me in the prayer like you did when I was saved, or do I simply pray it myself?"

"Doctor, I think you are completely ready to express your own passion for the baptizing, sanctifying fullness of the Holy Spirit," Estelle replied. "But before you do, I have one promise by Jesus that I want you to consider, which I think will help determine the way you ask for the fulfillment of this great promise. Listen to Jesus in Luke 11:13: **If you then, who are evil, know how to give good gifts to your children, how much more will the heavenly Father give the Holy Spirit to those who ask him!**"

Estelle put her New Testament down, paused for the doctor's response, and heard him begin, "Oh God! How thankful I am for Your mercy and grace in sending Your Son Jesus Christ to die for my sins. I thank You that a few months ago, when I confessed my sins and placed my faith in Jesus Christ alone for my salvation, You transformed my heart and adopted me into Your forever family. I thank You for Estelle's influence on my life, her prayers, and her clear teachings concerning the spiritual life. And now, Lord, You are looking into my heart, seeing my hunger to be sanctified holy and made into the likeness of Your Son, Jesus. Hear my request for the cleansing and empowering of the Holy Spirit! I ask now, and I believe now! You promised that if I would ask, You would give me the gift of the presence and power of the Holy Spirit. I know You keep Your Word. Thank you for giving me the baptism with the Holy Spirit and fire!"

The doctor's head remained bowed even after Estelle uttered, "O Lord, You have heard the doctor's prayer. You have filled him with the Holy Spirit. Now, in your own gracious wisdom, grant Him the witness of this special milestone in His walk of faith. We wait before You for whatever manifestations You are pleased to give."

Waiting for what seemed like a few minutes, the only sound was the ticking of the clock Sister Martha had left on the radio stand. Estelle looked at the doctor and could see a smile starting to form on his face, yet his head remained bowed. Feeling perfectly free to allow the seconds to tick away, she believed a special inner witness would be forthcoming to the doctor.

"Estelle!" the doctor blurted out. "Estelle!" he repeated. Trying to catch his breath, he said, "What peace is now sweeping over me mentally, emotionally, and even physically!" Then he stood and lifted both hands heavenward, and a string of the most beautiful praises Estelle had ever heard from another human being came forth in flowing streams and continued for three minutes by the clock. The doctor then sat down and, sighing in relief, said, "I knew it would be real, but the witness of the Spirit far exceeds anything I expected!"

On the way to the house, the doctor asked, "Estelle, do you think it might be in order for me to testify in your service to this mighty blessing that has come to me?"

"I can hardly wait for that!" Estelle exclaimed. "Indeed, I shall enjoy introducing you to our people and have you say whatever the Lord leads you to say. In fact, I feel as of now that all I need to do is open the service, call for a hymn or two, lead a prayer, and then introduce you. When you are through, I'll know whether to give an invitation, share a few spiritual thoughts, or pronounce a benediction. Yes, indeed, Doctor, plan to testify to the baptism of the Holy Spirit and fire in the morning. And don't be too concerned about preparing your speech. Just let the Holy Spirit lead you to say extemporaneously what you should. Feel free, and don't make it too short!"

Only about 40 people gathered on the beautiful spring Sunday morning, and Estelle was filled with anticipation but relaxed in her spirit as she followed the order that she had suggested to the doctor the evening before. The people warmed to the doctor, showing both respect for his profession and his excitement concerning his faith. It was clear to Estelle that the physician was not only brilliant and capable as a communicator but also sensitive to the Holy Spirit—he cared that people understood what he meant with his words. Estelle discerned the convicting presence of the Holy Spirit on six or eight believers as she studied their faces from where she sat facing the congregation. She knew that when the doctor was finished she was to extend the invitation to come forward and be filled with the Spirit.

Ten people, six men and four women, came forward to stand in front of Estelle to be prayed for. She anointed each one with oil and then called on Dr. Bonnhoffer to lead a prayer for the ten to be cleansed and filled with the Holy Spirit. What a prayer the doctor offered! As he finished his prayer, he went down the line and touched the shoulder of each one! Then he reversed his course and blessed each one on the other shoulder before he sat down. As soon as Estelle had pronounced the benediction, the ten swarmed around the doctor expressing their thanks; then the rest of the crowd took their turn. Jim was the first to say to him, "Thanks, Doctor, for a powerful testimony! It shore touched this old sinner's heart!"

About two hours after the doctor had departed for Hot Springs, Jim and Jake saddled the horses for an afternoon ride. Estelle asked Jeanette to watch the children, saying, "Set out the leftovers from the noon meal when Daddy returns, for I'll not be back from the cabin until about midnight. Tell Daddy to go on to bed."

Estelle had planned to work on messages for the Hot Springs event that evening. However, no sooner had she read a Scripture and knelt in prayer than the tears began flowing. *What thoughts must I give to these tears? I know they are from you, Lord! I didn't mean to come here to weep. What am I to weep over? Jim's lostness? Patsy's murder? The war with its casualties and destruction? The violent wickedness in the bottoms and the spiritual indifference on the prairie? The apparent ignorance of the American political leaders in Washington of the spiritual warfare behind the nations at war?*

Perhaps it was all of these things, Estelle was about to conclude, as she kept on weeping. Then after an hour, a burning thought came through: *The Holy Spirit is leading you to share the tears of Jesus over the lost of the earth, even as Hell is being populated by the millions who are dying over the earth.* "O, Lord! That I might be faithful! How blessed I am in my unworthiness to **share in your sufferings, becoming like you in your death, that if possible even I might attain to the**

resurrection of the dead." Having felt the Spirit confirm her conclusion, she was enabled by the Spirit to weep over Jim as never before. She was glad neither he nor anyone else could hear how the Spirit was leading her to pray for him. After praying a long time for Jim, she prayed for her seven children individually—about their spiritual needs, their vulnerabilities and temptations, their mental and physical development, and their sensitivity to the Gospel and to the will of God.

Estelle noticed that it was getting dark when she felt the freedom to rise from her knees and pace about the cabin. She continued to pour her heart out in intercession for all whom the Spirit brought to her mind—all of her relatives and all of Jim's, those in the community who professed to know Christ, and those who had not indicated a desire to know him. Then the Spirit laid it on her heart to pray for Martha Honeycutt and her travels to recruit prayer warriors for the great American revival so desperately needed.

Hours later, tired and weary, she felt free to lie down. Immediately upon reclining on the couch, she felt an incredible presence fill the room and calm her mind. There standing over her was the most scintillating figure she'd ever seen—glistening white and whispering a message she prayed for an understanding to grasp! Estelle rolled from the couch and instantly was on her knees before the mysterious being, crying out expressions of worship and praise. But she was interrupted. "Cease your words, dear one! I am not the Lord. I am an angel, a messenger of the Most High God, and I come to you with a word from on high. I am here to say this: *You are greatly loved and highly esteemed. I've been sent here to tell you that you shall have strength, wisdom, anointing, and power to be humble, to pray sacrificially, and to become a militant intercessor for a mighty, historic spiritual awakening that will sweep thousands into the Kingdom of God! I'm also to tell you to never be afraid—not because of your poverty, lack of education, or being unknown. Just go ahead as you are. You will be used mightily in Hot Springs, in Little Rock, and here in Arkansas County. And later, you are to move northward and be used mightily. As of now, you are not prepared for all that is planned for the transformation of wicked men in those bottoms and hundreds of seemingly upright people on these prairies! There will be a rending of the heavens! Your husband and children will be saved. All on your prayer list will confess the Savior.*

Now, get back on the couch, lie down, and rest. Sleep, dear one! Be blessed."

Even as Estelle lay back down on the couch, she knew that her wish for the angel to remain was in vain. Yes, the angel was gone, but she had heard enough. The Holy Spirit would be faithful to help her deny herself, become a living sacrifice in prayer, remember the message, and enter into the fellowship of Christ's intercession for a world revival. So *there would be a rending of the heavens!* She knew she was to sleep, but a euphoria swept over her for several minutes before she fell into a deep sleep.

Jim retired about ten o'clock, but he could not get to sleep. Jeanette had told him that her mother said she would not return until midnight, and that he was to go on to bed when he was ready. And she assured him that she had reminded Jake to check on their mother a few times before he went to bed. At the midnight hour, Jim got up and dressed and went over to the cabin. He knocked loudly and called Estelle's name, but there was no response. He then stood on the top step and peered through the glass.

He was amazed! Estelle appeared to be asleep on the couch, and a strange light was shining on her face. He could not figure out the source of the light, because the floor lamp at her end of the couch was not lit. The light appeared to be coming from above, but Jim knew there was no overhead light in the cabin.

What's goin' on here? Is she alright? Am I imaginin' that her face is aglow? Is this really a spiritual mystery? I'm shakin', and I can't hep myself. Why am I cryin'? God, are Ye in this at all?

Jim tried the door even though he knew it would be locked. He returned to the house and got the key. Back at the door, the mystery deepened when the lock would not respond to the key. The door simply would not open! *I reckon it's not supposed to.* Standing on the top step, Jim called out and knocked again and again, eventually giving up.

Finally, the door opened and there stood Estelle! "Oh, darling! I'm so glad to see you! I've had a visitor from Heaven, and when the angel left, it told me to sleep. What a wonderful sleep I've had, but I'm glad to see you!"

"Well, I knew somethin' happened to you, because I saw a light on yore face and couldn't figure out where it come from. I couldn't get the door open, even with the key."

"Let's go to the house and go to bed," Estelle said. When Jim reached for her, he was glad the aura had subsided. Even if an angel had visited her, he felt that she was wonderfully normal.

The weekend that Estelle was to speak at Dr. Bonnhoffer's club, the doctor had made their reservation at the Hot Springs Inn and promised that they would be comfortable. The inn was the nicest hotel that Jim and she had ever stayed in. After unpacking, Estelle suggested that they call Dr. Bonnhoffer to let him know they were settled in their room, since he and Maureen had expressed a desire to join them at the hotel for the evening meal. The doctor answered Estelle's call and welcomed her warmly, requesting that she and Jim meet them downstairs in the hotel dining room in two hours.

After a few minutes of thinking over his and Estelle's relating to Dr. and Mrs. Bonnhoffer, Jim asked, "Honey, are ye goin' to be comfortable with the doctor's wife? Now, I know ye made it fine with the doctor, but ye know they are in a class above us."

"Well, in a way they are," Estelle replied. "But, really, in the Lord's work I think there ought not be a feeling of one class over another. The doctor is far more educated than we are and thousands of dollars richer, but I don't feel inferior to him. I do not want either of us to become intimidated by them or anyone they might introduce us to. I do, however, feel the need to trust the Lord to keep me from any fear of being unable to speak with clarity and conviction to the people tomorrow and Sunday. And as for Mrs. Bonnhoffer, I just doubt that she is a snob, especially since she's found the Lord. Anyway, I want us to relax with them, and I think we'll see they can learn from us just as well as we can learn from them. I believe the Lord is giving me a confidence, a poise, and a passion to share His message with them."

"Aw, ye'll do fine!" Jim said. "Ain't no one gonna miss what ye say."

Estelle realized the moment she saw Maureen Bonnhoffer enter the dining room ahead of her husband that she could relax completely with her whether worshiping, dining, or visiting. The doctor introduced her to Jim and Estelle with a pride and simplicity that Estelle appreciated. Jim was the first to respond: "Why, how nice to meet the beautiful wife of our doctor friend!" But it was apparent that the doctor's wife was most anxious to meet Estelle—she ignored Estelle's outstretched hand, and soon the two women were in each other's arms. Looking deep into Estelle's eyes, Maureen said, "Dear Estelle, I know not how to express my appreciation for your transforming influence on Martin. He has shared with me the same Gospel, and we both have peace with God. Our marriage has never been happier!"

The receptionist was both listening and waiting, and when it seemed appropriate, she said, "This way, please, if you are ready." The four were seated in a lighted corner and each given a menu. After taking orders for coffee, she promised to return for their dinner orders.

"Well, Jim, how's fishing been this spring?" the doctor asked.

"A little above normal," Jim said. "We just hope the prices hold. Of course, we know that around this time each year they cut about twenty percent."

When Maureen noticed a pause in the men's conversation, Martin's questioning, and Jim's answers, she said to Estelle, "We can hardly wait to hear the truth you will give us in the morning at the club! I've told all the wives I know to be sure and come and invite their friends."

"Yes, we're all looking forward to what you'll have to tell us at the club, Estelle. I think I told you that they are all a worldly bunch. But I know you'll be relaxed and wade in on them with the Word of truth," the doctor said.

"She'll wade in on them alright," Jim said. "I've never seen her back down on any crowd when she felt she had somethin' to say from the Lord," Jim said. "Miz Bonnhoffer, I..."

"No, please, Jim! Just call me Maureen."

"Well, Maureen, I was gonna 'fess up and tell ye what I told the doctor—I'm not a believer like y'all are. I wanta be, though. And if Estelle has her way, the sooner the better. But I'm special deputy to the sheriff of Arkansas County, and it seems my way of life is contrary to the Bible. I don't wanta put off too long my comin' to the Lord, but I can't make the move until I'm more ready."

"Jim, you just relax around us," the doctor said. "Be sure, we are glad you are with us whether you are a believer or not. Maureen and I have been praying that the Holy Spirit will prepare your heart to receive salvation as a free gift of God's grace. But meanwhile, we have nothing but gratitude and pride in your accomplishments as a special deputy to the sheriff. In the past, we've seen your picture in the *Gazette,* and we've read of your feats with the help of your horse and dog. As far as I'm concerned, your work, even when it becomes your duty to shoot some dangerous outlaw, is not inconsistent with the Christian life. We hope you won't allow your work to keep you from confessing our Lord as Savior."

"Yes, Jim! That's exactly the way I feel, too!" Maureen said. "I think it would be a mistake for you to think you would need to resign your work with the sheriff when you become a believer."

Estelle thought it was time she also made her thoughts known. Addressing Jim at her side, she said, "Honey, I've never thought your work with the sheriff was displeasing to God. You've shot and killed men only when they were trying to kill you or the sheriff or someone in your party. As I've told you before, *that is not murder*! I, too, hope you don't allow your work to keep you from trusting the Lord for your salvation. And I'm so glad the Bonnhoffers feel as I do about that."

While they ate their meal, Maureen wanted to hear Estelle's testimony, including a description of Dr. Martha Honeycutt. Estelle enjoyed describing her mentor in terms that Jim found interesting. He felt free now and then to add his own impressions of her size and voice: "Sister Martha won't weigh a hundred pounds soakin' wet, I reckon, and I guess you'd say she has the voice of God—at least Estelle thinks so."

After the delicious meal, the doctor said, "The club will meet right here in this hotel at 9:00 in the morning in the Roosevelt Room! In fact, since we all seem to be through with our pie, let's go over there; I want to lead a prayer for God's blessing on the gathering and His anointing on Estelle." In less than two minutes, the four entered a large expensively furnished auditorium. Estelle judged that there were 400 seats with a wide dividing aisle and a platform with six chairs. Previous to this time she had been calm about facing the "worldly" crowd. Now she quietly rebuked the enemy who would have her fear the faces of unsaved people. The doctor prayed, "Now Lord, we thank You for the safe arrival of Jim and Estelle, for the delicious meal we have shared, and for the wonderful fellowship we have enjoyed. Even now, I ask that You prepare the men and women who will hear the powerful Gospel of Jesus Christ, and may they come under deep conviction and turn from their sinful, selfish lives to follow You as their Lord and Savior. Give Estelle an anointing that will carry over into the minds and hearts of needy souls and give her freedom over fear of people. Do a mighty work in this place in the morning, I pray!"

Even Jim joined in the other three's *Amen*!

The next morning, Bonnhoffers joined Jim and Estelle for breakfast at 8:00 in the dining room. According to the doctor, nearly a hundred club members were in the restaurant for breakfast. As they entered the Roosevelt Room behind the crowd of members, they could see that there would be standing room only. The doctor led Jim to a front row seat and then escorted Estelle to a seat on the platform. She prayed quietly for the crowd of men and women seated and being seated before her. It would be the largest crowd she had addressed with the exception of the time she had given her testimony at the camp meeting in Westfield, Indiana. She prayed, as the doctor had, for a needed freedom from the fear of people. Immediately, she longed to be on her feet to speak what the Lord had given her for this group.

At exactly nine o'clock, Dr. Martin Bonnhoffer stepped to the lectern microphone and called the meeting to order. After Dr. Richard Baylor prayed an invocation, an officer from Camp Robinson, near Little Rock, led in the pledge of allegiance to Old Glory. When the crowd had sat down again, a female soloist from Faith Presbyterian Church sang "God Bless America." Then back at the lectern, the doctor said, "This is a special meeting of this club, a meeting like we've never held before. Before it adjourns you might think you are in a revival meeting, because I want to tell you that you are going to hear one of the most spiritually powerful women I've ever met. She has been used of God to lead me into a saving knowledge of Jesus Christ, and she happens to fellowship with God and the angels. I've never known a person of miracles before. Her prayer life is an unending string of miracles. God uses her to save lives by her visions and dreams. She prays and gets YES answers from God. Maureen and I have been so impressed by her life and ministry that we have invited her to speak to the club today. Then tomorrow morning at 10:30, she'll be speaking at Faith Presbyterian Church here in Hot Springs. I know many of you are faithful in attending your own churches. But as you listen to Estelle this morning, many of you will no doubt wish to hear her again tomorrow morning. You will be welcome.

"Before Estelle speaks, I want you to meet her husband, Jim Tharp. If you read the *Arkansas Gazette* in past years, you have seen his picture and read about him and his horse Star and his dog Buck. According to the newspaper, Jim is the most accurate marksman in the nation. Whether he is shooting a shotgun, a rifle, or a pistol, Jim never misses. He's got the fastest draw of a pistol of anyone on record, and he has saved the life of the Arkansas County sheriff, as well as his own, many times by taking the outlaw out before he can touch his gun. I've hunted quail with this man, and I've spent time in his home. What a beautiful family he and Estelle have! I'm going to ask Jim to stand, and I want you to give him a warm Hot Springs welcome!"

Jim stood with a smile on his face and turned and waved to the crowd that was cheering, clapping, and whistling. It was clear that many of the men had read about him and knew just what the doctor was talking about.

"And now, I ask that you also give Estelle a warm Hot Springs welcome!" The doctor motioned for Estelle to come, and as she made her way to the lectern, the crowd stood, cheered, and clapped. Laying her Bible on the lectern, she placed a hand at each side of the lectern and smiled as she waited for the cheering to cease.

"Dr. Bonnhoffer and ladies and gentlemen, my husband, Jim, and I are delighted to be in Hot Springs with you this weekend. I've come to share the greatest story ever told, the Gospel of Jesus Christ, as recorded in the Holy Bible. It has never lost its credibility across its 2,000-year history, despite its many enemies and a few phony Christians. It is a story of love, God's love. **For God so loved the world that he gave his only Son that whoever believes in him should not perish but have eternal life. For God sent the Son into the world, not to condemn the world, but that the world might be saved through him. He who believes in him is not condemned; he who does not believe is condemned already, because he has not believed in the name of the only Son of God.**

"In 1930, over in Arkansas County, I heard the Gospel preached in an old brush arbor, and I believed in Jesus Christ as my Savior. I repented of my sins and placed my trust in Jesus Christ alone for my salvation. I found peace with God. God's Spirit came into my heart. I was born anew by the Holy Spirit, and I was adopted into God's redeemed family. I began discovering the power of prayer. The Lord sent a Bible scholar from a Bible college in Indiana to teach me and others in our community. Dr. Martha Honeycutt discipled me, teaching me about the Christian way. She led me into the Spirit-filled life and taught me how to relate to the Holy Spirit—how to let him cleanse, fill, empower, and guide my life. I was never right with God nor was I ever right with myself until I came to know Jesus Christ as my Savior and the Holy Spirit as my Sanctifier and Anointer. I never knew the power of prayer until I was filled with the Spirit.

"But I'm here in Hot Springs to share my vision of revival. Now, when I speak of revival, I'm talking about a great spiritual awakening! The people of God must undergo periodic renewals in an atmosphere of outpourings of the Holy Spirit. As a matter of fact, revivals are ordained of God as a means of preserving His Church and keeping His people alive in a fallen and depraved world. Apart from revivals, there will soon be little distinction between the church and the world. When Christian believers who make up the Church of Jesus Christ begin thinking and behaving like the world, the world reasons that there is no difference and that there is nothing real about Christianity. So people of the world soon refer to Christian believers as phony, hypocritical, and unreal.

"As I understand the history of revivals in America, it has been 80 years since we've had a significant outpouring of the Holy Spirit on believers in our nation which resulted in hundreds of thousands of unbelievers turning in saving faith to Jesus Christ our Lord.

"The first great awakening came to Colonial America in the years between 1720 and 1744. The most prominent leaders were Jonathan Edwards, the Puritan pastor in New England, and George Whitefield, the young British evangelist. The second great awakening came between the years of 1790 and 1810. The prominent leader was Francis Asbury, who had been commissioned by John Wesley to come to America and spread the teachings of evangelical holiness and revival. And then Timothy Dwight, president of Yale University, saw a mighty sweep of the power of God on that great educational institution. The third great awakening came between the years of 1821 and 1899. The three more prominent names associated with this revival in this 39-year period are Charles G. Finney, Jeremiah Lanphier, and D. L. Moody. Finney was converted to Christ as a young lawyer in upstate New York. Entire communities would turn to Christ under the preaching of this fiery evangelist. Jeremiah Lanphier, a Dutch Reformed minister in New York City, was instrumental in starting the phenomenal Laymen's Prayer Revival that filled the churches, theatres, and public halls of hundreds of cities with several millions calling on the Lord during the years of 1857 to 1859. Then came the influence of a layman by the name of D. L. Moody, who filled the largest auditoriums in the nation with his evangelistic crusades between the years of 1870 until his death in 1899. So we might say that the last great spiritual awakening in America lasted from the conversion of Charles G. Finney in 1821 to the death of D. L. Moody in 1899.

"My dear people, it's been too long since the heavens have opened on our nation and poured out the mercies and graces of God in revival power, cleansing the hearts and lives of believers and sweeping hundreds of thousands of sinners into the Kingdom of God. So, it is the burden of my heart to see revival in our times. I want the elderly in America, most of whom can hardly remember the days of revival, to see the glory of God once again in our land. I want the middle-aged to experience great movements of the Spirit with miracles of salvation, healing, and deliverance. I want the young to see revival—including my children and yours!

"I must say that it appears to me there is a moral and spiritual sickness in the land today, and I believe it is due to our prayerlessness and our loss of faith and interest in the God of the supernatural. I realize that many of the fundamentalists have already given up on the possibility of another moral and spiritual awakening. And who can deny that the sun might be already setting on Western civilization, that our sacred values of family life are eroding, and that the socioeconomic infrastructure is crumbling? I happen to believe that we are now living in that late hour of human history in which God declared that He would **shake the heavens and the earth**, and that such a judgment would extend to all the nations. But I am convinced that if Jonathan Edwards, Charles Finney, and D. L.

Moody were alive today, they would find a way to tell North Americans that all of the idolatry, immorality, and irreverence in this present darkness merely form the background and set the stage for the greatest revival in the history of the Church!

"But I want to close my message to you today by citing God's requirements on the part of His people to send revival. He spells out the terms in II Chronicles 7:14: **If my people who are called by my name humble themselves, and pray and seek my face, and turn from their wicked ways, then I will hear from heaven, and will forgive their sin and heal their land**.

"So revival begins with God's people who will in humility begin to pray and seek God's face and then turn from anything that displeases Him; then He promises to forgive and heal us. You see, most of our American churches are valleys of dry bones! But I want you to know I believe dead churches are going to come to life. Dry bones will live again!

"Before I pray a closing prayer, I want to say that after Dr. Bonnhoffer has adjourned the meeting, if anyone wants to come down here to my right between the first row and the platform, I'll be down on your level to talk or pray with you. Now let us pray."

Estelle led a short prayer asking the Lord "to speak to our hearts today, and give us a desire to prepare for the revival You want to give in our hearts and homes and churches and nation." The doctor adjourned the meeting by urging those who are drawn by the Spirit of God to come and visit and pray with Estelle.

Dr. Bonnhoffer assisted Estelle off the platform to receive the people, saying in departing from her, "Estelle, I was moved deeply by all that you said, and I believe others were also. Excuse me while I greet a few folks. Don't go to your room until Maureen and I have talked with you and Jim, for I know Maureen wants to have you at our place either for lunch or dinner today."

Estelle noticed some ladies a distance away heading toward her. While she waited, she saw that Jim had a crowd around him, some slapping him on the back in a friendly way. She was glad to see the way Jim was responding—shaking hands, nodding, and saying, "Thank you!"

The first lady to reach Estelle simply wanted to thank her for being used of the Lord to speak to her about her worldliness of life and coldness of heart. "Please pray for me to be renewed in the Spirit of Christ." As she turned to leave, Estelle put a hand on her arm and said, "May I pray a short prayer for you right now?" The lady's body language spoke an emphatic yes, so Estelle began, "Lord, I thank You that You've spoken to my sister's heart about her way of living and her cold heart. Now all You're asking her to do is to draw close to You, repent of the things You're convicting her of, and You'll come in a new heartwarming experience of peace and joy. May this happen this very day! In Jesus' name, Amen!" The "Amen" was echoed by a smiling lady as she said, "Thanks!" and cleared the way for others. After hearing ten others—four men and six ladies—there was only one person left in the entire front area, so Estelle said, "Sir, could we have a seat here on the front row, for I want to hear your concerns." As they sat down, Estelle said, "Please feel free to tell me what's on your heart."

"Well, I ain't been to church in two or three years. I don't like it when my wife, Mary, wants us to pray at meals or just before we go to bed at night. I know I'm in no spiritual shape to begin to pray for this revival you talked about, though I do confess that's what the people of God need."

When the middle-aged man paused, Estelle asked, "Sir, have you ever in your life asked for God's forgiveness, then confessed Christ as Savior from sin, and looked to Him as the One who died in full payment for all your sins? In other words, I'm asking, have you ever been born again?"

"Naw, and maybe that's my trouble."

"Well, Jesus said **unless you are born of the Spirit, you cannot enter the kingdom of God**. So if you are ready and willing, I will lead you in a prayer which you can repeat, and the Holy Spirit will bring you the assurance of peace with God. You can leave this place this afternoon knowing that Christ is your Savior, your name is written in the Lamb's Book of Life, and you are ready for Heaven."

"Okay, I'm ready and willing," the man said, with a smile.

"Then repeat this prayer after me: O God, I ask Your forgiveness for all my sins.... I thank You for sending Your Son Jesus to die on the cross for my sins.... I now confess Jesus Christ as my Savior, ... and I trust His death in full payment for all my transgressions.... Here and now I surrender my heart and life to Him, ... to follow Him for the rest of my days…. Help me to read and understand and obey the Bible…. Show me how to live day by day for the rest of life…. Amen!"

When they both raised their heads, Estelle saw that the penitent man's face was beaming and he was smiling. She said, "Sir, I don't know your name, but I do know you are now my brother in Christ and that you have been born again. It shows on your face, and I hope you know it in your heart!"

"Ma'am, my name is Bob McCorkle. I want you to know I do trust Jesus as my Savior, and I feel His peace and blessing upon me already! I thank you for prayin' with me!" As Bob stood up to leave, he added, "My wife is a member of Faith Presbyterian, and I plan to join her in attending church. We'll be there to hear you speak again in the morning. This is a great day in my life. I can't wait to get home and tell Mary!"

A few people were still talking with Jim, but seeing the doctor and Maureen waiting for them near the exit, Estelle made her way over to Jim and said, "Honey, I think the doctor and his wife are waiting for us."

"Yeah, I'm ready." The men around him reached out to shake his hand before they let him go.

"It's been a great morning!" the doctor said, as the four of them made their way to the hotel lobby. "Why don't you two catch a lunch here after awhile, and then Maureen and I want you at our place for the evening meal. I'll pick you up at 6:00."

In their hotel room, Jim said, "Well, wife, ye're quite a preacher! I hadn't known about the history of revivals in our country. I got a lot outa what ye said this mornin'."

"Well, thank you, my dear!" Estelle exclaimed, as she walked over and kissed him. "I'd say you had quite an admiration society around you this morning! When the doctor talked about you, it was good to see that a lot of the people already knew about your heroics as special deputy."

"I was kinda surprised. But I know I ain't in the important business that you and the doctor are, so he shouldn't take away from the purpose of our bein' here just to make me feel good."

"Now, honey, the doctor's only trying to compliment you and your good work. In my judgment, that's no distraction in our purpose here. He likes you, and he wants others to like you and appreciate the work you are doing, too. Just don't be surprised if he doesn't do the same thing in the morning at their church."

"Well, I'm kinda hungry," Jim said. "Wanta go down and eat, then maybe go shoppin' or drive by the racetracks?"

"I don't care that much about the racetracks, unless there are some beautiful horses to see. But I do have a few things I ought to get here, and I know you don't want to shop Monday morning. Now, it's only eleven o'clock, so let's lie down and rest awhile—or you can turn on the radio and listen to the news while I lie down. Then we'll go eat and you can drive past the tracks as we go downtown." Already she was slipping out of her shoes and taking off her dress.

Jim nodded his approval, turned on the radio, and found a familiar voice reporting on the wars in both Europe and the South Pacific.

Both enjoyed the drive around Hot Springs, which in the 1940s was the second largest city in Arkansas. Since no horses were in sight at the racetrack, Jim did not even slow down as he drove toward the downtown area. He got a haircut, shave, and tonic while Estelle shopped. He was ready to get back to the hotel when she showed up in the parking lot where he had asked her to meet him.

"My! But you look and smell good! Just like a city guy!" Estelle said, teasingly.

"Well, we are in the city, and we're hobnobbin' with city folks. When in Rome, we do as Rome does. Tomorrow, I'll bet ye're gonna wear that purty dress I bought ye when we wuz here last, ain't ye?" Jim asked.

"I guess I will," Estelle admitted.

Right at six, the doctor led Jim and Estelle to his new Buick Limited parked in the hotel driveway. Maureen met them at the door of their home dressed in the same nice outfit she had worn the day before. Immediately both Jim and Estelle admired their stately home. They knew from looking at the exterior as well as the interior of the Bonnhoffer home that they had never been in such an elegant house before. But both Martin and Maureen made them feel relaxed and free to answer as well as ask questions. The dinner, served on fine china, was great, but not any tastier than the Bonnhoffers would have enjoyed at the Tharps. The elegant chandelier over the lovely dining room table, the comfortable upholstered furniture in the living room, and the furnishings in every room cost thousands of dollars more than anything in the Tharp home. But the two couples obviously felt no distinctions between them as they dined, discussed, laughed, and prayed together for three hours.

Martin urged Estelle to give the same discourse on revival in the morning church service that she had given at the club. Before leaving the Bonnhoffer home, the four stood in a ring holding hands while Martin prayed for the service—that it would bring about "a turnaround and the beginning of spiritual renewal in Faith Presbyterian Church. Use Estelle mightily for Your glory." Jim and Estelle left knowing they had been in the presence of dear Christian friends. Estelle believed Jim had enjoyed the spiritual part of the fellowship almost as much as she had.

When Estelle woke up on Sunday morning, she went to the hotel window and looked out on a beautiful spring day. "Well, it looks like the Lord is smiling on all of us here in southwestern Arkansas!"

Jim was now stirring awake and getting out of bed, and he came over to look out on the beautiful morning with her. "I reckon the Lord wants to give ye a good day to preach revival to the Presbyterians."

"Well, it wouldn't matter if it were the Methodists, Lutherans, Baptists, or any other denomination. I do believe God wants to send revival to our nation. I just feel privileged to be here in Hot Springs and have the opportunity to speak to the Presbyterians. The Lord has made this possible, so I plan to humbly and heartily do my best. I'm just glad you are with me for moral support."

"I'm sure with ye," Jim said as he leaned over and kissed her. "But as soon as I can get dressed, I'm ready to go down and see what this outfit has for breakfast."

"Give me just a few minutes to comb my hair and get dressed," Estelle said.

The Bonnhoffers came by the hotel and picked up Jim and Estelle and drove them to Faith Presbyterian Church. All during the 20-minute ride, Estelle felt an excitement building within her about the service. *Lord, would You give me a special promise about this service, this day, this weekend. I am truly thankful for this opportunity to share Your word on revival. Let this people—at least a few—hear from Your Holy Spirit and know what they should do and what they are to say to their fellow members. Speak to Dr. Baylor. Help Dr. Bonnhoffer to know exactly what to say in the introduction. Lord, I want to be nothing, but I want You to be everything.* Jim was uncomfortable, not because he knew Estelle was praying, but because she was weeping. He was glad he had a fresh handkerchief in his pocket to hand her. She smiled her thanks, wiped the tears, and then handed the wet cloth back to him. When the doctor pulled up to the entrance of the grand edifice, Estelle was thankful that she was neither feeling overwhelmed by the grandeur of the church building nor frightened by the scores of well-dressed people walking across the parking lot. Never had she felt more certain of what she was to say and how she was to say it.

Just as they entered the grand vestibule, Estelle's mind powerfully and gratefully received the promise: **The Spirit of the Lord is upon me, because he has anointed me to preach good news to the poor. He has sent me to proclaim release to the captives and recovering of sight to the blind, to set at liberty those who are oppressed, to proclaim the acceptable year of the Lord**.

"Well, Jim, I guess here is where we trade partners for about an hour," Maureen said. "Martin will escort Estelle to the platform, and you may escort me to that second pew down front on the right, if you will." Jim nodded and positioned his arm, and Maureen slipped her arm in his as they went to their seat. After a few minutes, Maureen whispered, "Jim, this sanctuary is packed today! Martin and I have been members of this church for over twelve years, and I've never seen a crowd like this. I can't help but wonder what Dr. Baylor is thinking. I just believe the Lord is doing a new thing here today."

Jim noticed that Maureen had bowed her head, and he was sure she was praying. He sensed that both the doctor and Estelle were praying also as he looked at them on the platform. The organist began playing exactly at ten o'clock, and the crowd grew silent. Would Estelle be too nervous to speak her thoughts? She didn't seem to be yesterday, nor at any time this morning. She had been quiet ever since she stopped weeping in the car. She seemed confident and perfectly in control when Martin introduced her to the pastor. Jim wondered why he thought Estelle might not be her normally competent self today.

Jim noticed that the first item on the worship order was "A Call to Worship" by the sanctuary choir. As he watched the choir marching into a section to the right of the chancel, he guessed there must be at least 100 of them. The organist paused and then began playing the introductory notes of "Holy, Holy, Holy." The choir sang it more beautifully than Jim had ever heard it. The pastor came to the pulpit microphone and prayed a brief invocation after which a blond lady from the choir came to the pulpit and sang "The Love of God." Jim was reminded of Helen Rich's rendition of the same song. He liked the message, but preferred Helen's rendition.

While Jim was worrying about Estelle's emotional condition, she was digesting the promise the Lord had given her a few minutes before as she entered the building. She enjoyed studying the faces of the hundreds seated in the sanctuary. If the Lord had not said it, she would not have seen these nicely-dressed people as **poor and needy**, ready for **release as captives**, **blind and desperate for sight**, or **sorely oppressed**. Now she knew the Lord had sent her here this morning to tell them that Christ was their good news, their freedom, their wisdom, and their riches. She could hardly wait to get on her feet.

The offering was next, and before Jim realized that it was time, the pastor was presenting "Dr. Martin Bonnhoffer, who will introduce our special guest speaker this morning."

Jim was surprised when the doctor began his comments by first introducing "the husband of our special speaker today." It was a replay of yesterday's experience in the club meeting at the hotel. The same things about Jim were said. As Jim stood, the crowd exploded with applause for the hero the doctor had made him out to be.

As Jim sat down, the doctor went on, "And now I must confess that words fail me in seeking to tell you what our speaker today has meant to me and my wife, Maureen. When I went over a few months ago to quail hunt with Jim, I not only met a new friend in him, but I found a new life with Jesus Christ when I met Estelle. For the first time in my life, I learned that I was spiritually lost, unsaved, and unready for Heaven. Estelle gently and kindly shared the Gospel of Jesus Christ with me, and I begged her to pray for me. She said she would if I would pray also. She helped me pray the sinner's prayer and then patiently waited until the Holy Spirit gave me the assurance of salvation with a love, joy, and peace I had never felt before. Now I must confess that I'd been a member of the church for over 40 years, but I'd never before had the assurance of salvation. Now I know that when I die, I'll go to Heaven!

"Now, Estelle is not an ordained minister of the Gospel. But she is more deeply into the Bible as the Word of God than any theologian I've ever talked with. She is devoted to prayer and sees miracles happen. She has visions of things to come, and some of those visions save peoples' lives. Angels visit her. Oh, she'll not tell you this. But no one can be around her without realizing a tremendous presence of God on her life.

"Estelle carries a tremendous prayer burden for spiritual renewal in all of the churches of North America. She calls it revival. And no doubt she's going to talk about that today just as she did in the club meeting yesterday. I see a number of people here today who heard her there yesterday. Now, will you give Estelle a grand Faith Presbyterian welcome here this morning?"

Over one thousand people were on their feet clapping their heartfelt welcome to an unknown woman making her way confidently to the pulpit. She showed such poise as she spoke clearly and in a tone that caused Jim to breathe easily and forget all fear of any lack of success on her part. She began by addressing the two gentlemen on the platform, "Pastor Baylor, Dr. Bonnhoffer, and ladies and gentlemen: I come to you this beautiful Lord's Day morning, realizing my unworthiness of the grace and mercy of our gracious God. I'm thankful to be alive and bring good news in a war-torn world that causes so much sadness in many of our hearts and homes. At a time of war, I've come to share peace. In a day of fear, I've come to preach faith. During this age of destruction, I've come to preach salvation.

"Who can deny that over the last 50 years, our churches in North America have lost much of their spiritual fervor. Just as Jesus predicted, **because wickedness is multiplied, most men's love will grow cold.** I am certain that many of you good men and women here this morning once had a warm relationship with Jesus Christ, but today you are lukewarm, indifferent, and in great need of renewal. You hunger for a meaningful relationship with God and a prayer life filled with sweet communion and timely answers. And you desire the assurance that when you die you will go to be with the Lord. Please don't try to deny the vacuum that has developed since you stopped praying and ceased reading the Word of God. Stop pretending that you still enjoy the renewing presence of God.

"Well, this morning I've come to tell you that you don't have to continue in a meaningless religious experience. The Holy Spirit reveals to me just now in the words of the prophet Isaiah: **Remember not the former things, nor consider the things of old. Behold, I am doing a new thing; now it springs forth, do you not perceive it? I will make a way in the wilderness and rivers in the desert**."

With an unusual freedom Estelle had never experienced, she went on to describe how backsliders can be transformed into a people filled with the Holy Spirit, filled with the love of God, and filled with a hunger for holiness. She described the transformed community in lower Arkansas County, telling how murderers had found forgiveness, adulterers had found purity, and those who were empty had been filled with meaning and joy. Then she proceeded to tell how God is raising up an army of prayer warriors who are devoting themselves to militant intercession for a divine intervention in the lives of His defeated people. She went on for several minutes and then decided to spell out the terms of true biblical revival by quoting II Chronicles 7:14: "**If my people who are called by my name humble themselves, and pray and seek my face, and turn from their wicked ways, then I will hear from heaven, and will forgive their sin and heal their land**." Estelle finished the quote in tears, but when she paused to get her breath to finish her message, she realized she was not the only one in tears. People in nearly every section of the sanctuary were wiping tears and weeping silently, and many heads were bowed.

How should she finish? Estelle knew she must do a bold thing in closing, so she lifted the microphone from its holder on the pulpit desk, stepped down on the chancel step in front of the pulpit, and continued, "The Holy Spirit is mercifully present, dear people. Hearts are stirred deeply here this morning, even as you've never been visited before. You need not leave in sadness, emptiness, frustration, and longing. You can meet the Lord here this morning, and He will do a new thing in your heart and with your life. As Pastor Baylor comes to pray the benediction, I'm going to step down on the lower step here. You who wish to renew your faith in the Lord Jesus Christ come boldly, but quietly, and I'll lead you in a prayer of renewal. God will meet you here and revive your spiritual life; you'll never be the same again. Come on down, please!"

Estelle stepped up again to the pulpit to replace the microphone, but Pastor Baylor reached for her hand and the microphone before she could do it. She thought he had been weeping. Then he amazed her by speaking into the microphone: "My dear people of Faith Presbyterian Church, I plan to be among those of us who gather around Estelle and experience spiritual renewal this morning. Only as this dear woman began speaking from the Bible about renewal did I realize how cold my heart has grown and how distracted my life and ministry have become from the Gospel. So, elders, ministers, staff, and any or all, come on down and join us for a great time of refreshing from the Lord as we allow true revival to come to Faith Presbyterian Church!" With that he handed the microphone back to Estelle and said, "Take your freedom, Estelle; call us to faith and pray for us!"

Standing on the second step from floor level, Estelle watched the people coming from the balconies, from every section of the sanctuary, and even from the choir loft. Many were groaning or weeping. Estelle knew it would be easy and simple to instruct the hundreds of hungry hearts waiting and crying softly. Dr. Baylor, true to his word, was in the first row standing near the steps. The aisles were full of standing people, looking to Estelle to guide them in prayer. The Spirit came upon her as she tenderly, clearly, and excitedly instructed them to "bow your heads and confess your sins to the Lord, who promises to forgive. Now, forgive anyone who has ever hurt, offended, violated, or misused you in any way. Confess Jesus and His death on the cross as full payment for all your sins. Let your heart, mind, and will even now rely on Jesus and Jesus alone for your salvation. Ask Him to fill you with the Holy Spirit, and believe that He does. Now allow me to pray for you before we go." With humility, brokenness, and gratitude for all that God had done, Estelle wept her way through her blessing upon the hundreds who had registered their hunger for God and His way in their lives.

The crowd down front did not scatter quickly, even though the sanctuary emptied in the usual manner. Jim sat patiently for an hour and watched the people gather one by one around Estelle. Had he been a praying man, he would have prayed for God to give her a special strength to bear all their burdens and special wisdom to respond to all their questions. He saw the pastor step back a dozen times from speaking his thanks while she dealt with another inquirer.

At long last, the Bonnhoffers and the Tharps were en route to the hotel. Jim had agreed that they should remain another night to give Estelle the rest she needed for the trip home.

After breakfast with Martin and Maureen on Monday morning, Jim and Estelle checked out of the hotel and departed for home. Estelle was rested from the strain of the weekend, but she discovered a grief settling on her spirit. She felt it was caused by the fact that the spiritual deadness that had been prevalent in Faith Presbyterian Church was actually nationwide, and it included all of Arkansas—the towns they would drive through today such as Malvern, Sheridan, Dumas, and Gillette. For two hours, Estelle allowed the tears to roll as her spirit turned to God in intercession. Jim noticed, but he had learned to allow her the freedom to worship or intercede without question or comment. Estelle was so grateful for her union with the Holy Spirit that enabled her to pray with His empowerment. She believed He was transmitting her imperfect thoughts and petitions to the Throne of Grace, where her Great High Priest, Jesus, would personally represent her burdens and supplications, purified from all imperfections of selfishness and ignorance, to the heavenly Father. The Spirit even assured her that the answers were on the way. Estelle was filled with gratitude for all of God's power demonstrated in both services and for the way Jim was affected by the Bonnhoffers' and the people's responses to him both at the club and at the church.

Estelle enjoyed being home again with Jim and the children. She had a restful night, but she awakened early on Tuesday morning with a deepening of the grief she had felt over the backsliding and spiritual death of God's children. Oh how she missed Patsy! After getting breakfast and driving the children to school, she knew she must return to her times of supplication and intercession in the cabin. There she would tarry for several hours most days and many nights throughout the years of 1942 through 1945.

11   The Rending of the Heavens

Estelle planned to spend the day in the cabin just as she had for most of the last 500 days. When she started for the cabin, she was surprised at how warm it was outside. What was different about the atmosphere? Something was mysterious for sure! Instead of going directly to the cabin, she walked clear around the house. Looking into the sunlit White River bottoms to the east, she sensed a difference down in those woods. To the north across and beyond the orchard, the horizon was sparkling blue as far as she could see. Gazing west, she studied the grassy prairie clear to the wooded area, anticipating inspirational happenings beyond her ability to explain. The euphoria continued as she turned south and looked through and over the persimmon and cedar groves.

Are the heavenly hosts invading our prairie and river bottom communities? Is the Lord answering our prayers for the moving of His Spirit over Arkansas County? Am I stretching and reaching in my imagination for what is beyond reality? Well, it's time to get to the cabin and ask the Lord for a strong dose of reality. Enough of my dreams, imaginations, and fantasies!

In the cabin Estelle's mind dwelt on Ephesians 3:20: **Now to him who by the power at work within us is able to do far more abundantly than all that we can ask or think**. *So my time in the yard a while ago was not a walk of fantasy. Something is in the air. The heavenly hosts are on the move in these parts! Our prayers have been heard. Revival is coming!*

For more than an hour she engaged in a time of inspirational praise in a language of adoring worship. Her heart was strangely warmed, but no tears were falling. She was sure the Spirit was saying to her, **Stand still, and see the salvation of the Lord!** Soon a sweet peace swept over her spirit and body so that sleep was inevitable.

In her sleep, an angel said, *"Wake up and read Daniel 10! Now!"*

She awoke and read: **And behold, a hand touched me and set me trembling on my hands and knees. And he said to me, 'O Daniel, man greatly loved, give heed to the words that I speak to you, and stand upright, for now I have been sent to you … Fear not, Daniel, for from the first day that you set your mind to understand and humbled yourself before your God, your words have been heard, and I have come because of your words. The prince of the kingdom of Persia withstood me twenty-one days; but Michael, one of the chief princes came to help me, so I left him there with the prince of the kingdom of Persia and came to make you understand what is to befall your people….**

O Lord, thank You for clearing things up for me! Now I know my years of praying and weeping are not in vain. I'm not comparing myself to the prophet Daniel. But just as You heard his prayer, so You have heard mine and others, and You have sent Your angels Gabriel and Michael, Your mighty warriors, over the territories that demons sought to control. O Lord! I know we are now on the verge of a rending of the heavens!

Estelle was quite sure someone had knocked on the door, but she could not regret having been so taken up with the vision and the command to read from Daniel that she did not answer. Now she was free to see if someone was waiting.

She opened the front door to look outside and could see Linda talking with a man in the front yard. He was dressed like a cowboy and seemed to be in a hurry. Noticing Estelle at the door, Linda called, "I'm sorry I disturbed you by knocking, but I do believe this gentleman has something important for you to hear."

The man began talking as he walked toward Estelle. "Miz Tharp, my name is Jay Lawson, and I ride for the Whitman Ranch over across Merrisach Lake. My boss, Mr. Press Whitman, ain't been outa bed in three days. Miz Edith, his wife, sent me to get you to come pray for Mr. Press. She says he knows he'll die and go to Hell iffen he can't get some hep to find God. She says, please come and hep us. Can I go back and tell her you'll be comin'?"

"Yes, I'll come either tonight or in the morning." Estelle listened as he gave her instructions on how to get to the ranch.

"Thank ye, ma'am," he said as he ran to his pickup.

Returning to her prayer time, Estelle praised the Lord that there was some real evidence that His Spirit was moving over the prairie; she expected to see the same from the bottoms. For another hour she paced the cabin, praising God that He would be moving to save sinners, heal marriages, draw the young to Jesus, and heal the land. Jim would be saved!

Jim came in early, and after an early supper, Estelle told Jim about Press Whitman's needing to get right with God. "Could we drive over there tonight, or shall we take the children to school in the morning and then go over there?"

"That old hard-hearted soul does need to get right with God, but I'd prefer to go in the mornin'."

As Jim drove up to the Whitman house the next morning, he was admiring the prosperous ranch. "Estelle, Ole Press is one of the richest cattlemen on Little Prairie, but I hear he ain't always been honest. I reckon ye'll tell him God forgives it all."

"Of course I will, if he repents and trusts in Jesus for full payment of all his sins. That's the good news of the Gospel!"

Edith met them at the door. "Oh, Estelle! Thank you for comin'! You, too, Jim. Press ain't slept for so long, cuz he's just sure he's lost forever. Jim, have that seat over there by the window. I see you've got the news to read. Estelle, come with me." Edith led her into their bedroom and drew up a chair for Estelle by her husband's bedside. The rancher had pulled the covers over his head, but when Edith told him Estelle was there, he roused enough that they could see his tousled gray hair, bloodshot eyes, and unshaven face. Edith excused herself and left the room.

Estelle had not yet dealt with a man as hungry for God as Press was. She could tell he was full of fear. He listened to the Gospel as a child would listen to a bedtime story, all ears and heart. He was ready to repent and pray and trust God for His salvation because of what Jesus did on the cross. Estelle did not need to pump him for confession and assurance. Immediately, he began rejoicing in his newfound peace with God! "You mean to tell me my sins are washed away, my name's been written in Heaven's book, and I'm on my way to Heaven? Well, don't leave just yet, 'specially if Jim's out there. I wanta get outa this bed and get cleaned up. I'll have Edie make us breakfast or lunch and y'all can eat with us. Then I think Edie'll be ready to give her heart to Jesus, too. Would you please tell Edie to come back here?"

Edith went back in to Press, and she came out beaming. "Press is different. Thank you, Estelle!"

"No, thank the Lord! I merely gave him the good news of the Gospel, and he believed it."

"Well, we want y'all to stay and have a meal with us; then I want you to pray with me, Estelle. Press is gettin' cleaned up, and he'll be out to visit with Jim soon."

"In a few minutes, Press came bouncing out to greet Jim. "Jim, I believe I'm a new man! I feel forgiven, changed in my heart. I thank y'all fer comin'."

After breakfast for the Whitmans and lunch for the Tharps, Edith was as easy to lead to Christ as her husband had been. Before leaving, Estelle asked, "Press, do you and Edith usually go to church anywhere on Sunday?"

"No, we haven't been going to church, but now that we are Christians, I think we should begin somewhere."

Jim said, "Estelle teaches the Bible every Sunday morning over at Nady in the Menard schoolhouse. I've heard several preachers, but nobody I've ever heard makes the Bible more understandable than her. I know y'all would enjoy the service. Ye know Ross Morgan, Cleve Sweeney, and probably several others that go there. They'd all be glad to see ye."

"Press and Edith, why don't you come Sunday morning and sit with Jim. Then plan to come home with us for dinner."

"Edie, I just think we oughta go hear Estelle and then go eat dinner with them."

"Then, that's what we'll do."

Estelle left them a passage of Scripture to think on. She showed them Mark 8:34-38, which she had marked in red in the New Testament she presented to each of them. After Estelle had prayed for them, they all hugged as the Tharps put on their coats to leave.

The Sunday morning service was well attended. Several who knew Press and Edith Whitman were delighted to see them in church and greeted them warmly. After the service was opened with singing, prayer, and announcements, Estelle said, "I don't want to embarrass our new attendees, Press and Edith Whitman, but we do want to welcome them to our fellowship today. What I really want to say is that Jim and I had the privilege of witnessing their conversion to Christ a few days ago. I know we would all love to hear their testimony, and I believe it would strengthen their faith if they would tell us what the Lord has done for them."

Deciding he would go first, Press stood up. "Well, I shore never expected to be in a church service about to say what I hope will come out alright. Jim and Estelle found an awful sinner at our place last Friday morning. I just knew I was gonna die and go to Hell. In all my sinful years, I can't ever remember feelin' so lost or disgusted with myself. Estelle come and laid the Gospel on the line. She told me I'd have to quit my sinful ways, but she said God would change my heart and give me His Spirit to hep me. I believed her, and I believed God's Word. I plunged in, and folks, it works! I ain't cussed once, and Edie and I now act like we love each another—no fightin' and fussin'. It really feels good to be in church, too. We plan to keep comin'."

Press had no sooner sat down when Edith stood, letting all know she was not intimidated. "I was glad God spoke to Press, but I realized right away after he was saved that I needed salvation, too. Estelle did double duty—she helped both Press and me find the Lord. Then she and Jim invited us home with them today for dinner. I think we are winners all around. But, like Press said, we do feel good in this place this morning. I know we need this, so we'll just keep comin'."

After Estelle had taught the Bible lesson, she closed in prayer, bringing before the Lord the names of several people who had found Christ in the last few days. She encouraged the other believers to be sure to greet the new believers who were present and give them a word of encouragement. Several swarmed around the Whitmans. As Estelle greeted the Morgans and Sweeneys, she invited them to their home for the noon meal with the Whitmans.

Jim and Estelle felt the Lord used the noon meal to help the Whitmans bond with the other couples. When Press learned that Jim was not yet a believer, by his own admission, he urged him before leaving, "Don't keep puttin' it off, Jim! We need you doin' what you're doin' with Lloyd, but the Lord wants you in His service, too. Edith and me'll be prayin' fer ye."

384

After everyone left, Estelle left the kitchen duties to Linda, Jeanette, and Anniece and went to the cabin. She spent the first hour in praise and thanksgiving, expressing confidence in seeing the heavens open and the Holy Spirit convicting sinners and cleansing and empowering the saints. *Oh, for the salvation of Jim, Jeanette, Jake, and Anniece! Work mightily in Hot Springs, blessing the Bonnhoffers, Dr. Baylor, and the other Presbyterians. Deal with Mr. Jackson, Lloyd, and Irene. Now, Lord, here I am to be used of You wherever and whenever You please.*

Estelle knew it was getting late, but she felt a call from the Spirit to rest, a call that was as strong as her call to pray earlier. She reclined on the couch and was soon asleep. This was the way Jim found her. For some reason she had not turned the lock on the door. He stood just inside and listened to her breathing. Once he heard her say, "Yes, Lord!" Thinking she was waking up, he lingered awhile. He was about to give up, turn away, and slip out quietly when he saw something startling— amazing! Over Estelle's head was a fiery blaze, lighting her face. A pillar of fire moved over her feet. Jim lost track of time, unsure of how long he had gazed on Estelle with the mysterious light over her. Jim started trembling, unable to speak when he tried to call her name. He simply couldn't order a word! *What's happenin' to me? To Estelle? God, are ye tryin' to tell me somethin'? Is what Estelle prophesied comin' to pass? Is this Your light? Are You dealin' with me? Have I put off yieldin' my heart to You too long? Lord, do have mercy on me!*

He walked out the door to calm down. Outside in the twilight, Jim peered through the glass. The blaze was still over her head and the pillar of fire still over her feet. Now he could make a sound and speak her name. Relieved, but stirred deeply, he locked the door and went to talk to the horses and the dogs. A half hour later, he stopped by the cabin window and could see the lights were still there. Feeling she was secure, he went on to the house. Anniece had made coffee and had cut a piece of raisin pie for him, leaving it on the table.

Two weeks after Estelle led the Whitmans to Christ, Jim was driving home from the Arkansas River when he was flagged down by a rough-looking young man. Jim stopped, expecting him to want a ride out of the bottoms. He surprised him by asking, "Do you know Estelle Tharp?"

"I reckon I ought to—she's my wife. Why?"

"My partner and me, we been cuttin' timber over 'crost the river fer a mill down a ways. Ol' Shorty, he been actin' funny fer over a month. Ever mornin' he start out sayin' 'It's my time!' I put up with that a long time, 'til I say, 'Whudda ye mean?' He say, 'Cholly, I'm gonna meet me Maker; I ain't ready.' I say, 'I'm tard of hearin' it. I'm leavin' ye.' He met someone who say, 'See Miz Tharp if ye wanta get saved.' Mr. Tharp, can you take me to her?"

"Get in. She'll be home and listen to yer story. Where is this Shorty now?"

"At our camp downriver here a few miles."

"If my wife wants to go and help him, can we drive to him?"

"Looks like this rig oughta make it. Better roads in there than this one here."

"What's yore name, and where are ye from?"

"Cholly Glidden; I live in log camps or wherever I can get work. Right now we are camped in Yoncapin. I 'spect ye'd wanta cross on old Pendleton Ferry and go downriver from there."

"If Estelle decides to go, can ye guide us to the camp?"

"I sho 'nuff can! But I reckon Ol Shorty's worried 'bout the cost."

"I don't reckon he's got much of a worry there."

It was about two o'clock when the three arrived at the log camp located in a little clearing surrounded by cottonwood timber. Jim told Estelle to stay in the truck while he and Cholly went into the tent to meet Shorty and get him ready for her. Inside, a big dog jumped up on Cholly and then tried to climb on Jim, but Cholly knocked him down. Soon a short, stocky, red-headed young man emerged from his bed, and Cholly said, "Shorty, Miz Tharp's out there when ye're ready for her to come in."

In a few minutes he opened the tent flap and said, "Ma'am, I'm Shorty and I'm shore glad to see ye. He stepped back and knocked the dog out of a chair, wiped the seat off with his sleeve, and told her, "Sit down, please."

Jim said, "Shorty, why don't ye slide that bench there over by Estelle, and Cholly and me'll go out and get a little fresh air."

Estelle said, "Shorty, tell me a little about yourself—about your family and where you were raised."

"Ain't much to tell. My fokes and my two sisters drowned in the '37 flood. My brother an' me wuz stayin' with our aunt up in Helena, or I guess we'd a drowned, too. I only had three years of schoolin' when my aunt took us in. I been pullin' a saw since I wuz eight, so I been either sawin', snakin', or loggin' ever since."

"I'm sorry you lost your parents and sisters. Did you ever go to Sunday school or church? Have you been told about a God of love who will save those who will confess Jesus as their Savior and Lord?"

"No, ma'am. My daddy and mama wuz not church fokes."

"Well, Shorty, that's why I'm here. Cholly said you are afraid you're going to die."

"Ma'am, for the past several weeks, I been skeered like this. Late one Sunday night a month or so ago, I turned on the radio and heerd this preacher say God is gonna call saints and sinners to judgment. Sumpin' got holta me when he said that. Cholly and me wuz in Dumas one Sunday night havin' us a steak. Next to us wuz two sheriffs—one from Desha, and the other from over where y'all live. I reckon it wuz just 'posed to be, cuz I overheerd one say iffen a man wants to get right with God, he needs to see Estelle Tharp. 'Whar could I find her?' I ast the sheriff. He say, 'North and a little east of the Nady store.' That's all I knew. Cholly and me ast 'round and found out we had to cross the river to Medina and go west to the prairie. I reckon Cholly found ye awright. I bet ye'll have somethin' to tell me 'bout how to get right with God."

Estelle found his simple mind receptive and his spirit hungry. In no time he was crying and believing and praying. He believed the Scriptures she read, trusted the Savior she described, and found peace with God. She gave him a Bible and a booklet on how to begin living the Christian life.

Outside Shorty testified to Jim and Cholly and told Cholly, "Ye need what I got!" Since he was open to hearing, Estelle led Cholly to the Lord at the fender of their pickup. She prayed with both of them and gave Cholly a copy of the same two books she had given Shorty.

Before they left, Jim told the boys they oughta come over to Nady on Sunday and hear Estelle preach the Gospel. As Jim and Estelle neared Dumas, Jim said, "Well, wife, it looks like ye're gonna keep busy runnin' over both the prairies and down in the bottoms, leadin' people to the Lord."

"Sweetheart, I doubt that you can discern it, but the heavens are astir with the forces of Almighty God—heavenly hosts are invading this part of the world, convicting sinners and saints of their need of God. Many, many people are going to believe the Gospel and become transformed. I'm thankful that you are willing to drive me to places like this today."

"If what ye say is true, why do ye think just them two poor, ignorant boys wuz the only fellers that got the call to repent and get right with God?"

Before long, three women from the prairie came to Estelle and asked that she help them find the Lord. Then a whole family came from Garland Lake to find the Tharp home so that they could give their hearts to the Lord. Estelle begin feeling that it was time for her to contact Sister Martha. Estelle would ask her to consult with Dr. Smith about the possibility of forming an evangelistic party of preachers, singers, and musicians to come and have a Gospel meeting. Perhaps the Holy Spirit would use this to draw the multitudes to Christ. It made sense to her to have a focal point for a spiritual meeting where multitudes could come and hear the Gospel and get saved.

The next time Jim needed to go to DeWitt, Estelle asked to ride along. He dropped her off to visit Frank and Ola Fox while he went about his business. Frank was delighted with Estelle's suggestion that it was time to plan a Gospel meeting. Around DeWitt he had seen signs of spiritual hunger similar to what Estelle was reporting in her area.

Jim had driven Estelle into the bottoms twice in one week—once to a fish camp on a lake and the other to a log camp—to lead people to the Lord. During the trip home from the log camp, Jim remarked, "It seems to me my wife is in greater demand for preachin' the Gospel than Billy Sunday was when I was a growin' boy."

"That's why Pastor Fox and I agree that it's time to bring down some preachers and singers from Indiana to hold a Gospel meeting. Multitudes could then come and get saved in the meeting, rather than me and a few others combing these areas and leading people to the Lord on a much smaller scale."

Jim stopped at their mailbox. With his hands full of mail, he was climbing back into the pickup when Estelle said, "Honey, let's drive up to Tichnor."

"What for?" Jim wanted to know.

"I want to get to a telephone. I've started twice now to write Sister Martha, but I think maybe I'd better talk to her, and possibly Dr. William Smith, about a revival."

Jim seemed a bit disturbed as he drove on north. "What do ye mean, ye need to talk to them about a revival?" he asked, sounding angry.

"Quite frankly, I believe the many people recently finding the Lord is a sign that the revival is already beginning. Instead of you and me running all over Arkansas County, including the White River bottoms and the prairie, I feel we need to schedule a time and place for a meeting where the multitudes can come together and find the Lord!" Estelle explained.

"Listen, woman! I've heard ye talk a lot about revival, but would ye one more time try and tell me what ye're talkin' about?" Jim demanded.

Estelle swallowed hard and took a deep breath as she looked at Jim's red face. She remembered that, across the years, the only time he had addressed her as "woman" was when he was provoked or angry with her. As she took a few moments to respond, the Lord was revealing to her that Jim's anger was due to the enemy's opposition to his interest in spiritual things; it was a part of her husband's last holdout against the Spirit's convicting power in his life. So she patiently and kindly replied, "Honey, a revival is an invisible invasion of the Holy Spirit coming on a person, a family, a community, or a whole area with conviction of sin and a growing sense of need to come to the Lord in repentance and faith. We have now reached that point where we need the Lord's ordained messengers to proclaim the Gospel in the power of the Spirit."

"Well, ye ain't doin' so bad yerself, without a preacher heppin' ye. Just think back at how many places we've had to go to because ye've been sent for. And think of all the folks who've come to the house— mostly women, I guess—to get saved. Ye've shore been a busy woman! If what ye've done ain't preachin', I don't know what is."

"Yes, the Lord has helped me, and we've seen enough people saved to know that it is only the beginning of a mighty move of the Holy Spirit. But we need preachers called of God and skilled in the Word and trained singers and musicians. We need people like Sister Martha, Simeon and LaVaun Smith, Homer and Helen Rich, or whoever the Lord has in mind."

Jim was quiet, but his face was still red, and Estelle was quite sure she had not heard the end of his objections to plans for the revival meeting. "Where do ye wanta go here in Tichnor?" he asked.

"Go on up to Uncle Bob's. He has a phone in his little cubbyhole back there where I can have a little privacy," Estelle explained. "I have the number for Union Bible College, and I might be able to speak to Sister Martha there. I think I'll call the college first, and if I can't get her there, I'll try her home phone."

Inside, Uncle Bob was warm and friendly. After shaking hands with Jim, he said, "Estelle, it's nice to have you here with Jim today. What can I do for y'all?"

"Uncle Bob, I need to use your telephone to make a long distance call to Indiana, if I may, please," Estelle said.

"Why, of course, I'll show you where it is back there. Then Jim and I will drink a Coke and catch up on things," the old gentleman said, as he led the way to the back of the store.

"If I remember the way this works, Uncle Bob, I make the call, and then I can get the cost of the call from an operator so that I can pay you, right?"

"Yeah, that's the way it works, but don't worry 'bout payin' fer the call."

"Oh yes, I will pay for it. This call is important, and I'd never think of using your phone for a long distance call and leaving you to pay the bill."

When the old man was gone, Estelle bowed her head and silently asked the Lord to calm her from the disappointment she felt from Jim's attitude. She prayed for the ability to communicate with whoever answered the phone and to reach the person the Lord would provide to make her case for a team of workers to come and lead in the harvest of souls. With confidence, she picked up the phone, dialed the long distance number, and gave the number in Westfield, Indiana, to the operator. She heard the dial tone ring only three times and a man's voice answered, saying, "Union Bible College, William Smith speaking."

"Oh, Dr. Smith! This is Estelle Tharp down in Arkansas County."

"Well, Sister Tharp! How good to hear from you! Dr. Honeycutt and I were just talking this morning about you and the good things happening down there."

"Yes, Dr. Smith, that's why I'm calling. In the last month, my husband has driven me all over the prairie and down in the bottoms to about nineteen places! We've prayed with nearly thirty people who have given their hearts to the Lord. Most of them are coming to the Menard schoolhouse on Sunday morning to hear the Word, and they're growing in the grace of God. Several people have simply come to our house to say they were ready to find the Lord, and they've been saved and are worshiping with us at the schoolhouse. But, Dr. Smith, I'm calling to tell you that, after much prayer and thought, Brother Frank Fox and I agree that it is time to call you and request that you and Sister Martha Honeycutt put together a team of evangelistic preachers, musicians, and singers to come down for a special meeting. We are convinced that the revival has already begun, and we believe before it is over we shall see a mighty rending of the heavens!" Estelle decided to pause a few seconds to let her report sink into the dear old gentleman's heart and mind.

After a brief pause, she heard him say, "That's just wonderful, Sister Tharp! Sister Honeycutt and I agreed this morning before chapel that a call of this very nature would be forthcoming. So we are in agreement with you. May I ask you a few questions?"

"Of course, Doctor!"

"How many preachers and other workers do you think we should send? And for how long?"

"Well, I feel sure we need more than one preacher; I would think two or three. And I would hope that Sister Martha might be one of the three. But right now I feel we need at least one man with the gift of evangelism—someone gifted with discernment, eloquence, and a good deliverance to present the Gospel to the lost. I also believe we need a teacher or two who can help us with discipling new believers. Many who will come to God will need help to really get their feet down spiritually and be strong witnesses for the Lord. Of course, we need musicians and a good song leader."

"Sister, I am in full agreement with all you have requested."

"Doctor, do you have some men up there who can preach like John Wesley, George Whitefield, or Charles Finney?"

The old gentleman was chuckling as he answered her. "Sister, I know what you mean by mentioning those great anointed revivalists. I can't say that we have men who are exactly that caliber, but we do have some powerful preachers who will present the Gospel with the same great results. These I have in mind are not newcomers, but proven messengers of the Gospel who have seen some mighty outpourings of the Spirit in their ministry. And I know we can find musicians and singers for you. Sister Tharp, I know this is a bit delicate, but I need to tell you that the men I have in mind are people who have to work for a living. Now I know you folks down there are not well off financially. But if you want these workers for any length of time, do you think you might be able to come up with a fairly good financial offering that you could divide among the three or four people we would send?"

"Brother Smith, I've prayed a lot about offerings for the workers. I've been to the man who runs the general store in Nady and two others who run sawmills. I've told them what I believe God is going to do in this great revival—that it will change the character of our community; thieves will become honest and merchants, cattlemen, and farmers will stop losing hundreds of dollars in stolen merchandise, timber, and cattle. I've asked that they consider making a financial investment in this meeting. I've led one of the wealthiest ranchers and his wife to the Lord, and I've talked to him about an investment in the revival meetings planned. I know some prosperous fishermen and lumbermen who've found the Lord, and I will be speaking to them about investing. My husband and I plan to give $1,000. Please tell those people you plan to send down here that they'll leave from Nady with an amount greater than they might have earned up in Indiana. I make that promise in good faith after much prayer and preparation for a great offering for the Lord's servants.

"To answer your question about how long we'll need these people, I'm thinking the revival should run all spring and summer and into the fall! I believe it's God's housecleaning time for all these neighborhoods around here. I have over 300 names on my prayer list, and I just believe everyone of them will get saved, plus hundreds of others whom I don't even know about!"

"Wonderful! I believe you! But we might be talking about sending different groups at different times if you think we should go from April through October. Now, one other question: Do you think you can find safe, clean accommodations for these people?"

"Oh, yes, Doctor! I've given thought to that, too. Some of them will stay with us, and I will find good safe homes for the others. Now I do need to remind you that none of the homes in Nady have electricity. Nor do they have indoor plumbing and bathrooms. But I assure you that everyone you send will sleep on good clean beds, eat healthy food, and be protected from thieves, murderers, and rapists. My husband as special deputy to the sheriff of Arkansas County will see to that."

"Yes, and we know you will meet their needs! So one final question: When do you want to start this meeting?"

"Two weeks from this Sunday!" Estelle said.

"I'll have Sister Honeycutt write to you early in the week and give you the date of their arrival and the number of men and women in the party. Please give Frank and Ola our blessings, and also greet your fine husband for us. Goodbye, and we'll all be praying for the meetings!"

Estelle placed the phone down with a great sense of having accomplished the Lord's will. She believed in her heart that the coming evangelistic meeting would herald to those far and wide the wonders of God's grace upon a wicked area of Arkansas. As she returned to Jim and Bob Hibbard, she believed that a harvest was about to be reaped. She knew her next task was to pray for an understanding on how to get posters printed and placed in locations where they would be read.

"Well, did ye get yer call in to the preachers?" Jim asked. He turned to Bob and said, "Yeah, Estelle thinks everbody on the lower end of Little Prairie is gonna get saved!" The lighthearted way he said it caused Estelle inner pain.

"Yes, I talked to Dr. Smith. He agrees with me that the time is right for revival in this part of the world. He's sending a team of Christian workers—preachers, singers, and musicians—in about two weeks. We'll start the revival two weeks from this Sunday night, so we'll need to get the word around."

They had not driven far before Jim resumed his negative remarks. "I reckon ye're gonna try and pay them steak-and-chicken-eatin' preachers somethin' for their time here."

"Yes, indeed! They'll need money to live on while they are here. Honey, I'm disappointed that you resent our giving money to people like Sister Martha, Pastors Homer Rich and Frank Fox, and others like them who will come to preach the Gospel here! I've already talked with Ross and Cleve, and I've mentioned it to Press and Edith Whitman. They're all excited about chipping in generously to help pay for the expenses of this revival meeting.

"I want you to hear what the apostle Paul said about paying Christian workers who preach the Gospel. It'll take me just a minute to find the Scripture. Here it is in 1 Corinthians 9:14, and he is quoting Jesus. Now listen to it: **In the same way, the Lord commanded that those who proclaim the gospel should get their living by the gospel**. Now, I know this means that they should not have to farm, log, or fish in order to live while they preach and minister spiritually to the people. Again, in 1 Timothy 5:17 and 18: **Let the elders who rule well be considered worthy of double honor, especially those who labor in preaching and teaching; for the scripture says, 'You shall not muzzle an ox when he is treading out the grain,' and 'The laborer deserves his wages.'"** Estelle looked across at Jim, and she was glad that he seemed to be listening. She went on, "Now, you need to realize, along with Ross, Cleve, and the Whitmans, that this is the greatest event that has ever hit this part of the country, and we cannot treat this lightly nor deprive God's messengers of their financial needs. In fact, I believe that we should give $1,000!"

The pickup lurched, and Estelle looked over to see that Jim had lost control of the truck and of himself. She saw Jim's head roll back and his body stiffen as the vehicle headed into the ditch. Jim screamed, "Hell, woman! I ain't about to give that kinda money to this shindig you and Preacher Fox have cooked up!" Slamming on the brakes and gripping the steering wheel, he maneuvered the truck out of the ditch. He coughed, got his breath, and went on at Estelle's silence, "Now, I admit I like Sister Martha and Homer and Helen Rich. I don't begrudge anythang we ever give 'em. But I think ye're goin' overboard talkin' thousands of dollars for them preachers."

"Well, if they are here all this spring and summer and into the fall, it'll be more than six months. They've got bills to pay. Even if we feed them—and we will—they've got houses to keep up and families and bills back home to care for. And, honey, look how the Lord has blessed us! He's blessed Ross and the Whitmans! And He's blessed several others who will gladly contribute to the needs of this evangelistic party." Thinking she had said enough, she quit talking and just prayed as Jim drove along home.

As Jim parked the truck and shut off the ignition, he looked over at Estelle and patted her hand. "Honey, I think ye're a little high on yer budget for the revival, but I want ye to know I ain't as much agin it all as I might've sounded a while ago." With that he got out and waited for her to join him as they walked to the house.

Climbing the front porch steps together, she said, "Thanks, darling! I know the Lord has been blessing us for being generous for the last sixteen years. I'm glad for your willingness to tithe our prosperity and give special offerings. Just you wait and see what He's got in store for you, our whole family, and all the people in this part of the country who will heed His call!"

Estelle was so fulfilled and thankful for the response to her phone call to Dr. Smith. However, she felt the need to retreat to the cabin for a period of prayer and praise and rest in the Lord. Linda would have the children home by 5:00 o'clock. Since Anniece, 14 years of age, was so capable in the kitchen, her mother left her a note to cook the evening meal. She would prepare a supper as delicious as anything Estelle could prepare.

She spent a half hour studying the Bible and then an hour in prayer. She then felt the need to lie down and give herself to praise and meditation. *Lord, I thank You for the conversation with Dr. Smith and for helping me with Jim in his negative attitude. Lord, please use me to prepare the Nady believers for the coming meetings! Help me communicate with Pastor Fox all that was said and received from Dr. Smith. Help Dr. Smith and Sister Martha to agree with Your Spirit in selecting the workers. Please, Lord, send us the very messengers You will anoint to bring in the harvest. Oh, help us get the word out. Just lay it on the hearts of the people who don't hear of the meeting to just come on out to the schoolhouse. Bring them in! Lord, I come against the demonic forces that will seek to rally against what You want to do here. Evil spirits, I command in the strong name of Jesus that you depart into the regions of darkness and have done with the minds of all souls here in this area. Now, Father, invade the homes and hearts of all people, stirring their interests in salvation and causing them to think about their eternal destiny. Put a fear of You in their hearts that causes them to tremble. Inspire an interest that will make them want to come and search for You! Lord, would You cause our son Jake to want to come home from Wichita in time to get in on this revival and give his heart to You? Please help me Sunday morning as I announce the meeting. Help me make it a compelling thing, and may our people get excited about inviting everyone they know and those with whom they come in contact.*

Having already conferred with Pastor Fox, on Sunday morning Estelle announced revival services beginning April 14 and running many weeks through the spring and summer and possibly into the fall. The revival would involve several evangelistic parties coming down from Indiana as decided upon by a committee made up of Dr. William Smith, Sister Martha Honeycutt, and Pastor Homer Rich. "All of us need to be in prayer concerning financial support for these people, most of whom have to work for a living; they have families and homes to maintain back in Indiana even while they minister to us here. We'll also need places for these people to stay. However, our greatest need is prayer. We must have special prayer meetings in spiritual preparation for the Holy Spirit to convict and draw people to the services to hear the Gospel."

When Estelle, Jim, and the children, along with Martha Honeycutt, arrived at the Menard schoolhouse on a clear Sunday morning, April 14, 1946, Jim wasn't sure how far he would have to drive to find a place to park. At least 200 people were standing outside, which indicated they had not found seats in either of the two rooms inside. Jim let the others out at the front entrance, and he drove around the back of the building and beyond the men's outhouse to park along the fence dividing the Massey's property from the school grounds. He walked the 300 yards back to the schoolhouse. Meanwhile, Estelle had allowed the children to remain outside to wait for their father. She led her guest into the south room and found that Homer and Helen had reserved a place for them on the front seat near the stage. Homer had never used the stage as a platform from which to preach when he was their pastor. But all speakers and musicians would need to sit and remain on the large stage from this morning on because of the packed two rooms. The dividing partition had been raised upward, so that the two rooms were more like one. To make more room, eight men had been enlisted to lift the piano to the east end of the stage.

The musicians opened the service with "Revive Us Again," played by Helen Rich at the piano, accompanied by John Newby on the trombone, and R. H. Searcy and Preston Mitchell on guitars. Pastor Fox, Pastor Homer, and Sister Martha had decided that Estelle should greet the people, introduce Sister Martha, and call on Pastor Fox to lead a prayer. After several congregational songs led by John Newby with the accompaniment of the other musicians, Homer would introduce the Rev. Woody Shields, who would bring the morning message.

As Estelle walked toward the stage, she spied Dr. Bonnhoffer and Maureen and was pleased that they had come early to find a seat inside. She believed that prayer warriors in several states during the past seven years accounted for the electrified atmosphere. This crowd included over a hundred Arkansas County prayer warriors who had joined with her to pray for a great spiritual awakening.

She opened by saying, "Dear Friends, the hour has come! Thousands have prayed for what is beginning here today—**times of refreshing from the Presence of the Lord; the pouring out of God's Spirit upon all flesh; mighty works and wonders and signs which God shall do in our midst;** salvation, cleansing, **purifying of our hearts**, divine healings; **baptisms with the Holy Spirit and fire**; God's doing a new thing, **making the wilderness a river and the desert a blossoming of the rose**. Oh, dear people, we stand at the dawn of a new day! Please welcome God's appointed forerunner of this great spiritual awakening, a dear lady who came to our dark community several years ago and was sent of God as our John the Baptist to prepare the way for what our Lord is now about to do. Greet Sister Martha Honeycutt as she comes to lead us to the Throne of Grace!"

Inside the building, more than 200 people stood up and clapped, and many on the outside joined in on the deafening applause, which went on for at least two minutes. Knowing the crowd would be too large to fit inside, Pastor Fox had engaged the services of Fletcher Electronics in

DeWitt to come down and set up battery-operated loud speakers. With all of the windows completely open, the people outside crowded near each one and were pleased to be able to hear those speaking and enjoy the music.

Martha Honeycutt prayed a most moving prayer that brought all who knew her to tears. When Homer Rich emerged on the stage, and before he could introduce the speaker, the crowd inside burst into applause for him as their former pastor. He thanked the people for their expression of love for him and Helen, saying how great it was to be back and feel the presence of the Lord in this place. Then he said he wanted to introduce a younger preacher, who he was sure the congregation had never heard of. He declared Woody Shields to be one of the finest preachers he and Helen had ever met. He was a Baptist now turned Wesleyan with nothing but love and admiration for his Baptist brothers and sisters. The response of the crowd to the newcomer was honorable but noticeably modest compared to that for Sister Martha and Homer and Helen Rich.

Woody Shields captured the crowd immediately with his humor, but most of all with his knowledge of the Gospel of Jesus Christ. His persuasive illustrations of God's love and power held the attention of the people.

Recognizing that so many in his audience were new believers, he used his time to add to all that Estelle and Martha had said to build expectations and encourage faith in them concerning what the Lord wanted to do during the revival in bringing to pass the salvation of sinners. He declared that the people in Nady had never seen crowds like they would see at the services in the days to come, beginning tonight. People they had never seen or heard of and people who had never seen or heard of the Menard schoolhouse would be drawn here by the Holy Spirit to meet their spiritual destiny. They would become born again and begin a new life of discipleship with Jesus Christ as their Lord and King, all because God had willed it and believers had prayed His will to pass!

Woody Shields' message was short and to the point. He did not go on and on with words. After about 25 minutes, he closed with a brief but powerful prayer. He asked Homer to come and announce the service that evening and then pronounce the benediction.

Jim and Estelle and their guests enjoyed a wonderful time of fellowship over the noon meal. Estelle had invited the doctor and Maureen to come and meet Sister Martha and get to know her better. At his first opportunity to speak with Estelle after dinner, the doctor said, "I've never been in a gathering where I've felt the presence of the Holy Spirit on the same scale that I did this morning! And that's saying a great deal, because Faith Presbyterian Church has been visited by many of His outpourings ever since you and Jim were with us!"

On the way to the evening service, Estelle said, "I do hope Jake gets here from Wichita in time for this revival." Jim nodded his agreement and added, "Yeah, it'll be good to see our boy again."

Nearing the schoolhouse, Estelle said, "Look at the cars and trucks here already!"

When Anniece spied a tall young man standing at the entrance above the steps, she cried out, "Mama, that's Jake standing up there!" Estelle sucked in her breath, and after one glance at the person, she said, "Honey, you are right! Bless his heart! He has come home!"

"How do ye reckon he got here from DeWitt?" Jim asked.

"Well, there's Brother Fox's car, so he probably rode here with him. I'll guess he rode into DeWitt on the bus and then learned that Pastor Fox was coming to Nady."

Almost before Jim had stopped the car, Estelle and Anniece were on the ground and running to Jake. Jim said to Sister Martha, who was in the back seat, "I'm sure ye remember our oldest son, Jake. He's been workin' in Wichita, Kansas, for the last five months and livin' with my sister Hollis Krablin. If ye'll excuse me, I'll go and get my hug after Estelle and Anniece are through with him."

Jake, who would be seventeen in a few months, seemed taller than Jim had remembered. "Hello there, son! Glad ye got here when ye did!" Jim hugged his son with real feeling, and Jake delighted in his father's embrace. "Hi, Dad! How are you? It's sure good to see you again! I've missed all of you. Aunt Hollis sends her love."

Estelle brought Jake over to the car to see Sister Martha. She extended her hand and shook Jake's hand warmly. "Jake, you've grown up a lot since I saw you. I know your family is glad to have you home!"

"Thank you, Sister Martha. It's wonderful to see you again."

Estelle took Jake by the arm and led him inside the schoolhouse. "Son, I'm so glad you came home when you did. We are in the beginning of a great revival, and we are going to see some miracles. We had over 700 people here this morning—most of them were on the outside, of course. But we're expecting 1,000 tonight!"

"Brother Fox told me you had an unusual meeting this morning. I know you've been praying for years for what you are about to see. I guess I can use some spiritual help myself." Looking around to see if his dad was close, Jake lowered his voice and asked, "What is Dad thinking about all of this?"

"Son, he is so close to getting saved. He will probably make up his mind to yield to Jesus tonight," Estelle said as she wiped a tear. "And I want you to come to the Lord, too!" she added as she watched her oldest son look more serious.

Down near the stage, Estelle said, "Brother Fox, thank you for bringing my dear son home to us."

"We were so glad to, Estelle! Jake is a fine young man, and I know you're glad he came home for the first night of the revival."

Jim was glad to see other influential members of the community arrive early—George Best, Ross Morgan, Perry Plant, Jeff Wallace, Garland Coose, Cleve Sweeney, Oscar Shelton, and Jim's brother Henry. Jim motioned for all of them to go into a huddle with him.

"Fellows," Jim began, "Estelle thinks there will be a bigger crowd here tonight than we had this mornin'. Now all the people outside this mornin' I figured to be around 500, and they were orderly. But we don't know who might show up here tonight to make this place dangerous. Ye know how it's been when there's been dances, benefit suppers, and other events—brawlin', cussin', fightin', drinkin', shootin', and stabbin'. Well, I never felt the crowd needed patrollin' this mornin', but I think we'd better be ready for about anythang tonight. So, Ross, why don't ye put these men together in pairs of two to be ready to patrol for at least 30 minutes and then have two more takin' their turn. I'll be down front with Estelle, but if trouble breaks loose out here and I'm needed, come on down and get me. I'll be out here on a moment's notice, and I'll be armed and ready. I do expect the sheriff to be present, but whether Lloyd is here or not, I'll be ready for anythang that comes up."

"Fine, Jim," Ross said. "You go ahead, and if all the rest of you will stay, we'll get organized right now."

It was still an hour before the service would begin, but Jim could see riders on horseback, wagonloads of farm people, and carloads and truckloads of people driving in. As he started for the steps, he saw the sheriff and his wife drive up. He walked over and welcomed them, urging them to get inside before it would be too late to find a seat.

"It looks like the place will be packed," the sheriff said.

"Yeah, there were over 700 here this mornin'. Course, that means 500 or more were out here."

"Do you expect any disorder, Jim?" Lloyd asked.

"Depends on who shows up, Lloyd. Nothin' upsettin' happened this mornin'. But ye can't tell what might blow if them rowdies from the bottoms drop by. But I just talked with Ross and several of our men— we'll be patrollin' out here continually. They'll let me know if they need me," Jim assured the sheriff.

"I'm glad you've got it covered, Jim. I can't imagine your needin' me, but if you do, I'm right there with you."

"Thanks, Lloyd. Glad ye're here. You and Irene need to go on in while there are still seats available."

By 5:45 the south room was packed, and at 6:30 Jim noticed that the north room was almost full. Ross had stationed two men at the bottom steps to signal to women to come on inside and be seated. It was felt that if anyone had to remain outside, it should be men, even though several men were seated inside. At 6:45, Jim and Ross went outside to try and size up the kinds of people in the growing crowd. "Ross, there's already 'bout as many here tonight as was here this mornin'. I see some pretty rough characters here from the bottoms, and all we can do is keep an eye on 'em."

"Yeah, I guess we oughta be glad they're here, but we hope it's for the right reason," Ross said.

"Exactly!" Jim agreed.

Just as John Newby and Helen Rich played through a stanza of "Amazing Grace," Jim took his seat by Estelle. "Where's Jake settin'?" Jim asked.

"Yonder in the corner," Estelle said, pointing to their son seated diagonally across the room from them in the back.

Estelle had insisted that Homer take his place as the coordinating pastor of the revival meeting for as long as he could remain. Homer shared with her that he thought Pastor Fox should lead the opening prayer, John would lead the congregation in several songs, and then he would make announcements about the nightly services. John and Helen would have the special music, and then Woody Shields would preach. Estelle agreed.

Pastor Fox prayed passionately, and Estelle was so glad his and the other voices were amplified, especially for the people in the north room and outside. John announced the opening congregational hymn, "Victory in Jesus," and on the chorus he played his trombone.

After a stanza or two of powerful singing and music, Dr. Bonnhoffer leaned over to Estelle and whispered loud enough for her to hear, "God's Spirit is here even stronger than He was this morning! Don't be surprised if I start to shout!"

"Please don't quench the Spirit, Doctor. Express your heart however the Lord wants you to!"

Jim heard all that the doctor had said, even though Estelle was seated between them. He felt something, but he didn't understand it. He actually felt frightened, confused, and anxious. Suddenly Ross appeared, standing over him. "Jim, ye need to come and see what's goin' on outside. It ain't what ye might think. But ye oughta come see it and try to figger it out. Come! Please!"

As Jim followed Ross down the aisle, he could see there was standing room only in both rooms. *What was he about to face outside?* When they got outside, Ross said, "If ye think the Spirit of God is strong inside—and I know it is!—wait 'til ye see what's happenin' out here." Moaning, groaning, and outcries hit Jim's ears as he descended the steps. All across the school yard to the south men lay on the ground stretched out as if dead, while others were rolling, crying, and praying. When Jim turned and looked to the north, he saw the same thing! He estimated that about 200 people were either on their faces or on their sides, as though a tornado or a strong wind had toppled them. "Jim, I want to know what ye make of this."

"Ross, I guess there's only one answer: God is at work in a strange way!"

"That's my take on it! I've walked among 'em, Jim, and I'm telling ye—these are the lowest in them bottoms: moonshiners, bootleggers, murderers, liars, thieves, rapists, ambushers, and fellers of the worst kind. But it seems to me like God's come on them just like Estelle's been prayin'. What are we gonna do with them?"

"Well, that ain't fer me to decide, Ross. I reckon we'll know the answer to your question before the night is over, and we'll likely know it by the way they act as soon as they gain consciousness." Jim turned away from the amazing scene to return to the service. He met his brother Henry coming down the steps.

"I saw ye leave the service, Jim. Need any help?"

"Naw, but go have a look around and then tell me what ye think." In a daze, Jim climbed the steps and walked the aisle back down to the front and sat down by Estelle.

Woody Shields was weeping as he told of the suffering of Jesus for the sins of both the good and the bad people on earth. He seemed to have no knowledge of all that was happening outside the building. But Sister Martha was strongly impressed that she was to go outside, and she leaned over and shared her impression with Estelle. Jim had already told Estelle what he had found outside. When Martha stood up, Estelle also got up, and both ladies made their way down the aisle toward the door, with Jim following. Ross, George, Henry, and Garland also decided to go out one by one so as not to distract the preacher or the people who might become curious.

Estelle and Sister Martha stood on the lower step looking around and saw what Jim had reported. Openly, they wept and praised the Lord! "Slain in the Spirit!" was all that Sister Martha could say. "It's what the Lord showed me in a vision!" Estelle said excitedly. The two women and Jim returned to their seats to listen to the rest of the service.

"I'm not sure of all that is going on around us at this time," Woody Shields said, "but something supernatural is happening both inside and outside this building. I just want to remind us that when there is a visitation of the Holy Spirit in whatever form He chooses, He expects a gracious response on our part. So I want everyone of us to realize that God is not only a God of justice, He is also a God of mercy and grace. Mercy is a divine attribute in which God sees to it that we do not get what we deserve. We all deserve to go to Hell, because the Bible says, **All have sinned, and come short of the glory of God**. But grace is a divine attribute in which God gives us what we do not deserve—forgiveness of sin, salvation through Christ's atoning death, adoption into the redeemed family of God, and the gift of the Holy Spirit. Through the Holy Spirit we are given wisdom, strength, and understanding for living the Christian life.

"God's attention has been on this community for several years now. Just this very night He has chosen to come in a mighty, dramatic, mysterious way. So let all who hear me—inside and outside—as you hear and feel God drawing you to faith and salvation in Jesus Christ, get up from where you are and come down here for prayer. Don't be ashamed to accept God's loving grace and forgiveness. Many of you will come, but I want each one of you personally to know that God will hear your prayer, forgive your sin, and make you one of His children.

"As we all stand, I'll ask Helen to slip to the piano, and John will come and lead us in that great invitational hymn, "Just As I Am." As we sing, let's come and stand down front and in these aisles. God loves you and calls you to salvation through Jesus Christ. Come on and accept the grace of God!"

Ross and Henry were on the outside watching the people, and heard the preacher say, "As we all stand...." They would later report that nearly all of those who had been sprawled on the ground stood immediately, as if ordered by some strange voice. Sister Martha had spoken to Estelle a few minutes before the invitation had begun, suggesting that the two of them go back outside and urge those on the ground to come inside for prayer. But as they were ready to slip away, Estelle saw the tears in Jim's eyes and noticed his shaking. She knew it was his moment of salvation, so she said to Sister Martha, "Jim is about to be saved. Please go ahead; I'll assist Jim." Sister Martha nodded her approval and departed down the aisle.

From his standing position in the back of the south room, Jake could see his father's shoulders shaking. At first, he wondered why his dad would be laughing, then he realized it was not laughter that was causing his shoulders to shake. Jake caught a glimpse of his father's face as he stood up, and he could see the tears. Tears filled his own eyes, and he felt something mysterious in his own heart as he watched his mother and father move arm in arm out into the aisle and then kneel at the small altar bench in front of Woody Shields. Many others were coming and filling the space between the front rows and the stage on which the preacher stood.

A noise at the door caught Jake's attention. Sister Martha was motioning to a crowd of men following behind her. Their hair and clothes were in a disheveled state and some were shoeless, having removed their muddy shoes and boots on the walk outside. What caused Jake to notice them first was the noises they were making—all were crying and groaning, and some were cursing. *What gives?* he wondered. *Are these evil heathen going to try and break up this service? But they were being led and urged forward by Sister Martha, so surely they were sincere.* What Jake didn't know was that a supernatural work of the Holy Spirit had smitten these men. They had been lying on the ground for over 20 minutes as still as death, and they had all gained consciousness at the same time with an awareness they had never experienced—God was calling them to salvation! It had not been the sermon or the music or the voice of Sister Martha that had drawn them to follow her inside. As the men were on their way, they yielded to an instinctive compulsion to express their frustrations through profanity. A new hope was burning within them that there was a better way of life, and it was propelling them forward.

Sister Martha directed the men forward until the western aisle was packed. Jake could hear their sobbing, groaning, and praying until it drowned out the congregational singing. Only John Newby could be heard singing the verses of "Just As I Am." Then Sister Martha began herding a stream of penitent men from the outside to the eastern aisle until it was packed. The noise emanating from the western aisle was duplicated on the eastern one. The last of the men from outside were near Jake. He heard two of them talking. One said, "What the hell do we think we'll get in here anyway?" Then he heard the dirty-faced shorter man reply, "Just whut we need, I reckon—forgiveness and the grace of God, like the man say." Jake supposed they had heard more of the message than he would have guessed.

Woody Shields was motioning for the music and singing to stop. Then Jake saw his father's and mother's heads appear. They were both standing at the front of the crowded space. Woody spoke into the microphone: "Dear men and women, I am amazed, humbled, and thrilled at what God is doing in Nady, Arkansas, on this night of April 14, 1946! He has brought scores of you to a moment of repentance and faith. He is offering you salvation through Jesus Christ, who has already died in full payment for your sins. All of us have *sinned.* Some of you have *killed.* Some of you have *committed adultery.* Some of you have *stolen.* Some of you have *lied.* But **we have all sinned and come short of the glory of God.** Now, God is saying to us, **If we confess our sins, He will faithfully forgive our sins and cleanse us from all unrighteousness.** We can all leave here tonight forgiven, pardoned, cleansed in our hearts, and filled with faith to live holy and righteously because of the blood of Jesus Christ that was shed as an atonement for us. So if you are ready to turn from your old evil ways and take up your new way of life in Jesus, bow your heads and follow me—repeat after me—this prayer."

Jake could never remember having wept in church before. But as Woody Shields began "The Sinner's Prayer" with nearly 200 people repeating their confessions and embracing a new faith in God and in Jesus Christ, Jake found himself tearful and wishing that he had joined that number. *But I'll see how Dad gets along in his new faith. I'll talk to Mom and Sister Martha, and maybe I'll make this move, too.* Jake could see by the smile on his dad's face and the look on his mother's that his dad had already made his peace with God. No doubt his mother had made sure he prayed as he ought and trusted God's saving grace. *Yeah, it seems appropriate that Jim Tharp, my dad, should be the first one saved in this mighty revival that Estelle Tharp, my mom, has prayed to pass!*

Woody Shields had John Newby teach everyone a simple chorus, "Thank You, Lord, for saving my soul; thank You, Lord, for making me whole. Thank You, Lord, for giving to me, Thy great salvation so full and free." They repeated the few lines again and again. Jake was convinced that something must have really transformed most of those old boys, because they had their hands in the air in praise and worship. Some yelled out, "Yeah! Ain't it so!" and another of the former rowdies would answer, "Hell, yes!" Jake would have laughed if it had been appropriate, but he was still too much in awe of all that had taken place to be lighthearted. The whole scene was wrapped in a mysterious gravity, which he knew Mom and Sister Martha would attribute to the Holy Spirit.

While Woody Shields, Homer Rich, Martha Honeycutt, and Estelle sought to grasp all that had happened in the last two hours, Helen began playing "Nothing But the Blood of Jesus." Woody saw this as an opportunity to allow the Spirit to help the newly converted realize the glorious miracle of their spiritual transformation, so he signaled to John to lead out on another chorus, saying, "They'll pick it up after you sing it once!" And they did! They sang heartily, "What can wash away my sins? Nothing but the blood of Jesus! What can make me whole again? Nothing but the blood of Jesus!" None of the leaders could remember ever being in a more sincere celebration of the supreme sacrifice Christ paid for the sins of mankind. All were amazed as they watched these ignorant bumpkins come into faith and join the saints in their **joy unspeakable and full of glory**. Even when Newby decided to let the chorus die, those whose hearts had been made whole would not let it die; they led out again and again until John rejoined the joyous celebration.

The celebration was as great on the outside as it was on the inside. When the newly converted returned to their acquaintances on the outside, their testimonies were so powerfully convincing that the Spirit convicted another hundred people in a matter of minutes. When Sister Martha and Estelle agreed that Woody Shields was needed to address the crowd on the outside, Jim went to get him. The evangelist was amazed at the sincerity, reverence, and humility demonstrated by the spiritually hungry and penitent men. Their ignorance and brokenness did not affect their hunger and repentance at all, but made their transformation seem all the more glorious.

Not one soul departed the scene of celebration until one o'clock in the morning. The people finally started leaving, some in cars and trucks, others in horse-drawn buggies or mule-drawn wagons, and the rest on foot. The folks from the river bottoms were the last to leave, probably because they felt they had more to celebrate. At first a few cars and trucks left slowly. Then a parade of mule-drawn wagons and horse-drawn buggies passed slowly from the scene, followed by people on foot.

Jim put an arm around Estelle as they headed for the car. "Sweetheart, ye're takin' a new husband home with ye tonight!" They embraced in the darkness, and Estelle whispered, "Darling, I've always loved you, but I've never been more in love with you than I am now. Oh!

How I praise God that you've finally given Him your heart! I guess I knew all along that it would happen when we finally saw **a rending of the heavens**! And, wasn't it wonderful that you were the first one to respond to the call!"

Walking with Sister Martha from the car to the cabin, Estelle said, "Sister Martha, I know we both need to talk over all that has happened, but we also need to get some sleep. So, please sleep late. I'll prepare our breakfast about 10 o'clock. Then we'll come back to your cabin for prayer and discussion, if that is alright with you."

"Oh, yes, my dear Estelle! You are being very wise. Of course we will want to discuss what the Lord has done, and where we think He might lead us from here. In the coming days and nights, I don't know if we'll get anywhere close to the thing God did tonight. But if I'm here to counsel the team, we'll need to pray together and have the mind of the Lord. It would be good if we could meet early tomorrow night and pray with the brethren and Helen before the service. We all must operate in the Spirit to not get ahead of, or lag behind, what He has in mind. By the way, I'd never met this Woody Shields before the trip down here from Indiana. But I believe Brother Homer made the right choice, and Dr. Smith approved. Estelle, I know you agree that no one could have handled the meeting better than our Brother Shields did. Sleep well, and we'll talk about this some more at breakfast."

All over the lower end of Arkansas County, the talk on Monday had to do with the "mighty revival in Nady last night." All over DeWitt, Gillette, Tichnor, Weber, Sweeney's General Store at Nady, and down in the river bottoms, people were talking about "them that fell out under the power of God." A few laughed and said it was just a bunch of religious emotion. But every time such a remark was made, a voice was heard to reply, "Well, not all of it, cuz I know God done somethin' fer this ole sinner!" or "That's just whut you think, buddy; somethin' happened to this ole heart of mine, and I reckon I oughta know that I've been changed! I got peace in my heart!" The radically converted drunks, murderers, and liars shut the mouths of the critics and skeptics all over the prairie and in the towns. Even doubters felt a curiosity to check out what was going on at the Menard schoolhouse down at Nady.

By five o'clock on Monday night, there were 1,000 people gathered around the Menard schoolhouse. The doors were locked, and there was not a soul inside. The crowd was alive with praises and song. About a hundred took turns walking up to the top step of the entrance and giving testimony to what God had done in their hearts the night before. "I ain't cussed once!" one said. "I been praisin' God mosta the day," another said. "I been scared to take a nip of whiskey," still another said. "Sumpin' powerful shore happened to this ole bastard last night," said an old man. Every statement was met with loud clapping, cheers, and whistles. No one was in charge of the testimonies, so no one felt the need to ask permission to speak.

When Jim drove up and let Estelle, Sister Martha, and the family members out, it seemed to interrupt the testimonies. But when Estelle learned what had been happening, she urged the newly converted to "go right ahead with your testimonies. It will strengthen you in your faith when you tell others what Jesus Christ has done for you and what He means to you. So please continue to give your words for the Lord. The Bible says, **Let the redeemed of the Lord say so**! You have been redeemed by the blood of Jesus Christ, so come and say so!" When Estelle realized that Jim had unlocked the doors of the schoolhouse, she went inside followed by about 200 more people, most of whom were women.

When the singing began, Woody Shields walked outside holding a microphone, stood on the steps, and addressed the people, commending them for their decision to give their hearts to Christ. He announced a baptismal service the last Sunday afternoon in May in the Rice Canal at the Vansickle farm across the road from Fairview School, about seven miles north.

The Monday night service followed the pattern of the service the night before, but instead of nearly 200 people responding to the invitation to salvation, over 300 made their way down the aisles to pray and confess Christ as Savior and Lord. In that number were more unknown people from the bottoms and about 40 well-known folks from the prairie. Some were members of churches on the prairie and around the towns of DeWitt and Gillette.

During the service Jim went outside several times before it was time for preaching. He was satisfied with the order and respect he found. He was surprised to see Barney from the Arkansas River Bridge. "How are ye, Barney?" Jim asked as the two shook hands.

"I'm a right smart better than I wuz," Barney said with a smile. "Last night I give my heart to Jesus right over there under that giant oak tree. I laid out cold there fer 20 minutes. I guess God jes' knocked me down! Then I went inside for the sinner's prayer."

"I'm shore glad to hear it, Barney! I did the same, though I didn't fall out beforehand. But it's been a lot better bein' right with God today."

As Jim turned to climb the steps and return to the service, Barney called, "Hey, Jim, ye reckon that preacher'd be willin' to come down to the Bridge some afternoon and preach to a crowd on the riverbanks? I bet they'd line the banks on both sides, and he could preach to 'em from high up on the bridge."

"I'll ask him and let ye know, Barney," Jim promised.

Estelle and Sister Martha decided that there should be a meeting with the entire evangelistic team, including Pastor Fox from DeWitt and others who had a vested interest in the revival. Since Dr. and Mrs. Bonnhoffer had rented a room in Gillette for an indefinite period of time so they could attend all the services, they were invited to sit in on the meeting. The women involved provided a noon meal on Wednesday, after which Sister Martha opened the meeting by sharing her thoughts on the revival services. "I've been in some meetings where the Holy Spirit just took over, but I've never seen so many "slain in the Spirit," as we witnessed on Sunday night! But, I'm convinced an even greater work of the Spirit was done last night. I've read *The Works of Wesley* and *The Works of George Whitefield*, and what we experienced in Nady the last two nights comes closer to what those two men of God saw in England nearly 200 years ago than anything I've ever witnessed. We simply need to feel humble and grateful and make sure that God gets all the glory! I want to encourage Brother Shields to continue the clear Bible preaching of salvation by grace through faith, **and that not of good works**."

Jim brought up Barney's suggestion of a service down at the Arkansas River Bridge one day. Ross Morgan was moved deeply by the suggestion and urged, "Let's go down there and see the glory of God mow some more sinners to the ground!" Ross was to visit with Barney and suggest a Friday afternoon for the service.

Pastor Fox wondered if it might be wise to move the services to Camp Doughboy to accommodate more people. Sister Martha thought that might be a good idea for the month of May, when fresh workers—preachers and singers—would be coming down from Indiana. "However, I feel we should allow the Holy Spirit to finish what He has begun on the prairie and in the bottoms before we change the venue." The feeling was unanimous with the 20 people present, including Pastor Fox.

"How long ye reckon we'll be holdin' meetin's in Nady?" Jim asked.

"Well, when Estelle called Dr. Smith to arrange for an evangelistic party, she wanted us to prepare for all spring and summer and possibly into the fall," responded Sister Martha. "Dr. Smith and I met together and listed those we felt might participate. I understand that Brothers Rich and Shields are now willing to stay all of April, even though they had intended to remain for only a week."

Woody Shields said, "Since Homer and Helen have agreed to remain with Marj and me for all of this month, I'm willing to come back for the month of June if you need Marj and me. In fact, I have nothing I'd rather be doing for the rest of the summer and fall than seeing God at work here in Nady, Arkansas, or wherever he might want us to locate."

Dr. Bonnhoffer asked Estelle if he might say a word. "Indeed you may, Doctor!" Estelle wasn't sure everyone present had met the doctor and his wife, so she proceeded to introduce them.

"I feel so blessed to be among you dear people and to witness what God is doing in Nady in such a supernatural way! In fact, I've turned my cardiology work in Hot Springs over to my colleagues for an indefinite period of time so that Maureen and I can continue to pray and work among you as the Spirit directs. Ever since Estelle visited Faith Presbyterian Church in Hot Springs about three months ago, we've seen hundreds turn to Christ as Savior and Lord and a formal old church turn into a Pentecostal Upper Room. There's no doubt in my mind that even greater things are in store in this part of our state. I do think you are wise to continue in Nady for several more weeks. The word is getting out in Gillette and DeWitt—and no doubt all over the prairie—as to what God is doing. I'm sure the people are being drawn here by the Holy Spirit. But even if the crowds are coming out of curiosity, we are seeing people genuinely repent and turn to Jesus Christ. Whatever financial expense there will be in compensating our workers, I want you to know that

Maureen and I wish to contribute. And I'm sure we can tap more resources than just our own."

With tears in his eyes, Jim spoke up. "Ye know, Doctor, when Estelle told me we wuz gonna give $1,000 for the expenses of this meetin', I'm ashamed to say now that I just about had a fit! I lost control of the truck and went into a ditch. But now I just wanta say I'm glad we ain't passin' the plates, askin' the people comin' to help us pay the workers." Jim turned to Estelle to finish his speech, "Honey, God has saved this old sinner, and I reckon we jes' oughta give $2,000, even $3,000, cuz we can afford it, thanks to God's goodness and blessings!" Everyone joined in clapping, more to praise God for Jim's salvation than to rejoice over his generosity for the meeting.

A number of people gave testimonies and opinions on the services, including George Best, Henry Tharp, Ross Morgan, Oscar Shelton, Garland Coose, Spencer Sweeney, Henry Plemmons, Allen Freeman, and Perry Plant. The meeting concluded in a glorious prayer meeting. Estelle thought of Luke's account of the apostolic prayer meeting in Acts 4:31: **And when they had prayed, the place in which they had gathered together was shaken; and they were all filled with the Holy Spirit and spoke the word of God with boldness. Now the company of those who believed were of one heart and soul, and no one said that any of the things he possessed was his own, but they had everything in common. And with great power the apostles gave their testimony to the resurrection of the Lord Jesus, and great grace was upon them all.**

The service at the White River Bridge on a Friday afternoon in late April was quite a spectacle—500 people lined up on both the north and south banks of the river. A male trio, accompanied by an accordion, a guitar, and a mandolin, sang several Gospel songs, including "Amazing Grace." Woody Shields could be heard clearly by the 1,000 people as he powerfully preached on John 3:16, expounding on God's love for the lost and His power to forgive and transform a sinful human heart. At one point, a wave of sinners "went down" at the same time on both sides of the river. It was a breathtaking moment for all witnesses, both saints and sinners, to see the same miraculous demonstration of God's power as in the first Sunday evening service of the revival. The spiritual leaders present felt that it was God's purpose to use this amazing phenomenon to impress the human heart and mind. By the time Woody was ready to give the invitation, all who had "fallen" were on their feet. He challenged everyone listening to respond with an upraised hand if they wished to repent of sin, confess Jesus Christ as personal Savior and Lord, and begin a new life of following Him as His disciple. Barney was so overjoyed at the number of upraised hands that he offered drinks for everybody. Jim guessed that in the tubs of chipped ice there were at least 1,000 Coke, Orange Crush, and Pepsi drinks, because it appeared that everyone in the crowd filed by to get one and wave their thanks.

The meetings in Nady had continued nightly through April with attendance never falling below 1,200—with 1,000 outside, and 200 inside. The new evangelistic party sent from Indiana included Rev. Joseph Youmans and John Newby as preacher and singer, respectively. The results in attendance and conversions were no less than had been realized under the ministries of Woody Shields and the Riches. Estelle rejoiced again and again that "everyone on my prayer list has been saved including my own husband, sons, and daughters!" Both Jeanette and her husband, Don, had been among those who yielded their hearts to Jesus. No one knew exactly how many had come forward to pray for and claim salvation through Jesus Christ, but no one doubted that after one month of services, several hundred people had found the Lord. The people saved came not only from the lower end of Arkansas County but also from as far away in Arkansas as Hot Springs, Fort Smith, and Little Rock. A few that were converted said they were from Greenville, Mississippi, and Memphis, Tennessee.

Rev. Woody and Marj Shields volunteered to remain for the revival for an indefinite period of time. The team decided to call Dr. Smith and inform him that no new workers would be needed. Rev. Joseph Youmans had agreed to preach in Nady following the Camp Doughboy services, and Rev. Shields would succeed Rev. Youmans and preach to the end of the revival. Woody had already requested permission from the Committee to call his friend Charles Kercheval to come down from Indiana to assist in singing, leading worship, and preaching. His wife Iolene would also come. The request was granted unanimously, and they were to arrive the last of May.

Estelle and Sister Martha appreciated the wisdom and support of Dr. and Mrs. Bonnhoffer. Sister Martha suggested that if there was an interim between the services the last few days of May and the first of June that they probably could visit Faith Presbyterian Church in Hot Springs. They would need to check with the Bonnhoffers to find out if they thought it was feasible. She also said she felt the change of venue to Camp Doughboy would be wise, provided Pastor Fox could get the time cleared on his schedule, even if they needed to return to Nady for the remainder of the summer and part of the fall. Estelle had at first drawn back from the idea of an interim, feeling that something might be lost during the absence of nightly meetings. After further consideration, she told the team that since the outpouring of the Spirit was a divine plan, perhaps God would choose to use the lull to create an even wider range of interest throughout the whole county, especially if the team's vision included going to a more accommodating venue such as Camp Doughboy. She stressed that "we people of Nady must not feel that we have a monopoly on God, nor must we feel that we can contain His movements to our own small community."

Pastor Frank Fox was greatly encouraged by the team's openness to a change of venue. He was successful in getting the schedules cleared so that Camp Doughboy would be available to the revival meetings throughout the month of May and the first half of June. The Bonnhoffers worked with Pastor Baylor to set up weekend meetings at Faith Presbyterian Church in Hot Springs with Estelle and Sister Martha Honeycutt. They considered inviting Woody Shields, since he had been so effectively used of the Holy Spirit in the Nady meetings. But the Bonnhoffers offered the thought that since the Hot Springs community was already responsive to Estelle, they should limit the speakers to her and her mentor. Dr. Baylor agreed, and the two women consented to be the speakers. The Nady nightly services would cease temporarily on Saturday night, April 27. Estelle and Sister Martha would minister in Hot Springs the weekend of May 3-5. The revival nightly services would reopen in Camp Doughboy on Sunday night, May 12, and continue there through June 9. After an interlude of six days, nightly services would reopen in Nady on June 16 with Rev. Youmans

414

preaching. Woody urged the team to support the Grand Baptismal Service near Fairview on Sunday afternoon, April 28. The team agreed and encouraged Woody to promote it in the services each night.

Estelle and Sister Martha felt that the interest taken in the meetings by the *DeWitt Era Enterprise* and the *Arkansas Gazette* was no doubt a work of the Holy Spirit to widen the interest of the people in the remote areas of the state. Camp Doughboy could accommodate 4,000 people inside the facility; with the help of loud speakers, several more thousand outside would be able to hear the music and messages. If God was up to such a great thing, why should they shrink back out of fear of being in over their heads?

No one remembered ever seeing as many people on the highway as there were halfway between Tichnor and Nady on the beautiful Sunday afternoon of April 28. Woody Shields had announced the baptismal service every night in the services at Nady. He had run an invitation in both the *Enterprise* and the *Gazette*. The rice farmers on Lower Little Prairie knew they were to expect crowds in their communities. But no one had ever seen people from near and far crowd in by the thousands. Cars, trucks, wagons, and saddle horses lined both sides of the road near the Rice Canal for miles, north and south.

The road running east and west leading to the Camp Shed Methodist Church was lined with vehicles as well. Woody had things well organized. He had pastors from all denominations and independent churches represented to perform the baptisms: Friends, Assemblies of God, Church of the Nazarene, Southern Baptist, Free Will Baptist, Missionary Baptist, Methodist, Lutheran, Alliance, Presbyterian, Christian, Congregational, and three independent organizations. Each officiating pastor would be stationed on the canal 20 feet apart at water level, facing eastward. Someone would hold a sign identifying the pastor and the church. Woody would give a message on Baptism, which would be nonsectarian. Each pastor in a low voice would add any remarks he wished to the candidates as they entered the water. In no way did the rite of baptism make the candidate an official member of the respective church unless the pastor and candidate agreed otherwise.

Woody used the occasion with the amazing numbers present to proclaim the Gospel of Jesus Christ. He praised the Lord for what the Holy Spirit had been doing in the lower part of the county, attended by people from other communities. He remarked that he had not read or heard of anything in the history of revivals in America that could compare with the supernatural manifestations of the Holy Spirit as they had seen witnessed in the meetings in Nady and at the White River Bridge.

Woody explained what the rite of baptism does not do: "It does not save you (you've already been saved by confessing Christ as Savior); it does not perfect your character (you will come into the sanctifying experience and lifetime growth in the Lord by studying your Bible, praying daily, and obeying all that you understand as the Holy Spirit guides you, reaffirms your faith, and convicts you of sin. You will sometimes fall short of God's will, but you will confess your sin and be immediately forgiven to resume your fellowship with God in the Spirit); it does not exempt you from temptation (you will encounter the appeal to become selfish and choose the way of the world instead of the way Christ leads, but the Holy Spirit will help you to overcome).

"Baptism is a commitment to God and a testimony to the world that you have forsaken the ways of sin, selfishness, and evil to become a follower of the Lord Jesus Christ. You are now about to **be buried with Christ in baptism**—meaning that as you go under the water, you will come up, spiritually speaking, cleansed and enabled by the Spirit **to walk in newness of life**.

"We believe the oldest creed in the 2,000-year history of the church is the Apostles' Creed. Therefore, I shall read this wonderful old creed, and then I shall ask, *Will you be baptized into the truth of this Statement of Christian Faith?* When I have asked the question, together you will simply answer, *I will!*" Before he began reading, Woody saw and heard three small aircraft circling overhead, no doubt taking aerial shots of the great scene of a crowd of 5,000 people witnessing 1,213 people about to be baptized in the Christian faith, declaring their commitment to become followers of Jesus Christ. Everything before him—the pastors in their radiance, the candidates in their anticipation of a new spiritual experience, the joy of the crowd—caused him to feel an unquenchable, uncontrollable joy.

Woody began reading the Apostles' Creed: *"I believe in God the Father Almighty, Maker of heaven and earth; and in Jesus Christ, His only Son, our Lord; born of the Virgin Mary, suffered under Pontius*

416

Pilate, was crucified, dead, and buried; He descended into Hades; the third day He rose again from the dead; He ascended into heaven, and sitteth at the right hand of God the Father Almighty; from thence He shall come to judge the living and the dead. I believe in the Holy Spirit, the Church universal, the communion of saints, the forgiveness of sins, the resurrection of the body, and the life everlasting. Amen!

"To all believers who are ready for baptism, I now ask, *Will you be baptized into the truth of this Statement of Christian Faith? If so, answer, I will!*" The response must have pleased the Lord and His heavenly hosts, Woody thought, for it certainly blessed his heart and soul. On hearing the two-word response, he wiped tears and watched the pastors immerse their candidates and then help them emerge. Those witnessing the baptisms clapped in celebration as each one wiped the water from his or her eyes and returned to the arms of a loved one on the bank. Woody looked at his watch and decided it would take over an hour to baptize all 1,213 people. He made a mental note to schedule another baptism on June 9, thinking that perhaps there would be another 2,000 to 3,000 candidates! *Who but God knows what He is up to at this time in southeastern Arkansas!*

Knowing that prairie people this far south would not receive their copy of the Monday issue of the April 29 *Arkansas Gazette* until Tuesday, Woody and Marj Shields climbed into their blue Ford Coupe very early on Monday morning and headed out over the muddy, rutted, gravel county road to DeWitt to pick up the current issue. Sure enough, they were delighted to see that the GRAND UNITED BAPTISMAL SERVICE had made front-page news! Woody's picture was inserted over the large aerial view that captured the entire baptismal scene of the fifteen pastors and their respective groups.

"Praise the Lord! To God be the glory! Marj, I think it's just wonderful that the Lord moved somebody to make sure the whole world hears about what He's doing down here in this uncultured, unknown, ungodly region of the South! And the lady the *Gazette* assigned to write the story must have known something about the evangelical faith. I'm sure pleased with this excellent coverage."

"Woody, the folks down here may be plain, simple, and uneducated for the most part, but they are such precious people when you get to know them!"

"Of course, they are; and they will be, when they let Jesus into their hearts! We'll see what the DeWitt paper has to say when it comes out on Friday. Now, I hope the paper will also give the changes of location that have been announced and that the people will read and remember."

"Woody, I agree with Estelle and Sister Martha, that this whole event is a God-thing, that whether the papers get it right or not, the Holy Spirit will round up the people and get them to this Camp Doughboy location; I believe we'll see something unparalleled in the history of American revivals! I'm just so glad you made the decision to stay on through May, even through June if they need you. I want to be a part of this!"

"Good! I'm glad you feel this way, Marj. I know I want to be a part of it."

"I'm just thrilled at the way you are allowing the Lord to use you!"

When Jim, Estelle, and Sister Martha arrived in Hot Springs at 4:00 on Friday afternoon, the Bonnhoffers insisted that all three stay in their home for the weekend. It appeared that the entire city was talking about the Presbyterian Revival and the coming of Estelle Tharp! The *Hot Springs Herald* referred to her as "the female version of Billy Sunday." Estelle laughed, but Sister Martha said, "Well, that's quite a compliment. I've heard him preach the Gospel, but I know you'll be just as clear and effective as that well-known evangelist—and without using all the platform antics."

After they had finished the delicious dinner that Maureen served, they were off to Faith Presbyterian Church. Pastor Baylor had arrived early to greet the Tharps and Sister Martha. In his study, he expressed his appreciation for Estelle's willingness to return and said how delighted he was to hear all that had been happening over in Arkansas County. Turning to Sister Martha, he requested, "Please, my dear Sister Martha, tell me something of your background and experiences, and help me understand more clearly what we might expect from the Lord as we pray for outpourings of His Spirit. I need to tell you that I've not always been interested in these special manifestations of the Holy Spirit. But since Estelle was here a few months ago, God has turned me and my congregation rightside up! I'm having the time of my life praying, reading the great things about Wesley, Whitefield, Finney, and Brainerd and their special meetings. I'm so glad for the way you've taught Estelle, and we feel honored to have both of you with us for these services. Now I'll hush and let you share anything that's on your heart."

"Pastor Baylor, I grew up in Southern California. My parents were plain, simple, hardworking people, and they were Quakers, followers of George Fox. I'm sure you've read a great deal about George Fox. My parents prospered and, although their lifestyle was very frugal, they were very generous in supporting evangelical missions throughout the world. After graduating from high school, I went to a Friends University in Wichita, Kansas, and then completed a master's degree at Asbury Theological Seminary in Wilmore, Kentucky. I studied Wesleyan Theology at Drew Theological Seminary in Madison, New Jersey, and earned a doctorate. I'll admit that I wanted to pastor, but women pastors weren't in great demand in those days in either the Quaker or the Methodist Church—at least not as much as they might be today. So I decided to teach New Testament Studies in Cleveland Bible Institute. Then I ventured to Alaska and served as a missionary under the Central Indiana Yearly Meeting of Friends. Oh, I learned more things about a meaningful relationship with the Holy Spirit in those five years than I had learned in all eight years of studying in universities. When I returned to the Indianapolis area in 1933, I knew that I was to do an in-depth study on the subject of Revivals—Old Testament, Intertestamental (John the Baptist), the Messianic Revival (Jesus), the New Testament Revivals, the Revivals under the Early Church Fathers, the preRenaissance Revivals, the Protestant Reformation, the Wesleyan Revivals, the Finney Revivals, the Moody-Spurgeon Revivals, and the Wales Revival. Oh, Pastor, I'm so glad that the Lord led me in studying revivals; I filled notebook after notebook on what I learned, conferring here and there with revival historians and just praying my way through those three years. Following that study, I was invited to come and teach New Testament Studies at a small Bible college in Westfield, Indiana, by the name of Union Bible College. When Dr. William Smith, the president, learned of my studies in revival, he insisted that every senior in UBC have a course on Revival before graduating. Then in 1938, I was asked to be one of the speakers during a Summit Meeting on Spiritual Warfare Strategy in Westfield, Indiana. It so happened that Estelle and her husband were in attendance. That meeting resulted in a course on Spiritual Warfare that included Intercessory Prayer. In 1939, as part of testing the course, I took a sabbatical and went to Arkansas County and spent fourteen months teaching Estelle. What a hungry, passionate student she was! Then I spent a few months in DeWitt with Pastor Fox and his people. As some laymen attending the 1938 Strategy Summit in Westfield caught the vision, they set up a fund to have me, along with a musical trio, go to the various evangelical denominations in several states, organize prayer groups, and teach them militant intercessory prayer for revivals. Now, we are seeing in Nady the fruit of our labors and the faithfulness of the Holy Spirit in responding to sacrificial, prolonged, bold intercessory prayer."

Martha Honeycutt stopped speaking for a few seconds and drew a breath. "Pastor Baylor, look at this dear lady, Estelle. It was in divine order that she become my first student—and a model one at that. I've known no other Spirit-filled believer to dedicate his or her life to becoming a **living sacrifice** in prayer! She fasts, weeps, cries out, and pleads with the Lord for revival many hours a day. During the first revival service at the Menard schoolhouse when I saw 200 people lying on the ground, "slain in the Spirit" as though dead, I knew He was answering the prayers and rewarding the sacrifices of Estelle Tharp! Most of those people had never heard the Gospel; but as the Spirit raised them up to their feet, they came inside and confessed Jesus Christ as Savior and Lord. And, Pastor, I am so glad to hear what is happening here in your congregation in Hot Springs! I must say that we have been praying for the Presbyterians all over America. I believe your entire denomination will receive a great awakening. I am so glad to be able to accompany Estelle here and pray for her as she ministers."

"Thank you for coming, Sister Honeycutt! No doubt the Holy Spirit will also use you here. Our facilities will be packed here tonight, tomorrow night, and Sunday morning to hear Estelle. The Lord used her to change my heart, and then as I obeyed the Lord, crucified my pride, and witnessed to the members here, God has been resurrecting the dry bones in Hot Springs."

Looking at his watch, the pastor said, "We have about thirty minutes, so I'll explain what I've envisioned as our order of things tonight. But if either of you feel otherwise, please make your

420

suggestions. After our worship team has led us in several hymns and a prayer chorus, I'll lead a prayer. Dr. Bonnhoffer will then report on the mighty revival over in Arkansas County—about what he has heard and seen personally. Then he will introduce you, Sister Honeycutt, if you will allow this. I want you to speak definitively about revival for a few minutes. Then I'll introduce Estelle. Now, Estelle, please take all the time you need. The people can't get enough of you, dear lady! You were used of God to awaken all of us, and they'll hang onto your every word. Please give them a chance to pray about whatever they need to before you end! We don't mind if we're here until 10 or 11 o'clock tonight! We want to see this whole city turn to God. So we've rented the convention center for the closing service on Sunday night."

There was a knock at the door, and the pastor explained, "That knock means that Dr. Bonnhoffer and the worship leader are ready to join us for prayer." He called, "Come in," and soon the five were into a passionate period of calling on the Lord. They all laid hands on Estelle, and prayers went up that she would have freedom, boldness, and obedience in the Spirit. Pastor Baylor ended the period by also praying for Martin, Jeff, Sister Martha, and himself and their parts in the service. He asked the Holy Spirit to "arrest every saint and sinner on these premises here tonight!"

As the service began, Estelle recognized that the same Holy Spirit was as powerfully at work here as He had been for the last several weeks on the premises of the Menard schoolhouse in Arkansas County. When Martin began to report on the revival in Arkansas County, he knew he was free to tell all that the Spirit did in Nady on that glorious Sunday night of April 14. He told about the 200 people lying prostrate on the ground as if dead, how an hour later those who had been "slain by the Holy Spirit" were brought to life by the Spirit (no one roused them or bothered them at all), and how they all entered the service to confess Jesus Christ as their Savior. "Thousands have already been saved there! Miracles have been wrought through the preaching of Estelle and others. God is powerfully at work in various places in Arkansas County, and He is at work here in Hot Springs this weekend!" When the loud applause from the audience had lessened, he introduced "the Spirit-anointed scholar who mentored Estelle."

Martha Honeycutt came on, smiling, as the crowd stood and clapped. As it quieted down, she sweetly said, "This Quaker woman is so pleased to be among God's Presbyterian children, and we can all rejoice that He loves us all so very much! I'm so thankful for the way the Lord is using my cherished student Estelle Tharp!" She had to pause again because of the crowd's loud response, which reminded her that she was only a forerunner of the human star here tonight. "I wish you might have been present for the miraculous sights we saw in Nady on Sunday night, April 14, at the White River Bridge on Friday afternoon, April 26, and last Sunday afternoon at a Rice Canal on the prairie when the Rev. Woody Shields led in a baptismal service with fifteen pastors baptizing 1,213 new believers! Actually, you may have seen the pictures and read the story in the *Arkansas Gazette.* Oh, friends, the unity of the Spirit among all those different denominations and congregations was as sweet as the unity that I feel here tonight. I congratulate and bless your dear Pastor, Dr. Baylor, for his openness to the Holy Spirit and the influence God is giving him in this fair city for true spiritual awakening. I know we'll all be praying for all that the Holy Spirit has in mind for us this weekend both in this wonderful church and in the wider audience we'll be with come Sunday night." As Martha returned to her seat on the platform, she felt uplifted by the loud response from the audience.

Dr. Baylor preceded his introduction of Estelle with a personal testimony. "I am not the same person or the same pastor that I was before I met Estelle Tharp. But it was the way the Lord used her to influence Dr. Martin Bonnhoffer that convinced me that I must give Estelle a hearing. She patiently, wisely, and skillfully made her way into my mind and heart with the accompaniment of the Holy Spirit. He, not Estelle, convicted me of my lostness, my need of the new birth, my need of an anointing to do the work He called me to do. I yielded, and you know the rest of the story.

"We welcome Estelle back here for this amazing weekend. And how pleased we are to have Dr. Martha Honeycutt with her. And also, Estelle's husband, Jim Tharp! Please stand, Jim!" As Jim stood, the crowd clapped, whistled, and yelled like they would have greeted a hero coming home from war or their champion rodeo rider. Jim waved and sat down. As Estelle made her way to the podium, the crowd stood and clapped.

"Thank you, Dr. Baylor, for allowing me to come back to Faith Presbyterian Church and see first hand what God has been doing here! I know you will want to praise the Lord with me for what He is doing over in Arkansas County, up in Little Rock, and in many places throughout our state. The days of mighty, powerful revivals are not over! The best is yet to be! We shall see a glorious sweep of many of our cities and rural communities over the months ahead as we continue to humble ourselves, yield to the hunger the Spirit is building within our hearts, and add fasting to our prayers.

"I feel the Lord wants me to say a word to you here tonight. You have heard the testimonies of your pastor and fellow church members, but many of you have not experienced an excitement over what is happening in your church. Even though you are curious, there's something within you that doubts the reality of what you've been hearing. You sit here tonight filled with doubts, frustration, confusion, and a little anger. You are tempted to accuse those who are filled with the joy of the Lord of ruining your church by bringing emotionalism into a great old historic church.

"Even as I speak to you, the Holy Spirit witnesses to my spirit that I am to invite you to humble yourselves, crucify your pride, and come and ask God for the reality of His presence in your own heart. If you don't respond to His call, you'll go out of here with colder hearts and greater confusion, and you will run the risk of never hearing the call of the Spirit to repentance and eternal life. You have heard the testimony of both your pastor and Dr. Martin Bonnhoffer and others. Hundreds of your fellow church members have been transformed from coldness of heart to the glory of God's presence in their lives. Some of you are at the crossroads tonight. There's nothing more urgent on my heart than opening this service to those who are willing to give God an opportunity to reveal Himself to you." She knew it was pleasing to the Lord for her to cut short any more talking and get to the invitation.

"Come on down for prayer as Jeff comes to the podium to lead us all in a familiar invitational song." As Jeff and the organist signaled they were ready, Estelle called for everyone to stand and sing "Just As I Am." Again, she said, "Come on down, please!" Soon they were making their way down the aisle to the front, with many of them weeping and some praying out. Judging from the serious looks on their faces and their desperation for God's mercies, the same convicting power was evident in these well-dressed people as she had seen in the disheveled, barefooted seekers coming into the Menard schoolhouse a few weeks before.

The Spirit was directing Estelle to give leadership to their praying. At the end of the third stanza, she asked everyone to bow their heads. Then to the hundreds standing before her and filling the entire space between the platform and the front pews, she said, "Ask God to forgive your doubts about the reality of the revival this church is experiencing. Now beg His forgiveness for the unkind accusations of hypocrisy you've made against the pastor and those who have come alive in their spiritual lives. Ask Him to forgive your criticism and your gossip. Now, believe that He does. What you've done is sin. And His Word says, **If we confess our sins, He is faithful and just to forgive our sins and cleanse us from all unrighteousness**. Believe now that you are forgiven and that you are washed from your sins and made clean. Confess Jesus Christ as your Savior. Do it now in a prayer to God. You are about to enter into the spiritual reality of forgiveness, salvation, regeneration of heart. You are about to be adopted into the family of God as His transformed son or daughter. You'll know what Pastor Baylor and hundreds of others in this church, and thousands elsewhere, have been experiencing all through the past weeks. You have obeyed the Lord tonight in humbling yourselves and coming here to **taste and see that the Lord is good**; you are about to know that He is real, forgiving, gracious, merciful, and able to fill your heart with joy!

"Now, begin thanking the Lord for your salvation and for putting His Holy Spirit into your heart to give you the assurance of salvation. God is giving you peace, and I see joy on your faces. You're going to leave this service knowing that God is real. You'll receive power to live and walk with Christ and do His will. You will no longer have to rely on your own strength. What a great life awaits you as you trust the Lord and begin a life of prayer, worship, and Bible study! Let's all stand and join Jeff in singing our closing song."

As he led out, "Blessed assurance, Jesus is mine! O what a foretaste of glory divine! Heir of salvation, purchase of God, born of His Spirit, washed in His blood!" scores of hands were lifted in praise. As the song continued, the inspiration increased with the last two stanzas.

Estelle signaled to Pastor Baylor to come and give the benediction. Before he gave the closing prayer, the pastor congratulated the hundreds below him "for being forthright in dealing with your doubts and giving God the chance to prove to you that salvation is not a lot of hype and religiosity. I can see the joy on your faces as you now know for yourselves that God's gift of salvation is real! Now, Estelle and Sister Martha will be here at the front after we dismiss, if some of you wish to talk with them." After announcing the service for the following night and the schedule of services on Sunday, he pronounced the benediction.

The pastor was the first one to speak to Estelle. "Thank you for minding the Lord tonight and challenging the doubters. I had begun to wonder if the negative doubting might be the thing the devil would use to choke the movement of God. But you dealt with it head-on. I see they are lined up to have a word with you, but I hope they don't wear you out. Martha, maybe you could station yourself on the other end of this step from Estelle and let the people get in whatever line they wish. Thanks for being available for the people."

Many of them needed prayer, but most just wanted to shake their hands and thank them for the Word that spoke to their hearts. An hour and a half went by before those lined up to have their time with Estelle and Martha had left the church.

The Bonnhoffers decided the Saturday morning breakfast would be a good time to have a summit meeting to plan the strategy for the three closing services of the weekend. Pastor and Mrs. Baylor, Jeff Clements and his wife, Judy, the seven elders and their wives, and several key laymen were guests, along with the Bonnhoffers' three guests—twenty-nine in all. The meeting began with a prayer and welcome by the doctor. The pastor expressed appreciation for Estelle's prophetic word to negative thinkers in the congregation and praised the Lord for the results of the previous night's service. He then set forth his deep conviction that this was Faith Presbyterian's hour, saying "the spiritual tide is in, and let us immerse ourselves in God's plan for revival!"

Dr. Bonnhoffer announced that breakfast was ready to be served, and Dr. Baylor said they would resume the discussion afterward. Ten volunteer ladies from Women's Ministries began setting forth large platters of scrambled eggs, bacon, sausage, toast, and biscuits and gravy.

In the relaxed environment, Estelle studied faces and expressions. She spotted four people who she felt were out of harmony with the direction of the church at this time. She could not remember their having been among those who came forward the night before. Possibly they were very influential, and the pastor's plan was to seek to draw them in by inviting them to the breakfast meeting. *Lord, would You give me a word for them? Or do You wish to use someone else?* In less than a minute she knew how she was to approach them and exactly what she was to say.

When it appeared that all were finished eating and they had begun to visit with those nearest them, Dr. Baylor called the meeting to order. He asked that anyone who had thoughts about the conduct of the three coming services to share freely, acknowledging that "We know the Lord speaks to our Spirit-led laymen just as well as he does to the clergy."

The first five to speak were positive, three of whom gave testimony to a definite work of the Spirit in their hearts and lives in the service the night before. One person mentioned that it sounded like Estelle had been listening to their conversation in their homes. Then came an expression that began as something positive but soon turned into an outright denunciation of the direction in which the church was heading. Estelle was not surprised, because it came from a man across from her whom she discerned as being very upset; however, his response closed out with positive comments. Actually, Martha Honeycutt noted that no suggestions had been offered as to the conduct of the final meetings. She suspected the pastor had not actually expected any, but that he wanted everyone to feel free to give their input.

The pastor called on Jeff to lead the group in "We Are One in the Bond of Love." As Elder Swift closed the meeting with a spirited prayer, Estelle whispered to Sister Martha to pray for her as she dealt with two couples who were in opposition to the direction of the church.

When the group had been dismissed, the two couples Estelle had marked as negative did not turn to anyone for a friendly chat, so she made her way to them. They looked uncomfortable at her approach, so she asked the one who had spoken earlier, "Might I be able to have a word in the next room with you four?" She led the way to an empty room next door, probably a room for storing kitchen facilities. Immediately after requesting the meeting, Estelle had caught the pastor's eye and motioned for him to follow. Jim saw this and decided to follow Estelle without being invited.

With the door closed to the main meeting room, Estelle asked, "May I know your last names, please?"

"We are the Atkins," said the tall gentleman who had spoken in the breakfast meeting, "and these are the Halseys."

"Well, Mr. and Mrs. Atkins and Mr. and Mrs. Halsey, during breakfast I had a word from the Lord for you. You have quite an influence in this church, and the Lord is going to hold you responsible for misleading a lot of people here in Hot Springs. And…"

Art Atkins interrupted Estelle with loud words, "Estelle Tharp! You are nothing but a fanatical religious fraud! You come in here and think you're some kind of prophet. The reality of it all is that you are a witch with evil powers and…" He grabbed his chest, began gasping and coughing, and fell to the floor. At exactly that time, Martin Bonnhoffer opened the door and walked into the room followed by Maureen. *Thank You, Lord! Give the doctor wisdom and understanding to take charge here. I've obeyed You, and how can I help it if You've decided to intervene here much like You did in the case of Ananias and Sapphira?*

Dr. Bonnhoffer knelt by Art Atkins' side, could find no pulse, and shook his head. Looking up at Irene Atkins, he said, "I'm sorry, Irene; he's gone." The wife cried out and ran screaming to her dead husband. Estelle looked at the Halseys, and both were ashen and trembling. They looked at one another and then sat down in the only two seats in the room. Noticing that they were whispering to each other, Estelle was directed by the Spirit to approach them. She laid a hand on Mrs. Halsey's shoulder and said, "I know the Lord is speaking to you. But He has more in mind for you than the judgment of death here and now. If you humble your hearts, He will come to you with mercy, grace, and forgiveness. If you do not, God knows how to deal with you. May I pray for you right now?"

"Oh! Please do!" said Margaret Halsey, "but just a moment…" Turning to her husband, she said, "Mark, I know we've been wrong! What happened to Art should happen to us, too, but Estelle believes we can be saved. Don't we want to turn to the Lord and change our minds?" Mark nodded his head, and when he looked up at Estelle, tears were sliding down both cheeks. "Yes, Estelle, I know we've allowed Art and

Irene to influence us wrongly. If you believe the Lord will forgive us, we are willing to turn to Him with our whole hearts. Please pray for us." Even before she began the prayer, she was aware that Jim, the doctor, and the pastor were a part of the group. As Estelle began praying, the two penitent ones held hands.

"Father, we come to You at this solemn moment. We honor You not only for Your wisdom and power but also for Your grace. We are reminded of the judgment You visited on Ananias and Sapphira there in Jerusalem. Apparently You are dealing with Mark and Margaret so that they do not continue in rebellion against Your plan to visit their church and city with this great salvation. I thank You, Lord, that I can sense now their brokenness, their penitent hearts, and their readiness to surrender to your will and receive your Son Jesus Christ as their Savior and Lord! Come now and give them a new heart of faith, of love, of joy, and of peace. May they be strong to confess the truth in all things and become advocates of your Gospel instead of opponents. In Jesus' name I pray, Amen!"

Pastor Richard Baylor took charge immediately, for which Estelle was glad. He said, "Mark and Margaret, I'm so glad you have chosen Jesus Christ instead of continuing your dangerous path of opposing the revival God is giving to our church and city. I regret so deeply what just happened to Art. But, friends, it's serious business to fight against what God is doing, as Saul of Tarsus found out; but, like you, he repented and turned to Christ. Unfortunately, Art didn't, and what happened to Ananias and Sapphira in Acts 5 happened to him. We'll be praying for Irene; we don't yet know if she's going to wisely follow your course of turning to the Lord."

Dr. Bonnhoffer said, "Excuse me, dear ones. I have to go and speak to the coroner and see how Irene is doing. Please now, we must be strong in this. This will not be the end of this. No doubt, there'll be a hearing. We'll all need to answer questions, whether we are called in as a group or separately. We don't need to rehearse what we'll say. We'll just need to tell what we heard and saw. The Lord will be in charge. We have nothing to fear if we stay with the truth. Mark and Margaret, bless you! I know you will give accurate testimony to what you experienced. In fact, yours will be the most critical of all our testimonies, since you were for a time in sympathy with the Atkins. Well, I must go."

Martin returned to the scene of tragedy, sought to comfort Irene, and then went back to the coroner, Dr. Wills. The coroner asked, "Doctor, tell me what happened here, please."

"Dr. Wills, Faith Presbyterian Church is in a great spiritual revival. Many of us are turning back to life in the Holy Spirit for prayer, genuine Christian love, holiness, and victory over selfishness. Art Atkins has been a ring leader in opposing the direction of our church. Now, I'm just giving you the situation as I've come to understand it. This morning about 28 or 30 of us came together for a breakfast and for the purpose of discussing the three remaining services for this weekend. Pastor Baylor did invite at least two couples to the breakfast who oppose the direction of the church at this time. You might say he wanted to be fair and balanced. Estelle Tharp, who comes to us from over in Arkansas County, was invited here to lead us in spiritual renewal. Art confronted her this morning and called her "a fanatical religious fraud, a witch with evil powers." He really never finished all that he intended to say before he grabbed his chest, coughed, gasped, and fell down there where he is lying now. By the time I got to him, I could not get a pulse, so I just looked at his wife, Irene, and announced that he was gone. Now, we have at least 25 other witnesses to all that happened. I would think Irene and you and the sheriff would want an autopsy. I'm not Art's doctor, but I'm quite sure Art had a massive heart attack. I am available for any need you might have of me."

"Thanks, Doctor. We'll get Irene's consent to take him to the Medical Center for an autopsy. I'll report this to the sheriff, and he and I will take it from there. We'll be in touch. Nobody needs to stay around, but I would like to have the names of all who witnessed Mr. Atkins' collapse." The doctor nodded, then went back over to Irene, who was being attended by Maureen. For some reason that Martin could not understand, Maureen shook her head and had a solemn look on her face. Irene's eyes were closed, and she had laid her head back against the sofa where she was reclining.

"Irene had me call her daughter and tell her about Art," Maureen told her husband. "Her daughter and a friend will soon be here to drive Irene home."

"Then I'm sure you'll stay with Irene until her daughter comes. I'm going back over to where the Halseys are with Jim, Estelle, and

Martha. Come over when you are free here." Martin loved the look of joy on the faces of Mark and Margaret. He pulled the pastor aside and asked, "Don't you think the seven of us should spend a little time in prayer concerning the fallout of all this. We probably need to share our hearts even as we pray."

"Yes, how soon can we do this?"

"Well, Pastor, it's eleven o'clock, so I'd hope right away. We don't want to rush the Halseys off, but as soon as they leave, let's meet in the den." It wasn't long before the Halseys were saying goodbyes and assuring those around them that they would be available for any forthcoming questioning.

The seven—Baylors, Bonnhoffers, Tharps, and Sister Martha—gathered in the den for a time of sharing their hearts and prayers. "Well, we all witnessed what happened when Estelle graciously confronted the Atkins this morning. I thought she was in the Spirit all the way," the pastor said. "And I agree with her—this is another case of divine judgment on those who fight against God as did Ananias and Sapphira. But I'm so glad the Halseys took a different course. I'm worried about Irene, though. How's she doing?"

"Not well, I fear," Maureen answered. "Of course, she's in grief. But I sense that she is still angry over what Estelle had to say. And I agree totally with the pastor. Estelle is sent of God here to Faith Presbyterian. She's preached and prayed prophetically. It doesn't take a believer with the gift of discernment to realize that this morning she boldly, but graciously, took on the most determined opponent of this revival and became God's spokesperson. I applaud her courage and obedience. She has nothing to regret. She didn't expect God to strike Art dead any more than the apostle Peter expected God to strike Ananias dead in Acts 5. But as sad as we are about it all, we can't allow this to hinder the mighty moving of God here in Hot Springs. Satan wanted to use the Atkins and the Halseys and others to do just that. But, just like it turned out in Acts 5, this will put the fear of God in all of our hearts!"

"Right on, darling! I believe you've spoken for all of us in this room," Martin said.

"Then let's go to prayer for Irene, the hearing that will come, the three meetings to come yet, and Estelle and Sister Martha," the pastor said. Following the pastor's prayer, the other six continued with a brief prayer.

Maureen said, "If it meets with everyone's approval, the caterer will spread our dinner meal at 1:30, giving us all about an hour to get some rest. I know Estelle and Sister Martha should have at least that much time to rest."

"Thanks," Estelle said. "I think that will be enough time.

Jim and Estelle stretched out on the extra wide bed in the Bonnhoffer's guest room. Even as Jim was commenting on how the Lord had taken over Art Atkins in his anger, he noticed Estelle had slipped off to sleep and was soon snoring. Jim could not remember hearing her snore very many times in their 20 years of marriage. Jim soon felt rested, so he slipped out of bed without disturbing her. He had picked up the *Gazette* as they left the den and was reading it when Estelle suddenly stopped snoring and raised up in bed. "What time is it, honey?"

"My watch says 1:20," Jim said.

"I'll get up and comb my hair, and we'll go to the dining room. I'm sure they'll be ready to eat by the time we get there. I admit I'm hungry."

Later on, Sister Martha told Estelle that she thought she would attend the evening service until after the preliminaries; then she would slip away to the pastor's study and intercede for her as she preached. "Tonight, the enemy would like for all Hell to break loose. Instead, God wants to see to it that all Heaven breaks loose on saints and sinners. I need to be in prayer for this. May God give you a great anointing that will give you boldness and freedom!"

The church was packed and several hundred people were standing when the service began. Estelle could feel the spiritual opposition, and she was silently wrestling against the evil spirits urging people unknown to her to interrupt the services. She prayed against some violence being planned to disturb the service and commanded the devils behind it to "flee these premises and depart into the regions of darkness." Just as Sister Martha stood and touched her shoulder, whispering, "It will be alright," Estelle received the Spirit's assurance that all was clear, and that the Holy Spirit would have complete control of the service. When it was time to proclaim the Word, she went forth to read Ephesians 5:18, emphasizing the latter portion of the verse, ...**but be filled with the Spirit**.

She reminded believers that Jesus spent most of His teaching time with His disciples emphasizing their need to be filled with the Holy Spirit, who would be given after He had departed and ascended to the Father. She then felt led to give her personal testimony concerning how she was directed by the Spirit to become *cleansed and filled with the Holy Spirit*. After she had spent 10 minutes on her testimony, the Spirit signaled her that she was to give the invitation. She had prepared Jeff, with his beautiful voice, to personally sing the invitation, "Cleanse Me." The Spirit had been preparing the people, even as Estelle spoke. They were ready, and down the aisles they streamed; hundreds filled the space between the platform and the pews, waiting to be prayed for. When Jeff had sung the final stanza, Estelle knew it was time to pray. She directed the believers seeking the fullness of the Spirit to pray out all together. Before a volume of prayer had developed, she anointed Edith, a woman who stood closest to her, with oil and laid hands on her, asking, "Lord, would you come and do a mighty work in this sister? Cleanse, heal, fill, and anoint her for Your witness!" The Lord seemed to make an example of this woman. Edith fell to the floor, and Estelle could not sense that she was breathing. *What is happening here, Lord? This is too close to what happened to Art this morning! What do I do?* Suddenly, Estelle had an assurance that this was the opposite of what happened that morning; this was more in the spirit of the 200 who fell prostrate under the power of the Holy Spirit on the night of April 14 at Nady. In complete confidence, Estelle took the microphone and asked every believer who had truly been filled with the Holy Spirit to join with Jeff as he led in "The Comforter Has Come!"

With great joy, the 300 newly Spirit-filled joined in passionately singing their celebration of the Spirit of holiness, the Spirit of wisdom, and the Spirit of inspiration for directing their new way of life. When Estelle realized that Edith was coming around, she looked down and saw the glow on her face—"Estelle, the Lord visited me in great power and peace, and I've been delivered from a dark heart and given a new way to live! Praise the Lord!" She jumped up and hugged Estelle, and for a few seconds, she would not release her.

After the benediction, Pastor Baylor joined Jim and Estelle as they were walking out, and said, "There's someone here I want you to meet." A distinguished-looking gentleman appeared to be waiting for them in the foyer. Walking up to the smiling man, Dr. Baylor said, "Estelle and Jim, meet my friend, Dr. Brent Jones, pastor of the Little Rock Methodist Fellowship. And, Brent, this is Estelle's husband, Jim Tharp!"

"Jim, it's great to meet you!" Turning to Estelle, he said, "I've been waiting for this moment ever since Rich told me about how the Lord used you to bring revival to this church body. Now, I hope before you leave Hot Springs next week, you will feel clear in the Spirit to offer us a weekend date in Little Rock. I believe God wants to use you there among the Methodists just as He has used you here in Hot Springs among the Presbyterians! Please pray about it," he said, as he handed her his personal card with his address.

"Dr. Jones, it is a pleasure to meet you, and I do promise to pray about coming to Little Rock. Perhaps the Lord will clear my mind to offer a date. You know, a mighty revival fire is burning over in Arkansas County, and I'm committed there through the month of November. But right now we are on a break to allow the farmers to catch up with their work and the people to rest. We will be resuming nightly services in a few days. Perhaps at the end of June we'll take another break, and maybe then Jim and I can come to Little Rock for a weekend of services. If that sounds convenient for you, we'll talk about it Sunday night or perhaps at a breakfast on Monday morning before we leave." Estelle looked to Pastor Baylor to hear if this might work in with his schedule. Quickly he said, "Yes, let's plan a breakfast at 8:30 Monday morning. Maybe the Bonnhoffers will want to host it; but if not, we'll meet at the hotel. We can discuss our weekend services, and you and Brent can decide on the Little Rock date."

Saying "Good night!" Jim and Estelle headed to their room for a night of rest. Estelle slept well, awakening at sunup feeling excited and at peace about the day.

At breakfast, Maureen said she had just had a call from Irene Atkins' daughter reporting that her mother had been found dead in her bed that morning. Dr. Bonnhoffer prayed for the Atkins family in their grief, for the fallout from the deaths of Art and Irene, and for the guidance of the Spirit "as we all seek to glorify You in our response to questions."

Estelle asked, "Doctor, do you think we might be asked to attend a hearing?"

"I'm not sure, but I expect we need to be prepared. As Maureen attended Irene in her shock and grief over what happened to Art, Maureen heard her mumble some things against you 'and the evil curse that had been placed on Art.' Irene had kind of drifted off so no one can know how aware and clear she was about what she said. Now, what Irene discussed with family or others before retiring last night, we just don't know."

Jim asked, "Doctor, what about Art Atkins—was he a prominent businessman here in Hot Springs, with a lot of friends both in the church and in the city?"

"Art was the owner of Southwest Arkansas Steel Works and a very wealthy man. He had a lot of clients all over the state. He was a good supporter of Faith Presbyterian until a few months ago. How many members of our church he has influenced with his and Irene's thinking would be hard to say. They should know they are outnumbered by now, given the results of this weekend. As for the family of Art and Irene, we have seen little of them at church, but all three of their children are married and doing well and live in the area. I just can't say what we might expect from them. I say, let's just wait and see what the sheriff might have to say. I'm quite sure all of us at this table feel that their death is a judgment of God. I, for one, do not intend to pretend otherwise, not to myself nor to others. However, I do want to be prayerful and wise about what I say. And I know that Dr. Baylor feels the same way. Instead of Estelle putting a curse on them, she was offering them the way out of their bitterness and rebellion against the Lord; but, of course, it was God's decision to make a swift judgment on them, just as He did in the early church with Ananias and Sapphira."

Sister Martha spoke up, "I feel like we should be praying that the people of the church will follow you and the pastor in the attitudes that the early church took after that tragedy recorded in Acts 5. The apostles and believers in Jerusalem were not about to waste the impact of that tragedy. Luke tells us that because of the manner of the deaths of those two unfortunate people, **great fear came upon the whole church, and**

upon all who heard of these things. And then many signs and wonders were done among the people by the hands of the apostles....And more than ever believers were added to the Lord, multitudes both of men and women. I feel certain that the response to Estelle's message last night affirms this."

"Yeah, I agree," Jim said. "If we just let the Holy Spirit do the leadin' here, we could see the present revival reach new dimensions."

"Amen!" exclaimed Sister Martha. "A Sovereign, Omniscient, Omnipotent God is at work in Hot Springs. Let's just walk softly, humbly, and obediently and let Him do His work."

The morning service attracted more worshipers than anyone could ever remember at Faith Presbyterian. It followed the pattern of the service the night before, except Dr. Baylor presented Dr. Brent Jones before Estelle's message. The Little Rock pastor humbly and emotionally told of the spiritual hunger in his own life and ministry for the same thing that he had learned from his friend Pastor Baylor to be taking place in Hot Springs. He testified to "a cleansing and renewal received here last night as I prayed after the powerful message of Sister Estelle. I am glad to be here and taste and see what God is doing. Pray for us in Little Rock; we hope to have Estelle with us at the Little Rock Methodist Fellowship sometime this summer."

Estelle's message was a continuation of her emphasis on the Holy Spirit. She sought to make a case that "believers cannot succeed in becoming a New Testament Christian unless, and until, they are filled with the Holy Spirit. We must passionately desire and seek Him, and then continue to be filled with Him." The results were the same—hundreds readily responding, passionately seeking, rejoicing, and finding.

Before the benediction, Pastor Baylor urged that Faith Presbyterians members "arrive early tonight before 7:00 and help to greet the people. Remember, we are the hosts and the crowds will be our guests. We expect every seat at the Hot Springs Convention Center to be filled. Come praying!"

Jim expected Estelle to show some nervousness as they drove to the downtown Hot Springs Convention Center. Judging by Sister Martha's continual reassuring remarks to Estelle, Jim was sure she was thinking Estelle should be on edge as well. Then, as in many times before, Jim realized that *she has nothing to be nervous about. I know she has received from the Lord what she's supposed to tell this crowd, so why should she be worried about anythang! I reckon she's not even worried that the Atkins family might file a lawsuit charging her with bringin' about fear and shock resultin' in their deaths. I'm pretty sure they will file charges against Estelle, maybe the pastor, and perhaps even the church. I'll discuss this with Lloyd and see what he thinks. But I guess it's a waitin' game right now, like the doctor said.*

Parking attendants were on hand to direct Martin to the last row of cars in the field adjacent to the center. It would have meant a long walk for the ladies, so Maureen, Martha, and Estelle got out at the gate. Jim rode on with Martin to walk back with him. Inside they found the two pastors and Jeff in a circle for prayer. Estelle was relaxed all through the preliminaries, delighted with Dr. Brent's prayer, and fulfilled greatly by Sister Martha's 10-minute plea for prayer warriors to gear up for an invasion of evil spirits that sought to preclude the great revival on the way. Estelle could not have been more mentally, spiritually, and physically prepared to face the largest crowd to have ever packed the convention center, according to the word announced by Pastor Baylor. Nor could she have gotten a warmer reception anywhere. As she reached the podium, she went right to her text: "Amos 4:12: **Prepare to meet your God**. Tonight, I'm speaking to intelligent people who know how to prepare for many things: farmers know how to prepare for their crops— they break and disc the ground and get it in readiness to receive the seed they plant. Then the rains come and the sunshine warms the growing plant. At the right time, the farmers are ready to harvest the crops. We have learned how to budget our finances in order to feed the family, educate the children, fund our businesses, and retire with some assets. If we hear from the weather reports that a storm is on the way, we prepare for it by finding shelter for our families and our livestock and by taking other precautions against the wind, rain, snow, or lightning. If we feel we should become a professional—a schoolteacher, a doctor, an engineer, or whatever—we take certain courses in college and prepare ourselves academically for a career in that field.

"But, my dear friends, we are warned in the Word of God in the New Testament book of Hebrews, chapter 9, verse 27, of an appointment we all have, which we must prepare for above all other appointments.

Listen to the reading of this warning: **It is appointed unto man to die, and after that comes the judgment**. This is a warning to all of us—the greatest tragedy that any human being will ever face is to meet his or her Maker without being prepared! Each of us has an appointment with death. We do not know the day or the hour. It will happen to all of us; there's not one single exception. No one is prepared to meet God who has not believed in the Risen Son of God, Jesus Christ, and confessed Him as Savior and Lord. As exclusive as this may sound, I must tell you tonight—and Jesus said it: '**I am the way, and the truth, and the life, no one comes to the Father except by me**'! Only those who have received Jesus Christ will be saved and go to Heaven. Religion won't qualify you for Heaven. Good works, honorable deeds, and a good reputation will not prepare you for Heaven. Faith in Christ alone will prepare you for the kind of death that will result in passing the grade in the day of judgment.

"Over in Arkansas County, beginning the first week of this new year, I received many calls to pray with ranchers, fishermen, and loggers. They were calling to ask if I would come and help them get right with God. Most of the times, my husband accompanied me on those trips. I want to tell you what nearly every lost soul told me: 'Ma'am, I've been feeling for quite some time that I'm going to die and go to Hell. Can you help me know how to be ready to meet God?' The Holy Spirit has been moving down in the Arkansas and White River bottoms; He's been moving out on the prairies; He's been moving throughout the forests and in the towns. Thousands have gotten right with God through repentance and faith in Jesus Christ!"

"At this present time, we are seeing a mighty move of God here in the State of Arkansas to prepare many for getting right with God. You see, **He is not willing that any should perish, but that all might come to repentance**. That's exactly what this meeting is about here in this Hot Springs Convention Center. God's Spirit is conditioning your minds and hearts to get right with God by accepting His Son as Savior and Lord. Some of you have thought about it in times past, but you've been putting it off. But there is a special spiritual tide God is sending our way this season to stir hearts and cause us to ponder the question of where we might spend eternity. In a matter of a few minutes now, I'm going to ask you to stand; we will sing a great invitational hymn and ask hundreds of you to come forward to make your confession of faith in Christ. Please don't procrastinate and decide to do this some other time. The Bible says, **Today is the day of salvation, now is the accepted time**. If you come forward tonight, God promises to forgive you of your sins. If you will confess faith in Jesus Christ tonight, God promises to adopt you into His redeemed family and seal the transaction by putting His Holy Spirit into your heart so that you will know you are forgiven, saved, and on your way to Heaven. Thousands in various places in Arkansas are doing this very thing—walking down the aisles of small buildings as well as large auditoriums such as we are in here tonight. Would you please bow your heads with me as I lead a prayer for you? After the prayer, as Jeff sings 'Just As I Am,' don't hesitate to make your way down from where you are. Let's fill this open space in front of the platform with hundreds of you. After the prayer, I'll have a few words of instruction for you, and you'll be given a booklet to help you in your newly committed life to Christ. Coming down here to pray does not mean you are joining a church or subscribing to a system of Christian doctrine. It simply means that you have decided to confess Jesus as Savior and Lord and turn your life over to Him. He will direct you to a church body for baptism, fellowship, and growth in the grace and knowledge of our Lord Jesus Christ. Now let us pray."

Even before Estelle finished the prayer and Jeff began the song, she knew the crowds were coming. As Jeff began the last stanza, Estelle wondered if there would be enough room to accommodate all who were coming to confess the Savior.

Never had Estelle seen so many ready to pray the sinner's prayer in one setting. Nor had she ever led more than a family of five to Christ, with all of them repeating the prayer. Over at Nady, she had watched more than 200 come to the Lord the first night of the revival. But standing before her were already about 800, she supposed. She knew the Spirit was powerfully present. What did she need to worry about if He was here to help her and each penitent soul? Calmly and clearly, she led the crowd in a prayer of repentance, and their clearly given prayers sounded throughout the auditorium. Having finished, she said, "Now, let each one of you in your own words, either whispered or spoken aloud, give thanks for forgiveness of your sins through the shed blood of Jesus Christ. Then receive with thanksgiving the peace the Spirit puts in your hearts as He comes into your inner being assuring you of eternal life. Some young people will come among you and give you a booklet that will help you find certain scriptures and make suggestions to help you get started in living a new life in Christ. We hope the congregation will join us in singing "Blessed Assurance," after which Dr. Richard Baylor, Pastor of Faith Presbyterian Church here in Hot Springs, will come and pronounce our benediction. What a great night this has been!" The people evidently agreed with her because there was a loud and long period of applause, beginning among the 800 who had come to the Lord and then caught up by the more than 3,000 standing in the auditorium.

12   "A Time to Dance"

No one in Arkansas County could remember such a beautiful October; the leaves on the trees and shrubs had already turned to the beautiful orange and red colors of fall. Estelle, Anniece, Linda, and Oda had prepared a delicious breakfast meal for the three carloads of people departing for Indiana. Following breakfast, the hosts gathered just outside the Tharp's front gate to say goodbye to Charles and Iolene Kercheval, Woody and Marj Shields, Homer and Helen Rich, Joe and AnnaBelle Youmans, John Newby, Bob Eubanks, and Sister Martha. It was obvious that neither hosts nor guests were anxious to bring an end to 24 weeks of glorious outpourings of the Spirit which resulted in the salvation of a few thousand lost souls. Entire communities had turned from the shame of wickedness to the beauty of holiness. Peoples hearts were transformed, marriages salvaged, families united, and neighbors reconciled.

A certain degree of sadness had suddenly come over all of them in the last few minutes. No one was weeping, but each person, including the Tharp children, felt a sense of impending loss. Jim and Estelle, followed by Jim, Jake, and Anniece, were the last ones to embrace each of the eleven guests, ending with Sister Martha. Estelle stood with bowed head, feeling downcast and wondering ... *Lord, You see us standing around these cars like zombies, tempted to be sad. And I know that we should be praising You that You have done all we have asked in this part of our county, and You've gone beyond to other counties, cities, and communities all over our state. Let us bid these Your anointed servants goodbye, committing them to greater ministries elsewhere. Help us to continue to trust You to be with us to build on the foundation laid and see Your glory spread until every soul in the state is touched by Your grace. Lord, I don't know how to break this impasse at this moment. I think that either Sister Martha or I should lead a prayer. Lord, I'll just wait for Your guidance.*

To everyone's relief, Sister Martha spoke, "Well, dear ones, we all feel a deep gratitude to God for His marvelous demonstration of power in answering our seven long years of intercession by sending over this and many other communities a mighty **rending of the heavens**, pouring out His Spirit on saints and sinners, bringing salvation and manifold miraculous blessings. We'll join in singing the Doxology, led by our brother John Newby, after which we'll ask Estelle to say a prayer."

Estelle prayed, "Father God, look down upon us Your children here this morning and receive our worship, praise, and thanksgiving for all we have beheld from Your merciful, gracious hand here in our state over the past six months! Lord, You have answered our prayers. As Your Word declares, **There is a time to weep, and a time to laugh; a time to mourn, and a time to dance**. Lord, You were with us and heard us in our weeping; now be with us in our dancing, our rejoicing, our celebrating. May Your glory be upon us in moving on to preserve the fruit the harvest has produced. Continue to show Your glory in revival all over our state, and may it spread throughout our nation and to the entire world. Now, do bless these dear ones who have blessed us over the last six months. Grant them traveling mercies homeward, and may they find their families and loved ones in good condition. In Jesus' name, Amen."

The sadness Estelle had felt before her prayer was completely gone. With unspeakable joy, she waved to the ones in the three departing cars, realizing that everything she had prayed for had been granted. Now that she had learned the importance of prayer, she knew she must give it the great place in her life that the Spirit of God was calling for.

Later in the cabin alone, she read: **Then the eyes of the blind shall be opened, and the ear of the deaf unstopped; then shall the lame man leap like a hart, and the tongue of the dumb sing for joy. For waters shall break forth in the wilderness, and streams in the desert; the burning sand shall become a pool, and the thirsty ground springs of water; the haunt of jackals shall become a swamp, the grass shall become reeds and rushes. And a highway shall be there, and it shall be called the Holy Way; the unclean shall not pass over it ...they shall not be found there, but the redeemed shall walk there. And the ransomed of the Lord shall return, and come to Zion with** singing; everlasting joy shall be upon their heads; they shall obtain joy and gladness, and sorrow and sighing shall flee away.

Then her eyes fell on the passage to which her Bible had opened, Psalm 30:11-12: **Thou has turned for me my mourning into dancing; thou hast loosed my sackcloth and girded me with gladness, that my soul may praise thee and not be silent. O Lord my God, I will give thanks to thee forever.**

Estelle began, "Thank You, Lord! I believe You are anointing me now for praise! My soul is dancing in celebration for all You have done. Thank You that my long night of mourning has ended, though I know You will allow me more times of weeping the tears of Jesus over the lost and the backsliding. Please give me the topic for the message Sunday morning...**The Holy Way!** Is that it, Lord? Yes, I believe so. Help me to have freedom and power in preaching it. Oh, bring all those back who have truly found You—the ones down in the bottoms and out here on the prairies—and give me something for them. Come in power, Lord! Although the visiting evangelists, singers, and musicians are gone, help us who serve to be effective for You."

When Jim knocked on the cabin door, Estelle was delighted to see him. "Come in, dear; let's talk awhile and then pray together. I'm still getting used to having a Christian believer as a husband. I'm so proud of you!"

"Well, I'm glad to be livin' for the Lord, and I'm shore glad to have ye as my Christian wife! No man could be more blessed with his wife and children than I am. I know ye're gonna miss them fokes from Indiana, but let's jes' pull our family in closer and try to encourage all the newcomers to the faith."

"You're thinking exactly as I am, dear! I do want us to pull our children closer to us and to the Lord as we pray and talk together. Let's get the older children's thoughts on things. And, yes, I think maybe we ought to visit those new to the faith on the prairie and down in the bottoms—maybe a night or two each week for awhile. You and Henry might want to ride down in the bottoms and talk to Jay Reddon, Barney, and some of the others who probably need your influence pretty badly in the new life they are trying to live. I think the Lord just gave me something to say Sunday morning, and I hope they'll all be in the service."

"But, honey, I have something else to tell you," Estelle continued. "I'm pretty sure we are going to have another baby!"

"Really? Well, I shore thought we were through with that. How long's it been since Martha Jean was born?"

"We had her over a year ago—July 15, 1945. And about five years before that, Shirley arrived on October 1, 1940. So Martha will be one and a half when this one comes early in 1947. I'm really pleased, darling, and I don't want you to be disappointed."

"Like I said before, I don't want ye givin' birth to so many children that your health is affected."

"Honey, let's get back to the subject of our responsibility concerning the new converts. There is something on my heart about preserving the fruit of the great revival. Since I seem to be in charge of spiritual matters here on the lower end of Little Prairie, I'd like to suggest that you and Ross ride down into the bottoms—say to the two Bridges, Garland and Johnson Lakes, and elsewhere among the camps and tents, to see how the new converts are doing. You could visit and pray with them and remind them of the services at Nady on Sunday morning at 10:00."

In the middle of October, Jim and Estelle went to the White River Bridge to visit with Barney. The former owner of the bar was delighted to see that Estelle had come with Jim. Before they got into the matter of Bible studies, Barney had something else on his mind that he wanted to talk to Estelle about.

"Estelle, there's a woman here at the Bridge who is 'bout to leave, cuz she cain't make a livin' down here like she used to. Most of the men around here who've been visitin' her has got saved and don't come around anymore. So there just ain't no way fer her to make it without their money. Now, I need to tell ye, I ain't been one of her customers! Aside from her sleepin' with men, she's got a lotta good in her. Alice would make me a good waitress here, but then Sylvia would be out of a job. I been thinkin' you just might be able to find her some work out there on the prairie. Also, I wanta see her get saved and know the Lord. Would you and Jim be willin' to knock on her cabin door, talk to her awhile, and see if she'll let ye pray with her?"

Even though she sensed that Jim might be hesitant, Estelle replied, "We sure will, Barney. She's precious in God's sight, and He'll forgive her adultery if she will trust Jesus. Jim, you'll go with me today to call on Alice, won't you? We'll know right away whether she is ready to pray or not."

"Yeah, I guess so," Jim said. "It's the right thang to do, I know."

Finding Alice's cabin, Estelle knocked lightly, and a nicely dressed woman opened the door, appearing surprised to see the couple. She stood waiting, probably to hear the reason for their call.

"Alice, I'm Estelle Tharp and this is my husband, Jim. May we come in and have a friendly talk for a few minutes?"

"I guess so." She opened the door wider, stepped aside for the two to enter, and said, "Please have a seat over there on the couch."

The cabin was cleaner and neater than Estelle had expected it to be. Seated comfortably and watching Alice sit down in a rocker across from them, Estelle prayed silently, *Lord, give me a love for Alice that overlooks her past, and may she feel that love. And give me the words to say as I try to give her the gospel.*

"Well, folks, is there some reason ye're here that ye want to talk 'bout?" she asked, but not in an unfriendly manner.

"Yes, ma'am," Estelle said. "We just learned from Barney that you might be moving away from the community here. And there is something I want to tell you. We've been seeing hundreds of lives changed out in our community by the power of God in what we call a spiritual revival. I thought while we were visiting Barney, who gave his heart to the Lord out at Nady several weeks ago, I wanted you to know that I am praying for you. I'm wondering if you would like to open your heart to the Lord and let Jesus come in, give you a new heart, and help you with a new way of life. Don't you think, Alice, that it's time you prayed to God and put your trust in His Son, Jesus Christ, as your Savior?"

"Ma'am!" said Alice. "I reckon this old sinner woman oughta do somethin' like that, but it ain't very common fer a woman like me to find God's hep. That revival meetin' ye had out on the prairie there jes' about done me in—changed all my men friends' desires. So I'm not shore what I'll do now."

"Alice, the Bible says, **God so loved the world that he gave his only Son, that whoever believes in him should not perish but have everlasting life**. Now, **whoever** means just that—anyone of us—**for we've all sinned**, and we all need a Savior in order to receive a new heart and walk with God and go to Heaven when we die. Alice, I think God is trying to tell you that it's time for you to turn to Him in prayer, receive His forgiveness, and trust His Son Jesus' death on the cross for the full payment for your sins. But this requires a decision on your part, a commitment of trust. It is by faith that we ask His forgiveness and then make the confession to God in prayer when we are ready to turn to Jesus by faith and become a follower of His. We call this being saved. I feel as I talk to you that you are about ready to do that, aren't you?"

"Well, ma'am, I do feel somethin' I never felt before. I wondered when y'all come in here iffen ye was the law to arrest me fer my whorin' here at the Bridge. Then when ye started talkin' 'bout God and gettin' saved, I started thinkin' maybe it's what I need and maybe it's time. I ain't never been religious. But whut about the way I been livin'? Ye mean God might forgive me?"

"My dear Alice, there's no doubt about it! I'm going to read you something right out of this Holy Book. Now, you listen, because these words in I John 1:9 are for all of us. **If we confess our sins, he is faithful and just, and will forgive our sins and cleanse us from all unrighteousness**. If you are ready to do that now, I can lead you in a prayer of confessing your sins and placing your trust in the Lord Jesus Christ, who died on the cross to pay for your sins and for mine. If you will repeat the prayer after me, God will hear you, and He'll put His Spirit in your heart, and give you a peace by which you will know you are forgiven. Just ask Barney and all the other people around the Bridge who have been saved, and they will tell you what I've just said. Wouldn't you like for me to lead you in a prayer before we go?"

"Yes'm, I reckon so. I do believe that's whut I need to do," Alice said, and Estelle thought she saw a tear fall down her cheek.

Estelle prepared Alice to follow her in short phrases and sentences even as she had with scores of others. The deeper they got into the prayer of repentance and faith and surrender to the Lord, the more emotional Alice became. After praying the sinner's prayer with Alice, Estelle said, "The Lord has given you a new heart and a new spiritual nature with new desires. Now, I'll be praying that the Lord will open a new way of life for you." She presented Alice with a Bible and some other helpful literature for new Christians and urged her to read the Gospel of John first.

Before leaving, Estelle said, "Would you be interested in living with a couple with children to do their cooking, cleaning, and helping in and around the house with a few household chores, as well as gardening, yard work, and caring for animals? I don't have a job offer at this time, but if you would be interested, I might be able to find one for you out on the prairie between Nady and Tichnor or even around DeWitt."

"Yes ma'am, I thank you! I figger I ain't got no book learnin' or no trainin' fer much more than I been a doin'. I'd be glad to hep someone the way ye said."

"Then let's pray." Estelle told the Lord that she knew He was looking down upon Alice, now forgiven of sin and made a new person in Jesus Christ, who would read God's word and seek to please Him. "Father, Alice needs a new way of making a living. You love her and promise to provide for her. Would You provide a job for her in which she'll be fulfilled and blessed, so that she can earn her living the way You want her to? In Jesus' name I ask this, Amen!"

Estelle went across the room and embraced Alice. This woman with the tear-stained face was surprised that a stranger wanted to hug her, but she responded and enjoyed the feeling of Estelle's arms enfolding her. "If we learn of work for you, we'll come and tell you," Estelle promised.

Alice walked out on the pier with Jim and Estelle, and as they stepped off the plank onto the ground, she called, "Ma'am, I feel that peace ye said would come! I do thank ye both for comin'!" Waving and smiling, Estelle said, "My husband and I will be praying for you every day. Now read your Bible and pray to God. He'll hear you, now that you're His child!"

Barney served Jim and Estelle cold drinks as they rejoiced together about Alice finding the Lord. "Ye know, Jim and Estelle, she seems like a clean woman and pretty well dressed. I'll bet she would make somebody ye know a good housekeeper."

"I told her we'd try to find her work with a family somewhere," said Estelle.

Before Jim started the motor, he said, grinning, "Now, ye wouldn't be thinkin' of hirin' this Alice for yeself, would ye?"

"Well, I must confess it did cross my mind. But I wasn't about to do it before I talked it over with you. Like Barney said, she does look clean, and I noticed her cabin was neat and clean, at least the part we saw. The Lord has forgiven her for her past, and I don't think we could please the Lord and deny her the job, if we thought she was suited to the work we need to have done. What do you think?"

"Well, I reckon ye could use her, and that would give Linda, Anniece, Miriam, and Oda more freedom for their own lives. I agree with ye that we shouldn't hold her past against her; the Lord can hep her live right, just like He's heppin' Barney and the rest of us fellers around here. What would ye offer her, and what would yore job description be for her?"

"I guess that's something we ought to pray about and decide."

"Well, then we'll be goin', though I thought if our minds was made up on it, you could go back over there and tell her now, 'fore she takes off for someplace else."

"No, if we think she's the one after we've prayed and talked more about it, then it'll be worth another trip back." Jim nodded, untied the boat, cranked the engine, and they were on their way back to their pickup at the Mouth of LaGrue.

The last Sunday of October attracted the largest crowd at the Menard schoolhouse since the nightly revival services. The people both on the prairie and down in the bottoms took Estelle seriously about coming and saying a few words of praise and thanksgiving to God for their transformed lives.

Press and Edith Whitman believed they should come forward and lead off the time of testimonies. Edith stood by Press as he told the people how Estelle and Jim had come to their home after he had been stricken with illness, under deep conviction, and could hardly get out of bed. When Estelle explained God's plan of salvation, he was astounded that it was to be a gift, already paid for by the blood of Jesus in His death on the cross. He said that day was a double blessing because Edith wanted and found the same peace with God that he had found. He told how the Holy Spirit had led him to make restitution for wrongs done to some of his former workers and had convicted him about paying money he owed to people he had cheated. Now he felt a love for people he once hated, and he was able to forgive those who had wronged him.

Edith told how their marriage had turned from tension, fighting, stress, and disappointment into peace, sweetness, and happiness. It seemed amazing to her that they even enjoyed praying together. They were also thankful that their eleven children were showing an interest in spiritual things. Edith told them that words could not express what the services in Nady had meant to both of them. "Estelle, Press and I have learned so much from you! Thank you for making the Bible come alive for us."

Barney Stevens needed to tell about the night that "most of us bottoms fellers were struck down by the power of God. Why, I never knowed any such power as that existed in this universe. I knowed about electrical power, the power of a gas-burning engine, and mule power, of course. But, fokes, 'til I was struck down right out there near those big oak trees, I had been arguin' they ain't nuthin' to religion but talk. Now, fokes, let me tell ye, I knowed when I come to and got up from the ground out there that I needed to repent of my ways, my thinkin', the way I feel about people, my take on about everthang! I tell ye, when I walked through that door right yonder, I wuz tremblin', shakin' like a sheet in the wind, and scared to death of Almighty God and the judgment I deserved. But as I listened to that preacher, somethin' sprung up in me to believe whut he said. An' I knowed he got it from this Holy Book. Cuz when I said that prayer he led, a peace swept over me that I still can't get over! I ain't been the same since. I ain't nevah been one to read much, and nevah the Bible. Can't get enough of it now. Now, afore I set down, I just wanta tell y'all, a lotta people 'round that White River Bridge ain't the same no more! I want y'all to pray that we get more Bible teachin' down there like we hear from Miz Estelle up here."

Jay Reddon had let Estelle know before the service that he wanted a few minutes to tell what the Lord had done for him. He began with a startling self-denunciation: "Fokes, I'm the most unfittin' person in all these parts. I don't deserve the company of such people as you. When I look at Miz Estelle here, Miss Linda, and Miz Oda, I'm so ashamed of myself! Back before that night out there in the church yard that Barney done told about, I was worse than a dumb, wild, mean beast.

Jim Tharp shoulda killed me a long time ago for the thangs I tried to do to Miz Estelle and the other women fokes there at the Tharp property! I've begged their forgiveness, cuz I know God's done forgive me. That night when I could get up from the ground out there, I wuz pulled in here by some strange force, and like Barney said, I heerd that preacher give us hope—God would forgive us and cancel out our sins. Fokes, I had tons of 'em to confess. Shore 'nuff! That peace come into me jes' like it did Barney and a many others! I've gotta lot of thangs to make right, and ever week I'm goin' about doin' just that. I shore need y'alls prayers and help. Thank ye, Miz Estelle, fer yore forgiveness. Hep me pray I'll behave myself from here on!" With bowed head, the penitent soul shook hands with well-wishers all the way down the aisle. Leaving the building, he found the spot in the church yard where on that fateful night seven months before he discovered the incredible power of God. There he sat, listening to the sound of testimonies of others coming through the windows.

Fifteen more men and women from the prairie or near DeWitt and Gillette told how they too had been forgiven, not from outward acts such as murder, rape, or thievery, but from things dictated by their selfish nature—unbelief, self-righteousness, unreasonable demands they had imposed on their mates and children, and attitudes that tore their marriages apart and created tension in their family. They all testified to the power of the Gospel and the beauty of Jesus Christ in His power to make them whole and at peace.

As Estelle closed the service, she realized that she must find a way to help the hundreds of new Christians to deepen their faith, increase in love, and grow in the knowledge of the grace of God. She was glad that she had announced a "dinner on the grounds here" following the service the next Sunday. "If the weather is bad, we'll stack the chairs in both rooms and eat inside; but if it's nice, we'll eat out under the oak trees in the northwest corner of the church yard."

On the way home she reminded Jim that they needed to talk about hiring Alice to help her with her work, "so I can give more time to prayer and helping the new Christians grow in the Lord."

"Yeah, I know ye need help, and maybe we just oughta get that settled before we go to bed tonight. I'm gonna check on the cattle this afternoon and grease up some more traps to set out this winter. But we oughta talk after supper tonight."

"Are you putting out lots of traps this winter?"

"Yeah, about 200. I don't know what the fur market will be like, but we've gotta do what we can. Henry will be puttin' out 100, and George said he'd do 150; that's more than they put out last year."

"Are the cattle doing alright? I guess you have plenty of hay for the winter, right?"

"Yeah, we're in good shape there. But I've been wantin' to ask how we're doin' on our balance in the bank after sellin' the cattle last month? I know we gave a lot on the revival. We didn't do so well from the orchard, but we still paid Linda what we promised. We shore had some heavy repair bills, but I guess they're all paid."

As soon as they got back to the house, Estelle got the checkbook and sat down with Jim to continue their discussion on finances. "Jim, it's not such good news here as I had hoped. But I surely do not regret all we've given. Even after giving $3,000 on the revival and paying all our bills, including the repairs on the equipment and settling with Birdie, we still have almost $5,000 in the bank. You'll probably bring in enough from your trapping to meet our winter's expenses. And we need to decide what we'll pay Alice, if we ask her to come. Have you thought it over?"

"I've just decided to leave that up to you," Jim said. "If ye think she's reliable and will do what ye want done, I don't have any objections. Where will she live? I don't reckon ye wanta put her in the cabin, do ye?"

"No, I think we should keep it open for my place to pray and for a place to put your hunting guests. I think we should give her Jeanette's room, and Anniece and Shirley can manage in the same room. I've thought a little about what we should pay her. If she turns out as well as I think she will, I'd like to pay her $25.00 a week and her room and board. What do you think about that?"

"Well, that's about what I pay extra hands—$5.00 a day—when I need 'em in the cotton, or orchard, and when they help me seine. So if she turns out okay, I guess we can afford that."

"When can we make a trip down and talk to her about it?"

"How about Saturday mornin', if it's not rainin' or snowin'?"

"Let's plan on it. I doubt if she has all that many things to bring with her. Unless she has a piece of furniture or something, I'd guess she can get everything in a couple of suitcases. If that's the case, we can bring everything in the boat, can't we?"

"I reckon so. Hope she ain't got a table, a bunch of books, or a lot of other stuff."

"If she's ready to come home with us and she has more stuff than we can get in the boat, then we'll need to go back in the spring and get the rest of her things."

Saturday morning was almost as warm as if it were September, instead of nearly November. The trip down the White River was pleasant. Jim and Estelle decided to go about sunup and have breakfast at Barney's. Over ham and eggs and hot coffee, Jim told Barney that they were going to ask Alice if she would like to live with them and work for Estelle. Barney expressed his appreciation to Estelle for making a place for Alice. "Barney, we're hopin' she don't have much more than her clothes and personal stuff," Jim said.

"She ain't got more'n ye can get in yer boat, I know."

Seeing Jim and Estelle walking toward her cabin, Alice flung her door open. "Shore glad to see ye! Hope ye gonna offer me a job of housekeepin' fer someone like we talked about 'while back. Come on in and sit down."

"Yes, Jim and I want to offer you the job of being our housekeeper, at $5.00 a day—we figure $25.00 a week, plus room and board. You'll have your own room there in our house. Right now we have seven children at home, but I'm expecting another baby probably in January. It might get a little noisy at times. We also have quite a bit of company, so at times there'll be a lot of people to cook for besides our family."

"Miss Estelle, I'm so glad ye want me to live with ye and hep ye care for ye chillins. How old are they?"

"Our oldest son is seventeen, and our youngest daughter is one year old. We have four boys and three girls still at home. Our oldest daughter is married and lives several miles north of us."

"It's been so long since I wuz 'round kids, but it'll be fun to get to know 'em all."

"Alice, tell us a little about your background—your parents, where you were raised, how you did in school, and what interests you have in life," Estelle said.

"Well, Miss Estelle..."

"Now, Alice," Estelle interrupted, "I'd just like you to call me Estelle, okay?"

"I reckon, ma'am ... Estelle. But I feel ye're a much better woman than me, and..."

Estelle interrupted again. "Now, Alice, I'm a sinner saved by grace. No doubt our backgrounds are much different. I'm sorry if your background and upbringing did not prepare you for a better quality of life than you have known. But your past is forgiven by God and by all of us who know you; we will never bring up your past. You are precious in God's sight and in ours. We will be thinking of you as our Christian sister and just as good as we are. We'll try to help you understand your Bible and live a good Christian life. We hope you'll go to church with us on Sundays and join us in family prayer. By the way, I hope you are enjoying your Bible and your walk with the Lord. Are there things you want to ask about?"

"I really do feel different, and I know somethin' has happened to me on the inside of my heart. I talk to God a lot. I thank Him that you and Mr. Jim come by here and prayed with me. I thanked Him a lot that you wuz thinkin' 'bout findin' me work. And I wuz shore overjoyed that ye come back to tell me I could finally get away from this place!

"Now, as fer my Ma and Pa, they been dead a few years. I ain't got but one brother livin', and I ain't heard from him fer a long time. I don't write very good, but I read a little. I only got a second year of school, but I 'spect I'll be able to learn a lot from you."

"Alice, we'll help you all we can, but I know you'll be helping us a lot. Now, are you prepared to leave with us today? And if so, how many things will you be wanting to take along?"

"I ain't got nuthin' but a few clothes, and I don't own a stick of furniture. If not fer Barney and the old feller who owns this cabin, I wouldn't have use of these things ye see here. Naw, we can carry everthang I got in a suitcase and a pasteboard box. I thought ye'd be comin', so I'm all packed and ready to go."

452

Barney came out to the pier as the three were getting into the boat. "I'll be seein' y'all on Sunday mornin's. Alice, I wish you well in yore new job." He stood on the river bank and waved goodbye as they headed up the river.

Estelle showed Alice her room and told her to make herself at home. She was free to use the living room and to take books to read from the shelf. Alice seemed pleased with everything Estelle showed her or said. Even though she was quite reserved, she smiled a lot and nodded approval often. She seemed familiar with all the equipment in the kitchen and remarked that "It's shore nice to see a big table like that and a big stove and a big fridge. Estelle took her out to the smokehouse and pointed out their food supplies, the shelves of canned fruits and vegetables, and the laundry room.

"It shore seems like the Good Lord's blessed y'all with a good life," Alice said.

"He has, indeed! And we love sharing it with others, too."

Estelle was pleased with Alice's adjustment to the family and her work during her first week. She credited this as much to Alice's ability to listen well and catch on quickly as to her own clarity and patience in explaining to Alice what the family wanted and how things worked in the kitchen and elsewhere. She liked her new employee's even-tempered nature and quiet acceptance of things. Estelle appreciated the respect Alice showed her and Jim and noticed how she remembered each child's name. She went about cooking the meals with no questions, except to ask for the main menu for each meal. Rarely did she need to ask a second question about any procedure, but caught on quickly to where things were and how the stove burners and oven worked. She soon proved that she was worth all Estelle planned to pay her. Once she was comfortable with the household duties, other tasks would be added. Estelle wondered whether Alice could drive a car; if so, could she depend on her to drive the children back and forth to school? Would she do as well in the garden, in the smokehouse, and in the yard as she did in the living quarters? How willing would she be to shovel snow? All would be clear in a matter of weeks. For now, Estelle just hoped the dear woman would be happy in her new environment. Helping her grow spiritually was even more important to Estelle than how well she did in her work.

Estelle decided one afternoon to go over and visit Linda. She felt free and joyful as she trudged through the light snow that had just fallen. Going past the orchard bare of leaves, Estelle rejoiced in the seasons. She thought of the warmth of the Buchannons' friendship and the changes that had come in Linda's and the children's lives since they had become neighbors—their turning to Christ, their buying the farm, Jack's enlistment in the Army and then his death at sea, their recovery from grief, and their growth in their relationship with God. *Lord, what do You have in mind for Linda? She seems too young and pretty to stay single for the rest of her years. Would You be pleased to bring a true Christian gentleman into her life, one who would be a good father image for her children and a good provider?* Estelle smiled as she prayed about a possible mate for Linda, not thinking of how soon the answer might come. Just before reaching the top of the incline to the Buchannon house, she saw a Jeep parked near the gate. At first she hesitated to go on to the house. Linda had company, and perhaps she should not intrude. Then her instincts would not free her to turn back. At her first knock on the door, Linda opened it. "Why, Estelle! Come in! I'm so glad to see you. I'm sure you know Jay Reddon." Jay walked toward her with a smile, and she extended her hand.

"Miz Tharp, it's good to see you. I wuz just tellin' Linda some thangs on my mind, and I'd shore be glad for you to hear 'em, too!" Jay said as he returned to his chair.

"Estelle, let me have your coat. Take off your boots and sit here on the couch with me. I want you to hear what Jay is gonna tell me. You see, he's been visitin' here about one evenin' a week for the last month. I think you know that Jay's not the same man we all had trouble with once."

"Well, Linda, I'll sit a moment, but I sure don't want to intrude on you. Jim is picking up the children in a little while, so I'll need to get going soon."

"Estelle, you're not intrudin'! There's no one I'd rather have with me as I hear what's on Jay's mind. Go ahead, Jay."

Jay leaned forward, "Well, I just thank the Lord that He's give me the chance to come to you ladies without Mr. Jim killin' me. I done begged his forgiveness, and it seems like he was real decent 'bout it. I know I begged God's forgiveness for what I tried to do to y'all." He was looking at Estelle as if he was not sure about her approval of him.

"Jay," Estelle began, "we are all so thankful you have found the Lord and His forgiveness. You need not worry about our attitude toward you. You are no longer the same person that I once had to rebuke and order to shut up and be still! I thought about the power of God in your life last Sunday when you were telling us what all the Lord has done for you. We love and appreciate you now as a brother in Christ."

"Well, Linda and me—I've been here a few times lately, and we've been talkin'. I wuz about to tell her I think it's time there's more for us than just my stoppin' in 'bout once a week, eatin' a bite, prayin' together, and then me gettin' back to camp. See, Linda and Miz Tharp, I ain't gonna make whiskey the rest of my life. Fact is, there's good news I ain't even told Linda 'bout. My uncle, who owns the bizness down there in them bottoms, is in prison. I went to see him, and I told him what happened to me—the same thang that happened to Henry Tharp, who worked for him. 'Fore I left, my old uncle got down on his knees, prayed for forgiveness, and confessed Jesus as his Savior. Thang is, he'll get a parole in a few months. Then he claims he's gonna put us outa bizness down there. I think it's downright funny—the old man that used to shoot and kill them prohibition agents for tryin' to blow up his still now wants to come down there and blow it up hisself! Now, ain't that somethin'!"

"Praise the Lord!" Estelle said. Linda said, "Amen!"

"Yeah, my uncle's gonna put us outa bizness. And I'm kinda glad. Ye know, Linda, we've got pretty well off from that old still. I oughta be ashamed to tell you that my uncle and me are rich men. But it ain't the kind of life I wanta stay with anymore. I can go into 'bout any kinda retail bizness I want, serve people, and give to the Lord.

"Linda, I wanted to tell you that I ain't never felt about any other woman like the way I feel about you. And I shore think the world of yore kids, too. I reckon I first oughta ask ye if I can come a callin', like a feller who has more in mind than just a date or two." Jay paused, looking at Linda. She looked at him, then looked down.

Estelle felt she should be going. "Linda, I feel you and Jay should be alone to discuss your relationship. Before I go, however, may I lead a prayer for you?" Linda nodded as Estelle was rising and reaching for her coat and boots. She prayed for the Lord's guidance in "the lives of these two children of Yours, whom You've changed by Your grace and mercy. If it is You leading Jay and Linda together, may their love for You only be enhanced by their love for each other. Bless them as they share together today." All three said, "Amen." Estelle shook hands with Jay, hugged Linda, and said, "Honey, you can tell me later however much you want me to know. But be assured that Jim and I want the best for you and your family, and we'll support you however the Lord leads you!"

"Oh, how wonderful of you to say that!"

After Linda closed the door behind Estelle, she sat back down and smiled at Jay. "Go ahead, Jay, and tell me what is on your heart. Then it will be my turn."

After supper, Estelle followed Jim to the smokehouse. "Well, I figger ye got somethin' on yer mind," Jim said. Why don't we sit down here on the bench before I start stretchin' these hides." Seated together, Estelle told Jim what she had seen and heard at Linda's that afternoon.

"Then I reckon that was his Jeep I saw still there when I dropped off the kids," Jim said. "Well, if the man keeps on like he's goin' now, I reckon he could make Linda a good husband and be a great provider. But I'm glad ye heard him say he wanted out of the liquor bizness. Yeah, he apologized to me, and if he proves hisself, we'll wanta be good neighbors for them and support Linda if she decides to marry him."

"Well, honey, that's the way I feel, and I'm glad we are enabled by the Spirit to forgive and forget. Linda is like our own family, and she deserves the best. To think that at one time Jay was a man you thought you'd have to kill. Now, God has worked a great change in him, and it's like he'll be a member of our family. Oh, and guess what else Jay told us before I left?" Seeing Jim was waiting to hear, she went on. "His uncle who owns the still got saved when Jay went to visit him in prison, and he's coming down there when he gets out on parole and blow up the operation himself! Imagine that! Oh, what the Lord has done!"

"Yeah, well, maybe I'd better get up and see Lloyd in a few days and find out what's happenin' with Jay's uncle. I'm shore glad he got saved, but I'm surprised he's gonna be on parole so soon."

"Perhaps the Lord is in this, and maybe He'll use his testimony more powerfully out of prison than in. Let's just trust the Lord to work it out His way."

"Yeah, I'm in agreement with that." Then Jim got up and began attending to the hides.

It was Linda's turn to take the children to school the next morning. While picking up Burl, Russ, and Carroll, she told Estelle she'd be back by after awhile to talk with her.

As Estelle expected, Linda knocked on the cabin door about nine o'clock. After removing her coat and sitting down on the couch, she said excitedly, "Estelle, Jay and I are really in love!"

"Well, Linda, I'm happy for you both! You are like family to Jim and me and the children, and your happiness makes us happy. I know you've prayed about this and feel that Jay is settled enough in the Lord that you can trust him to seek to please the Lord and make you a wonderful Christian husband, as well as a trusted father to your children."

"Yes, to all of that! I wasn't sure he had love and marriage in mind until last night. Well, you heard what he said. After you left, he told me he felt sure that in his heart he loved me. He said he had never loved anyone before, but he did admit that he had known a few women intimately. He said he hoped I could come to love him eventually and would be willing to marry him." By this time, Linda was wiping a few tears and needed to pause and get her breath. "Estelle, I had already come to believe that I had feelings for Jay; I just hadn't felt free to tell him because last night is the first time I was sure he had feelings for me. I haven't told him yet that I love him, but I believe I do. Isn't it amazing that the evil man who tried to rape me, who cursed us, and who called us such ugly names, could get right with God and become the kind of person I could fall in love with and want to marry and have as a daddy to my kids? Well, Estelle, tell me if you think we are crazy and that I am making a wrong decision."

When Estelle was sure that Linda had finished pouring out her heart and mind, she responded, "No, Linda, I don't think that you and Jay are crazy. And I don't think it is the devil who is prompting Jay to come to you for the wrong reasons. No, I believe you and Jack sincerely yielded your hearts to the Lord. And since you've lost Jack, you've continued to live for the Lord and He has blessed you. Nor do I discern anything insincere about Jay. I was impressed greatly with all that he had to say Sunday. However, I would say that it would be wise to give your relationship a few more weeks or even months before you marry. You'll discern a restraining of the Spirit if you are not to go ahead with the marriage. I'll be praying that you will know the mind of the Lord about this. And, Linda, Jim fully supports your relationship with Jay."

"Oh, Estelle, that means so much! And I know what that will mean to Jay to know that Mr. Jim approves of the relationship! Jack and I never knew what it was to have any amount of money at all; we just skimped by most of the time. Only after we moved over here and got to know you and Mr. Jim did we really make ends meet fairly well. You've helped us so much! Then after losing Jack, I still can't believe how generous y'all have been to the children and me. I know Jay is going to want to know what I owe on the place, and he says he has plenty of money. Though, please believe me when I tell you, that has nothing to do with my feelings for him. But it will be good to be able to buy what we need, give the children a good education, and pay you and Mr. Jim all we owe you. When the government finally settles with me on the insurance for Jack, I do think that I can pay off this farm. Then I feel the rest of it, if there's any left, oughta be put away for the kids' college."

"Don't think for a moment that we'll ever let you lose your place if you want to keep it. I know you well enough to know you would never marry any man for his money, but I'm glad Jay is able to take good care of you and the children."

After a time of prayer, Linda left in even higher spirits than when she came because she knew she and Jay had Jim's and Estelle's blessing.

When Estelle informed Jim about the situation between Linda and Jay Reddon, he said, "Well, there's another sign of the grace of God at work in our midst, I reckon. The old boy seems to have truly allowed God to turn his life around since he's been saved. I hope he's on the level; if he isn't, he's got you and all the rest of us fooled and this could be the biggest mistake Linda could ever make. Why don't we have 'em over for a meal some night to show our approval and support?"

"What a good idea, honey!" Estelle exclaimed. "Let's make it next Friday night. I'm sure Jay will be back to see her before then."

Estelle could hardly wait until she could extend the invitation to Linda. She did so the next morning when Linda picked up the children for school. "Why, Estelle, that's just great! I know Jay will be pleased, too!"

After church on Sunday, Linda told Estelle that they were looking forward to Friday night, but that Jay was really sobered by the thought of facing Jim again. "But he knows Jim is 'truly a brother in Christ' and will not force his hand on anything. He really trusts Jim, but he's finding it hard to believe his own life is so different."

Jim was glad to see that Jay seemed cool and at ease all during the Friday night preliminaries and through the meal. He talked of his future, with "Uncle Fred gettin' free to take the operation back over and blowin' the thang up." He recognized Jim's and Estelle's concerns for Linda's and the children's future and sought to reassure them that he had the resources to take care of them and all their needs even after settling with his uncle. He guessed he oughta consult with people in the know about making investments with the "millions I got stored up in a safe down there in the bottoms." He knew that Linda still owed something on the farm. They hadn't yet decided whether they would keep the farm. He wasn't sure he would make a good cotton farmer, but he liked the idea of taking over Jim's orchard and developing significant markets for fruit across that part of Arkansas.

"That sounds interestin', Jay," Jim said. "If ye don't care to farm, I'll be glad to take it back. But if ye want to farm and need and want to hire someone, Birdie Washington—the finest colored man ye'll ever meet—is one of the best. Linda knows him and his wife and family well, and she'll vouch that he's a reliable source of information when it comes to cotton farmin'. We'll shore be glad to have y'all as neighbors. We want things to continue like family, just like it was with Linda, Jack, and the kids. Those three young people are some of the finest, and they deserve a good education."

"Yeah, I agree. We might need to move up to Little Rock or down to Hot Springs to live near a good college, cuz it won't be long 'fore they're ready for more learnin'."

Before Jay, Linda, and the children left, Estelle thanked the Lord for their relationship and prayed for divine direction for them as a promising family "who will become a part of a growing body of Christ wherever providence places them."

The sheriff could not explain Fred Reddon's parole and was concerned about the terms. "We might need to keep an eye on him, even though I know he will be assigned an officer to report to. He shore ain't served near enough time to be paroled, in my opinion."

"Should we just wait and ask him what the terms are?" Jim asked.

"Well, if the uncle has the same genuine religion you think his nephew's got, I reckon he wouldn't lie. I just need to know whether he'll bear watchin'."

Linda told Estelle that Jay's uncle was due to be released just any day. She did not know any of the terms. Linda wanted to have Fred and Jay over for a meal during that time. She said Jay thought his uncle would want to see Henry Tharp so they could rejoice in the Lord together; they had both been converted since their time together in the bottoms a few years ago.

The arrival of Fred Reddon in the White River Bottoms caused the sheriff to consider consulting the Governor and the Attorney General. Fred had already served time for his crimes, but he had done more and knew more than he had confessed a few years ago when he was convicted. "How many more of them fellers in the bottoms have had a part in violatin' the law, even if they ain't been as mean as Fred?" Lloyd asked Jim.

"Lloyd, I have no idea, but I would say ye'd be wise to get some counsel on this. I reckon I still figger ye oughta talk with Fred before ye go see the Governor though. Ye might figger it all out yerself. I'll hep ye any way I can—I know I can set up a meetin' between the two of ye."

"Ye know, we might do well to have Fred and Jay meet us at Barney's place there at the Bridge someday. Seems like we always have good success at Barney's, don't we?"

"Yep, Barney's been downright hepful," Jim agreed.

Before Sheriff LaFargue had a chance to meet with Fred Reddon at Nady or at the Bridge, Fred and his nephew showed up at his office in DeWitt. The parolee showed the sheriff his papers, saying, "Yeah, I reckon I'd been a good boy, and since they wuz real crowded up there, they let me go. I'll still need to report to you pretty often, they tell me."

"Since it says it's up to me how often, I won't require ye to come here every week, which is the way it usually is. I am making it once a month. Now, Fred, it also says here that there must be a hearing after one year."

"Does that mean I'm a free man after a year?"

"Not necessarily, Fred. I expect it will be decided mainly by the report. I need to hear from ye each month and have no negative reports on ye from anyone. The hearing results will determine whether or not ye continue on parole or if ye will have served yore time and be free."

"Sheriff, I shore hope it'll be what ye said last there."

Fred Reddon walked over to Jim's place on an evening when Jay was visiting with Linda. He wanted to see Henry, but he also wanted to ask Estelle if he might give his testimony in a service as she had allowed Jay and others to do a few weeks before. She assured him that she would love for him to do that the next Sunday. Then he asked where Henry lived. He went back over to Linda's to get Jay's Jeep and drove down to Nady where Henry lived. The two former moonshiners talked for two hours, rejoicing in what God had done for them and lamenting together about the way they used to drink, carouse, curse, and even kill. But as Henry put it when Fred was leaving, "Now that we know the Lord, we are brothers. We pray for one another and bear one another's burdens, and we witness to anyone who will listen to us about the love and grace of God through our Lord Jesus Christ!"

Fred saw a light on in Jim's living room when he returned from visiting Henry, so he knocked on the door. When Jim opened the door, Fred asked, "Is it too late to drop in a moment? I hear that ye have Alice here working for ye now."

"Come right in, Fred."

Seeing Alice sitting near the window, Fred said, "Alice, it's been years since I laid eyes on ye!" Alice stood and said, "Well, Fred I learned you were out, and it's good to see you." When Fred walked over to her and reached out to hug her, she walked right into his arms.

"Have a seat over there, Fred. We didn't know you and Alice were acquainted."

"Yeah, I used to visit Barney's Hole before Alice came down there. We go back a ways. Alice, do ye think it might be possible to go to DeWitt together some time and have supper at a restaurant or maybe take in a picture show?"

Alice hesitated for a second or two as she looked in Estelle's direction. "I'll think about that, Fred. Maybe Miss Estelle will let me get away for an evening."

"Of course, Alice. You can have an evening off now and then if you wish to get away. That will probably do you good."

Rising to leave, Fred told them he expected to see them on Sunday. He walked over and kissed Alice on the cheek and said, "Alice, I was thinkin' 'bout one week from tonight—next Friday night. Ye can tell me Sunday if that night is in the clear with you. Good night!"

"We'll see you Sunday, Fred," Estelle called as he went out the door.

In bed an hour later, Jim said, "Hey, Estelle, we just may see the Reddons reduce our family around here—uncle and nephew each takin' our housemaid and neighbor."

"Well, I'm a bit surprised. It seems like Fred and Alice might have had a relationship down at the Bridge a few years ago."

"Yeah, I thought that when Fred walked over and kissed her before he left. I wouldn't be surprised if he didn't visit her place a lot of times during those years of makin' whiskey and killin' prohibition agents."

"I just hope Alice will grow in the Lord a little more before we lose her, if we do. I know she is learning her Bible. I've helped her some with her English and quite a bit with her numbers. She really does love the Lord and seeks to know how to please Him. Fred seems quite a bit older than Alice, but if the Lord is in this, I guess they can work that out. But, like with Linda, we've just got to let go of Alice when she is making decisions about dating, going here or there, or even marrying Fred—if it should come to that."

"Yeah, I agree with ye as usual," Jim said, chuckling.

Jim and Estelle invited 45 people for a 1947 New Year's Party. The weather was cold, but clear. Estelle was far enough along in her ninth pregnancy that she realized she would need a lot of help for this occasion. She knew she could count on Anniece, BettyLee, Jeanell, Linda, Susan, and a few others for organizing, planning, and preparing food. The guests would include some bottoms and prairie people and close friends from DeWitt, Hot Springs, Little Rock, and Pine Bluff. Estelle had also invited her beloved brother Theo Hughes and his wife, Elsie.

With Bible readings, testimonies, and Gospel songs, the celebration was almost like a camp meeting. Dr. Martin Bonnhoffer gave a 10-minute message from Romans 12:1-2. A mixed trio from the Wesleyan Evangelical Fellowship (WEF) in Little Rock sang a number of moving songs. The pastor, Rev. Agnes Diffee, prayed a closing prayer which the Holy Spirit used to melt the hearts of all present.

Many left the party saying, "This was more like a revival than a New Year's Party!" Estelle's response was, "Just imagine what it will be like at the Marriage Supper of the Lamb! Well, God enjoys partying with his people in this life in preparation for the eternal party that's coming. Yes, indeed, it's a time to dance as we see all that God has done here in the state of Arkansas, especially in the communities around here."

On January 23, 1947, Estelle gave birth to her ninth baby, a boy whom she named Joseph Wayne. Again, Dr. Whitehead attended her with the help of BettyLee, Dee, and Oda. Since Alice was very preoccupied with her coming wedding, Dee moved in for two weeks and helped Estelle and Alice keep things moving as usual.

Linda and Alice were planning a double wedding in April. They had asked Estelle to perform their weddings, but she reminded them that she was what was known as a "lay preacher." Because she was neither ordained nor licensed as a minister, she couldn't perform the ceremony; she recommended Rev. Frank Fox. Fred and Jay Reddon and Linda had been invited to come early on the night of the New Year's Party, so that the two couples could meet and talk to Rev. Fox about officiating at their weddings in DeWitt on the first Sunday afternoon in April. Estelle and Henry were to serve as matron of honor and best man for both couples. It would be a simple ceremony in the Friends Church. Alice would remain as helper to Estelle. Fred would alternate in working for Jay and Linda on the farm and orchard and then with Jim in logging and farming; now and then, he would help Birdie. "I wanta work for a low wage, since I shore don't need the money," he said.

Alice looked to Estelle for guidance in preparing for her
wedding and marriage. "Fred is 59 and I'm 42, so I reckon I'm gonna
have to pray to God to help me. For so long I was a bad girl, and now I
need to live like a good girl with a good husband. I shore wanta make
Fred a good wife."

"Alice, you're not alone in your efforts to be a good person and a
good wife; the Lord is with you. He's provided Fred to be your husband,
and He'll help you both to be a blessing to each other. And I'm very
thankful you'll continue to help me."

"You know, Estelle, I was surprised when Fred became
interested in marriage, but when I learned that we could still live nearby
and I could help ye, that settled it for me; I knew then that I should try to
make a go of marriage."

The 1946-47 trapping season was the least profitable one in
about 10 years for Jim and the other trappers in Arkansas County. The
winter and early spring fishing period was also less profitable than the
last 10. Not only had cattle dropped in price since the war, but diseases
peculiar to cattle increased, which made the last two years
disappointingly unprofitable. Jim had to increase his work in timber to
break even.

"I thought our generous givin' would cause the Lord to bless us
more financially, but it seems to work the other way," he said to Estelle.
"And then all them cattle died! But the timber's savin' us."

"I just think we should look at this as a time of trial," Estelle
said. "We are going to make it alright, and look at what we still have. We
are out of debt, we still have over half the herd we had a few years ago,
and we still have the land, with the exception of the 80 acres we sold
Linda. You still have your work with the sheriff. Our oldest child is
happily married, and she and Don have given us two sweet
grandchildren. Our son Jake is growing in the Lord and is in the process
of answering a call to preach—already preaching on the streets of towns
here in our county and for us on some Sundays. Our daughter Anniece is
an amazing girl and really close to God, the other children are doing fine,
and we still have the Lord and each other! What more can we ask?"

Jim smiled and said, "Dear woman, you always know how to
cheer me up!"

"I'm so thankful that you know the Lord yourself; you are now a praying man and learning to **grow in the grace and knowledge of our Lord Jesus Christ**. I'm proud of you! I know that if we face some hard times, you are not going to give up your faith or your efforts to improve things around you."

A letter from Sister Martha inquiring about the aftermath of the revival touched Estelle deeply, especially her concern that "the spiritual leaders in the Nady church might want to consider moving beyond the traditions of the Friends Church." She was not recommending that the Nady church disaffiliate with the Friends, but she acknowledged that since the great baptismal service—which had stretched Pastors Fox and Rich to cooperate—"it might be time to consider associations with the WEF." This growing movement was spiritual, revivalistic, and more in keeping with the phenomenally growing evangelical movement in America and Canada, while holding steadily to the holiness teachings of Jesus, the apostle Paul, and John Wesley. She was, herself, considering participating in the ordinances of Water Baptism and the Lord's Supper. While the Friends had stubbornly excluded those ordinances from their practices, she felt they were both tremendous means of grace. Wesley, like Jesus, had declared the importance of both ordinances. In her departure from their traditions, she was not ready to denounce the Friends, but to bless them. She would be resigning her position at Union Bible College out of respect for Dr. William Smith and all that the Friends Church had meant to her and her loved ones in years past.

It seemed providential that Estelle received Sister Martha's correspondence just before two other letters: an invitation from Dr. Brent Jones invited her to return to the Methodist Fellowship Center in Little Rock "early this fall, perhaps no later than the latter part of October, and lead us in a renewal of the great revival that a good number of congregations experienced here one year ago." Pastor Agnes Diffee wrote to ask that she "come and preach for the WEF here in Little Rock some Sunday morning in October." The WEF pastor also hoped they could spend time and prayer together about "preserving the fruits of the great revival you've had down there in Nady."

Not since her seven-year period of weeping, fasting, and interceding for the great revival God had given a few months before had Estelle entered into such burdened, passionate, and sacrificial praying.

Three things were the focus of her intercessory prayers—a possible change in church affiliation, the invitation to return to Little Rock, and a freedom to respond to Pastor Diffee's request to meet about preserving the fruit of the Nady revival.

Estelle spent the days and parts of the nights in March in the cabin. She felt the same heavy burden for direction for the future as she had felt for the divine outpourings of the Holy Spirit during the previous seven years. She could now share some of this with Jim, who often joined her in prayer during the night hours. She was pleased with Jim's openness to her thoughts about changing from the traditions of the Friends Church, while still holding to the same New Testament Gospel. Jim said, "Honey, I'm so glad you aren't stubbornly seekin' to make Quakers out of us who have found the Lord. Remember how the Holy Spirit anointed and blessed Woody Shields just as greatly as He anointed and blessed Sister Martha, Frank Fox, and Homer Rich. And don't ever forget how God poured out His blessin' so powerfully on that great baptismal service last April!"

One April evening, after working all day with the sheriff tracking some cattle thieves, Jim returned home tired and hungry. As he headed to the house for supper, he heard cries and sobs coming from Estelle in the cabin. He paused at the cabin door and was about to go in without knocking when he saw the light—a bluish glow lingered over her head lighting her tear-washed face. He froze with his left foot on the second step and his hand on the doorknob. Then he heard an amazing voice that wasn't Estelle's: *Dear one, you are highly esteemed for your faithfulness and obedience. I have come to tell you that there are going to be times of change in your life and ministry. Read the Word prayerfully. Obey the Spirit's leadings specifically, and do not be afraid of new ways, new places, and new things when you are certain they are of the Lord.*

The voice ceased, but the light remained. Jim's heart was pounding. He wanted to rush to Estelle and kneel by the couch on which she lay. But the light seemed to restrain him, as did an inner voice whispering that he was only to see and hear for now. He would need to listen to her understanding of it all later.

Jim turned and went to the house where Alice served him a late supper. "Alice, it looks like Estelle is holding late hours with the Lord these days."

"Yessir, she shore 'nuff is! I ain't never seen anybody pray so much and get so much from the Lord, Mr. Jim. She takes up so much time with Him that I jus' figger I'm supposed to go on with thangs here the best way I can. I shore hope she ain't forgot about the weddin' comin' up in about 10 days."

"I don't think she'll forget that, Alice. She cares about you and Linda too much to forget and let y'all down," Jim said, trying to reassure their housekeeper.

"Can I set down here and talk to you a minute, Mr. Jim?" Alice asked.

"Of course, Alice! Pour yerself another cup of coffee and sit down and tell me what's on yore mind."

"Well, Fred will be off parole and free in a short while, and we've been thinkin' 'bout buildin' a house, maybe over on Linda's place. But we also wondered if maybe we might set up a tent. We'd like to live close to our work; I wanta still work for y'all, and Fred will probably be workin' for both you and Jay. Whadda ye think?"

"We'd be glad to have y'all live close here. Either way—a house or a tent—is fine."

Estelle wrote Dr. Jones in Little Rock and offered him a date in late September. Then she wrote Pastor Diffee and accepted her invitation to speak in her church on the Sunday following the time with the Methodists.

In the meantime, Estelle was taking the angel's message seriously—*do not be afraid of new ways, new places, and new things*—and felt comforted and assured. She prayed, "Lord, thank You for giving me and Jim a willingness, even a desire, to venture out to new places in ministry. Please help me hear and learn the things that You would use to broaden our vision and deepen our passion." Estelle called together Spencer Sweeney, Garland Coose, Allen Freeman, and Oscar Shelton and asked them to pray about teaching a Sunday school class before the usual Bible study led by her. The purpose was to teach the Bible to the new Christians, some of whom had never been to church or Sunday school. She promised them teaching materials to help guide them as instructors in the Word. In two weeks she would have their materials, and then they would have three weeks to study for their first lesson. They would have their class wherever there was any space—in the cloak room, the lunch room, the entrance area, and perhaps even under the large shade trees when the weather permitted them to be outside. Estelle was also grateful for Jake's growth in the Lord and pleased with the results of his messages on the few Sunday mornings when he had spoken in her place.

The double wedding in DeWitt was attended by over 100 people, more than half of them being from Nady. Lettie Kronz was the coordinator and Leora Brown, the soloist. Estelle read Scriptures from both the Old and the New Testament. Pastor Frank Fox's ceremony included appropriate admonitions to the grooms and the brides, all of whom appeared inspired and sincerely dedicated to the serious vows they made. Estelle was asked to close the ceremony with prayer. The ladies from Nady had prepared a wedding feast following the ceremony, after which the two couples departed in separate automobiles for different hotels in Little Rock. Jim and Estelle had volunteered to keep the Buchannon children until Linda and Jay returned from their honeymoon.

Oda and Miriam helped Anniece with the cooking and housework during Alice's week of absence for her honeymoon. Their help allowed Estelle to continue with her praying, studying, and preparing the teachers for their Sunday classes. She decided to add two more Sunday school classes; she asked Thelma Bonner to teach a class of adult women and Dorene Freeman to teach a class of children. Estelle believed Spencer Sweeney and Allen Freeman should take her place teaching during her two Sundays in Little Rock the last of September and the first of October. She was amazed at Spencer's spiritual growth and his grasp of the needs of the people in the community. Allen seemed gifted in speaking to the needs of those struggling with weakness and unbelief. He had a way of emphasizing both the love and patience of God and divine holiness that required commitment and obedience from His children.

Jim and Estelle prayed together daily for the summer Sunday classes and the services that followed. Each week the people continued to come and worship, learn, and grow in the Lord. It was with delight that Jim and Estelle would host several families every Sunday for the noon meal and then spend the rest of the Lord's day visiting, playing games, and praying with them. "Estelle, I can't ever remember this community ever fellowshipin' together like this," Jim said, as two carloads of people were following them home on the first Sunday of September.

Jake and Anniece were both in high school at Gillette, catching the bus each morning at 7:45 out on the county road near their mailbox. Jake was in the 11th grade and Anniece in the 10th. Jake had missed a year of high school and was returning for his junior year at Gillette High School. Estelle encouraged him to be thinking of studying for the ministry after graduation from high school in 1948. She suggested he should consider attending either Union Bible College in Westfield, Indiana, Moody Bible Institute in Chicago, Illinois, or Marion College in Marion, Indiana.

She was also concerned that Anniece, with her devotion to Jesus and her instrumental and vocal gifts, not fail to get the kind of education and training that would prepare her for whatever the Lord had in mind for her. Estelle made sure she set aside at least a half hour each week to pray with and encourage Jake and Anniece in an effort to overcome the enemy's attempts to distract, discourage, and mislead them in their critical teen years.

Jake accompanied Jim and Estelle to the Little Rock Revival of 1947. His parents gladly secured his excused absence from school, because they wanted him to experience a moving of the Holy Spirit among larger gatherings than those at the Menard schoolhouse in Nady. Nor were they disappointed! Before the weekend of meetings, Miss Agnes Lockhart—the same reporter who had covered the events both in Hot Springs and in Little Rock—had driven out to the Tharp home, interviewed Estelle, and taken pictures of the whole family. The resulting story had been timed to appear in the *Arkansas Gazette* only a few days before the renewal services. Both Little Rock KARK and KLRA, clear-channel radio stations, carried the announcements of the services. Also, Dr. Jones had run large invitational announcements in both Little Rock dailies, urging that "once again, let all in the Little Rock communities forego the pleasures of vacations and remote trips during this season. Let us **seek first the Kingdom of God and His righteousness** by attending the Spiritual Renewal Services led by Revivalist Estelle Tharp. She was with us one year ago, during which time we saw great outpourings of the Holy Spirit. We urge believers of all Christian denominations to join us as we demonstrate faith and unity and a passion for a mighty spiritual awakening in our city. We also invite those beyond our city to join us for this time of spiritual renewal!"

Estelle went to the WEF, confident of the Spirit's renewal upon her and of the message she was to deliver. On Monday morning after the event at a breakfast meeting with Jim, Estelle, and Jake, Pastor Agnes Diffee said the crowds at the meeting set a new record attendance for the WEF. "Estelle, my sister, I am blessed and encouraged with all that has happened since I met you—the meetings in Hot Springs, and now these two events in Little Rock, and the reports of the great and marvelous things God has done down at Nady. My burden now is to learn what you feel about the spiritual future of the communities around Nady and what God would have you do to preserve the quality of the spiritual lives of the hundreds who have turned to the Lord." She paused and waited for Estelle's response.

"Sister Agnes, I am open to the changes the Lord would bring about to help these hundreds grow into true Christian disciples. Many of them have come out of a life of sin and crime and ignorance. I have nothing but love and appreciation for Pastors Frank Fox and Homer Rich and for the Friends Church with which we are affiliated. However, one night a few weeks ago I had a special visitation from the Lord; He spoke to me about preparing for change. As you know, we experienced a mighty outpouring of the Holy Spirit on that great united baptismal service led by Brother Woody Shields, when more than a thousand new believers were baptized. Baptism, as well as Communion, is not practiced by the Friends. After hearing from Sister Martha, Brother Shields, and Pastor Homer about some doctrinal and practical differences they are feeling, I am not sure that we are to remain in our affiliation with the Friends. We need to be open to God's leading in new directions."

"Sister Estelle, believe me when I say that I have no sectarian motive in commending you for your openness to a new theological direction for what's ahead for Nady and the surrounding communities. I want to pledge to you my daily prayers for God's will. I am happy spiritually and theologically with the WEF, and I've brought a *Manual* and some materials containing the history and polity of our movement, which I ask you to study. And for now, we'll leave it at that. I shall not be initiating any communications with you for the purpose of seeking your affiliation. However, here is my card with my address and telephone number; when I can be of help to you by answering any questions that may arise, I am available. Perhaps when you, as well as a few of your established lay people, are ready to learn what it would mean to affiliate with the WEF, you might want to request an exploratory meeting with the appropriate administrative leader of our district here in Arkansas."

On the drive back home from Little Rock, Jim asked, "Did ye feel that Pastor Diffee was too pushy in tryin' to get us to become members of the WEF?"

"No, I did not. In fact, since Woody Shields, Joshua Stauffer, Homer Rich, Joseph Youmans, and John Newby have all joined the WEF, and it appears that Sister Martha will be joining also, I am open to that change as well. I did not feel Sister Agnes was out of order at all." Turning to Jake, she asked, "Son, what did you think about Sister Agnes' attitude and suggestion that some of us might want to meet with an official of the WEF?"

"Mama, I agree with you that the pastor was merely interested in being helpful and following the Lord's plan for the new converts in Nady. Since Woody Shields suggested that I read about John Wesley, I've learned where his differences lie with the Calvinists. And I happen to know that the Church of the Wesleyan Evangelical Fellowship is the largest denomination advocating Wesleyan-Arminian teachings. I hope you do talk to Spence Sweeney, Uncle George, Uncle Henry, Ross Morgan, Oscar Shelton, Garland Coose, Al Freeman, and perhaps a few others, and then request a meeting with a WEF leader. Study their Articles of Faith and find out what is required of individual members and expected of local churches. Know something about the local, district, and general policies and functions. Then put a lot of prayer behind it and obey the Lord."

471

"Hey, Jake, that's quite a speech! And if I must say so, it sounds like good advice. I believe you've just spoken the will of the Lord for me. Jim, I agree with everything our boy has told us."

"Mama and Daddy, I have been listening to Sister Diffee on the radio almost ever since I got saved. Also, on Saturday I listen to Dr. Oliver, one of their scholars in the church, as he explains the International Sunday School Lesson. He's definitely a brilliant Wesleyan scholar, and he makes the Bible come alive. Every Sunday school teacher should listen to him on Saturday before they try to teach the lesson, if they are following the same materials. By the way, Mama, did you know that the WEF in Little Rock owns that clear-channel station KLRA? Sister Diffee told me that when I told her how much I appreciated their broadcasts."

"No, son, I didn't know that."

"I guess that's why the church can afford so much air time," Jim said.

"I think I'll tune in to this Dr. Oliver," Estelle said.

"Yeah, Mama, you'll enjoy him, and I think you'll agree with him, too! There's one other thing I've been wanting to ask you, Mama," Jake said. "I think I know part of the answer to this, but in what way are Calvinists and Wesleyans alike, and in what ways are they different?"

"Well, son, like John Wesley, I feel we should guard against stressing our differences. But I'd like to begin with the ways in which we are alike. Both Wesleyans and Calvinists believe in the authority of the Scriptures, in the deity of Jesus Christ, in Christ's atoning death on the cross for our sins—the only hope of any human being ever being saved—and in the Second Coming of Christ. Both are Trinitarian, meaning they believe in One God in three Persons: Father, Son, and Holy Spirit. There are more things in which we believe alike. But let me say that *all* Calvinists and Wesleyans who are filled with the Holy Spirit *live alike, pray alike, love alike, and live holy lives.*

"The only difference I wish to mention is that it seems to me like our Calvinistic brothers and sisters in Christ tend to become *presumptuous about the doctrine of perseverance of the saints.* But not all of them! Some Calvinists believe that any sin they would be tempted to commit is already forgiven, so they feel free to sin. While we Wesleyan-Arminians believe that the obedient believer is enabled to resist the sin and by the Spirit deny self. But there are many Calvinists who are sensitive to the Holy Spirit's conviction of their shortfall in holiness, and they immediately repent of their sins and seek a fresh filling of the Holy Spirit so that they might continue in fellowship with God."

"Thanks, Mama! The way you see it makes me feel good, because I just don't like it that God's people are all divided up theologically and fight over Christian doctrines, especially since the Bible says there is only **one church, one Lord, one faith, one baptism, and one God and Father of all who is over all and through all and in all!**"

"Yes, son! And I hope you will always pray to allow that truth to soften your heart in love for all of God's people everywhere. I think nothing grieves the Holy Spirit more than believers fighting over their differences. It seems like most of us are convinced we are right and that everyone who happens to disagree with us is wrong."

The two newlywed couples returned from Little Rock with joyful excitement. Linda rejoiced over seeing her children again and whispered to all three, "You're gonna love yore new daddy! He's wonderful, thoughtful, and will do a lot of good things for us."

Alice pulled Estelle aside and said, "Oh, Miss Estelle, it's wonderful to be married to this man! My husband's got a way of makin' me know I ain't no whore no more!"

"Of course, you're not! All of your sins are under the blood of Jesus, and God has decreed to never remember them against you anymore. You are now a new creation in Jesus Christ! You are ordered of Him to enjoy your married life. Don't forget the Scripture in Hebrews 13:4, which reads, **Let marriage be held in honor among all, and let the marriage bed be undefiled; for God will judge the immoral and adulterous**. Just praise God for grace for a new beginning in life—with the Lord, with a good husband, and with a new spiritual family."

With Alice and Linda pitching in to help, Estelle prepared a feast for the evening meal. As they all sat down to eat together, peace settled over all three homes represented at the table.

Jay and Linda and the three teenagers left with the promise that they would like to return in the morning to pay off Linda's farm and to share their thinking about their future.

The Reddons were more generous in paying off the farm than Jim and Estelle required. Jay reasoned that he wanted to make up for Jim's generosity in carrying Linda when she couldn't make ends meet. Jim insisted the four of them go to the clerk's office in DeWitt that day and legally record the transaction.

"Jim, would you consider selling Linda and me yore farm, orchard, house, cattle, and all yore equipment?" Jay asked.

"Well, Jay, let Estelle and me have a little time to think and pray about the orchard and the cattle. Ye know I don't own all the land we've got cattle on; I lease some of that acreage from Anderson-Telly. If y'all are interested in buyin' me out—the whole outfit—I think we'll need to have a little time to decide on that."

"Yeah, I reckon so," Jay replied. "Now, money ain't no problem! I'll have to have the land, the equipment for planting, cutting, and baling the hay, and all that goes with it—the whole outfit, iffen you're willing to sell. I'd also want yore nice Pontiac sedan and yore tractors and trucks, 'specially the big trucks and the new pickup.

When Jim told Estelle what Jay suggested, her eyes lit up. Then a sadness seemed to creep over her. Finally she said, "Honey, it seems to me the Lord is preparing us for change; this may be of the Lord, but I'm not sure yet. Let's just tell Jay and Linda that we'll need time to pray about this. For one thing, I'm not sure how well you'll adjust to a new way of life without your fishing, trapping, logging, hunting, and running cattle. And besides, there's your work with the sheriff."

"I ain't gonna pretend I won't miss most of it. But I might be more ready for a change than ye know. At least I ain't had to kill anybody since I got saved—haven't even put a hole in anyone's ear. I kinda like that way of livin'. Course, I been heppin' Lloyd some, but on stuff that ain't been so dangerous. No, let's just pray and see how the Lord leads us. I trust Him enough to know it's always best goin' His way."

Estelle praised the Lord silently for Jim's determination to live the new life. She simply nodded in agreement and said, "We'll know what we are to do in a week or so, and then you can give Jay and Linda our answer."

In a meeting with Sheriff LaFargue in early November, Lloyd remarked, "Well, Jim, what we didn't have to do to bring the lower end of Arkansas County back into bein' a law-abidin' area, it seems like the Lord has done—conquered all them outlaws who thought nothin' of murderin', rapin', lyin', and stealin'. I think we owe a great deal to your wife, Estelle, and those she had prayin' with her. At least I've heard her claim that the credit for the great revival belonged to God and His prayin' intercessors."

"Yeah, she's said that a lotta times," Jim said. "I wish ye could see and hear them fellers we once thought were hopeless tell how God has made the difference in their lives. They now study their Bibles, attend the house of God, get up and pray and testify, and even tell their sinner friends that they need to get right with God. Lloyd, I know the same God who changed them has changed me. Now, I never felt good about killin' those men who would have killed you or me, and I don't know if I should go on servin' as your special deputy much longer. Of course, if ye say ye need me, it would be hard for me to up and quit ye."

"Well, Jim, we now have a patrolable situation down in yore area. It would be easier to let ye go now than it ever has been before. But I'd like to keep ye on as my special deputy for as long as I'm sheriff or as long as ye would be willin' to serve. The county owes ye a lot, and I'm sure in yore debt. Ye've saved my life several times. Never think that I'm ungrateful, Jim."

On a cold, snowy winter evening, Estelle hosted a dinner meeting to which she invited as special guests Dr. Paul S. Rees, General Superintendent of the Wesleyan Evangelical Fellowship, and Pastor Agnes Diffee, Pastor of the First Wesleyan Evangelical Fellowship in Little Rock. Also included were her husband, Jim, and her son Jake, as well as six others from the fellowship of believers: Thelma Bonner, George Best, Spencer Sweeney, Morgan Tharp, Garland Coose, and Ross Morgan. Pastor Diffee introduced Dr. Rees, explaining that she had been wanting their principal international leader to visit her church in Little Rock. She thought bringing the fruit of the great revival in Nady into the right fellowship was important enough that, besides inviting him to fill her pulpit one Sunday, she arranged for Dr. Rees to explain to a committee in Nady the purpose and mission of the WEF.

After a delicious dinner, they all retired to the living room where Dr. Rees began by saying, "I do remember Jim and Estelle Tharp from a special meeting called at Union Bible College in Westfield, Indiana, back in 1938. And it is a special privilege to be in your home and to rejoice with you in the great outpouring of the Holy Spirit here last year, bringing hundreds of new believers into the Kingdom of God. I have nothing but love and respect for the influence of the Friends Church and Dr. Martha Honeycutt and Pastors Frank Fox and Homer Rich, under whose guidance the body of Christ has been operating in Nady. However, I do respect the small differences in the beliefs and practices of the Friends and the WEF. For a period of time in my earlier years, I worshiped with the Friends, but I felt the Spirit's leadership in shifting to the WEF. With your permission, I shall present the Articles of Faith and explain the theology of the WEF; then, you might have questions about some of the points.

"I'll begin with our Articles of Faith—The Bible, The Holy Trinity, The Deity of Christ, The Holy Spirit, The Atoning Death of Jesus Christ and His Resurrection from the Dead, Salvation by Faith, Sanctification by Faith, Called Unto Holiness, The Second Coming of Christ, The Great Commission, The Church of Jesus Christ, The Ordinances, and The Divine Judgments."

Ross asked, "Dr. Rees, what are the differences of beliefs between the Friends Church and the WEF?"

"The only differences that I can note are in the ordinances of Water Baptism and the Lord's Supper or Holy Communion. While the Friends see them as unnecessary, we believe the Lord Jesus commanded us to observe them as a memorial to Him and as "a means of grace." Both organizations embrace Wesleyan theology in stressing that believers must respond to the call to holiness by totally surrendering their hearts and lives and asking for the cleansing and filling of the Holy Spirit. We feel that this practice helps us avoid the presumption that our Calvinistic friends fall into in their teaching on *the perseverance of the saints*. Calvin taught that in the new birth the believer is forgiven of all past, present, and future sins; we teach that in the new birth we are forgiven of all past and present sins. While we do not teach sinless perfection, we do insist that when a believer sins, he or she must confess the sin and that immediately he or she is forgiven and restored to fellowship. What we believe is that by not confessing our sins, believers break fellowship with God and will eventually willfully forfeit eternal life. While many Calvinists teach that once we have been born again we cannot possibly be lost, neither the Friends nor the WEF embrace this tenet of Calvinism. Other than the two ordinances I have mentioned, your beliefs and practices as a fellowship in the body will remain practically as it was in the Friends Church. I'll present to Estelle a *WEF Manual* for your further study.

"I understand that I am invited to preach to you this coming Sunday morning, and I'm pleased that Pastor Diffee and her husband will be with us. Everyone is invited to come and perhaps get a better understanding of what WEF services are like. I suspect you'll find there is no difference from the way you have worshiped in the Friends Church. Then on Wednesday night, we'll begin a series of meetings in Pastor Diffee's church in Little Rock and conclude next Sunday night. Pastor Diffee, do you or Estelle wish to take charge at this time to perhaps give our brothers and sisters here an opportunity to express themselves before a vote is taken on the direction you desire to go?"

Pastor Diffee responded,"Dr. Rees, I'd like to say that while I am highly recommending that the communities affiliate with WEF, Dr. Rees and I are not here to twist arms or to try and proselyte members. We simply want to help preserve the fruit of the great revival. I would remind you that we are here at the urging of Dr. Honeycutt, the Reverends Woody Shields and Homer Rich, and Dr. Joshua Stauffer. Estelle, you might want to tell us about Sister Martha's concerns for the future of the body of Christ here in Nady."

"Yes, thank you, Pastor Diffee. I can assure all of us here tonight that it is Sister Martha's desire that we join with WEF instead of remaining with the Friends. I am opening this meeting for any feelings pro or con on this matter before we take a vote."

Garland said, "Estelle, I do love the spirit of this gathering tonight, but I must say that I've been perfectly happy with the teachings and practices of the Friends and would be disappointed to break with it."

Thelma Bonner said, "I understand how my brother Garland feels, but I'm more inclined to believe that our future lies with WEF. I've listened to Dr. Oliver on the Little Rock radio station for years, and I've heard Sister Agnes Diffee preach the new birth and Christian holiness in a most biblical fashion. And I do want to see new Christians baptized in water as well as in the Holy Spirit, and I enjoy taking Communion every once in awhile. So I urge us to prayerfully consider joining the WEF."

Ross spoke next. "Thelma has expressed my feelings perfectly. Even our spiritual parents, the Riches, the Youmans, the Shields, and others have joined WEF, and they are urging us to do the same. I'm ready. Let's join WEF."

Spencer Sweeney stood and said, "First of all, I'm a firm believer in my Lord Jesus Christ, but I have the utmost confidence in my sister Estelle. She's carried the burden for the great revival and is continuing to carry great concerns for hundreds of us who were born of the Spirit during those meetings. I listen to her teach the Word Sunday after Sunday, and I feel her concern that we affiliate with a powerful Biblical movement that will help us preserve what the Lord has birthed. I have thoroughly enjoyed Dr. Rees's presentation here tonight and look forward to his message on Sunday. I'm ready to cast my lot with WEF."

Feeling that Spencer had clinched the debate in favor of WEF, Estelle continued: "Alright, is there an expression from Uncle Morg, or George, or Jim?" All three shook their heads indicating they did not wish to comment. "Then I want to pass out secret ballots, and after we have prayed, you will vote. You'll write either YES, meaning you're voting to unite with WEF; or you'll write NO, meaning you're voting to remain with the Friends. I do appreciate and respect Garland's wish to remain with the Friends. I should tell you that Jim and I went to DeWitt and visited with Pastor Fox concerning this meeting tonight. I invited him here, knowing that he hoped we would remain with the Friends. He does know that the majority here is likely to vote to join WEF, but I wanted him to feel free to express his heart."

Estelle passed out blank slips of paper and then prayed that "we shall have divine guidance in making a choice that will please the Lord in what is best for believers in this part of our state." Jim and Ross were asked to gather and count the votes. There were six votes YES and one vote NO. Estelle closed the meeting by announcing, "This means we will inform Pastor Fox about our decision to disaffiliate with the Friends Church. Then we shall invite the proper authorities from WEF to come and organize a WEF congregation here in Nady. Let's be in prayer for a great service with Dr. Rees this Sunday morning."

Pastor Diffee and her husband spent Friday and Saturday nights with Ross and Flossie Morgan, and Dr. Rees stayed in the Tharp's cabin. The Sunday morning service was well attended despite the weather being cold and snowy. Sister Diffee announced that a committee representing the congregation had voted to disaffiliate with the Friends Church and unite with the WEF. Dr. Rees spoke on "The Body of Christ" and spelled out its purposes and gave some history of the WEF. There seemed to be a friendly and interested atmosphere. After the closing prayer, Estelle invited the people to come forward and get acquainted with their two guests.

In the following weeks, uniting with the WEF seemed to be a favored direction by most of the community. Two or three remarks had been made to the contrary, but Estelle did not believe they were significant enough to be concerned. She wrote Pastor Fox of the decision and extended an open invitation to come and begin disaffiliation procedures.

Jim was glad when the trapping season ended, because for several years in a row trapping coons and minks had become less profitable. Also he no longer looked forward to new fishing seasons for the same reason. They had decided to sell out to Jay and Linda. About the middle of March, the Reddons could count on farming their new land, taking over the orchard, and having control of the cattle and equipment.

Jim was glad he had allowed Estelle to influence his thinking about moving north. "Well now, how far north do ye think we might move—to DeWitt, or clear up near the Canadian border?" Jim asked.

"Honey, I'm thinking maybe even as far north as Central Indiana, but I can't really say at this point," Estelle said. "You should have as much say in this as I do. We need to consider how a move will affect our children, how we can make a living, and—most of all—what the Lord has for us to do."

"Well, if we are to leave here, I don't think of any place else in this state I would want to live. So if it's Indiana, that's okay with me, except I don't know how I would make a livin' there. I'm sure trappin', fishin', and timberin' are not a part of my future if we move there. But maybe I'm supposed to do somethin' else. Right now, we've got to find another place to live, cuz Jay and Linda are buyin' this whole place."

"Well, I may have the answer to that," Estelle said. "Mama just told me that she is getting married to a fine Christian gentleman, a Mr. Castetter from Noblesville, Indiana, and she's moving there and taking her mother, my Grandma Best, with her. She's wanting us to move down on her place. I told her I would talk to you about it and let her know."

"Then if we moved on her place, I could be closer to fishin' the Arkansas River and closer to the lakes we seine in the summer. But I'd miss the trappin' up here."

"You could still drive up here and trap the same areas you've been trapping for years. You don't own that trapping territory anyway," Estelle reminded him. "And if you want to keep Flash and the buckskin, you'll have barn space at Mother's place."

"Yes, I'd like to keep the horses for now. It might be time to sign off with Lloyd. Lots of changes comin', I reckon.

"Yes, darling. No doubt some of these changes will be painful. But if we're in the Lord's will, He'll help us work it out."

Jim spent the first week of 1948 visiting first with Ross, then with Uncle Henry Purdy, and finally with Uncle Hay. He thought Ross was more realistic about the price of cattle, land, and equipment than were the other two. He talked it over with Estelle and on a Friday night the first part of March, they invited Jay and Linda to come for supper.

After supper, Alice and Anniece cleaned up the kitchen while Jim and Estelle and Jay and Linda went over to the cabin to talk business. Estelle had made a list of the number of cattle Jim and Jake had counted, the number of acres and their location, each farm implement and motor vehicle, and the number of each kind of fruit trees in the orchard—apple, peach, pear, and plum.

"Well, folks, we wanta buy the whole thang—lock, stock, and barrel," Jay said. "I don't care what y'all are askin'."

"Jay and Linda," Jim said, leaning forward and looking at them both, "I've consulted with three different people whose judgment I've relied on across the years, and I've took the suggestion of the one who was the lowest price. He pretty well knows land, cattle, and equipment." Turning to Estelle, he said, "Honey, tell them what I think is a fair price for all of this."

Estelle picked up a third page and read the figure written at the top.

Jay looked at Linda, and said, "Hey! Linda, they're lower than I told ye they'd be!"

"Yeah, well, Mr. Jim and Miz Estelle, we don't expect ye to give yore property away just because ye love us like family," Linda said.

"No, we're not makin' any cuts cuz y'all are like family," Jim said. "This is what we believe is a fair price right now, given the way the postwar economy is goin' here in the country. But Jay I want you to have Flash and the buckskin at no additional cost. They are good for a few more years yet, and they will come in handy working with the cattle. If ye need to put some of this price on a loan, I'm sure we can come to reasonable terms."

"Naw! We're able to pay cash. But I hope ye'll take a check for the full amount. I can assure you I'm worth millions, and I've got many times more in the DeWitt First National Bank than whut yore askin' fer all this." Jay pulled his checkbook out of his shirt pocket and started writing a check. He explained, "They tole me to wait thirty days 'fore I drawed any of it out, but it's been a little longer. So ye won't have any trouble gettin' yer money anytime ye wanta cash this. And another thang—Linda and me don't want y'all feelin' ye gotta move outa here real soon. Take yore time and wait 'til summer if ye wanta."

13   Going Home

After selling their place and everything else Jim and Estelle didn't need, they moved to her mother's place at Nady. The location was ideal for the family to go to Sunday worship and for the children to attend school. The property was near the river where Jim fished.

One last thing stood in the way of their remaining in Arkansas—despite Alma Wallace's desire to sell her place to Estelle and Jim, family members objected. More and more it seemed to Jim and Estelle that they were to move to Indiana. There they could be near two of their married children and Estelle's mother.

Estelle missed the cabin where she had prayed several hours a week, but on her mother's place she found the wooded area between the house and the hayfield on the west a desirable spot to walk and pray. She spent no less time in prayer there than she had before their move. She placed a comfortable chair out there to sit in when she was not pacing. She kept her Bible and books beside the chair in a waterproof metal suitcase to protect them from the elements. She also kept in contact with the Bonnhoffers and Dr. Baylor in Hot Springs, Dr. Jones and Pastor Diffee in Little Rock, and Sister Martha in Indiana; she enjoyed covering their ministries in intercession.

Another concern Estelle had that delayed their move to Indiana was a threatening division among the believers in the Nady congregation. An ultraconservative group had come in from Pennsylvania and had begun a program of worship promoting their views on sanctification and "standards of holiness." This grieved Estelle, especially since Henry, Jim's brother, embraced their teachings wholeheartedly. She risked a break in fellowship with her brother-in-law by saying, "Henry, the Scriptures should be our guide in a dress code for women—modesty, humility, and decency should dictate our outward appearance. Your requirements that your women style their hair and wear their dresses to a certain length will lead to legalistic extremes that will grieve the Holy Spirit and divide families and congregations. Please don't fall into a judgmental attitude that will cause division and make a mockery of true biblical holiness!"

Jim and Estelle were delighted when the spiritual authorities of WEF assigned a Spirit-filled young pastor to the Nady Church. Pastor and Mrs. Brad Huntley and their two small children arrived in early April from Allentown, Pennsylvania. Pastor Brad had only been out of seminary five years, and during that time he had planted a church in eastern Pennsylvania that had become a powerful congregation. But he felt led of the Spirit to come to a more primitive community and take up the work of discipling many new believers and preserving the fruit of the great revival of 1946. He had been made aware of a growing interest among several believers in the Nady church to organize another congregation that would hold to stricter dress codes for women. Being a man of prayer and determined to follow the leadership of the Holy Spirit, Pastor Brad became an example in practicing what he preached: "In essentials, unity; in nonessentials, liberty; in all things, charity."

Seeing the preservation of the fruit of the revival and growth in the WEF, Jim and Estelle felt released to begin planning their move. Estelle believed that the Lord had made it clear that they were to move *northward.* "Now, Jim, we have two married children living in Central Indiana. I feel it would please the Lord for us to take our younger children and trust the Lord to help us make a new life and have a new ministry in that part of Indiana. I'd enjoy fellowship with Sister Martha, the Riches, the Shields, the Kerchevals, and the Youmans. We'd find a body of believers to worship with and help advance God's kingdom. I might even be able to teach militant intercession and see revival in Indiana."

Estelle told Jim they would have another baby in the spring of 1950, probably the middle of April. Jim said, "Honey, this will make our tenth child, won't it? I think it ought to be the last one."

"No doubt it will be, dear. But I'm just as excited about this one as I was the first."

Paul Arnold, their tenth child, was born April 15, 1950.

Four years had gone by, and Jim began pressing Estelle to set a date for leaving Arkansas County. "If I'm to unbuckle my gun and give away my traps and nets, then I've got to get where I can develop a new way of makin' a livin'. We've got a good amount in the bank, but it won't last forever. It's now 1954. I'm 48 years old and ye're 46. We've got four married children: Jeanette, Jake, Anniece, and Russ; and six still at home. I reckon we oughta get to Indiana! It will be good to be near our older children, but we don't want to impose on them in any way."

"Honey, we won't have to do that. We've got money to either buy a house or rent, whichever we want to do. Let's not worry over finances. The Lord has helped us in our 28 years of marriage here, and He will help us for however long we have left. He'll be faithful to us in Indiana. I know you will find something to do that will be fulfilling and rewarding financially. You're intelligent, hardworking, and reliable. The Lord will provide you a place and a good situation. I have a witness from the Spirit on that!"

"Alright then, set the date, and then ye'd better tell Pastor Huntley. He said he wanted ye to give a farewell message before we leave. He puts a lot of stock in ye; he knows that, with the Lord's help, ye held the people together durin' yore years of leadership after the great revival. I'm sure he has felt yore influence in holdin' most of the people in the WEF."

"Darling, I think I can be ready in a week. Why don't we tell Pastor Huntley that next Sunday night will be our last service. We'll see how far we get in disposing of things during the next few days. We'll need to spend some time with your parents, BettyLee and George, Tassy and Garland, and Henry and Oda. Of course, you've got to take care of the milk cows. Then you need to get a shell for the pickup so that the children will be out of the weather on our trip to Indiana. Burl says he's staying here to finish high school. Carroll insists he's going, and then he changes his mind and says he wants to stay here so that he can fish, trap, and hunt. So we need to help him decide."

"I'm sure glad that a few years ago Uncle Henry Purdy agreed to take good care of Star and Buck until they died a natural death. That shore beat what I thought I'd have to do with 'em. Let's go to DeWitt tomorrow so that I can tell Lloyd goodbye."

When Jim told the sheriff they were moving to Indiana within a week, Lloyd called a photographer to come to his office to take their picture together. He explained to the photographer, "I'm writin' a story for the *Gazette* and *Era Enterprise* and sayin' goodbye to Jim Tharp, wishin' him and Estelle a good new life up in Indiana." Knowing they had a lot to do to in a short length of time, Jim said they needed to be on their way. Shaking hands with Jim, Lloyd said "the State of Arkansas, and especially Arkansas County, owe you more than we could ever pay you. Thank you, and may God bless you! And, Estelle, that goes for you, too!"

As Estelle was praying in her special place later that day, the Holy Spirit revealed what she should say to the Christians in the prairie and bottoms communities on Sunday night. Pastor Huntley had made the communities aware of the Tharps' farewell through the *DeWitt Era Enterprise*. When Jim and Estelle arrived at the new church building that had been erected, it was packed and hundreds were on the outside. People were there from Hot Springs, Little Rock, and many remote areas of the county. It appeared that most, if not all, of the new converts from the bottoms were present.

Pastor Huntley introduced Estelle with a few appropriate remarks and then said, "Welcome a woman of God who has been instrumental in birthing the great revival through travailing prayer until we've seen a mighty rending of the heavens. I know God has given her a final word for us that we will want to hear and heed." The applause on both the inside and the outside was deafening and prolonged.

In the early part of her discourse, Estelle spoke humbly about "nights of weeping" in sacrificial intercession for the mighty outpouring of the Holy Spirit. Then she praised God for the hundreds who had been saved and rejoiced over the way the Spirit had helped in preserving the fruit of the revival. She expressed confidence in the WEF and Pastor Huntley's anointing to hold believers together in spiritual unity in the Nady communities.

Estelle requested prayers that she and Jim and the children would find the Lord's will for a continuing ministry in Indiana. Then she said, "I leave you with five commands—imperatives from the Word of God. I believe the Lord wants me to emphasize that they are absolutely essential if this community experiences divine blessing and approval in the years to come. The key word is CONTINUE!

"CONTINUE to **be filled with the Spirit** (Eph. 5:18). "Keep on being filled with the Spirit" is the true meaning of the text. **Keep in step with the Spirit, Do not grieve the Holy Spirit, Do not quench the Spirit**. Maintain your relationship with Him. When you are convicted of falling short of the will of God, repent—ask His forgiveness and begin again with a renewal of obedience.

"CONTINUE **steadfastly in prayer** (Col. 4:2). Pray about your prayer life. Plan to meet with the Lord for a time each day. Spend part of some nights in prayer. Pray with the family. Pray with brothers and sisters in Christ. Pray about everything. No matter how gifted, how intelligent, how sincere we are, we simply cannot stay filled with the Spirit if we grow weak in prayer. If you allow Satan to defeat you in this, he can defeat you anywhere.

"CONTINUE **in one accord** (John 17:21). Jesus prayed **that they may all be one; even as thou, Father, art in me, and I in thee, that they also may be in us, so that the world may believe that thou has sent me**. We will not all agree even in Christian doctrine or in our understanding of the Bible, but we can all love one another, bear one another's burdens, and pray for one another. The Spirit simply will not work powerfully among a congregation, or even in a community, where there is dissension, criticism, and backbiting. We cannot win our loved ones and our neighbors to Jesus when we professing Christians do not love one another.

"CONTINUE **to make disciples** (Matt. 28:19). Don't leave it all up to the pastors and church staff; we are all called to be Christ's witnesses. This is the main task of the church. Let's train our new Christians to understand the simple Gospel story so that they can share it with any loved one, friend, or neighbor, without having to call the pastor to come and lead them to Christ. We should all be winning people to Jesus! I am not an educated woman. I do not have a seminary degree. And yet in the early months of 1946, it was my privilege to lead over 50 people to Jesus in their homes or in our home. And I see some of them here tonight. So make sure you share the Gospel and win people to Jesus; then, see that they become discipled in the Word of God and the ways of the Lord.

"CONTINUE **to seek holiness of heart and life** (Heb. 12:14). The WEF has been faithful from its beginning to emphasize that God has called us to a state of grace in which we are totally yielded to Jesus Christ as Lord, fully cleansed, filled with His sanctifying Spirit, and consistently anointed to bear **the fruit of the spirit**. Never be ashamed of being molded into the likeness of Jesus Christ. Holiness is Christlikeness in our daily lives. We are called to bear the fruit of the Spirit: **love, joy, peace, patience, kindness, goodness, faithfulness, gentleness, and self-control**.

And now I leave with you my final admonition, taken from the apostle Paul in Philippians 4:8-9: **Finally, brethren, whatever is true, whatever is honorable, whatever is just, whatever is lovely, whatever is gracious, if there is any excellence, if there is anything worthy of praise, think about these things. What you have learned and received and heard and seen in me, do; and the God of peace will be with you**."

As Estelle sat down with Jim and the children on the front seat, the applause began. After several seconds, people began standing. It was the longest period of applause Pastor Huntley had ever witnessed. He went to the platform and said, "We have heard powerful words from our dear sister who has been a model among us in all we have heard from her. I want to call on Pastor Frank Fox to come and lead a prayer as we gather around Jim, Estelle, and the children and commit them to the Lord for all that He has planned for them in the years ahead up in Indiana. Jim and Estelle, come and form a circle, and put your children in the circle. As many as can fill the aisles, put your hands remotely on them by touching those ahead of you, who will eventually be touching those of us immediately around them. After Pastor Fox prays, we'll sing the Doxology and then you'll have an opportunity to personally say goodbye to them at the door as you leave. So hold steady, dear people. It's not late. Let's take time to honor these who have meant so very much to us!"

The next morning, Jim divided his nets and traps between George and Henry, declining their offer to pay him for them. He borrowed Ross's truck and hauled three milk cows to Uncle Hay's place in Tichnor, asking him to put the cows on the market when convenient, deduct his commission, and send him a check for the balance to his daughter Anniece's address. After shaking hands with the old feeble gentleman, Jim returned Ross's truck and went home. "Well, Estelle, I'm ready to go. We've given everythang away, and tonight we'll sleep on these beds for the last time. Tomorrow after we're gone, the people will come and get the beds, mattresses, and other things we've marked for 'em."

On the second Tuesday of May of 1954, Jim, Estelle, and five of their children—Carroll, Shirley, Martha, Joe, and Paul—left Nady for their two-day drive to Zionsville, Indiana. They would spend a few nights there with their daughter Anniece and her husband, Don, until they could rent or buy a place of their own. On the second day of their journey after they had eaten breakfast in Carthage, Missouri, Estelle said, "Honey, I've been praying about your future work, and I know the Lord wants to provide something that you'll be fulfilled and happy in doing. What do you think you'd like to do up in Indiana?

"Well, since I know I can't go into farmin' and raisin' cattle or fishin', timberin', and trappin' like I'm used to doin', I've thought about somethin' else I'd like to do. You'll remember that when we bought the place from Tom Monk, we had Henry buildin' the barn, smokehouse, cabin, and sheds. Well, I hepped some, and I really admired Henry's ability to draw things out, follow his plan, and put things together. I enjoyed watchin' him and wished I had the same ability. So, here's what I been thinkin'. I know a lot of buildin' is goin' on up there. If I found a contractor I liked, talked to 'im, and felt he took a likin' to me, I'd ask 'im if he would take me on as a learner buildin' houses, barns, or whatever. I would learn how to frame buildin's, pour concrete, do drywall and plaster, lay block and brick, and do rafters and roofin'. I'd tell 'im to pay me a low wage to start, and then as I learned to do things the way he wanted and improved my skills, maybe he'd raise my hourly wage to where I could make a good livin'."

"Sweetheart, I believe the Lord will provide the person you are to meet to help you become a first-class carpenter and earn a good living. I just have this feeling that as we pray, we won't be in Indiana very long before you'll meet the right builder who will like you and take you on with the terms you set forth. I also feel we'll find the right Christian fellowship in the right community, where we can rent or buy a good house. Carroll will find the right kind of friends, and we'll be able to put the girls in good schools. Eventually, you and I can start a prayer ministry!"

"Well, with you prayin' the way ye do, I got a feelin' we'll see good things happen."

"Honey, you mean with *both of us praying*! Oh, I thank God you have now been praying *with* me for eight wonderful years!"

"Yeah, and I plan to keep on prayin' with ye, too!"

When Jim and Estelle and their children arrived in Zionsville and felt the welcome and warmth of their daughter Anniece and their son-in-law Don, their spirits were lifted. Estelle and Jim were delighted to get acquainted with their six-month-old granddaughter, Diana. Anniece and Don were anxious to be helpful and wanted them to know they need be in no hurry to rent a house. Right away, and with Jim's consent, Estelle asked Anniece to try and find the nearest Wesleyan Evangelical Fellowship in the phone book. The church they chose would help determine where they lived.

The nearest WEF was in Kirklin, about 22 miles from Zionsville. The next morning after their arrival, Jim and Estelle left the children with Anniece and drove north to Kirklin. They found the WEF on Main Street and met the pastor and his wife, Rev. and Mrs. Barse, who were warm in their reception. When Jim and Estelle asked if they knew about any houses for rent, they told them about one that was probably large enough, but it didn't have indoor plumbing. They also learned the location of the high school where Shirley would attend and the school in Kirklin where Martha and Joe would attend.

Estelle had hoped for an indoor bathroom and running water, but since the house was large enough for their family and clean, they decided to rent it. When they went to the landlord's home to pay the rent, Jim met the next-door neighbor, Henry Reynolds, and learned that he was a building contractor. "Mr. Reynolds, I don't know if ye're in need of another hand in carpentry or not, but I'd be interested in workin' for ye."

"Have you had experience in carpentry?" the middle-aged builder asked.

"No, but here's my story. We just moved up from Arkansas, where I farmed and raised cattle and spent a great deal of time in commercial fishin' and trappin' for minks. I made a good livin' for my family. When I got ready to put up some buildin's on my place—a log cabin, large barns, implement sheds, and a smokehouse—I didn't know how to build 'em, but I helped the fellers I hired. And I thought then how good it would be to learn buildin' skills. Now I'm not an educated man, and I don't care to work in a factory—but I'm a hard worker. I would like to find a builder who would take a chance on me, startin' me at low pay, if necessary. As I learn the skills needed to do the construction jobs, I would hope he would be fair with me and raise my pay so that I could make enough money to support my family."

Hank Reynolds said, "Jim Tharp, I like the looks of you and I like the way you talk. In two weeks I will begin on two houses right out here just off Route 38 between Kirklin and Frankfort. I'd like to have you begin two weeks from today. I'll start you at $5 an hour, and when you improve in skills and abilities, I'll be fair with you. Write down on this sheet of paper your name, address, date of birth, and Social Security number, and fill out the other information. Drop it off here sometime before nine o'clock tonight, and I'll look for you on Monday morning at eight o'clock, two weeks from now."

When Jim and Estelle left the small town of Kirklin at four o'clock in the afternoon to head back to Anniece's home, they had found a church, schools for the children, and a house to rent. Jim had also found work, and they had opened a bank account and applied for a telephone.

Their oldest daughter, Jeanette, and her husband, Don, lived about 15 miles away from Zionsville. Anniece invited them to come for supper the second day after her folks had arrived. That evening, the two daughters came up with items of furniture that left Jim and Estelle only beds, a stove, and a refrigerator to buy. They purchased these and other needed items the next day; four days from their arrival they were in their own home and looking forward to visiting their son in the east. Jake and his wife, Maxine, had moved to Pennsylvania to pastor a church, and he had told his parents that as soon as they could get settled in Indiana, he wanted them and his siblings still living at home to come there for a visit. "We've got ten days before I go to work," Jim said, "so let's call Jake and see if it's convenient for us to go east now so that I can get back in time to go to work."

Jake and his friend Johnny Bright came to pick up the family in Johnny's new Chrysler. As they traveled across the country, Jim, Estelle, and the older children enjoyed the scenery in Ohio, West Virginia, and Pennsylvania; they had never seen high mountains. Arriving after dark in Hellertown, Pennsylvania, they were welcomed by Maxine and the three children: Deborah, Steve, and Priscilla. They enjoyed seeing the historic sights in Philadelphia, got their first glimpse of the Atlantic Ocean, saw the Statue of Liberty, and were actually glad to get out of New York City and head back through New Jersey to eastern Pennsylvania. Back in Indiana, Estelle reported to Jeanette and Anniece that the highlights of the trip east were "being with Jake, Maxine, and the grandchildren; hearing Jake preach; and seeing the historic sights of Philadelphia, the Atlantic Ocean, and the Statue of Liberty."

On the first Sunday of June in 1954, the Tharp family was introduced to a small group of 40 people gathered to worship at the WEF in Kirklin. Jim and Estelle were accustomed to worshiping in Nady, Arkansas, with several times the number of people and a church body that was much more alive spiritually. But both felt led to be patient and prayerful and faithful to the Lord and to their praying ministry.

Pastor Barse soon learned of Estelle's prayer life and her experience in revival work. He invited her to join the church staff as an unpaid prayer leader to organize prayer groups, teach the church body the biblical conditions for revival, and lead sessions on intercessory prayer. Estelle was excited about organizing and preparing the Kirklin WEF for a spiritual awakening.

Jim found his work with Hank Reynolds fulfilling, and within six months he was making the same as Hank's best-paid workers—even the masons who laid blocks, tile, bricks, and stone. One night Jim told Estelle, "I never thought I would say it, but I no longer miss settin' traps, seinin' lakes and rivers, and raisin' cattle. Aw, I would enjoy saddlin' Star and takin' him and Buck for a few hours in the bottoms or on the prairie, but that's all behind me and I ain't lookin' back. I reckon I ain't makin' the money I did in Arkansas, but I ain't havin' to shoot bad men's ears or hearts."

"Honey, we are making ends meet, and you are learning the building work. We are seeing the church grow—people are getting saved, we now have 15 prayer warriors praying for revival, and the little building is packed three times a week. Now, the church board and pastor are searching for land to build so we can accommodate the crowds."

"Are the children and you happy?" Jim asked.

"Carroll is determined to not go to high school, but he is helping us garden and doing some work for the market downtown. He's listening to us about keeping good, clean company. The four in school are doing well. And little Paul is growing up fast, as you can see.

"My mother and her husband are a joy to be with, when we can get together. Of course, Anniece and Jeanette, their husbands, and our grandchildren are a blessing. So, honey, while I miss your mother and we miss Burl, George and BettyLee, and the Nady fellowship, I think we are right where God wants us."

"Well, that's what I wanted to hear, cuz I'm shore happy here."

"I am too, honey. I've been over to Union Bible College and visited with Dr. William Smith and Dr. Simeon and LaVaun Smith. They've asked me to speak in Chapel twice next month. And Dr. Hertel has invited me to speak on revival in Chapel at the Frankfort College."

The 1960s saw several changes in the lives of the Tharp children. Burl finished high school in Gillette, Arkansas, and then moved to Kirklin to live with his parents in the early 60s; a few years later, he married a Kirklin girl. Russell, during his time in the U.S. Army, met and married a girl from Colorado. Carroll married a girl from Indiana. Shirley finished high school and then married the son of a WEF pastor. Martha graduated high school and college, and then married a WEF pastor. Joe married an Indiana girl.

The 1970s brought both joy and sorrow into the lives of Jim and Estelle. Jim retired from carpentry work, after which he did some quail hunting with his sons Burl and Paul; eventually, Jim took up work as caretaker of several cemeteries. He also enjoyed growing large gardens with Estelle and the children.

The spiritual changes in the Kirklin WEF congregation, as influenced by the prayer ministries of Jim and Estelle and the many trained prayer warriors under Estelle's influence, resulted in true revival in Central Indiana. The Kirklin WEF outgrew its facility and then built and dedicated a new church building, which was packed to capacity in most services.

In the summer of 1971, Jim and Estelle lost the youngest of their ten children. Paul was killed in Vietnam while serving as a military policeman with the U.S. Army. Just before his death, Paul had written letters to his parents telling of his joy in finding Christ as his Savior. He assured them that if he did not return to them after the war, he would be meeting them in Heaven. Jim said, "Well, if it took Vietnam to help our son make up his mind to come to the Lord, then I'm glad he went there."

On Sunday, August 29, 1976, more than 500 people gathered at Jim and Estelle Tharp's home in Kirklin, Indiana, to celebrate their 50th wedding anniversary. The guests included their children and grandchildren, other relatives from a number of states, many believers Jim and Estelle had influenced for Christ, and their neighbors. Some of the leaders of the great Arkansas County Revival of 1946 were present— Rev. and Mrs. Homer Rich, Rev. and Mrs. Woody Shields, and Mr. and Mrs. Charles Kercheval. Scores left that event declaring, "This has been like attending a great camp meeting where the Holy Spirit has poured out on all of us, and we have a fresh filling of His power!"

Before Jim could allow the family of George and BettyLee Best to leave for Arkansas after the reunion, he approached his nephew Buddy. "Son, I just feel like I need to strongly urge ye to make up yore mind to surrender yore life to Jesus! I love ye, and I can't stand sayin' goodbye to ye without sharin' my concern. Come aside over here under the shade; I wanta pray for ye."

Buddy was weeping as he followed his uncle across the yard. He knew as he listened to his Uncle Jim's tearful prayer, he would make up his mind to serve the Lord! "Uncle Jim," he said, "I promise you and the Lord that by this time next month, I'll be completely yielded to Christ and trusting Him to help me get my life straightened out."

Failing health and old age did not prevent Jim and Estelle from intensifying their prayer ministry throughout the 1980s and 1990s. For a few years they had talked about the possibility of moving to a larger house. Their children discussed going together and purchasing them a larger dwelling on one floor. One was found on Perry Street in Kirklin. The large screened-in front porch was made usable for both summer and winter, and it became their powerful prayer room. They did not attempt to lessen the volume or passion of their praying. The Front Porch Power

House became known all through Central Indiana as the place to attend or send prayer requests for the two hours of prayer every Tuesday morning! Billy Graham and other renowned spiritual leaders credited much of their anointing from the power generated from the Kirklin Tuesday morning prayers offered up by Jim and Estelle and those who prayed with them. Pastors from various denominations would join them from time to time. Spiritual leaders traveling through Central Indiana would time their trip so they could be with Jim and Estelle in their praise, intercession, weeping over the lost, and believing for revival in America.

Sometimes their burdened hearts would not allow them to close their praying at 10:30. Often they would lay hands on a sick person and pray for their healing. Occasionally, they would receive a report that a congregation was being invaded by division and backbiting or that a spiritual leader had gone astray. With tears in her eyes and an ache in her heart, Estelle would say, "We just can't close until we have gone to the Throne of Grace with this brother's case." Then, like her Lord, **during the days of his flesh,** Estelle would **offer up prayers and supplications with loud cries and tears to him who was able**. They received many phone calls and letters confirming answers to their prayers. Estelle kept accurate accounts of requests and answers, usually sharing them in the early moments of the praying sessions. One night after a great day of praying, Estelle told Jim, "Honey, I just read where Oswald Chambers said, 'Don't just use prayer to prepare you for a greater work for God; *prayer IS the greater work!*' I may not know a lot, but I thank God for what He has taught me about prayer!"

January 18, 1996 dawned cold and clear. It was Estelle's 88th birthday. When Jim woke at daylight and realized Estelle was still asleep, he slipped out of bed and made himself toast and coffee. At 8:00, Jim went back into the bedroom to find Estelle getting dressed. "Coffee's hot, and I'll put toast in for ye. Burl will be by at 8:30 to pick me up. He wants me to look at some land he may buy or lease. He kissed Estelle and said, "Don't expect us back 'til tonight."

Estelle ate her toast and drank her coffee, all the time thinking of how good the Lord had been to her and Jim. Their children and grandchildren were all doing well. Even before opening her Bible and spending an hour in prayer, as she was accustomed to doing after breakfast, Estelle said, "Father, how I praise You for Your gracious care of Jim and me and for Your provision for our children and grandchildren! Be with each of us this morning, helping us with burdens that seem too heavy to bear. May we each know that You are present and ready to help us." She paused and wept, thinking of two sons and several grandchildren who had strayed from the Lord. She called their names out to the Lord, praying, "Give them a sense of urgency to call upon the name of the Lord and be saved!"

A little after 9:00, Estelle walked to the window, looked out on a cold and sunlit morning, and praised God for such a beautiful day. She cleared the table, turned off the coffee pot, and went into the living room. After sitting down in her comfortable chair and resting her feet on the matching ottoman, she reached for her Bible and opened the Word: **He who dwells in the shelter of the Most High will rest in the shadow of the Almighty. I will say of the Lord, He is my refuge and my fortress, my God in whom I trust**.

She knew to not continue reading. *Lord, I feel so secure in You this morning—I have joy unspeakable, an inner peace deeper than I've ever known, and a courage to go on and finish my course without doubting or fearing any opposition by humans or demons. I don't fear death, just kind of long for it. I do want to see You, Lord! I think I need to get into prayer.*

Twenty minutes into praying for Jim, their nine living children and their spouses, and their grandchildren and great-grandchildren, she could only rejoice in a new faith that swept over her. The Lord *really would save her lost sons and grandchildren* and strengthen those who were weak and floundering!

Was that a knock at the door? Then she thought she heard someone say, "Estelle!" She heard the door open and gentle footsteps coming through the kitchen. *There! No! It can't be!* A white-robed Being with hands outstretched stood in the living room doorway smiling, hands outstretched. He spoke, **Peace, Estelle! Don't be afraid! We must visit a little while**.

He walked over to Jim's chair across the room from her and sat down. As He sat, Estelle caught a glimpse of the scar in His right hand.

How can this be? she wanted to ask. *How unworthy I am to have Your Presence here in my humble home!*

Still! Quiet! O, Estelle, We've looked forward to Our visit with you. Please, now! Just sit back, relax, and hear what We have to say.

Can I dare look at Him? Is this a reality or a dream? A few minutes ago I wanted to see Jesus. Now, He's here. Or have I lost my mind? I need to relax and try to listen to what He says.

As He had commanded, she sat back to listen, afraid at first to look directly at the white-robed Man. She started by noticing His feet—*sandals, brown, sparkling*; His robe—*spotlessly white, seamless, glistening*; His face—*smiling*, and as the apostle John wrote, **like the sun shining in all its brilliance**; His eyes—**like blazing fire!**

Estelle was trembling, weeping, waiting, and wanting Him to speak. *How can I, a weak mortal, stand the overwhelming Presence of such Glory! Such Holiness! Such Majesty!*

Then He spoke. *O the sound of His voice! Yes, I've heard that voice before! In the cabin in Arkansas. Now comes His command:* **Still! Quiet!** *It was taking effect. I'm no longer afraid. I want to hear Him.*

He was leaning forward. She sensed He had been waiting for her fears to subside. **Estelle, We—the Father, the Spirit, and I—feel We want to visit you and prepare you for your homegoing. We're here to tell you that before long it will be time to call you home to be with Us.** He paused, smiled, sat back in the chair, and waited.

"Well, Lord…, I am ready, but I have only one concern: my husband, Jim. Forgive my concern, Lord, but if I'm gone, no one can take care of him. I know I'm ready to go and be with You, but Jim will grieve and be miserable without me here to care for him."

The Lord was smiling and leaning forward again. **Estelle, We knew you would say this. My dear one, you are highly esteemed in the celestial world, particularly by Us and the archangels. So We are gladly and freely granting your request to remain here a little longer. But before We leave, We assure you that your prayer life since before the Arkansas Revival represents what We long to see among the redeemed—a living sacrifice! You have overcome many obstacles—poverty, ignorance, and an environment of depravity. You have overcome much opposition. You have fought a good fight** against principalities, powers, rulers of darkness, and hosts of wicked spirits in the heavenlies. **Your faithfulness in prayer drew Our release of heavenly hosts over the prairie and river bottom communities down in Arkansas and now here in Central Indiana. We promise you, there is laid up for you a crown of righteousness, which I Myself, the Righteous Judge, shall award you on that Day. And now, before We leave you, I want to come and bless you with My touch. Please remain seated.**

He stood. But He never walked any steps toward her. *He was just there standing before her.* She could hear Him breathing. She heard the crisp rustle of His garment as He raised His hand to reach out and touch her. *His hand was on her shoulder!* A burning sensation traveled over her and raced to her heart. He was unhurried. Finally, He uttered, **Estelle, rest in Me. We will overshadow you in your few years of physical weakness and pain. Continue to offer up sacrifices of praise, committing your dear ones to Us. We know your grief over some of your children and grandchildren. We've heard your cries for their deliverance, and We've seen your tears. Do not fear, fret, or fight with them; just keep loving and interceding. We are not deaf, nor are We indifferent. We shall move upon them. Now, tell your preacher son to get Our Word out to Billy Graham and his other associates to PRAY IN THE SPIRIT, DIE OUT TO SELFISH DESIRES, AND EXPECT THE GREATEST OUTPOURINGS OF OUR SPIRIT FROM HERE TO THE END. THE TIME IS SHORT. IT WILL NOT BE LONG!**

Estelle, We'll suffer the weakness and pain with you. Then We'll come. There's nothing to fear in death; I've conquered it all. We'll come for Jim first, then a little later for you. Until then, We look forward to our continued fellowship in prayer. I'm a good listener, and the Father loves what we tell Him. Goodbye, faithful one. Our Blessings!

Suddenly Estelle realized His hand was no longer on her shoulder. Estelle opened her eyes and looked up. He was gone, but she heard no receding steps nor the opening or closing of doors. She stood and went to the window, even though she knew she would not see Him. She walked back to her chair to sit down, but changed her mind and decided to sit where He had sat.

She closed her eyes. *Did I just imagine that Jesus visited me for an hour? And am I just imagining that all the pain in my neck, shoulders, and joints is now gone? O, Lord! Help me remember everything You said. You will come for Jim first and then, after a little while, for me. We'll continue to fellowship in prayer. You are a good listener, and the Father loves to hear what we tell Him. Until my dying day, Lord, I shall be grateful for Your visit!*

Jim awakened her about sundown, asking, "Are you alright? Have you slept long? Is anything wrong? I feel something must have happened around here today."

Estelle wanted to say that Jesus had been there and spill out all He had said, but she felt an inner restraint outweigh the strong compulsion. Maybe at the appropriate time she would tell him. So she said, "Nothing's wrong. It's been a wonderful day!"

"I guess ye mean ye've been talkin' to the Lord!"

She nodded and wanted to say, "Yes, *face to face!*" But that could wait. She did say, "I'll get dressed and broil some chops and make a salad. Then how about coffee and a piece of coconut cake?"

"Sounds good! Can't wait!"

As the weeks passed, Estelle was surprised that she had not felt free to tell Jim, Anniece, or any of the others about the Visit. Even though she was given a message for Jake, she sensed she was not to call him but that, in time, she'd be given the opportunity to deliver the message in person.

Then Jake called. He would be flying into Indianapolis the next Wednesday, renting a car, and driving to Saginaw, Michigan, for a School of Prayer. He'd likely arrive in Kirklin in time for the noon meal. Jim was working in the garden when Jake drove in. They visited a few minutes before Jim said, "Son, go on in and visit with Mama. Allow me to finish these two rows. It'll be time to eat soon, and I'll be in."

"Take that chair there!" Jake's mother ordered, pointing to the chair his father usually sat in. Of course Jake sat down where she designated. She was sitting in her regular chair across the room, both feet stretched across the ottoman. Jake looked at her smiling face and sparkling eyes as she leaned forward in her chair.

What's going on here? What's this burning sensation crawling up my body and now settling around my heart? Could it be imagination?

498

I'd better listen to what Mama is saying. It seems important. Oh, yeah, she's got a message from the Lord for me. He listened.

"Son, I hope you won't think your mother has lost her mind, but I've got something to tell you that may shock you. Last Thursday morning was my 88th birthday, as you know. And Jesus came in person to visit me! He stayed an hour and sat in that very chair in which you are sitting!" Estelle paused to see how her son was taking this.

"Mom, you seem sure about this…, but …" He looked away, got up and walked to the window, and looked out at his father stooped over some plants he was hoeing. Returning to his seat, he waited…. *There it was again! A warming from his hips upward and then a burning around his heart.* "Mom, I believe you! I sat here a moment ago and felt a burning sensation. It should have convinced me that I was sitting where Jesus had physically sat. When I was standing at the window, I asked God that if this really happened as you said it would happen again. And, Mom, the same burning has come again! I know you are not imagining the visit. It really happened!"

"Yes, it did! After Jesus left, I sat there where you are and had the same warming, burning sensation you are feeling. I needed that, too! Son, Jesus came to prepare me for my homegoing. But when I said I could not see how your Dad could exist without me, He said, **'We (meaning the Father, the Son, and the Holy Spirit) knew this would be your request. So We will take Jim first, then a little later We will come for you.'** This will be the sure way you can know if Jesus actually visited me—your father will die first, and then I'll die later—whether a few days or a few years, I don't know."

"Yes, Mom, Dad will go first and then you. Now, what else can you share with me that Jesus said?"

"Son, the Lord counseled us concerning our dear ones—children and grandchildren—who have chosen a different way of life. Hear what He said: **'YOU ARE NOT TO FEAR, FRET, OR FIGHT OVER CHILDREN AND GRANDCHILDREN WHO HAVE CHOSEN A DIFFERENT COURSE IN LIFE. JUST CONTINUE YOUR INTERCESSION FOR THEM, AND SMOTHER THEM WITH LOVE AND KINDNESS.'**

"Jake, I know you are terribly burdened over some close loved ones. But I want you to believe this with me—Jesus was telling me that

They (the Holy Trinity) with Their Divine Love will find a way to target their darkness, delusion, rebellion, and unbelief. The Spirit of God will mercifully reveal to them their lostness, hardness, and self-justification and create within them a startling condition of longing to embrace a God of love and compassion Who has graciously prepared for their salvation in Jesus Christ. Son, I'm counting on a Gracious, Merciful God to give our erring loved ones a spirit of repentance and faith so that they will **call on the Lord and be saved!**"

Both mother and son were weeping by this time. Jake had not had so much relief concerning those dear to him who argued against the Christian faith with such bitterness and hostility. He was nodding and wiping tears, as Estelle went on speaking. "Son, Divine Love, Divine Sovereignty, and Divine Wisdom will penetrate their darkness, delusion, rebellion, unbelief, and pride. They will experience a growing inner vacuum, unrelenting doubts, and a haunting sense of the eternal consequences of missing the truth, which will eventually explode in brokenness—resulting in a biblical faith that will lead them to repentance and a confession of faith.

"Now, Jake, I must say this: When our loved ones come to Jesus, we must make sure we do not get in their way with our traditional and conventional expectations and directions. We must not usurp the role of the Holy Spirit to lead their believing hearts. Our loved ones may not become a part of the institutional church, but we must be satisfied that they have accepted the Gospel of Jesus Christ and confessed Jesus as Savior, the One who died on the cross in full payment for their sins. We must trust the same Holy Spirit who lives within us to live within them in conviction, counsel, and comfort. We must never impose on them the traditions, rituals, and practices within the WEF that we observe. However, they must know that we embrace and accept them as fully in Jesus Christ!"

"Amen!" Jake said. "Oh, Mom! It's time to hear what Jesus told you to tell me!"

"Jesus said, '**TELL YOUR PREACHER SON TO TELL BILLY GRAHAM AND HIS OTHER ASSOCIATES IN MINISTRY TO PRAY IN THE SPIRIT, DIE OUT TO FLESHLY DESIRES, AND EXPECT THE GREATEST OUTPOURINGS OF**

THE HOLY SPIRIT IN THESE END TIMES THAN IN ALL OF THE HISTORY OF THE CHURCH.'"

Estelle and Jake sat a few seconds in holy silence, and then they stood and embraced. Finally, Estelle said, "Well, I hear your father cleaning up in the bathroom, so I'd better get the food on the table. When do you need to leave?"

"In about two hours."

When his father came in from the garden, Jake said, "Dad, you're looking well, and I noticed you were working pretty hard out there."

"Well, I don't think I'm doin' too bad for an old man of 90!"

"Well, Dad. I am so glad you are healthy and happy and full of the joy of the Lord!"

In August of 1996, Jim and Estelle celebrated their 70th wedding anniversary in Frankfort, Indiana, in connection with the annual Tharp-Best Family Reunion. Because of an announcement made on ABC's Paul Harvey news by the famous newsman himself, many television, radio, and newspaper reporters showed up with their camera crews and notepads. Attendees numbered in the hundreds, despite the absence of scores who had joined the Church Triumphant over the passing years of association and acquaintance with Jim and Estelle. Congratulatory messages were read from President Bill Clinton, Evangelist Dr. Billy Graham, and Governor Evans of Indiana.

Soon after the celebration, Estelle began noticing pain in her left hip. She kept this to herself for awhile, but one day when Anniece, a nurse, was visiting her, she noticed her mother's slight limp. She was able to get her mother to acknowledge she was having pain and eventually convinced her mother to get medical treatment. A doctor ordered an X-ray and an MRI, and these resulted in her being scheduled for a hip replacement procedure at St. Vincent's Hospital in Indianapolis. Following the surgery, Estelle's blood pressure elevated critically, and her pain level became excruciating, which all led to a major stroke. A few days later, she was admitted to the Indiana Rehabilitation Hospital not far from St. Vincent's. Jim practically lived at Estelle's bedside until her condition improved, and eventually she was allowed to go home.

For several months her daughter Shirley and daughter-in-law Judy were able to care for her in her home. But there came a day in 1998, a heartbreaking day for Jim and the family, when Estelle's needs for care were greater than what could be given at home. She was admitted to the Clinton County Nursing Home in Frankfort, 12 miles from their home in Kirklin.

After Jim had spent the day with his darling wife, he went home to an empty house and hit an emotional low. Needing someone to comfort him, he decided to call his preacher son. As they began talking, Jim wept out his grief, saying, "Son, I never thought the Lord would allow thangs to get to this place! I no longer want to live. Your mother is the finest, holiest, most precious person in the world, and I just can't stand another day of seein' her suffer." Jake spent over an hour listening, often interrupting his father with promises of God's grace. Finally, his father began listening, believing, and accepting that the Holy Spirit within him was the Spirit of Comfort and Wisdom and Grace, and that **we are to know that in everything God works for good with those who love him, who are called according to his purpose**. It took Jim a few seconds after hearing this truth to get ahold of it, believe it, and rest in it. From that night on, Jim seemed to suffer in silence, receiving God's grace for each new day. He had given up driving voluntarily, but he visited Estelle daily. Burl and Pat, Russ and Judy, Joe and Judy, Martha and Garry, Don and Anniece, and Shirley were all faithful to get him to Estelle's bedside every morning, and he often stayed late into the night.

At the nursing home the evening of April 8, 1998, Jim was dreading the good-night ritual. Anniece was waiting for her father to indicate his readiness to return home, but she slipped to the ladies room to allow her parents some privacy. When she returned, Jim was kneeling by Estelle's bed, and they were holding hands. Jim had finished praying as Anniece walked into the room. Estelle began praying, "Father God, thank You for my dear Jim, for his love and faithfulness to me, and for Your salvation and blessings all across our 72 years together. You've kept Your promise to be with us to the very end. Bless and comfort Jim as he goes home tonight. Let him remember that he is not alone, and that I am not alone in this bed. Come for us when You are ready for us. Give

Jim a good night's rest, and manifest Your presence to comfort his heart. Amen."

Jim and Estelle were both weeping as they kissed good night. Anniece was in tears also, wondering: *Is this their last moment together? Lord, maybe You'll decide to take Dad before Mother, for how will he be able to bear the grief of losing her?*"

"I'm ready, Anniece. Let's go," Jim said as he finished putting on his coat and moved toward the door. He turned and looked at Estelle and said, "Now, darlin', go to sleep and get a good night's rest. I'll see ye in the mornin'!" He blew her a kiss, and when his darling returned it, he smiled and led the way through the door.

Anniece parked the car and walked her father to the house. Inside she said, "I love you, Dad! You're the greatest father in the world." Then she prayed, "Lord, give both Dad and Mother a good night's rest and a special comfort in their being apart, for we know they'll be together soon in perfect happiness. Amen."

"It won't be long, Anniece," Jim said as he hugged his daughter good night and thanked her and Don for all they had done for him and Estelle.

Jim waited for Anniece's car to back out before he turned out the porch light. As he was undressing for bed, he felt that he was having a premonition. *I don't guess I ever felt this way before. Not in a shootout down in Arkansas and not when Dr. Whitehead warned me that time that I might not make it. But, Lord, I believe I've covered everythang with You, and my sins are under the blood. Sure wish my boys wuz livin' for Ye. I'd shore like to see Estelle one more time.* Then Jim's mind was flooded with joy and hope. *I'll see her agin, maybe real soon. Do I leave a note sayin' I knew I would die tonight and I'm all okay with God? No, I'll just write Burl's phone number here. Well, good night Lord. I'm ready for You!* After writing down Burl's number and putting it on the bedside table, Jim crawled into bed and was soon asleep.

In a predawn hour, Jim went into a very impressive dream. On a crisp autumn morning, he, his horse Star, and his dog Buck were with Sheriff Lloyd LaFargue in the White River Bottoms tracking an escaped convict by the name of Joel Jackson. The sun was shining in the bottoms as they tethered their horses between Elm Ridge and Elbow Slough where they could feed on Yellowtop.

When they had walked near Elbow Slough, Jim stopped Buck and talked in whispers to Lloyd. "We are on track. He's only 200 yards away, but because of dense timber, we can't see 'im. I'm quite sure I know where he'll try to ambush us. So here's the plan: Buck and me will go to the right here a little higher up on the ridge and move to the north." Jim pointed, making sure Lloyd knew the way of north. "Slip through the woods to our left, go a hundred yards, and then turn north. Stop when you get to a hackberry grove. Stay behind the biggest one and wait. It'll be only 75 yards from where I'm guessin' our man is—hid behind a big oak at the edge of a bunch of buck brush. Don't get in a hurry to close in. With Buck, I'll close in on 'im, even if I never catch sight of 'im. I reckon ye want him alive?"

"I'd prefer that. But, Jim, you're free to do what's best. If the murderer gets too stubborn 'bout surrenderin', let him have it through the heart—forget the ear!"

"One more thang, Lloyd. When and if ye hear me call 'im out, wait a second or two and make a noise from that hackberry grove. Don't be exposed to his sight, but hit the side of the tree with yore gun barrel or stomp in the leaves, givin' me a chance to challenge him as he steps out from where he's hidin'. Don't leave that hackberry grove, cuz I don't want ye in my line of fire."

Before departing, Lloyd walked over and shook Jim's hand and said, "Thanks, Jim, for comin' outa retirement to hep me catch this most-sought-after criminal!"

"Sure! Glad ye called for me!" Jim said, as he watched his friend disappear into the woods. He then signaled the direction he wanted Buck to lead them. Within an hour of slipping and stopping, Buck had led them within 50 yards of the huge oak bordered by buck brush where Jim had suspected their man lurked. Jim chose a large bunch of huge oaks to take his stand. He watched Buck's ears and heard a sniff and a whispered yelp. He knew he was right.

When Buck looked at Jim, gave a smothered yelp, and then looked back at the big oak 50 yards away, Jim called, "Jackson! Come out with yore hands up! Ye're surrounded. We'd prefer to return ye to prison instead of killin' ye here! Come on, make up yore mind!"

Jim watched. Soon he heard the sound of Lloyd's rifle barrel striking the clear solid bark of the hackberry tree, followed by a second sound of him stomping leaves. Just as he had guessed, Jackson partially emerged from the oak, looking in Lloyd's direction. Jim could have easily killed him with a soft-nosed bullet from his .30.30 that would have blown his side out.

Instead, watching him bow one knee and bring up his rifle in the direction of the sound Lloyd had made, Jim stepped out, and with his gun ready, called, "Right here, Jackson! Either throw down yore gun or get ready to die." Knowing what Jackson would do, Jim had positioned his rifle, and as the criminal turned around to shoot him, Jim pressed his rifle's trigger, knowing the bullet would pierce Jackson's heart.

The instant that Jim pressed the trigger in his dream, he wakened with an excruciating pain in his own chest, which he immediately knew was a massive fatal heart attack. He was able to reach the light switch and turn it on and then punch in the seven digits of Burl's phone number.

At 3:05 in the morning of April 9, 1998, Burl answered the phone, thinking it might be his dad. "Yes, Dad! What's wrong...? I'll be right there! Just lay back and relax! I'm comin'!"

Burl dressed quickly, grabbed his wallet, found his car keys, and within 12 minutes he was walking through the unlocked door of his parents' home. His father was dressed and waiting for him in his chair in the living room. "What's happenin', Dad?"

"Son, I ain't never had such pain! It's takin' my breath! Won't let up! My left arm's numb! I know it's a massive heart attack. It's the end of the line for me, son. But it's okay."

"I'm callin' 911 and gettin' ye to St. Vincent's."

"Burl, I ain't gonna make it, maybe not even to the hospital."

"Don't say that, Dad! I just can't stand to lose ye!"

"Well, I'm sorry to leave Mama and y'all, but I want ye to promise me ye'll meet us over there."

"Dad, I do wanta see y'all over there! I'll try not to put off too long turnin' to the Lord."

"Don't put it off, Burl! We love ye, and Mama and me don't want to enjoy Heaven without ye!"

"I hope that ambulance will get here soon! I know ye're hurtin', Dad."

"Yeah, real bad, son. I'll walk around some, 'til they get here."

At 5:40, they loaded Jim into the ambulance. Burl had to talk persuasively to the driver, who had tried to insist that they would have to take Jim to Frankfort, the nearest hospital. Giving in to Burl, they headed for St. Vincent's in Indianapolis.

It was noon when the cardiologist came out to report to the family: their father's condition was terminal; the end would come within a few hours. He might regain consciousness soon, and then they would be allowed to visit him briefly.

Burl had phoned all of his siblings living in the area, and they were in the room when their father regained consciousness. They heard him say, "Kids, I'm not hurtin' like I was, but I know I won't make it. I want to meet all of ye in Heaven. Burl and Joe, don't keep puttin' off gettin' right with God. Take the news to Mama that I'm ready to go and I wish I could've seen her one more time, but tell her I'll see her over there." Remembering that Don was critically ill, he started to ask about his son-in-law. "Anniece, how's..." Suddenly alarms went off, and all his children were asked to leave the room.

Two hours later, some of the children were allowed back in Jim's room. Just before sundown, with only his son Joe in the room, Jim raised his head and his eyes widened as he struggled to speak. He simply breathed hard, and his head fell back on his pillow. Joe knew that his father was gone.

All six children who lived in Indiana—Anniece, Burl, Russell, Shirley, Martha, and Joe—went to the nursing home in Frankfort and interrupted Estelle's dinner. Seeing their sad faces, she knew their report. "Oh, children, you've come to tell me that my darling has gone to be with the Lord!" she cried. When they nodded, she pushed her food away, rolled over with her face toward the wall, wailed softly for a few minutes, but soon grew quiet. Each of the six tried in their own way to comfort her.

Before the children left, she said, "We said our goodbyes last night, and as my sweetheart left, I felt we had had our last time together. Now you know that Bob Stubbs is to officiate at both of our funerals. You children please meet tonight and come up with the outline of your Dad's funeral. Bring it to me in the morning, and I'll consider it and possibly make a few changes. Also, I'll tell you then what suit to have your father wear."

The next morning, Anniece and Shirley presented their mother with a suggested outline for their father's funeral. Estelle said, "It looks fine, but I want to include some time for Bob to open the service for expressions from the people concerning Jim's influence on their lives. Also, I want the Williamsons to sing early in the service and once more just before the closing prayer."

The First WEF building in Frankfort, Indiana, was packed to its capacity for the funeral of Jim Tharp. All five sons—Jake, Burl, Russ, Carroll, and Joe—had transported Estelle from the nursing home to the church and then arranged her comfortably on the front row. All nine children surrounded her during the service.

Rev. Bob Stubbs opened the service with prayer. He then expressed his gratitude for being privileged to be in the Tharp family by marrying Jim's and Estelle's niece Paulette Menard. He stated that he had never learned the importance and power of prayer until they had moved to Kirklin, Indiana, and he had joined in their Tuesday morning prayer meetings. When the Williamsons sang, a camp meeting spirit filled the sanctuary; all present who knew Jim and Estelle understood that the spirit matched the spirit of their lives.

Bob spoke from Romans 12:1-2 and sought in his eulogy to identify Jim as being influenced by Estelle, who had helped him make his prayer life a **living sacrifice** for the rest of his years. He then called for expressions from those whose lives had been powerfully touched by Jim Tharp.

Several WEF officials paid tribute to Jim's life as an organizer and motivator for the kingdom of God. However, it would be the tribute paid by Mrs. Darlene Pratt that would be long remembered: "My name is Darlene Pratt, postmistress of the Kirklin Post Office. Jim would come into the post office to get his mail, and if he could see that I was not busy with a customer, he would come by the window and we would talk about gardening. I learned a lot from him. He would also tell me what the Lord was doing through their WEF congregation. On one particular day, he said, 'Darlene, God is doing wonderful things here in Central Indiana. We call it revival! And, Darlene, you and I have talked about gardening, weather, and a little politics; but I want to ask you if you have ever made your peace with God by confessing His Son Jesus Christ as your personal Savior?' When I said, 'I guess not,' he led me step by step through the Gospel and helped me put my faith in Christ alone for my salvation! And that was not the end of our relationship; he and Estelle visited me in my home, prayed with me, and helped me find fellowship and strength in joining the WEF in Kirklin. So why shouldn't I stand here at Jim's funeral and thank God for such a faithful witness for our Lord Jesus Christ!"

Bob sensed that after that tribute, it was time for the Williamsons to sing the closing song, "Going Home," and then have the benediction.

For several months after Jim's funeral, it appeared that Estelle had checked out mentally, emotionally, and even spiritually. She seemed to notice no one, asked for nothing, and barely responded to even one of her children. The meals might be late or the room too cold or too hot—it did not seem to matter to her. She was almost never seen reading her Bible or heard praying.

Anniece, who knew her mother better than any of her siblings, told them, "Please understand, the Lord is allowing our mother to enter a period of rest from grief over the death of her husband of 72 years and the end of a most amazing love relationship. She's also resting from decades of passionate suffering with Christ for revival in our nation, from concerns in our family and other relatives, and from hundreds of churches and more than a thousand believers across the world who need cleansing and renewal. Now I know the Lord wants us to keep coming and visiting her. But He wants us to respect what He is doing with our dear mother even in these silent months. Let's not worry about her lack of interest in things—in us, in the churches, in the nation, and in the world. But I do feel we need to watch for a time when she does grow more sensitive and alert to all that is going on around us and to each of us personally. In my opinion, that will mean we won't have her with us much longer. I don't have to tell you that Estelle Tharp has lived a life of unusual intimacy with God, resulting in the kind of spiritual power that most of us will never know. She has fought a good fight and kept the faith. Our own father, who is in Heaven with the Lord today, knows that Mother's persistent, intercessory praying got results.

"And now, my dear brothers and sisters, when the Lord is ready for our mother, let not one of us beg Him to keep her here with us a single day longer. For she wants to go and be with Jesus, with Dad, with Paul, and with her parents and grandparents, as well as hosts of others whom she has led to the Lord." In tears, her children embraced each other and celebrated in praise to God for their wonderful heritage.

Just a few days before Christmas, Shirley drove to Frankfort to visit her mother. She sat down by her mother's bed, leaned over and kissed her, and was delighted to see a clearer look in her eyes. Then came a more inquisitive conversation initiated by her mother. "It seems I've been away a long time. I remember that your Daddy is gone to be with Jesus, but I'm not sure where I am and what is wrong with me. Why am I here in this bed? What month of the year are we in? How are all the children and grandchildren? And what about our Arkansas loved ones?"

"Mom, today is Monday, December 21, 1998, four days before Christmas. You had a stroke at St. Vincent's Hospital in Indianapolis a few years ago. We took care of you at home until we realized you were not getting the care you needed. Even though it nearly killed Daddy for us to have to bring you here, he allowed the Lord to help him. He visited you every day! Several months ago, on April 9, 1998, Dad had a massive heart attack early in the morning and he died about 18 hours later that evening in St. Vincent's Hospital. All six of us who live in this area—Anniece, Burl, Russell, me, Martha, and Joe—got to be with him before he died. Jeanette and Don live in Doniphan, Missouri; Jake and Maxine live in Bozeman, Montana; and Carroll lives in Pineville, Missouri. Our Arkansas loved ones are all okay. They call often, telling us they are praying for you. And, oh, Mom! This whole county is asking about you! You're a VIP where Wesleyans, Friends, United Methodists, Church of God, and most evangelicals are concerned. So many are crediting you for the revivals in their churches, the salvation of their loved ones, and for thousands of answered prayers. The phones are continually ringing for us to tell you of their love and prayers!"

"Shirley, that kind of credit belongs to God alone, and I won't touch His glory by taking you seriously. Now that I feel more alive—and I do realize that I am partially paralyzed—I want to show you something I found in my notes yesterday that I had underlined from a book by Andrew Murray. It is addressed to believers: *'Don't use prayer to prepare you for a greater work for God; prayer IS the greater work!'* I realize that I don't know a lot, but oh how I thank God for what He has taught me about prayer! Shirley, will you do something for me?"

"Of course, Mom! Gladly! Just tell me what you want."

"The next time you come, bring me a list of the names of all my children and their mates, each of their children, and then their mates and children—all listed by their order of birth. You know, I've always enjoyed praying for the family by their names and ages. Will you do that for me, please?"

"Sure, Mom! I might have to make a few phone calls and get the names of the latest great-grandchildren for you, but I'll bring that before Christmas," Shirley promised.

The first few weeks of 1999 was a time of renewal for Estelle. With her new list of loved ones, Estelle began her final period of intercession, much like she had prayed in the cabin during her "night of weeping." She feasted on the memory of Jesus' personal visit. "Oh, Lord, I long now for Your coming for me! Thank You for taking Jim first! He won't have to grieve over my death, but rather he will greet me there with You in a few days!"

The doctors and nursing staff had been kind and thoughtful. Estelle thanked them and prayed for them, asking God's blessing on them. Jeanette, Jake, and Carroll, who now lived a distance away, would come and spend a few hours to bring her personal joy in seeing their faces, hearing their voices, and enjoying their prayers with her.

Anniece, Shirley, and Martha visited their mother on her 91st birthday, January 18, 1999. Rev. Bob Stubbs and his wife, Paulette, came in to see her that day as well. Estelle reminded Bob that at her funeral he was to preach to the living and say the least possible about her—that Jesus should get all the glory from anything good that might have come from her life. Paulette said, "Well, Grandma, there's no way Bob can be fair to you without praising God for all that He has done through you. I know Bob will honor your wishes, but you'll have to allow him to praise the Lord for your praying God's will to pass in giving revivals in Arkansas and here in Central Indiana."

On a Friday morning in the middle of February, Anniece arose with a strong feeling that she should clear most of her day to spend with her mother. Estelle seemed wide awake and comfortable, but quiet. "Mother, is there anything you need or want this morning?" Anniece asked.

Estelle smiled, "Just to see my dear children and have as many of them as possible near me today."

"Well, I know Martha is coming. Perhaps Burl, Joe, and Russ will show up, too. I know Jake was by several days ago. Jeanette called yesterday and said she regrets so much that she can't slip in here every day and be with you a little while."

"Oh, I know and understand they would come if they could, but I'm thankful for the visits of you who are close by."

In late afternoon, Bob and his wife, Paulette, came, followed a little later by Shirley and then Martha and her husband, Garry. Toward evening, both Burl and Joe decided to visit their mother on their way home from work. Shirley particularly noticed Joe's communication with his mother. After kissing her, Joe stood gazing into her eyes for several seconds. Shirley believed he was silently communicating love, appreciation, gratitude, and sorrow that she might not be with them long. She noticed her brother's sad and moist eyes as he said goodbye and left the room.

Anniece needed to get home. She led a prayer of thanksgiving for "the love and influence of a Godly, Spirit-filled mother." Why was she so reluctant to leave? She walked to the bed and kissed her mother, saying, "Thank you, Mother, for your love, prayers, and powerful influence on all of us, on our churches, and on our communities. I love you!" Estelle returned the expression of love, wiped a tear, and waved to her dear daughter. Anniece stood at the door thinking, *Maybe you won't be here tomorrow when I plan to visit.* "Good night, Mother!"

Bob needed to leave for an appointment, so Shirley promised to drop Paulette off on her way home. Burl departed when Bob left.

"They will bring Mother's dinner in a few minutes," Shirley said. "So, Martha and Paulette, I'll go get us a sandwich and a drink. We'll visit with Mother a little while, but we probably shouldn't stay too late, so she can get her rest. What would you two like?"

Martha and Paulette gave their orders, and Shirley left for the deli.

Estelle asked Martha and Paulette to sing something, an old favorite, "Tell It to Jesus."

"Which verse?" Martha asked.

"Well, there are four verses, but I don't need you to sing the last one, for it asks, 'Are you troubled at the tho't of dying?' I'm not troubled at all. In fact, I'd love to go home! I guess maybe the first verse, though it does not fit perfectly. 'Are you weary, are you heavyhearted? Tell it to Jesus; tell it to Jesus. Are you grieving over joys departed? Tell it to Jesus alone.'"

Martha led out on the first verse, and Paulette sang along. Estelle only smiled and hummed. She hummed the loudest on the refrain, "Tell it to Jesus; tell it to Jesus. He is a friend that's well-known! You've no other such a friend or brother. Tell it to Jesus alone." Estelle even sang aloud the words "He is a friend that's well-known!" As Martha and Paulette finished the refrain, Estelle's hand was in the air waving, as she often did when blessed while praising the Lord. As the girls finished, Estelle's head suddenly raised up several inches from her pillow and her eyes widened and gleamed. Without a word, she fell back and her head rolled to one side. Her daughter and niece knew she had gone to be with the Lord.

On Tuesday morning, February 23, 1999, an hour before Estelle's funeral service began, the First WEF building in Frankfort, Indiana, was packed. By the time the service began, several hundred people were gathered around the building, spilling over into the parking lots.

Pastor Bob Stubbs opened the service with a passage from Psalm 116:15: **Precious in the sight of the Lord is the death of his saints**. He then went on to say, "The hundreds of you gathered here this morning to celebrate the life of Estelle Tharp will agree that she is one of the outstanding saints of modern times. She is now with the Lord, and we are here to glorify God for making her life count for eternity." Bob then led a prayer for God's comforting and convicting presence. The Williamsons—a family of four who Jim and Estelle had led to the Lord when they were neighbors—sang three numbers, climaxing their portion of the service with an appropriate number entitled, "Going Home."

Bob continued the service by giving some specifics that Estelle had insisted he share at her service: (1) The absolute requirement of the new birth for anyone who would go to Heaven, (2) The call to holiness on the heart and life of every believer, (3) The conditions for renewal and revival in every believer's heart and in every congregation's membership—sacrificial prayer, and (4) An opportunity to surrender one's life to the Lord in this service. Bob closed then by asking for

512

bowed heads while he called for anyone present who would like to accept Estelle's Savior Jesus Christ to indicate by holding up a hand. He acknowledged the hands of many and prayed for their sincerity, encouraging them to become a part of a Bible-believing church and to counsel with their pastors.

For several minutes after Bob's prayer of benediction, hardly anyone left the auditorium. All of Estelle's nine children were kept busy for more than an hour receiving those who wished to express their appreciation for Estelle's life and influence—college students, individuals, younger and older couples, whole families, pastors representing congregations, and denominational officials who had called on Estelle to address their gatherings.

The nine children gathered at the Tharp home in Kirklin for prayer and to go through hundreds of messages and greetings from people all over the world. They enjoyed recalling the things their parents had said and done both in Arkansas and in Indiana.

A few days after his mother's funeral, Jake resumed his ministry schedule and left for Laurel, Delaware, to conduct a School of Prayer. He checked into the hotel, enjoyed a short nap, and went to the hotel dining room for dinner.

Having ordered a steak and salad, Jake relaxed in the comfortable booth and began reflecting on his mother's life and influence. *She was fatherless at age five; her mother was left a penniless pauper with four children. Her grandparents opened their home to them for a few years. While still in grade school, Estelle was sent to live with her Aunt Mertice and Uncle Tom to do the household duties of cooking, cleaning, and laundry. In her teens, she was allowed to get one year of high school. When Aunt Mertice failed in health, Estelle gave up schoolwork and assumed all household duties for a small salary. She read extensively. At 18, she met and married 20-year-old Jim Tharp—a fisherman, hunter, trapper, and timberman. The influence of her mother, Alma, and her Grandmother Best led her to believe she could know God in a personal relationship. Before marrying Jim, she let him know that her main purpose in life would be finding God and discovering His will for her life. Four years after their marriage, she found the Lord in a "brush arbor" revival in Nady, Arkansas, totally surrendering her life to*

Him. The Lord sent a Spirit-filled Bible scholar to mentor her in Christian holiness, anointed prayer, and outpourings of the Holy Spirit in revivals. She believed an outpouring of the Holy Spirit in Pentecostal power to be the only remedy for the lostness of her own loved ones and the depravity of a wicked community in southeastern Arkansas. So, through prayer, she was "crucified with Christ" and became "a living sacrifice" in intercessory prayer. She lived to see a "rending of the heavens" in both Arkansas County and Central Indiana.

It was only when the waitress served Jake's steak dinner that he recovered from his reverie. Even as he began cutting his steak, he returned his thoughts to his mother's influence. While she greatly influenced the North American portion of the WEF, he rejoiced that she was inclusive in her understanding of the universal Kingdom of God. She loved worshiping with Calvinists or Wesleyan-Arminians, as well as Pentecostals or Episcopalians. And she could do this freely, whether in a tent revival or in a metropolitan cathedral.

After finishing his meal, Jake suddenly thought of his friend Dr. Paul S. Rees, the General Superintendent of the WEF, Vice President of World Vision, and former President of the National Association of Evangelicals. Had Paul heard of his mother's passing? Paul was one of the few people Jake had told of Estelle's visit from Jesus on her 88th birthday. To Jake's delight, Paul said, "Jake, I knew your mother, and I have no problem believing that Jesus actually visited her in person. I realized when I prayed with her that she entertained angels!"

Back in his hotel room, Jake was leafing through his address book to find Paul's number when his phone rang. The hotel operator said, "Mr. Tharp, please hold for a connection with a Dr. Paul Rees, please." He soon heard the stately voice of his friend. "Oh, Jake! It's so good to hear your voice and have the opportunity to express my condolence in the passing of your saintly mother! I just flew in from the Orient and picked up the special issue of your *Journal* on Estelle's death. I want to write about her life in a future issue of *World Vision* magazine."

"Thank you, Paul! I gladly give you my permission."

"When will you arrive back in Bozeman, Montana?"

"In about five weeks."

"Then shortly after your arrival you will find my article about your mother in the coming issue. Please allow me to pray for you and your loved ones before we disconnect." Paul's tender voice led out in a prayer of thanksgiving for the great influence of "The Pentecostal Prophetess Estelle Tharp" on her husband, children, and grandchildren and on needy hearts around the world. He asked God's blessings on Jake's ministry and said "Good night."

The School of Prayer with Pastor Ken Deusa and his people in Laurel, Delaware, turned out to be a series of outpourings of the Spirit in all of the nightly sessions and the closing worship service on Sunday morning. On Monday morning, Jake went to his next assignment where he experienced similar outpourings of the Spirit. A month later, he drove to Baltimore, turned in his rental car, and caught a flight to Denver, where he changed for a flight to Bozeman.

Jake had been looking forward to what Dr. Rees had written about his mother. He slit open the *World Vision* magazine envelope and was excited about what he was about to read:

> Estelle Tharp, a simple, uneducated, unknown woman was chosen by Almighty God to prove His power and reveal His grace and love through a life of sacrificial, prolonged, militant intercessory prayer. At her Grandmother Best's knee, she learned that a God of love longs for a relationship with each one of us. She purposed in her heart to reach that moment in time when God would become real to her through faith in Jesus Christ, the only One He had designated to suffer and die for our sins.
>
> Unlike so many who profess to find Christ as Savior, Estelle, finding peace with God through forgiveness of sin and the gift of the Spirit's assurance of eternal life, decided to go on for the **fullness of God**. Then she learned on the road to **the baptism with the Holy Spirit and with fire** that there is the experience of becoming **crucified with Christ**. She told me the time and place and the when and where that it happened.

She also told me that after this happened she felt *the call to a life of prayer.* God spoke to her from Romans 12:1: **I appeal to you ... to present your body as a living sacrifice, holy and acceptable to God, which is your spiritual worship.** She said that the Spirit impressed her with the phrase **a living sacrifice.** She said the Lord told her, "You can only become **a living sacrifice** in *a life of Spirit-anointed praying.*"

The Lord sent Dr. Martha Honeycutt to review with Estelle the great revivals of church history. During those months, Estelle caught the vision of the great Arkansas County Revival which began under her ministry early in 1946 after seven long years of sacrificial, militant intercession. The caliber, velocity, and impact of those outpourings supersede anything this editor ever heard or read about since the European awakenings under John Wesley and George Whitefield and the American awakenings under Charles G. Finney! As witnessed by her husband and hundreds of others, scores of people were "slain in the Spirit," which brought fear and trembling on multitudes who would then humbly repent and trust in Jesus Christ as their Savior.

Estelle introduced me to a cardiologist whom she had led to the Lord. Dr. Martin Bonnhoffer told me that after being discipled by Estelle and observing the way the Holy Spirit used her in Arkansas County and then in Hot Springs and Little Rock, his title for her was "The Pentecostal Prophetess." He claimed that nearly all of Hot Springs turned out and packed their largest public arena to hear her. Sister Agnes Diffee told me how God used her mightily among the Wesleyans, United Methodists, and Baptists in Little Rock.

The last conversation I had with Estelle and her husband was on the campus of Indiana Wesleyan University in Marion, Indiana. While eating dinner together, we discussed the revival fires that were burning around the Indiana cities of Westfield, Frankfort, Kokomo, Lafayette, and Marion. Most of the pastors presented in the event in Marion credited Estelle's influence for the revival in Central Indiana during the 1960s through the 1980s. Many referenced the Tuesday morning prayer meetings hosted by Jim and Estelle on their front porch in Kirklin.

After meeting Estelle and hearing her testimony and listening to a multitude of witnesses of her spiritual life and powerful ministry, I have not one doubt about our Lord's personal visit with her on her 88th birthday. The world and the church is poorer since Estelle's passing. She has closed her eyes upon the earthly scene, and along with her faithful husband, has opened them upon celestial glory. But we who remain are still beholding terrestrial scenes—a depraved world, a paralyzed church, and the conflict of good and evil operating relentlessly in this present darkness.

Considering Estelle's amazing example of holiness and power through prayer, I resolve to dedicate my remaining time on earth to praying for the same passion that burned in the heart of "The Pentecostal Prophetess," prompting her to become **a living sacrifice** in prayer. May we also remember with her that **God did not give us a spirit of timidity but a spirit of power and love and self control**. Let us therefore go the same route as Estelle: *dying to self and asking, believing, and receiving fresh fire and fresh faith from renewed fillings of the Holy Spirit to keep us praying the will of God to pass in our lives, in our ministries, and in our world!*

Jake finished reading in tears. Looking at the clock, he felt the call to his prayer trails a few miles away from Bozeman in the Hyalite Mountains. On his way, he prayed, "O God, please help me to have the Spirit of prayer—as Jesus had, as Estelle Tharp had!" Then he remembered the struggle of one of his spiritual heroes, Jim Elliot, who finally prayed, "*Father, let me be weak that I might lose my clutch on everything temporal—my reputation, my possessions, and all selfish dreams. Let me lose the tension of a grasping hand.... Rather, open my hand to receive the nail of Calvary—as Christ's was opened—that I, releasing all, might be released for all you have planned for me."*

Working his way up an incline that would eventually allow him to overlook the city, Jake sat on a rock and prayed for the Spirit's influence on his thoughts while he rested. *"O God, let the same fire burn in me that burned in Mama so that I can tear away from this world's interests and cares of life and give myself to prayer even as she did. May I be as passionate as she was to see the church aflame and the world transformed. May I become as yielded, broken, cleansed, and filled with Your Spirit so that You can pour into my mind and lay on my heart the burdens of our Interceding Savior. May the Holy Spirit be just as free to pray through me as He was to pray through Estelle Tharp, groaning through my spirit, weeping through my eyes, and believing through my heart to* **see great and mighty things** *for Your glory!*

"Even as Estelle entered into the fellowship of Your intercession for revival, I beg of You, baptize me now into the fires of that same Spirit of intercession. Lord, just as You sent revivals in Indiana and in Arkansas, DO IT AGAIN! Do it on a grand scale that will cause the world and the church to exclaim as in Elijah's day, **'THE LORD, HE IS GOD! THE LORD, HE IS GOD!'"**

518

About the Author

James W. Tharp was born and raised in Arkansas during the events in this book. His mother's persistent love, unwavering faith, and steadfast prayers for revival inspired him to write ESTELLE, a story of the remarkable spiritual awakening he witnessed, which impacted thousands of people in every walk of life not only in his immediate location but also in surrounding counties.

Tharp was ordained in the Church of the Nazarene in 1957. He has pastored churches in Indiana, Pennsylvania, California, New Mexico, Washington, and Montana. His ministry is dedicated to preparing the Church through prayer for another great spiritual awakening.

In 1979, he began working with the Billy Graham Evangelistic Association, assisting the evangelist in his telephone counseling ministry. He was the personal guest of Billy Graham for the 10 days of "Amsterdam '86".

From 1979-1981, Tharp lectured on the Holy Spirit for California Graduate School of Theology in their doctorate program. He pursued further studies at Olivet Nazarene University in Kankakee, Illinois, and at Seattle Pacific University. Since 1994 he has been devoted to speaking in camp meetings, revivals, and pastoral institutes and conducting the School of Prayer, helping thousands to improve their prayer lives and deepen their Christian walk.

Tharp is the founder and president of CHRISTIAN RENEWAL MINISTRIES based in Bozeman, Montana (formerly in Dothan, Alabama). He is the editor of a quarterly publication, *Christian Renewal Journal.* Some of his daily radio broadcasts from *A Word On Revival* can be heard on the ministry's website, www.crmin.org.

OTHER BOOKS BY JAMES W. THARP

REVIVAL MUST COME!

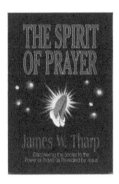

THE SPIRIT OF PRAYER

Ordering information at

Christian Renewal Ministries website

www.crmin.org